The Copper Beech
&
A Week in Winter

The Copper Beech
&
A Week in Winter

Maeve Binchy

First published in Great Britain in 1992 by Orion Books,
an imprint of The Orion Publishing Group Ltd
Carmelite House, 50 Victoria Embankment
London EC4Y 0DZ

An Hachette UK Company

1 3 5 7 9 10 8 6 4 2

A CIP catalogue record for this book is
available from the British Library.

ISBN (Trade Paperback) 978 1 4091 7212 3

Printed in Australia by Mcpherson's Printing Group

www.orionbooks.co.uk

The Copper Beech

For Gordon, who has made my life so good and happy,
with all my gratitude and love.

SHANCARRIG
SCHOOL

Father Gunn knew that their housekeeper Mrs Kennedy could have done it all much better than he would do it. Mrs Kennedy would have done *everything* better in fact, heard Confessions, forgiven sins, sung the *Tantum Ergo* at Benediction, buried the dead. Mrs Kennedy would have looked the part too, tall and angular like the Bishop, not round and small like Father Gunn. Mrs Kennedy's eyes were soulful and looked as if they understood the sadness of the world.

Most of the time he was very happy in Shancarrig, a peaceful place in the midlands. Most people only knew it because of the huge rock that stood high on a hill over Barna Woods. There had once been great speculation about this rock. Had it been part of something greater? Was it of great geological interest? But experts had come and decided while there may well have been a house built around it once all traces must have been washed away with the rains and storms of centuries. It had never been mentioned in any history book. All that was there was one great rock. And since Carrig was the Irish word for rock that was how the place was named – Shancarrig, the Old Rock.

Life was good at the Church of the Holy Redeemer in Shancarrig. The parish priest, Monsignor O'Toole, was a courteous, frail man who let the curate run things his own way. Father Gunn wished that more could be done for the people of the parish so that they didn't have to stand at the railway station waving goodbye to sons and daughters emigrating to England and America. He wished that there were fewer damp cottages where tuberculosis could flourish, filling the graveyard with people too young to die. He wished that tired women did not have to bear so many children, children for whom there was often scant living. But he knew that all the young men who had been in the seminary with him were in similar parishes wishing the same thing. He didn't think he was a man who could change the world. For one thing he didn't *look* like a man who could change the world. Father Gunn's eyes were like two currants in a bun.

There had been a Mr Kennedy long ago, long before Father Gunn's time, but he had died of pneumonia. Every year he was prayed for at mass on the anniversary of his death, and every year Mrs Kennedy's sad face achieved what seemed to be an impossible feat, which was a still more sorrowful appearance. But even though it was nowhere near her late husband's anniversary now she was pretty gloomy, and it was all to do with Shancarrig school.

Mrs Kennedy would have thought since it was a question of a visit from the Bishop that *she*, as the priests' housekeeper, should have been in charge of everything. She didn't want to impose, she said many a time, but really had Father Gunn got it quite clear? Was it really expected that those teachers, those lay teachers above at the school-house and the children that were taught in it, were really in charge of the ceremony?

'They're not used to bishops,' said Mrs Kennedy, implying that she had her breakfast, dinner and tea with the higher orders.

But Father Gunn had been adamant. The occasion was the dedication of the school, a bishop's blessing, a ceremony to add to the legion of ceremonies for Holy Year, but it was to involve the children, the teachers. It wasn't something run by the presbytery.

'But Monsignor O'Toole is the manager,' Mrs Kennedy protested. The elderly frail parish priest played little part in the events of the parish, it was all done by his bustling energetic curate, Father Gunn.

In many ways, of course, it would have been much easier to let Mrs Kennedy take charge, to have allowed her to get her machine into motion and organise the tired sponge cases, the heavy pastries, the big pots of tea that characterised so many church functions. But Father Gunn had stood firm. This event was for the school and the school would run it.

Thinking of Mrs Kennedy standing there hatted and gloved and sorrowfully disapproving, he asked God to let the thing be done right, to inspire young Jim and Nora Kelly, the teachers, to set it up properly. And to keep that mob of young savages that they taught in some kind of control.

After all, God had an interest in the whole thing too, and making the Holy Year meaningful in the parish was important. God must want it to be a success, not just to impress the Bishop but so that the children would remember their school and all the values they learned there. He was very fond of the school, the little stone building under the huge copper beech. He loved going up there on visits and watching the little heads bent over their copy books.

'Procrastination is the thief of time' they copied diligently.

'What does that mean, do you think?' he had asked once.

'We don't know what it means, Father. We only have to copy it out,' explained one of the children helpfully.

They weren't too bad really, the children of Shancarrig – he heard their Confessions regularly. The most terrible sin, and the one for which he had to remember to apportion a heavy penance, was scutting

4

on the back of a lorry. As far as Father Gunn could work out this was holding on to the back of a moving vehicle and being borne along without the driver's knowledge. It not unnaturally drew huge rage and disapproval from parents and passers-by, so he had to reflect the evilness of it by a decade of the Rosary, which was almost unheard of in the canon of children's penances. But scutting apart they were good children, weren't they? They'd do the school and Shancarrig credit when the Bishop came, wouldn't they?

The children talked of little else all term. The teachers told them over and over what an honour it was. The Bishop didn't normally go to small schools like this. They would have the chance to see him on their own ground, unlike so many children in the country who had never seen him until they were confirmed in the big town.

They had spent days cleaning the place up. The windows had been painted, and the door. The bicycle shed had been tidied so that you wouldn't recognise it. The classrooms had been polished till they gleamed. Perhaps His Grace would tour the school. It wasn't certain, but every eventuality had to be allowed for.

Long trestle tables would be arranged under the copper beech tree which dominated the school yard. Clean white sheets would cover them and Mrs Barton, the local dressmaker, had embroidered some lovely edging so that they wouldn't look like sheets. There would be jars of flowers, bunches of lilac and the wonderful purple orchids that grow wild in Barna Woods in the month of June.

A special table with Holy Water and a really good white cloth would be there so that His Grace could take the silver spoon and sprinkle the Water, dedicating the school again to God. The children would sing 'Faith of Our Fathers', and because it was near to the Feast of Corpus Christi they would also sing 'Sweet Sacrament Divine'. They rehearsed it every single day, they were word perfect now.

Whether or not the children were going to be allowed to partake of the feast itself was a somewhat grey area. Some of the braver ones had inquired but the answers were always unsatisfactory.

'We'll see,' Mrs Kelly had said.

'Don't always think of your bellies,' Mr Kelly had said.

It didn't look terribly hopeful.

Even though it was all going to take place at the school they knew that it wasn't really centred around the children. It was for the parish.

There would be something, of course, they knew that. But only when the grown-ups were properly served. There might be just plain bits of bread and butter with a little scraping of sandwich paste on them, or the duller biscuits when all the iced and chocolate-sided ones had gone.

The feast was going to be a communal effort from Shancarrig and so they each knew some aspect of it. There was hardly a household that wouldn't be contributing.

'There are going to be bowls of jelly and cream with strawberries on top,' Nessa Ryan was able to tell.

'That's for grown-ups!' Eddie Barton felt this was unfair.

'Well, my mother is making the jellies and giving the cream. Mrs Kelly said it would be whipped in the school and the decorations put on at the last moment in case they ran.'

'And chocolate cake. Two whole ones,' Leo Murphy said.

It seemed very unfair that this should all be for the Bishop and priests and great crowds of multifarious adults in front of whom they had all been instructed, or ordered, to behave well.

Sergeant Keane would be there, they had been told, as if he was about to take them all personally to the gaol in the big town if there was a word astray.

'They'll have to give some to us,' Maura Brennan said. 'It wouldn't be fair otherwise.'

Father Gunn heard her say this and marvelled at the innocence of children. For a child like young Maura, daughter of Paudie who drank every penny that came his way, to believe still in fairness was touching.

'There'll be bound to be *something* left over for you and your friends, Maura,' he said to her, hoping to spread comfort, but Maura's face reddened. It was bad to be overheard by the priest wanting food on a holy occasion. She hung back and let her hair fall over her face.

But Father Gunn had other worries.

The Bishop was a thin silent man. He didn't walk to places but was more inclined to glide. Under his long soutane or his regal-style vestments he might well have had wheels rather than feet. He had already said he would like to process rather than drive from the railway station to the school. Very nice if you were a gliding person and it was a cool day. Not so good however if it was a hot day, and the Bishop would notice the unattractive features of Shancarrig.

Like Johnny Finn's pub where Johnny had said that out of deference to the occasion he would close his doors but he was not going to dislodge the sitters.

'They'll sing. They'll be disrespectful,' Father Gunn had pleaded.

6

'Think what they'd be like if they were out on the streets, Father.' The publican had been firm.

So much was spoken about the day and so much was made of the numbers that would attend that the children grew increasingly nervous.

'There's no proof at all that we'll get *any* jelly and cream,' Niall Hayes said.

'I heard no talk of special bowls or plates or forks.'

'And if they let people like Nellie Dunne loose they'll eat all before them.' Nessa Ryan bit her lip with anxiety.

'We'll help ourselves,' said Foxy Dunne.

They looked at him round-eyed. Everything would be counted, they'd be murdered, he must be mad.

'I'll sort it out on the day,' he said.

Father Gunn was not sleeping well for the days preceding the ceremony. It was a great kindness that he hadn't heard Foxy's plans.

Mrs Kennedy said that she would have some basic emergency supplies ready in the kitchen of the presbytery, just in case. Just in case. She said it several times.

Father Gunn would not give her the satisfaction of asking just in case *what*. He knew only too well. She meant in case his foolish confidence in allowing lay people up at a small schoolhouse to run a huge public religious ceremony was misplaced. She shook her head and dressed in black from head to foot, in honour of the occasion.

There had been three days of volunteer work trying to beautify the station. No money had been allotted by CIE, the railways company, for repainting. The stationmaster, Jack Kerr, had been most unwilling to allow a party of amateur painters loose on it. His instructions did not include playing fast and loose with company property, painting it all the colours of the rainbow.

'We'll paint it grey,' Father Gunn had begged.

But no. Jack Kerr wouldn't hear of it, and he was greatly insulted at the weeding and slashing down of dandelions that took place.

'The Bishop likes flowers,' Father Gunn said sadly.

'Let him bring his own bunch of them to wear with his frock then,' said Mattie the postman, the one man in Shancarrig foolhardy enough to say publicly that he did not believe in God and wouldn't therefore be hypocritical enough to attend mass, or the sacraments.

'Mattie, this is not the time to get me into a theological discussion,' implored Father Gunn.

7

'We'll have it whenever you're feeling yourself again, Father.' Mattie was unfailingly courteous and rather too patronising for Father Gunn's liking.

But he had a good heart. He transported clumps of flowers from Barna Woods and planted them in the station beds. 'Tell Jack they grew when the earth was disturbed,' he advised. He had correctly judged the stationmaster to be unsound about nature and uninterested in gardening.

'I think the place is perfectly all right,' Jack Kerr was heard to grumble as they all stood waiting for the Bishop's train. He looked around his transformed railway station and saw nothing different.

The Bishop emerged from the train gracefully. He was shaped like an S hook, Father Gunn thought sadly. He was graceful, straightening or bending as he talked to each person. He was extraordinarily gracious, he didn't fuss or fumble, he remembered everyone's name, unlike Father Gunn who had immediately forgotten the names of the two self-important clerics who accompanied the Bishop.

Some of the younger children, dressed in the little white surplices of altar boys, stood ready to lead the procession up the town.

The sun shone mercilessly. Father Gunn had prayed unsuccessfully for one of the wet summer days they had been having recently. Even that would be better than this oppressive heat.

The Bishop seemed interested in everything he saw. They left the station and walked the narrow road to what might be called the centre of town had Shancarrig been a larger place. They paused at the Church of the Holy Redeemer for His Grace to say a silent prayer at the foot of the altar. Then they walked past the bus stop, the little line of shops, Ryan's Commercial Hotel and The Terrace where the doctor, the solicitor and other people of importance lived.

The Bishop seemed to nod approvingly when places looked well, and to frown slightly as he passed the poorer cottages. But perhaps that was all in Father Gunn's mind. Maybe His Grace was unaware of his surroundings and was merely saying his prayers. As they walked along Father Gunn was only too conscious of the smell from the River Grane, low and muddy. As they crossed the bridge he saw out of the corner of his eye a few faces at the window of Johnny Finn Noted for Best Drinks. He prayed they wouldn't find it necessary to open the window.

Mattie the postman sat laconically on an upturned barrel. He was one of the only spectators since almost every other citizen of Shancarrig was waiting at the school.

The Bishop stretched out his hand very slightly as if offering his ring to be kissed.

Mattie inclined his head very slightly and touched his cap. The gesture was not offensive, but neither was it exactly respectful. If the Bishop understood it he said nothing. He smiled to the right and the left, his thin aristocratic face impervious to the heat. Father Gunn's face was a red round puddle of sweat.

The first sign of the schoolhouse was the huge ancient beech tree, a copper beech that shaded the playground. Then you saw the little stone schoolhouse that had been built at the turn of the century. The dedication ceremony had been carefully written out in advance and scrutinised by these bureaucratic clerics who seemed to swarm around the Bishop. They had checked every word in case Father Gunn might have included a major heresy or sacrilege. The purpose of it all was to consecrate the school, and the future of all the young people it would educate, to God in this Holy Year. Father Gunn failed to understand why this should be considered some kind of doctrinal minefield. All he was trying to do was to involve the community at the right level, to make them see that their children were their hope and their future.

For almost three months the event had been heralded from the altar at mass. And the pious hope expressed that the whole village would be present for the prayers and the dedication. The prayers, hymns and short discourse should take forty-five minutes, and then there would be an hour for tea.

As they plodded up the hill Father Gunn saw that everything was in place.

A crowd of almost two hundred people stood around the school yard. Some of the men leaned against the school walls but the women stood chatting to each other. They were dressed in their Sunday best. The group would part to let the little procession through and then the Bishop would see the children of Shancarrig.

All neat and shining – he had been on a tour of inspection already this morning. There wasn't a hair out of place, a dirty nose or a bare foot to be seen. Even the Brennans and the Dunnes had been made respectable. They stood, all forty-eight of them, outside the school. They were in six rows of eight; those at the back were on benches so that they could be seen. They looked like little angels, Father Gunn thought. It was always a great surprise the difference a little cleaning and polishing could make.

Father Gunn relaxed, they were nearly there. Only a few more moments then the ceremony would begin. It would be all right after all.

The school looked magnificent. Not even Mrs Kennedy could have complained about its appearance, Father Gunn thought. And the tables were arranged under the spreading shade of the copper beech.

The master and the mistress had the children beautifully arranged, great emphasis having been laid on looking neat and tidy. Father Gunn began to relax a little. This was as fine a gathering as the Bishop would find anywhere in the diocese.

The ceremony went like clockwork. The chair for Monsignor O'Toole, the elderly parish priest, was discreetly placed. The singing, if not strictly tuneful, was at least in the right area. No huge discordancies were evident.

It was almost time for tea – the most splendid tea that had ever been served in Shancarrig. All the eatables were kept inside the school building, out of the heat and away from the flies. When the last notes of the last hymn died away Mr and Mrs Kelly withdrew indoors.

There was something about the set line of Mrs Kennedy's face that made Father Gunn decide to go and help them. He couldn't bear it if a tray of sandwiches fell to the ground or the cream slid from the top of a trifle. Quietly he moved in, to find a scene of total confusion. Mr and Mrs Kelly and Mrs Barton, who had offered to help with carrying plates to tables, stood frozen in a tableau, their faces expressing different degrees of horror.

'What is it?' he asked, barely able to speak.

'Every single queen cake!' Mrs Kelly held up what looked from the top a perfectly acceptable tea cake with white icing on it, but underneath the sign of tooth marks showed that the innards had been eaten away.

'And the chocolate cake!' gasped Una Barton, who was white as a sheet. The front of the big cake as you saw it looked delectable, but the back had been propped up with a piece of bark, a good third of the cake having been eaten away.

'It's the same with the apple tarts!' Mrs Kelly's tears were now openly flowing down her cheeks. 'Some of the children, I suppose.'

'That Foxy Dunne and his gang! I should have known. I should have bloody known.' Jim Kelly's face was working itself into a terrible anger.

'How did he get in?'

'The little bastard said he'd help with the chairs, brought a whole gang in with him. I said to him, "All those cakes are counted very carefully." And I did bloody count them when they went out.'

'Stop saying bloody and bastard to Father Gunn,' said Nora Kelly.

'I think it's called for.' Father Gunn was grim.

'If only they could have just eaten half a dozen. They've wrecked the whole thing.'

'Maybe I shouldn't have gone on about counting them.' Jim Kelly's big face was full of regret.

'It's all ruined,' Mrs Barton said. 'It's ruined.' Her voice held the high tinge of hysteria that Father Gunn needed to bring him to his senses.

'Of course it's not ruined. Mrs Barton, get the teapots out, call Mrs Kennedy to help you. She's wonderful at pouring tea and she'd like to be invited. Get Conor Ryan from the hotel to start pouring the lemonade and send Dr Jims in here to me quick as lightning.'

His words were so firm that Mrs Barton was out the door in a flash. Through the small window he saw the tea pouring begin and Conor Ryan happy to be doing something he was familiar with, pouring the lemonade.

The doctor arrived, worried in case someone had been taken ill.

'It's your surgical skills we need, Doctor. You take one knife, I'll take another and we'll cut up all these cakes and put out a small selection.'

'In the name of God, Father Gunn, what do you want to do that for?' asked the doctor.

'Because these lighting devils that go by the wrong name of innocent children have torn most of the cakes apart with their teeth,' said Father Gunn.

Triumphantly they arrived out with the plates full of cake selections.

'Plenty more where that came from!' Father Gunn beamed as he pressed the assortments into their hands. Since most people might not have felt bold enough to choose such a wide selection they were pleased rather than distressed to see so much coming their way.

Out of the corner of his mouth Father Gunn kept asking Mr Kelly, the master, for the names of those likely to have been involved. He kept repeating them to himself, as someone might repeat the names of tribal leaders who had brought havoc and destruction on his ancestors. Smiling as he served people and bustled to and fro, he repeated as an incantation – 'Leo Murphy, Eddie Barton, Niall Hayes, Maura Brennan, Nessa Ryan, and Foxy Bloody Dunne.'

He saw that Mattie the postman had consented to join the gathering, and was dangerously near the Bishop.

'Willing to eat the food of the Opium of the People, I see,' he hissed out of the corner of his mouth.

'That's a bit harsh from you, Father,' Mattie said, halfway through a plate of cake.

'Speak to the Bishop on any subject whatsoever and you'll never deliver a letter in this parish again,' Father Gunn warned.

The gathering was nearing its end. Soon it would be time to return to the station.

This time the journey would be made by car. Dr Jims and Mr Hayes, the solicitor, would drive the Bishop and the two clerics, whose names had never been ascertained.

Father Gunn assembled the criminals together in the school. 'Correct me if I have made an error in identifying any of the most evil people it has ever been my misfortune to meet,' he said in a terrible tone.

Their faces told him that his information had been mainly correct.

'Well?' he thundered.

'Niall wasn't in on it,' Leo Murphy said. She was a small wiry ten-year-old with red hair. She came from The Glen, the big house on the hill. She could have had cake for tea seven days a week.

'I did have a bit, though,' Niall Hayes said.

'Mr Kelly is a man with large hands. He has declared his intention of using them to break your necks, one after the other. I told him that I would check with the Vatican, but I was sure he would get absolution. Maybe even a *medal.*' Father Gunn roared the last word. They all jumped back in fright. 'However, I told Mr Kelly not to waste the Holy Father's time with all these dispensations and pardons, instead I would handle it. I told him that you had all volunteered to wash every dish and plate and cup and glass. That it was your contribution. That you would pick up every single piece of litter that has fallen around the school. That you would come to report to Mr and Mrs Kelly when it is all completed.'

They looked at each other in dismay. This was a long job. This was something that the ladies of the parish might have been expected to do.

'What about people like Mrs Kennedy? Wouldn't they want to . . . ?' Foxy began.

'No, they wouldn't want to, and people like Mrs Kennedy are *delighted* to know that you volunteered to do this. Because those kinds of people haven't seen into your black souls.'

There was silence.

'This day will never be forgotten. I want you to know that. When other bad deeds are hard to remember this one will always be to the forefront of the mind. This June day in 1950 will be etched there for ever.' He could see that Eddie Barton's and Maura Brennan's faces were beginning to pucker; he mustn't frighten them to death. 'So now. You will join the guard of honour to say farewell to the Bishop, to wave goodbye with your hypocritical hearts to His Grace whose visit you did your best to undermine and destroy. *Out.*' He glared at them. '*Out* this minute.'

Outside, the Bishop's party was about to depart. Gracefully he was moving from person to person, thanking them, praising them, admiring the lovely rural part of Ireland they lived in, saying that it did the heart good to get out to see God's beautiful nature from time to time rather than being always in a bishop's palace in a city.

'What a wonderful tree this is, and what great shade it gave us today.' He looked up at the copper beech as if to thank it, although it was obvious that he was the kind of man who could stand for hours in the Sahara desert without noticing anything amiss in the climate. It was the boiling Father Gunn who owed thanks to the leafy shade.

'And what's all this writing on the trunk?' He peered at it, his face alive with its well-bred interest and curiosity. Father Gunn heard the Kellys' intake of breath. This was the tree where the children always inscribed their initials, complete with hearts and messages saying who was loved by whom. Too secular, too racy, too sexual to be admired by a bishop. Possibly even a hint of vandalism about it.

But no.

The Bishop seemed by some miracle to be admiring it.

'It's good to see the children mark their being here and leaving here,' he said to the group who stood around straining for his last words. 'Like this tree has been here for decades, maybe even centuries back, so will there always be a school in Shancarrig to open the minds of its children and to send them out into the world.'

He looked back lingeringly at the little stone schoolhouse and the huge tree as the car swept him down the hill and towards the station. As Father Gunn got into the second car to follow him and make the final farewells at the station he turned to look once more at the criminals. Because his heart was big and the day hadn't been ruined he gave them half a smile. They didn't dare to believe it.

MADDY

When Madeleine Ross was brought to the church in Shancarrig to be baptised she wore an old christening robe that had belonged to her grandmother. Such lace was rarely seen in the Church of the Holy Redeemer – it would have been more at home in St Matthew's parish church, the ivy-covered Protestant church eleven miles away. But this was 1932, the year of the Eucharistic Congress in Ireland. Catholic fervour was at its highest and everyone would expect fine lace on a baby who was being christened.

The old priest did say to someone that this was a baby girl not likely to be lacking in anything, considering the life she was born into.

But parish priests don't know everything.

Madeleine's father died when she was eight. He was killed in the War. Her only brother went out to Rhodesia to live with an uncle who had a farm the size of Munster.

When Maddy Ross was eighteen years old in 1950 there were a great many things lacking in her life: like any plan of what she was going to do – like any freedom to go away and do it.

Her mother needed somebody at home and her brother had gone, so Maddy would be the one to stay.

Maddy also thought she needed a man friend, but Shancarrig was not the place to find one.

It wasn't even a question of being a big fish in a small pond. The Ross family were not rich landowners – people of class and distinction. If they had been then there might have been some society that Maddy could have moved in and hunted for a husband.

It was a matter of such fine degree.

Maddy and her mother were both too well off and not well enough off to fit into the pattern of small-town life. It was fortunate for Maddy that she was a girl who liked her own company, since so little of anyone else's company was offered to her.

Or perhaps she became this way because of circumstances.

But ever since she was a child people remembered her gathering armfuls of bluebells all on her own in the Barna Woods, or bringing home funny-shaped stones from around the big rock of Shancarrig.

The Rosses had a small house on the bank of the River Grane, not near the rundown cottages, but further on towards Barna Woods which led up to the Old Rock. Almost anywhere you walked from Maddy Ross's house was full of interest, whether it was up a side road to the school, or past the cottages to the bridge and into the heart of town, where The Terrace, Ryan's Commercial Hotel and the row of shops all stood. But her favourite walk was to head out through the woods, which changed so much in each season they were like different woods altogether. She loved them most in autumn when everything was golden, when the ground was a carpet of leaves.

You could imagine the trees were people, kind big people about to embrace you with their branches, or that there was a world of tiny people living in the roots, people who couldn't really be seen by humans.

She would tell stories, half wanting to be listened to and half to herself – stories about where she found golden and scarlet branches in autumn and the eyes of an old woman watching her through the trees, or of how children in bare feet played by the big rock that overlooked the town and ran away when anyone approached.

They were harmless stories, the Imaginary Friend stories of all children. Nobody took any notice, especially since it all died down when she went off to boarding school at the age of eleven. Shancarrig school was much too rough a place for little Madeleine Ross. She was sent to a convent two counties away.

Then they saw her growing up, her long pale hair in plaits hanging down her back and when she got to seventeen the plaits were wound around her head.

She was slim and willowy like her mother but she had these curious pale eyes. Had Maddy had good strong eyes of any colour she would have been beautiful. The lightness somehow gave her a colourless quality, a wispy appearance, as if she wasn't a proper person.

And if anyone in Shancarrig had thought much about her they might have come to the conclusion that she was a weak girl who had few views of her own.

A more determined young woman might have made a decision about finding work for herself, or friends. No matter how complex the social structure of Shancarrig you'd have thought that young Maddy Ross would have had some friends.

There were cousins of course, aunts and uncles to visit. Maddy and her mother went to see families in four counties, always her mother's relations. Her father's people lived in England.

But at home she was really only on the fringe of things. Like the day they had the dedication of the school, the day the Bishop came.

Maddy Ross stood on the edge with her straw sunhat to keep the rays of the sun from her fair skin. She watched Father Gunn bowing his way up the hill towards the school. She watched the elderly Monsignor O'Toole in his wheelchair. But she stood slightly apart from the rest of Shancarrig as they waited for the procession to arrive.

The Kellys with their little niece Maria, all of them dressed to kill. Nora Kelly should have worn a hat like Maddy had, not a hopeless lank mantilla that made her look out of place in the Irish countryside.

Still it would be nice to belong somewhere, like the Kellys did. They had come to that school and made it their own. They were the centre of the community now while Maddy, who had lived here all her life, was still on the outside.

She accepted her plate of cakes, all served for some reason sliced and on a plate, rather than letting people choose what they wished.

Mrs Kelly looked at her speculatively.

'I think the time has come to get a JAM,' she said.

Maddy was mystified. 'I hardly think you need any more,' she said, looking at her plate.

'A Junior Assistant Mistress,' Mrs Kelly explained, as if to a five-year-old.

'Oh, sorry.'

'Well, do you think we should talk to your mother about it?'

Maddy began to wonder was the heat affecting all of them.

'I ... think she's a bit set in her ways now ... she mightn't be able to teach,' she explained kindly.

'I meant you, Miss Ross.'

'Oh. Of course. Yes, well ...' Maddy said.

It proved how little she must have been planning her life. She had *no* immediate plans.

There had been much talk that year of visiting Rome. It was the Holy Year. It would be a special time. Aunty Peggy had been, the pictures were endless, the stories often repeated, the lack of good strong tea regretted over and over.

But Mother could never make up her mind about little things like whether to have strawberry jam or gooseberry jam for tea, so how could she make up her mind about something huge like a visit to Rome? The autumn came, the evenings started to get cooler, and everyone agreed that there would be grave danger of catching a chill.

It was just as well they hadn't gone to all the trouble of getting passports and booking tickets. And as Mother often said, you could love God just as well from Shancarrig as you could from a city in Italy.

Maddy Ross had been disappointed at first when the often discussed plans looked as if they were coming to nothing. But then she didn't think about it any more. She was good at putting disappointments behind her, there had been many of them even by the time she was eighteen.

Her best friend at school, Kathleen White, hadn't even told Maddy when she decided to enter the convent and become a nun. Everyone else in the school knew first. Maddy had been shaking with emotion when she challenged Kathleen with the news.

Kathleen had become unhealthily calm, too serene for her own good.

'I didn't tell you because you're so intense about everything,' Kathleen said simply. 'You'd either have wanted to join with me or you'd have been too dramatic about it. It's just what I want to do. That's all.'

Maddy decided to forgive Kathleen after a while. After all, a Vocation was a huge step. Obviously Kathleen had too much on her mind to care about the sensibilities of her friend. Maddy wrote her long letters forgiving her and talking about the commitment to religious life. Kathleen had written one short note. In two months' time she would be a postulant at the convent. She could neither write nor receive letters then. Perhaps it would be better to get ready for that by not beginning a very emotional correspondence now.

And there had been other disappointments that summer. At the tennis club dance Maddy had thought she looked well and that a young man had admired her. He had danced with her for longer than anyone else. He had been particularly attentive about glasses of fruit punch. They had sat in the swinging seat and talked easily about every subject. But nothing had come of it. She had gone to great trouble to let him know where she lived and even found two occasions to call at his house. But it was as if she had never existed.

Sometimes when Maddy Ross went for her long lonely walks up the tree-covered hill to the Old Rock that stood guarding the town she felt that she handled everything wrong. It was all so different to things that happened to girls in the pictures.

Maddy had always known that there wouldn't be the money to send her to university, so she had thought it just as well that she didn't have any burning desire to be a professor, or a doctor or lawyer. But there was nothing else that fired her either. Other girls had gone to train as nurses, some of them had done secretarial courses and gone into the bank or big insurance offices. There were others who went to be radiographers, or physiotherapists.

Maddy, the girl with the long pale hair and the slow smile that went all over her face once it began, thought that sooner or later something would turn up.

Probably at the end of the holidays.

Mrs Kelly had been serious on that hot day, and in the very first week of September Mr and Mrs Kelly from the school came to see Mother.

Shancarrig's small stone schoolhouse was a little way out of the town. That was to make it easier for the children of the farmers, it had been said. Mr and Mrs Kelly had come as newly marrieds to the school in answer to Father Gunn's appeal. The last teachers had left in some disarray. Maddy had heard stories about drinking and dismissals, but as usual, only a very edited version of events, filtered through her mother. Mother never seemed to grasp the full end of any stick.

Mr and Mrs Kelly were a strange couple. He was big and innocent-looking, like a farmer's boy. She was small and taut-looking, her mouth often in a narrow line of disapproval.

Maddy Ross had looked at her more than once, wondering what it was about Mrs Kelly that had attracted the big, simple, good-natured man by her side. They were only about ten years older than she was.

She wondered if Mrs Kelly had looked about her and then, finding nobody more suitable, settled for the teacher. She certainly looked as if something had displeased her. Even when they came uninvited to see Mother they both looked as if they were going to issue some complaint.

Maddy found nothing odd about their asking Mother rather than asking her. After all, it was the kind of thing Mrs Ross would have a view on. Perhaps she thought her daughter Madeleine was intended for something more elevated than working in Shancarrig school. It was better to sound out the opinions before making a direct approach.

But Mother thought it would be an excellent idea. 'Fallen straight into their laps' was the way she described it when the cousins came to supper the following day.

'And won't Madeleine need to be trained to teach?' the cousins asked.

'Nonsense,' said Mother. 'What training would anyone need to put manners on unfortunates like the young Brennans or the young Dunnes?'

They agreed. It wasn't a real career like the cousins' children were embarking on: one in a bank, one doing a very advanced secretarial course, with Commercial French thrown in, which could lead to any kind of a position almost anywhere in the world.

To her surprise Maddy loved it.

She had neither the roar of Mr Kelly nor the confident firm voice of his wife. She spoke gently and almost hesitantly but the children responded to her. Even the bold Brennan children, whose father was Paudie Brennan, drunk and layabout, seemed easy to handle. And the Dunnes, whose faces were smeared with jam, agreed quite meekly to having their mouths wiped before class began.

There were three classsrooms in the little schoolhouse, one for Mrs Kelly's class, one for Mr Kelly's, and the biggest one for Maddy Ross. It was called Mixed Infants and it was here that she started the young minds of Shancarrig off on what might be a limited kind of educational journey. There would be some, of course, who would advance to a far greater education than she had herself. The young Hayes girls, whose father was a solicitor, might well get professions, as might little Nuala Ryan from the hotel. But it was only too obvious that the Dunnes and Brennans would say goodbye to any hopes of education once they left this school. They would be on the boat abroad or into the town to get whatever was on offer for children of fourteen years of age.

They all looked the same at five, however. There was nothing except the difference of clothing to mark out those who would have the money to go further and those who would not.

Before she had gone into the school Maddy Ross barely noticed the children of her own place. Now she knew everything about them, the ones that sniffled and seemed upset, the ones who thought they could run the place, those that had the doorsteps of sandwiches for their lunch, those who had nothing at all. There were children who clung to her and told her everything about themselves and their families, and there were those who hung back.

She had never known that there would be a great joy in seeing a child work out for himself the letters of a simple sentence and read it aloud, or in watching a girl who had bitten her pencil to a stub suddenly realise how you did the great long tots or the subtraction sums. Each day it was a pleasure to point to the map of Ireland with a long stick and hear them chant the places out.

'What are the main towns of County Cavan? All right. All together now. Cavan, Cootehill, Virginia ...' all in a sing-song voice.

There were two cloakrooms, one for the girls and one for the boys. They smelled of Jeyes Fluid, as the master obviously poured it liberally in the evenings when the children had left.

It would have been a bleak little place had it not been for the huge copper beech which dwarfed it and looked as if it was holding the school under its protective arm. Like she felt safe in Barna Woods as a child, Maddy felt safe with this tree. It marked the seasons with its colouring and its leaves.

The days passed easily, each one very much like that which had gone before. Madeleine Ross made big cardboard charts to entertain the children. She had pictures of the flowers she collected in Barna Woods, and she sometimes pressed the flowers as well and wrote their names underneath. Every day the children in Shancarrig school sat in their little wooden desks and repeated the names of the ferns, and foxgloves, cowslips and primroses and ivies. Then they would look at the pictures of St Patrick and St Brigid and St Colmcille and chant their names too.

Maddy made sure that they remembered the saints as well as the flowers.

The saints were higher on Father Gunn's list of priorities. Father Gunn was a very nice curate. He had little whirly glasses, like looking through the bottom of a lemonade bottle. Now the school manager he was a frequent visitor – he had to guard the faith and morals of the future parishioners of Shancarrig. But Father Gunn liked flowers and trees too, and he was always kind and supportive to the Junior Assistant Mistress.

Maddy wondered how old he was. With priests, as with nuns, it was always so hard to know. One day he unexpectedly told her how old he was. He said he was born on the day the Treaty was signed in 1921.

'I'm as old as the State,' he said proudly. 'I hope we'll both live for ever.'

'It's good to hear you saying that, Father.' Maddy was arranging a nature display in the window. 'It shows you enjoy life. Mother is always saying that she can't get her wings soon enough.'

'Wings!' The priest was puzzled.

'It's her way of saying she'd like to be in heaven with God. She talks about it quite a lot.'

Father Gunn seemed at a loss for words. 'It's wholly admirable, of course, to see this world only as a shadow of the heavenly bliss Our Father has prepared for us but ...'

'But Mother's only just gone fifty. It's a bit soon to be thinking about it already, isn't it?' Maddy helped him out.

He nodded gratefully, 'Of course, I'm getting on myself. Maybe I'll start thinking the same way.' His voice was jokey. 'But I have so much to do I don't feel old.'

'You should have someone to help you.' Maddy said only what everyone else in Shancarrig said. The old priest was doddery now. Father Gunn did everything. They definitely needed a new curate.

And it wasn't as if the priests' housekeeper was any help. Mrs Kennedy had a face like a long drink of water. She was dressed in black most of the time, mourning for a husband who had died so long ago hardly anyone in Shancarrig could remember him. A good priests' housekeeper should surely be kind and supportive, fill the role of mother, old family retainer and friend.

It had to be said that Mrs Kennedy played none of these roles. She seemed to smoulder in resentment that she herself had not been given charge of the parish. She snorted derisively when anyone offered to help out in the parish work. It was a tribute to Father Gunn's own niceness that so many people stepped in to help with the problems caused by Monsignor O'Toole being almost out of the picture, and Mrs Kennedy being almost too much in it.

Then the news came that there was indeed a new priest on the way to Shancarrig. Someone knew someone in Dublin who had been told definitely. He was meant to be a very nice man altogether.

About six months later, in the spring of 1952, the new curate arrived. He was a pale young man called Father Barry. He had long delicate white hands, light fair hair and dark, startling blue eyes. He moved gracefully around Shancarrig, his soutane swishing gently from side to side. He had none of the bustle of Father Gunn, who always seemed uneasily belted into his priestly garb and distinctly ill at ease in the vestments.

When Father Barry said mass a shaft of sunlight seemed to come in and touch his pale face, making him look more saintly than ever. The people of Shancarrig loved Father Barry and in her heart Maddy Ross often felt a little sorry for Father Gunn, who had somehow been overshadowed.

It wasn't *his* fault that he looked burly and solid. He was just as good and attentive to the old and the feeble, just as understanding in Confession, just as involved in the school. And yet she had to admit that Father Barry brought with him some new sense of exhilaration that the first priest didn't have.

When Father Barry came to her classroom and spoke he didn't talk vaguely about the missions and the need to save stamps and silver paper for mission stations, he talked of hill villages in Peru where the people ached to hear of Our Lord, where there was only one small river and that dried up during the dry seasons, leaving the villagers to walk for miles over the hot dry land to get water for the old and for their babies.

As they sat in the damp little schoolhouse in Shancarrig, Maddy and Mixed Infants were transported miles away to another continent. The Brennans had broken shoes and torn clothes, they even bore the marks of a drunken father's fist, but they felt rich beyond the dreams of kings compared to the people in Vieja Piedra, thousands of miles away.

The very name of this village was the same as their own. It meant Old Rock. The people in this village were crying out to them across the world for help.

Father Barry fired the children with an enthusiasm never before known in that school. And it wasn't only in Maddy Ross's class. Even under the sterner eye of Mrs Kelly, who might have been expected to say that we should look after our own first before going abroad to give help, the collections increased. And in Mr Kelly's class the fierce master echoed the words of the young priest, but in his own way.

'Come out of that, Jeremiah O'Connor. You'll want your arse kicked from here to Barna and back if you can't go out and raise a shilling for the poor people of Vieja Piedra.'

When he gave the Sunday sermon Father Barry often closed his disturbing blue eyes and spoke of how fortunate his congregation were to live in the green fertile lands around Shancarrig. The church might be full of people sneezing and coughing, wearing coats wet from the trek across three miles of road and field to get there, but Father Barry made their place sound like a paradise compared to its namesake in Peru.

Some of them began to wonder why a loving God had been so unjust to the good Spanish-speaking people in that part of the world, who would have done anything to have a church and priests in their midst.

Father Barry had an answer for that whenever the matter was raised. He said it was God's plan to test men's love and goodness for each other. It was easy to love God, Father Barry assured everyone. Nobody had any problem in loving Our Heavenly Father. The problem was to love people in a small lonely village miles away and treat them as brothers and sisters.

Maddy and her mother often talked about Father Barry and his saintliness. It was something they both agreed on, which meant they talked about him more than ever. There were so many subjects which divided them.

Maddy wondered would there be the chance for them to go out to Rhodesia to Joseph's wedding. Her brother was marrying a girl from a Scottish family in Bulawayo. There would be nobody from the Ross side of the family. He had sent the money, and the wedding was during the school holidays, but Mrs Ross said she wasn't up to the journey. Dr Jims had said that Maddy's mother was fit as a fiddle and well able to make the trip. In fact, the sea journey would do nothing except improve her health.

Father Gunn had said that family solidarity would be a great thing at a time like this and that truly she should make the effort. Major and Mrs Murphy who lived in The Glen, the big house with the iron railings and the wonderful glasshouses, said that it was a chance of a lifetime. Mr Hayes the solicitor said that if it was his choice he'd go.

But Mother remained adamant. It was a waste, she said, to spend the money on a trip for such an old person as she was. She would soon be getting her wings. She would see enough and know enough then.

Maddy was becoming increasingly impatient with this attitude of her mother's. The wings theory seemed to apply to everything. If Maddy wanted a new coat, or a trip to Dublin, or a perm for her light straight hair, her mother would sigh and say there would be plenty of time for that and money to spend on it after Mother had gone.

Mother was in her fifties and as strong as anyone in Shancarrig, but giving the aura of frailty. Maddy did the housework, because until Mother had got her wings there would be no money to spend on luxuries like having a maid. Maddy's own wages as a Junior Assistant Mistress were so small as to be insignificant.

She was twenty-three and very restless.

The only person in the whole of Shancarrig who understood was Father Barry. He was thirty-three and equally restless. He had been called to order for preaching too much about Vieja Piedra, by no less an authority than the Bishop. He burned with the injustice of it. Monsignor O'Toole was doting, and knew nothing of what was being preached or what was not. Father Gunn must have gone behind his back and complained about him. Father Gunn was only a fellow curate, he had no authority over him.

Father Brian Barry roamed the woods of Barna, swishing angrily against the bushes that got in his way. What right had men, the pettiest and most jealous of men, to try to halt God's work for dying people, for brothers and sisters who were calling out to them?

If Brian Barry's own health had been better he would have been a missionary priest. He would have been amongst the people of Vieja Piedra, like his friend from the seminary, Cormac Flynn, was. Cormac it was who wrote and told him at first hand of the work that had to be done.

In the Church of the Holy Redeemer there was a window dedicated to the memory of the Hayes family relations who had gone to their eternal reward. There had been many priests in that family. On the window the words were written *The Harvest is Great but the Labourers are Few*. There it was, written in stained glass, in their own church, and the mad parish priest and the selfish complacent Father Gunn were so blind they couldn't see it.

In one of these angry walks Father Barry came across Miss Ross from the school, sitting on a tree trunk and puzzling over a letter. He calmed himself for a minute before he spoke. She was a gentle girl and he didn't want to let her know the depth of his rage and resentment in the battle for people's souls, and all the obstacles that were being put in his way.

She looked up startled when she saw him, but made room on the log for him to sit down.

'Isn't it beautiful here? You can often find a solution in this place, I think.'

He reached through the slit in his cassock to take cigarettes out of his pocket and sat beside her without speaking.

Somehow, she seemed to understand the need for silence. She sat, hugging her knees and looking out ahead of her, as the summer afternoon light came in patches between the rowan trees and beeches that made up Barna Woods. A squirrel came and gazed at them, inquisitively looking from one to the other before he hopped away.

They laughed. The tension and the silence broken, they could talk to each other easily.

'When I was young I'd never seen a squirrel,' Father Barry said. 'Only in picture books, and there was a giraffe on the same page so I always thought they were the same size. I was terrified of meeting one.'

'When did you?'

'Not until I was in the seminary ... someone said there was a squirrel over there and I urged everyone to take cover ... they thought I was mad.'

'Well, that's nothing,' she encouraged him. 'I thought guerrilla warfare was sending gorillas out to fight each other instead of people.'

'You're saying that to make me feel good,' he teased her.

'Not a bit of it. Did they all laugh or didn't any of them understand?'

'I had a friend, Cormac. He understood. He understood everything.'

'That's Father Cormac out in Peru?'

'Yes. He understood everything. But how can I tell him what's happening now?'

As the shadows got longer they sat in Barna Woods and talked. Brian Barry told of his anguish over the work that had to be done and the burden of guilt he felt about the people of this place that seemed to call to him, but what did he do about Obedience to superiors? Maddy Ross told of her brother Joseph who had sent money and expected his mother and sister to come and be there for the happiest day of his life.

'How can I find the words to tell him?' Maddy asked.

'How can I find the words to tell Cormac there'll be no more support from Shancarrig?' asked Father Barry.

That was the day that began their dependence on each other – the knowledge that only the other understood the pressures, the pain and the indecision. The very thought that somebody else understood gave each of them courage.

Maddy Ross found herself able to write to her brother Joseph and say that she would love to come to his wedding, but that Mother did not consider herself strong enough to travel. It meant a lot of silences and sulks at home, but Maddy weathered it. She assembled a simple wardrobe and made her bookings.

Eventually her mother relented and began to show some enthusiasm for the trip. She didn't take this enthusiasm to the point of going with her daughter, but at least the stony silences ended and the atmosphere had cleared.

Father Barry too showed courage. He spoke directly to Father Gunn, and said that he accepted the ruling of the diocese that there was not to be exceptional emphasis on the missions in general or on one mission field in particular. He agreed that other themes such as tolerance and charity on the home front and devotion to Our Blessed Lady, Queen of Ireland, be brought to the forefront.

He also said that in his spare time, if he could run sales of work, he could set up charitable projects in aid of Vieja Piedra. He felt sure that there could be no objection. To this Father Gunn, with a sigh of pure relief, said that there would no objection.

In the summer of 1955 Maddy Ross and Brian Barry wished each other well, she on her journey to Africa, he on his fund-raising efforts so that Cormac Flynn would not be let down. When they met again in the autumn they would tell each other everything.

'We'll meet in the woods with the giant squirrels,' said Father Barry.

'Watching out for the military gorillas,' laughed Maddy Ross.

They were both looking forward to the meeting even as they were saying goodbye.

They were very much changed when they met again. They knew this just from the briefest meeting in the church porch after ten o'clock mass. Father Barry was rearranging the pamphlets that the Catholic Truth Society published, which were in racks for sale, but were always mixed up whenever he passed them by. The problem was that everyone wanted to read 'The Devil at Dances' and 'Keeping Company', but nobody wanted to buy them. Copies of these booklets were always well thumbed and returned to some position or other.

He saw Madeleine come out with her mother. Mrs Ross spent a lengthy time at the holy water font, blessing herself as if she were giving the *Urbi et Orbi* blessing from the papal Balcony in Rome.

'Welcome back, stranger. Was it wonderful?' He smiled at her.

'No. It couldn't have gone more differently than was planned.'

They looked at each other, both surprised by the intense way the other had spoken. Father Barry looked over at Mrs Ross, still far enough away not to hear.

'Barna Woods,' he said, his eyes dark and huge.

'At four o'clock,' Maddy said.

She hadn't felt like this since gym class back at school, where they did the wall bars and all the blood ran to her head, making her feel dizzy and faint.

When she found herself deliberating over which blouse to wear she pulled herself up sharply. He's a priest, she said. But she still wore the striped one which gave her more colour and didn't make her look wishy-washy.

When her mother asked her where she was going, she said she wanted to pick the great fronds of beech leaves in Barna Woods. They could put them in glycerine later and preserve them to decorate the house for the winter.

'I'll look for some really good ones that have turned,' she explained. 'I might be some time.'

She found him sitting on their log with his head in his hands. He told of a summer where everything he had done for Vieja Piedra had been thwarted, not just by Father Gunn, who had turned up dutifully at the bring and buy sale, at the whist drive and the general knowledge quiz, but because the interest simply wasn't there. And since he could no longer use the parish pulpit to preach of the plight of these poor people he didn't have the ear and the heart of the congregation any more. His face was troubled. Maddy felt there was more he wasn't telling. She didn't push him. He would tell what he wanted to tell. Now he asked about her: had her brother Joseph been delighted to see her?

'Yes, and no.' Her brother's fiancée was of the Presbyterian faith and had only agreed to be married in a Catholic Church to please Joseph. Now that his mother wasn't coming to the wedding Joseph had decided that he shouldn't put Caitriona through all this since, really and truly as long as it was Christian, one service was the same as another in the eyes of God.

So Maddy had gone the whole way to Africa to see her brother commit a mortal sin. There had been endless arguments, discussions and tears on both their parts. Joseph said that since they hardly knew each other their tie as brother and sister was not like a real family. Maddy had asked why then had he paid for her to come out to see him.

30

'To show people that I am not alone in the world,' he had said.

Oh yes, she had attended the ceremony, and smiled, and been pleasant to all the guests. She had told her mother nothing of this. In fact, she was worn out remembering to call the priest Father McPherson rather than Mr McPherson, which was the name of the Presbyterian minister who had married the young couple, in a stiflingly hot church under a cloudless sky – a church with no tabernacle, and no proper God in it at all.

They walked together to find the kind of sprays she wanted. She explained that she had made a sort of excuse to her mother for going to the woods. Then she wished she hadn't said that – it might appear to him as if she needed an excuse for something so perfectly innocent as a meeting with a friend.

But, oddly, it struck a chord with him.

'I made an excuse too, to Father Gunn and Mrs Kennedy, of course. I told him that I wanted to make a couple of parish calls, the Dunnes and the Brennans. Both of them are sure to be out, or at any rate unlikely to invite me in.'

They looked at each other and looked away. A lot had been admitted.

Speaking too quickly she told him about how you preserved flowers and leaves, and how the trick was to put very few in a vase with a narrow opening.

Speaking equally quickly he nodded agreement and perfect understanding of the process, and said that parish calls were an imposition on the priest and the people, everyone dreaded them, and how much better it would be to spend our life in a place where people really needed you rather than worrying had they a clean tablecloth and a slice of cake to give you. His face looked very bitter and sad as he spoke and she felt such huge sympathy for him that she touched him lightly on the arm.

'You *do* a great deal of good here. If you knew how much you touch all our lives.'

To her shock his eyes filled with tears.

'Oh, Madeleine,' he cried. 'Oh God, I'm so lonely. I've no one to talk to, I've no friends. No one will listen.'

'Shush, shush.' She spoke as to a child. 'I'm your friend. I'll listen.'

He put his arms around her and laid his head on her shoulder. She felt arms around her waist and his body close to hers as he shook with sobs.

'I'm so sorry. I'm so foolish,' he wept.

31

'No. No, you're not. You're good. You care. You wouldn't be you unless you were so caring,' she soothed him. She stroked his head and the back of his neck. She could feel his tears wet against her face as he raised his head to try to apologise.

'Shush, shush,' she said again. She held him until the sobs died down. Then she took out her handkerchief, a small white one with a blue flower in the corner, and handed it to him.

They walked wordlessly to their tree trunk. He blew his nose very hard.

'I feel such a fool. I should be strong and courageous for you, Madeleine, tell you things that will console you about your brother's situation, not cry like a baby.'

'No, you *do* make me feel courageous and strong, really, Father Barry ...'

He interrupted her sharply. 'Now, listen here. If I'm going to cry in your arms, the least you can do is call me Brian.'

She accepted it immediately. 'Yes, but Brian, you must believe that you have helped me. I didn't think I was any use to anyone, a disappointment to my mother, no support to my brother ...'

'You must have friends. You of all people, so generous and giving. You're not locked up in rigid rules and practices like I am.'

'I have no friends,' Madeleine Ross said simply.

That afternoon there wasn't time to tell each other all the millions of things there were still to tell – like how Brian had a letter from his great friend Cormac Flynn in Peru saying for heaven's sake not to be so intense about Vieja Piedra, it was just one place on the globe – Father Brian Barry hadn't been born into the world thousands of miles away with a direct instruction to save the place single-handed.

Father Brian Barry had been more hurt than he could ever express by that letter. But when he told Maddy and she tumbled out her own information about Kathleen White and how she had begged Maddy, her friend, not to write to her so intensely, they saw it as one further common bond between them.

She learned about his childhood – his mother who had always wanted a son as a priest, but who had died a month before his ordination and never received his blessing.

He heard of life with a mother who was becoming increasingly irrational – of a life lived more and more in fantasy – in a world where her cousins were people of great wealth and high breeding – where all

32

kinds of niceties were important, the wearing of gloves, the owning of a coach and horses in the old days, the calling with visiting cards. None of it had any basis in reality, Maddy said, but Dr Jims said it was harmless. Lots of middle-aged women had notions and delusions of grandeur, and those harboured by Mrs Ross were no worse than a lot of people's, and better than most.

Their meetings had to be more and more conspiratorial. Maddy would stay late in the school, decorating her window displays. Father Barry would call with some information for the Kellys and happen to see her in the classroom. The door would be left open. He would sit on the teacher's desk, swinging his legs. If Mrs Kelly were to look in, and her anxious face seemed to look everywhere, then she would see nothing untoward.

But when they walked together in Barna Woods away from the eyes of the town they walked close together. Sometimes they would stop by chance at exactly the same time and she would lay her head companionably on his shoulder, and lean against him as they peeled the bark from a tree or looked at a bird's nest hidden in the branches.

Night after night Maddy lay alone in her narrow bed remembering that day he had cried and she had held him in the woods. She could remember the way his body shook and how she could feel his heart beat against her. She could bring back the smell of him, the smell of winegums and Gold Flake tobacco, of Knight's Castile soap. She could remember the way his hair had tickled her neck and how his tears had wet her cheeks. It was like seeing the same scene of a film over and over.

She wondered did he ever think of it, but supposed that would be foolishly romantic. And for Father Barry ... for Brian ... it might even be a sin.

Because of this new centre to her life Maddy Ross was able to do more than ever before. She could scarcely remember the days when the time had seemed long and hung heavily around her. Now there weren't enough hours in the week for all that had to be done. She had long back hired young Maura Brennan from the cottages, a solemn poor child who loved stroking the furniture, to do her ironing and that worked out very well. Now on a different day she got young Eddie Barton to come and do her garden for her.

Eddie was a funny little fellow of about fourteen, interested in plants and nature. He would often want to talk to her about the various things that grew in her garden.

33

'What do you spend the money on?' she asked him one day. He reddened. 'It doesn't matter. It's yours to spend any way you like.'

'Stamps,' he said eventually.

'That's nice. Have you a big collection?'

'No. To put on letters. Father Barry said we should have a pen-friend overseas,' he said.

It was wonderful to think how much good Father Barry was doing. Imagine a boy with wiry sticky-up hair like Eddie, a boy who would normally be kicking a ball up against a house wall, or writing messages on it, now had a Catholic pen-friend overseas. She gave him extra money that day.

'Tell him about Shancarrig, what a great place it is.'

'I do,' Eddie said simply. 'I write all about it.'

When Eddie got flu and his mother wouldn't let him out, Foxy Dunne offered to do the chore.

'I believe you're a great payer, Miss Ross,' he said cheerfully.

'You won't get as much as Eddie – you don't know which are flowers and which are weeds.' She was spirited and cheerful herself.

'Ah but you're a teacher, Miss Ross. It'd only take you a minute to show me.'

'Only till Eddie comes back,' she agreed.

By the time Eddie was better and came back to fume over the desecration he claimed Foxy had done in the garden, Foxy had got himself several odd jobs, mending doors, fixing locks on an outhouse. Her mother didn't like having one of the Dunnes around the place in case he was sizing it up for a job for himself or one of his brothers.

'Oh Mother! They shouldn't all be tarred with the same brush,' Maddy cried.

'You're nearly as unworldly as Father Barry himself,' said her mother.

There had once been a Dramatic Society in Shancarrig but it had fallen into inactivity. There was some vague story behind this, as there was behind everything. It had to do with the previous teacher having become very inebriated at a performance and some kind of unpleasantness was meant to have taken place. Nellie Dunne always said she could tell you a thing or two about the play-acting that went on in this town. It was play-acting in every sense of the word, she might say. But though she threatened she never in fact did tell anybody a thing or two about what had gone on; and whatever it was had gone on long

34

before Father Gunn had come to Shancarrig. And Monsignor O'Toole wasn't likely to remember it.

Maddy thought that very possibly the members of whatever it had been were sufficiently cooled to start again. She was surprised and pleased at the enthusiasm – Eddie Barton's mother said she'd help with the wardrobe; you always needed a professional to stop the thing looking like children playing charades. Biddy, the maid up at The Glen, said that if there was any call for a step dance she would be glad to oblige. It was a skill which her position didn't give her much chance to use, and she didn't want to get too rusty. Both Brian and Liam Dunne from the hardware store said they would join, and Carrie who looked after Dr Jims' little boy said she'd love to try out for a small part, but nothing with too many lines. Sergeant Keane and his wife both said it was the one thing they had been waiting for and the Sergeant pumped Maddy's hand up and down in gratitude.

So Maddy started the Shancarrig Dramatic Society and they were always very grateful for the kind interest that Father Barry took in their productions. Nobody thought it a bit odd that the saintly young priest with the sad face should throw himself whole-heartedly into anything that was for the parish good. And of course the proceeds went to the charity of the missions in South America. And it was just as well to have Father Barry, everyone agreed, laughing a little behind Father Gunn's back, because poor Father Gunn, in spite of his many other great qualities, didn't know one side of the stage from the other, while Father Barry could turn his hand to anything. He could design a set, arrange the lighting, and best of all, direct performances. He coaxed the townspeople of Shancarrig to play everything from *Pygmalion* to *Drama at Inish*, and the Christmas concerts were a legend.

Only Maddy knew how his heart wasn't in any of it.

Only she knew the real man, who hid his unhappiness. Soon she found she was thinking of him all the time, and imagining his reaction to the smallest and most inconsequential things she did. If she was telling the story of the Flight into Egypt to the Mixed Infants at school she imagined him leaning against the door smiling at her approvingly. Sometimes she smiled back as if he were really there. The children would look around to see if someone had come in.

Then at home, when she was preparing her mother's supper, she would decorate the plate with a garnish of finely sliced tomato, or chopped hard-boiled egg and fresh parsley. Her mother barely noticed, but she could see how Brian Barry would respond. She would put

35

words of praise in his mouth and say them to herself.

She spent her time in what she considered was a much more satisfactory relationship than anyone else around her. Mr and Mrs Kelly were locked in a routine marriage if ever she saw one. Poor Maura Brennan of the cottages, who married a flash harry of a barman, was left alone with her Down's syndrome child to rear. Major Murphy in The Glen had a marriage that defied description. They never went anywhere outside their four walls. In any other land they would have been called recluses, but here, because The Glen was the big house, they were admired for their sense of isolation.

There was nobody that Madeleine Ross envied. Nobody she knew had as dear and pure a love as she had known, a man who depended on her utterly and who would have been lost to his vocation if it had not been for her.

And then one night all of a sudden, when she least expected it, came a strange thought. It was one of those sleepless nights when the moon seemed unnaturally bright and visible even through the curtains, so it was easier to leave them open.

Maddy saw a figure walking past going to the woods. She thought first that it was Brian, and she was about to slip into some clothes and follow him. But then she saw at the last moment that it was Major Murphy, on goodness knew what kind of outing. It was easy to mistake them, tall men in dark clothes. But Brian was asleep in the presbytery, or possibly not asleep, maybe looking at the same moon and feeling the same restlessness.

That was when it came to Maddy Ross that Father Barry should leave Shancarrig.

He could no longer be wasted passing plates of sandwiches, rigging up old curtains, praising a tuneless choir, welcoming yet another bishop or visiting churchmen. There was only one life to be lived. He must go on and live it as best he could, serving the people of Vieja Piedra. The whole notion of there being only one life to live buzzed around in her head all night. There was no more sleep now. She sat hugging a mug of tea, remembering how her brother Joseph had said those very words to her, all that while ago when she had gone to Rhodesia for his wedding, about there being only one chance to live your life.

And Joseph, who had been given the same kind of education as she had had, and who came from the same parents, had been able to seize at the life he wanted. Joseph and Caitriona Ross had children out in

Africa. Sometimes they sent pictures of them outside their big white house with the pillars at the front door. Maddy had never told her mother that these little children weren't Catholics and might not even have been properly baptised. She and Brian had agreed that it was better not to trouble an already troubled mind with such information.

If Joseph Ross had only one life so had Maddy Ross and so had Brian Barry. Why couldn't Father Brian leave and go to South America? After a decent interval Maddy could leave too and be with him.

For part of the night as she paced the house she told herself that things need not change between them. They would be as they were here, true friends doing the work they felt was calling across the land and sea to them. And Brian could remain a priest. Once a priest always a priest. He wouldn't have to leave, just change the nature and scope of his vocation.

And then as dawn came up over Barna Woods Maddy Ross admitted to herself what she had been hiding. She acknowledged that she wanted Brian Barry to be her love, her husband. She wanted him to leave the priesthood. If he could get released from his vows by Rome so much the better. But even if he could not Maddy wanted him anyway. She would take him on any terms.

It was a curious freedom realising this.

She felt almost light-headed and at the same time she stopped playing games. She took her mother breakfast on a tray without fantasising what Brian would say if he had been standing beside them looking on. It was as if she had come out of the shadows, she thought, and into the real world.

She could barely wait to meet Brian. No day had ever seemed longer. Mrs Kelly had never been sharper or more inquisitive about everything Maddy was doing.

Why was she putting greetings on the blackboard in different languages? Spanish. And French, no less. Wasn't it enough for these boneheaded children to try and learn Irish and English like the Department laid down without filling their heads with how to say good day and goodbye in tongues they'd never need to use?

Maddy looked at her levelly. Normally, she would have seen Brian in her mind's eye standing by the blackboard, congratulating her on her patience and forbearance, and then the two of them wandering together in Barna Woods crying 'Buenos dias Vieja Piedra, we are coming to help you.'

But today she saw no shadowy figure. She saw only the small

quivering Mrs Kelly, who was wearing a brown and yellow striped dress and looked for all the world like a wasp.

Maddy Ross was a different person today.

'I'm putting some phrases in foreign languages on the blackboard, Mrs Kelly, because, despite what you and the Department of Education think, these children may well go to lands where they use them. And I shall put them on the blackboard every day until they feel a little bit of confidence about themselves instead of being humble and content to remain in Shancarrig pulling their caps and saying *good morning* in Irish and English until they are old men and women.'

Mrs Kelly went red and white in rapid succession.

'You'll do nothing of the sort, Miss Ross. Not in the timetable that is laid down for you.'

'I had no intention of doing it in school time, Mrs Kelly.' Maddy smiled a falsely sweet smile. 'I am in the fortunate position of being able to hold the children's interest *outside* school hours as well as when the bell rings. They will learn it before or after school. That will be clearly understood.'

She felt twenty feet tall. She felt as if she were elevated above the small stone schoolhouse and the town. She could hardly bear the slow noise of the clock ticking until she could go to Brian and tell him of her new courage, her hope and her belief that they had only one chance at life.

She met him at rehearsal under the eyes of the nosey people in town.

'How is your mother these days, Miss Ross?' he asked. It was part of their code. They had never practised it; it just came naturally to them, as so much else would now.

'She's fine, Father, always asking for you, of course.'

'I might drop in and see her later tonight, if you think she'd like that.'

'She'd love it, Father. I'll just let her know. I'm going out myself, but she'd be delighted to see you, like everyone.'

Her eyes danced with mischief as she said the words. She thought she saw the hint of a frown on Brian Barry's face, but it passed.

Miss Ross left the rehearsal and she imagined people thinking that she was a dutiful daughter, and very good also to the priest, to go home and prepare a little tray for her mother to offer him. As Maddy walked home, her cheeks burning, she thought that she had been a bloody good daughter for all her life, nearly thirty years of life in this small place. And come to think of it she had been good to the priest too. Good for him and a good friend.

Nobody could blame her for wanting her chance at life.

She sat in the wood and waited on their log. He came gently through the leafy paths. His smile was tired. Something had crossed him during the day; she knew him so very well, every little change, every flicker in his face.

'I'm late. I had to go into your mother's,' he said.

'What on earth for? You know I didn't mean ...'

'I know, but Father Gunn said to me, this very morning, that he thought I should see less of you.'

'What!'

Brian Barry was nervous and edgy. 'Oh, he said it very nicely of course, not an accusation, nothing you could take offence at ...'

'I most certainly do take offence at it,' Maddy blazed. 'How dare he insinuate that there has been anything improper between us. How *dare* he!'

'No, he didn't. He was very anxious that I should know he wasn't suggesting that.' He walked up and down as he talked, agitated, and anxious to get over the mildness of the message, the lack of blame and the motive behind it. It was just that Father Gunn wanted to protect them both from evil minds and idle wagging tongues. In a place this size when people had little real news to speculate about they made up their own. It would be better for Father Barry not to be seen so obviously sharing the same interests as Miss Ross, for both of them to make other friends.

'And what did you say, Brian?' Her pale eyes had flecks of light in them tonight.

'I said that he had a very poor opinion of people if he thought they would give such low motives to what was an obvious and proper friendship.'

But it was clear that Brian Barry had not found his own answer satisfactory. He looked confused and bewildered. She had never loved him more. 'I am sorry, Maddy, I couldn't think of what else to say.' He had never called her Maddy before, always Madeleine like her mother did.

She moved over to him and closed her arms around his neck. He smelled still of cigarette smoke, but his soap was Imperial Leather now, and he hadn't been eating the winegums. It was the chocolate cake given to him, Maddy realised, by her mother.

'It was perfect,' she whispered.

He looked very startled and moved as if to get away.

'What was perfect?' he asked, his eyes large and alarmed.

'What you said. It is a proper friendship and a proper love ...'

'Yes ... well ...' He hadn't raised his arms to hold her.

She moved nearer to him and pressed herself towards him. 'Brian, hold me. Please hold me.'

'I can't, Maddy. I can't. I'm a priest.'

'I held you years ago when you had no friend. Hold me now; now that I have no friend and they are trying to take you away.' Her eyes filled with tears.

'No, no, no.' He soothed her as she had stroked him all that time ago. He held her head to his shoulder and comforted her. 'No, it's not a question of being taken away ... it's just ... well, you know what it is.'

She snuggled closer to him. Again she could hear his heart beat in the way she had remembered so often from that first time. He was about to release her so she allowed sobs to shake her body again. He was so clumsy, and tender at the same time. Maddy knew that this was her man, and her one chance to take what life was presenting.

'I love you so much, Brian,' she whispered.

The answering words were not there. She changed direction slightly.

'You are the only person who understands me, who knows what I want to do in the world, and I think I'm the only person who knows what is best for you.' She gulped as she spoke so that he wouldn't think the storm was over, the need for consolation at an end. In the seven years since they had first held each other in these woods times had changed; when he offered her a handkerchief now it was a paper tissue, when he sat down beside her on their log to smoke it wasn't the flaky old Gold Flake, it was a tipped cigarette.

'You've been better to me than anyone in the world. I mean that.' His voice was sincere. He *did* mean it. She could see his brain clicking through all the people who had been good to him, his mother, some kind superior in the seminary possibly. She was the best of this pathetic little list. That was all. Why was she not his great love? She would have to walk very warily.

'I have wanted the best for you since the day I met you,' she said simply.

'And I for you. Truly.'

This was probably true, Maddy thought. Like he wanted the best for the people of Vieja Piedra, wanted it in his heart but wasn't able to do anything real and lasting about it.

'You must go there,' she said.

'Go where?'

'To Peru. To Father Cormac.'

He looked at her as if she was suggesting he fly to the moon. 'How can I go, Maddy? They'll never let me.'

'Don't ask them. Just go. You've often said that God isn't worried about some pecking order and lines of obedience. Our Lord didn't ask permission when he wanted to heal people.'

He still looked doubtful. Maddy got up and paced up and down beside him. With all the powers of persuasion she could gather she told him why he must go. She played back to him all his own thoughts and phrases about the small village where people had died waiting for someone to come and help them, where they looked up to the mountain pass each day hoping that a man of God would come, not just to visit but to stay amongst them and give them the sacraments. She could see the light coming to his eye: the magic was working.

'How would I get the fare to go there?' he asked.

'You can take it from the collection.' To her it was simple.

'I couldn't do that. It's for Vieja Piedra.'

'But isn't that exactly where you would be going? Isn't that why we're raising this money, so that they'd have someone to help them?'

'No, I don't believe that would be right. I've never been sure about the end justifying the means ... remember we often discussed that.' They had, here in this wood, sitting in her classroom, having coffee after the rehearsals for the plays.

She looked at him, flushed and eager in the middle of yet another moral dilemma, but not moved by the fact that he had held her close to him and felt her heart beat, her hair against his face, her eyelashes on his cheek. Was he an ordinary man or had he managed to quell that side of himself so satisfactorily that it didn't respond any more? She had to know.

'And when you go you can write and tell me about it ... until I come there too.'

His eyes were dark circles of amazement now. 'You come out there, Maddy? You couldn't. You couldn't come all that far and you can't be with me. I'm a priest.'

'We have only one life.' She spoke calmly.

'And I chose mine as a priest. You know I can't change that. Nothing will change that.'

'You can change it if you want to. Just like you can change the place

41

you live.' There was something in the direct simple way she spoke that seemed to alarm him. This was not the over-excitable intense Maddy Ross he had known, it was a serious young woman going after what she wanted.

'Sit down, Maddy.' He too was calm. He squatted in front of her, holding both her hands in his. 'If I ever gave you the impression that I might leave the priesthood then I must spend the rest of my days making up for such a terrible misunderstanding ...' His face was troubled as he sought some response in hers. 'Maddy, I am a priest for ever. It's the one thing that means anything to me. I've been selfish and impatient and critical of those around me, I don't have the understanding and generosity of a Father Gunn, but I do have this belief that God chose me and called me.'

'You also have the belief that the people of Vieja Piedra are calling you.'

'Yes, I do. If there was a way to go there I *would* go. You have given me that courage. I won't take the money that the people of Shancarrig raised. They didn't raise it for their priest to run away with.'

The moon came up as they talked. They saw a badger quite nearby, but it wasn't important enough for either of them to comment on. Brian Barry told Madeleine Ross that he would never leave his ministry. He had a few certainties in life. This was one of them. In vain did Maddy tell him that clerical celibacy was only something introduced long after Our Lord's time, it was more or less a Civil Service ruling, not part of the Constitution. The first apostles had wives and children.

'Children.' She stroked his hand as she said the word.

He pulled both hands away from her and stood up. This was something he was never going to think about. It was the sacrifice he had made for God, the one thing God wanted from his priests: to give up the happiness and love of a wife and family. Not that it had been hard to give up because he had never known it, and now he was heading for forty years of age so it wasn't something he would be thinking of, even if he weren't a priest.

'A lot of men marry around forty,' Maddy said.

'Not priests.'

'You can do anything. Anything.'

'I won't do this.'

'But you love me, Brian. You're not going to be frightened into some kind of cringing life for the rest of your days by a silly warning from Father Gunn, by Mrs Kennedy spying, by a promise made when you were a child . . . when you didn't know what love was . . . or anything about it.'

'I still don't really know.'

'You know.'

He shook his head and Maddy could bear it no more. She reached out for him and kissed him directly on the lips. She moved herself into his arms and opened her mouth to his. She felt his arms tighten around her . . . He stroked her back and then because she pulled away from his clasp a little he stroked the outline of her breasts. She peeped through her closed eyes and saw that his eyes were closed too.

They stood locked like this for a time. Eventually he pulled away.

They looked at each other for moments before he spoke. 'You've given me everything, Maddy Ross,' he said.

'I haven't begun to give you anything,' she said.

'No but you have, believe me. You've given me such bravery, such faith. Without you I'd be nothing. You've given me the courage to go. Now you must give me one more thing . . . the freedom.'

She looked at him with disbelief. 'You could hold me like that and ask me never to be in your arms again?'

'That is what I'm begging you. *Begging* you, Maddy. It was my only sure centre. The only thing I knew . . . that I was to be a priest of God. Don't take that away from me or all the other things you have given will totter like a house of cards.'

This man had been her best friend, her soul mate. Now he was asking her permission and her encouragement to leave her life entirely, to step out of it and away from Shancarrig to the village that they had both dreamed about and prayed for and saved for all these years.

Such monstrous selfishness couldn't be part of God's plan. It couldn't be part of any dream of taking your chance in life. Maddy looked at him, confused. It was all going wrong, very very wrong.

He saw her shock, he didn't run away from it. He spoke very gently.

'Since I came to Shancarrig and even before it I've known that women are stronger than men. We could list them in this town. And I know more than you because I hear them in the Confessional. I'm there at their deathbeds when they worry not about their own pain but about how a husband will manage or whether a son will go to the bad. I've been there when their babies have died at birth, when they bury a man who was not only a husband but their means of living. Women are very strong. Can you be strong and let me go with your blessing?'

She looked at him dumbly. The words would not come, the torrent of words welling up inside her. She must be able to explain that he could not be bound by these tired old rules, these empty vows made at another time by another person. Brian Barry was different now, he had come into his kingdom, he was a man who could love and give. But she said none of these things. Which was just as well because he looked at her and the dark blue of his eyes was hard.

'You see, I want to go with your blessing, because I'm *going* to go anyway.'

They didn't meet again in Shancarrig without other people being present.

There were no more walks in the woods, no visits to the classroom. The rehearsals had to do without the kind help of Father Barry, Shancarrig Dramatic Society was told. He had been advised to take it easy. Somehow that was the hardest place, the place she missed him most. They had started these plays together; she didn't know how she would have the heart to continue. In fact, she feared the whole organisation would fall apart without him.

The Shancarrig Dramatic Society continued to thrive without Father Barry. In many ways his leaving gave them greater scope. They were able to do more comedies. They had never liked to suggest anything too light-hearted when Father Barry was there, he was so soulful and good it seemed like being too flippant in his presence.

In the weeks that seemed endless to Maddy the society decided to enter the All Ireland contest for the humorous one-act play.

'Poor Father Barry. He'd have loved this,' said Biddy from The Glen, who was going to play a dancing washroom woman in the piece.

'Go on out of that,' said Sergeant Keane's wife, 'we'd be doing a tragedy if poor Father Barry was here. Not that I wish the man any harm, and I hope whatever's bothering him gets better.'

The rumour was that he had a spot on his lung. Heads nodded. Yes, it was true he did have that colour, the very pale complexion with occasional spots of high colour that could spell out TB. Still, the sanatorium was wonderful and anyway it hadn't been confirmed yet.

He didn't avoid her eye, Maddy realised. He was totally at peace with himself, and grateful to her that she had nodded her head that night in Barna Woods and left without trusting herself to speak a word.

He thought she had seen his way was the only way.

The days were endless as she waited to hear that he had gone. It was three whole months before she heard what she had been waiting for. Father Gunn, visiting the school in his usual way, had asked her pleasantly if she could drop in at the presbytery that evening. Nothing in his face had given a hint of what was to be said.

When she arrived she was startled to see Brian sitting in one of the chairs. Father Gunn motioned her to the other.

'Maddy, you know that Father Barry is going to Peru?'

'I knew he wanted to.' She spoke carefully, but smiled at Brian. His face was alive and happy. 'You mean, it's settled? You're going to be able to go, officially?'

'I'm going with everyone's blessing,' Brian said. His face was full of love, love and gratitude.

'The Bishop is very understanding and when he saw such missionary zeal he said it would be hard not to encourage it,' said Father Gunn.

It had always been impossible to see Father Gunn's eyes through those glasses, but they seemed more opaque than ever. Maddy wondered had Father Gunn told the Bishop that Vieja Piedra alone and on Church business was infinitely preferable to another alternative.

'I hope it's every bit as rewarding for you as you and I have always believed it would be.' Her voice choked slightly.

'I wanted to thank you, Maddy, for all your help and encouragement. Father Gunn has been so wise and understanding about everything. When I told him that I wanted you to be the first to know he insisted that we invite you here, to tell you that it has all finally gone through.'

Maddy looked at Father Gunn. She knew exactly why she had been invited to the presbytery, so that there could be no tearful farewells, implorings and highly charged emotion in Barna Woods, or anywhere on their own.

'That's very kind of you, Father,' she said to the small square priest, in a very cold tone.

'No, no, and I must just get some papers. I'll leave the two of you for a few minutes.' He fussed out of the room.

Brian didn't move from his chair. 'I owe it all to you, Maddy,' he said.

'Will you write?' she asked, her voice dull.

'To everyone, a general letter in response to whatever marvellous fund-raising you do for me ...' He smiled at her winningly as he had smiled at so many people. As he would smile at the poor Peruvians in the dry valley, who had been calling out for him. She said nothing.

And for the first time in seven years they sat in silence. They willed the time to pass when Father Gunn would have found his letters and returned to the sitting room of the presbytery. The sitting-room door had been left open.

The farewells were endless. Father Barry wanted no present, he insisted. He didn't need any goodbye gift to remind him of Shancarrig, its great people and the wonderful years he had spent here. He said he would try to describe what the place was like, their namesake on the other side of the world.

He cried when they came to see him off at the station. Maddy was in the back of the crowd. She wanted to be sure he was actually going. She wanted to see it with her own eyes. He waved with one hand and dabbed his eyes with the other. Maddy heard Dr Jims saying to Mr Hayes that he was always a very emotional and intense young man. He hoped he would fare all right in that hot climate over there.

And the time went by, but it was like a summer garden when the sun has gone, and although there's daylight there's no point in sitting out in it. More children came and went in Mixed Infants. They left Miss Ross and went up to Mrs Kelly. They still learned how to say *bonjour* and *buenos dias* in their own time. Maddy Ross had won that victory hard from Mrs Kelly – she was not going to give it up.

The fund-raising continued, but Ireland was changing in the sixties. There was television for one thing ... people heard about other parts of the world where there was famine and disaster. Suddenly Vieja Piedra was not the only place that called to them. Sometimes the collections were small that went in the money order to the Reverend Brian Barry at his post office in a hill town some sixty-seven miles from Vieja Piedra.

Yet his letters were always grateful and warm, and there were stories of the church being built, a small building. It looked like a shed with a cross on top, but Father Barry was desperately proud of it. Pictures were sent of it, badly focused snapshots taken from different angles.

And then there was the wonderful help of Viatores Christi, some lay Christians who were coming out to help. They were invaluable, as committed in every way as were the clergy.

Maddy heard the letters read aloud, and wondered why could Brian Barry not have become a lay missionary. Then there would have been the same dream and the same hope but no terrible promise about celibacy.

But she cheered herself up. If he had not been ordained as a priest he would never have come to Shancarrig, she would never have known him, never had her chance in life.

There had been five years of walking alone in Barna Woods, five plays in Shancarrig Dramatic Society, five Christmas concerts, there had been five sales of work, whist drives, beetle drives, treasure hunts. There had been five years of raffles, bingo, house to house collections. And then, one day, Brian Barry telephoned Maddy Ross.

'I thought you'd be home from school by now.' He sounded as if he were down the road. He couldn't be telephoning her from Peru!

'I'm in Dublin,' he said.

Her heart gave an uncomfortable lurch. Something was happening. Why had the communication not been through Father Gunn?

'I want to see you. Nobody knows I'm home.'

'Brian.' Her voice was only a whisper.

'Don't tell anyone at all. Just come tomorrow.'

'But why? What's happened?'

'I'll tell you tomorrow.'

'Tomorrow? All the way to Dublin, just like that?'

'I've come all the way from Peru.'

'Is anything wrong? Is there any trouble?'

'No no. Oh Maddy, it's good to talk to you.'

'I haven't talked to you for five years, Brian. You have to tell me why are you home? Are you going to leave the priesthood?'

'Please, Maddy. Trust me. I want to tell you personally. That's why I came the whole way back. Just get the early train, will you? I'll meet you.'

'Brian?'

'I'll be on the platform.' He hung up.

She had to cash a cheque at the hotel. Mrs Ryan was interested as usual in everything. Maddy gave her no information. Her mind was too confused. She knew there would be no sleep tonight.

For five years she had slept seven hours a night.

But tonight she would not close her eyes. No matter how tired and old she might look next morning Maddy knew that there was no point in lying in that same bed where she had lain for years, seeking sleep.

Instead she examined everything in her wardrobe.

She chose a cream blouse and a blue skirt. She wore a soft blue woollen scarf around her neck. It wasn't girlish but it was youthful. It didn't look like the ageing school teacher grown old in her love for the faraway priest.

Maddy smiled. At least she had kept her sense of humour. Whatever he was going to tell her he would like that.

He didn't seem to have got a day older. He was boyish, even at forty-five. His coat collar was up so she couldn't see whether he still wore his roman collar, but she had told herself not to read anything into that. Out in the missions priests wore no clerical garb and yet they were as firmly priests as ever they had been.

He saw her and ran to her. They hugged like a long-separated brother and sister, like old friends parted unwillingly, which is probably what they were. She pulled away from him to see his face, but still he hugged her. You can't kiss someone who is hugging the life out of you.

The crowd had thinned on the platform. Some caution seemed to seep back into him.

'There was no one from home on the train, was there?'

'Where's home?' She laughed at him. 'In all your letters you say Vieja Piedra is home.'

'And so it is.' He seemed satisfied that they weren't under sur-veillance. He tucked her arm into his and they walked to a nearby hotel. The lounge was small and dark, the coffee strong and scalding. Maddy Ross would remember for ever the way it stuck to the roof of her mouth when Brian Barry told her that he was going to leave the priesthood and marry Deirdre, one of the volunteers. It was like a patch of red-hot tar in her mouth. It wouldn't go away as she nodded and listened and forced her face to smile through tales of growth, and understanding and love and the emptiness of vows taken at an early age before a boy was a man, and about a loving God not holding people to meaningless promises.

And she heard how there was still a lot to be decided. Deirdre and he had realised that laicisation took such a long time, and brought so much grief, destroying the relationships of those who waited.

But in South America the clergy had understood the core values. They had gone straight to the heart of things. They knew that a blessing could be given to a union of which God would patently approve. What was the expression that Maddy herself had used so many years ago? Something about thinking in terms of the Constitution rather than in petty Civil Service bye-laws.

And he owed it all to Maddy. So often he had told that to Deirdre, who wanted to send her gratitude. If Maddy hadn't proven to him that he could be courageous and open up his heart to the world and to love, this might never have happened.

'Did you ever love me?' Maddy asked him.

'Of course I love you. I love you with all my heart. Nothing will destroy our love, not my marrying Deirdre or you marrying whoever you will. Maybe you have someone in mind?' He was roguish now, playful even. She wanted to knock him down.

'No. No plans as yet.'

'Well you should, Maddy.' Gone was the light-hearted banter, now he was being serious and caring. 'A woman should get married, and have children. That's what a woman should do.'

'And have you and Deirdre decided to have children?' She tried to put the smile back in her voice. It was so easy to let a sneer creep in instead, to let him know how she could sense that Deirdre was already pregnant.

'Eventually,' he told her, which meant imminently.

He was going to leave Vieja Piedra, and they were going to a place further down the coast of Peru. He would teach in a town, there was just as much work needed there, but they had found a native born priest, a real Peruvian, to look after the valley of Vieja Piedra. He talked on. Nothing would be said to Father Gunn. The fund-raising would take a different style. Nothing would be said to anyone really. In today's world you didn't need to explain or to be intense. It was a matter of seizing what good there was and creating more good. It was taking your chance when it was offered.

The only person who *had* to be told face to face was Maddy. That's why he had taken Deirdre's savings to come back and tell her, to thank her in the way that a letter could never do for having put him on this road to happiness.

'And did Deirdre not feel afraid that once you saw your old love you might never return to her?' Maddy's tone was light, her question deadly serious.

But Brian hastened to put her anxieties at rest. 'Lord no. Deirdre knew that what *we* had wasn't love. It was childlike fumblings, it was heavy meaning-of-life conversation, it was part of growth, and for me a very important part.' He wanted to reassure her about that.

The train back to Shancarrig left in fifteen minutes. Maddy said she thought she should take it.

49

'But you can't go *now*. You've only been here an hour.' His dismay was enormous.

'But you've told me everything.'

'No, I haven't told you anything really. I have only skimmed the surface.'

'I have to go back, Brian. I would have, anyway, no matter what you told me. My mother hasn't been well.'

'I didn't know that.'

'Of course you didn't. You didn't know a great many things, like Mrs Murphy in The Glen died, and that Maura Brennan brings her poor son around with her and he sits in every house in Shancarrig while she cleans floors and does washing. There are many things you don't know.'

'Well, they don't tell me. *You* don't tell me. You don't write at all.'

'I was ordered not to. Don't you remember?'

'Not ordered, just advised.'

'To you it was the same once.'

'If you'd wanted to write to me enough you would have,' he said, head on one side, roguish again.

She closed her mind to his disbelief that she would return on the next train. He had thought she would spend the whole day, if not the weekend, in Dublin with him. What was he to do now? No relations were meant to know he was back.

'Did I do the wrong thing coming back to tell you?' He was a child again, confused, uncertain.

She was gentle. She could afford to be. She had a lifetime ahead of her with little to contemplate except why her one stab at living life had failed. She reached out and held his hand.

'No, you did the right thing,' she lied straight into his face. 'Tell Deirdre that I wish you well, all of you. Tell her I went back to Shancarrig on the train with my heart brimming over.'

It was the only wedding present she could give him.

And she held the tears until the train had turned the bend and until she could no longer see his eager hand waving her goodbye.

MAURA

W hen the time came for Maura to go to school any small enthusiasm that there had ever been in the Brennan family for education had died down. Maura's mother was worn out with all the demands that were made on her to dress them up for this May Procession and that visit from the Bishop. Not to mention communion and confirmations. Mrs Brennan had been heard to say that the Shancarrig school had notions about itself being some kind of private college for the sons and daughters of the land-owning gentry rather than the National School it was, and that nature had always intended it to be.

And the young Maura didn't get much encouragement from her father either. Paudie Brennan believed that schools and all that were women's work and not things a man got involved with. And since Paudie Brennan was not a man ever continuously in work he couldn't be expected to take an interest financially and every other way in each and every one of his nine living children, and Maura came near the end of the trail. Paudie Brennan had too much on his mind what with a leaking roof missing a dozen slates, and a very different and worrying kind of slate altogether above in Johnny Finn Noted for Best Drinks, so what time was there to be wondering about young Maura and her book learning?

Maura had never expected there to be an interest. School was for books, home was for fights. The older brothers and sisters had gone to England – the really grown-up ones.' They went as soon as they were seventeen or eighteen. They came home for holidays and it was great at first, but after a day it would wear off, the niceness, and there would be shouting again as if the returned sister or brother was an ordinary part of the family, not a visitor.

One day, Maura knew, she would be the eldest one at home – just herself and Geraldine left. But Maura wasn't going to England to work in a shoe factory like Margaret, or a fish shop like Deirdre. No, she was going to stay here in Shancarrig. She wouldn't get married but she would live like Miss Ross, who was very old and could do what she liked and stay up all night without anyone giving out or groaning at her. Of course, Miss Ross was a school teacher and must earn pots of money, but Maura would save whenever she started to work, and keep the money in the post office until she could have a house and freedom to go to bed at two in the morning if the notion took her.

Maura Brennan often stayed on late at school to talk to Miss Ross, to try to find out more about this magnificent lifestyle in the small house with the lilac bushes and the tall hollyhocks, where Miss Ross lived. She would ask endless questions about the dog or the cat. She knew their names and ages, which nobody else at school did. She would hope that one day Miss Ross might drop another hint or two about her life. Miss Ross seemed puzzled by her interest. The child was in no way bright. Even taking into account her loutish father and timid uneducated mother, young Maura must still be called one of the slower learners in the school. Even the youngest of that Brennan string of children, Geraldine, with the permanent cold and her hair in her eyes, was quicker. But Maura was the one who hung about, who found excuses to have meaningless little conversations.

One day Miss Ross let slip that she hated ironing.

'I love ironing,' Maura said. 'I love it, I'd do it all day but the one we have is broke, and my da won't pay to have it mended.'

'What do you like about it?' Miss Ross seemed genuinely interested.

'The way your hand goes on and on ... it's like music almost ... and the clothes get lovely and smooth, and it all smells nice and clean,' Maura said.

'You make it sound great. I wish you'd come and do mine.'

'Of course I will,' said Maura.

She was eleven then, a square girl with her hair clipped back by a brown slide, a high forehead and clear eyes. In a different family in another place she might have had a better chance, a start that would have brought her further along some kind of road.

'No, Maura, you can't, child. I don't want the other children to see you rating yourself as only fit to do my ironing. I don't want you making little of yourself before you have to.'

'How could that be making little of myself?' The question was without guile. Maura Brennan saw no lack of dignity in coming to the teacher's house to do household chores.

'The others ... they don't have to know, Miss Ross.'

'But they do, they will. You know this place.'

'They don't know lots of things, like that my sister Margaret had a baby in Northampton. Geraldine and I are aunts, Miss Ross. Imagine!' Maura had told the family secret easily, as if she knew that there was no danger that Miss Ross would pass on this titbit. There was the same simplicity as when she had spoken of ironing.

'Once a week, and I'll pay you properly,' Miss Ross had said.

'Thank you, Miss Ross, I'll put it in the post office.' It was the beginning for Maura Brennan. She warned young Geraldine not to tell anyone. It would be their secret.

'Why has it to be a secret?' Geraldine wanted to know.

'I don't know.' Maura was truthful. 'But it has.'

So if ever Mrs Brennan asked what was keeping Maura above at the school, Geraldine said she didn't know. It seemed daft to her, all this sucking up to Miss Ross. It wasn't as if Maura ever got anywhere at her books. She was slow and was always asking people to help her, Leo Murphy or Nessa Ryan, girls from important families, big houses. Geraldine would know better than to talk to them or their like. Maura was half daft a lot of the time.

When Maura started doing the ironing Miss Ross gave her a doll as well as the money. She said she had seen Maura admiring it and even taking off its crushed pink dress and giving it a good press. Anyone who thought that much of a doll should have it. Maura always told Geraldine that it was on loan. Miss Ross had lent it to her until the time Miss Ross married someone and had children of her own.

'Sure Miss Ross is a hundred. She'll never marry and have children,' Geraldine cried.

'People have them at all ages. Look at Mammy, look at St Elizabeth.'

Geraldine wasn't so sure about her ground on St Elizabeth, but she knew all about their mother. 'Mammy started having them and she couldn't stop. I heard her telling Mrs Barton. But after me she stopped all of a sudden.' Geraldine was nine and she knew everything.

Maura wished she had those kind of certainties.

The doll sat on a shelf in their bedroom. It had a china face and little china hands. When Geraldine wasn't there to laugh at her Maura would hug it and speak reassuring words, saying the doll was very much loved. Sometimes Miss Ross gave Maura things to wear, a nice coloured belt once, a scarf with a tassel.

'I never wore them in the school, Maura, no one will know they're mine.'

'But what would I mind if they knew?' Again the question was so honest and without guile that Miss Ross seemed taken aback.

'I wish I could help you with your lessons, Maura. I wish I could, but you don't really have the will to concentrate.'

Maura was eager to reassure her. 'I'll be fine, Miss Ross. There's no point in trying to put things into my head that won't go in, and what would I need with all those sums and knowing poems off by heart? It wouldn't be any use to me at all.'

'What's to become of you, though ... off to England like Deirdre and Margaret with no qualifications ... ?'

'No, I'm staying here. I'm going to get a house like this one, and have it the way you do, lovely and shiny and clean, and coloured china on a dresser and a smell of lavender polish everywhere.'

'It'll be some lucky man if you are going to do all that for him.'

'I won't be getting married, Miss Ross.' It was one of the few things she had ever said with conviction.

Her sister Geraldine believed her too, over this.

'Why don't you go the whole hog and be a nun?' Geraldine wanted to know. 'If you're so sure you're not going to get a fellow, hadn't you better be in a convent, singing hymns and getting three meals a day?'

'I can still pray in a house of my own. I'll have a Sacred Heart lamp on a small wooden shelf, and I'll have a picture of Our Lady, Queen of May on a small round table with a blue table cloth and a vase of flowers in front of it.'

She didn't say that she was going to buy a chair for the doll too.

Geraldine shrugged. She was twelve now, and much more grown up than her sister of fourteen, who would be leaving school this year. Geraldine's confirmation was coming up and between wheedling and complaining she and her mother had managed to get Paudie Brennan to put up money for a lovely confirmation dress. This was the first item of clothing that had ever been bought new to celebrate the confirmation of any of his nine children. The dress hung on the back of the bedroom door and had been tried on a dozen times. Maura had managed to persuade Geraldine to keep the hair from hanging over her eyes.

Geraldine was going to look gorgeous on her confirmation day. She had written to her sisters and brothers in England telling them of this event and, getting the hint, they had sent a pound note or a ten-shilling note in an envelope with a couple of lines scrawled to wish her well. Maura hadn't done that and she looked with envy at the riches coming in. It took a lot of ironing in Miss Ross's house to make anything like that amount of money.

Three days before confirmation Paudie Brennan, on a serious drinking bout, found himself short of ready cash and, deciding that the Lord couldn't possibly be concerned what clothes young Christians decked themselves in for confirmation ceremonies, managed to take the new dress to a pawnbroker in the big town and raise the sum of two pounds on it.

The consternation was terrible. In the middle of the shouting, tears and accusations being hurled backwards and forwards, Maura realised that this was all that would happen. Bluster and hurt, disappointment and recriminations. There was no question of anyone getting the dress back for Geraldine. That kind of money could not appear by magic. Credit had been arranged in the first place to buy it. There was no possibility of more funds being made available.

'I'll get it for you,' Maura said simply to a red-eyed, near hysterical Geraldine who lay on her bed railing at the unfairness of life and the meanness of her father.

'How can you get it? Don't be stupid.'

'I have that saved. Just get the ticket from him. We'll go on the bus, but you must never tell them, never never.'

'Where will they think we got the money? They might say we stole it.' Geraldine didn't care to believe that there was a way out.

'Da's not going to be able to say much one way or the other after what he did,' said Maura.

On the day, Paudie Brennan was dressed and shaved and his neck squeezed into a proper shirt and collar for the visit of the Bishop. It was a sunlit day, and the children from Shancarrig looked a credit to their school, people said, as they gathered for the group photograph outside the cathedral in the big town. Geraldine Brennan, resplendent with her shiny blonde hair and her frilly white dress, caught the eye of a lot of people.

'You have dressed her up like a picture. She's a credit to you,' said Mrs Ryan, of Ryan's Hotel. Her own daughter Catherine looked far less resplendent. It was easy to see that she was mystified and even put out that the young Brennan girl, daughter of a known layabout and drunk, should look so well.

'Ah, sure, you have to do your best, Mrs Ryan, Ma'am,' Maura's mother said. Maura felt her heart harden. If her mam had been the one in charge Geraldine would have stood there in some limp handout dress that had been begged from a family who might not have used all its castoffs. There had been no word of apology from her father, no question of any promised repayment from Geraldine. No questions, no interest.

Any more than anyone had asked what Maura would do when she left school in a few short weeks' time. She wouldn't be going to the convent in the town like Leo Murphy and Nessa Ryan. There were no plans for her to go into the technical school. She wasn't smart enough to be taken on as a trainee in one of the shops, or the hairdressing salon.

Maura was going to work as a maid, the only question was where – and this, she realised, was something she would have to work out for herself as well as everything else. Maura would really have liked a job where she could live in. In a lovely big house, with beautiful furniture in it. Somewhere like The Glen, where Leo Murphy lived.

She would call and ask them had they a place. It wasn't fair to ask Leo at school and embarrass her in case the answer was no. Or she could possibly get a place in the kitchens of Ryan's Commercial Hotel, or as a chambermaid. She wouldn't like that as much. There was nothing beautiful to touch and polish.

'Are you thinking about your own confirmation, Maura?' Father Gunn from Shancarrig was standing beside her.

'Not really, I'm afraid, Father. I was thinking about where I'd go to work.'

'Is it time for you to leave school already?' He was a kindly man with very thick glasses that made him look vaguer and more confused than he was. It seemed impossible for him to believe that another of Paudie Brennan's brood was ready for the emigrant ship.

'It is. I'll be fifteen soon,' Maura said proudly. Father Gunn looked at her. She was a pleasant open-faced child. Not a pretty face like the one being confirmed today, but still easy enough on the eye. He hoped she wouldn't fall for a child the way the elder sister had in Northampton. There were few secrets kept from a priest in a small community.

'You'll be needing a reference I suppose,' he sighed, thinking of the numbers of young people that he had written about, praising their honesty and integrity to anonymous English employers.

'I suppose they'll all know me in Shancarrig,' she said. 'I'll be looking for a job as a maid, Father. If you hear of anyone, I'm great at cleaning altogether.'

'I will, Maura, I'll keep my eyes open for you.' He turned away, feeling unexpectedly sad.

Maura went first to the back door of The Glen and waited patiently as the dogs raced around her, barking the news of her arrival, but nobody came to see what was her business. She had seen two figures sitting in the front room. Surely they must have heard. After a lot of thought she went around to the front and Leo, tall and confident, came running down the stairs.

'Maura, what on earth are you doing?' she asked.

'I came wondering do your parents want anyone to work for them in the house, Leo,' she said to the girl who had been sitting beside her in school for eight years.

'Work?' Leo seemed startled.

'Yes, like I have to have a job working somewhere, and this is a big house. I wondered ... ?'

'No, Maura.'

'But, I know how to turn out a room ...'

'There's Biddy here already.'

'I meant as well as Biddy, under her of course.'

Leo had always been nice at school. Maura couldn't understand why she spoke so brusquely. 'It wouldn't work. You couldn't come here and clear up after me.'

'I have to clear up after someone. Wouldn't your family be as nice as anyone else's? Let me ask them, Leo.' She didn't say the place could do with a clean. She didn't plead. She had always been quick to recognise when something was impossible. And a look at Leo Murphy's face told her that this was now the case.

'Right then,' she said cheerfully. 'I had to ask.'

She knew Leo was standing at the door with the dogs as she walked down the avenue. Maura thought that she should have been allowed to talk to the people of the house, rather than being sent off by her own schoolfriend. Still, Leo had the air of being the one who made the decisions in that house. They mightn't have hired her if they knew Leo disapproved.

Imagine being able to make the decisions at nearly fifteen. But then Maura told herself that that's what she was doing herself. There were very few decisions made in Brennans' by anyone except herself.

Maura went then to Mrs Hayes. Mr Hayes was a solicitor so the Hayes family were very wealthy. They had a big house covered with virginia creeper, and a lovely piano in the drawing room. Maura knew this because Niall Hayes went to the same school. He was very nice. He told her one day how much he hated the piano lessons that his mother arranged for him twice a week, and Maura told him how much she hated going to the pub to tell her father his dinner was ready on Saturday and Sunday lunchtimes. It was a kind of bond between them.

But Mrs Hayes didn't want a young girl, she told Maura. She'd need someone older, someone trained.

She went to Mrs Barton, Eddie Barton's mother, who ran a dressmaking business, but Mrs Barton said it was hard enough to put food on the table for herself and Eddie, without trying to find another few shillings for a child to be playing at pushing a brush around the floor. She had said it kindly, but the facts were the facts.

And Dr Jims said that he had not only Carrie to look after his son but there were many good years left in Maisie as well. So, everything now depended on going to the Ryans in the hotel. Maura had left that till last because she thought Mrs Ryan was very strong willed. She was a woman whom it might be easy to annoy.

She got the job, chambermaid. Mrs Ryan said she hoped Maura would be happy but there were three things they should get straight from the start – Maura was not to speak to Nessa just because they knew each other at school – Maura was to live on the premises, they didn't really want her going back to the cottages every night – and lastly, if there was a question of flirting or making free with any of the customers there would be words with Father Gunn about it and Maura would leave Shancarrig without a backward glance.

It suited Maura not to live at home. Her father was increasingly difficult these days. Geraldine had her friends in and out of the place, giggling in the bedroom. It would be nice to have a place of her own, a small room certainly, like a nun's cell, but all to herself.

Maura began work at once, and in her time off she did the ironing still for Miss Ross and she polished silver for Mrs Hayes, sitting quietly in the kitchen on her afternoon off from the hotel. She never spoke to Niall when he came home on holidays from his boarding school. Nobody would ever have known they had been schoolfriends and even companions in a kind of way too. If Niall ever saw her there he didn't seem to take any notice.

Not even as the years passed and Maura Brennan developed a small waist and began to look altogether more attractive. If you were born square and dull-looking in appearance you didn't ever think that things would change. Maura knew that her sister Geraldine was pretty but she didn't feel jealous. It was good that Geraldine had got a job up in the sawmills; they liked someone nice with a bright smile around the office. Maura never thought that it was bad luck to be square and making beds behind the scenes in a hotel.

In fact, she was so used to being square and dull-looking she was quite unaware that she had changed and had begun to look very attractive indeed.

The men who came to stay in Ryan's Commercial Hotel noticed, though. Maura had many an occasion to raise her voice sharply and speak in clear firm tones when men asked for an extra blanket, or complained of some imaginary fault in their rooms, just in order to give her a squeeze.

By the time she was eighteen years old, Mrs Ryan suggested to her husband that they put her behind the bar. She'd be able to attract custom. To their surprise, Maura refused. She'd prefer to continue the work she was doing, she had no head for figures. She would need a lot of smart clothes if she was to be in the public eye. She would be happier making beds and helping in the kitchen.

'At least, wait on the tables,' Mrs Ryan asked. But no, if her work was satisfactory she would prefer to keep in the background.

Breda Ryan shrugged. They had tried to better her, a girl from the cottages, poor Paudie Brennan's child, and yet she wouldn't seize the opportunity. Mrs Ryan had always thought that if the whole wealth of the world was taken back and divided out equally, giving the same amount to each person, you'd find in five years that the same people would end up having money and power and the same people would end up shiftless and hopeless. In a changing world, she found this view very comforting.

Maura didn't want to change because her life suited her just the way it was. She had three square meals a day. She could even choose what she wanted to eat in a hotel, which she mightn't have been able to do in a private house. She had the excuse which she could give her mother and father that the hotel needed her night and day. As a barmaid or waitress she might be expected to live out. And she wanted nothing to interfere with her savings and her plans.

Whenever she took the children she minded for walks she would always go the same way, past the places that she would buy when she had the money. There was the little gate lodge to The Glen. It was totally disused. People had lived there once, but now the ivy grew in the windows. That would be her first choice. Then there was the little house near where Miss Ross lived. It was painted a wishy-washy grey, but if Maura had it she would paint it pink and have window boxes full of red geraniums on each side of the hall door.

*

61

There wasn't much time for talking to friends these days. Not if you had to save as hard as Maura did. And she didn't go dancing – dances cost money, lots of money. First you had to buy something to wear, then the price of the bus fare to the town, and the admission to the dance hall, and the minerals. It would run away with your savings.

Maura had never been to a dance by the time her young sister Geraldine was ready to leave Shancarrig and join their sisters in England.

'Come on, just as my goodbye,' Geraldine had urged.

'I've nothing to wear.'

The sisters had remained friendly over the years as Maura had worked on in the hotel and Geraldine had worked in the office in the sawmills.

'I've plenty,' Geraldine said.

And indeed she had, Maura discovered. The bedroom they had once shared would never have held a second bed these days, with all the clothes strewn around it. Maura looked in wonder. 'You must have spent everything you earned on these,' she said.

'Don't be mean, Maura. There's nothing worse than a mean woman,' Geraldine said.

Was she mean? Maura wondered. It would indeed be terrible to be a mean woman. Yet, she didn't think she was mean. She gave a pound a week out of her wages to her mother and she always brought a cake or a half pound of ham when she came home to tea. She seemed to be giving Geraldine the price of the cinema for as long as she remembered. All she had been careful about was not spending on herself.

But perhaps that too was mean.

She fingered the dresses. A taffeta dress with shot silk in green and yellow colours, a red corduroy skirt, a black satin with little bits of diamanté at the shoulders. It was like Aladdin's cave.

'Do all your friends have clothes like this?' she asked.

'Well, Catherine Ryan from the place you work, she'd have different things. You know, well-cut, awful-looking garments you wouldn't be seen dead in. Some people have a ton of stuff. We swap a bit. What'll you wear?'

Maura Brennan wore the black satin with the diamanté decorations and set out for the dance in the big town. She looked at herself in the mirror of the ladies' cloakroom. She thought she looked all right. It was hard to tell what fellows would like, but she thought she'd get asked up to dance and not be left a fool by the side of the wall.

The first man who came over was Gerry O'Sullivan, the new barman in Ryan's Hotel.

'Well, don't tell me you're the same girl that I see in the kitchen in the back of beyond where we work,' he said, stretching out his arms to her.

And then the night flew by. They danced everything, sambas and tangos, and rock and roll, and old-time waltzes. She couldn't believe that it was time for the National Anthem.

'I have to find my sister and her friends,' she said.

'Aw, don't give me that. I've the loan of a car,' he said.

He was very handsome, Gerry O'Sullivan, small and dark with black hair and an easy laugh. But there was no question of it. They had all given five shillings to get their lift there and back in a big van.

'I'll see you tomorrow in the hotel,' she said, thinking that might cheer him up. She was wrong.

'Tomorrow you won't be looking like this, you'll be dressed like a streel and emptying chamber pots,' he grumbled, and went off.

Maura said very little on the way home. Geraldine's friends passed around a bottle of cider, but she shook her head. She supposed he was right: that was the way she dressed and that was what she did for a living.

'I'll write from England,' Geraldine said. Maura knew she wouldn't, any more than the others had.

A few days later Gerry O'Sullivan found her alone.

'I only said that because I was so mad wanting to be with you. I had a very bad mouth and I'm sorry.' He was so handsome and so upset. Maura's face lit up.

'I didn't mind a bit,' she said.

'You should have minded. Listen, will you come to the dance again, on Friday? I'll bring you there and back. Please?' She looked doubtful, because this time she literally didn't have anything to wear. Geraldine had taken her wardrobe across the sea to England. 'I'll be very nicely mannered all night long,' he said with a grin. 'And it's Mick Delahunty's Show Band and he won't be back this way for a good bit.'

She decided she could take the cost of one party dress from her savings. And the following week she took another, and the price of shoes and a nice bag. She'd never have her house at this rate, Maura told herself. But she found herself saying that you only live once.

Gerry O'Sullivan told her that she was the loveliest girl in the dance hall.

'Don't be making a jeer of me,' she said.

'I'll show you I'm not making a jeer of you.' Gerry was indignant. 'I'll not dance with you and see how you'll be swept away...' Before she could say anything he picked a girl from the waiting line and began to dance.

Red-cheeked and unsure Maura was about to step aside but from three directions arms were stretched out and faces offered a dance. She laughed, confused, and picked the nearest one. He had been right. She *was* the kind of girl men danced with.

'What did I tell you,' he murmured in the back of the car that night. He seemed excited by the thought of other men wanting Maura and not being able to have her. His own intention of having her had now become a near reality. No protestations were going to be any use, and in honesty Maura didn't want to protest any further.

'Not in the car, please,' she whispered.

'You're right.' He seemed cheerful. Too cheerful, in fact. From his pocket he took out one of the hotel keys.

'Room Eleven,' he said triumphantly. 'There'll be no one there. We'll be fine as long as we keep the light off.' Maura looked at him trustingly.

'Will it be all right?' she asked in a whisper.

'I'll not let you down,' Gerry O'Sullivan said.

She knew he spoke the truth. She knew it again five months later, after many happy visits to Room Eleven and even Room Two, when she told him she was pregnant.

'We'll get married,' he said.

Father Gunn agreed that it should be as speedily as possible. His face seemed to say that it would be no better or worse than a lot of marriages he was asked to officiate at with speed. And at least in this case they seemed to have a deposit for a house, which was more than you might have hoped for in some cases. Father Gunn talked about it to Miss Ross.

'It could be a lot worse, I suppose,' he said.

'She'll never settle in a poor house. She wanted to be well away from those cottages. She had her eyes on great things,' the teacher said.

'Well, faith and she should have her eyes on being grateful the fellow married her and putting her mind to raising the child and being glad they have a roof over their heads.' Father Gunn knew he sounded like a stern old parish priest from thirty years ago, but somehow the whole thing had him annoyed and he didn't want to hear any fairy stories about people having their eyes set on great things.

Maura decided to work until the day before the wedding. She looked Mrs Ryan straight in the eye and refused to accept any hints about the work being tiring in her condition. She said she needed every penny she could earn.

Mrs Ryan was cross to be losing a hard-working maid, and at the same time having an attractive barman marry beneath him because of activities obviously carried out under her own roof. She began to look more sternly at her own daughters, Nessa and Catherine, lest anything untoward should happen in their lives.

Nessa, the same age as Maura, had been all through Shancarrig school with her. 'What should I give her as a present?' she said to her mother.

'Best present is to ignore it and the reason for it,' Mrs Ryan snapped.

This reaction ensured, of course, that Nessa would go to great trouble to find a nice present. She rang Leo Murphy up in The Glen. Maura, putting away mops and buckets in the room at the end of the corridor, heard Nessa on the phone.

'Leo, she *was* in our class. We have to do something. Of course it's shotgun. What else could it be? You choose something, anything at all. Poor Maura, she expects so little.'

That's not true, Maura thought as she put away the cleaning equipment. She didn't expect so little, she expected a lot and mainly she got it. She had wanted to stay in Shancarrig rather than emigrating like the rest of her brothers and sisters, and here she had stayed. She had wanted the one handsome man that she ever fancied in her life, and he had wanted her. He was standing by her now and marrying her.

She had got more than she expected. She certainly hadn't thought that she would be having a baby and yet there was one on the way. The very thought of it made her pleased and excited. It took away the ache of sorrow about the place they would be living in.

With Gerry and a baby it wouldn't matter anyway.

Leo Murphy and Nessa Ryan gave her a little glass-fronted cabinet.

She couldn't have liked it more. She stroked it over and over and said how lovely it would look on a wall when she got her own treasures to put in it.

'Have you any treasures yet?' Nessa asked.

'Only a doll. A doll with a china face and china hands,' Maura said.

'That'll be nice for the baby...' Leo gulped. 'If you ever have one, I mean,' she said hastily.

'Oh, I'm sure I will,' Maura said. 'But the baby won't be let play with this doll. It's a treasure, for the lovely cabinet.'

She could see that the girls thought their money had been well spent, and she was touched by how much they must have given for it. As part of her continuing fantasy about a house, Maura used to look at furniture and price it. She knew well that this cabinet was not inexpensive.

Maura hoped that Geraldine would come home from England. She even offered her the fare, but there was no reply. It would have been nice to have had her standing as a bridesmaid, but instead she had Eileen Dunne, who said she loved weddings and she'd be anyone's bridesmaid for them. And with a great nudge that nearly knocked Maura over she said she'd do godmother as well, and laughed a lot.

Gerry's brother came to do the best man bit. His parents were old and didn't travel, he said.

Maura saw nothing sad or shabby about her wedding day.

When she turned around in the church she saw Nessa Ryan, Leo Murphy, Niall Hayes and Eddie Barton sitting smiling at her. She was the first of their class to get married. They seemed to think this was like winning some kind of race rather than having been caught in a teenage pregnancy. When they went to Johnny Finn's for drinks Mr Ryan from the hotel came running in with a fistful of money to buy them all a drink. He said he came to wish them well from everyone in Ryan's Commercial Hotel.

There was no word of the haste or the disgrace or anything. Maura's father behaved in a way that, for Paudie Brennan, could be called respectable. This week he happened to be friendly with Foxy Dunne's father, so the two of them had their arms around each other as they sang tunelessly together in a corner. If it had been one of the weeks when they were fighting, things would have been terrible – insults hurling across Johnny Finn's all afternoon.

And Father Gunn and Father Barry were there smiling and talking to people as if it were a real wedding.

Maura didn't see anything less than the kind of wedding day she had dreamed about when she was at school, or when reading the

66

women's magazines. All she saw was Gerry O'Sullivan beside her, smiling and saying everything would be grand.

And everything *was* grand for a while.

Maura left her job in the hotel. Mrs Ryan seemed to want it that way. Possibly there would be social differences now that Maura was the wife of the popular barman, instead of just the girl from the cottages cleaning the floors and washing potatoes. But Maura found plenty of work, hours here and hours there. When it was obvious that she was expecting a child many of her employers said they would be lost without her. Mrs Hayes, who hadn't wanted her in the start, was particularly keen to keep her.

'Maybe your mother could look after the child, and you'd still want to go out and work?' she said hopefully.

Maura had no intention of letting any child grow up in the same house as she had herself, with the lack of interest and love. But she had learned to be very circumspect in her life. 'Maybe indeed,' she said to Mrs Hayes and the others. 'We'll have to wait and see.'

It seemed a long time to wait for the baby, all those evenings on her own in the little cottage, sometimes hearing her father going home drunk, as she had when she was a child. She polished the little cabinet, took out the doll and patted the bump of her stomach.

'Soon you'll be admiring this,' she said to the unborn baby.

It was Dr Jims Blake who told her about the baby boy. The child had Down's syndrome. The boy, who was what was called a mongol, would still be healthy and loving and live a full and happy life.

It was Father Gunn who told her about Gerry, and how he had come from the cottage to the church and told the priest he was going. He took the wages owing to him from the hotel, saying his father had died and he needed time off for the funeral. But he told Father Gunn that he was getting the boat to England.

No entreaties would make him stay.

Maura remembered always the way that Father Gunn's thick round glasses seemed to sparkle as he was telling her. She didn't know if there were tears behind them, or if it was only a trick of the light.

People were kind, very kind. Maura often told herself that she had been lucky to have stayed in Shancarrig. Suppose all this had happened to her in some big city in England where she had known nobody. Here she had a friendly face everywhere she turned.

And of course she had Michael.

67

Nobody had told her how much she would love him because nobody could have known. She had never known a child as loving. She watched him grow with a heart that nearly burst with pride. Everything he learned, every new skill – like being able to do up his buttons – was a huge hurdle for the child, and soon everyone in Shancarrig got used to seeing them hand in hand walking around.

'Who's this?' people would ask affectionately, even though they knew well.

'This is Michael O'Sullivan,' Maura would say proudly.

'I'm Michael O'Sullivan,' he would say and, as often as not, hug the person who had asked.

If you wanted Maura to come and clean your house you took Michael as well. And as they walked from job to job each day Maura used to point out the houses that she loved to her son – the little gate lodge, ever more covered with ivy and choked with nettles, that stood at the end of the long avenue up to The Glen, and there was the one near Miss Ross which she was going to paint pink if she ever bought it.

At night she would take the doll with the china hands and face out from its cabinet and the two cups and saucers she had been given by Mrs Ryan. There was a little silver plate, which had EPNS on the back, that Eileen Dunne had given when she stood as godmother to Michael. She said that this meant it wasn't real silver, but since the S stood for silver Maura thought it deserved a place in the cabinet. There was a watch too, one that belonged to Gerry. A watch that didn't go, but might go one day if it were seen to, and would hang on a chain. When Michael got to be a man he could call it his father's watch.

Most people forgot that Michael ever had a father; the memory of Gerry O'Sullivan faded. And for Maura the memory began to fade too. Days passed when she didn't think of the handsome fellow with the dark eyes who had cared enough to marry her, but hadn't got the strength to stay when he knew his child was handicapped. She had never hated him, sometimes she even pitied him that he didn't know the great hugs and devotion of Michael his son, who grew in size but not greatly in achievement.

Maura had got glances and serious invitations out from other men in the town, but she had always told them simply that she wasn't free to accept any invitation. She had a husband living in England and really there could be no question of anything else.

Her dream remained constant. A proper little home, not the broken-down cottage where only the hopeless and the helpless lived, where she had grown up and wanted to escape.

Then the Darcys came to Shancarrig. They bought a small grocery shop like the one Nellie Dunne ran, and they put in all kinds of new-fangled things. The world was changing, even in places like Shancarrig. Mike and Gloria Darcy were new people who livened the place up. No one had ever met anyone called Gloria before and she lived up to her name. Lots of black curly hair like a gypsy, and she must have known this because she often wore a red scarf knotted around her neck and a full coloured skirt, as if she was going to break into a gypsy dance any moment.

Mike Darcy was easy-going and got on with everyone. Even old Nellie Dunne who looked on them as rivals liked Mike Darcy. He had a laugh and a word for anyone he met on the road. Mrs Ryan in the Commercial Hotel felt they were a bit brash for the town, but when Mike said he'd buy for her at the market as well as for himself she began to change her tune.

It was good to see such energy about the place, she said, and it wasn't long before she had the front of the hotel painted to make it the equal of the new shopfront in Darcy's. Mike's brother, Jimmy Darcy, had come with them. He was a great house-painter and Mrs Ryan claimed that even the dozy fellows from down in the cottages, who used to paint a bit when the humour took them, seemed to think Jimmy did a good job. Mike and Gloria had children, two tough dark little boys who used to get up to all kinds of devilment in the school.

Maura didn't wait to see whether the town liked the Darcys or not; she presented herself on the doorstep the moment they arrived.

'You'll be needing someone to work for you,' she said to Gloria.

Gloria glanced at the round eager face of Michael, who stood holding his mother's hand. 'Will you be able to make yourself free?' she asked.

'Michael would come with me. He's the greatest help you could imagine,' she said, and Michael beamed at the praise.

'I'm not sure if we really *do* need anyone...' Gloria was polite but unsure.

'You do need someone, but take your time. Ask around a bit about me. Maura O'Sullivan is the name, Mrs Maura O'Sullivan.'

'Well, yes, Mrs O'Sullivan...'

'No, I just wanted you to know, because you're new. Michael's daddy had to go and live in England. You'd call me Maura if you had me in the house.'

'And you'd call me Michael,' the boy said, putting both his arms around Gloria's small waist.

'I don't need to ask around. When will you start?'

The Darcys were better payers than anyone else in the town. They seemed to have no end of money. The children's clothes were all good quality, their shoes were new, not mended. The furniture they had was expensive, not lovely old wood which Maura would have enjoyed polishing, but dear modern furniture. She knew the prices of all these things from her trips to the big town, and her dreams of furnishing the house that she'd buy.

Back in the cottage she had hardly anything worth speaking of. The small slow savings were being kept for the day she moved into the place she wanted. Only the glass-fronted cabinet with its small trove of treasures showed any sign of the gracious living that Maura yearned for. Otherwise it was converted boxes and broken second-hand furniture.

The Darcys had been in lots of places. Maura marvelled at how quickly the children could adapt.

They were warm-hearted too. They didn't like to come across Michael cleaning their shoes. 'He doesn't have to do that, Missus,' said Kevin Darcy, who was nine.

'I'm doing them great,' Michael protested.

'Don't worry, Kevin, that's Michael's and my job. All we ask you to do is not to leave everything on the floor of your bedroom so as we have to bend and pick it up.'

It worked. Gloria Darcy said that Maura and her son had managed to put manners on her children, something no one in any house had ever done before.

'Don't you find it hard, Mam, all the moving from place to place?'

Gloria looked at her. 'No, it's interesting. You meet new people, and in each place we better ourselves. We sell the place at a profit and then move on.'

'And will you be moving on from here too, do you think?' Maura was disappointed. She wouldn't ever get the kind of hours and payments that the Darcys gave her from anyone else. Gloria Darcy said not for a while. She thought they would stay in Shancarrig until the children got a bit of an education before uprooting them.

And their business prospered. They built on a whole new section to the original building they had bought and they expanded their range of goods. Soon people didn't need to go into the big town for their shopping trips. You could buy nearly everything you needed in Darcy's.

'I don't know where they get the money,' Mrs Hayes said one day to Maura. 'They can't be doing that much business, nothing that would warrant the kind of showing off they're doing.'

Maura said nothing. She thought that Mrs Hayes was the kind of wife who might well disapprove of Gloria's low-cut blouses and winning ways with the men of Shancarrig.

It was around this time that Maura became aware of financial problems in the Darcy household. There were bills that were being presented over and over to them. She could hear Mike Darcy's voice raised on the phone. But at the same time he had bought Gloria some marvellous jewellery that was the talk of Shancarrig.

'She has me broke,' he'd say to anyone who came into the shop. 'Go on Gloria, show them that emerald.'

And laughing, Gloria would wave the emerald on the chain. It had been bought in the big town in the jeweller's. She had always wanted one. And it was the same with the little diamond earrings. They were so small they were only specks really, but the thought that they were real diamonds made her shiver with excitement.

Shancarrig looked on with admiration. And the Darcys weren't blowing or boasting either. Nessa Ryan had been in the big town and checked. They were the real thing. The Darcys were new rich, courageous and not afraid to spend. With varying degrees of envy the people of Shancarrig wished them good luck.

The tinkers came every year on the way to the Galway races. They didn't stay in Shancarrig. They stayed nearby. Maura was struck with how Gloria looked like the Hollywood version of a gypsy, not the real thing. The real women of the travelling people looked tired and weather-beaten, not the flashing eyes and colourful garb of Gloria Darcy, and certainly not the real diamonds in the ears and the real emerald around her neck.

But this particular year people said some tinker woman must be wearing the jewels because, at the very time they were encamped outside Shancarrig, Gloria Darcy's jewellery case was stolen.

All hell broke loose. It could only be the tinkers.

Sergeant Keane was in charge of the search, and the ill will created was enormous. Nothing was found. No one was charged. Everyone was upset. Even Michael was interrogated and asked about what he had seen and what he had touched in his visits to the Darcy house. It was a frightening time in Shancarrig; there had never been a robbery like this before.

There had never been anything like this to steal before.

A lot of tut-tutting and head-shaking went on. It was vulgar of the Darcys to have displayed that jewellery; it made people envious. It put temptation in the way of others. But then, how had the gypsies known about it? They had only just come to camp. They hadn't been given dazzling displays of the glinting emerald on the chain around Gloria's throat.

'I'm sorry if the guards frightened Michael,' Gloria said to Maura.

'I don't mind about that. Sergeant Keane has known Michael since he was in a pram, he wouldn't frighten him,' Maura said. 'But I'm sorry for you, Mrs Darcy. You put a lot of store by those jewels. It won't be the same without them.'

'No, but there will be the insurance money ... eventually,' Gloria said. She said they weren't going to buy emeralds and diamonds again. Maybe put the money into paying off the extension and getting the place rewired and better stocked.

Maura remembered some of the conversations she had heard about the need to pay builders' bills. She went back over those financial difficulties she thought she had been aware of. Possibly the insurance money was exactly what the Darcys needed at this stage.

Indeed, it could be said to come at exactly the right time.

Maura had been used to keeping her own counsel for as long as she could remember. She had seen what the wild indiscretions of her own family had brought on themselves and everyone else around – her father's blustering revelations of any bit of gossip he knew, her mother's trying to play one member of the family off against the other.

Maura said very little.

She had sometimes suspected over the years that the envelope Father Gunn gave her each Christmas, saying that it was from Gerry O'Sullivan from no fixed address in England, actually came from the priest himself. But she never let Father Gunn know of her suspicions. She thanked him for acting as postman.

She sometimes wondered why she had become so secretive and close. When she was a youngster she had been open and would talk to everyone. Maybe it was just the whole business of Gerry and having

72

to be protective of Michael. And because there had never been a real friend to talk to.

The robbery of the jewels had been a nine-day wonder. Soon people stopped talking about it. There were other things to occupy their minds.

There was always something happening in Shancarrig. Maura never knew why people called it sleepy or a backwater. Only people who didn't know the place would have used words like that. Maura and Michael helped at the Dramatic Society and there was a drama a week there from the time that Biddy who worked at The Glen started to dance and went on like something wound up until no one could drag her from the stage. And there was all the business about Father Barry not being well, and then going off to the missions.

There was Richard, that handsome cousin of Niall Hayes, who had come to The Terrace and broken a few hearts – Nessa's maybe – and Maura thought there might be a bit of electricity between him and Mrs Darcy, not that she would ever mention a word of it. Yet Nellie Dunne hinted of it too so that rumour might well be going around the place. Eddie Barton had opened all their eyes with his unexpected romance, and the news of Foxy Dunne from London was always worth people pausing to discuss.

There was plenty to distract the minds of Shancarrig from the missing emerald and diamonds.

Maura O'Sullivan and her son Michael went from house to house – the ironing for Miss Ross, who had lines set in her face now, and had begun to look like a waxwork image of her old mother – there was the silver polishing for Mrs Hayes – the two hours on a Saturday for Mrs Barton – but mainly, the Darcys.

There was a lot to be done in a house where there were two boys and where the parents were hardly ever out of the shop. Maura didn't wait to be asked to do things. She had her own routine.

She was doing the master bedroom, as Gloria called it, when she found the jewellery. It was on top of the wardrobe in a big round hat box. Maura had been dusting the top of the wardrobe with sheets of newspapers spread below to catch the falling dirt. She saw a neater way to stack the suitcases, but it involved lifting them down. Michael stood willingly to take them from her. And it was only because the hat box rattled that she opened it. It was as if there was a big stone in it. She didn't want whatever it was to fall out.

It was a red silk scarf with two small black velvet bags wrapped up in it.

Michael saw her stop and hold the wardrobe top for support.

'Are you going to fall down?' he asked anxiously.

'No, love.' Maura climbed down and sat on the bed. Her heart was racing dangerously.

There was no way that she could have accidentally discovered the lost and much-mourned jewellery. There would be no cries of delight if the gems were recovered and the insurance claim had to be cancelled.

She also knew that they had not got into the hat box by accident. The description had been given over and over. The emerald on its chain had been in a box on the desk downstairs, and the little earrings in their black velvet bag beside them. The room they were in, the sitting room, had a pair of glass doors opening on to the small back garden. A light-fingered, light-footed tinker boy could have been in and out without anyone noticing.

That was how the story went.

In all her time cleaning in this house Maura had never known the valuables kept in this hat box. It was not a place someone would have put them and forgotten about them.

'Why aren't you speaking?' Michael wanted to know.

'I'm trying to think about something,' she said. She put her arm around his shoulder and drew him close.

She seemed to sit there for a long time, yellow duster in hand, her feet squarely on the spread newspaper, her son enclosed in her arm.

That evening Maura put the two little black velvet bags in her cabinet of treasures. She had to think it out very cleverly. She mustn't do the wrong thing and end up the worse for this great discovery.

Weeks went by before she brought up the subject of the lost jewels. She waited until she had Gloria in the house on her own. She had left Michael playing with the chickens outside.

'I was thinking, Mam, Mrs Darcy ... what would happen if someone found your emerald chain say ... thrown in a hedge by the tinkers?'

'What do you mean?' Gloria's voice was sharp.

'Well, now that you've done all the renovations here ... and got used to not having it and wearing it round your neck ... wouldn't it be bad for you if it turned up?'

'It won't turn up. That lot have it well sold by now, you can be sure.'

'But where would they sell it? If they brought it into a jeweller's shop, Mrs Darcy, wouldn't people know it was the one that was stolen from you? They'd call the guards, not give them the money.'

'That crowd travel far and wide. They could take it to a shop miles from here.'

There was a silence.

Then Gloria said, 'Anyway, it hasn't been found.'

'My head is full of dreams, Mrs Darcy. I go walking by the hedges. I often find things ... what would happen if I were to find it?'

'I don't know what you mean.'

'Well, suppose I did find it, would I take it to Sergeant Keane and say where I came across it, or would I give it to you ... ?'

Gloria's eyes were very narrow.

Maura saw her glance towards the stairs as if she were about to run up and check the hat box.

'This is fancy talk,' she said eventually. 'But I suppose the best would be, if you *were* to find it, to give it to me quietly. As you say, the insurance money was really more use to us than the jewellery itself at this stage.'

'What about a reward?' Maura looked confused and eager.

'We'd have to see.'

Maura went out to the chickens to find Michael, but she paused before she closed the door behind her and heard the light sound of Gloria Darcy's feet running up the stairs, and the sound of the suitcases being thrown from the high wardrobe to the floor.

Nothing was said.

It wasn't as hard for Maura as it might have been for others, because after a life of keeping her thoughts and opinions to herself it was relatively easy to work on in the house where Gloria and Mike Darcy obviously walked on a knife edge of anxiety around her.

They offered her cups of tea in the middle of her cleaning. They found things for Michael in the shop as gifts, but Maura said he mustn't be allowed to think of the shop as a wonderland where he could stroll and take whatever bar of chocolate he wanted. It would be very bad for him, and she had spent so much time trying to make him see what was his and what wasn't.

When she said this Maura O'Sullivan looked Mike and Gloria straight in the eye. She could see that she had them totally perplexed.

It was Gloria who broke eventually.

75

'Remember you were saying that you were a great one for finding things, Maura?'

'Yes indeed. I prayed to St Anthony for that good Parker pen of Mr Darcy's to turn up and didn't it roll out from behind where we keep the trays stacked in the kitchen.' Maura was proud and pleased with the results of her prayers.

'I was thinking about what you said ... and in our business, well ... we get to know a lot of people. Now, suppose you were to find the stuff that the tinkers took somewhere ...?'

'Yes, Mrs Darcy?'

'Do you know what the very best thing to do with it would be ...?'

'I do not. And I've been wondering and wondering.'

'You see, the insurance money has been paid and spent improving the shop, providing work for people, even for you in the house.' Maura held her head on one side, waiting. 'So, if it did turn up and you were able to give it to me I could get it sold for you, and give you some of it ...' Her voice trailed away.

'Ah, but if I knew the right place to sell it myself, then I could get plenty of money. Because, as you say yourself, you got the insurance money out of it already. You wouldn't want to be getting things twice over ... it wouldn't be fair.'

'But why would it be fair for *you* to get it all?'

'If I found it in a hedge, or wherever I found it, it's finders keepers, isn't it?'

'But no use of course if you didn't know where to sell it.'

This was the deal. They both knew it.

'I'll be going to the big town next week, Mrs Darcy.'

'Yes, for your Christmas shopping. Of course.'

'I get this envelope from Michael's father, through Father Gunn. I'll be spending whatever there is ...'

'I know.'

'And I was thinking, suppose I found the lost jewels by then, I'd be able to sell the emerald on the chain and I could give you back the diamonds, on account of you taking me straight to the right place, and that way ...' She let the sentence hang there.

'That way would be better, I suppose, than any other way.' Gloria's face was grim.

Niall Hayes was surprised when he heard that a Mrs O'Sullivan wanted to see him particularly. People usually wanted to see his father, Mr

Hayes Senior, the real solicitor as he had heard him described.

He was more surprised when he discovered that it was Maura Brennan from the cottages. He welcomed the two of them into his office – hardly anyone in Shancarrig had ever seen them apart.

'How have you been keeping, Maura?' he said, always a kind open fellow, despite his sharp snobby mother.

'I couldn't be better, Niall,' she said. 'We've had a bit of good luck. Michael's father always sends a bit to help out at Christmas time, and this year he was able to send a lot more.'

'Well, that's good, very good.' Niall couldn't see where the conversation was leading.

'And I'll tell you what we'd love, Niall . . . You know the cottage at the gate of The Glen?'

'I do, indeed. And they're putting it up for sale.'

'I'd like to buy it for Michael and myself. Would you act for us?'

Niall paused. How could Maura have enough to buy and renovate a place like that?

'I'll talk to Leo,' he said.

'No, talk to me. Tell me what's fair to offer her. Fair to her, fair to me.'

That was the way Niall Hayes liked to do business. There wasn't enough of it around. People were changing, attitudes were different. They wanted sharp dealings here and there.

He patted Maura's hand. It would be done.

Maura told Father Gunn that Michael's father had given them a great deal of money this year, much more than other times. If the priest was surprised he didn't show it.

'I think that's the last payment, Father.' She looked into the priest's eyes behind the thick round glasses. 'I don't think you'll be getting any more envelopes to give out at Christmas.'

He looked after them as they went down the road – Maura and Michael, soon to be householders, soon to go into a place of dreams, and paint it and tidy it and fill it with treasures.

He knew that the longer he lived in this parish the less he would understand.

EDDIE

Eddie Barton only had a birthday once every four years, which was highly unusual. In fact, he thought he was the only person in the world in this situation. It came as a shock to him that other children had been born on this day. He was ten before he accepted it properly. Up to that he had thought he was unique.

Miss Ross, who was so nice at school, had told them all about Leap Year. Mr Kelly had frightened the wits out of him by saying that if a woman proposed to you on February twenty-ninth you had to say yes, even if she was the most terrifyingly awful person in the world. Mr Kelly had laughed as he said it but Eddie wasn't sure if it was a real laugh or not. Mr Kelly often looked sad.

'Did Mrs Kelly propose to you on my birthday?' Eddie asked fearfully. If the answer was yes then this indeed was another bad aspect of growing up.

But Mr Kelly had put his finger on his lips in a jokey sort of way and said, 'Nonsense and don't let Mrs Kelly hear a whisper of this or there'd be trouble.' It was to be a secret between them.

'I thought you said it was a well-known fact?' Eddie was confused.

'I did,' the teacher sighed. 'I did but I keep forgetting, even after all my years in a classroom, how dangerous it is to say anything, anything at all, to children.'

When Eddie's tenth birthday was coming up, his mother said he could be ten on the day before or the day after.

'I'd better wait until the day after,' he told Leo Murphy, who walked home after school with him because she lived in the big house, The Glen, up the hill, and Eddie lived in the small pink house halfway up the road. Leo had said that Eddie's house reminded her of a child's drawing of a house. It had windows that looked as if they were painted on. Eddie didn't know whether this was praise or not.

'What's wrong with that?' he had asked ferociously.

'Nothing. It's nice. It looks safe and normal, not like a jungle,' Leo had replied.

That meant she liked it. He was pleased.

Eddie liked Leo Murphy. If *she* were to ask him to marry her when he had a real birthday he wouldn't say no. The Glen would be a great place to live, orchards and an old tennis court. Fantastic.

Leo took things seriously.

'Why wait until March first?' she asked Eddie about his birthday. 'Suppose you died on the night of the twenty-eighth then you'd have missed your birthday altogether.'

It was unanswerable.

Eddie's mother said she didn't mind which day he had it just so long as he knew there'd be a cake and an apple tart and no more. He could have ten people or he could have two.

Eddie measured the cake plate carefully. He'd have three and himself. That way they'd have lots. He invited Leo Murphy and Nessa Ryan and Maura Brennan. They were the people he sat beside at class and liked.

'No boys at all?' Eddie's mother was a dressmaker. She was rarely seen without pins in her mouth or a frown of concentration on her face.

'I don't sit near any boys,' Eddie said.

His mother seemed to accept this. Una Barton was a small dark woman with worried eyes. She always walked very quickly, as if she feared people might stop her and detain her in conversation. She had a kind heart and a good eye for colour and dress fabrics in the clothes she made for the women of Shancarrig and the farmers' wives from out the country. They said that Una Barton lived for her son Eddie and for him alone.

Eddie had hair that grew upwards from his head. Foxy Dunne had said he looked like a lavatory brush. Eddie didn't know what a lavatory brush was. They didn't have one in their house, but when he saw one in Ryan's Hotel he was very annoyed. His hair wasn't as bad as that.

He liked doing things that the other boys didn't like doing at all. He liked going up to Barna Woods and collecting flowers. He sometimes pressed them and wrote their names underneath, and then stuck them on a card. His mother said that he was a real artist.

'Was my father artistic?' Eddie asked.

'The less said about your father's artistry the better.' His mother's face was in that sharp straight line again. There would be no more said.

He had to make a wish when he cut the cake. He closed his eyes and wished that his father would come back, like he had wished last year and the year before.

Maybe if you wished it three times it happened.

Ted Barton had left when his son was five. He had left in some spectacular manner, because Eddie had heard it mentioned several times when people didn't know he was listening. People would say about something, 'There was nearly as much noise as the night Ted Barton was thrown out.'

And once he heard the Dunnes in their shop say that if someone didn't mind himself it would be another case of Ted Barton, with the suitcase flung down the stairs after him. Eddie couldn't imagine his mother shouting or throwing a suitcase. But then again she must have.

She told him everything else he asked, but never told him about his father. 'Let's just agree that he didn't keep his part of the bargain. He didn't look after his wife and son. He doesn't deserve our interest.'

It was easy for her to say that but hard for Eddie to agree. Every boy wanted to know where his father was, even if it was a terrible father like the Brennans' or a fierce one like Leo Murphy's, with his moustache and being called a Major and everything.

Sometimes Eddie saw people getting off the bus and dreamed that maybe it was his father coming for him – coming to take him on a long holiday, just the two of them, walking all round Ireland, staying where they felt like. And then he'd imagine his father saying, with his head on one side, 'How about it, Eddie son, will I come home?' In the daydream Eddie's mother would always be smiling and welcoming and there would be less work to make her tired because his father would be looking after them now.

After tea they played games. They had to play on the floor of Eddie's bedroom, because Mrs Barton needed to bring her sewing machine back on to the table downstairs.

They said if only Eddie had a birthday in the summer they could all have gone up to Barna Woods. Eddie showed them some of the pressed flowers.

'They're beautiful,' Nessa Ryan said.

Nessa never said anything nice just to please you. If Nessa Ryan said they were good then they must be.

'You could even do that for a living,' she added.

At ten they usually didn't think as far ahead as that, but today there had been a talk on careers in school and an encouragement to think ahead and try to get trained for something rather than just gazing out the window and letting the time pass by.

'How could I get trained to press flowers?' Eddie was interested, but Nessa's momentary enthusiasm had passed.

'We'll have another go at blow football,' she said.

It had been Eddie's birthday present. His one gift. He hadn't really wanted it but his mother had heard from the Dunnes in the shop that it was what every child wanted this year and she had paid it off over five weeks. She was pleased the game was being used. Eddie secretly thought it was silly and tiring and that there was too much spit trying to blow a paper ball through paper tubes that got chewy and soggy.

When the party was over he stood at the door of the pink house in the moonlight and watched Leo skipping up the hill to her home. You could see the walls of The Glen from here. She waved when she reached the gate.

Nessa and Maura went downhill, Maura to the row of cottages where she lived. Eddie hoped that her father wouldn't be drunk tonight. Sometimes Paudie Brennan fell around the town shouting and insulting people.

Nessa Ryan had run on ahead. She lived in Ryan's Hotel. She could have anything she wanted to eat any time. She had told that to Eddie when he had explained about the cake and the apple tart. But there must have been something of an apology in his face because Nessa had said quickly that she didn't get as much *cake* as she liked. It was really only chips and sandwiches.

The moon was shining brightly, even though it was only seven o'clock. His mother's sewing machine was already whirring away. There she would sit surrounded by paper patterns and the big dummy which used to frighten him when he was a child, always draped with some nearly finished garment, as she listened to the radio. She would smile at him a lot, but when he came upon her alone he thought her face looked sad and tired. He wished she didn't have to work so hard. And it would keep whirring until he slept. It had been like that as long as he remembered. Eddie wondered was his father looking at the moon somewhere. Did he remember his son was ten-years-old today?

That night Eddie wrote a letter to his father.

He told him about the day and the pressed flowers that Nessa Ryan had admired so much. Then he wondered would his father think that bit was sissy so he crossed it out. He told his father that there was a big wedding in the next town and that his mother had been asked to do not only the bride's dress but the two bridesmaids and the mother and aunt of the bride as well. The whole church nearly would be dressed by Mrs Barton. And that his mother had said it came just in the nick of time because something needed to be done to the roof and there wasn't enough money to pay for it.

Then he read that last bit again and wondered would his father think it was a complaint. He didn't want to annoy him now that he had just found him.

With a jolt Eddie realised that he hadn't found his father, he was only making it up. Still, it was kind of comforting. He crossed out the bit about the roof costing money and left in the good news about the wedding dresses. He told his father about the careers lecture at school and about there being lots of jobs for hard-working young fellows over in England when he got old enough. He thought that maybe his father might be in England. Wouldn't it be marvellous if he met him by accident over there in a good job with prospects.

He wrote often that year. He told his father that Bernard Shaw had died, in case he might be somewhere where they didn't get that kind of news. Mr Kelly at school had said he was a great writer but he had been a bit against the church. Eddie asked his father why people would be against the church.

His father didn't answer, of course, because the letters were never sent. There was nowhere to send them to.

It wasn't that Eddie was all *that* lonely and friendless. He did have friends, of course he did. He often went up to The Glen to play with Leo Murphy. They used to hit the ball across the net to each other on the tennis court, and Leo had a great swing on a big oak tree. She hadn't known it was an oak tree until he told her and showed her the leaves and the acorns. It was extraordinary to have all those trees and still not know what they were.

Eddie often took oak leaves and traced around them. He loved the shape – there were so many more zig-zags than in the leaves of the plane trees, or the poplar. He liked the chestnut leaves too, and he never played the silly game that the others did at school – peeling away the green bits to see who could have the most perfect fillet, like a fish with no flesh, only bones. Eddie liked the texture of the leaves.

He didn't write any of this to his father, but he did tell him when de Valera got back again and Nessa Ryan had said there had been a terrible shouting match one night in the hotel and they had to send for the guards because some people didn't agree that it was great he was back. He went on writing and told a lot of fairly private things.

Still, he didn't mention that he was afraid of someone proposing to him on his birthday when he was twelve. It seemed such a stupid thing to be afraid of. But Eddie had great fears of Eileen Dunne at school, who had a terribly loud laugh and about five brothers who would deal with him if he refused her.

'You weren't thinking of asking me to marry you on Friday, were you?' he asked Leo hopefully. She had just raised her head from a book.

'No,' Leo said. 'I was thinking about the King of England being dead and my father being all upset about it.'

'Would you?' he asked.

'Would I what? Be all upset?'

'No. Ask me to marry you.'

'Why should I? You never asked *me* to marry you.'

'It's the day, you see. It's the day women can.'

'Men can every other day of the year.'

Eddie had worked that out. 'Suppose I asked you now, and we were engaged, then if anyone asked me on Friday I could say that I wasn't free.'

He looked very worried. Leo wasn't concentrating one bit. She was reading her book. She always had a book with her. This time it was *Good Wives*. It seemed a fine coincidence to Eddie.

'What *is* it, Eddie?'

'Just say yes. You don't have to.'

'Yes, then.'

Eddie was flooded with relief. He wasn't having a party for his twelfth birthday, he was too old. He was getting a bicycle, a second-hand bicycle. His mother had told him he could cycle to school on the day. He thought he'd keep it until next day, he said. His mother looked at him affectionately. He was such a funny little thing, quirky and complicated but never a moment's trouble to her, which was more than she could have hoped the day that bastard had left her doorstep.

People sometimes said it must be hard for her to bring a boy up all on her own. But Una Barton thought they had a reasonable life together. Her son told her long rambling tales, he was interested in helping her cook what they ate and would dry the dishes dutifully. She wished there was more money or time to take him to the seaside or to Dublin to the zoo. But that wasn't for their kind. That was for boys who had fathers that didn't run away.

Eddie didn't want to remind anyone it was his birthday, just in case Eileen Dunne might get it into her head, or Maura Brennan's young sister Geraldine. But nobody seemed to have realised the opportunity they had of proposing to Eddie, or to anyone. They were far more interested in Father Barry, who had come to give them a talk about the missions and to show them a Missionary magazine which had competitions in it and a Pen-Friends Corner. There were people in every part of the world who wanted to exchange ideas with young Irish people, he said. They could have a great time writing to youngsters in different lands.

Father Barry was very nice. He seemed kind of dreamy when he spoke and he sometimes closed his eyes as if the place he was talking about was somehow nearer than the place where he was. Eddie liked that. He often thought about being out with trees and flowers when he should have been thinking about the sums on the blackboard. Father Barry pinned up the page with names of the boys and girls who wanted pen-friends. They could all speak English. They lived in far lands. One of them said he liked botany, flowers and plants. His name was Chris and he lived in Glasgow, Scotland.

'That's not very far to be writing,' Niall Hayes said dismissively. He had picked a boy in Argentina.

'There's more chance he might write back if he's not too far away,' Eddie said.

'That's stupid,' said Niall.

In his heart Eddie agreed that it was. Maybe the boy in Scotland wanted someone more exotic, not from a small town in Ireland. But the real reason he had picked Chris Taylor was that Scotland wouldn't be too dear a stamp and because he had said he liked plant life. Eddie had always thought botany was a kind of wool. He checked with Miss Ross. He didn't want to get involved in writing about knitting or sheep or anything. Not that a boy would like knitting. Miss Ross said botany was plants and things that grew.

He wrote to Chris, a long letter. It was extraordinary to be writing one that would actually go into the post box. Other twelve-year-olds might have had to suck their pens and think of something more to say to use up another sheet of paper, but not Eddie Barton. He was well used to writing long letters about the state of the world in general and Shancarrig in particular.

The letter came back very quickly but it came addressed to Miss E. Barton. It had a Glasgow postmark on it. Eddie looked at it for a long time. It must be for him. His mother's name was Una. But why had Chris Taylor called him Miss? Burning with shame he opened the letter.

Dear Edith,

    I couldn't read your name properly and maybe yours is an Irish name, but I hope I'm right in guessing Edith.

The letter went on, a friendly interesting letter, lots about Scottish fir trees and pine cones, a request to send some pressed flowers, an inquiry about whether it might be good to learn the Latin names of things in case it was going to be easier to find them when you looked them up – Chris had gone to the library and spent two hours looking up a very ordinary maple and couldn't find it because he didn't know it was called *Acer*.

Eddie read on, delighted. It was nice of Chris to take so much trouble to write, especially since he obviously thought that Eddie was a girl, and a girl called Edith. Ugh. He even asked what kind of a convent was it if the teachers were called Miss Ross and Mrs Kelly and weren't nuns.

Then on the last page Eddie got an even worse shock. Chris was closing in hope that there would be a letter soon, and saying that he was delighted to find a kindred spirit on the other side of the sea, and then signed his name

Christine

Chris was a girl.

He went hot and cold thinking about the stupid mistake. She wouldn't write to him any more once she knew he didn't go to a convent school like she did, once she knew he was a twelve-year-old boy with baggy trousers and spiky hair. It was a great pity because that was just the sort of person he would have liked to write to. And it was her fault. Not his. She was the one who had the name that could have been anything. He had a perfectly normal male name, Eddie. He could imagine what they'd say at school if they knew he had got himself a *girl* in Scotland as a pen-friend when they were all finding fellows in India or South America.

Typical sissy Eddie Barton, they'd say.

He'd love to have sent Chris, whether it was a boy Chris or a girl Chris, some of the pressed flowers. All of a sudden Eddie realised that's what he'd do, he'd *pretend* to be a girl. Just get her not to put the Miss on the envelopes any more.

And for four years Eddie Barton and Christine Taylor wrote to each

88

other, long long letters, pouring out their hearts in a way that neither of them could to anyone else.

Chris told how her mother had this dream of moving out of the city and into a house on an estate, a place with a garden and a garage, even though they didn't have a car. Chris hated the idea, she would be miles from the library and the art gallery and the places she went to when school was over. The girls at school didn't want to do anything except go to the sweet shop and talk about the fellows. Chris sent a picture of herself in school uniform and wanted Edith to send one too. In desperation Eddie sent one of Leo which he stole from The Glen when he was visiting there.

Chris wrote and said she hadn't thought of him as tall like that. She had a feeling from what he wrote that he was short and stocky and had hair that stood up. Eddie trembled when he read this as if she had found him out. He thanked the heavens that Scotland was so far away and that she would never visit. It would have been better still if she had been in Argentina, then the thought needn't have crossed his mind.

It was hard to keep up the fiction of school life when he had left Shancarrig school at the age of fourteen and now went to the Brothers in the big town every day on the bus. He told Chris that truly he wasn't happy at school and he preferred to talk about other things in his letters, like the rowan tree, like the fact that his mother was getting headaches from working too hard, like he wondered was there any way of finding out where his father was, so that he could just let him know what things were like.

He wrote about Father Barry and how he had been preaching about this village in Peru called Vieja Piedra and then had to stop, and people said the Bishop didn't like money going out of the diocese to foreign places instead of being spent at home. Chris seemed to understand. She asked him why didn't he help his mother with the sewing – it wasn't hard, they could share it.

Eddie burned with frustration over that. He realised he had made himself sound selfish and unhelpful while his only crime was that he was a boy. Everyone knew boys didn't do sewing.

He was getting on very badly at school, but he couldn't tell Chris. How could he tell of Brothers who were loud and rough with him, who often hit him with a belt when he least expected it, and one who even mocked his stutter?

Chris asked him for another picture when he was sixteen. He had none of Leo. He couldn't bear to ask her personally so he wrote her a note.

'For a long complicated reason which I'll explain to you some time, I need a photograph of you. I want you to know that it has nothing at all to do with that promise of marriage I once forced you to give. You are free from that vow, but could I have a picture next week?'

She didn't reply, but then just before his sixteenth birthday he met her unexpectedly in the middle of the town.

'Did you forget the picture?' he asked.

Leo looked distracted. She hadn't remembered.

'Please Leo, it is very important. You know I wouldn't ask you unless it were. Can I come to the house and see if you have one?'

It *was* important. Chris had sent him a picture of herself on *her* sixteenth birthday a month back. A dark girl with big eyes and a nice smile.

'*No.*' He had never known her so adamant.

'Well then, will you bring me one?'

She looked at him, as if deciding what would be the way that would cause less interference in her life.

'Oh God, I'll bring you one,' she said.

He looked hurt. 'I thought we were friends in a sort of a way,' he said.

'Yes, yes of course we are,' she relented.

'So, don't bite my head off. It's got nothing to do with being engaged.'

'What?'

Eddie decided that Leo Murphy never listened to anything anyone said. She wasn't like Chris Taylor who cared about everything.

Except of course that she thought Eddie was a girl, a fellow conspirator in life. Eddie had been forced to write and say that yes he had got his periods when he was eleven. He had managed to say that he fancied the film star Fernando Lamass and that he liked red tartan as a colour for a winter skirt.

But mainly Chris wrote about interesting things – she only descended into these female things every now and then. It always gave him a start.

He posted the photograph and waited.

He knew that she would write with a card for his birthday, usually flowers and bows and entirely unsuitable things he couldn't show to anyone. This year it was a small envelope.

'Do not open until Wednesday 29th,' it said.

Eddie took it away to read when he was on his own. He had explained to his mother that he had this pen-friend, a boy in Scotland.

'What does the Scots boy say?' his mother asked him from time to time.

'Not much. All about flowers and trees,' Eddie would say.

'Keeps you out of harm's way, I suppose,' Mrs Barton would say.

Eddie knew she sounded gruffer than she was.

In his bedroom he opened the letter from Chris and got such a shock that he had to sit down.

'I always told myself that when we were both sixteen I would tell you that I have known since the very beginning that you were a boy. I was afraid to tell you that I knew in case you'd stop writing. I *like* you being a boy. You're the nicest boy I ever met in my whole life. Happy birthday dear Eddie and thank you for your friendship.'

His first feeling was shame. How dare she have made a fool of him for four years? Then bewilderment. *How* did she know? He had agreed to having periods, being at a convent, wearing a red plaid skirt. Then came an entirely different feeling. A feeling of excitement. She knew he was a boy, and she liked him. She was afraid she'd lose him. He went to the drawer where her letters were. He read bits over and over.

'You are so easy to talk to. You really understand. You have a marvellous mind, people here are so ignorant.'

Eddie Barton was sixteen years old and in love. He went to Barna Woods. It was icy cold but he didn't care. He found an old log which he sat on, and thought about the new turn of events in his life. He must put a letter in the post to her before six o'clock. There was no question of going to school, there was far too much to think about.

Through the day he felt overwhelming regret about some of the things he had written, whole paragraphs that she must have known were lies. Then he was swept with an irritation. Why had she asked him to help his mother with the sewing when she knew he was a boy? But he mainly wanted his letter to her to be perfect and to say what he felt without frightening her off. He took the picture out again. Huge dark eyes, like an Italian. Then his heart lurched. She had no idea what he looked like. She thought he looked like Leo Murphy. Well, no she didn't, but she had no idea. Eddie wished he was tall and strong, that he looked like Niall Hayes' cousin, Richard, who had come to visit.

Everyone said he was so handsome. Eddie wished more than ever that he could find his father and ask his advice.

But his father didn't turn up on Eddie's sixteenth birthday any more than he had on any other anniversary, so he knew he would have to write it alone.

He decided to go to Miss Ross and her mother and ask if he could write the letter there. It would be warm and dry. There would be no fear of his mother asking him what he was doing, saying something that was bound to irritate him. He often did some work on the garden for Miss Ross, who wouldn't mind him coming in on a wild cold day like this.

She was just coming back from the school for her lunch when he arrived. She wore a belted raincoat which swished as she walked along. Eddie wondered if Chris wore a raincoat like that. He might ask her but somehow it seemed a bit personal, that swishy sound. Something he didn't want her to know about, and the feeling it gave him.

Miss Ross looked tired and pale. She said he was an answer to prayer. If he would just chop a few logs for her not only could he sit by the fire and write for the afternoon, she would give him a big bowl of soup as well.

'It's my birthday, Miss Ross. That's why,' he said.

She seemed to find the explanation perfectly satisfactory, and asked nothing about why he had absented himself from the Brothers without any permission. She couldn't imagine Brother O'Brien saying to a lad of sixteen that he should celebrate the day.

'What kind of a letter? Is it an application for a job?' Miss Ross asked.

'No. It's more a letter to a friend.' He was scarlet as he spoke.

'Yes, well if the friend's in a convent boarding school don't forget the nuns might read it.' Miss Ross was full of wisdom.

'No, the friend's not in a boarding school.' Eddie knew he sounded stiff.

'Well, you're all right then.' Eddie thought Miss Ross sounded as if she was trying to be cheerful for his sake. And maybe a little envious.

Eddie looked around the room before he began his letter. He had never noticed the house very much before, thinking of it as a place to take off his shoes before he came in from the garden. He remembered that Maura Brennan, who had been his friend at Shancarrig school, had always said she loved this house and that when she got old she would have one just like it, with lovely pieces of furniture that she would polish until they shone and china ornaments on shelves and thick rich velvet curtains. Eddie admired the colours; everything seemed to match with everything else, not like in his own home where the carpet was brown and the curtains were yellow and the table cloth was green; it looked as if everything was chosen to clash with everything else. He knew this was not the case, it was because they didn't have enough money to get things that would look nice. His mother had great taste in the clothes she made. She was always advising her customers what went well with their eyes or their complexion.

But still, that didn't help him to write to Chris Taylor.

He sat for a long time, the old grandfather clock ticking. Miss Ross had gone back to Shancarrig school; her mother was having her afternoon rest upstairs.

'Dearest Chris,' Eddie wrote. 'I can't tell you how good it is to be able to write as myself. I wanted to so often but once I had begun with the silly lie I had to keep it going in case you stopped writing. Your letters are the most important thing in my life. I couldn't bear them to stop.'

And then it was easy. Page after page. He tried to imagine himself sitting in this small house in Glasgow. She called it a two up two down, meaning the number of rooms. Her mother had never realised the dream of moving to an estate. Her father kept pigeons and hadn't much interest in anything else. Her two brothers were at sea and only came home for a very short visit now and then. She wanted to go to a school of art but she wasn't good enough. Her mother said to get a job in the florists and be grateful for it; most people had to do work they hated. At least Chris liked flowers so she'd be ahead of the game.

What would this girl like to read from Eddie, now revealed as a man? He knew one thing. There must be no more pretence.

'I'm small and square and have hair that sticks up. I don't think I ever told you properly about school and how much I hate it, because when I was meant to be a girl I couldn't tell you how rough they are there and how they think I'm as thick as the wall. I don't think I am, and your letters make me think I have something.'

There was no trouble finding the words. When he read it over he thought she would think it was a fair explanation for his years of deceit. Not too much apology, more setting the record straight.

He was surprised when Miss Ross came back from school.

'That's a letter and a half, Eddie,' she said approvingly.

'Would you have said I was thick, Miss Ross?'

'No, I wouldn't, and you're not,' she said.

He grinned at her and ran off. She looked out the door and saw him heading for the post office, skipping and jumping over puddles.

The letters came fast and thick. They wrote to each other about hopes and fears, about books and paintings, about colours and designs. They kept nothing back.

'If we ever meet I must show you the ferns of Barna Woods,' he wrote once.

'What do you mean "if we ever meet"? It's "when we meet"!' she wrote back, and his heart felt leaden because he knew he had made Shancarrig sound too beautiful, too exciting, too romantic for Christine Taylor.

'That boy must have nothing to do but write letters,' his mother said one day when the usual fat envelope arrived from Scotland.

'It's not a boy, it's a girl.' Eddie knew he'd have to explain some time.

'What do you mean? Did he turn into a girl all of a sudden?' Mrs Barton didn't like the sound of it being a girl.

'No, it's a different one.' Eddie didn't feel that any further explanation would help.

'Why Scotland?' his mother said.

'It's nice and far away,' he grinned. 'If I have to be writing to a girl, Ma, isn't it better that I write to one in a far off country?'

'At your age you shouldn't be writing to a girl at all. There'll be plenty of time for that later. Too much time if you're your father's son.'

There had been much mention over the years of Ted Barton's interest in women, always vague and generalised, never specific and detailed. Eddie had long given up the hope of getting any more information than the sketchy amount he already had. His father had been thrown out because of a known association with another woman. When he had left Shancarrig that night the woman had not gone with him. She might even be someone he knew. Someone he had spoken to. If only it was someone nice like Miss Ross then maybe she could have told him more about the man who had left their lives.

'Did my father ever like Miss Ross?' he asked his mother suddenly.

'Maddy Ross?' His mother looked at him in surprise.

'Yes. Could she have been his love?'

'Well, given that she was about twelve or thirteen when he left town

94

it isn't entirely likely, but that doesn't say it should be ruled out either.' His mother had even managed a wry smile as she said this.

Eddie thought she was less bitter. He must remember to tell this to Chris when he wrote; they had no secrets. She told him about her father being laid off in the shipyard and her mother getting an extra shift in the factory. Chris was doing Saturdays in the local flower shop. It wasn't like she thought it would be, working with flowers. It was very mechanical, stiff little arrangements and awful cheaty ways of making flowers look alive when they were almost dead.

They wrote to each other when they should have been trying a last desperate effort at their books. Christine said that they were snobby in her convent and didn't like the girls whose mothers worked in factories. Eddie wrote that the Brothers had a down on anyone with a bit of soul at all and that they had him written off as a no-hoper. The results of the exams were a foregone conclusion to them both.

In the summer of 1957 they wrote and told each other of poor results, bad marks and limited futures.

'I had a word with Brother O'Brien. He doesn't think it worth trying to repeat the year,' Eddie's mother said glumly. She had taken the bus into the big town to buy materials, threads, zip fasteners and spare pieces for the sewing machine. She had used the opportunity to visit the school.

It hadn't been a happy encounter.

'I told him that other boys had fathers who could pay for this kind of thing, but that we weren't in the lucky position to know where your father is or has been for the last dozen years.' Her face had that old bitter look which Eddie hated.

'Ma, you threw him out. You asked him to go. You can't keep blaming him for everything after he went, only for what he did before he went.'

'And that was plenty for one lifetime, let me assure you.'

'You always *assure* me these things but you never explain them.'

'Oh, you've words at will, just like him.'

'And was Brother O'Brien sympathetic? I bet he wasn't. He couldn't care about anyone's father, or mother, or anyone at all.'

His mother gave him an odd look.

'He wasn't sympathetic. Neither to you nor to me. But I think he does care about people. He said there was no point in my lamenting the absence of a husband, that it was mainly women who did all the consulting whether their husbands were alive or around or whatever.'

'And what else?'

'He said that you had got it into your head you were too good for the school, above them and their plain ways. And that would have been fine if you were a real artist burning to paint or to write, but the way things were he didn't know what would become of you. He sounded sorry.'

To Eddie it had the ring of truth. That was exactly the way Brother O'Brien would speak, and there was some truth in it. He could see the big man with his red face regretting that he couldn't find a place for the boy. Brother O'Brien loved his boys to get into banks and insurance offices, the Civil Service, and the very odd time even into a university.

There would be nowhere for Eddie Barton.

If he hadn't had his lifeline of letters to hold him together as support and strength Eddie would have been very depressed that summer. But Chris wrote every day. She said they must get themselves out of this situation. She would not work in a factory like her mother, nor would she train to be a florist.

They had begun to talk of love now, they ended each letter with more and more yearning and wishes that they could meet. Eddie said that perhaps he had made Shancarrig sound too attractive. Maybe they could meet in some foreign land where there would be warm winds and palm trees. Chris said that nobody could love anybody if they met in the grey streets around her home. She was all for somewhere exotic too.

The world of fantasy became an important part of their letter-writing. It almost took over from the practical side. Chris Taylor went to work in a department store in Glasgow. She hated it, she said. It was very tiring. Her legs ached more than usual. Eddie wrote and asked did her legs usually ache, she had never mentioned it before. But she didn't mention it again so he thought it must have been just a phrase.

Eddie Barton went to work in Dunne's Hardware. He hated it. He wrote to Chris about the days talking to farmers who came in to buy chicken wire and plough parts. He said he was sick of harrows and rakes and if he had to talk about linseed oil or red oxide for painting a barn again he thought he might actually lie down and die. He wrote about how ignorant the Dunnes were. Their aunt, Nellie Dunne, ran a small grocery shop and she gave people credit which was the only reason why anyone shopped there. Eddie worked for old Mr Dunne and his sons Brian and Liam. Eileen, who was his own age, worked in Ryan's Hotel, but was always giving him the eye when she came in.

'I tell you this...' he wrote to Chris, 'not to make myself sound great or to make you jealous, but to remind myself how lucky I am that stupid girls like Eileen with her forward pushy ways form no part of my life now that I know what love is. Now that I have you.'

Sometimes she wrote about going to a dance, but she said she sat in a seat on the balcony most of the time and thought about what he had said in his last letter.

Sometimes Nessa Ryan and Leo Murphy came into the shop to talk to him. The Dunnes never minded him talking to them because they were as near to the Quality as Shancarrig possessed. If Maura Brennan came in, or anyone else from the cottages, it would be different. But old Mr Dunne seemed to take positive pleasure out of a visit from young Miss Ryan of the hotel and young Miss Murphy from The Glen.

'And how goes the good Major?' he would ask Leo about her father.

'Talking to himself as usual,' Leo muttered once and they all giggled. Mr Dunne didn't like such disrespect.

'And how are they all in Ireland's leading hostelry?' he would ask Nessa Ryan about her family's hotel.

Nessa always said it was doing fine thank you.

Eddie wrote to Chris about how strained and worried Leo Murphy looked when she should have had no worries in the world. She had got six honours in her Leaving Certificate. She had all the money in the world; she could have gone to university in Cork or Galway or Dublin, yet she always seemed to be biting her lip.

Chris wrote back and said you never knew what worries people had. Perhaps Leo wasn't well, maybe it was her health. What did she look like? In shame Eddie wrote and said that Leo looked like him, or rather, the pictures he had sent of him when he was meant to be a girl were of Leo.

'She's very good-looking,' Chris wrote back anxiously.

'I never noticed it,' he wrote. 'Perhaps I should have stayed a girl.'

'No. You're lovely as you are,' she said in the next letter.

They knew that they must talk. Neither household had a phone but Chris could use the public phone and Eddie could be in Ryan's Hotel waiting for the call. They rehearsed it in letters for some weeks.

'We mightn't like each other's voices,' Chris wrote. 'But it's important to remember that we like each other so the voice doesn't matter.'

'What do you mean we *like* each other?' wrote Eddie. 'We love each other. That's what we must remember on Saturday night.'

They made it Saturday so that they could look forward to it all week. He dressed himself up and put on a clean shirt.

'On the town again I suppose.' His mother hardly seemed to look up but she had taken in that he was smartly turned out.

'Aw, no, Mam. There's nowhere much to go on the town in Shancarrig.'

'Well, where are you going if I might ask?' Her tone wasn't as sharp as the words. She was aching to know.

'Just down to Ryan's Hotel, Mam, for a cup of coffee.'

'Eddie ...?'

'Yes, Mam.'

'Eddie, I know I'm nagging you but you won't ...'

'Mam, I told you I don't drink. I didn't like the smell of it or the taste of it the once I tried.'

'I don't mean drink.' She looked him up and down, a boy setting out for a date, for romance.

'What do you mean?'

'You wouldn't get involved with that Eileen Dunne, now would you? They'd be bad people to get on the wrong side of ...'

'Who are you telling! Don't I work for them?'

'But Eileen ...?'

He knelt beside his mother and looked up into her face.

'If she were the last woman in Ireland I wouldn't want her.'

Anyone would have known that he was speaking the truth. Eddie's mother waved him off with a lighter heart.

Chris was to ring at eight. Eddie positioned himself in the hall. The telephone would ring at the reception desk, then whoever was on duty would look around and say, 'Eddie Barton, I don't know ... oh yes, *there* he is,' and she'd motion Eddie to go into the booth. Then he would speak to her. To the girl he loved.

Another good thing about it being a Saturday was that awful Eileen Dunne wouldn't be working at the desk. She was in the dining room on Saturdays, her dress tight across the bottom and the bosom, and a small white apron making no attempt to cover her at all.

Eddie's heart was beating so strongly it reminded him of the big clock in Shancarrig school and the thudding sounds it made as the seconds ticked on.

Soon, soon. Ten minutes. Nine.

He jumped a foot in the air when he heard the phone ring. He hadn't noticed that Eileen Dunne *was* working at Reception tonight. Please may she not make any remark, may she not say something stupid that Chris would hear all the way away in Scotland.

'Yes, he's here. Hold on. *Edd . . . ie?*'

He was at the desk.

'Yes?'

'There's someone on the phone for you. Will you take it here at the desk? God, you're looking like a dog's dinner tonight.'

'I'll go into the box,' he said, his face red with fury.

'Right. Hold on till I get this bloody thing through. There's more plugs and wires than a hedgehog's backside. Are you going in to town to the dance?'

He ran in to the dark phone booth, his hands trembling. Damn Eileen Dunne to hell. Please may Chris not have heard.

'Hello?' he said tentatively.

It must be the Scottish telephone operator on the line. He could hardly understand her. She was saying something about difficulty in getting through.

'Can you put me on to Chris, please?' He knew his voice was shaky but it had been a bit of luck that she hadn't come straight through. She wouldn't have heard that stupid stupid Eileen. Any moment she'd talk to him.

'This *is* Chris,' he managed to decipher from the strange speech. 'Do you mean you canna hear me?'

It wasn't Chris's voice. It was like someone imitating a Scottish comedian. Every word was canna and wouldna.

'That's never you, not you yourself, Chris?' he said. She must be playing a joke.

'Och, Eddie, stop putting on that Irish blarney bit. You're like the fellows they have at Christmas concerts in the church, with their afther doing this and afther doing that.'

There was silence. They realised that neither of them was putting on an act. This is the way they were. The silence was broken by their laughter.

'Oh God, Eddie . . . I forgot. I had you talking normally in my mind.'

His heart was full of love. This strange way she spoke didn't matter a bit. 'I thought you'd be like a real person too,' he said.

Then it was back to the way they were in letters. Until the three minutes ran out.

'I love you, Chris, more than ever.'

'And I love you too,' she said.

They lived for Saturdays, and yet as they wrote to each other the phone calls were never as good as they expected. Sometimes they literally didn't understand what the other was saying and they wasted precious time explaining.

They were desperate to meet. The time was very long.

'We'd better meet soon before we're too old to recognise each other,' she wrote.

'While we still remember what we wrote to each other.'

They each kept their letters in shoe boxes. It seemed a small thing but a bond ... another bond. Yet they hesitated each to ask the other to their town. Eddie couldn't bear the explanations, the doing up of the spare room, the questioning from his mother, the eyes of Shancarrig.

Chris said that if he had found it hard to understand her voice then her family and her neighbours in Glasgow would be incomprehensible.

She obviously yearned for Barna Woods and the hill with the big rock on it, the rock that gave its name to the town. She wanted to see Eddie's pink house and meet his mother.

He wanted her here and he didn't want her. He wanted to leave Shancarrig for ever, and yet he couldn't. One man had left his mother already, Eddie couldn't go.

Then at last he heard himself inviting her. He didn't really intend to, it just came out.

It had been a long hard day in Dunne's when nothing had gone right. Old Mr Dunne was like a devil, Liam had been scornful, Brian had been giving him orders, and to make matters worse their cousin Foxy who had been in Eddie's class at school had come back for a visit.

Foxy worked on the buildings in England. He was doing well by all accounts. He had started by making billycans of tea for Irishmen working on the lump, building the big roads over in Britain. He came home every year, eyes bright and darting around him as usual.

Normally Eddie was pleased to see Foxy, he had a quick wit and was always ready with a joke.

Today it hadn't been like that. 'Don't let him speak to you like that,' Foxy said to Eddie when Mr Dunne had called him an ignorant bosthoon.

'Fine words, Foxy. He's only an uncle to you, but he pays my week's wages.'

'Still and all, you're letting him walk over you. You'll be here for the rest of your life with a shop coat on you stuck behind a counter.'

'And what are you going to be?' Eddie had flared back.

'I've got the hell out of here. I wouldn't sit here listening to my uncle mumbling and bumbling, and my Aunt Nellie letting people run up bad debts because they're Quality. I'm in England and I'll make a pile of money. And then I'll come back and marry Leo Murphy.'

It was the longest speech that Foxy had ever made. Eddie had been surprised.

'And will Leo marry *you*?'

'Not now, she won't. Not the way I am. No one would marry either of us, Eddie. We're eejits. We have only one good suit each with an arse in the trousers of it. We have to *do* something with our lives instead of standing round here like fools. What class of a woman would want the likes of us?'

'I don't know. We might have a charm of our own.' Eddie was being light-hearted but he felt that Foxy was right.

Foxy turned away impatiently. 'I can see you in twenty years still saying that, Eddie. This place makes us all slow and stupid. It's like a muddy river dragging us down.'

Eddie had been thinking about it all day. He didn't dress up for the phone call that night. It was his turn to call the Glasgow phone box.

'Come over to Ireland. Come to Shancarrig,' he said when Chris answered the phone.

'When? When will I come?'

'As soon as you can. I'm sick of being without you,' he said. 'There's nothing at all else in my life except you.'

Their letters changed tone. It was confident now. It was 'when' not 'if'. It was definite. The love was there, the need, the surprise that one other person could feel exactly the same about everything as another.

There were the details.

Chris would take her two weeks holidays from the flower shop. Eddie could take his two weeks off from Dunne's. She would get the boat from Stranraer to Larne, and the train to Belfast maybe?

'Will I come to meet you there? I've never been to the North of Ireland. It'll be familiar to you, red buses, red pillar boxes. Like England.'

'Like Scotland,' she corrected him. She had never been to England in her life.

Or would she take a train to Wales, and get the boat from Holyhead? Maybe that would be a nicer way to go. She could see Dun Laoghaire and a bit of Dublin before taking the train to Shancarrig.

'I don't want you wandering around on your own, meeting Dublin fellows. I'll come and meet you off the boat,' he suggested.

Chris said no, she wanted to arrive in Shancarrig on the train herself. She knew about the station, and the flowers that now spelt out the word Shancarrig. He had written that long ago to her.

Eddie could be on the platform.

He prayed that it would be a fine fortnight, that the sun would shine into Barna Woods between the branches, that there would be a sparkle on the River Grane. He knew you shouldn't pray for something bad to happen to another human but he hoped that somehow Eileen Dunne would be in hospital when Chris arrived, and that Nessa Ryan wouldn't be superior towards him, and that he'd be free of Brian and Liam Dunne and their bad-tempered father because he was on holidays.

He hoped most of all that his mother would be nice to Chris. They had never had anyone to stay, and Eddie had distempered the walls, and painted the woodwork in the small stuffy room they had called a box room up to now. His mother had been curiously quiet.

'What kind of a girl is she?' was all she had asked.

'A girl I write to, I write to her a lot. I like her through the post and on the telephone. I've asked her to come over here so that ... well, so that I wouldn't be the one going off on you.'

His mother looked away so that he wouldn't see the look of gratitude in her face. But he saw all the same.

'I'll make curtains for the room,' she said.

Please let them like each other.

They had got ham for tea, cooked ham and tomatoes, and a Fullers chocolate cake with four chocolate buttons on the top.

His mother had cleared the sewing away so that the place would look like a normal house. There were blue curtains on the window of the box room, and a matching bedspread. On the makeshift dressing table there was a little blue cloth and Eddie had gathered a bunch of flowers.

It was nearly time. The train would be in at three. Only four hours. Three. Two. It was time.

*

Liam Dunne was on the platform; there was a delivery coming down with the guard on the train.

'What are you doing?' Liam asked. 'Aren't you meant to be on your holidays? If you're doing nothing you could give me a hand...?'

'I most definitely *am* on my holidays and I'm meeting a friend,' Eddie said firmly.

The train whistled and came around the corner. She got off. She carried a big suitcase, square with little firm bits over the corners like leather triangles to preserve it.

She had a red jacket and a navy skirt, a navy shoulder bag and a huge bright smile.

He had been afraid for a moment that she might think Liam Dunne was him. Liam was taller and good-looking in a rangy sort of way. Eddie felt like a barrel. He wished his spine would shoot up and make him willowy.

He started to walk towards her and saw her foot. Chris Taylor had a big built-up shoe. He willed his eyes away from it, and on to her smiling eager face.

Liam was busy with the guard, hauling things from the luggage van, and nobody was watching them.

Eddie had never kissed anyone in his life apart from fumbles at dances. He put his arms around Chris.

'Welcome to Shancarrig,' he said first, then he kissed her very gently. She clung to him.

'I didn't tell you about my foot,' she said, her face working anxiously.

'What about your foot?' He forced himself not to look at it again to see how bad it was. Could she walk? Did it drag? His head was whirling.

'I didn't want you to pity me,' she said.

'Me? Pity *you*? You must be mad,' he said.

'I can walk and everything, and I can keep up. I'll be able to see every bit of Barna Woods with you after tea.'

She looked very young and frightened. She must have been worried about this for ages, like he worried about the place not being as nice as he described.

'I don't know what you're going on about,' he tried to reassure her, but he knew it wasn't working.

'My leg, Eddie. I've got one shorter than the other, you see. I wear a special shoe.'

He could read how hard it was for her to say this. How often she must have rehearsed it. He urged himself to find the right words.

He looked down at her foot in its black shoe with the big thick raised sole and heel.

'Does it hurt?' he asked.

'No, of course not, but it's the way it looks.'

He took both her hands in his. 'Chris, are you mad?' he asked her. 'Are you off your head? It's me. It's Eddie, your best friend. Your love. Do you think for a moment that it's part of the bargain that our legs had to be the same length?'

It was, as it happened, exactly the right thing to say. Chris Taylor burst into tears and hugged Eddie to her as if she was never going to leave him go. 'I love you, Eddie.'

'I love you too. Come on, let's go home.' He carried her case and they walked to the gate of the station.

Chris was still wiping her eyes. Liam Dunne stood watching them.

'Don't mind him.' He nodded in Eddie's direction. 'That fellow's as thick as the wall. He's always upsetting people and making them cry. There's plenty of real men in Shancarrig.'

She gave him a bright smile.

'I bet there are. I've come all the way from Scotland to investigate them.' She tucked her arm into Eddie's and they went out the gate.

Eddie felt ten feet tall.

'Who was that?' she whispered.

'Liam Dunne. Desperate . . .'

'Don't tell me. I know all about him. The younger son, the one that'll take over if Brian goes to England and the old man dies.'

'You know it all,' he said in wonder.

'I feel like I'm coming home.'

As they walked up the road and he pointed out Ryan's Hotel where he had sat waiting for the phone calls, and the church where Father Gunn waved to him cheerfully, the pubs and Nellie Dunne's grocery, he knew that in many ways she had come home. He knew that he had been right, she was the centre of his life. It would be fine when he brought her home to his mother.

Afterwards nobody could ever tell you exactly how and why Chris Taylor came to live in Shancarrig. One day she had never been heard of and then the next there she was, as if she had been part of the place all her life.

If people asked Mrs Barton about her they were told that she was a marvellous girl altogether and a dab hand at the sewing. There was nothing she couldn't turn her hand to. Look at the way she had made them go into furnishings, for example. Chris Taylor had loved the curtains and bedspread in her little room the day she arrived. Her praise was unstinting. Mrs Barton was a genius.

Eddie never thought of his mother's dressmaking as anything except a way to make a living; he knew she didn't particularly like some of the women whose dresses she made. He hadn't realised that the work was artistic in itself.

Chris opened his eyes for him. 'Look at the way the ribbon falls, look at the colours she's put together... Eddie, it's easy to see where you got your artistic sense from...'

His mother reddened with pleasure. There were no derisory remarks about his father. In fact, Chris was able to introduce the first reasonable conversation about the long-departed Ted Barton that had ever been held in this house.

'I suppose he was a restless kind of a man. Better for him to be gone in a lot of ways.'

And to his surprise Eddie heard his mother agreeing. Things had really begun to change around here.

Chris was part of Shancarrig.

They knew her coming in and out of Dunnes to see Eddie or to give him a message, they knew her in the hotel where she became friendly with Nessa Ryan. No one ever spoke dismissively to Chris Taylor as people had been known to do to Eddie Barton. She talked furnishings and fabrics to Nessa's mother. There was going to be a grant for the hotel to make it smarter, the kind of a place where tourist visitors might stay as well as commercial travellers.

They couldn't stay in Ryan's the way it was. Chris seemed to know the way it should be – pelmets, nice wooden pelmets covered in fabric, she had seen it all in an American magazine, you stuck the fabric to the plywood, and then the curtains draped properly down below. And, of course, bed covers to match.

Nessa Ryan and her mother were very excited.

'How would we get it started? Would we need to call someone in from Dublin? Who'd do it?'

'We would,' Chris said simply.

'We?'

'Mrs Barton and I. Let us do one room as a sample and see.'

'Wooden pelmets...? You couldn't do that...?'

'Eddie could, he could get the plywood. Liam Dunne could help him...'

The room was a huge success. The whole hotel would be done the same way. They had chosen a fabric which would tone in with Eddie's pressed flowers, with his large bold designs, flowers from Barna Woods, a place in the locality, especially commissioned from a local artist.

'You can't call me a local artist,' Eddie had protested.

'You are local. You live here, don't you?' she said simply.

The plans were afoot. Chris and Eddie's mother would be able to do it between them, but they needed someone to organise it, someone who would go and choose the right fabrics, someone with an eye for colour, someone whose pictures were already on the wall.

Flushed and happy Chris told Eddie the plan.

'You can leave Dunne's. We'll have a business, all of us...'

'I can't leave ... if we get married I have to support you.'

'What's this *if*? Are you changing your mind? I've come over here and lived with you, set myself up shamelessly in your house and you say "if"?'

'I want to ask you something properly.'

'Not here, Eddie. Let's go up to the woods.'

Eddie's mother stood by the window and watched the two of them walk together, the limping figure of this strange strong Scottish girl, the stocky figure of her own son, who had grown taller since Chris had arrived.

She knew nothing about the kind of family over in Scotland who let their daughter wander away to another land without seeming to care.

She cared little now about the past. Once she had lived in it and felt burdened by it, now she thought only about the future, the proposal that was going to be made in Barna Woods and accepted, the new life that was ahead of all of them.

DR JIMS

I n Shancarrig they only knew him as Dr Blake for about six weeks. Then they all started to call him Dr Jims. It had to do with Maisie, of course. Maisie who couldn't pronounce any name properly, not even one as ordinary as James. She had been asked to call Dr James to the telephone and in front of the whole waiting room she had said that Dr Jims was wanted. Somehow, the name had stuck. James Blake was too young a man to be given a full title, not while the great Dr Nolan held sway in Shancarrig.

Jims Blake got very accustomed to people asking for the real doctor when they came to The Terrace, and if a call came in the night which Dr Jims answered, the gravest doubts were expressed. He learned to say that he was only holding the fort for the real doctor, and Dr Nolan would be along at a more convenient hour to give his approval.

But it was a good partnership – the wise old man who knew all the secrets of Shancarrig and the thin eager young man, son of a small farmer out the country. The old man who drank more brandy at night than was good for him and the young man who stayed up late reading the journals and reports ... they lived together peaceably. They had Maisie doting on both of them and resenting the fact that people kept getting sick and needing to disturb the two men in her life, the great Dr Nolan and poor young Dr Jims.

Dr Nolan was always saying that Jims Blake should find a wife for himself and Maisie was always saying that there was plenty of time.

Matters came to a head in 1940 when Dr Nolan was seventy and Dr Jims was thirty. It had been a busy time. There was a baby to be delivered in almost every house around them. A little girl Leonora up at The Glen, a first daughter to the Ryans at the hotel, another Dunne to the cottages, a son for the wife of wild Ted Barton, another Brennan to add to Paudie's brood.

Dr Jims would come back tired to the big house in The Terrace – the tall house, one of a line facing the hotel. It formed the centre of the town in a triangle with the row of shops. The bus stopped nearby and the movement of Shancarrig could be charted from any of the windows. Dr Jims' work took him to the far outlying districts as well, but the centre of life remained this small area around the place where he lived.

Even though it was comfortable there were ways in which it was not a real life. Dr Nolan was able to put it into words. 'I'm not going to let you make the same mistake as I did,' the old man said. 'A doctor needs a wife, really and truly. I had my chances and my choices in the old days, like you do now. But I was both too set and too easy in my ways. I didn't want to disrupt everything by bringing a woman in. I didn't really need a woman, I thought.'

'And you didn't either,' Dr Jims encouraged him. 'Didn't you have a full life ... where was there room for a wife? I've seen too many doctors' wives neglected, left out ... maybe the medical profession should take a vow of celibacy, like the clerics. It might be something we could bring up at the Irish Medical Association.'

'Don't make a jeer out of it, Jims. I'm serious.'

'So am I. How could I marry? Where would I get the stake for a house? I still send a bit home to the farm. You know that. I have to be averting my eyes for a bit, in case I think I might want a wife.'

'And who are you averting them from?' The old man drank his brandy, looking deep into the glass and not at his partner.

'Not anybody in particular.'

'But Frances Fitzgerald, maybe?'

'Ah, come on out of that. What could I offer Frances Fitzgerald?'

But Jims Blake knew that the old man had seen through him. He most desperately wanted to advance things with Frances, to go further than the games of tennis with other people present, the card evenings at The Glen or in Ryan's Hotel.

He'd hoped it hadn't been as transparent to other people.

Yet again Dr Nolan seemed to read his mind.

'Nobody would know but myself,' he said reassuringly. 'And you could offer her half a house here.'

'It's your house.'

'I won't be here for ever. It's taking more of this stuff to ease the pain in my gut.' He raised his brandy glass to show what he was referring to.

'The pain in your gut would be less if you had less of that stuff.'

'So you say, with the arrogance of youth... We'll get the top two floors done up for you. The Dunnes can come in on Monday and lean on their picks and shovels and we'll see what they can do. Frances will want her own kitchen ... she won't want Maisie traipsing around after her.'

'Charles, I can't ... we don't even know if Frances is interested...'

'We do,' said Dr Nolan.

Jims Blake didn't even wait to let that sink in.

'But I can't afford...' he began.

Charles Nolan's face winced with pain and anger. 'Stop being such a defeatist, such a sniveller... I can't this, I can't that... Is that how you made yourself a doctor...?'

His face was red now proving his point.

'Listen here to me, Jims Blake, why do you think I took you on here? Think about it. It wasn't for your great moneyed connections and class. No. I took you on because you were a fighter, and a dogged little fellow. I liked your thin white face and your determination. I liked the way you forced them to let you study, and took jobs to make up the extra money that they couldn't give you. That's what people need in a doctor – someone who won't quit.'

'I could pay you so much a month for it, I suppose. I could take on more of the work.'

'Boy, aren't you doing almost all the work already. I'm only giving you what's fair...'

And it was settled like that. Dr Jims was to have the upstairs part of the house. Everyone said it was very sensible. After all, Dr Nolan wasn't getting any younger. Wasn't it sensible that a bedroom be built for him on the ground floor?

Maisie sniffed a bit, especially since it became known that Dr Jims was now courting Miss Fitzgerald.

The Dunne brothers were in regularly, wondering should the kitchen be facing the front or the back of the house. It might be good to have it looking out on the town. There was a nice view of Shancarrig from upstairs in The Terrace. But then, traditionally a kitchen was at the back. They puzzled at it.

Before they came to any solution their work was rendered unnecessary. Dr Charles Nolan died of the liver complaint he had been ignoring for some years, and he willed his house to his partner Dr Blake.

Before he died he spoke of it to Jims. 'You're a good lad. You'll keep it all going fine here, if only you'd learn to...'

'You've got years yet. Stop making a farewell speech,' Jims Blake said to the dying man.

'What I was *going* to say, if only you'd learn that there are people, myself included, who are quite glad to be coming to the end of their lives, who don't *want* to be told that there are years of pain and confusion ahead of them...'

Jims held his partner's hand – it was a simple gesture of solidarity where no words would have worked.

'That's more like it,' said Dr Nolan. 'Now, will you promise me to have a family and a real life for yourself? Don't be forced to leave this place to some whippersnapper of a junior partner, like I am!'

'You can't leave it all to me . . .' He was aghast.

'I was hoping to leave it to Frances as well. Tell me you've made some move in that direction . . .'

'Yes. We were hoping to marry . . .' His voice choked, realising that his benefactor wouldn't now be at the wedding.

'That's good, very good. I'm tired now. Get me into hospital tomorrow, Jims. I don't want to die in the house where she's coming as a bride.'

'It's your house. Die wherever you want to,' Jims blazed at him.

The old man smiled. 'I like to hear you talk that way. And where I would like to die is the hospital. Tell that young Father Gunn to come up there to me, not to be upsetting Maisie by coming here. And move that brandy bottle back to my reach.'

It didn't take Shancarrig long to recognise Dr Jims as the real doctor. Everything had changed. There was no old Dr Nolan any more to know their secrets so they told them to Dr Jims instead. He was a married man now, of course, and his wife a very gentle person – one of the Fitzgeralds who owned a big milling business.

It had been a good match – that's what outsiders thought. But they only knew the surface. They didn't know about passion and love and understanding. Frances, with her gentle solemn face transformed so often with a quick smile that lit up her whole being, was a wife that he never dreamed possible.

She would creep up behind him and lock her arms around his neck. She would feed him pieces of food from her plate when Maisie wasn't looking. When he was called out at night Frances sometimes left a note on his pillow saying, 'Wake me up. I want to welcome you home properly.' In every way she made him grow in confidence. Jims Blake walked with a lighter step and a smile in his eyes.

The fact that Dr Nolan had left him the house made Dr Jims even more respected in the community. If the old doctor had thought so much of him then this must be a good man. Sometimes Jims Blake felt unworthy of all the respect he got in Shancarrig.

When he visited his dour family on their small bleak farm and saw the lifestyle that he would have been condemned to had he not fought so hard to study medicine, he felt guilty. He was saddened that they had so little, and even the money he gave them was stored under a mattress, not used to buy his mother and father a better standard of life.

He had tried to explain this guilt to Frances but she calmed him down. He had done everything he could for the family. Surely that was as much as anyone was expected to do – he couldn't do any more.

Frances said that *they* were a family now she and Jims and the baby they were expecting. There was no tie that bound them to the bleak family of Blakes in the small wet farm, or the distant, undemonstrative Fitzgeralds wrapped up in their business affairs. They were a little unit in themselves.

And so it was for a while.

Jims often thought that the spirit of old Dr Nolan would have been pleased to hear the way that Number Three The Terrace rang with laughter. First Eileen was born, then Sheila. No son and heir yet, but as people said, God would send the boy in his own good time.

There were many attempts for the boy – all ending in miscarriage.

Frances Blake was a frail woman – the efforts to hold a child to full term were taking a great toll on her health.

Several times Jims asked himself what would the old doctor have advised if he had been involved in a family where this had been the situation. He could almost hear Dr Nolan's voice.

'This is a thing you could work out between the pair of you... Now the good God up in heaven doesn't have a book of rules saying you must do this or that, and so many times... The good God expects us to use our intelligence...'

And he might go on to explain some of the most elemental details of times of high fertility and low fertility, suggesting the latter as the wiser time to indulge in what he called the business of marriage.

But always he would urge the couple to talk to each other.

Jims Blake somehow found it hard to talk to his own wife.

The problem was all the greater because he loved her so much. He desired her *and* he wanted to protect her. A combination of that was hard to rationalise. He had worked out her ovulation as carefully as he could, they had tried to make love at the times she was least likely to conceive. He had held her face in his hands and assured her that his two little girls were plenty, they didn't need to try for a son. Let them live their lives without putting her to any additional strain, without placing her health in danger.

Sometimes she looked sad, he didn't know if it was because she feared that he didn't desire her as much as he once had. Perhaps it was because she really did yearn to give him a son. He found it impossible to believe that two people who loved each other so much could still have areas of misunderstanding. And yet, whenever he approached her she seemed so receptive and willing that he had to believe this was what she wanted too.

When Frances became pregnant again in 1946 the girls Eileen and Sheila were five and four – two cherubs sitting in their Viyella nightdresses and red flannel dressing gowns while he read them stories. This time he hoped for a son to join them.

In the coldest winter that Ireland had ever known Frances Blake gave birth to her son. And in the house with log fires burning in every room, with a midwife from the hospital in the big town in attendance, as well as her husband who had, even at the age of thirty-seven, delivered thousands of children into the world … she died.

They had never even discussed what to call the baby. They hadn't dared to hope it would live, nor had they dared to hope it would be a boy.

Father Gunn, arriving at the house to the news of the birth and death, enquired if the child was sickly, and whether there should be an emergency baptism.

'I think the child is healthy enough.' Jims Blake's voice was empty.

'Well, we'll leave it for a while then. It'll bring some cheer to the household to have a baptism.' Father Gunn was optimistic. He tried to see some light at the end of the seemingly endless dark tunnels of this particular winter. He had been burying far more than he baptised.

'Maybe you could get it over with, Father.' The young doctor looked white and strained.

'Not now, Jims. Wait a bit. Give the lad a start, find godparents for him. Think of a name. He has a life to live, Frances would want that for him.'

'He mightn't live, let's do it now.'

Something about the face of Jims Blake made Father Gunn know that this was not so. But he couldn't close the doors of heaven to a little soul.

He still had his stole on.

'Bill Hayes is downstairs, he could be the godfather. What about a godmother?'

'Maisie will stand for him…'

'But later, the boy might like to...'

'It doesn't matter what the boy might like later on. Will we do it or will we not?'

Father Gunn said the words of baptism while pouring the holy water on the head of Declan Blake. He had asked was there to be any other name – people usually had two.

'Declan will do,' said Jims Blake.

Maisie, her face red from crying, her voice almost inaudible from a heavy chest cold, made the vows together with Bill Hayes, the local solicitor – they would look after the spiritual welfare of this child.

Bill Hayes, the local solicitor in Shancarrig, had children the same age as Jims Blake's, including a newly born baby girl, safely delivered from a living wife not four weeks previously.

Never short of the right word in terms of the law, Bill Hayes found himself totally unable to give any meaningful sympathy at a time like this.

'If you were a drinking man I'd get you drunk, Jims,' he said.

'But you're not a drinking man either, Bill.'

'Still, I could become one if it would help you.'

The doctor shook his head.

He had seen too many people opting for this solution.

'Would I sit with you downstairs by the fire?'

Poor Bill Hayes was truly at a loss for the comforting small talk that came to him so easily in his office when consoling those who had been cut out of wills or who had lost a court case. Nothing seemed appropriate to say.

'No. Go home, Bill. I beg you. I'll sit by myself. There's a doctor coming in from the town. He'll be staying in the spare room tonight ... in case I get a call-out. He'll do it for me tonight. I wouldn't be much good to anyone.'

'Did Frances know she had a son?' Bill Hayes asked. He knew his wife would want to know – it wasn't the kind of question he would normally ask.

'No. She knew nothing at all.'

'Well, well. He'll grow up a credit to you both. I know that.'

Jims tried to remember that he had a son, a boy who would grow in this house, as the girls had grown. A baby who would be fed with a bottle, and who would cry in the night. A baby who would smile and flail with little fists. A baby boy who would sit in a dressing gown and want to hear stories read aloud to him.

Suddenly it was all too much for him. He could see other pictures crowding in. A little boy with a school satchel, struggling along the road to Shancarrig school. A boy with a hurley going to a match. He almost felt dizzy with the responsibility of it all.

A wave of loneliness swept over him. There would be no Frances ever again. No Frances so proud of the girls in their little powder-blue coats, going up the church with them at mass. No Frances to talk to in the evening. She was lying ice-cold already. Tomorrow she would be taken to the church and then the whole of Shancarrig would process to the churchyard.

His father and mother would come, his sisters and his brother, rosary beads dangling from their hands, nudging each other, whispering. No help or support to anyone.

The Fitzgeralds would come, the women in hats looking down at the Blake women in headscarves. There would be stiff and stilted conversation in the house.

Not one of them knew how terrible it was that his wife had died, and that he felt responsible. If it hadn't been for that time ... the time they must have conceived the child ... Frances would be alive and well tonight.

He said goodbye to Bill Hayes, who left with some relief. And then Jims Blake sat down at his fire and tried to count his blessings, like he always urged his patients to do.

He listed a good marriage with Frances as a blessing. Nearly seven years of it. Great passion, great friendship, a happy time full of hope.

He listed his little girls, he listed the big house in The Terrace, left to him by his good, kind partner. And a big steady doctor's practice. He counted in having escaped from his own family as a blessing, and he added his own good health. He did not include his son, the baby not yet one day old.

Everyone said that it was the worst funeral they were ever at – the rain lashing against the church, the traces of old snow slippery on the ground, a freezing east wind as they walked to the cemetery.

Jims Blake insisted that the girls be taken home after the mass. In fact, as he stood shaking hands with the congregation of sympathisers, many of them with heavy colds and flu, he begged them not to come to the grave.

'Things are bad enough already, don't get pneumonia,' he urged them.

But in Shancarrig people felt it was only right and respectful to accompany a funeral to the final resting place. They stood, a wretched group, as the wind caught the coats of the grave diggers and blew the few flowers away from the top of the coffin, hurtling them in a macabre sort of dance around the gravestones.

Back in The Terrace they asked in hushed tones how he would manage. What was he going to do? The loss of Frances wasn't just that of a wife, it was the loss of the person who managed the home. Three little children. Every time they said three he got a shock.

He thought of Eileen and Sheila with their little faces. He had forgotten about the baby.

This wasn't at all healthy, he told himself. And as his relations and friends drank sherry and ate plates of sandwiches in the rooms downstairs he went up wearily to look at his son.

The child was sleeping as he went into the room.

Tiny and red as all children, he seemed swamped and smothered by the bedding, his tiny perfect little fists with their minuscule nails on the pillow. Was it his imagination or did the baby look more helpless and alone than any other child? As if he knew he was motherless from the moment he had come on earth.

'I'll do my best for you, Declan,' he promised aloud. It was curiously formal and he felt himself remote as he said it. It was like a contract or a bargain between strangers, not a father to his infant son.

He hadn't heard anyone come into the room they called the nursery, but turned to find Nora Kelly, the young schoolmistress married to the master.

'Can I pick him up?' she whispered softly, as if she were in a sickroom.

'Of course, Nora.'

He saw the woman who had been aching to have her own child lift the tiny baby and hold him to her breast.

She said nothing, just walked around the room.

Her stance was that of a woman who had always nursed a child. Her hold on the baby was sure, her love obvious. No one except Jims Blake would know the amount of examination she had undergone to try and discover why she could not conceive.

He watched, almost mesmerised, as she walked to and fro crooning a very soft sound to the baby boy.

He didn't know how long they were there – the strange tableau of the doctor, the teacher and child. But he felt this slow urge coming over him to give away his baby son. He wanted more than anything in the world to say to Nora Kelly: 'Take him home, you have none, you never will have any. I don't want this child that killed Frances . . . Bring him back home and rear him as your own.'

In a more civilised society that's what people would have done. Why would it be the scandal of Shancarrig, the talk of the county and, moreover, a crime against the law of the land, for someone to walk out of this room with the child they so desperately wanted, taking him from a home where he wasn't needed?

Then he pulled himself together.

'I'll go on down, Nora. Stay here a bit if you want to.'

'No, I'd better come down too, Doctor,' she said.

He knew that the same solution had crossed her mind, and she was banishing it, as he had.

It was on occasions like this that Mrs Kennedy, the mournful bleak-looking housekeeper to Father Gunn, came into her own. She slid almost invisibly into the house of the bereaved, suggesting, helping and organising. She would arrive with a supply of gleaming white table cloths to hand them, then in a trice sum up what the house would need in order to give hospitality to those who would come to sympathise. A quick word with the hotel across the road from The Terrace about extra cups, glasses and plates while Maisie listened to it all wringing her hands. Mrs Kennedy had the authority of the clergy because she had worked with them for so long.

She never interfered, she just guided.

Maisie wouldn't have known about the need for good hot soup to serve with the sandwiches, nor that a room should be cleared for people's coats and umbrellas. Mrs Kennedy managed to imply that she was the voice of order and sanity in sad circumstances like these. And in houses rich and poor all over Shancarrig people had gone along with her, feeling a sense of overpowering relief that someone was taking charge.

Jims Blake greeted people, accepted their condolences, poured them more drinks, inquired about their health, but he did so with only part of his brain. He was working out what arrangements he was going to make. He did so by elimination. He would not have either of his unmarried sisters to live in the house, and he must make that clear before any offer was made. He would not have anyone from the Fitzgerald side of the family either, though they were less likely to present themselves.

Maisie couldn't manage a baby. It would be too expensive to have a live-in nurse. What was he to do?

As he had done so often, he asked himself what old Charles Nolan would have done. Again the voice came to him, booming as it would have been. 'Isn't the countryside crawling with young girls dying to get out from under their parents? Any one of them will have brought up a rake of brothers and sisters. They'll be well able to look after one small baby.'

He felt better then, and was even able to smile at Foxy Dunne, one of the boldest of the entire Dunne clan from the cottages – a red-haired boy in raggy trousers who had come to the door to sympathise.

'I'm sorry for your trouble,' Foxy had said, standing confidently in the cold outside Number Three The Terrace.

'Thank you, Foxy. It was good of you to call.'

The boy was looking past him to the table where there was food and orange squash.

'Well then...' Foxy said.

'Would you like to come in and ... sympathise inside?'

'That's very good of you, Sir,' said Foxy, and was past him and at the table in two seconds.

Maisie looked disapproving and was on the point of ejecting him. Mrs Kennedy frowned heavily.

Dr Jims shook his head.

'Mr Dunne has come to sympathise, Maisie. Mrs Kennedy, can you please give him a slice of cake?'

The nurse was booked to stay for a month and Jims Blake began his search for the girl who would bring up his son. It didn't take long.

He found Carrie, a big-boned, dark-haired girl of twenty-four, living on the side of a hill, deeply discontented with a life that involved cooking for six unappreciative brothers. He had been to the house on several occasions, usually to deal with injuries from threshing machines or otherwise around the farm. He had never treated the girl, but when he was called to their place to stitch the father's head after yet another violent altercation with some farm machinery, it occurred to Jims Blake that Carrie might be glad of the offer of a place, and a better situation.

They walked to the farmyard gate and he told her what he had in mind.

'Why me, Doctor? I'd be a bit ignorant for the kind of house you run.'

'You'd be kind. You could manage a child. You managed all this lot.' He jerked his head back at the house where she had looked after brothers, older and younger than herself, since her own mother died.

'I'm not very smart,' she said.

'You're fine. But here's a few pounds anyway, in case you want to buy yourself some clothes to travel in.'

It was a nice way to put it. He knew the travelling which meant taking a few belongings on the next lift she could get to the town wasn't important, but it covered the fact that she hadn't an outfit to wear.

Maisie sniffed a bit at the news of the new arrival, but not too much. After all, the poor young doctor was still in mourning, and mustn't be upset. And it had been very clear from the outset that Carrie would help Maisie in the house. There would be no question of meals on a tray for a fancy nurse.

Declan Blake was only ten days old when Carrie took him in her arms.

'He's a bit like my own,' she said quietly to Dr Blake.

'You had one of your own?' The world was full of surprises. She had never consulted him about the pregnancy.

'Up in Dublin. He's given away, it was for the best. He's three now, somewhere.'

'As you say, it would have been hard to have reared him.' His voice held its usual gentle sympathetic tone, but it came from the heart. This gawky girl wouldn't think it was at all for the best that her three-year-old had been given away.

'I'll do a good job minding this little fellow, Dr Jims,' she said.

It reminded him of his own vow to the child. Everyone was promising this tiny baby some kind of care, as if the baby feared he wouldn't get any.

The summer eventually came that year, and Dr Jims took his little daughters by the hand up to Shancarrig school.

He walked around the three classrooms with them, and showed

120

them the globe and the map of the world. He pointed out the ink wells in the desks and told them that soon they'd be dipping their own pens in there and doing their exercises. Solemnly they all studied the charts showing the Irish lettering for the alphabet.

'You'll be able to speak Irish when you leave here,' he promised them.

'Who would we speak it to?' Eileen asked.

Mrs Kelly was standing at the door and gave one of her rare smiles.

'It's a good question,' she said ruefully.

Dr Jims had sent her to Dublin again for further tests, none of the results being remotely helpful. There was no reason that specialists could find why the Kellys were not conceiving a child. He remembered his strange urge to bundle the baby into her arms on that unreal day back at The Terrace. He knew how near he had been to saying something so unsettling that it could never have been unsaid.

Again, this time she seemed to be thinking along the same lines.

'How is Declan?' she asked the children. 'It won't be long now until you'll be bringing him along to school with you.'

'Oh, he'd be useless. He never says anything at all,' Eileen said.

'And he'd wet the floor,' Sheila added, in case there was any question of enrolling the baby.

'Not now. The child's only ten weeks old on Friday. You were the same at that age.' Mrs Kelly spoke in her stern teacher's voice. Eileen and Sheila drew back in awe.

Jims Blake noted that Nora Kelly remembered the exact age of the baby boy he had wanted to give her.

If he had been asked he couldn't have said without counting back to the April day when Frances had died.

'Come on now, girls. We mustn't delay Mrs Kelly.' He began to shepherd them home.

'I'm sure you're dying to be back to him,' she said.

'Yes. Yes, of course.' His voice sounded false and he knew it.

As they closed the school gate he wondered was he unnatural not to hurry home to see a sleeping infant? He didn't think so. When Eileen and Sheila were babies he didn't see them for hours on end, and then only when presented with them by Frances after bathtime. Surely that was the way most men felt?

He mustn't dwell on that one highly charged moment on the day of his wife's funeral. Rationally of course he had no intention of giving away the baby that she had died bringing into the world. It was foolish to keep harking back to it with guilt.

He had perfectly normal feelings towards this child, and the hiring of Carrie had been inspired. She had indeed a natural instinct of motherhood, and she seemed to know that they wanted as little sign of a baby about the house as possible.

The girls went to the nursery each evening to play with him and to hear stories of Carrie's wild brothers, and the desperate injuries they had endured. She told them nothing of the child born in Dublin and given away. She sat rocking the substitute baby Declan in her arms.

Jims Blake called in from time to time. Not every day.

He knew that Mrs Kelly at the school would find this unbelievable.

That evening he went into the nursery.

Carrie was sitting at a table with pen and ink and several sheets of screwed-up paper.

'I was never one for writing, Doctor,' she said.

'We're all good at different things. Aren't you marvellous with the child?'

'Anyone would love a baby.' She shrugged it off.

'Yes,' he said.

Something in his voice made her look up. 'Well, it's different in your case ... I mean, being a man and everything, and your poor wife dying giving birth to him.'

'I don't blame him for that.' It was true. Jims Blake blamed himself, not his son, for the death of Frances.

'You'll grow to love him. Wait till he starts to call you Daddy ... and clings to your legs. They're lovely at that age.'

She must have been thinking about her brothers, he realised. She didn't see her own child grow.

He changed the subject. 'Could I help you at all with the writing ... or is it private?' He saw Carrie look at him. In many ways he had the same status as Father Gunn, a man who knew secrets, a man who could be told things.

Carrie had a brother in gaol. None of the rest of the family wrote to him. She wanted him to feel that he wasn't forgotten, that there'd be a place for him when he got out. It was told trustingly and simply.

He sat down at the table and took out his pen.

He wrote a letter to the boy, whose head he had stitched some years back, as if the letter came from Carrie. He told of the changes in the farm, the new barn, the way they had let the lower field go to grass. He told how Jacky Noone had got a new truck, and how Cissy had married. He said that Shancarrig looked fine in the summer sunshine and would be waiting to greet him when he came home.

Haltingly Carrie read it aloud, and tears came to her eyes. 'You're such a good man, Doctor. You knew what I wanted to say, even though I didn't know myself.'

'Here. You can have my fountain pen as a present. You'll get into less of a mess with it than trying to dip that thing there.' The baby began to cry and the doctor stood up. He walked to the door without going to see the child. 'Copy that out, Carrie, yourself. It's no use sending the boy my letter. You copy it and next time I'll give you more ideas.'

She picked the child up and looked at him with a face confused. A man so kind as to spend time writing a letter to her gaol-bird brother, a man who would give her his own good pen, but wouldn't pick up his son who was ten weeks old.

When Declan Blake was three Carrie had a cake for him with three candles and there was a party in the nursery. Maisie made special drop scones for the occasion. The girls got him presents of sweets and they all sang 'Happy Birthday' before he blew the candles out.

Jims Blake looked at the small excited face of his son, the snub nose and the straight shiny hair washed especially for the day. He was wearing a new yellow jumper which Carrie must have bought in the town. He left money for the children's clothes with Carrie and for the food with Maisie. Together they ran his house very well for him.

He had a curious empty feeling when the birthday song was over, as if something were expected of him.

It was only ten years ago in this house that Charles Nolan had urged him to marry. Ten years of visiting people and hearing their troubles and learning their hopes, realistic or wildly beyond their reach. He didn't know what his own hopes were. He had never had time to work them out, he told himself.

The children were still looking at him.

In his mind he asked old Charles Nolan what to do and he heard himself saying...

'Why don't we sing "For He's a Jolly Good Fellow"...?'

Their eyes lit up, Carrie's face softened, the girls shouted the chorus and Declan clapped his hands to be the centre of such attention. Jims Blake felt the moment frozen for a long time.

The day came sooner than he ever thought it would when Declan should be brought to school.

'A great day for you, Doctor, to see your son setting out with a satchel,' Carrie had said.

Jims Blake looked at the child. 'It's a great day all right. Isn't it, Declan?'

Declan looked up at him solemnly, as if he were a stranger. 'It is, yes.' He spoke shyly, and half hid himself behind Carrie, scuffing his new shoes a little on the ground, and seeming awkward.

Probably all children that age are awkward with their fathers, the doctor told himself. He watched from the window as his son went off to school on wobbly legs.

The doctor meant to ask how the day went, but he was out on calls when Declan came home, and the next morning there wasn't time to talk either. It was a week before he even knew that there was a problem about Carrie delivering Declan to the school.

'The other children call him a baby,' Carrie explained.

'He's too young at five to walk all that way by himself,' his father protested.

'Other children do. All the young Dunnes come up from the cottages on their own...'

'Those Dunnes aren't children at all, they're like monkeys. They were climbing trees barefoot when they were two years old.'

Jims Blake was indignant that there should be any comparison.

'But it's terrible to have him made a jeer of. Maybe he could go with the girls...?'

'The girls say they don't want him traipsing after them. They have their own friends...'

Carrie looked at him as if he had let her down. Jims Blake felt a wave of self-pity sweep over him. Why was he always made out to be in the wrong? He thought he was doing his best for all of them, not loading Eileen and Sheila down with dragging their baby brother, and now he was the worst in the world as a result.

None of his patients challenged what he said. They took their tablets, drank their medicine bottles, changed poultices and dressings, made journeys into hospitals for tests, without ever doubting him.

Only at home did his every action seem suspect.

Later, when he was helping Carrie with her letters, as he did every week, underlining a spelling mistake lightly in pencil, she looked at him, troubled.

'You're a very good man, Doctor.'

'Why do you say that?'

'You correct me without insulting me. I write "yez" meaning "you all" and you just say, "Wouldn't it be better to put you all, it might be clearer" ... You don't say I'm pig ignorant!'

'But you're *not* pig ignorant.'

'Maybe you shouldn't be teaching me all the time. Maybe you should be doing pot hooks with Declan.'

'Pot hooks?'

'It's how they teach them to write.'

'I don't want to be cutting across Mrs Kelly and her ways.'

He did look at Declan's copy book though, and asked him knowledgeably, 'Are these pot hooks, then?'

'Yes, Daddy.'

'Very good. Very good, keep at them,' he said. There was the familiar feeling that it hadn't been the right thing to say.

Since he had organised them all to sing 'For He's a Jolly Good Fellow' when Declan was three, there had hardly been a time when he was sure that the right thing had been said.

Eileen and Sheila always asked about his patients, ever since they had been very young.

'Is Mrs Barton going to die?' They liked the quiet dressmaker who lived with her only son in the pink house on the hill.

'No, of course not. She's only got the flu.'

'Is Miss Ross going to have a baby?' They had seen her knitting and thought the two went together.

'Was there much blood in the car crash?'

He parried their questions, kept the secrecy and diffused the sense of drama, and always he was aware that his son never asked him questions.

As the years went by he was even more aware of it. The girls left Shancarrig school and went to be boarders at a good convent school fifty miles away. There was now only the doctor and Maisie and Declan left in the house.

Carrie had given her own notice when Declan made his first communion.

'He's seven now, Doctor. He's a grown lad. He can dress himself, keep his room tidy, do his homework and all. You don't need me.'

'And maybe you're thinking of getting married?' There was nothing Dr Jims didn't see or know.

'I'm not going to say much about it.'

'And is it the father of the little lad?'

'Yes, it is. Thanks to you, Doctor, I was able to write to him a bit, tell him things, speak my mind. You're a great man for getting people to say things out. There's far too many round here who bottle it all up.'

He was pleased at her praise. 'You'll have another child. I know you'll never forget the first one, but you'll be a family now.' He was full of happiness for this dark-haired angular girl, who had such a poor start in life.

'And you'll have a chance to get to know your son more, maybe, when I'm gone.'

'Ah, that will come, that will come. I was thinking of getting a desk up here for him to do his homework.'

'The girls always did it downstairs, you know, more in the hub of things.'

'But he'd like it here. More independent. Wouldn't he?'

'He might feel a bit shut away.' Her eyes were troubled.

'Not a bit of it, it would let him concentrate. Anyway, enough of such things. You'll come back and see us?'

'Of course I will. It was the best seven years of my life. I grew up properly in this house. I was very privileged.' He tried to brush it away. 'I mean it, Doctor Jims. I wouldn't even have been able to use a word like privileged when I came here. Isn't that living proof?'

When she was gone he made deliberate efforts to get involved in his son's world.

Always he seemed choked off.

Declan did his homework silently up in the room that used to be called the nursery, then he would come down and sit with Maisie in the kitchen while she prepared the supper. Dr Jims was out so often it seemed only sensible for the boy to eat with Maisie, after all he had eaten his meals with Carrie when she was there to look after him.

He tried to think of things to interest Declan. 'Are you on to fractions yet, lad?'

'I don't know.'

126

'You must know. Either you are or you aren't.' His voice was suddenly impatient.

'We might be. Sometimes you call things one thing and they call it another at school.'

'And how's your friend, Dinnie?'

'Vinnie.'

'Yes, Vinnie. How is he?'

'He's all right, I think, Dad.'

'Well, surely you know whether he's all right or not?' Again the impatience arising without control, the tone of his voice changing.

'I mean, I haven't seen him for ages.'

'Aren't you friends any more?'

'I don't know. We might be. He's living in the town, I'm here.'

Guilt then. Had he not listened? Had he ever been told? Surely other parents had this confusion about their children's friends.

And of course, girls were easier too, anyone knew that. There had never been any trouble about Eileen and Sheila. He knew who their friends were. They talked about them, they brought them to The Terrace. When they came home from boarding school they always sought out Nessa Ryan from the hotel, and Leo Murphy, the daughter of Major Murphy up at The Glen.

Boys were hard to fathom. They lived in a secretive world of their own, it seemed. Jims Blake looked back on his own childhood, on the small bleak farm with the dour uncommunicative father who had hardly ever thrown him a word. He was behaving so differently from that silent man, and still meeting rebuff, it seemed.

The girls talked to him very easily. Eileen came and sat on a footstool in his study, hugging her knees. 'Leo Murphy's got all odd and snooty this year,' she complained.

'Is that a fact?' Jims Blake had his own worries about the mental health of Miriam Murphy, the girl's mother.

'Yes. She wouldn't let me in when I went up to The Glen, just said she couldn't play today. *Play*, as if I was a child or she was a child.'

'I know, I know.' He was soothing.

'And Nessa Ryan says the same thing about her, snooty as anything. She won't let you into her house, as if anyone wanted to go.'

'Maybe Maisie could make you a nice tea here...'

'She doesn't want to go to anyone else's house either, Nessa says.'

'At least you have Nessa,' he said consolingly.

Eileen flounced. 'Yes, and who needs Leo Murphy and her big house? Ours is much smarter than theirs anyway.'

'Don't be boasting about our good fortune in having a nice house,' he said.

He had tried to tell them all about the good fortune in being given a house of such quality by the late Dr Nolan, but his loyal daughters dismissed it. They thought their father was worth it and more, they said.

Eileen was going to go to university if she got a lot of honours in her Leaving Certificate. She would be an architect. She would love that. The nuns said she had all the brains in the world and by the time she was qualified the world, and indeed Ireland, would be moving to the point where women architects would be quite acceptable. It would be the 1960s after all. Imagine.

And Sheila wanted to do nursing, so he was already sending out feelers for her to the better training hospitals in Dublin.

Declan would do medicine, of course, so the main thing was to get him into a good boarding school. He had spoken to the Jesuits, the Benedictines, the Vincentians and the Holy Ghost Fathers. There were advantages and drawbacks in all of them. He checked the records, the achievements, the teaching records and he chose the one that came out best overall. The bad side was that it was further away than any other school.

'You won't be able to go and see him much there,' Eileen said.

'He'll come home in the holidays.' Dr Jims knew he was being defensive. Again.

'But it's lovely to have visitors at school. We loved you coming on Sundays.'

He used to go every second week, a long, wet drive in winter. He had never taken Declan. At first he would have been too young and restless for the drive, and the girls would have hated him to be troublesome when he arrived in the parlour. Then later, it didn't seem the right thing to suggest.

A ten-year-old boy wouldn't *want* to be dragged off to a girls' school of a Sunday even if he had been invited. It would be a sissy sort of thing for a boy.

He intended to spend more time with the boy during the summer before Declan went to boarding school, but there was so much to do. There was the whole business of Maura Brennan's child for one thing.

He had always liked Maura, the only Brennan girl to stay in Shancarrig. The others had long gone to unsatisfactory posts in England.

Maura had a dreamy quality about her, an acceptance of what life had to offer. He remembered the day he had confirmed her pregnancy.

'He'll never marry me, Dr Jims,' she had said, big tears waiting to fall from her eyes.

'I wouldn't be sure of that. Aren't you a great catch for any man?' He had said it but his heart wasn't in the words. He had thought Gerry O'Sullivan would disappear but he had been wrong, Gerry stayed. There had been a wedding, he had gone in to Johnny Finn's to drink their health.

And then when he had delivered her child it was he who saw the epicanthic folds around the eyes. It was he who had to tell Maura O'Sullivan, as she so proudly called herself, that her son was a child with Down's syndrome.

He remembered how he had held the girl in his arms and told her it would all be all right. Even when Father Gunn had told him that Gerry O'Sullivan, father of the boy, had taken the train from Shancarrig station and was gone before the baptism, he remembered the sense of hearing his own voice mouth the words of comfort, telling Maura that everything would be fine.

And he had been right to say that she would always love young Michael with an overpowering love. That much had been true even if Gerry O'Sullivan was never seen in the streets of Shancarrig again.

There was a human story everywhere he turned ... in the small houses and in the big ones.

There was something seriously wrong up at The Glen and he didn't know how to cope with it. Frank Murphy, a quiet man who bore his war injuries bravely, had something much more serious on his mind than the bad leg he dragged after him so uncomplainingly.

Jims Blake thought it had to do with his wife. But Miriam Murphy was someone he had never examined. She assured him she was as strong as a horse. She was an attractive woman with a dismissive manner if crossed, and he had liked her red-gold hair and her effortless way of looking elegant while walking around the big gardens with a shallow basket, an old silk scarf draped over her shoulders.

People in Shancarrig had long grown accustomed to the fact that Mrs Murphy never came down to the shops. There were accounts in the shops and the delivery boys who called on bicycles always got a friendly wave from the mistress of The Glen. They would deal with Biddy the maid, or with the Major himself.

But this summer there was something different about Miriam. A vacancy in her eyes that was more than disturbing. And a cautious protective look in Frank's that hadn't been there before. Charles Nolan had told him often enough about families who guarded their secrets, who kept their unstable people hidden. Often it was better not to pry.

Jims Blake wondered what old Charles would have made of the situation in The Glen. Not only was the Major in a state of distress, but their daughter Leo, who had been such a close friend of his daughters, had also begun to show signs of strain. He met the girl when driving past Barna Woods.

'Do you want a lift back up to the house, Leo?'

'Are you going that way?'

'A car goes whatever way you point it.'

'Thanks, Doctor.'

'Have you lots of new friends for yourself this summer, Leo?'

She was surprised. No, it turned out she hadn't any. Why did he ask? Without putting his own children in the role of complainers he hinted that she hadn't been around.

'We went on a bit of a holiday, you see, to the seaside.'

That was true. He had heard Bill Hayes say that the Major had packed dogs and all into the car and driven off without warning.

'Ah, but you're back now, and still no one ever sees you. I thought you'd gone off with the gypsies.' They had just driven in the gate of The Glen as he said this. She looked at him, as white as a sheet. 'It's all right, Leo. I was only joking.'

'I hate jokes about the gypsies,' she said.

He wondered had they frightened her in the woods. Dark, suspicious and always on guard, they had given him a pheasant once, when he had delivered a child for them. Unsmiling and proud they had handed him the bird, wrapped in grass, to thank him for the skill they hadn't sought, but had used because he was passing near during a difficult birth.

The Major appeared at the door. 'I won't ask you in,' he said.

'No, no.' His reputation as a discreet man who could be told anything rested on ending conversations when others wanted to. He never probed a step further, but his face was always open and ready to hear when others wanted to tell.

His son Declan never wanted to tell anything.

'Will you like being at the school do you think, Declan?'

'I won't know, not really, until I get there.'

Had there ever been a boy so pedantic, so unwilling to talk?

*

Maisie wanted to know had he settled in? Was the bed aired? Were there any other boys from this part of the world there?

Dr Jims Blake could answer none of this. His only memory was his son's hand waving goodbye. He wasn't clinging, like one or two other lads were, loath to leave mothers go. Nor was he chatting and making friends as some of the more outgoing boys seemed to be doing.

They had to write letters home every Sunday. Declan wrote of saints' days, and walks, and doing a play, making a relief map. Jims Blake knew that these letters were supervised by the priests, that they were intended to give a good impression of the school and all its activities. Sometimes the letter lay unopened on the hall table along with the advertising literature from pharmaceutical companies that was sent to all doctors on a mailing list.

Declan didn't write to Eileen, now in a hostel in Dublin while she studied architecture in University College. He didn't write to Sheila, now nursing in one of Dublin's best hospitals. He sent a birthday card to Maisie, but they knew very little about his world at school.

The reports said that he was satisfactory, his marks were average, his place in the class was in the top end of the lower half.

His school holidays seemed long and formless. The doctor got the impression that he was dying to be back at school.

'Would you like to ask any of your friends to stay?'

'Here?' Declan had been surprised.

'Well, there's plenty of room. They might like it.'

'What would they do, Daddy?'

'I don't know. Whatever they do, whatever you do anywhere.' He was irritated now. It was this habit of answering one question with another that he found hard to take.

It never came to anything, that suggestion. Nor the invitation to go to Dublin.

'What would I do in Dublin for two days?'

'What does anyone do in Dublin? We could see your sisters, take them out to lunch. That would be nice, wouldn't it?' He realised he sounded as if he was talking to a five-year-old, not a boy of fifteen. A boy who had grown apart from Eileen, now nearly qualified as an architect, from Sheila, now almost a qualified nurse.

The visit never happened. Neither did the outing to the Galway races, which had been long spoken of as a reward when Declan's Leaving Certificate was over.

Jims Blake said he could put his hand on his heart and swear that he had made every move to try and get close to his son, and that at every turn he was repelled.

It wasn't a thing that he would normally talk to another man about, but he did mention it to Bill Hayes. 'Do you find it like ploughing a hard field trying to get a word out of your fellow, Niall, or does he talk to you?'

'Niall would talk to the birds in the trees if he thought they'd listen. He has a yarn for every moment of the day. Not much knack of dealing with clients, though.'

Bill Hayes shook his head gloomily. His son too seemed a slight disappointment to him. Although a qualified solicitor he showed no signs of being able to attract new business or, indeed, cope with the business that was already there.

'And does he talk to *you*?' Dr Jims persisted.

'When he can get me to listen, which isn't often. I don't want to hear rambling tales about the mountains and the lakes when he goes out to make some farmer's will for him. I want to hear that it's been done properly, the man's affairs are settled and everything's in order.'

Dr Jims sighed. 'With me it's just the opposite. I can't even get him to talk about enrolling up at the university. He keeps making excuses.'

'Talk to him at a meal. Don't serve him until he answers your question... That'll get an answer out of him. Boys love their food.'

Jims Blake was ashamed to say why this wouldn't work, to admit that his son still ate meals in the kitchen with Maisie, out of habit, out of tradition. No point in laying up two places in the dining room. Who knew when the poor doctor would have to be called out?

But the summer of 1964 was moving on. Arrangements would have to be made, fees must be paid, places in the Medical School reserved, living quarters booked.

'Declan? No one would ever think we lived in the same house, lad...'

'I'm always here,' the boy said. It wasn't mutinous or defensive, it was said as a simple fact.

Jims Blake was annoyed by it.

'I'm always here too,' he said. 'Except when I'm out working, as you will be.'

'I'm not going to do medicine, Dad.'

Somehow, it came as no surprise. He must have been expecting it.

'When did you decide against it?' His voice was cold.

'I never decided *for* it, it was only in your mind. It wasn't in mine.'

They talked like strangers, polite but firm.

Declan would like to join an auctioneering firm. His friend Vinnie O'Neill's father would take him on. He'd like the life. It was the kind of thing that appealed to him, looking at places, showing them to customers. He was good at talking to people, telling them the good points of a place. There'd be a very good living in it for him. Vinnie was going off to be a priest. There was no other boy in the family, only girls. Mr O'Neill liked him, got on well with him.

Jims Blake listened bleakly to the story of a man he didn't know, a man called Gerry O'Neill, whose estate agent's signs he had seen around the place. A man who got on well with Declan Blake and regarded him as a kind of son now that his own was going to enter the priesthood. Silently he accepted the plans, plans that involved Declan going to live in the big town. He could have Vinnie's room, apparently. It would be easier to have him on the spot, and the sooner the better.

Vinnie was going to the seminary next week. Declan thought he'd move in at the weekend.

Jims Blake heard that Maisie wouldn't miss him because so much of her life was now centred around the church. And she had got used to him being away at school.

'And what about me?' Jims Blake said. 'What about my missing you?'

'Aw, Dad, you're your own person. You wouldn't miss me.'

It was said with total sincerity, and when the boy realised that there actually was loneliness in his father's face, he seemed distressed.

'But even if I were going to be doing medicine wouldn't I be away all the time?'

'You'd be coming back to help me in the practice, and take over. That's what I thought.'

There was a silence. A long silence.

'I'm sorry,' Declan said.

Later Jims wondered should he have put his arm around the boy's shoulder. Should he have made some gesture to apologise for the coldness and distance of eighteen years, to hope that the next years would be better. But he shrugged. 'You must do as you want to,' he said. And then he heard himself saying, 'It's what you've always done.'

He knew it was the most final goodbye he could ever have said.

Sometimes when he was in the town Jims Blake called in to O'Neill's. Like someone probing a sore tooth he was anxious to see the man and the home where Declan Blake felt he belonged. Gerry O'Neill, a florid man with a fund of anecdotes about people and places, regarded himself as a great raconteur. Jims Blake found him boring and opinionated. He sat and watched unbelievingly while the man's wife and daughters and Declan laughed and encouraged him in these tales.

The eldest girl was Ruth, a good-looking girl, her Daddy's pet. She was doing a commercial course in the local secretarial college so that she could help in the business. They talked of O'Neill's Auctioneers as if it was a long-established and widely respected family firm, instead of a Mickey Mouse operation set up by Gerry O'Neill himself on the basis of being a fast talker;.

'Invite Ruth to The Terrace some time, won't you?' Jims asked his son.

He could see that Declan was very attracted to the dark-eyed girl in his new family.

'I don't think so . . .'

'I'm not asking you to live there, I'm just asking you to bring the girl to Sunday lunch, for God's sake.' Again, the harsh ungracious words that he didn't mean to speak. His son looked taken aback.

'Yes, well. Of course . . . some time.'

Jims Blake contemplated getting an assistant. He realised now how the lonely old Charles Nolan must have relished him coming to stay in that house all those years ago. How he had felt able to will him the place, as well as the practice. Jims had thought the same thing would have happened with Declan. He had foreseen evenings like he had had with Charles, discussing articles in the *Lancet* and the *Irish Medical Times*, wondering about a new cure-all cream with apparently magical qualities that had come from one of the drug firms.

There was a phone call every week from Sheila in her Dublin hospital, and a letter every week from Eileen, now working in an architect's practice in England.

He had almost forgotten what Frances had looked like, or felt like in his arms. He should not have felt like an old man, after all he was only in his late fifties, yet he had the distinct feeling that his life, such as it was, was over.

Declan did bring Ruth to lunch eventually. And the girl chattered easily and eagerly, as she did in her own home. She asked questions, seemed interested in the answers. She asked Maisie about doing the flowers for the altar. Maisie said she was a girl of great breeding, and that Declan was very lucky to have met her and not some foolish fast girl, like he might well have met in the town.

On her third visit she took the initiative and leaned over to kiss him goodbye.

'Thank you, Dr Jims,' she said. She smelled of Knight's Castile soap, fresh and lovely. He was not surprised his son was so taken by her.

He was horrified when he saw Declan some weeks later. The boy arrived on a Thursday afternoon, Maisie's half day. He was ashen white, but the circles under his eyes were deep purple shadows.

He paced the house until the last patient left. 'Will there be any more?'

'I have to go out the country. One of Carrie's brothers. Do you remember Carrie?'

'Of course I do. Can I come with you?'

Somehow Jims Blake found the right silences and didn't choose the wrong words. He didn't ask what had the boy out on a working day, and looking so terrible. Instead he smiled and opened the hall door for him. They walked together to the car, father and son, down the steps of Number Three The Terrace, as he had always wanted to walk with a son.

They talked of nothing during the drive out to the farm where one of Carrie's brothers had impaled himself on yet another piece of rusting machinery. Declan watched wordlessly as his father cleaned the wound and stitched it.

The talk came on the way back.

They stopped under the shadow of the Old Rock, the big craggy monument from which Shancarrig took its name. They walked a little in the crisp afternoon with the shadows of the trees lengthening.

Jims Blake heard the story. The terrible tale of a boy invited into a good man's house. How Gerry O'Neill would lie down dead when he knew Ruth was pregnant. How her brother Vinnie, studying to be a priest, would never forgive such a betrayal.

The boy had not slept or eaten for a week, and presumably neither had the girl. It was the end of the road. Declan wanted them to run away, but Ruth wouldn't go, and in his saner moments he realised that she was right.

'You realise how bad things are, if I had to tell you,' he said to his father.

Jims Blake bit back the retort. At another time he might have made the remark that would drive the boy back into the shell from which he had painfully dragged himself. He didn't ask what Declan wanted of him. He knew that Declan himself barely knew. So instead he did what he had been intending to do all his life, he put his arm around his son's shoulder.

He pretended not to notice the flinching in surprise. 'I'll tell you what I think,' he said. His voice was calm, almost cheerful. He could feel his son's shoulders relaxing under his arm. 'I have this friend up in Dublin, we did our training together. He's in gynaecology and obstetrics. A specialist now. Quite a well-known man ... I'll recommend that young Ruth go to see him for a D and C ... Oh, don't worry, these names are always very alarming. It's called a dilatation and curettage, just an examination under anaesthetic of the neck of the womb. Clears up any disorders. A lot of girls have them ...'

Declan turned to look at him.

'Is that ...? I mean is that the same as ...?'

Jims Blake had decided how to play it. 'As I was saying to you, there's no knowing what names all these things go by, the main thing is that Ruth will go in there and be out in a day or two and it can all go through this house and this address without having to bother anyone else.'

They walked back to the car and drove to Shancarrig. The mood was not broken.

His son came in to Number Three The Terrace and sat with him as they lit a fire, because the evening was getting chilly. Declan had a small brandy and some of the colour had returned to his face.

Jims Blake remembered how old Dr Nolan had often said to him that the ways of the world were stranger than anyone would ever believe. Dr Jims Blake agreed with him as he sat there and realised that the only companionable evening he had ever had with his son was the evening he had arranged to abort his own grandchild.

NORA KELLY

Nora and Jim Kelly had no pictures of their wedding. The cousin with the camera had been unreliable. There was something wrong with the film, he told them afterwards.

It didn't matter, they told him.

But to Nora it did. There was nothing to mark the day their marriage began. It hadn't been a very fancy wedding. During the Emergency of course people didn't go in for big flashy do's, not even people with more class and style than Nora and Jim. But theirs had been particularly quiet.

It took place in Lent, because they wanted to have a honeymoon in the Easter Holidays, the two young teachers starting out life together. Nora's mother had been tight-lipped. A Lenten wedding often meant one thing and one thing only, that the privileges of matrimony had been anticipated and that an unexpected pregnancy had resulted.

But this was not the case, Nora and Jim had anticipated nothing. And the pregnancy that her mother feared might disgrace the whole family did not result, even after many years of marriage.

Month after month Nora Kelly reported to her husband that there was no reason to hope for a conception this time either. They shrugged and said it would happen sooner or later. That was for the first three years. Then they consoled each other in a brittle way. Why should two school teachers who had the entire child population of Shancarrig to cope with want to bring any more children into the world?

Then they decided to ask for help.

It was not easy for Nora Kelly to approach Dr Jims. He was a courteous man and kind to everyone. She knew that he would not be coy, or too inquisitive. He would reach for his pad and write, as he nodded thoughtfully.

Nora Kelly was pale at the best of times and this was not the best of times. She was a slight young woman with flyaway fair hair. She did it in a braid, which she rolled loosely at the back of her neck.

Nobody in Shancarrig had seen her with hair loose and flowing. They thought her expression a little stern, but that was appropriate for the school mistress. Her big husband looked more like a local farmer than the master – it was good to have some authority written on the face of the family.

Someone who had known Nora before she married said she was one of three young girls always dashing about and riding precarious bicycles, in a town some sixty miles away. They were three young harum-scarums, it was said. But it didn't sound likely.

She had no relations there now, she had no identity or past. She was just the school mistress – a sensible woman, not given to fancy dressing or notions. Not too fancy a cook either, to judge by what she bought in the butcher's, but a perfectly qualified woman to be teaching their children. It was of course a terrible cross to bear that the Lord hadn't given her children, but who ever knew the full story in these cases?

As she had expected, Dr Jims was kindness itself. The examination was swift and impersonal, the advice gentle and practical – some very simple, maybe even folk, remedies. Dr Jims said that he never despised wisdom handed down through the generations. He had got a cure from the tinkers once, he told her. They knew a lot of things that modern medicine hadn't discovered yet. But they were a people who kept their ways to themselves.

The old wives' advice hadn't worked. There were tests in the hospital in the big town. Jim had to give samples of his sperm. It was wearying, embarrassing, and ultimately depressing. The Kellys were told that, as far as medical science could determine in 1946, there was no reason why they should not conceive. They must live in hope.

Nora Kelly knew that Dr Jims found it hard to deliver this news to her, in an autumn where his own wife was pregnant again. Their little girls were already up at the school, this was another family starting. She saw his sympathy and appreciated it all the more because he didn't speak it aloud. It wasn't easy to be a childless woman in a small town; she had been aware of the sideways glances for a long time. Nora knew that the ways of God were strange and past understanding by ordinary people, but it did seem hard to understand why he kept giving more and more children to the Brennans and the Dunnes in the cottages, families who couldn't feed or care for the children they already had, and passing her by.

Sometimes when she saw the little round faces coming in to start a new life at school the pain she felt in her heart was as real as if it had been a physical one. She watched their little wobbly legs and the way the poorest of them came in shoes that were too big and clothes that were too long. If she and Jim had a child of their own they would look after it so well. It seemed every other woman in the village only had to think about conception to become pregnant – women who claimed to have enough already, women who sighed and said, 'Here we go again.'

When the doctor's baby son was born, in the coldest winter that Shancarrig ever knew, the year that the River Grane had frozen solid for three long months, his wife died at the birth.

Nora Kelly held the infant child in her arms and wished that she could take the little boy home. She and Jim would rear him so well. They would take out the baby clothes, bought and made many years ago, now smelling of mothballs. He would grow up in their school. He would not be over-favoured in front of the others just because he was the teachers' son.

For a wild moment that day in the doctor's nursery, when she had come to sympathise at the funeral, she thought that the doctor was going to give her the baby. But of course it was fantasy.

Nora had heard that couples who didn't have children often grew very close to each other. It was as if the disappointment had united them and the shared lifestyle, without the distractions of a family, made it easier for them to establish an intimacy.

She wished it had happened in her case, but in honesty she couldn't say that it had.

Jim grew more aloof. His walks of an evening became longer and longer. She found herself sitting alone by the fire, or even returning to the schoolroom to draw maps for the next day.

By the time she was twenty-eight years old her husband reached towards her to make love very rarely.

'Sure what's the point?' he said to her one night as she snuggled up to him. And after that she kept very much to her own side of the bed.

They had agreed not to say it was anyone's fault, but Nora looked to her side of the family. Her own two sisters had given birth to small families; one had only two, the other had an only child, while the sisters and sisters-in-law of Jim Kelly seemed to breed like rabbits.

Her sister Kay, who lived in Dublin, had two little boys. Sometimes they came to stay. Nora would feel her heart lurch when she saw how eagerly Jim reached for them and how happily he took them on walks. It was different entirely to the way he taught the children in the school. In the classroom he was patient and fair, but he was formal; there was no happy wildness like with her nephews. He used to take the small boys by the hand, and let them wade through the shallows of the River Grane and bring them to pick mushrooms up near the Old Rock, or to prowl through Barna Woods looking for bears and tigers.

Nora's sister never failed to say: 'He's a born father, isn't he?' Nora's teeth never failed to be set on edge.

She had more contact with her twin sister Helen, even though Helen lived on the other side of the world in Chicago.

She had sent grainy photographs of the baby, little Maria. Helen had gone to Chicago when Nora went to the training college. She didn't have the brains, she said, and she wanted no more studying. She wanted to see the world and make sure she didn't end up in some one-horse town like the one they'd come from.

In fact, Shancarrig was a much smaller one-horse town than their native place. Nora was sure that Helen must pity her. What had she got with all her brains? Marriage, to the increasingly silent Jim, school mistress in a tiny backwater, and no children.

Helen's life had been much more exciting. She had worked as a waitress in Stouffers. It was a coffee house – one of the many coffee houses of that name – and they had restaurants as well. She met Lexi when he was delivering the meat from the yards.

Big, blond, handsome Lexi, Polish Catholic, silent, whose dark blue eyes followed her everywhere she went. Helen had written about how he asked her out, how she had been taken to meet his family. They spoke Polish in the home, but in broken English told Helen she was welcome.

When they married in one of the big Polish churches in Chicago no one of Helen's family was there to give her courage. Who could afford a journey halfway across the world in 1942, when that world was at war?

And then Maria was born in 1944, baptised by a Polish priest. There were potato cakes served at the christening party, except they called them latkes, and there was a terrible soup called polewka, which they all drank at the drop of a hat.

Maria was beautiful. Helen wrote this over and over. Nora knew from experience that there wasn't much point in believing old wives' tales – they certainly hadn't been much use in her predicament – but she did believe that twins sort of knew about each other, even when they were almost five thousand miles apart.

She read and reread Helen's letters for some hint of what was troubling her, because Nora Kelly knew that life on Chicago's South-side was not as it was described in the very frequent letters.

On an impulse she wrote to her one spring day in 1948.

'I know it sounds like a tall order, but why don't you bring Maria over to see us in the summer? When the school closes Jim and I have all the time in the world and there's nothing that would please us more.'

Nora wrote warmly inviting Lexi too, but the implication was that he would not be able to take the time. Helen, working only part time in the restaurant now, could arrange leave.

Nora described the flowers and the hedges around Shancarrig. She made the river sound full of sparkle and the woods as if they were on the lid of a box of chocolates.

Helen replied by return of post. Lexi wouldn't be able to make the trip, but she and Maria would come to Shancarrig.

Nora could hardly wait. Their elder sister Kay said that Helen must have money to burn if she could just leap on a plane and fly off to Dublin on the spur of the moment. But Nora felt that it might well have taken a lot of explanations and excuses, as well as unimaginable scrimping and saving. She kept quiet about this. She would hear everything when Helen came home.

It was a relief to the twins when, after the big reunion in Dublin, they were able to leave Kay and travel together on the train to Shancarrig. They held hands and talked to each other, words tumbling and falling, finishing each other's sentences and beginning new ones ... and mainly they said that the camera had not done the little girl justice.

Maria was beautiful.

She was four and a half, with a smile that went all the way around her face. She sang and hummed to herself, and was happy with the piece of cardboard and colouring pencils which Nora had brought to greet her.

'Aren't you great!' Helen exclaimed. 'Everyone else gives her these ridiculous ornaments or lacy things that she breaks or tears up.'

'Everyone else?'

'The Poles,' confessed Helen, and they giggled like the children they had been when they said goodbye so many years ago.

The sun shone as the train pulled into Shancarrig. There on the platform stood the master, Jim Kelly, waiting to meet his sister-in-law and little niece.

Maria took to him straight away. She reached up with her small chubby hand and he held it firmly while carrying the heavy suitcase in the other.

'Oh Nora.' Helen's eyes were full of tears. 'Oh Nora, you're so lucky.'

As they left the station and walked down to the row of shops where of late she had felt that she had been an object of pity, the childless school teacher Nora *did* feel lucky.

Nellie Dunne looked out of her door.

'Aren't you looking well today, Mrs Kelly!' she said.

'This is my sister, Miss Dunne.'

'And you have a little girl, do you?' Nellie Dunne asked. She wanted to have all the news for whoever came in next.

'That's my Maria,' said Helen proudly.

When Nellie was out of hearing Nora said, 'It'll be a nine days wonder in the place that someone belonging to me produced a child.'

Helen laid her hand on her twin sister's arm.

'Shush now. We'll have weeks on end to talk about all that.'

They walked companionably through Shancarrig, and home to make the tea.

But Nora Kelly did not have weeks on end to talk to her twin sister about life in Chicago and life in Shancarrig. Five days after she arrived Helen was killed when a runaway horse and cart went across the path of the bus which, swerving to avoid them, hit Helen, killing her outright.

Nora Kelly was in Nellie Dunne's with Maria when it happened. The child was trying to decide between a red and a green lollipop, holding them up against her yellow Viyella dress with the smocking on it, as if somehow one would look better with the outfit than the other.

The sounds were never to leave Nora's mind. She could hear them over and over, each one separate, the wheels of the cart, the whinnying of the horse, the irregular sound of the bus scraping the wrong way, and the long scream. Then silence, before the cries and shouts and everyone running to see what could be done.

Afterwards people said there was no scream, that Helen made no sound.

But Nora heard it.

They took her into Ryan's Hotel. She was given brandy, people's arms were around her, everywhere there were running footsteps. Someone had been sent up to the schoolhouse for Jim. There was Major Murphy from The Glen, a military man trying to organise things on some kind of military lines.

There was Father Gunn with his stole around his neck. He had run from the church to say the Act of Contrition into the lifeless ear of the dead woman.

'She's in heaven now,' Father Gunn told Nora. 'She's there, praying for us all.'

A great sense of the unfairness of it all rose in Nora. Helen didn't want to be in heaven praying for them all, she wanted to be here in Shancarrig telling the long complicated tale of a strange marriage to a silent man who drank, not like the Irish people drink, but differently. She wanted to arrange that her daughter came to Ireland regularly rather than grow up speaking Polish, hardly noticed amid the great crowds of other children in the family. Lexi's brothers and sisters had produced great numbers of new Chicagoans, apparently. Helen had begun to fear that Maria might get lost and never know a life of her own, be a personality and character in her own right like all the children in Shancarrig were. Nora had told her about the children who filled the classrooms during term time, each one with a history and a future.

Nora could not take it in. It couldn't have happened. Every minute seemed like half an hour as she sat in the lounge and a procession advanced and retired.

The voice of Sergeant Keane seemed a hundred miles away when he spoke of the telegram to Chicago, or the possibility of a phone call.

'We can't wire that man and say Helen is dead.' She heard her own voice as if it was someone else's. The words sounded unreal. The Sergeant explained that they could send a telegram asking him to phone Ryan's Hotel and someone would be here to give the message.

'I'll stay,' said Nora Kelly.

No one could dissuade her. It was not three o'clock in the afternoon in Chicago, it was early morning. Lexi was on his meat delivery rounds. It might be many hours before he got the telegram. She would be in the hotel, whatever time he phoned. Mrs Ryan organised a bed to be brought to the commercial lounge; the commercial travellers would understand that this was an emergency, that Mrs Kelly had to be near the phone, day or night.

She drank tea and they brought jelly for Maria. Red jelly, with the top of the milk. Every spoonful seemed to be in slow motion.

Then, at ten o'clock at night, she heard them coming to tell her that the call had been put through. She spoke to the man with the broken English. She had lain on the bed with the curtains pulled to keep out the evening sunlight of Shancarrig. And now it was almost dark. She spoke as she had drilled herself to speak, without tears, trying to give him all the information as calmly as possible.

'Why do you not weep for your sister?' He had a broken English accent, like a foreigner in a film.

'Because my sister would want me to be strong for you,' she said simply.

She asked did he want to speak to Maria, but he said no. She told him that Helen's body would be brought to Shancarrig church the next night, and the funeral would be on the following day, and that Mr Hayes had found out about flights. He had been on the phone to Shannon Airport all day...

She was cut short. Lexi would not come to the funeral.

Nora was literally unable to speak.

The slow voice spoke on. It would not be possible, they were not people who had unlimited money. Who would he know to walk with him behind his wife's coffin? There would be prayers said for her in his own parish, in his church. He returned again to the accident and how it had happened. Who was at fault? What part of Helen had been hurt to kill her?

The nightmare continued for what Nora Kelly thought was an endless time. It was only when the operator said six minutes that she realised how little time had actually passed.

'Will you ring again tomorrow?' she said.

'To say what?'

'To talk.'

'There is nothing to talk about,' he said.

'And Maria...?'

'Will you look after her until we can come for her?'

'Of course ... but if you are going to come for her, could you not come for Helen's funeral?'

'It will be later.'

The days of the funeral passed without Nora being really aware of what was going on. Always she saw Jim, his big hand stretched out to little Maria, whose crying for her mama grew less and less. They told her Mama was with the angels in heaven, and showed her the holy pictures on the wall and in the church to identify where her mother had gone.

And as the days passed Nora went through her sister's possessions, while Jim took little Maria up to Barna Woods to pick flowers.

Nora sat on her bed and looked at her sister's passport and official-looking cards for work and insurance. She could find no return air ticket. Was it possible that Helen had intended to stay here and not to return? There were letters from a solicitor 'regarding the matter we spoke of'. Could this solicitor have been arranging an American divorce? Did the strange tone of voice mean that Lexi was too upset to talk? Or that all love and feeling had gone from his marriage with Helen? Her head was whirling. Why had they not talked at once, she and Helen? It had been part of the slow getting back to knowing each other, the delighted realisation that each had only to begin a thought and the other could finish it.

What a cruel God to have taken this away from them five days after they had found it.

Kay the eldest sister was as usual practical.

'Don't grow too fond of the child,' she warned Nora. 'That unfeeling lout will be back for her the day it suits him.'

What did people mean ... don't grow too fond of? How could anyone put a limit to the love she felt for this little girl with the big dark blue eyes, the head of curls and the endearing habit of stroking her cheek?

After a week Nora found herself saying to Jim, 'Is the child asleep yet?' and realised she was certainly coming to regard Maria as her child.

His reply was tender. 'I read her a story but she wants another from No, she says No has better stories.'

He was smiling at her affectionately, like before. He didn't turn away from her in bed any more, he reached for her like before. It was as if Maria had made their life complete.

'I suppose Kay's right about not getting too fond of her,' Nora said one summer evening, as they sat watching Maria play with the three baby chickens that Mrs Barton, the dressmaker, had brought along in a box as something to entertain the little girl.

'I keep hoping he won't want her back,' Jim said. It was the first time in four weeks it had been mentioned.

'We shouldn't get up our hopes ... any man would want his only child.'

'Any man would have come to his wife's funeral,' Jim said.

Nora wrote letters regularly. She described the funeral, the flowers, the sermon. She told about the grave under a tree in the churchyard, and how on Sundays she went there with Maria to lay flowers on it.

In a year a stone would be put up, Lexi must let her know what he would like written on the tombstone.

She told him about the bus driver who would never be the same again after the accident; the man who walked alone up to Shancarrig Rock. Everyone had told him that it had not been his fault. No one could have faulted him, it was an Act of God that the horse had shied at that very time. But he said that he would never drive again, and had come with flowers to the grave when he thought no one was looking.

She wrote that Maria said God Bless Daddy and a lot of other names every night, so she assumed that these were grandparents or relations. She didn't want him to think that that side of the family had been forgotten. She said that when the term started in September Maria would join the Mixed Infants. She was almost five – five was the age the children began coming to school.

She wrote and told him about the place, the huge big copper beech tree in the playground, and the maps on the schoolroom walls. She stopped saying 'until you come for her' and 'for the present time'. Instead she just wrote as if it was all agreed that Maria would stay here for an unspecified amount of time.

The children accepted her totally. They never thought it odd that she called Mrs Kelly 'No'. They thought it was just because she was babyish and younger than they were. Geraldine Brennan from the cottages decided to be her protector. Nora Kelly had to watch carefully in case part of the protecting might also mean eating Maria's little sandwich lunch.

The communications from Lexi were minimal. He wrote to say that he was grateful for her letters. His hand was not educated, and his grasp of grammar poor. He told her little or nothing about his intentions. He asked many times about the accident, what court case had resulted and whether the compensation had arrived. Once he inquired whether Helen had any valuables with her that needed to be looked after.

In Shancarrig too, people began to think of Maria as belonging to Jim and Nora. She was even called by their name.

'Hey, Maria Kelly, come over here and see the tadpoles!' Nora heard one day during dinner hour, when they played in the yard. Her heart soared with pleasure.

By accident she did have a child, a child of her own.

A child who had a fifth birthday party with a cake and candles. A child who had her first Christmas in Shancarrig and sang carols by the crib in the church.

'Do you remember the church back in Chicago at Christmas?' Nora asked, as she wrapped the child up in a warm scarf before taking her back up the road home from the church.

Maria shook her curly head. 'I can't think,' she said, and Nora smiled in the dark. The less Maria thought, the greater seemed the likelihood of her remaining with them.

Mr Hayes, father of Niall, an easy-going boy often put upon by the others, came to see her.

'My wife says he's being bullied by the other boys. Your husband will probably say it'll make a man of him. I wonder would you and I be better able to reach some kind of consensus?' he asked.

Nora Kelly smiled at him. It was typical of the way he did things, seeing was there a gentle way around things before you went in guns blazing.

'I think he needs to make a friend of Foxy Dunne,' she said after some thought.

'Foxy? That little divil from the cottages?'

'He's as smart as paint, that Foxy. He'll get himself out of that place, and away from the mess he's growing up in.'

'How should he make a friend of this fellow, so? Ethel would be afraid he'd lift the silver.' Bill Hayes looked rueful.

'He won't. He'd be a good ally for Niall. Niall's gentle. He doesn't need another gentle friend like Eddie, he needs a fighter in his court.'

'You can solve it all, Mrs Kelly.'

'I wish I could. I wish I knew how to keep my sister's child. I wish I believed that possession is nine tenths of the law.'

'You're too honourable for that.'

'I think my sister was going to leave her husband. I have letters from a solicitor... They don't say much, though.'

'They never do,' Bill Hayes admitted ruefully.

She sighed. He was telling her what Father Gunn and Dr Jims were telling her. Do nothing. Live in hope. If the man hadn't come over in six months it was a good sign.

When a year had passed it was even better.

When the time came for the Holy Year ceremonies at the school and the big dedication ceremony, Maria Kelly was part of their family and part of Shancarrig. She called Jim Daddy and she called Nora Mama No.

'It sounds like something from Japan, or from *Madam Butterfly*!' Jim said to Nora. He was always good-natured these days.

'She can't call me Mother, she remembers her mother,' Nora said.

'She seems to have forgotten her father though.' Jim spoke in a whisper.

At night Maria's prayers included a litany of friends at school, and the chickens – now hens – that Mrs Barton had given her. She prayed for all kinds of unlikely people, like little Declan Blake, who was pushed in his pram by that strange, abstracted maid, Carrie. Maria loved Carrie and Declan, and often asked Mama No if they could have a baby like Declan to play with. She prayed for Leo Murphy's dog, Jessica, which had broken its paw, and she prayed that Foxy Dunne would give her one of his worms in a jam jar. But the Polish names and her father's name had gone from the list.

It didn't take her long to realise she was in a privileged position being the daughter of the school.

'What would happen if you didn't know your tables?' Geraldine Brennan asked with great interest. 'Would you get your hand slapped like the rest of us?'

'No, she wouldn't.' Catherine Ryan from the hotel knew everything. 'She can grow up knowing nothing if she likes.'

'That's very unfair,' Geraldine Brennan complained. 'Just because my mam and dad aren't teachers I can get belted to bits, but you can do what you like.'

Marie Kelly didn't like Dad and Mama No being criticised. She worked harder than ever.

'Go to bed, child. You'll hurt your eyes,' Jim Kelly said, as Maria was learning her poem by the light of the oil lamp.

'I have to know it, I *have* to. It's much worse on me than any of the others. If I'm not word perfect I *must* be beaten, or else they'll be giving out about you and Mama No.'

Jim and Nora Kelly spoke in whispers that night. No child of their own could have brought them greater pleasure and happiness. It was as if she had been given to them as a gift from God in 1948, five long years ago.

*

Mattie, the postman, had delivered good and bad news to every house in Shancarrig. He knew when the emigrants' remittances arrived, he knew when a letter was unwelcome. He always hesitated slightly before handing Mrs Kelly any letter with a Chicago postmark.

When he was delivering an envelope with American stamps that was bigger and bulkier than usual, and looked more serious than the short scrappy-looking ones which had come before, Mattie asked if he could come in for a drop of water. Mrs Kelly poured him a cup of tea.

'I don't want to be in the way or anything ... it's just in case it was bad news. I know that you're on your own today. Hasn't the master taken the children up to the Old Rock?'

It was true. Early in each summer term Jim organised an outing. The whole school would go – all fifty-six children. Father Gunn used to go too, and bring the elderly Monsignor O'Toole when he felt able. The old Monsignor liked to know that the children didn't think of the Old Rock as some kind of pagan place. That was the trouble with ancient monuments that dated back to before St Patrick ... people didn't relate them to God.

Nora Kelly had decided not to go today, and here, as ill luck would have it, was the news from Chicago. Could they be legal papers? Her hand trembled. She opened it. There were newspaper cuttings, a description of how Maria's father Lexi, had opened his own shop, his own butcher's place, a beautiful meat shop. He wanted his daughter to know this, to be proud of him.

Would Nora please show them to Maria? And perhaps she might write. 'She is a big girl now, it is strange that she does not write.' Nora Kelly put her head in her hands and wept at her kitchen table.

Mattie, who bitterly regretted not dropping the letter on the table as he would have done ordinarily, reached out and patted her heaving shoulders.

'It'll be all right, Mrs Kelly. You were meant to have her,' he kept saying, over and over.

Nora Kelly pulled herself together, washed her face and combed her hair. She put on her summer hat, a black straw one, and set off down the road to The Terrace, the row of houses in Shancarrig where Dr Jim Blake and Mr Bill Hayes, the solicitor, lived.

Nellie Dunne, looking out her open door over her counter, saw the school mistress walking briskly, cheeks flushed, face determined. Maybe she was heading for the doctor's? She might have news for him. They often said when you stopped worrying about having a child of your own that was the very time you conceived.

But Nora Kelly went up the steps to the Hayes household. Her business was legal, not medical.

Mr Hayes seemed to notice a change in her, a determination to have the compensation settled and done with.

'Has anything happened, Mrs Kelly?' he asked gently. 'It's just that up to now you were the one to put it on the long finger, saying that money couldn't bring your sister back and that the child lacked for nothing.' He was polite but questioning.

'I know,' Nora Kelly agreed. 'That's what I did think. But now I think my only hope is to get the compensation, whatever it is, and give it to him.'

'Him?'

'Her father. He's not interested in anything else, believe me.'

'But the compensation is for Maria as well as for him.'

'We'll give it all to him if he'll let us keep the child.'

'Ah Nora, Nora...' Normally Niall Hayes' father didn't call her by her first name. He seemed upset.

'What are you trying to say to me, Mr Hayes?'

'I suppose I'm saying that you can't buy the child.'

'And I'm saying that that's exactly what I'm going to do,' she said, face flushed and eyes bright, much too bright.

Wearily Bill Hayes took out the file and together they went through the letters from CIE – the transport company – the solicitors for the insurance, and copies of his own to them. There was a sum. It would be agreed eventually. At most it would be £2,000, at the least £1,200. If they agreed to take something nearer the lower figure it would be sooner rather than later. But perhaps, after all this time, they should hold out for more.

'Take whatever you can get, Mr Hayes.'

'Forgive me, but should your husband perhaps...?'

'Jim is as desperate to keep her as I am. More so, if that's possible.'

'There is absolutely no guarantee...'

'I know, but I have to have *something* to offer him. He's written to say he owns a shop. He's as proud as punch of it. Now he's started wanting her to write to him...' Her lip was trembling.

'Perhaps this is the first time he feels able to. You know Americans, they set a lot of store on having their own business...'

'Please don't stand up for him. I could have borne it if he had come over and taken her away at once. Not now. Not all those years of ignoring and neglect and now...'

'She might come for holidays...'

Nora Kelly's mouth was a thin line. 'You mean very well, Mr Hayes, but it's not a help.'

'Fine, Mrs Kelly. I'll get it moving, inasmuch as anything ever moves in the law.' Bill Hayes waved his hand around shelves filled with envelopes and documents tied up in pale pink tape.

'Will you write a little note to your father?' Nora asked Maria that night.

'What for? To thank him for the day up at the Old Rock?' She looked surprised.

Nora swallowed, and could hardly speak. Maria thought of Jim as her father. The man who was so proud of the new shop selling best meats in Chicago didn't even exist for her.

A few days later she brought it up again.

'We've had a letter from your Papa Lexi in Chicago. He wanted you to see the pictures of his new meat shop.'

Maria took the newspaper cutting.

'Ugh! Look at the dead animals hanging there,' she said, handing it back.

'That's his job. Like Jimmy Morrissey's father.' Nora wished she could leave it, but she knew that she dare not. 'Anyway Maria, it would be good to write him a letter and say the shop looks very nice.'

'It doesn't!' Maria said, giggling her infectious laugh.

Her hair, long now but still curly, was tied with a coloured ribbon. She always had her head in a book – the early years of long bedtime story sessions had paid off. She was tall and suntanned and strong. She was nearly ten years old, a girl that anyone would love to claim as a daughter.

'But he'd like to hear,' Nora insisted.

'It would only be pretending.' She pulled the newspaper cutting towards her again and looked, as Nora knew she must, at the picture of the tall, handsome man standing beside his shop.

'Is this him?' she asked.

'Yes.'

She looked uneasy, her dark blue eyes seeming troubled.

'What will I say?'

'Oh. Whatever you think. Whatever comes into your mind to say. I can't be dictating it for you.'

'But, nothing comes into my mind to say. I don't know. I don't feel safe when I think about ... all this.'

Nora Kelly put her arms around Maria. 'We'll make you safe, pet. Believe me, we will.'

Maria wriggled away. It was too emotional.

'Yes. Fine. Okay, I'll say something. Will I say "you look fine and rich"?'

'*No*, Maria. Whatever else you say, I beg you not to say that.'

'Ah Mama No, I don't know what to say. I think you are going to have to dictate it to me.'

'I think I am,' agreed Nora.

They kept the letters respectful and distant, telling little about life in Shancarrig, mentioning nothing of the Kellys who were her real parents, but giving vague sentiments of goodwill to a stranger in Chicago.

Nora noticed with delight how briefly and casually Maria read the stilted letters which came back, each one beginning 'My dear daughter Maria'.

The man had little to say, and said it badly.

'He's not much at spelling, is Papa Lexi,' Maria said.

'Now, now!' Jim corrected her.

'Is he a secret? Do people know about him?'

'Of course he's not a secret, love. Why do you think that?'

'Because we don't talk about him. And nobody else has another papa miles away.'

'We do talk about him, and you write to him. Of course he's not a secret.' Nora was very anxious to take any glamour or mystery away.

'Do you write to him, Mama No?'

'I do, love. But about business.'

'The meat business?' She was genuinely puzzled.

'No. Legal things, you know, after your mother's accident ...'

'Why do you have to write about that?'

'Oh, you know. Red Tape. Formalities. All that.' Nora was vague.

Maria lost interest. Instead she wanted to tell Mama No about Miss Ross.

'I saw her climbing the tree this morning,' she said, giggling at the thought of the elegant Miss Ross actually getting her leg up on the lower branch and hauling herself up into the higher parts of the tree.

'Nonsense! You imagined it.'

'No, I didn't. I was looking out my window at six o'clock this morning, and she came into the school yard. I swear she did.'

'What on earth could she have been doing at that hour?'

'Well, I saw her. She'd been up all night. She was coming back from Barna Woods.'

'I think you've been reading too many stories – you can't tell what's true from what's made up.'

Nora shook her head. The very idea of Miss Ross climbing the beech tree. Really.

'Miss Ross?'

'Yes, Maria.'

'Miss Ross, did you climb the beech tree yesterday morning?'

Miss Ross's face was red. 'Did I what, child?'

'It's just ... it's just, I told Mama No, and she said "nonsense".'

'That's what it is too, Maria. Nonsense.'

Miss Ross turned and walked away.

Nora heard the conversation. There was something about the way the young teacher spoke that didn't ring true.

'I was wrong about Miss Ross,' Maria said.

'Maybe it was the light. It's full of odd shadows at that time of morning.' Nora spoke kindly.

They exchanged a glance and somehow Maria seemed to know that Nora knew it wasn't something that had been made up. That it was something which might indeed have happened.

'I never thanked you properly for putting us right about that young divil, Foxy Dunne,' Mr Hayes said to Nora Kelly when she called to see him next time. 'It was absolutely the right thing for young Niall. Foxy taught him to catch rabbits – we have six of them out in the back. All male. Foxy taught him how to work that out too.'

Nora laughed. 'There's not much that fellow doesn't know.'

Bill Hayes looked out his window at the back garden. 'Look at that. He showed Niall how to build a proper little house for them, and put up a wire run from the hutch. It's very professional, and he's only a child.'

'He'll go far,' Nora said. She knew too that visiting The Terrace had a civilising effect on Foxy Dunne. He combed his hair and washed his hands without being asked to. He ate slowly, like his hosts. He was a fast learner.

Nora liked talking to Bill Hayes. He was a quiet man and people who didn't know him well might think he was a little too precise and fussy. But nobody's life was easy. Nora Kelly knew it was not a bed of roses living with the gloomy Ethel Hayes, who hadn't smiled for a long time. She knew that everyone's business was safe and secret in Number Five The Terrace. And that she would get the best advice that she could be given.

'Well now, you didn't come to talk to me about rabbits and hutches. I'm being very remiss.' He moved back to his desk and picked up some papers. 'We do have an offer now ... they're delighted to be able to close the file after five and a half years.'

'How much?'

'Thirteen hundred. Now we could get...'

'That's fine, and here's a note from Jim saying he agrees too, in case you think I'm doing all this on my own.'

'No, no...' But he took the note.

'I'll write tonight. When would we have the money?'

'Oh, in a week or two.'

'And would there be a certain percentage legally for him and for Maria?'

'I'd advise that half be for her, to be invested...'

'You do know what we are going to do with her portion, don't you?'

'Yes, and I must say again how very unwise it is from every point of view. Suppose the child does stay with you, will she thank you for handing away what is her legal inheritance?'

Nora Kelly wasn't listening ... she would write tonight.

She went to the post office to get a stamp, and Katty Morrissey looked up from behind the grille.

'Well, isn't that the coincidence! There was a telegram for you half an hour ago. I was going to get Mattie to go out with it.'

Nora felt cold. Her hand trembled as she opened the envelope, and in full view of Katty Morrissey and Nellie Dunne, who had materialised as usual when any drama was about to unfold, she read that Lexi was arriving in Shannon Airport on Friday morning and would be with them on Friday afternoon.

'Would you like a glass of water, Mrs Kelly?'

'No, Miss Dunne, thank you very much. I would like nothing of the sort.' Nora Kelly gathered every ounce of strength and walked out of the post office, leaving Nellie and Katty to say to each other, before they said it to the rest of Shancarrig, that the school teachers' time was up. The real father was on his way from the United States to take his child home.

'You don't look well, Mrs Kelly.' Maddy Ross had come up behind her as she crossed the bridge on the way back up home.

'Neither do you, Miss Ross,' Nora countered. There would be no sympathy from this young teacher who had her life before her – a life with marriage and children in it.

'I'm fine. A little tired. I don't sleep at night. I walk a lot in the woods – it clears my head.' She had a strange, almost wild, look about her.

Jim had said, over and over, that it was essential for Shancarrig school to keep Miss Ross. Her salary was small, as the Department would only pay the minimum. And only Maddy Ross, who had a house, and a mother with private means of a sort, would be able to live on what went into her envelope every month.

But sometimes Nora thought that Miss Ross had a giddiness and light-headedness that none of their silliest fourteen-year-old girls had ever managed to reach. And more than once she thought, God forgive her, that Miss Ross was almost flirting with young Father Barry. Nora kept her own counsel about this, not even confiding to Jim.

'Do you sometimes feel the world is bursting with happiness?' Maddy Ross asked her as they walked together up the road.

Nora Kelly, who could well have done without this feverish conversation, replied tersely that she didn't think that at all, and particularly not today. So if Miss Ross would excuse her she would like to be left to her own thoughts.

She saw Maddy Ross shrink away like an animal that has received a blow.

Still, there was no time to think about that now, the young teacher's nonsense could be dealt with later. Right now she had to cope with the event that she had dreaded since the week after her sister died – the arrival of her brother-in-law in Shancarrig to take his daughter home.

She walked like a woman in a dream. Not since the time of Helen's death had Nora felt this sensation of being outside her body, as if she was watching another being going through the motions – of filling a kettle, of setting a table.

When Jim came in she was sitting motionless at the table. He saw the telegram and needed to ask very little.

'When is he coming?' he said.

'Friday.'

'Nora. Oh Nora, my love. What are we going to do?'

He put his hands over his face and wept like a baby.

She sat there stroking his arm, listing the possibilities. Could they leave Shancarrig and hide somewhere? No, that was ridiculous, he would get the guards. Could they pretend that Maria was too sick to travel? Could they get Mr Hayes to brief a barrister in Dublin who would fight a case against her being taken away from them? Each solution was more unlikely than the one which had gone before.

They could ask Maria to beg him. No. They must never do that.

Perhaps for the child it *was* the best. A comfortable living in the New World. A whole lot of cousins, a ready-made family, a welcome home as if the five years since she left Chicago airport in 1948 were just a pause in her real life.

Nora and Jim Kelly realised that this was one occasion when they could do absolutely nothing. They would have to wait for Friday and all it would bring.

By the time they showed Maria the telegram they had calmed each other sufficiently to speak without letting their emotions show.

'Is he going to take me away from here?' Maria asked.

'Well, we don't know what he plans, do we? After all, he just says "arriving to visit you". He doesn't say anything about . . . anything after that.'

'I don't want to go.'

'Now, that's not the way to start,' Jim Kelly said.

'Well, what *is* the way to start . . . ?' Maria was flushed. They hadn't realised how independent she had become, how strong in her own views. 'This is my home. You are my parents. I don't want to go away with someone I don't remember, someone who didn't come for me when my real mother died.'

'He couldn't. And you mustn't begin by making him an enemy.'

'He *is* an enemy. I don't want to meet him, I'll run away.'

'No, Maria, please. Please, that would be the worst thing.'

'What would be the best thing?'

'I suppose it would be to reason with him, tell him how much you think of Shancarrig as your home, and of us as your ... well, your people.'

'My parents,' Maria said stubbornly.

'He won't want to hear that,' Nora said.

'I don't care what he wants to hear. Why should I have to beg him to let me stay in my own home?'

'Because life isn't fair, and you're only ten years of age.'

Maria ran out the door through the yard, and across the fields towards Barna Woods.

When she came home later that night, she was very silent. And pale. Nora, who knew every heart-beat of this child, knew that it was something else, something not to do with what was going to happen on Friday.

'Did something happen to frighten you?'

'You know everything, Mama No.'

'Was it something you saw?'

'Yes.' She hung her head.

Nora's cheeks burned. How could life be so cruel, that someone must have exposed himself to the little girl on this of all days?

'You can tell me,' she said.

'Not really. It's really very bad. You won't believe me.'

'I will. I always do.'

'I saw Miss Ross and Father Barry kissing each other.' She blurted it out.

Immediately Nora knew she was telling the truth. Without a shadow of a doubt she realised that this was indeed what had been going on under her eyes.

A priest of God and their Junior Assistant Mistress.

But even the scandal, and the need to tell Father Gunn tactfully, and the whole attendant list of complications, faded away compared to the shock that it had all given to Maria.

'Do you remember when you told me Miss Ross had climbed the tree? I didn't really believe you, but I did later. And I most certainly believe you now. But Maria, we have so much to worry about, you and I. Let us put this to the very back of our minds, right back behind everything, and later we'll talk about it. Just you and I. It's best to tell nobody, nobody at all. These things have explanations.'

159

'Don't send me to Papa Lexi.'

'You'll be strong and good when he comes. I'll help you every step of the way. We'll ask him can you share your time between us. Hey, wouldn't that be great? Two countries. Two continents. And we all want you. Not everyone has that.'

'Will it work?'

'Yes,' said Nora Kelly, knowing that she had never spoken such an untruth in her whole life.

They survived the four days to Friday.

People were very kind, which they expected, but also very tactful which they hadn't expected. They did practical things.

Mrs Ryan in the hotel looked up the time of the flight, and since it would be arriving in the early hours of the morning, worked out what time he could be expected in Shancarrig. Maybe lunchtime. If it would be easier they could have lunch at Ryan's Commercial Hotel, she suggested, a private room.

Mr Hayes, the solicitor, offered to take him through the steps of the settlement one by one, pointing out how it had been the best thing to do.

Dr Jims dropped by with sleeping tablets in case they were finding the nights long.

Leo Murphy, daughter of the Major up at The Glen, said that Maria could come up and hit a ball around on the tennis court if she liked. Even though she was four years younger it would be all right, because of things being difficult.

Young Father Barry said, with eyes of glazing sincerity, that God was a God of Love above all, and that he would open this man's heart to see the love the Kellys had for Maria.

Nora Kelly preferred not to think too deeply about the God of Love that Father Barry interpreted, but she thanked him all the same.

Father Gunn said that Polish Catholics were very devoted to Our Lady, and that Mrs Kelly should show him the plaque on the wall, where the school had been dedicated to the Blessed Virgin.

Foxy Dunne said he had heard there was a bit of a problem, and he knew some very tough people, or his brothers did, if reinforcements were called for. Jim Kelly put on his sternest face when refusing this offer, but gripped Foxy by the arm and told him he was a great fellow for all that.

Eddie Barton told his mother that the gypsies were coming again —

wouldn't it be great if they were to kidnap Maria and then for her to be found and brought back after the man had gone back to Chicago.

Mrs Barton was altering Nora Kelly's best dress for her, with a trim of lace down the front, and on the collar and cuffs. She wanted to look the equal of anyone in Chicago for the visit. 'I only tell you what Eddie said, just in case. It might work,' she said, mouth full of pins.

'God bless you both,' Nora Kelly said, looking at her pale reflection in the mirror.

In many ways it was like a Western where they are all waiting for the gunmen to come to town. Down by the station Mattie the postman happened to be waiting with his bicycle, just waiting, looking into the middle distance as it were. Sergeant Keane was sitting on a window sill by the bus stop, throwing the odd word to Nellie Dunne who had come out from behind her counter to stand at her doorway.

The Morrisseys in the butcher's shop were making frequent sorties out on to the street, and Mrs Breda Ryan from the hotel seemed to find a lot of activity that took her to the entrance porch of their premises.

Although none of them would have admitted it, and no one pretended to see the curtains of the presbytery move as Mrs Kennedy watched from one window and Father Gunn from another ... they were all waiting.

Someone would let the Kellys know the moment the man came into the town. They never thought he would arrive by car, and because it was an ordinary car, not a big American Cadillac, nobody knew it was Lexi when he drove into Shancarrig and looked around him to see where the schoolhouse was.

Not seeing it in the centre or near the church he took the road over the Grane and arrived at a huge copper beech tree, where the one-storey building had the notice Shancarrig National School.

Behind was the small stone house of Jim and Nora Kelly. They were sitting waiting for the message that would tell them by which route he had arrived. They certainly had not expected the man himself.

He was big and handsome, fair curly hair around his ears, eyes dark blue. He must be thirty-six or thirty-seven. He looked years younger – he looked like a film star.

Nora and Jim stood in their doorway, their sides touching for strength. She longed to hold her husband's hand, but it would look too girlish. It wasn't in their manner to do a thing like that; hip to hip was enough.

'I am Alexis,' he said. 'You are Nora and Jim?'

'You're very welcome to Shancarrig,' Nora said, the untruthfulness of the words hidden, she hoped, by the smile she had nailed on her face.

'My daughter Maria?' he said.

'We thought it best that she go to a friend's house. We will take you to her whenever you like.' Jim spoke loudly to try and hide the shake in his voice.

'This house of her friend?' he asked.

'It's ten minutes' walk, maybe two or three minutes in your car. Don't worry. She's there, she knows you're coming,' Jim said. He thought he could sense suspicion in Lexi's voice.

'We felt it would be more fair on you not to have to tell her in her own home ... what she thinks of as her own home.' Nora looked around the kitchen of the small house where she had spent all her married life.

'Tell her?'

'Well, talk to her. Meet her, get to know her. Whatever it is you want to do.' Jim knew his voice was trailing lamely. These monosyllables from Lexi were hard to cope with. Somehow he had expected something totally different.

'It is good that she is not here for the moment. May I sit down?'

They rushed to get him a chair, and offer him tea, or whiskey.

'Do you have poitín?' he asked.

Nora's warning bells sounded. She remembered her sister Helen telling of this morose drinking, this silent swallowing of neat alcohol.

'No. The local teacher has to set a good example, I'm afraid. But I *do* have a bottle of Irish whiskey that I bought in a bar, if that would do.'

He smiled. Lexi, the man who had come to take their daughter, smiled as if he was a friend. 'I need a drink for what I am to tell you.'

Their hearts were like lead as they poured the three little glasses, lest he think them aloof. They proposed no toast.

'I am going to marry again,' Lexi told them. 'I am to marry a girl, Karina, who is also Polish. Her father owns a butcher's shop too, and we are going to combine the two. She is much more young than I am, Karina. She is twenty-two years of age.'

'Yes, yes.' Nora was holding her breath to know what would come next.

'I tell you the truth. It would be much more easy for our marriage if Karina and I were to start our own family ... to begin like any other couple. To get to know each other, to make our own children ...'

Nora felt the breath hissing between her teeth. She gripped her small glass so hard she feared it might shatter in her hands. 'And you were wondering ... ?' she said.

'And I thought that perhaps, if my daughter Maria is happy here ... then perhaps this is where she might like to be ... But, you see, it is not fair that I leave her with you ... you have your life. You have been so good to her for so long ...'

The tears were running down Nora's face. She didn't even try to wipe them away.

Lexi continued, 'I have made many inquiries about the finances because I want you to have the money to do so. But always when I talk of the money you do not reply. I fear there may be no money. I fear to give you money in case you think I am trying to give you a bribe ...'

Jim Kelly was on his feet. 'Oh Lexi, sir, we'd *love* to keep her here. She'll always be your daughter. Whenever you want her she'll go on a holiday to you ... but it's our hearts' desire that she stay with us.'

Nora spoke very calmly. 'And maybe she would see you as Uncle Lexi more than Papa Lexi, don't you think?' She didn't know where she found the strength to say the words that Lexi wanted to hear. She didn't dare to believe that she had got them right until she saw his face light up.

'Yes, yes. This would be much better for Karina, that she think of her as a niece, not a daughter. Because, in many ways now, that is what she is.'

Nora saw, out of the corner of her eyes, a shadow move on the beech tree in the school yard. It was Foxy Dunne, hovering. He had seen the car and guessed the driver.

'Foxy!' she called. He came swaggering in. This man was an enemy, he wouldn't be civil to him. 'Foxy, could you do us a favour? Maria is over at The Glen with Leo Murphy. Would you go over and tell her to come home, and tell her everything's fine.'

'It's a long journey over to The Glen,' Foxy said unexpectedly.

'It's ten minutes, you little pup,' said Jim Kelly.

'It'd be easier if you let me drive over for her.' He looked at the car keys on the table.

'Hey, how old are you?' Lexi asked.

'I've driven everything. That's dead easy.'

'He's thirteen and a half,' said Nora.

'That's a grown man,' said Lexi. 'But don't you put a scratch on it. I have to take it back to Shannon airport tonight.' He threw him the keys.

Tonight. The man was going back to his new life tonight. Without Maria.

The sunlight streamed into the kitchen as they talked, as they sat as friends and spoke of the past and the future, until Maria arrived, white-faced from the journey. Foxy had driven her three times round Shancarrig to get value from the drive, and then spotted Sergeant Keane so had put his foot down to get her back to the schoolhouse.

Nora put her arms around the girl.

'We've had a great chat, my love,' she said. 'This is Lexi, maybe even Uncle Lexi. He'll be going back to America tonight, and he wants to meet you and get to know you a little bit before he goes.'

Maria's eyes were wide trying to take it in.

'Before he goes off and leaves you here with us. Which is what we all agreed is where you want to be,' said Nora Kelly, who had told her daughter Maria that everything would be all right, and had now delivered on her promise.

NESSA

It was Mrs Ryan who wore the trousers in Ryan's Commercial Hotel. Everyone knew that. And just as well, because if Conor Ryan had married a mouse the place would have gone to the wall years ago.

Conor Ryan certainly hadn't married a mouse when he wed Breda O'Connor. A small, thin girl with restless eyes and straight black shiny hair, she was a distant cousin of the Ryans. They met at a family wedding. Conor Ryan told her that he was thinking of going off to England and joining the British army. Anything to get out from under his parents' feet – they ran this hole-in-the-wall hotel in a real backward town.

'What do you want going into the army? There might be a war and you'd get killed,' she said.

Conor Ryan implied that it mightn't be a huge choice between that and staying put with his parents.

'They can't be *that* bad,' Breda said.

'They are. The place is like the ark. No, the ark was safe and dry and people wanted to get into it. This is like a morgue.'

'Why don't you improve it?'

'I'm only twenty-three, they'd never let me,' he said.

Breda O'Connor decided there and then that she would marry him. By the time Britain declared war on Germany they were already engaged.

'*Now*, aren't you glad I didn't let you join the army?' Breda said.

'You haven't lived with my father and mother yet,' he said, with a look of defeat and resignation that she was determined to take out of him.

'Nor will I,' she said with spirit. 'We'll build a place of our own.'

Conor Ryan's father said that he had picked a wastrel, a girl who thought they were made of money, when the outhouse was converted into a small dwelling for the newlyweds.

Conor Ryan's mother said there would be no interfering from a fancy young one who thought she was the divil and all because she had a domestic science diploma. Conor reported none of these views to the bride-to-be. Breda would find out soon enough what they were like. She had assured him that she had been given fair warning.

As it happened she never really found out how much they had resented her coming to their house, and marrying their only son while he was still a child.

Breda never heard how his parents prophesied that when she had a few children out in that cement hut she was getting built for herself in the yard it would soften her cough.

The Ryan parents fell victim to a bad flu that swept the countryside in the winter of 1939.

Two weeks after the winter wedding of Conor and Breda the same congregation stood in the church for the double funeral of the groom's parents.

There was a lot of head-shaking. How hard it was for a young girl to step in like that. It would be too much for her. She was only a little bit of a thing. And you'd need to light a bonfire under Conor Ryan to get any kind of action out of him. It was the end of Ryan's Commercial Hotel for Shancarrig.

Never were people so wrong.

Breda Ryan took control at once. Even on the very day of the funeral. She assured the mourners that they would be very welcome to come back to the hotel bar for drinks rather than going up to Johnny Finn's pub, as they thought they should do out of some kind of respect.

'The best respect that you could give my parents-in-law is to come to their hotel,' Breda Ryan said.

Within a week she made it known that she didn't like to be referred to as the *young* Mrs Ryan.

'My husband's mother has gone to her reward, and the Lord have mercy on her she is no longer here to need her name. I am Mrs Ryan now,' she said.

And so she was. Mrs Ryan of Shancarrig's only hotel, a part of the triangle that people called the heart of the town – one side The Terrace where the rich people like the doctor and Mr Hayes the solicitor lived, one side the row of shops – Nellie Dunne's the grocery, Mr Connors the chemist, the other Dunnes who ran the hardware business, the butcher, the draper – the few small places that got a meagre living from Shancarrig and its outlying farms. The third side of the triangle was Ryan's Hotel.

Not very prepossessing, dark brown throughout, floors covered in linoleum. The rooms all had heavy oak fireplaces, the pictures on the walls were in dark heavy frames. Most of them were of unlikely romantic scenes with men in frock coats, never seen in Shancarrig or even in the county, offering their arms to ladies in outfits similarly unknown.

There were some religious pictures in the hall ... the one of the Sacred Heart had a small red lamp burning in front of it. The sideboards in the hall and dining room were stuffed with glass never used on the table, and Belleek china.

Mrs Ryan had plans to change and improve it all but first she must see that people came to it as it was.

She made sure that the smell of cooking didn't meet guests at the hall door by putting heavy curtains outside the kitchen doors. She installed a glass-fronted noticeboard near the reception desk and put up details of concerts, hunt balls or other high-class events in neighbouring towns.

She intended to make the hotel the very centre of Shancarrig, the place where people would come to look for information. The bus and train times were there too for all to see, in the hopes that it would encourage travellers to come and have a drink or a coffee as they waited.

Her plans had only just begun when she realised she was pregnant.

Her first child was born in 1940, a little girl, delivered by young Dr Jims because the baby arrived in the middle of the night and Dr Nolan was getting too old to come out at all hours.

'A lovely daughter,' he said. 'Is that what you wanted?'

'Indeed it's not. I wanted a strong son to run the hotel for me.' She was laughing as she held the baby.

'Well, maybe she'll run it till she gets a brother.' Dr Jims had a warm way with him.

'It's no life for a woman. We'll find a better job for Vanessa.' She held the child close.

'Vanessa! Now there's a name.'

'Oh, think big, Doctor. That's what I always believed.'

Conor Ryan poured a brandy for the doctor, and the two men sat companionably in the bar at 4.30 a.m. to drink to the new life in Shancarrig.

'May Vanessa live to see the year two thousand,' said Dr Jims.

'Won't Nessa only be a young one of sixty then! Why are you wishing her a short life?' said the new father.

She was Nessa from the start. Even her strong-willed mother was not able to impose her will on the people of Shancarrig on this point. And

169

when her sister was born the baby was Catherine, and the third girl Nuala. There were no strong sons to run the hotel. But by the time they realised there never would be, the women were so well established in Ryan's that the absence of a boy wasn't even noticed.

Nessa always thought she had got the worst possible combination of looks from her parents.

She had her mother's dead-straight hair. No amount of pipe cleaners would put even the hint of a wave or a kink in it. And she inherited her father's broad shoulders and big feet. Why could she not have got his curly hair and her mother's tiny proportions? Life was very unfair. Everyone admired people with curly hair.

Like Leo's hair.

Since Nessa could remember she had been best friends with Leo Murphy. Leo was the girl who lived up at The Glen. She was almost an only child. Lucky thing. Not a real only child like Eddie Barton, the son of the dressmaker, but Leo's two brothers were very old and didn't live at home.

Nessa had even known Leo before the day they both started at Shancarrig school. Leo had been invited to come and play with her. Mrs Ryan had said she wanted Vanessa to have a proper friend before she started in there and had to consort with the Dunnes and the Brennans.

'What's consorting?' Nessa asked her mother.

'Never mind, but you won't be doing it anyway.'

'That's why you're off to school, to learn things like that,' said Conor Ryan, folding back the paper at the race card to see could he pick a likely winner in the afternoon races.

The first day at school Nessa Ryan sat beside Maura Brennan. Together they learned to do pot hooks.

'Why are they called pot hooks?' Nessa asked, as the two girls slowly traced the S shapes in their headline copy books.

'They look a bit like the hooks that hang over the fire. You know ... to hold the pots,' Maura explained.

Nessa told this information proudly to her mother.

'What! Have they got you sitting next to one of the Brennans from the cottages?' she said crossly.

'Don't be putting notions into her head. Isn't the poor Brennan child entitled to sit beside someone? Isn't she a human being?' Nessa's father was defending Maura Brennan for something. Her mother was still in a bad temper about it, whatever it was.

'That's not what you say when her father comes in here breaking all before him, and swearing like a soldier.'

'He takes his trade to Johnny Finn's after what you said to him that time...'

'You sound as if you're sorry, as if you miss that good-for-nothing drunk. It was a fine day for this house when I shifted him out. You agreed yourself.'

'I did, I did.'

'So what are you going on about?'

'I don't know, Breda...' He shook his head. Nessa realised whatever it was ... her Daddy really didn't know. He didn't know about things like her mother did. About running a hotel, and being in charge.

'Will I not sit beside her?' Nessa asked.

Her mother's face softened. 'Don't mind me, your father is right. The child's not to be blamed.'

'We don't have pot hooks, do we?'

'No. We have a range, like any normal person would. The Brennans cook over an open fire, I expect. Did you not see Leo Murphy at school today?'

'She was sitting beside Eddie. They got told off for talking.'

'What else happened? Tell me all about it.'

'We played a game around the tree, you know, like a big ring o' roses.'

'I did that myself,' said her father.

She saw her mother going over and putting her arm around his shoulder. They were smiling. She felt safe. Maybe her mother *did* love her father even if he didn't know how to run a hotel. When anyone came to the hotel they asked for Mrs Ryan, not for Mr, that's if they knew the place. Otherwise it was a delay while Mr Ryan sent for his wife.

Nessa grew up knowing that she should get her mother, not her father, in any crisis. At the start she thought this was the same in all families.

But she learned it wasn't always the case. She discovered that Leo Murphy's mother didn't know where anything was, that Major Murphy and Biddy the maid ran The Glen between them. Leo never had to consult her mother about anything. It was a huge freedom.

She learned that Maura Brennan's mother had to go out begging because Mr Brennan drank whatever money he got. When Nessa wondered why Mrs Brennan didn't stop him with a word or a glance as her mother would have, Maura shrugged. Women weren't like that, she said.

Niall Hayes said that his mother didn't have any say in the house. His father paid all the bills, and dealt with things that happened. Foxy Dunne said that his mother hadn't been known to open her mouth on any subject, but of course his father had never been known to close his, so that made up a pair of them.

Only Eddie, whose father was dead or had gone away or something, said that his mother was in charge. But she didn't like being in charge, he said. She kept thinking there should be a man around the place.

Sometimes they even made jokes about Nessa's mother, about how different she was from the other women in Shancarrig. Nessa didn't like that very much but in her heart she had to admit it was true. Her mother was rather too interested in her for her liking. She wanted to know everything that happened.

'Why do you want to know so much?' Nessa asked her once.

'I want to make sure you don't make the same mistakes that I made. I want to try and help your childhood.' Her mother had seemed very simple and direct in that answer, as if she was talking to someone her own age, not talking down.

'Leave the child alone,' her father said, as he said so often. 'Aren't they only children for a very short time? Let them enjoy it.'

'I don't know about the very short time,' Nessa's mother said. 'There are quite a few people around here who never grew up.'

When people stopped to admire young Nessa Ryan on the street they often asked, 'And whose pet are you?' It was only a greeting, not a question, but Nessa took it seriously.

'Nobody's,' she would say firmly. 'There's so much work in a hotel there's no time to have pets.' People laughed at the solemn way the child spoke, in the parrot fashion she must have heard at home.

Her mother didn't approve. 'You're the most petted child in the country. Stop telling people that there's no one spoiling you,' she said.

But Nessa didn't think this was so. She wondered was she a foundling. Had the dark gypsies, the families who came through every year, left her on the hotel doorstep? Had she been found up at the Old Rock, left there by a wonderful kind noblewoman with long hair – someone who was in great secret trouble and left her baby while she escaped?

Nessa didn't know exactly what she wanted but she knew very definitely that it was something different from what she had got. She

172

would never be able to please her mother, no matter what she did, and her father was too soft and easy-going for his views to count.

Sometimes when she was feeling particularly religious and near to God she used to ask him to make her popular and loved.

'I'm not asking to be pretty, God, I know we're not meant to pray for good looks. But I am asking to be liked more. People that are popular are very very happy. They can go around doing good all the time. Honestly God, even children. I'd be a great child and a great grown-up. Just try it and see.'

The years of Nessa Ryan's childhood saw a great change in Ryan's Commercial Hotel.

After endless rationing and petrol shortages brought about by the war in Europe, suddenly cars appeared on the road again. Instead of the hotel's visitors arriving at Shancarrig railway station and walking across to where Ryan's stood taking up one side of the three-cornered green that formed the centre and heart of the place, they now drew up outside the door. Most people were loath to leave their cars in the street, even though this was the best part of Shancarrig. Visitors didn't know that The Terrace where Dr Nolan and then Dr Jims lived in Number Three and where the Hayes family lived in Number Five was about the best address in the county. They wanted safe parking for their cars.

The hotel was no longer dark brown. The dark colours had been replaced by cream and what Breda called a lovely restful *eau de nil*. She had toured other smarter hotels and discovered that this pale greenish shade was high fashion.

The more sober of the heavy-framed pictures had been relegated to the master bedroom, out of view of any visitors.

More bathrooms had been installed, chamber pots were hidden discreetly in bedside cupboards rather than being placed expectantly under beds.

The women who served in the dining room of Ryan's Commercial Hotel wore smart green dresses now, with their white aprons and little white half caps. The days of black outfits were over. There were comfortable chairs in the entrance hall encouraging guests to think of it as it used to be.

When Nessa and her sisters, Catherine and Nuala, were young they were kept well out of sight of the hotel visitors, but were trained to say good morning or good evening to anyone they encountered, even

173

scarlet-faced drunks who might not be able to reply.

Nessa's mother had cleared up the hotel yard. Old and broken machinery was removed, outhouses were painted. No longer was the place used as a dumping ground. Guests were told that ample parking facilities existed.

And the visitors changed too.

A trickle of American servicemen who had got to know Europe during the days of war, returned again in peacetime bringing their wives, particularly if there was any Irish heritage in the family tree. They would stay in hotels around the country and try to find it out. They became a familiar sight, sometimes still in uniform, and looking very dashing as they would book into Ryan's Commercial Hotel.

Father Gunn said he was worn out tracing roots from old church records.

There were the commercial travellers too. The same people coming regularly, once a month – once a fortnight sometimes. Usually two or three rooms would be booked by the various representatives coming to take orders in Shancarrig and outlying areas.

Nessa's mother treated them with great respect. They would be the backbone of their business, she told her husband. Conor Ryan shrugged. He often thought them a dull crowd, abstemious too, no bar profit from them. Pale, tired men, anxious about their sales, restless, uneasy.

It was Nessa's mother who insisted on the commercial room, and lighting a fire there. There were a few tables strewn around, they could fill their order books and smoke there. They could bring in a cup of tea or coffee.

Conor Ryan thought it a waste. Why couldn't they sit in the bar like any other person? He had noted that few of them followed either horses or dogs, there was little conversation with them at the best of times.

At school everyone was always interested in the hotel and its goings on. They always asked about what the farmers ate for breakfast on the fair days once a month, and whether any of the beasts had ever backed into the windows and broken them, as happened once down in Nellie Dunne's grocery when she forgot to put up the barriers.

Nessa told of the huge breakfasts served all morning, and of how fathers and sons would take turns, one to mind the animals while the other would eat bacon and eggs heaped high on plates.

'Who was your best friend when you were young?' Nessa asked her mother when Breda Ryan was brushing the dark shiny hair which she persisted in admiring so much despite all Nessa's complaints.

'We didn't have time for best friends then. Stay still, Vanessa.'

'Why do you call me Vanessa? Nobody else does.'

'It's your name. There, that looks great.'

'I look like the witch in the school play.'

'Why are you always saying such awful things about yourself, child? If you think these stupid things, other people will too.'

'That's funny. That's what Leo said too.'

'She's got her head screwed on her shoulders, that one,' Mrs Ryan said approvingly.

'We'll be going into the convent together next year, every day on the bus. Maybe she'll be more my friend then.'

In a rare moment of affection Nessa's mother held her eldest daughter close.

'You'll have plenty of friends. Wait and see!' she said.

'It had better start soon. I'm nearly fourteen,' Nessa said glumly.

In magazine stories Nessa had read of girls whose mothers were like friends. She wished she had a mother like that, not one so brisk and so sure of everything. Nessa had never known an occasion when her mother had been wrong, or at a loss for a word. Her father now, that was different, he was always scratching his head and saying he hadn't a clue about things. But Nessa felt her mother was born knowing all the answers.

On their last day at Shancarrig school Nessa Ryan stood between Niall Hayes and Foxy Dunne during the school photograph. Mrs Kelly always liked to have a picture taken on that day, and they were urged to dress themselves up well so that future generations could see how respectable had been the classes that had gone through these schoolrooms.

It had become a tradition now. The formal photograph taken under the tree outside the schoolhouse door. The very last moment of the year, organised to calm them down after the other tradition of name carving and the boisterous racing around the classroom collecting the books and pencils while singing:

No more Irish, no more French
No more sitting on a hard school bench
Kick up tables, kick up chairs
Kick the master and the mistress down the stairs.

That there had been no French ever learned in Shancarrig and that there were no stairs in the schoolhouse were details that didn't concern them. All over the world children sang that song on the last day.

Those who were only thirteen, and would have to return to school after the summer, looked on enviously. This was the day when they wrote their names on the tree. The boys had brought penknives. Everyone was busy digging at the wood of the old beech tree.

Nessa wished she could enjoy this like the others did. They all seemed very intense. Maura Brennan had been planning for weeks where she would put her name. Eddie Barton said he was going to carve his in a drawing of a flower so that it would look special in years to come. Foxy was saying nothing, but looked knowing all the same.

Nessa took the extra knife from Master Kelly and wrote Vanessa Ryan, June 1954. She felt there was more to say, but she didn't know what it was.

The sun was in their eyes as they squinted at Mrs Kelly's camera.

'Stand up straight! Stop fidgeting there!' She spoke knowing these were the last commands she would ever give them.

Foxy Dunne stroked Nessa's hair, which hung loose on her shoulders. 'Very nice,' he said.

'Take your hands off me, Foxy Dunne,' she snapped.

'Just admiring, Miss Bossy Boots. Admiring, that's all.' He didn't look the slightest bit put out.

Imagine Foxy, from that desperate house of Dunnes, daring to touch her hair.

'It is very nice, your hair,' Niall Hayes said. Square, dependable, dull Niall, who had never had an original thought. He said it as if he were trying to curry favour with Foxy and excuse him for his views.

'Well,' she said, at a loss for words. To her surprise she felt her face and neck redden at the praise. Nessa Ryan hadn't known a compliment from a boy before. She put her hand up to her face so that they wouldn't see her flush.

'Smile, everyone. Nessa, take your hand away from your face at once. Leo, if I see you put your tongue out once more there's going to be trouble. Great trouble.'

Everyone laughed, and it was a happy picture for the schoolhouse wall.

As they walked together for the last time from Shancarrig school, Nessa and Leo were arm in arm and Maura Brennan walked with them. Maura would get a job as a maid or in a factory, she had said she didn't want to go to England like her sisters. Nessa felt a flash of sympathy for the girl who hadn't the same chances as she had. Nessa's father had said about the Brennans and the Dunnes from the cottages that they had a poor hand dealt to them, very few aces there.

'Don't describe everything in terms of cards,' Mrs Ryan corrected him.

'Right. Then I'd say that the bookie's odds against the Brennans and Dunnes were fixed,' he said, grinning.

But Maura Brennan never complained.

She was always very agreeable and quiet, as if she had accepted long ago that her father was a disgrace and her mother was always asking for handouts. Foxy Dunne was different, he behaved as if his family were dukes and earls instead of drunks and layabouts. You'd never know from looking at Foxy Dunne that his father and brothers were barred from almost every establishment in the town. They weren't even allowed into their Uncle Jimmy's the hardware shop.

Foxy neither apologised for them nor defended them. It was as if he regarded them as separate people.

Nessa wished she could be like that sometimes. It hurt her when her mother was sharp to her easy-going father. It annoyed her when her father just shrugged and took none of the responsibility.

'There's a gypsy telling fortunes. They say she's terrific,' Maura said.

'Will we get our fortunes told?' Leo's eyes were sparkling.

Nessa knew that her mother would be very cross indeed if they went anywhere near the tinkers' camp. So would Leo's mother, but Leo didn't care. It would be wonderful to be as free as that.

'She'd only tell you back what you'd tell her,' Foxy said. 'That's what they do. They ask you what you want to be and then they tell you two minutes later that this is what's going to happen to you.'

'But that's dishonest,' Niall Hayes objected.

'That's life, Niall.' Foxy spoke as if he knew much more of the world from his broken-down cottage than did Niall Hayes, the lawyer's son who lived in The Terrace.

'So? Will we go?' Leo was on for any excitement.

'We could read palms to know what's going to happen to us,' Eddie said suddenly.

That seemed much safer to Nessa. Her mother need never know of this. 'How could we do it?' she asked.

'It's easy. There's a life line and a love line, and a whole lot of ridges for children.' Eddie sounded very confident.

'Where did you learn all this?' Foxy asked.

'I got interested in it through a friend,' he said.

'Is that your pen-friend?' Leo asked. He nodded.

A wave of jealousy flooded over Nessa. How did Leo know everything about everyone else and hardly anything about Nessa, who was meant to be her best friend?

'If we're going to do it, let's do it.' Nessa spoke sharply.

They walked up through Barna Woods, up towards the Old Rock.

No one needed to lead the way or decide where they were going. Once anything of importance had to be done, it was always at the Old Rock.

Eddie showed them their life lines. Everyone seemed to have a long one.

'How many years to the inch, do you think?' Foxy asked.

'I don't know,' Eddie admitted.

'Lots, I'd say.' Maura wanted to believe the best.

'Now. This is the heart line.' These varied. Nessa's seemed to have a break in hers.

'That means you'll have two loves,' Eddie explained.

'Or maybe love the same person twice. You know. Get your heart broken in the middle and then he'd come back to you,' Maura suggested.

'I might break *his* heart, whoever he is.' Nessa tossed her head.

'Yeah, sure. It doesn't say. Back to the lines.' Eddie moved away from troubled waters.

Foxy's heart line was faint.

So was Leo's. 'Is that good or bad?' Leo asked.

'It's good.' Foxy was firm. 'It means that neither of us will have much romance until it's time for us to marry each other.'

They all laughed.

Eddie moved to children. You'd know how many you were going to have by the number of tiny lines that went sideways at the base of your little finger. Maura was going to have six. She giggled. She'd be like her mother, she said, not knowing when to stop. Leo was going to have two. So was Foxy. He nodded approvingly. Eddie and Niall didn't look as if they were going to have any. They kept searching their hands and uttering great mock wails of despair.

Nessa had three little lines.

'That's three fine little Ryans to bring into the hotel with you,' Foxy said approvingly. He had already pointed out to Leo that they each had a matching score of two on their hands.

'Not Ryans,' Nessa corrected him sharply. 'They'll be my husband's name.'

'Yeah, but if you're anything like your ma they'll be thought of as Ryans,' Foxy said.

Nessa wouldn't let him see how annoyed she was. She fought back the tears of rage at his mockery.

'Don't let him upset you,' Leo said. 'Let it roll off.'

'It's all right for you. You don't care about your family,' Nessa snapped.

The others were still counting their future children. Leo and Nessa sat apart.

Although Nessa's eyes were bright, she would not allow herself to cry. She felt she had to keep talking, it might stop her starting to weep. 'If anyone says anything about your mother or father, Leo Murphy, you just laugh.'

'It wouldn't matter *what* they say, Nessa you eejit. It's only important if it upsets you, otherwise it's just words floating around in the air.'

Leo had lost interest as usual.

She went off to join the others, who had discovered the line in your hand that meant money. It looked as if the only one who would have any wealth to speak of was Maura Brennan from the cottages, the least likely one of them all.

Nessa didn't wait around to hear how her own future was mapped out in terms of wealth. Maybe Foxy would make some joke about her father's love of horses and greyhounds. It was so unfair, she raged. You couldn't answer back. You couldn't say that Foxy Dunne's father was even barred from Johnny Finn's, which meant he must have done something spectacular in terms of drunkenness.

Nor could you say that Foxy had one brother in gaol, and one who had got on the boat to England an hour ahead of the posse before *he* was in gaol too. It seemed that by being so really desperate Foxy's family had put themselves above being spoken badly of.

And yet she got annoyed at home when her mother would say those very things about the Dunnes. She found herself defending her friends in her home and defending her family when she was with her friends.

She couldn't bear it when Maura Brennan wiped her nose on her sleeve, because she knew her mother would sigh and shake her head.

179

But it was just as bad and even worse if Eddie and Niall were around when her mother would speak sharply to Dad, and tell him to clear the papers away, put on his jacket and make some pretence of running a hotel. She had seen them exchange glances once or twice at her mother's sharpness of tongue.

She longed to explain that it was needed, that Dad would sit there for ever telling long pedigrees of dogs and horses in far-away race tracks, while people waited to be served. She wished they knew that her father didn't take offence like other men might.

Nessa wanted her friends to be interested in tales she told about what her parents discussed over supper at home, but no one could care less. She wanted her mother and father to listen to stories about Foxy being mad enough to fancy Leo, without sniffing and saying something dismissive about both of them.

Up to now, she had felt safe in her family. It was one of the many bad things about growing up that you began to feel it wasn't as safe as it used to be.

A few days after the end of term the convent where Nessa would go to school sent a message saying that they would like to see the new pupils in advance.

'We'll dress you up smartly. It's important to make a good impression,' her mother said.

'But they're not going to refuse me, are they?'

'Will you ever learn? You want them to treat you as someone important, then *look* like someone important.'

'They're nuns, Mam. They don't look at things in that snobby way.'

'They don't, my foot.' Her mother was adamant.

They had a good outing. Leo went in her ordinary clothes, she hadn't dressed up at all.

'She doesn't need to,' Nessa's mother had said when they saw Leo arriving in her ordinary pink cotton frock, with its faded flower pattern and frayed collar.

'Why?'

'Because she is who she is.'

It was a mystery.

Leo was in great form that day, she and Nessa laughed and giggled at everything. They laughed all the more because they had to keep such solemn faces in the convent.

The corridors were long and smelled of floor polish. Little red lights burned in front of statues and pictures of the Sacred Heart, little blue lights in front of Our Lady.

Mother Dorothy, the Principal, spoke to them very earnestly about the need to behave well in school uniform. She told them that it would all be very very different from Shancarrig. She made Shancarrig sound as if it were on the back of the moon.

'Are you two great friends?' Mother Dorothy asked.

'Everyone's friends in our school,' Leo shrugged.

The nun's bright eyes seemed to take it all in.

Leo was all for exploring the town.

'We'd better go back,' Nessa said. 'They'll be wondering where we are.'

Leo looked at her in surprise. 'We're nearly fifteen, we've gone to see the convent where we are going to be imprisoned for the next three years. What can they be worried about?' she asked.

'They'll find something,' Nessa said.

'You're a scream.' Leo was affectionate.

And then, about three weeks later, Leo became almost a different person as far as Nessa was concerned. She was never around, and seemed unwilling to stir from The Glen at all. She'd gone off mysteriously for a holiday with her mother and father and the two great stupid dogs without even telling anyone where she was going.

The summer was endless. There was nobody to play with. Maura Brennan had gone around asking everyone could she be a maid in their house, and eventually Nessa's mother had given her a job, as a chambermaid in the hotel. Maura slept in, which was stupid because it was only ten minutes' walk to the cottages. But then again, Mother had said would Maura want to sleep in that place, and would you want to have her sleeping there?

Eddie Barton was lost in his old pressed flowers, and writing letters. Niall Hayes was complaining all the time about the school he was going to start in next September. He seemed to want reassurance that it was going to be all right.

Nessa wished that Leo was more like Niall, dependent on her, asking for advice. She thought Niall should be more like that tough little girl up in The Glen, able to survive on her own, fight her own battles.

Her mother noticed, like she always did.

'I've told you a dozen times, lead and they'll follow.'

'I could lead a thousand miles and Leo would never follow.' Nessa wished she hadn't admitted it, but it was out before she knew it. Breda Ryan sighed, she looked disappointed. 'I'm sorry, Mam, but it's different for you. You were always a born leader. Some people just have it in them.'

Her mother looked at her thoughtfully.

'I've been thinking about your hair,' she said unexpectedly.

'Well, don't think about it,' Nessa cried. 'Don't always think about how everyone else could do things better if only they did them like you.'

'Nessa!' Her mother was shocked at the outburst.

'I mean it. I'm fifteen. In some countries I could be married and have my own family. *You* always know best. *You* know Dad can't talk about greyhounds. *You* know that we can't call anyone a fella because you think it's vulgar, we have to say boy or man or something that no one else says.'

'I try to give you some manners. Style, that's all.'

'No. That's not all. You don't let us be normal. Maura is below us for some reason. Leo Murphy's family is above us because they live in a big house. You're *so* sure of everything, you just *know* you're right.' Nessa's face was red and angry.

'What brought this on, may I ask?'

'My hair. I was having an ordinary conversation with you and suddenly you said you wanted to talk to me about my hair. I don't care *what* you want, I won't do it. I won't do it. I'll go and tell Dad you want me to cut it or dye it or put it in an awful bun like yours. Whatever you want I won't do it.'

'Fine, fine ... if that's the way you feel.' Her mother stood up to leave the sitting room.

Nessa was still in a temper. 'That's right. You'll go down now to Daddy and frighten him. You'll tell him I'm being so difficult you don't know how to handle me, and then poor Dad will come and plead with me, and ask me to apologise.'

'Is that what you think I'm going to do?' Her mother looked distant and surprised.

'It's what you've done for years.' She was in so far now it didn't matter what she said.

'As it happens I was *going* to tell you about your hair. That it never looked better, that you should get a good cut. I was going to suggest that we went to Dublin together and I took you to a good place that

I asked about.'

'I don't believe you!'

'Well, believe what you like. The address is here on a piece of paper. I was going to say we could go on the cheap excursion on Wednesday. But go on your own.'

'How can I go on my own? I've no money.'

'I was going to ask your father to give you the money.'

'But you're not now. I see. You mean I lost it all by being badly behaved.' Nessa gave a mirthless laugh to show she knew the ways of adults.

'Ask him yourself, Nessa. You're too tiresome to talk to any more.'

Nessa didn't ask her father, so he mentioned it on Tuesday night. Why didn't she take the day trip up to Dublin and have a nice hair cut. She said she didn't want to go, she said her mother hated her, she said her mother was only making her feel guilty, she said her hair was horrible, that it was like a horse's tail.

She said she wouldn't go to Dublin on her own.

'Take Leo. I'll stand you both,' he said.

'You can't, Dad.'

'Yes, I can. I make some of the decisions around here.'

'No, you don't.'

'I do, Nessa. I make the ones I want to.' There was something about his voice. She believed him utterly.

Leo went to Dublin with her.

The hairdresser spent ages cutting and styling. 'You should come back every three months.'

'What about in five years?' Nessa said.

'Don't mind her,' Leo interrupted. 'She looks so great now they'll have her up every week.'

'Do I really?' Nessa asked.

'Do you really what?'

'Look great? Were you just saying it to be polite to her?'

'But you're terrific-looking. You *must* know that. You're like Jean Simmons or someone.' Leo said this as if it was as obvious as that it was day rather than night.

'How would I know? No one ever told me.'

'I'm telling you.'

'You're just my friend. You could be telling me just to keep me quiet,' Nessa complained.

'Ah God, Nessa. You can be very tiresome sometimes,' Leo said.

It was the same word as her mother had used. She had better watch it.

It was an up and down relationship with her mother all the years that Nessa Ryan went to school every day in the big town.

It was no use talking to Leo because Leo didn't seem to consider her own mother as any part of her life. If Nessa couldn't go to the pictures it was because her mother wanted her to clean the silver. If Leo couldn't go to the pictures it was only because Lance and Jessica – the dogs – needed to go for a run, or because her father wanted help with something.

Mrs Murphy was never mentioned.

Nessa heard that Mrs Murphy of The Glen was not a strong woman and possibly suffered from her nerves, but this wasn't talked about much in front of children. Leo seemed very distracted, as if there was something wrong at home, but even in the cosiest of chats she couldn't be persuaded to talk about it.

And there were so few other people to talk to.

She wasn't encouraged to talk to Maura Brennan who worked as a chambermaid in the hotel. Every time she stopped in a corridor to speak to Maura, Maura looked around nervously.

'No, Nessa. Your mother wouldn't like us to be chatting.'

'That's bull, Maura. Anyway, I don't care what she wants.'

'I do. It's my bread and butter.'

And there was no answer to that.

Sometimes Mrs Ryan was terrific, like when she got them all dancing lessons – Leo, Nessa and her young sisters Catherine and Nuala, the two Blake girls. It had been the greatest of fun.

Sometimes Mother was horrible – when she had asked Father to leave the bar the night he won eighty-five pounds on a greyhound. 'I just didn't want to lose *two hundred* and eighty-five pounds, Nessa,' she had explained afterwards. 'He was going out in to the streets looking for greyhounds, or anything that approached them in shape, to buy them drinks.'

Nessa had fumed over it. Her father should have been allowed his dignity. He should have had his night of celebration.

Her mother had been wonderful about the record player, and Nessa built up her own collection – 'Three Coins in the Fountain', 'Rock Around the Clock', 'Whatever Will Be Will Be'. But by the time she bought Tab Hunter's 'Young Love' her mother had become horrible again, saying that Nessa was now leaving school with a very poor Leaving Certificate.

There was no question of university, no plan for a career, nothing except the usual refuge of those who couldn't think what to do – the secretarial course in the town.

Nessa became very mulish that summer. Several times her father asked her for the sake of peace to try and ensure they had a happy house.

'You're so weak, Daddy,' she snapped at him one day. She was sorry instantly. It was so like something she felt her mother would have said.

'No, I'm not weak actually. I just like a quiet life without the people I love fighting like tinkers, that's all.' He spoke mildly.

'Why do you nag me so much?' she asked her mother. 'I mean, it's not going to make either of us happier, and it's upsetting Daddy.'

'I don't think of it as nagging. I think of it as giving you courage and strength to live your own life. To be full of courage. Honestly.' She believed her mother too when she said that.

'Did you always have courage?'

'No I did not. I learned it when I came to this house. When I had to cope with the pair on the wall.'

'The what?'

'Your sainted grandparents,' her mother said crisply.

Nessa looked up in shock at the elderly Ryans who had always been spoken of with such admiration and respect in this house.

'Why did it need courage to cope with them?' she asked.

'They would have liked your father to have lived in a glass case and they could have thrown sugar at him,' Mrs Ryan said.

When she said things like this she seemed very normal, like someone you could talk to, but she didn't say them often enough.

So, the summer she was eighteen Nessa began her course in shorthand and typewriting with a very bad grace.

Leo Murphy wouldn't come with her, a series of vague and unsatisfactory excuses about being needed up at The Glen. It was a confused time in Shancarrig.

Eddie Barton was so depressed working in Dunne's that he could hardly raise his eyes when you went in to talk to him. Niall Hayes was in Dublin setting up his plans to study law. Foxy was in England on the building sites. The Blake girls were studying in Dublin. She wasn't meant to talk to Maura. Her mother asked so many questions about who she went to the pictures with in the big town it sometimes seemed hardly worth the whole business of going.

She was ready for something exciting to happen the weekend Richard Hayes came to town.

He was very handsome, not square like Niall. He was tall and slim and very grown up, seven or eight years older than Nessa – twenty-five or twenty-six. He had been sent away from Dublin because of some disgrace with a girl.

Everyone knew that.

He had been banished to Shancarrig. Where apparently there would be no girls. Or no girls worth looking at.

Nessa dressed herself very very carefully until she caught his eye.

'Things *are* looking up,' he said. 'I'm Richard Hayes.'

'Hello, Richard,' Nessa said in a voice she had been practising for weeks.

His smile was warm but it made her nervous. She longed to run away and ask someone for advice, and as it happened at that very moment her mother called for her.

'Now I know your name,' he said.

'Only my mother calls me Vanessa,' she said.

But she was glad to escape.

Her mother had seen it all. 'What a handsome young man,' she said.

'Yes.' Nessa bit her lip.

'You have absolutely no competition,' her mother assured her. 'That's a man who likes pretty girls, and you are the prettiest girl in Shancarrig.'

The next time he met her he suggested that she take him for a walk.

'I'd love to do that but I'm practising my awful grammalogues,' said Nessa.

'Shorthand is going out of fashion, it'll all be machines soon,' he said.

'You may very well be right, but not before I do my Certificate exams. So maybe I'll see you later in the evening,' she said. She could see by his eyes that she had done the right thing. He was more interested than ever before.

'Absolutely, Vanessa,' he said with a mock bow.

She took him for long walks around her country.

She brought him up to the Old Rock and told him all its legends. She brought him to the school and showed him the tree where they had carved their names. She took him to the graveyard and pointed out the oldest tombstones to him. She showed him the children fishing in the river, and explained how you caught little fish with your hands if you could trap them in the stones.

She told him about Mattie the postman, who didn't go to mass but could deliver any letter to anyone if it just had their name and Shancarrig on it. She brought him to meet Father Gunn and Father Barry, saying that she was being a guide. Mrs Kennedy, the priests' housekeeper, looked very disapproving so Nessa just laughed and sat up on her table, saying that she had brought Richard Hayes here especially to taste one of Mrs Kennedy's scones. They were legendary.

Privately she told Richard they were legendary because they were as heavy as stones.

Nessa took Richard Hayes to visit Miss Ross in her house, she brought him to Nellie Dunne's shop, she took him to every nook and cranny in about three days.

'It's your introduction,' she said to him cheerfully. 'So that you'll never say you weren't shown the place properly.' She could sense that he was delighted with her, that he thought her a confident, bright young woman.

And indeed, that is what she was.

She was proud of her dark thick hair, her clear skin, her bright yellow and red blouses, and most proud of all that she wasn't silly and giggling like so many others were with him. Her mother had given her this gift, this belief that she was the equal of any Adonis who came to Shancarrig.

But Nessa would not settle for a weaker man like her mother had done. She wouldn't take second best, which was obviously how her mother must regard her father. There would be no dull, plodding, average fellow for Nessa. Not now. Not now that she had seen the admiring glance of a man like Richard.

He was the kind of man who came through a town like this once every fifty years. She was lucky to have caught his eye, she must be absolutely certain not to lose it again. This was the kind of man you could dream about night and day, someone who would occupy all your thoughts. But for some reason she didn't really allow herself to think about what she felt for him, this charming attentive Richard Hayes, who seemed to want to spend every free minute he had in her company. Yes of course she wanted to think that he really liked her, but some warning voice made her think that she could only keep his attention if she didn't seem to care.

It was an act.

Life shouldn't be an act. Yet she felt that they were unequal somehow. She must play this one very carefully.

Of course she heard a lot of stories about why he had come to help his Uncle Bill in the office. Some people said that Mr Hayes was getting too busy to manage on his own and that he had little hopes of his son Niall ever learning enough about the business. Niall was off to University in Dublin where he would serve his time in a solicitor's office as well. It would be four or five years before he'd qualify – old Bill Hayes was quite right to take this bright young man into his firm.

There were others who said that Richard had been sent to Shancarrig to cool his heels – there had been talk of an incident in Dublin, an incident involving a judge's daughter. There was another story about a broken engagement and a breach of promise action settled at the last moment.

In the stories Richard Hayes, cousin of the solid Niall, was always shown as a playboy.

The feeling was that Shancarrig would be very small potatoes indeed for someone who had seen and done as much as this handsome young man of twenty-five or so who had taken the place by storm.

'Isn't he fantastic?' Leo had said when she saw him for the first time.

'He's very easy to talk to.' Nessa was quick to let her best friend know just how far she was ahead in the race which every woman in Shancarrig seemed to have joined.

'I wish he'd come into the bar more,' Nessa's mother said. 'He's such an attractive kind of fellow he'd be a great draw.'

'I'd say that boyo has been asked to leave more bars than a few,' Conor Ryan said with the voice of a man who has seen it all and knew it all.

Unexpectedly Gerry O'Sullivan, their personable young barman, agreed.

'Real lady killer,' he said. 'The kind they'd go for each other's throats over.'

'That's what we don't need,' Mrs Ryan said firmly. 'Maybe it's just as well he's not in here every night.'

'Who is there in Shancarrig that would cut anyone's throat over a fellow? There's not that kind of passion and spark around the place at all.' Conor Ryan was back reading the forecasts for race meetings in towns he would never visit, on courses he would never walk.

Breda Ryan looked thoughtfully out at the front desk where Nessa was painstakingly practising her typing. They were meant to do an hour a day homework, and she had covered up the keys of the hotel machine with Elastoplast so that she couldn't see the letters.

Nessa's hair was shiny, her eyes were bright, her neckline low. They didn't have to look far for any passion and spark as far as Richard Hayes was concerned.

Nessa fought off three attempts by her mother to talk about sex.

'I *know* all that, didn't you tell me that years ago when I got my periods first.'

'It's different kind of telling now, there are other things to be taken into consideration ... please, Nessa.'

'There are no other things, I don't want to talk about it.' She wriggled away.

She didn't want to hear her mother say anything coarse or frightening. She was terrified enough already. These were problems that no mother could solve.

Richard Hayes told Nessa that she was beautiful. He called into the hotel and sat up on the reception desk to talk to her. It was the middle of the afternoon, a time when hotel business was slack and when Richard very probably should have been in his uncle's office.

He told Nessa that she had wonderful dark looks and she reminded him of Diana the mistress.

'Was she good or bad?'

'She was beautiful. Don't you know about her?'

'No, the nuns sort of dwelt more on the New Testament. She was the one that was extremely chaste, wasn't she?'

'That's her story and she's sticking to it,' he laughed, and she reddened. It seemed to her that he was eyeing her as if he was thinking along those lines himself.

He stroked her cheek thoughtfully.

'What happens if a girl is less than extremely chaste here?' he asked.

'They go to their grannies or to England.' She hoped that her cheeks didn't still look so red. It was just that he was looking at her breasts and appreciating her in a way that a man might if he wanted to make love.

Or maybe she was just fancying it. Nessa didn't know these days if anything was real or whether she was imagining a whole series of looks and gestures and feelings that didn't exist at all.

'I'd be very careful if we were ... to do anything that might cause a trip to your Granny's,' he said. 'You know, really careful. There would be no danger at all.'

From somewhere she found a confident answer.

'Ah but there wouldn't be any question of that, Richard,' she said.

He was more interested than ever.

'Are you afraid?'

'No. There could be other reasons why people might say no to you.'

'But you do like me, that I know.' He was playful.

'But do I *love* you, and do you love *me*? That's what you'd have to ask yourself before going wherever people go.'

'Like up to the Old Rock?'

He had only been in Shancarrig ten days and already he knew where the lovers went. To the little hollow in Barna Woods where the road to the Old Rock began.

'If only we knew what love is, Vanessa Mary Ryan, then we could rule the world.' He sighed a heavy mock sigh.

'And would we rule it well, Richard Aloysius Hayes?' she laughed.

'How did you know that?'

'I asked Niall what the RAH stood for on your tennis bag.'

'And he told you? The swine!'

They were fencing now, and laughing. He caught her by the wrist.

'I'm not joking, you're the loveliest girl for miles around.'

'You haven't seen any others.'

'Excuse me but I have. I went on a tour of inspection, brought my tennis bag up to The Glen, got no game, and no great joy out of your so-called best friend, little bag of nerves with a frizzy head, she is.'

'Don't speak like that about Leo.'

'And I studied Madeleine Ross.'

'She's ancient.'

'She's three years older than I am. And let me see who else. Pretty little Maura Brennan who works in Ryan's Ritz, but I think she's been to the Old Rock with a young Mr O'Sullivan. We'll have wedding bells there if I'm not greatly mistaken.'

'Maura? Pregnant! I don't believe it.'

He held up his hands defensively.

'I could be wrong,' he said.

'She's a fool. Gerry O'Sullivan will never marry her...' Nessa had let it slip out.

'Aha ... so it's not just a question of loving each other. It's a question of the chap marrying the girl, is it?'

Nessa had lost that one. 'I must be off,' she said.

She barely made it upstairs on shaking legs and went into her room. There she found her sisters Catherine and Nuala starting up guiltily from the dressing table where they had been reading her diary.

'I thought you were meant to be at the reception desk,' Catherine said, flying immediately to the attack.

'We hadn't read anything private really,' begged Nuala, who was younger and more frightened.

Frightened she had reason to be.

Nessa Ryan, eighteen and desired by the most handsome man in Ireland, drew herself up to her full height.

'You can explain all that later,' she said, taking the key out of the inside of the door. 'I'm locking you in until I find Mother.'

'Don't tell Mam,' roared Nuala.

'Mam won't like what you've been up to,' Catherine threatened.

But Nessa had the upper hand. She had written nothing in her diary, it was all in the back of her shorthand notebook which never left her side.

She had been coming up to write more, to tell herself of the passion in his voice, the tingles she had felt when he held her wrist, how he had said that he could love her.

She ignored the pleas and lamentations from her room and set off to find her mother.

In the corridor she met Maura Brennan carrying sheets.

'Is everything all right, Maura?' she asked.

'Why do you ask?'

'Well, I don't know. You look different.'

'I *am* different. I'm getting married next week to Gerry. I haven't told everyone else. It was only just arranged.'

'Married?'

'I know. Isn't it great!'

Nessa was dumbfounded. Perhaps there was a different set of rules, perhaps fellows *did* marry you if you went to the Old Rock with them.

Maybe her mother and the nuns and Catholic Truth Society pamphlets had it all wrong. She pulled herself together.

'That's great, Maura,' she said. 'Congratulations.'

Nessa found her mother, and told her of the two criminals locked in the bedroom.

'Give them a very bad punishment,' she ordered.

'Did they find anything to read, anything they shouldn't have?' Her mother's eyes were anxious.

'If I have to say to you once more that there is nothing to find, nothing to discuss, I will go *mad.*' The words were almost shouted.

To her surprise her mother looked at her admiringly.

'You know, I think Richard may be good for you after all. You're getting to be confident at last. You'll be a leader yet.'

It was true. She did feel more in control. She was delighted to find that her mother took such a strong stand with Catherine and Nuala. And so, unexpectedly, did her father.

'A person must be allowed to have their private life and their dreams,' he told the two sulking girls, who were allowed no outings for a week. 'It's a monstrous thing to invade someone's life of dreams.'

'There was nothing there,' Catherine said.

'To say that is making it worse still.'

The two girls were startled.

There was Nessa, usually the one in trouble, Nessa who had been making calf's eyes at Niall Hayes's cousin, and all she was getting was praise for doing something as dangerous as locking them in a bedroom.

'Suppose there had been a fire?' Catherine even suggested as a possibility.

She got little support.

'Then you would have burned to death,' said their mother.

Eddie Barton came in sometimes for a chat.

'Are you doing a line with Richard Hayes?' he asked Nessa.

'What's a line?'

'I don't know, I often wondered. But are you?'

'No I'm not. He comes in and out. He's very handsome, probably too handsome for me.'

'I know what you mean,' Eddie said unflatteringly.

'Thanks a lot, friend.'

'No, I didn't mean that. You're fine-looking and you've got much better-looking than when we were all young, honestly . . .' Eddie was flustered now and he saw he was making gestures to show how much better-looking Nessa had got. Gestures that indicated a bosom and a small waist. But she didn't seem offended. 'Looks are important, aren't they?' He seemed anxious.

'I suppose so, though people keep saying they're not.'

Eddie was running his hand through his spiky hair. 'I wish fellows improved, all fellows, like all girls seem to.'

'Aren't you a grand-looking fellow, Eddie?' Her voice was encouraging and light, she thought.

'Don't make fun of me.' His face was red.

'I'm not.'

'Yes you are. I've hair like God knows what, I'm pushing a brush around bloody Dunne's all day. Who'd look at me?'

He banged out of the hotel, leaving Nessa mystified. As far as she knew Eddie had never asked any girl in Shancarrig out, and had shown no interest at all in any of the females around the place. He did come in from time to time to make mysterious phone calls to Scotland. It was too hard to understand, and anyway she had far more important things on her mind.

Richard took Nessa to the pictures in the town in his uncle's car.

'He lets you drive this?'

'He doesn't go out at night.'

'Niall never drove it.'

'Niall never asked.'

Niall Hayes was staying with a schoolfriend of his. Together they were going to a three-week course in book-keeping. They hated it. Niall had sent several letters and postcards to Nessa saying how dreary it was. He hoped university would be better.

'I think Niall fancies you desperately,' Richard said as he kissed Nessa in his uncle's car.

She drew away.

'I don't think so,' she said, cool, ungiggly. Her mother was right. She had grown up a lot since Richard had come to Shancarrig.

'Oh I think he does. Doesn't he take you to the pictures? Doesn't Niall plan journeys to the Old Rock with you like I do?' He repeated his own words about his younger cousin.

'Niall never asked,' said Nessa.

'Niall will be back tomorrow, Ethel was telling me,' Mrs Ryan said to Nessa.

'That should shake the town to its foundations,' Nessa said.

'You and he were always good friends.' Her mother's voice was mild so Nessa became contrite.

'That's true, we were. He's got very mopey though, Mam. Not easy to talk to.'

'Everyone doesn't have the charm of his cousin Richard.'

'Richard's normal. He's nice to people, he's pleasant. He's not always grousing and groaning about things the way Niall is.'

'Maybe Niall has something to grouse and groan about.'

'What? What any more than the rest of us?'

'Well, his best girl is starry-eyed about his cousin, his place in the firm isn't nearly as secure as it used to be ... *and* he doesn't have a wonderful understanding mother like you do. He has dreary old Ethel.'

They laughed as they sometimes could nowadays like sisters, like friends.

'What would *you* do for Niall if you were his friend?' Nessa asked. She thought she saw her mother watching her very carefully, but she couldn't be sure.

'I'd encourage him to fight for his place over there. He's Bill's son. It's *his* business. I'd tell him that there are only a few chances and you should take them. Oh, I suppose I'd go on a bit about letting grass grow under your feet.'

'He mightn't listen to me.'

'No. People often don't listen when others are out for their good.'

'Did Dad listen to you?'

'Ah, yes. But that was different, I loved your father. Still do.'

'I don't *love* Niall, but I am very fond of him.'

'Then don't let him get walked on,' said Breda Ryan.

Nessa invited Niall to come over to the hotel and have a drink with her. It felt very grown up.

'You look great,' he said.

'Thanks, Niall. You look fine too.'

'I meant *pretty* like ...' he said.

'What work are you doing in the office?' She changed the subject.

'Filing! Taking things out of torn envelopes and putting them into non-torn envelopes. God, Dinny Dunne could do that on one of his good days.'

Niall was full of misery and Nessa was full of impatience. Why hadn't he the fire to get up and go, the sheer charm of his cousin?

They were the sons of brothers, after all. Richard's father must have been the one with the spirit.

Richard had told his uncle that a younger man should go around on home visits, which meant that he had the use of the car and could be out all day. Who knew how long it took to make a will or to get the details in a right-of-way claim? Who could measure how many hours it might involve talking to a publican about the extinguishing of a licence or to a woman about a marriage settlement involving a farm?

Richard was sunny and cheerful to everyone.

If he had been asked to do the files he would have made it into the most prestigious job in the office. Why could Niall not see this? Why did he hunch his shoulders and look defeated? Why didn't he throw back his head and laugh?

'Did you see much of Richard while I was away?' Niall asked, cutting across her thoughts.

'He's been around, he's been very lively.'

'He's not reliable, of course,' Niall said.

'Don't be such a tell-tale, Niall.' Her lightness of voice hid her annoyance. She wanted to hear nothing that would puncture her idea of Richard Hayes, no silly family story of shame or disgrace.

'It's just that you should know.'

'Oh, I know all about him,' she said airily.

'You do?' Niall seemed relieved.

'A girl in every town. We even had that Elaine down from Dublin last week. No, there are no secrets.'

'Elaine was here? After all that happened!'

'Right in front of your house. Dropped him off from a real posh car.'

'There'll be hell to pay if anyone knows that. She was the one.'

'The one?'

'The one that had the ... the one who got into ... the one.'

'Oh yes, I supposed she was.' Nessa's heart was leaden. Niall didn't have to finish any of his sentences. The stories had gone before, the judge's daughter who was reported to have been pregnant.

Imagine her coming down to Shancarrig, pursuing Richard after all that.

She must be pretty desperate.

'So that's all right.' Niall looked at Nessa protectively, as if he was relieved that he didn't have to rescue her from a quagmire of misunderstanding.

'We're all fine here, it was a lovely summer. *You* sound as if you had a terrible time.' She led him into a further catalogue of his woes so that she could follow her own line of thought. Surely Richard couldn't still be involved with this girl. Then of course it was known that this girl, unlike Nessa, would go to bed with him. And had.

Is this all he wanted? Surely he wanted other things – fun and chat, and kissing, and a girl who was seven years younger than him who looked like Diana the mistress?

If only there was someone to ask. But there was no one.

On Maura Brennan's wedding day Leo suggested they go to the church.

'Maura won't like it. She doesn't want to mix because of working in the hotel.'

'That's pure rubbish,' Leo said. 'It's just your mother who doesn't want her to mix. Let's go.'

As they sat waiting for the sad little ceremony to begin Nessa was pleased to see Niall Hayes and Eddie Barton come in as well.

'I got an hour off from the desperate Dunnes,' Eddie whispered – he worked for the more respectable branch of the family in Foxy's uncle's hardware shop. He seemed very miserable about it.

'I'm allowed out from sticking labels on envelopes,' Niall said.

'I'm meant to be at the typing course but I told my mother we had a day off. I'm watched like a hawk,' Nessa complained.

'We weren't the most successful class ever to come out of Shancarrig school, were we?' asked Leo with a little laugh.

'Well, at least the rest of us . . .' Nessa stopped. She had remembered before that Leo had looked very upset when she had been referred to as a lady of leisure.

Leo flashed her a smile of gratitude. They sat in supportive silence, the four of them, as they watched their schoolfriend Maura, pregnant and happy, marry Gerry O'Sullivan, small, handsome, with one best man but no other friend or family in the church.

'He doesn't look very reliable,' whispered Niall.

'Jesus, Mary and Holy Saint Joseph, who do you think *is* reliable these days?' Nessa hissed.

'*I* am, for what it's worth.' He looked at her and suddenly she saw that he did like her, much more than in the sort of hang-dog dependent way she had thought. Niall Hayes was keen on her. It didn't give her the kind of boost that she had thought it might. In the days when nobody fancied her she would love to have had a few notches on her gun, affections to play with, hearts to break.

But Niall was too much of a friend for that.

'Thank you,' she said very simply in a whisper.

Maura was delighted with the present they bought her, a little glass-fronted cabinet. Leo had remembered Maura saying that she would love to collect treasures and display them in a cabinet. There were tears of joy in her eyes when they delivered it to the cottage where she would be living – only a stone's throw from where her father still fell home drunk every night.

'You're great friends,' she said, her voice choked.

Nessa felt a blanket of guilt almost suffocate her. For years Maura had been working in Ryan's Hotel and hardly a sentence exchanged between them. If only she had the courage of a Leo Murphy she would have taken no heed of offending her mother, of crossing boundaries of familiarity between staff and owners.

But she *did* have courage these days and she would show it, use it. When she got back to the hotel her mother asked where the festivities were going to be held.

'You know that it will be a few drinks in Johnny Finn's and whatever bit of cold chicken poor Maura managed to put out on plates for those that will drag themselves back to her cottage for it.'

'Well, she should have thought of all that...' her mother began.

'No she shouldn't, she should be having a reception here by right. She was my schoolfriend, she and Gerry both work here. Anyone with a bit of decency would have given them that at least.'

Breda Ryan was taken aback.

'You don't understand...'

'I don't like what I do understand. It's so snobby, so ludicrous. Does it make us better people to be seen to be superior to Maura Brennan from the cottages? Is this what you always wanted, a place on some kind of ladder?'

'No. That's not what I always wanted.' Her mother was calm and didn't show the expected anger at being shouted at in the front hall of the hotel.

'Well, what did you want then?'

'I'll tell you if you take that puss off your face ... and stop shouting like a fishwife. Come on.' Her mother was talking to her like an equal. They walked into the bar.

'Conor, why don't you take a fiver from the till and go up to Johnny

197

Finn's to buy a few drinks for Gerry and Maura?'

Nessa's father looked up, pleased.

'Didn't I only suggest...?'

'And you were right. Go on now while they're still sober enough to know you're treating them. Nessa and I'll look after the bar.'

They watched as Conor Ryan moved eagerly across to the festivities, hardly daring to believe his good luck. Nessa sat still and waited to be told. Mrs Ryan poured two small glasses of cream sherry, something that had never happened before. Nessa decided to make no comment; she raised the glass to her lips as if she and her mother had been knocking back drinks for years.

'People want things at different times. I wanted a man called Teddy Burke. I wanted him from the moment I saw him when I was sixteen until I was twenty-one. Five long years.' Nessa looked at this stranger sipping the sherry; she was afraid to speak. 'Teddy Burke had a word for everyone, but that's all it was ... a word... I thought it was more. I thought I was special. I built a life of dreams on it. I couldn't eat. I lost my health and my looks, such as they were. They sent me away to do a domestic economy course.

'Do you know, I can't really remember those years. I suppose I must have followed the course – I got my exams and certificates – but I only thought of Teddy Burke.' She paused for such a long time that Nessa felt able to speak.

She spoke as a friend, as an equal. 'And did he know, did he have any idea...?'

'I don't think so, truly. He was so used to everyone admiring, I was just one more.' Her mother's eyes were far away as she sat there in the empty hotel bar, her dark hair back in a loose coil with a mother-of-pearl clasp on it. Her pale pink blouse had its neat collar out over her dark pink cardigan – she looked every inch the successful businesswoman. This story of a thin frightened girl loving a man for five years – a man who didn't know she existed – was hard to believe.

'So anyway, one day I was told that Teddy Burke was going to marry Annie Lynch, the plainest girl for three parishes, with a bad temper and a cast in her eye. Everything changed. He was marrying her for her land, for her great acres running down to the lakes and over green valleys, for the fishing rights, for the stock. A man as handsome and loving as Teddy Burke could trade everything for land.

'It made me wonder what I really wanted.

'And I went to a cousin's wedding and met your father and I decided that I wanted to go far from where I lived, where I would remember Teddy Burke's laugh and his way with people. I decided that I wanted to make your father strong and confident like Teddy was when he got the land, like Annie Lynch always was because she had the land... I put my mind to it.'

There was a long silence. Nessa was taking it in.

'Were you ever sorry?'

'Not a day, not once I decided. And hasn't it turned out well? The hotel has survived, the pair out in the pictures in the hall would have let it run into the ground, and they'd have let your father go off to the British army.'

'Why are you telling me this now?'

'Because you thought that all I wanted was to put ourselves above other people. I may have done that by accident but it wasn't what I set out to do.'

'Does Dad know about Teddy Burke?'

'There was nothing for him to know but a young girl's silliness and dreams.'

Mattie came in, his sack of letters delivered.

'This town is going to hell, Mrs Ryan,' he said. 'A wedding party bawling "Bless this House" above in Johnny Finn's and the women of the house sipping sherry in Ryan's.'

'And no one to pour a pint for the postman,' laughed Nessa's mother.

The moment was over, it might never come again.

Nessa began to look at other people in a new light after this. Perhaps everyone had a huge love in their life, or something they thought was a huge love. Maybe Mr Kelly up at the school had fancied a night-club singer before he settled for Mrs Kelly. Maybe Nellie Dunne had once been head over heels in love with some travelling salesman who had come many years ago to Ryan's Commercial Hotel, but who had married someone else. Maybe one of those old men in the commercial room had been Nellie's heart's desire.

It wasn't so impossible.

Look at Eddie Barton, falling in love with someone in Scotland. It had never been exactly clear how he had got in touch with her in the first place, but apparently he had been writing to Christine Taylor for ages, and phoning her from the hotel.

And then she had arrived over and was living with his mother.

Nessa was amazed at the change in Eddie. He was speaking to the Dunnes, cousins of Foxy, as if he was their equal. He was in the hotel with Christine discussing improvements and ways to decorate the bedrooms.

Love did extraordinary things to people.

Eileen Blake from The Terrace said that she was stopping for a coffee in Portlaoise on her way back from Dublin and who was there but Richard Hayes and a girl, and they were booking in. As man and wife.

Young Maria Kelly from Shancarrig schoolhouse was reported to have been at a dance with him in the big town, but her parents didn't know because she had climbed in and out her window through the branches of the old copper beech tree that grew in the yard.

Nessa Ryan heard all these facts in the space of three days. She came across them accidentally, they were not brought in as deliberate bad news to her door.

She felt, not as she had feared she might – no sense of cold betrayal, no rage that a man should tell her she was special and he wanted her to be his girl, and yet behave the same way with half the country. Very clearly and deliberately she felt her infatuation with him end. Perhaps she *was* her mother's daughter much more than she had ever believed. She was not ready to give him up but she would have him in her life under different terms.

Richard came into the commercial room of the hotel. There were no travellers staying and so Nessa was using the room to do her shorthand homework.

'I have to go into town tomorrow. I could pick you up outside your college,' he offered.

She could imagine the eyes of her classmates when Richard Hayes leant across to open the door of the car for her.

'And where would we go then?' she asked.

'I'm sure we'd find somewhere,' he said.

Nessa looked back into the bar where her mother and father were standing, well out of earshot.

'They're not listening.' Richard was impatient. But that wasn't what concerned Nessa. She looked at them and saw her mother stroke Dad's face gently, lovingly.

She saw that it really never mattered who talked to the men from the brewery, the biscuit salesmen, who hired or fired the barmen. It wasn't important that Sergeant Keane dealt with her mother over the licensing laws, not her father. Mother had forgotten Teddy whatever he was, he'd have been no good to her. She had found what she really wanted, someone she could share her own strength with. Nessa saw for the first time that her mother had got what she wanted. It wasn't a case of settling for second best.

And with a shock of recognition she felt that she was going to follow exactly the same path. It wouldn't be a question of aiming high and searching for fireworks. There might be an entirely different way to live your life. Unbidden, Niall's worried face came to mind. She longed to calm him and tell him it would all be all right.

She looked straight at Richard, right into his eyes.

'No thanks,' she said. 'No to everything. Thank you all the same.'

It wasn't at all easy to do.

But she would not live in fear of him and how he would react. Nothing was worth that.

'Well, well, well.' He looked around the room scornfully. 'So *this* is all you are ever going to amount to. A second-rate shabby hotel ... a grown woman still a prisoner to her mother.' He looked very angry and put out. People didn't usually speak to Richard Hayes like this. Girls certainly didn't.

Nessa was furious.

'It is *not* a shabby hotel. It's my home. *My* home. I live here and I choose to live here. You can't even live where you want to because they run you out of town. Don't come down here and start criticising us. It doesn't sit well on you. And answer me one thing: how would I amount to any more if I were to go off to the glen with you and roll around for five minutes on the ground?'

'It would be longer than five minutes,' he said mischievously. She hadn't lost him. He fancied her all the more because she was refusing him.

What a wonderful power.

It was the making of Nessa Ryan.

She didn't flirt with him like every other woman within a hundred-mile radius seemed to. She did not want to be known as his girl.

It was as if she had turned around the relationship, made it businesslike, affectionate but in no way exclusive. She teased him about his latest conquests, real and supposed, she knew that her very lack of jealousy was driving him wild. She was happy in the knowledge that he desired her. When she met him it was always with other people.

She finished her course at the college and went to work full time for her mother and father.

It was she who decided to lift the hotel on to a higher level. She contacted the tourist board about grants, and organised that they got money advanced to improve their facilities. She asked visiting Americans to write letters to their local papers praising Ryan's so as to get them further custom.

She told her mother to drop the word Commercial from the title.

'Ryan's makes it sound like a pub,' her mother complained.

'Call it Ryan's Shancarrig Hotel,' said Nessa.

A few eyebrows were raised. Nellie Dunne presided over several conversations about the Ryans having notions.

'That young one is the cut of her mother,' said Nellie. 'I remember when Breda O'Connor came in and took the whole establishment from Conor's mother and father. That Nessa will do the same.'

But Nessa Ryan showed no signs of friction with her mother and father. She would laugh with her mother about the Sainted Grandparents who glared from the picture on the wall. She told her father that he looked handsome in a jacket and begged him to have nice framed pictures of racehorses on the wall, so that they might attract a few of the horsey set and give some legitimacy to her father's constant topic of conversation.

Catherine and Nuala were mystified by her. The most handsome man around seemed to be waiting on their sister Nessa and she barely gave him the time of day. They watched uncomprehending as Nessa became more and more attractive-looking, her dark shiny hair always loose and cut with a fringe. A style that owed nothing to the hairdresser but a lot to a picture in a children's book she had seen, a picture of Diana the mistress.

Nessa got on well with her mother. The two of them often drove to Dublin to look for fittings and fabrics. At an early age she seemed to have their trust, and to be allowed a lot of freedom that was later denied to the more spirited Catherine and Nuala.

'Why can't we go to Galway on our own? Nessa did,' Catherine complained.

'Because you're both so unreliable and untrustworthy you'd probably go under a hedge with the first pair of tinker boys you met,' Nessa said cheerfully to them. They felt it a great betrayal, there should be *some* solidarity between sisters. Imagine mentioning going under hedges in front of their mother, putting ideas in her mind.

'I have no solidarity with you,' Nessa said. 'You steal my make-up, you wear my nylons, you spray yourself with *my* perfume. You don't wash the bath, you do nothing to help in the hotel, you can't wait to get away from here. *Why* should I help you?'

Put like that it was hard to know why.

'Flesh and blood,' Catherine suggested.

'Overrated,' Nessa told her.

'Would you try for hotel management, do you think?' her mother suggested. 'It would teach you so much. There's a great course in Dublin.'

'I'm happy here,' Nessa said.

'I don't ask you about Richard . . .' her mother began.

'I know, Mother. It's one of the things I love about you.' Nessa headed her off before she could start.

She wondered how long would be his exile in Shancarrig, and on Niall's behalf she worried lest he had made too permanent and important a niche for himself with his Uncle Bill.

Mr Hayes came in to drink in Ryan's Shancarrig Bar with Major Murphy, Leo's father, sometimes. Nessa served behind the bar from time to time. She said it helped her to know what the customers wanted. Mr Hayes dropped no hint of how long his nephew would stay, but to Nessa's distress he showed little enthusiasm about his son's return.

'Hard to know what he learned up there, you couldn't get a word out of him,' she heard him say to Dr Jims Blake one evening. She didn't want to join in the conversation but later she brought up the subject.

'Niall seems to be enjoying university and studying hard,' she said.

'Divil a bit of a sign he gives of either.'

'Oh now. All fathers are the same. Still, business is good. There'll be plenty for Niall to take on when he comes back.'

'Oh, I don't know. What with Richard . . .' He let his voice trail away.

'But Richard won't be here for ever?' Her voice was clear and without guile.

Bill Hayes looked at her directly. 'There's something keeping him here. I had a notion it might be yourself?' he said.

'No, Mr Hayes, I'm not the girl for Richard.' There was no play-acting, nothing wistful – she seemed to be stating a fact.

'Well, something's keeping him here, Nessa. It's not the pay, and it's not the social life.'

'I expect he'll move on one day, like he moved in.' Her voice was bland, expressionless.

'I expect so.' He sounded troubled.

Niall was home the following week.

'I hear they're giving you a car for your twenty-first birthday,' he said to Nessa.

'It's meant to be a surprise, shut up about it,' she hissed.

'I didn't know it was a secret. Isn't it great though? A car of your own.'

'You could have one too.'

'How, might I ask? I'm not the doted-on daughter of the house.'

'No, but you're the eldest son of the house, and you never show the slightest interest in your father's business.'

'I'm only qualifying as a bloody solicitor, that's all.' Niall was offended.

'But what kind of a solicitor? You don't even ask him what's going on. You don't know about the competition.'

'Richard, I suppose.'

'No, you fool. He's the family, he's on your team. The competition. You know Gerry O'Neill the auctioneer in the town? Well, he has a brother who's taking a lot of the conveyancing, even out this way. You have to fight back.'

'I didn't know that.'

'You don't ask.'

'When I do ask can I help I'm told to tear up files and put labels on envelopes.'

'That was three years ago, silly.' She put her arm around his shoulder. 'Bring your father in here for a pint, treat him as an equal.'

'He wouldn't like that.'

'I used to be like that, I spent my whole childhood thinking my mother wouldn't like this or that. I was wrong. They want us to have minds of our own.'

'No. They want us to be reliable,' Niall insisted.

'Yes, well. You and I *are* reliable, so they've got that much. Now they want us to have views, opinions, be out for the common good.'

He looked at her with great admiration.

'Have you . . . ?' he began.

She knew he wanted to say something about Richard.

'Yes?' Her voice stopped him asking.

'Nothing,' Niall said.

'See you and your father tonight.'

When Nessa Ryan got her car for her twenty-first birthday she first took her mother and father for a drive around Shancarrig, waving to everyone they passed. She caught her mother's eye in the driving mirror more than once and they smiled. Friends. People who understood each other. She was doing the right thing. Thanking them publicly, showing Shancarrig that Breda O'Connor had come here twenty-two years ago and made a triumph of her life.

It was six o'clock and the angelus was ringing as she headed back home. People would be coming in to Ryan's Shancarrig now for a drink. There would be autumn tourists to check in – the coach buses arrived in the evening.

As they passed Eddie Barton's house Eddie and his Scottish Christine were in the garden. Nessa screeched to a halt.

'I'll come back for you later. I'll pick up Leo, Niall and Maura and take you all for a spin,' she called.

'Just Eddie,' Christine said. 'So it will be like old times.'

'You too.'

'No. Thanks, but no.'

'She knows what she's doing,' Nessa's mother said approvingly.

'Like all women, it seems to me,' Conor Ryan said. His sigh was happy, not resigned. Nessa knew this now. Once she thought he was yearning to be free, now she believed that her father had the life he wanted.

Maura wouldn't come, Nessa knew that, but she would love to be asked. She would be so pleased for the car to pull up at her cottage and for a group of the nobs, as Mrs Brennan would call them, to get out and beg her to join them.

But she would stay and mind Michael – her little boy, two-and-a-half-years old, a loving child, a child who never knew his father. Gerry O'Sullivan the handsome barman had been reliable enough to marry Nessa, but not reliable enough to stay when the child had been born handicapped.

Nessa ran up the steps of Number Five The Terrace. The door was never locked.

'Hello, Mr Hayes. I've come to take your right-hand man out for a drive in my new car,' she said.

'Congratulations, Nessa. I heard of the birthday and the car. Richard should be with you in a minute,' he said.

'I meant Niall,' she answered.

'Oh yes,' he said.

'I don't know *why* you're not out playing golf yourself, Mr Hayes, with all the help you have in here.' She was playful, confident, she knew he liked her. Three years ago she wouldn't have raised her glance to him, let alone her voice.

'Oh, my wife wouldn't like that,' he said.

Nessa thought of Niall's mother, a solid glum-looking woman, dressed always in browns or olive green. No spark, no life. Mr Hayes would have been better with a woman like Nessa's mother, or Nessa herself.

Niall had heard her voice. 'Did the car arrive?'

'It did. And I've come to drive you off in it.' She linked her arm in his and appeared not to notice as Richard arrived out of the other door, straightening his tie and assuming that all the fuss in the hall meant someone had called for him.

Richard Hayes was standing at the top of the steps as Nessa ushered Niall into the front seat.

'Didn't you want . . . ?' Niall began.

'Yeah. I wanted you but I waited till after six not to annoy your father. Let's pick up Eddie.'

If Niall had been going to say anything about Richard he didn't now. He settled back happily in the front seat. Eddie came, on his own. Chris had things to discuss with his mother. They drove up the long drive of The Glen. Leo was at the door waiting to meet them.

'Will I show the car to your parents?' Nessa asked.

'No. No, I'd rather not,' Leo said.

Possibly Leo's mother and father might not have been able to afford a car for her. Or maybe her mother wasn't well. Nobody had seen Mrs Murphy in ages, and Leo's brothers, Harry and James, never came home from wherever they were. Biddy their maid was as silent as the grave, as if she were defending the family. Perhaps they had their secrets. Nessa didn't mind.

Not nowadays.

And she was right about Maura. Maura wouldn't come out with them, but she had a cake and they ate it together companionably in

206

her cottage. The glass-fronted cabinet had a few items in it – a spoon in a purple velvet box, a piece of Connemara marble, and one of Eddie's pressed flowers that he had done under glass as a christening present for the baby Michael.

There was a picture of Gerry O'Sullivan in a small frame on the mantelpiece.

'Isn't it great how we all stuck together,' said Maura. And they nodded, unable to speak. 'All we need is Foxy to come home and we'd be complete.'

'He's doing very well,' Leo said unexpectedly. 'He'll be able to buy the town the way things are going.'

'Does he want to buy the town?' Niall asked.

'Well, he'd like to be a person of importance here, that's for certain,' Leo said.

'Wouldn't we all?' Niall said.

'You *are*, Niall. You're a solicitor. If ever I have any business I'll bring it to you,' Maura said.

They laughed good-naturedly, Maura most of all.

'But remember when we did our fortunes *you* were going to be the one who was going to be wealthy, not Foxy. Maybe you *will* have business,' Eddie Barton said. They all remembered the day they left Shancarrig school. It was seven years ago – it seemed a lifetime.

Nessa drove them up to the base of the Old Rock. They left the car and scampered up as they had done so often before.

It was hard to read their faces, but Nessa thought that Eddie's future seemed certain, bound up with the Scottish Chris who had come in some unexplained way into his life.

She knew that Maura would never consider herself unlucky. She would like a better house, maybe she was saving for one – there was no sign of her hard-earned wages in the cottage they had visited.

Leo would always be unfathomable but it was Niall, good dependable Niall, that Nessa was thinking about today. Leo and Eddie wandered off to stand on the stone where you were meant to be able to view four counties. Sometimes it was easier in this evening light. You could see a steeple that was in one county, a mountain that was in another.

Niall sat beside her, his jacket too small for him, his shirt crumpled. His hair was the same soft brown-black as his cousin Richard's, but jagged and not lying right. His eyes were troubled as he looked at her.

'We'll be very happy, Niall,' she said to him, patting his hand.

'I hope you will.' His voice was gruff with generosity and wishing her well, and loneliness. She could hear it, as her mother must have heard the eagerness in Conor Ryan's voice all those years ago, and coped with it.

'You and I,' Nessa said. 'We will get married, won't we? You will ask me eventually?'

'Don't make fun of me, Nessa.'

'I was never more serious in my life.'

'But Richard?'

'What about him?'

'Don't you . . . ?'

'No.'

'Well, didn't you . . . ?'

'No.'

'I thought that you didn't even *see* me,' he said.

'I've always seen you. Since the day you told me my hair was nice, the day we left Shancarrig school.'

'I wrote your name on the tree,' he said.

'You what?'

'I wrote JNH loves VR, very low down near a root. I did then, and I do now.'

'John Niall Hayes, Vanessa Ryan. You never did!'

'Will we go and see it?' he said. 'As proof.'

They had their first kiss in the sunset on her twenty-first birthday, on the hill that looked down over the town. Nessa knew that there would be a lot of work ahead. She would have to fight the apathy of his glum mother, the refusal to relinquish power by his father. She would have to decide where they would live and how they would live. Richard would move on sooner or later. Possibly sooner, now that this had all been planned.

Over the years she would reassure Niall Hayes that there had never been anything to fear from Richard, he was not a lover, nor even a love. He was someone who came in when she needed it and gave her the surge of confidence that her mother had never been given.

And yet, the reason that she felt so sure had a lot to do with being her mother's daughter.

RICHARD

R ichard hated the sight of the Old Rock. It meant that they were back in Shancarrig for their miserable summer holiday. Back in Uncle Bill and Aunt Ethel's dark gloomy house, with the solicitor's office on the ground floor and the living quarters upstairs. Bedrooms with heavy furniture, nothing to see, nothing to do. A one-horse town and a pretty poor horse at that.

For as long as he could remember they had come here for a week in July. All through the war years, or the Emergency as it was called, they had travelled down from Dublin on a train fuelled by turf. If the weather was anyway bad the turf was bad and the journey was endless.

Richard's father would walk every night for miles with Uncle Bill. They both carried blackthorn sticks and pointed happily to places they had played when they were children – the gravelly shallows of the River Grane where they had caught their fish, the great Barna Woods which had got so small since they were young, the huge ugly heap of stones they called the Old Rock.

They would stand outside Shancarrig school and marvel at the old copper beech where they had carved their initials in 1914, twin boys aged fourteen, KH and WH – Kevin and William. It made Richard sick to see them so full of happy memories over nothing.

He was a handsome boy and a restless one. He thought this week of enforced idleness in his father's old village a waste of time. Even when he was very young he had asked if they really needed to go.

'Yes of course, we need to go. It's only one week out of fifty-two,' his mother had said.

It gave him hope that she didn't like it either. But she wasn't the soft touch on this as she was on other things. She was adamant.

'Your father doesn't ask much from us. Just this one week. We will do it and do it with a good grace.'

'But it's so boring, and Aunt Ethel is so awful.'

'She's not awful, she's just quiet. Bring something to entertain yourself – books, games.'

He noted his mother brought knitting. She usually managed to get two jumpers finished in their week in Shancarrig.

'You're a powerful knitter,' Aunt Ethel had said once.

'I love it. It's so restful,' his mother had murmured. Richard noticed that she didn't say that she hardly produced the needles and wool at all when she was in Dublin. She regarded Shancarrig as her knitting time – her purgatory on earth.

Uncle Bill's children were all very young; the eldest boy Niall was a whole seven years younger than Richard, a child of five when Richard was twelve and looking for company.

By the year 1950 Richard was seventeen. It would be his last holiday in this terrible place.

As he stood at an endless school dedication with bishop and priest and self-important people from around he vowed he would never come back. It made him feel claustrophobic, as if he was being choked.

Richard Hayes was leaving his Jesuit boarding school that year. He would get his Leaving Certificate and Matriculation and go to university to study, not medicine like his father, but law. Next summer he could legitimately be away on some study course or be abroad.

They would never drag him to this village again. Let his sisters come, they seemed perfectly happy to play with the village children and run free. Richard Hayes had done his stint.

There was only one good-looking girl at the ceremony, in a blue and white dress, and a straw hat with the same material around the brim. She was shading her eyes from the sun and listening intently to the speeches. She was slim with a tiny waist and a pretty if pale face.

'Who's that, Uncle Bill?' he asked.

'Madeleine Ross. Nice girl, a bit under her mother's thumb though, and will probably go on that way.'

'She's going to stay here all her life?' Richard was horrified.

'Some of us do that willingly.' His uncle sounded huffy.

'Oh I know, Uncle Bill, I meant she seems so young.'

'I was young when I decided to come back here to live, all those years ago. If old Dr Nolan had wanted someone in the practice at that time then your father would have come back too. It's home, you see.'

Richard shuddered at the very thought.

The Dublin Hayeses lived in Waterloo Road, which was ideal for anyone with children at university. Richard was within walking distance of his lectures and, even more useful, within walking distance of all the night-time activities that went with being a student. The pubs in Leeson Street were literally on his way home, the student dances nearby, the parties in Baggot Street where fellows had flats only a stone's throw away.

Richard Hayes offered to do up the disused basement of his parents' house so that he could live there. To study, he said. To be out of the way.

His father and mother never heard or saw any sign of anything untoward. They were pleased with their son who was unfailingly charming as he came to sit at their table for supper at six and for weekend lunches. He was always smiling politely as he passed his bag of laundry to Lizzie to wash, and managed to make his own part of the house off limits.

'You've enough to do up here, honestly. I'll keep my own place tidy below,' he had said with his boyish smile. So without anyone realising it he had got his own little self-contained flat down in the basement. At eighteen years of age he had a freedom undreamed of by other undergraduates.

His parents had no idea that their son brought a series of girlfriends home and that not all of them left before morning. He had posters on his walls, chianti bottles that had been turned into lamps, coloured Indian bedspreads over chairs and sofas and his own bed.

There were very noisy studenty parties with loud songs and crashers. The kind of parties that Richard Hayes gave were usually for two people, and sometimes for four. There were two rooms in his little basement flat, and all you had to do was to leave confidently and authoritatively, as if you had every right to be there.

'Don't slink in and out,' Richard warned one girl. 'Walk out of the gate as if you had been delivering a note in my door. They wouldn't in their wildest dreams believe anything else.'

And he was totally correct in his belief that his parents knew nothing of his private life. They told their friends, and Richard's Uncle Bill down in Shancarrig, that the law studies seemed to be going very well, and that unlike a lot of young tearaways their son seemed to be a homebird, which was all they could have wanted for him and more.

So it came as a complete shock when shortly before Richard's finals there was the unpleasant business of Olive Kennedy and her parents.

It appeared that Olive was pregnant and that Richard Hayes was to blame.

Richard felt that the scene was like a play, a film of a court case. Nobody seemed to be speaking the truth.

Not Olive, who was crying and saying that she had thought it would be all right because Richard loved her and they were getting married. Not the Kennedy parents who said their daughter had been ruined. Not his own parents who kept protesting that their son could never have done anything like this. He lived at home for heaven's sake, he was under their watchful eye.

Olive made no mention of the many nights she had spent in the basement in Waterloo Road – perhaps she didn't want her family to know that. The location of the conception was not discussed, only the responsibility for it. And what was to be done now. Richard spoke clearly. He was very very sorry. He denied nothing, but he said that he and Olive were far too young to consider marriage. They had never committed themselves to it. He seemed to think that this was all that was needed.

His manner, respectful and firm, won the day. It now became a matter of negotiation: Olive was to go to England and have the child; she would return having given the baby for adoption and resume her studies. Some financial contribution should be expected for this. It was agreed between the fathers.

'Olive, I wouldn't have had this happen for the world,' Richard said as they left.

'Thank you, Richard.' She lowered her eyes, pleased that he still respected her and loved her even if they were too young to marry.

That was when Richard Hayes, as he let his breath out slowly in relief, began to realise that he must be by some kind of accident a bit of a lady-killer.

Richard kept his head down and studied hard for months after this event. He invited his parents down to his flat on several occasions so that they could see every sign of a blameless life and a hard-working son.

Bit by bit, without his having to tell any story, they began to see this Olive as a scheming wanton girl who had set out to get their Richard. They began to think he had behaved decently in the face of such temptation.

They watched proudly as he received his parchment, was admitted to practise as a solicitor and got a job in a first-rate office in Dublin. Even before his first month's salary they gave him money for clothes – he went to a tailor and his real good looks were obvious to everyone he met.

Particularly Elaine, one of the apprentices in the office. She was a niece of the senior partner, and the daughter of a judge. She wore the most expensive of twin-sets, her pearls were real ones, her handbags and silk scarves came from Paris. They looked a very elegant couple when they were seen together.

But they were rarely seen together because Richard said he wasn't a suitable escort for her. A penniless young solicitor starting off ...

'You're not penniless, my uncle pays you a fortune ...' She used to cling to his arm as if she never wanted him out of her sight.

'But we're too young, you and I ...' he begged, knowing that she found him all the more irresistible the more he protested.

'We could grow up,' she said, looking at him directly.

So Richard Hayes saw a lot of Elaine the judge's daughter, but always in his flat where nobody else saw them.

For three years they lived a hidden life, behaving perfectly correctly to each other in the office, wrapped around each other passionately all night. It amazed him how easily she was able to tell her parents that she was staying with girlfriends.

As she stood in the sunlight barebottomed, wearing only the top of his pyjamas and frying eggs for their breakfast, he marvelled at his luck, that such a beautiful and clever girl should make him her choice in this way.

'Do you love me at all, Richard?' she asked as she turned the eggs on the pan.

He lay back on his bed, luxuriating and waiting for the breakfast that would be brought to him on a tray before they got up and dressed and made their separate ways to the office. He loved the very clandestine nature of it all, the fact that nobody in the office knew.

'What an extraordinary question! Why do you ask?' he said.

'It's always dangerous when people answer questions with another question.' She laughed, pretty Elaine with the golden hair and the expensive clothes thrown on the floor of his flat.

'No seriously, we loved each other twice last night and once this morning ... and you ask me an odd thing like that?' He seemed puzzled.

'No, I meant real love.'

'That's real love. It seemed pretty real to me.'

'I'm pregnant,' she said.

'Oh shit,' he said.

'I see where we stand.' Elaine threw the plate of fried eggs into the sink and picked up her clothes.

'Elaine wait ... I didn't mean ...'

From the bathroom he heard over the running water her voice call back.

'You're so bloody right, you didn't mean it. You didn't mean any bloody word you said.'

She was out of the bathroom, dressed and furious. He came towards her.

'Don't touch me. You've said what you wanted to say.'

'I've said nothing. We have to talk.'

'You've talked. You said "shit". That's what you said.'

It was awkward in the office. She wouldn't catch his eye or agree to meet. Then she went missing for four days.

At home alone Richard didn't dare to let his thoughts follow the train they were heading down. Was it possible that she could have gone to have an abortion?

In the Dublin of 1958 such things were not unknown. There had been stories, none of them pleasant, of a nurse ... He headed away from that thought. Elaine wouldn't have done that on her own.

But then, had he not shown how he didn't want to be involved? He telephoned her house; when he gave his name to the maid he was told that Elaine didn't want to speak to him.

This time there was no carpeting, no council of war as there had been in the case of Olive Kennedy. This time he was told by the senior partner that his position with the firm was now being terminated.

'But why?' Richard cried.

'I think you know.' The older man, Elaine's uncle, stood up and turned away.

It was the coldest gesture that Richard had ever seen. Now to explain to his parents.

He wanted to try to get another job first: to tell his parents that he had decided to change offices. This way it might not appear so bald. He had reckoned without the power of the senior partner, brother of the judge, and the smallness of Dublin legal circles. The word was out about him. He didn't know which word it was but it must have had something to do with being unreliable, a seducer of young women, someone unwilling to pay for his pleasure.

There were no jobs for Richard Hayes, whose record in the law was not so staggering that it would override the other considerations.

He told his parents.

It was not an easy conversation. There were very few solutions, and to his horror he realised that the only one which seemed possible was Shancarrig.

In July of 1958 he installed himself in Number Five The Terrace. He wandered disconsolately around the village, looking without interest at the church with its notices of upcoming events, like whist drives in aid of some villagers in South America who apparently needed a church ... just like this one.

He walked hands in pockets across the River Grane and up towards the school where he remembered going to some tedious ceremony years ago. The place hadn't changed at all. Nor had the ill-kept river bank with its row of shabby dwellings, nor the clumps of trees they so proudly called Barna Woods. He couldn't bear to make the climb he had done so often as a child to the Old Rock. He came home shoulders hunched wearily and crossed the bridge back into the town.

A group of youngsters were playing on the bridge and turned to look at him as he passed. He realised that whatever he did in this village would be under the scrutiny of hundreds of eyes. It was an appalling thought.

Everything about Shancarrig depressed him.

The small fat beady-eyed priest welcoming him, and saying it would be a pleasure to have him in the congregation – what could he mean? And the wraith-like priests' housekeeper with a face like the Queen of Spades – a sour woman called Mrs Kennedy who looked straight through him and seemed to read his inner soul. She nodded dryly on being introduced, as if to say she knew his type and didn't like it.

His uncle's home offered little joy to him. Although Uncle Bill was a pleasant enough man and an efficient solicitor he had managed to encumber himself with such a mournful wife. Aunt Ethel saw little to celebrate in the world. And the children were not going to rate high on any ladder of companionship.

Niall was now about eighteen and at an age when he should have been full of the joys of spring, but he appeared disconsolate and without any fire. It didn't occur to Richard that his cousin Niall might merely be lacking in self-confidence; Richard had never known that state. He wondered why the boy didn't ask to borrow his father's Ford which was parked outside The Terrace. That way he could have toured the countryside and found wider horizons. There must be *some* social life for a boy in this place, but Niall had seemingly never found it; he stayed around the house, moving between The Terrace and Ryan's Hotel.

Richard looked at the bedroom he had been given – a huge heavy dark mahogany wardrobe which despite its great size found it difficult to hold the suits and coats of the young solicitor down from the city.

His Aunt Ethel had proudly shown him the hot and cold running water; he had the only room with a hand-basin. The bed would never welcome a companion. To manoeuvre a girl up those stairs past offices, kitchens, sitting rooms and bedrooms would be a feat that few would undertake. It would be celibacy, or else find someone else with a place of their own, which didn't look at all likely in Shancarrig.

There were, of course, pretty children.

Like Nessa from the hotel. He saw the huge interest in her eyes, the eagerness and shyness, the trying to please, the fear she was boring him.

He was not arrogant, he was realistic about this kind of response. If you were nice to girls, if you smiled at them and listened to them, just *liked* them, they opened up like flowers.

He supposed it helped being reasonably good-looking, but he truly thought it was a matter of liking them. Many a man in Dublin who had envied Richard's success had been so anxious for the conquest that he forgot to enjoy the chase. That must be where the secret, if there were a secret, lay.

He spent a lot of time wooing Vanessa Ryan. She was the best in town. He had been on an exploratory mission.

There was Madeleine Ross the school teacher, very intense and spiritual, deeply caught up in this attempt to convert some Spanish-named place that apparently meant Shancarrig in Peruvian or whatever. He suspected that she might harbour longings for the rather fey-looking priest, but he was very sure that neither of them had done anything about this hothouse passion if it existed.

There was a tough little girl who came from a falling-down Georgian mansion called The Glen, frizzy hair, good legs, strong face. There was some secret there too. Money, maybe, or a mad relative. He had called and been discouraged from calling again.

There were a few others, unsatisfactory.

Nessa with her clear eyes and dark good looks was the only one. To his surprise he didn't wear her down. He must be losing his touch, he thought. His winning Dublin ways didn't work here.

He threatened her that they wouldn't see each other any more ... gentle loving threats of course, but she got the message ... She said no.

And continued to say no.

It was a constant irritant to see her across the road in her parents' hotel, growing more attractive and confident by the week. Her dark hair shining as it hung framing her face, she wore clear yellows and reds that set off her colouring. She laughed and joked with the customers; he had even seen American men look at her approvingly.

The years passed slowly.

They were not as bad as he feared his years of exile would be, but still he yearned to be back in Dublin.

Elaine came to visit him.

'I'm getting married,' she told him.

'Do you love him?' he asked.

'You'd never have asked that question a few years ago. You didn't think love existed.'

'I know it exists. I haven't come across it, that's all.'

'You will.' She was gentle.

'About the baby ... ?'

'There never was a baby,' she said.

'*What?*'

'There never was. I made it up.'

The colour drained from his face.

'You sent me here, you got me drummed out of Dublin on a lie.'

'There *could* have been a child, and your response would have been exactly the same. "Oh shit." That's all you would have said if we created a child between us.'

'But *you* ... why did you let yourself be seen in that light by every-one ... tell your father and your uncle ... and let people think ... ?'

'It seemed worth it at the time. It's a long time ago.'

'And why are you telling me *now?* Is the interdict lifted? Is the barring order called off? Can I crawl back to Dublin and they'll give me a job?'

'No, it's much more selfish. I wanted to tell you so that you'd know there never had been a child, no child born, no child aborted. I wanted you to know that in case ...'

'In case what?'

'In case ...' She seemed lost for words. He thought she was going to tell him that she worried lest he was thinking about this child, in case he felt ashamed. He had never thought of it as a child, real or imaginary as it now proved to be.

'In case Gerald ever heard. In case you might ever say ...'

He realised she was more frightened of Gerald knowing about her past than anything to do with him.

'Tell Gerald you're white as the driven snow,' he said. He had been so right not to marry this devious lady.

It was around this time that his young cousin Niall asked him for advice.

'You sort of know everything, Richard.'

'Oh yeah?'

'Well, I know you're good-looking and everything but you know how to be nice to people and make them like you. Is there a trick?'

Richard looked at him, his hair unkempt, the jacket expensive but out of fashion, the trousers baggy. Mainly the boy's stance was what held him back: his shoulders were rounded, he looked down and not at the people he was talking to; it came from a natural diffidence but it made him look feeble and untrustworthy.

At another time and in another place Richard might have given the boy some brotherly advice; after all Niall *had* asked, which could not have been easy.

But this was the wrong time.

The business with Elaine had ruffled him. He began to doubt his own success with women, and there was also the fact that that little madam, Nessa Ryan across the road in the hotel, had become altogether too pert and self-confident. Richard Hayes didn't feel in the mood to give out advice.

'There's no trick,' he said gruffly. 'People either like you or they don't. That's the way it goes through life.' He looked away from the naked disappointment on the boy's face.

'You mean people can't get better, more popular, or successful?'

Richard shrugged. 'I never saw anyone change, did you?'

Niall had said nothing.

He looked increasingly mopey at meals in The Terrace. Richard wondered what work they would find for the lad to do when he came back to Shancarrig full time, as he undoubtedly would. It might make more sense for him to cut his teeth in a solicitor's office somewhere else. But this was his father's firm. He should come back and claim his inheritance lest Richard take it over from him. Not that Richard was going to stay here for ever. After Elaine's revelations he thought that it might well be time for him to go back to Dublin.

But that was when he got to know Gloria Darcy.

The Darcys were newcomers. This meant they hadn't been born and raised here for three generations like everyone else. They had been considered fly-by-nights when they came first, but that was before their small grocery shop became a larger grocery shop, and before they started selling light bulbs, saucepans and cutlery and began to bite into the profits of Dunne's Hardware. Mike and Gloria Darcy always smiled cheerfully in the face of any muttering.

'Isn't there plenty for everyone?' Mike would say with his big broad smile.

'This place is only starting out, it'll be a boom town in the middle sixties,' Gloria would say with a toss of her long dark curly hair and her gypsy smile.

She often wore a handkerchief tied around her neck so that she looked like a picture of a gypsy girl – not like the tall silent tinker girls who came into Shancarrig when they camped each year at Barna Woods, more like an illustration from a child's story book.

Bit by bit they were accepted.

Gloria was flashy, the women all agreed this. Richard heard his Aunt Ethel tut-tutting about her to Nellie Dunne and to Mrs Ryan, but there was nothing they could put their finger on. Her neckline wasn't so low as to raise a comment nor were her skirts too short. It was just that she walked with a swish and a certainty. Her eyes roamed around and lit up when they caught other eyes. There was nothing demure about Mrs Gloria Darcy.

Richard met her first when he bought a packet of razor blades. He didn't like the fussy Mr Connors the chemist – a small man with bad breath who was inclined to keep you half the day. When he saw packets of razor blades in the window of Darcy's he regarded it as a merciful escape.

'Anything else?' Gloria asked him, her smile wide and generous, her tongue moving slightly over her lower lip.

If it weren't for the fact that her husband stood not a foot away Richard would have thought she was flirting, being suggestive.

'Not for the moment,' he said in exactly the same tone, and their eyes met.

He warned himself not to be stupid as he walked back to The Terrace. This would be the silliest thing that a human could do.

What he must do now was sort out a new job in Dublin, and leave this town without having committed any major misdemeanour. He had been saving his salary quite methodically over the three years of his exile in the sticks. There was no point in buying finery to be paraded here, there were no places for meals, no going to the races. He had learned a lot about the rural practice, for all the use it would be to him in the future. But human nature was the same everywhere: perhaps his stay here might have been a better apprenticeship than he had ever thought possible.

It was early closing, the day his Uncle Bill usually walked up to The Glen and went for a stroll with the old Major Murphy. What the two of them talked about it would be hard to know. But today Bill Hayes was still in his office.

'I'm in a quandary,' he said to Richard.

'Tell me about it.' Richard sat down, legs stretched, face enthusiastic and receptive. He knew his uncle was pleased to be able to talk.

There was no one else in the house, not dour Aunt Ethel nor sulky Niall.

'It's up at The Glen. Miriam Murphy keeps telephoning me, saying she wants to set her affairs in order.'

'Well?'

'Well, Frank says not to take any notice of her – she's rambling.'

'She is a bit daft, isn't she?' Richard encouraged his uncle to speak.

'I suppose so, I mean it's not the kind of thing you'd ask a man. Not something that you'd talk about to a friend.' Bill Hayes looked troubled.

Richard thought that it should be the most important thing you might talk to a friend about, whether your wife was going off her head or not, but the more he heard of marriage the less likely anyone seemed to do anything normal within its bonds.

'So what do you think you should do?' he asked, expert as always in finding out what the other man wanted before giving his own view.

'You see, I think she has something pressing on her mind, some crime, even ... imaginary, of course.'

'Well, if it's imaginary ...'

'But suppose it's not, suppose it's something she wants to make restitution for?'

'You're not Father Gunn, Uncle Bill. You're not Sergeant Keane. All you have to do is make her will, or not be free to make it if that's what you'd prefer for Major Frank's sake.'

'It's worrying me.'

'Why don't I go and see her? Then you won't have failed either of them.'

'Would you, Richard?'

'I'll go today while you and Major Murphy take your constitutional.' His smile was bright.

'I don't know what I'd do without you, Richard.'

'You'll have a son of your own to help you in no time. You won't need me, I'll head off to Dublin soon.'

'Not too soon.'

'All right, not too soon, but soonish.' He stood up and clapped his uncle on the shoulder.

What was one more mad old bat of a woman confessing to the Lord knew what!

He had his lunch in the dark dining room of The Terrace; they talked of other things and he waited until his uncle and the Major would be well clear before he went to The Glen.

He didn't even have to go into the house to find her. Mrs Miriam Murphy half lay, half sat across the rockery. She was wearing a long white dress, possibly a nightgown; her hair streaked with grey was loose on her shoulders.

She was crying.

There was some garden furniture strewn about. Richard Hayes pulled up a chair for himself.

'I'm from Bill Hayes's office, I'm his nephew. He says you're anxious for us to sort something out for you.'

'You're too young,' she said.

'Ah no, Mrs Murphy, I'm older than I look. I'm twenty-eight, well on my way to thirty.' His smile would have broken down the reserve of any woman in Ireland, but Miriam Murphy's mind was miles away.

'That's what he was, twenty-eight, if you could believe him,' she said.

Richard was nonplussed. 'Well, what do you think we should do?' he said.

He knew his uncle wanted the woman to say that she had changed her mind, that she wanted no will made, no affairs sorted out. He must try to lead her in that direction.

'It's too late to do anything. It was done,' she said. He nodded uncomprehendingly.

There was a long silence between them. She seemed quite at ease lounging, half lying over the rock plants and the jagged edges of the stones that made up the rockery. He didn't suggest that she sit somewhere more comfortable – he knew that this was irrelevant.

'So perhaps we should leave things as they are?' He looked at her, pouring out reassurance.

'Is that enough?' she asked.

'I think it is.'

'You don't think we should leave them the place, The Glen, for themselves whenever they come this way?'

'Leave it to who exactly?'

'The gypsies.'

'No, no. Definitely not. People are always trying to leave them places. They want to be free,' he said.

'Free?'

'Yes, that's what they like best.' He stood up, anxious to be away from the mad staring eyes. It wasn't healthy for that girl Leo to stay here all the time. Why didn't she get a training, a job?

'If you think so.' Mrs Miriam Murphy didn't look relieved, she looked only resigned.

He walked down the long drive and was about to head down the hill to Shancarrig. God, the sooner he was out of a place like this the better. Walking along the road towards him was Gloria Darcy.

'Well, well, well. You have had a shave, I see.' She looked directly at his face.

'What do you mean?'

'I sold you razor blades this morning, don't tell me you've forgotten me already?' She was most definitely leading him on. Her laugh was unaffected, she could see the impression that she was making on him.

'No, Mrs Darcy, I imagine that very few people forget you,' he said. He was being equally gallant and flattering, giving as good as he got.

'And were you going to walk straight home down the hill or go the better way through the woods?'

He knew he stood at a crossroads. He could have said that he was needed back at the office, that he had work to catch up with, that he had to make a phone call to Dublin. He might have said anything.

But he said, 'I was hoping to find some attractive company to walk me through Barna Woods, and now I have.'

They laughed as they walked. She teased him about his city suit, he said she was dressing deliberately like a pantomime gypsy. She asked what he had been doing at The Glen, he said that there was a secrecy like the seal of Confession about matters between lawyer and client. He asked if the Darcy's had a proper title to their shop, they hadn't bought it through his uncle's firm . . . She said the same seal of

Confession applied to business deals.

By the time they came out into the sunshine again, and walked by the cottages to the bridge, they were well aware of each other. Much more than attractive faces and winning ways. They were people who could talk and play. They were a match for each other.

So when he went to buy things there he went knowing that it was a move, a degree of courtship. He bought more razor blades.

'My, what a strong beard we must have,' she said. Again within her husband's hearing.

When he bought a pound of tomatoes she asked him was he going on a picnic in the woods. Mike Darcy was serving another customer.

'No, my aunt wants some more, that's all.'

'No, she was in this morning and bought plenty,' said Gloria, eyes dancing and full of mischief.

The teasing visits and banter went on for some days.

'It's lovely of you to come and see me so often,' she said, pressing her body towards the counter. She wore a chain around her neck, the pendant was between her breasts, the eye followed it down as it was intended to.

'Yes, it's lovely of me, you never come to call on me,' Richard said.

'Ah, but I can't make excuses about civil bills and statements of claim,' she said. 'You can invent all the tomatoes and razor blades in the world.'

'So we'll have to meet on neutral ground,' he suggested.

They met two days later at the church when they both attended the funeral of Mrs Miriam Murphy.

It was pneumonia, Dr Jims Blake had said. Brought on by exposure, someone else had said, Mrs Murphy had taken to sleeping out on the rockery of their garden. It was a sure fact that money and position didn't bring you happiness.

Richard Hayes looked at the small wiry Leo as she walked down the church supporting her father. Two strange men, the brothers from abroad, had come for the funeral. They looked military, they knew hardly anyone.

There was a gathering in Ryan's Hotel. Young Nessa had done up one of the downstairs rooms as a special function room. It was exactly what was needed for this occasion. Coffee and sandwiches and some drinks. Those who wished to adjourn to the bar could do so. It had never been done before in Shancarrig; you either went back to someone's house or you went to the pub. This was a new respectability.

'Very clever of you to have thought this up, Nessa,' he said admiringly. Genuinely so.

'Leo is my friend. It's not easy for her to have people at the house.' Nessa hadn't time to talk to him – these days she was great with young Niall, and already the boy was beginning to look the better for it. His hair was smarter, he had got a new jacket. Somehow he even seemed to walk taller.

Gloria and Mike Darcy were in the gathering though somehow Richard wondered had they been invited in the strict sense of the word.

As people moved around offering sympathy and trying to place Harry and James who had long left Shancarrig, Gloria found herself next to Richard.

'So now we're on neutral ground,' she said.

'Yes, but very crowded neutral ground,' he said, shaking his head in exaggerated sorrow.

'Have you any suggestions for somewhere that's not crowded?' She couldn't have been more direct. Had she asked him to make love to her she could not have said it more clearly.

'Well, since your place, my place and this hotel are out of the question, let's think of somewhere that might be deserted at this moment.' He wasn't serious. There was nowhere they could go in Shancarrig, literally nowhere.

'There's The Glen,' she said. She saw the look of revulsion on his face. They were sympathising over the death of the woman who had lived all her life in The Glen; Gloria could not possibly be considering going there to use the empty house. 'Not the house, the gate lodge,' she said.

'How would we get in?' Already he had bypassed any moral objections to a place in the grounds. That was different.

'The back window is open, I checked.'

'Twenty minutes?' he asked. It would take him ten to say his goodbyes, two to go back to his room for condoms.

'Fifteen,' she said, and again she ran her tongue along her lower lip. His goodbyes were courteous and very swift.

There was a crotchety old farmer who lived out that direction. If he was asked he could say he got a message to visit him but then he had turned out not to be there. But why was he taking these kind of precautions? No one would ask him. Nobody would dream he was about to do what he was about to do.

She was there before him, lying on a divan covered with a rug. The place smelled musty but not of damp.

'Did you bring anything?'

'Yes, that's what delayed me. I had to go back to my room for them. I don't carry them always just in case,' he laughed, patting his pocket.

'Now don't be so unromantic. I meant champagne, something like that.'

'No, I'm afraid not.' He looked crestfallen.

'Never mind, I did.' Her white teeth flashed as she bit the foil from the top of the bottle, there were cups on the dresser. They laughed as they drank it too quickly so that the fizzy liquid went up their noses. And they kissed.

'Did you go back to the shop for this?' He marvelled at her speed.

'No. I had it with me in my big shoulder bag.' She laughed at her own wickedness and the confidence that it would have needed.

'Let me take off these dark respectable clothes. They don't suit you,' he said.

'Well, it was a funeral. I couldn't wear my red skirt but ...' She was wearing a red petticoat, trimmed with white lace, she wore no brassiere, just a gold chain around her throat. She looked so abandoned and wild as she lay there laughing up at him he could scarcely bear the moments of waiting.

'I've longed for you, Richard Hayes,' she said. And he sank into her as if he had known her all his life.

After that it was always urgent and never easy. If only the Murphys lived a more regular life, Richard groaned to himself. If he could know they would stay in the big house, or stay out of it, then the gate lodge would have been the ideal place for his meetings with Gloria. But they could never be sure; they would have no excuse if they were seen going in and out of the window.

It took them weeks to work out some kind of a pattern to the curious ways of Leo and her father.

Leo eventually started a secretarial course which involved going to the town on the bus. This gave her day a shape. The Major, who walked the long avenue with his old dogs, that he kept calling Lance and Jessie, was less predictable. Richard tried to find out more of his movements by asking his uncle, but it seemed that a friendship of twenty-five years was based on Bill Hayes knowing nothing whatsoever about Frank Murphy. It was hard to believe, but that was the way it was.

And there was the time that Hayes and Son, Solicitors, were asked to see to a property. Richard and Gloria had many happy meetings there in the guise of showing it to clients.

Gloria could get away so easily it was almost frightening.

'Does Mike never ask where you're going?'

'Lord no. Why should he?'

'Well, if I had a beautiful wife like you I wouldn't let her wander off . . . to do the devil knows what . . .' He squeezed her and held her to him again.

'Then you wouldn't be a husband, you'd be a gaoler,' she laughed. He thought about it.

There was some truth in what she said. If you married someone just to guard her like a possession it was like an imprisonment. But look at it the other way, if Mike was more careful and caring about his wife then surely Gloria wouldn't wander free as she was.

Sometimes he spoke about her children, her little boys, Kevin and Sean.

'What is there to say?'

'Aren't you afraid they'll find out, that they'd hate you for this?'

'Darling Richard, you are riddled with guilt. I think we should make a regular thing of visiting Father Gunn together after we meet.'

'Don't tease me. I only say these things because I love you.'

'No, you don't.'

'I do. I never said it to anyone before.'

'We say it at the moment we make love, because at that moment everyone loves. But you don't love me in an everyday sort of way.'

'I could.'

'No, Richard.' She put her fingers on his lips and then into his mouth, and then she kissed him and soon the words were forgotten.

She was the ideal lover. He could never have dreamed of anyone so passionate and responsive, a beautiful woman who found him desirable and wasn't afraid to say so. A witty, flowing, secret love whose dark eyes flashed at him when they met in Ryan's Hotel, in the shops or at the church.

After years of girls wanting more from Richard here was someone who wanted no more at all. Not public recognition, not a commitment, and obviously because of the heavy band she already wore on her finger, not an engagement ring. For quite a time it was the perfect romance.

And then he began to notice small changes in his own attitude. He couldn't say that Gloria had changed, she had always been light-hearted in their daring and the fear of discovery ... and enthusiastic about the pleasure they gave each other.

No. It was Richard who changed.

He couldn't bear to see her holding her little boys by the hand. He thought back to his own mother and father, the respectable Dublin doctor and his busy bridge-playing wife. Theirs had been a house of stability as he grew up in Waterloo Road. His mother had always been there for them. Suppose she had been someone who sneaked out to the arms of a lover while his father worked? He dismissed the thought as some kind of guilty fantasy.

There had been no way in which he had compared his life with that of his parents before, why was he holding up their staid and plodding existence as some kind of example now? Gloria was a wonderful mother to Kevin and Sean. What she had with Richard was something totally different, something separate entirely.

Then Richard found himself uneasy about Mike, big handsome Mike Darcy with his teeth as white and even as his wife's, who stood long hours in the grocery shop they were so busy building up together. Mike, who would go to endless trouble to find something Richard ordered, furrowing his brow to think where they might get that particular chamois leather Richard wanted. He didn't like the man being so generous with his time and help for him. Mike's innocent face was a reproach to Richard Hayes.

Gloria only laughed when he mentioned it. 'What Mike and I have is different to what you and I have ... Let's keep them separate,' she said.

'But I know about him, he doesn't know about me.'

'Why do men have to think everything's a game, with rules?' she laughed.

And then there were times when he wondered if he *did* know about Mike and Gloria and what they had together. He would see the way they leant towards each other in the shop when they thought no one was looking. He saw the way Mike Darcy sometimes stroked his wife's body.

A very unfamiliar feeling of raging jealousy came over him when he saw them touch.

'You don't do this with Mike, do you?' he begged her one afternoon in their gate lodge.

'Nobody could do what you and I do. This is ours.'

'But does he want to ... ? I mean do you and he ... ?'

'You're so handsome when you look worried, Richard,' she said.

'I must know.'

Suddenly she sat up, eyes flashing. 'No, you must not know. There is no must about it. We are not master and slave ... you have no right to know anything that I do not wish to tell you. Do I ask you any such questions ... ?'

'But there's nothing to know about me.' He was wretched.

'That's because this is the way I choose to see things. I am not curious, suspicious, asking where I should ask nothing.' Her voice held an ultimatum.

Accept things as they were or there would be no more to accept. He longed to know if she had known other men since her marriage to Mike, if they failed at this test and had been sent away.

He would have killed any man, any traveller who walked into Ryan's Hotel, if he had said he shared a bed with Gloria Darcy. Yes, he would have taken this man by the throat and shaken him to squeeze out his life, uncaring about what onlookers or the law would say or do. Why then was Mike able to stand and fill bags with sugar and other bags with potatoes and not wonder where his beautiful wife went to in the afternoons?

It was becoming more difficult too for Richard to be free in the afternoons since young Niall had joined the firm. The boy had definitely gained a new confidence, which Richard suspected was due to the blossoming of a friendship and even courtship with the glossy young Nessa Ryan from the hotel.

Gone were the days when Niall Hayes was happy with the menial jobs, the work of a glorified clerk. Now he wanted to learn, to share, to study Richard's ways with clients. 'Can I come with you to the place that there's all the fuss about the title?' he would ask.

This was one of Richard's mythical excuses for being out of the office. He had described a difficult old farmer set in his ways who had to be cajoled and flattered into revealing his documents.

'No, Niall. It wouldn't work out ... this fellow is as mad as a wasps' nest. You wouldn't know what he'd do if I brought anyone else. I've only got as far as I have because I go on my own and put in endless bloody hours with him.'

'Well, can I see the file on him?' Niall asked.

'Why? What do you want to bother yourself with that old fart for, there's plenty of other work to do ...'

'But won't we need to know when ... ?'

The words remained unfinished, the sentence hung in the air – when ... Richard went back to Dublin – something they all knew would happen. There wasn't room for two partnerships in the firm. The business simply wasn't there; even two salaries was beginning to strain Bill Hayes. Niall was the son of the family.

Surely Richard would be going back any day now.

Only Richard knew that he could never leave Shancarrig and the woman he loved.

'I *do* love you,' he said defensively to Gloria, as they sat smoking a cigarette by their little oil stove one cold evening in the gate lodge.

'I know.' She sat hugging her knees.

'No, you don't know. You said we shouldn't talk of love, that I only felt it at the moment of taking you. That's what you said.'

'Stop sounding like a schoolboy, Richard.' She looked beautiful as she sat there in the flickering light.

'What are you thinking about?' he asked.

'About you and how good you make me feel.'

'What are we going to do, Gloria?'

'Well, get dressed and go home, I imagine.'

'About everything?'

'We can't solve everything, we can only solve things like not letting the light be seen through the windows and not getting our death of cold in all the rain.'

'What will you say ... about where you've been?'

'That's not your concern.'

'But it is, you are my concern.'

'Then let me handle it.' Again he saw the warning in her eyes, and he felt frightened.

They had met in late summer and continued through autumn and a cold wet winter; soon it would be spring. Surely some solution would have to be found.

But for Gloria spring meant that she could wear fresh yellow and white flowery dresses, and white sandals and take her lover to hidden parts of Barna Woods, to dells with bluebells and soft springy grass. Again an ache came over him. How did she know where to find such places? She hadn't grown up in this place – had other men taken her here? Not only could he never ask, he must never think about it. He hated that the shop was doing so well, he wanted to be her provider and give her things but she would never take them.

'What would I say, Richard? I mean I could hardly say that the handsome young solicitor who drops in to buy an inordinate amount of razor blades bought me a silver bracelet, now could I?'

But with increased prosperity Mike Darcy bought his wife jewellery. There was an emerald pendant, there were diamonds. Nobody in Shancarrig had ever known such extravagance. Quite unsuitable, Richard's Aunt Ethel had said, shaking her head about it.

Richard agreed from the bottom of his heart but was careful not to express this.

To his surprise young Niall had the opposite view.

'What do people work for if it isn't to get themselves what they want?' he asked.

'I hope you wouldn't throw your money away on emeralds for Gloria Darcy and her like,' his father said in ritual dismissive vein to his son.

These days Niall Hayes answered back. 'I'm not sure what you mean "her like", but if I loved someone and I earned my money lawfully I would feel very justified in spending it on presents for her,' he said.

Suddenly the room was silent and drab. Aunt Ethel looked at her son in some surprise. On her cardigan there was no jewellery; there never had been any except the engagement ring, wedding ring and good watch. Perhaps life might have been better if Bill Hayes had visited a shop and looked at jewels.

'Let's celebrate our anniversary,' Richard said to Gloria.

'Like what? Dinner for two in Ryan's Shancarrig Hotel, a bottle of wine?'

'No, but let's do something festive.'

'I find what we do is fairly festive already.' She laughed at him.

'You must want more, you must want more than creeping around.'

She sighed. It was the weary sigh of a mother who can't explain to a toddler how to tie his shoe laces. 'No, I don't want any more,' she said resignedly. 'But you do, so we'll do whatever you like for the anniversary.'

It was hard to think what they could do. The mystery was that they had spent a year as lovers without being discovered. In a place of this size and curiosity it was a miracle.

Perhaps they could go to Dublin. He would find an excuse and she would surely be able to think of some reason to go away as well.

Before he suggested it he would plan what they would do, otherwise she would shrug and say that they might as well stay here. He wanted to take her into Dublin bars, restaurants, he wanted people to admire her and be attracted by her beautiful face and sparkling laugh. He wanted to see her against some other background, not just the grey shapeless forms of Shancarrig. In all his years there Richard had never been able to like the place, it was lit up only by Gloria and he wanted to take her away from it.

He planned the visit to Dublin, how he would meet her off the train in Kingsbridge in his car – he would have gone up the day before so that there would be even less suspicion – how he would show her the sights – she didn't know Dublin well, she had told him. He would be her guide.

They would check into one of the better hotels. He would check out the room first, make sure it was perfect ... they would walk arm in arm down Grafton Street. If they met anyone from Shancarrig they would all laugh excitedly and say wasn't it great coming to Dublin how you ran into everyone from home.

The more he thought about it the more Richard realised that he did not want Gloria in Dublin just for one night, he wanted her there always. He didn't want them in a furtive hotel room, he wanted them in a home of their own. Together always.

There were the most enormous difficulties in the way. The biggest, most handsome and innocent was Mike Darcy, smiling and welcoming with no idea that his wife loved another.

There were the children. Richard loved the look of them, dark boys with enormous eyes like Gloria. They had their father's slow, lopsided grin too, but it was silly to work out characteristics and assign them to one parent or the other.

He wished he could get to know the children, but it had been impossible. If he could get to know them then they would find it easier to come as a little family to Dublin to live with him. Richard realised suddenly that he was no longer planning an illicit trip to celebrate an anniversary, he was planning a new life. He must take it more slowly.

He must not rush things and risk losing her.

*

233

The anniversary was all that he could have wanted and more.

The hotel welcomed them as Mr and Mrs Hayes with no difficulty. Gloria's large rings did not look as if they had been put on for the occasion, they had a right to sit on her hand.

They had champagne in their room, they walked the city. He showed her places that he had loved when he was a boy, the canal bank from Baggot Street to Leeson Street. It thrilled him to be so near Waterloo Road. It was quite possible that his father could walk by on his way to the bookshop on Baggot Street Bridge, or his mother going to the butcher's shop to say that last Sunday's joint had not been as tender as they would have expected and the Doctor had been very disappointed.

He didn't see his parents but he did see Elaine pregnant and contented-looking, getting out of her mother's car. She hadn't seen him, and under normal circumstances he would have let her go on without stopping her. But these were not normal times. He wanted to show her Gloria, he wanted her to see the magnificent woman on his arm.

He called and she waddled over.

'Oh, Mummy will be sorry to have missed you,' she said. He had waited carefully until her mother had driven off. He didn't think his name was held in any favour in that family.

'I'd like you to meet Gloria Darcy.' The pride in his voice was overpowering.

They talked easily. Gloria asked her was it the first baby. Looking Richard straight in the eye Elaine said yes it was, she was very excited.

Gloria said she had two little boys of her own, and that you wished they'd never grow up and yet you were so proud of every little thing they did. She was saying all the things that Elaine wanted to hear. She also told her that the old wives' tales about labour were greatly exaggerated – it was probably to put people off having children before they were married.

'Oh, very few of us would be foolish enough to do that,' Elaine said, looking again at Richard.

He realised with a shock that he had been a monster of selfishness. Suddenly he was glad that Elaine had lied to him, that she had never carried his baby. But Olive Kennedy had. She had gone to England and given birth to their child. Where was this child now? A boy or girl in an orphanage, in a foster family, adopted.

How could he have not cared before? He felt his eyes water.

They had drinks in the Shelbourne Bar, and lunch in a small

restaurant near Grafton Street that he had heard was very good.

He managed to meet three people he knew slightly. That wasn't bad for a man four years in exile from the capital city. He had chosen the place well.

'Did you love that girl Elaine a lot?' Gloria asked.

'No, I have never loved anyone except you,' he said simply.

'I thought you looked sad when you left, your eyes were full of tears ... but it's not my business. I'd be very cross with you for asking prying questions,' she said, squeezing his hand warmly.

He could barely speak.

'I'll die if I can't be with you always, Gloria,' he said.

'Shush now.' She put her finger in the little glass of Irish Mist that she was drinking and offered it to him to suck. Soon the familiar desire returned, banishing for the moment the sense of loss and anxiety about returning her to real life in Shancarrig. They went back to their hotel and celebrated their anniversary well and truly.

He never asked what excuse she had made to Mike, whether it was shopping, or a visit to a hospital, or seeing an old friend. He knew she didn't want him to be a party to her lies. It could not have been hard to lie to Mike, his enthusiasm and simplicity wouldn't take into account the deviousness of the world around him, a wife who would betray him, a casual friend Richard Hayes walking in and out of his shop not for the errands he pretended but to feast his eyes on Gloria, to remind himself of the last time and look forward to the next time.

Kevin Darcy was at Shancarrig school. Sometimes Richard stopped him on the road just for the excuse to talk to him.

'How's your mammy and daddy?' he'd say.

'They're all right.' Kevin hadn't much interest.

'What did you learn at school?' he might ask.

'Not much,' Kevin would say.

One day Richard saw him with a cut head. He fell off the tree, Christy Dunne explained. Richard went to the shop to sympathise. Mike was out in the yard supervising the building of the new extension. Darcy's was now almost three times the size it was when they had bought it first.

'Oh, for God's sake, Richard, it's only a scrape. Don't be such a clucking hen,' Gloria said.

'He was bleeding a lot, I was worried.'

'Well, don't worry, he's fine. I put a big plaster on him, and gave him two Crunchies, one for him and one for Christy. There wasn't a bother out of him.' He looked at her with admiration. How was she so calm, so good and wise a mother as well as everything else?

He was still more admiring when the burglars came the following week and stole all the jewellery that Mike Darcy had bought for his wife.

Sergeant Keane was in and out of the place, inquiries were made everywhere, tinkers had been in Johnny Finn's pub, you couldn't watch the place all the time.

Gloria was philosophical. It was terrible, particularly the little emerald, she loved the way it glowed. But then what was the alternative? You watched them day and night, you made the place into something like Fort Knox. It would be like living in a prison; she shivered. Richard remembered how she had once said that to be married to a suspicious husband who checked up on her would be like living with a gaoler. She needed to be free.

Maura O'Sullivan, who minded the Darcy children and cleaned the house for them, also worked in his aunt's house. He tried to find out more about the household, but Maura, unlike the rest of Shancarrig, was not inclined to gossip.

'What was it exactly you wanted to know?' she would say in a way that ended all inquiries.

'I was just wondering how the family were getting over the loss,' he said lamely.

Maura nodded, satisfied. She always brought her son with her, an affectionate boy called Michael who had Down's syndrome. Richard liked him and the way he would run towards whoever came into the room.

'Daddy?' he said hopefully to Richard.

The first time he had said this Maura explained that the child's father had had to go to England, and that consequently he thought everyone he met was his father.

'Daddy, my daddy?' he asked Richard again and again.

'Sort of, we're all daddys and mammys to other people,' Richard said to him.

Niall had heard him.

'You're very kind, Richard. It comes naturally to you. I mean it, you're terribly nice to people, that's why you're so successful.' Richard was surprised, the boy had never made a speech like this.

'No I'm not. I'm quite selfish really. I'm surprised it doesn't show.'

'I never saw it. I was jealous of you of course with women, but I didn't think you were selfish.'

'Not jealous of me any more?'

'Well, I only like one person and she assures me that she's not under your spell ... so ...' Niall Hayes looked happy.

'She never was. I thought she was lovely like anyone would, but it was admiration from afar, I assure you.'

'That's what she says.' Niall sounded smug and content.

'I'm not cramping your style in work here, am I?' Richard wanted to have it out. This seemed a good time.

'No. No of course not, it's just that I suppose we expected ... everyone thought that sooner or later ...'

'Yes, and one day I will but ... not just yet.'

'You're saving, I know.' Niall was understanding.

'How do you know?'

'Well, you never go anywhere, you only have a shabby car. You don't buy jazzy suits.'

'That's right,' Richard admitted. 'I'm saving.' This was his cover, he realised. He was putting together a stake to buy a practice in Dublin.

The months went on. Gloria bought him a silk tie.

'You said no presents.' He fingered the cream and gold tie lovingly.

'I said you weren't to buy *me* any, that's all.'

'I want to buy you a piece of jewellery. Not an emerald, a ruby – a very small ruby. Let me,' he begged.

'No, Richard. Seriously, when could I wear it? Be sensible.'

He bought it anyway. He gave it to her in the gate lodge.

Their Wednesday afternoons there were totally secure. Major Murphy walked with his uncle rain or shine, and Leo had got a job working in the office of one of the building contractors' firms in the town. It seemed an unlikely job, but Gloria told him that she heard Leo was still in touch with that mad Foxy Dunne, who was going from strength to strength on the building sites in England. The word was that he would come back and set up his own firm. The word was that he and Leo had an understanding.

'Foxy Dunne, son of Dinny Dunne?'

'Oh, Foxy Dunne is like the papal nuncio in terms of respectability compared to his father. You know him falling out of Johnny Finn's most nights.'

'Well, well, well.' He realised he was getting a small-town mentality;

he was finding serious difficulty in believing that Major Murphy of The Glen would let his daughter contemplate one of the Dunnes from the cottages. He was glad however that it meant Leo worked far away. It left the coast much more clear.

Gloria looked at the ruby for a long time.

'You're not angry?'

'How could I be angry that you spent so much on me? I'm touched, but I'll never wear it.'

'Couldn't you say ... ?'

'We both know there's nothing I could say.'

'You could wear it here with me.'

'Yes, I will.'

She took the ruby away and had it made into a tie pin, then she gave it back to him. 'I'll put on a chain to wear it when I am with you, but for the rest of the time you keep it. Wear it on the tie that I gave you, then you'll think of me.'

'I think of you always,' he said.

Too much perhaps.

It was the beginning of the withdrawal. He saw it and blinded himself to it. He feared that someone else had come to town, but he knew there could be no one. She didn't dream up schemes to meet him for five minutes any more, and although she lay and took his loving she didn't implore him to love her as she once had, begging, encouraging and exciting him to performances that he had thought impossible.

He felt it was the place, it was getting too much for them. There had been endless complications about builders' suppliers, and the building of the extension, and the hostility of the Dunnes who said that they weren't anxious to build the place that was going to be direct competition with them. There had been delays over the insurance money for the jewellery. There was a problem about the newspaper delivery they planned, Nellie Dunne had created difficulties.

In his uncle's office Niall was restless and urging that he be involved in more cases, have consultations with clients and barristers, and in general learn his trade. Richard felt he was putting him off at every turn.

It was time to take Gloria away.

He began to explain it and for once he wouldn't listen when she tried to stop him. 'No, I've shushed enough. We have to think. It's been nearly two years. We must have our own home, our own life together. I don't wish Mike any harm but he has to know, he has to be told. He's a decent man, he'll agree to whatever we suggest. Whatever's for the best ... he can come to Dublin to see the boys, we'll never hide from them who their real father is ... he'd prefer to be taken into our confidence from the start ... well, not exactly from the start but from now ...' His voice trailed away as he looked at her face.

They sat in the gate lodge. They hadn't undressed. Their cigarettes and the little tin they used as an ashtray and cleaned after each visit sat between them on the table. It was an odd place to be talking about their future. It was an odd expression on her face as she listened. It showed utter bewilderment and shock.

He thought first it was the enormity of what they were about to do ... coupled with the disruption for the children. He must reassure her. 'I've been looking at houses in Dublin, a little out of the city so that we could have privacy and so that Kevin and Sean would have a local-type school, not somewhere huge like the big Christian Brothers in the city ...' He stopped. He had not read her look right.

She didn't want reassurance, she wanted him to stop talking straight away. 'None of this is going to happen, you must know this. Richard, you *must* know.'

'But you love me ...'

'Not like this, not to run away with you ...'

'Why have we been doing all this ... ?' He waved his hand wildly around the room where they had made love so often.

'It had nothing whatsoever to do with my leaving here. That was never promised, never on the cards.'

He was the one bewildered now, and confused. 'What was it all about?' he asked, begging to be told.

She stood up and walked around the room as she spoke. She had never looked more beautiful. She spoke of a happy time with Richard, how he had made her feel wonderful and needed, how she had given him no undertaking, no looking ahead.

She said that her future was here in Shancarrig or very possibly another small town. They might sell up to the Dunnes and move. She and Mike liked starting a place from scratch. They had done that in other places. It was a challenge, it kept everything exciting, new.

Richard Hayes listened amazed as she spoke of Mike with this respect and love.

She was totally enmeshed with Mike in a way Richard had never understood. Her concern had nothing to do with a fear that Mike might be hurt or made to suffer. It was much more an involvement, a caring what he would do and decide and where he would want to go.

'But you don't love him!' he gasped.

'Of course I love him, I've never loved anyone else.'

'But why ... ?' He couldn't even finish the sentence.

'He couldn't give me everything I wanted. No one can do that for anybody. I love him because he lets me be free.'

Richard realised she spoke the truth. 'And does he know ... ?'

'Know what?'

'About me, about us. Do you tell him?' His voice grew angry and loud. 'Is this what gets him excited, your coming home and telling him what you and I did together?'

'Don't be disgusting,' she said.

'You're the one who is disgusting, out like an alley cat and then pretending that you're the model wife and mother.'

She looked at him reproachfully. He knew it was over.

In the years when he had wriggled out of relationships and escaped from affairs he had not been as honest as she was being, he had been devious and avoided face-to-face contact except when it was utterly necessary. His heart was heavy when he thought of Olive Kennedy, and the way he had disowned her in front of her parents.

If only he could have his time all over again. He hung his head.

'Richard?' she said.

'I didn't mean it about the alley cat.'

'I know you didn't.'

'I don't know what to do, darling Gloria. I don't know what to do.'

'Go away and leave this place, have a good life in Dublin. One day I'll meet you there, we will talk in a civilised way like you and the girl in Baggot Street, the one who was having the baby.'

'No.'

'That's what you'll do.' She spoke soothingly.

'And if you go to another town will you find someone new?'

'I won't go out looking for anyone, that I assure you.'

'And will he ... will he put up with it, turn the other way ... ?' He couldn't even bear to speak Mike Darcy's name.

'He'll know I love him and will never leave him.'

There was nothing more to say.

There was a lot to be done.

He would go back to the office and telephone some solicitors' offices in Dublin. He would ask his mother if he could go back to the basement flat in Waterloo Road. He would work day and night to clear his files, and leave everything ship-shape for Niall. He could shake off his years here and start again.

They tidied up the little house that they were visiting for the last time. As usual they emptied the cigarette butts and ash into an envelope. They straightened the furniture to the way it had been when they first found the place. They left by the window as they had always done. They rearranged the branches that hung to hide it.

She wouldn't bring anyone else here after he had gone, he felt sure of that. With a little lurch he wondered had she ever brought anyone before.

But that was useless speculation.

'Now that we're legitimate we can walk home together,' he said.

'Why not?' She was easy and affectionate, as she was with everyone.

'The long way or the short way?' He offered her the choice.

'The scenic route,' she decided.

They went up past the open ground that led to the Old Rock, and back through the woods, past Maddy Ross's house where she sat at her little desk, maybe writing letters to that priest who had gone to the missions, the one that she might have fancied. Richard felt a huge wave of sympathy for her. What a wasted love that must have been. Compared to his own great passion.

They came to the bridge, children still playing there as they had been the day Richard Hayes had come to town five long years ago.

Different children, same game.

Imagine, only an hour ago he had been planning for Gloria's children to go to school in Dublin. He thought he had taken over a family.

And now everything was over.

Now they were free to talk to each other there was nothing to say. His thoughts went up the road to the old schoolhouse, to the big beech tree which was covered with people's initials and their names.

In the first weeks of loving Gloria he had gone there secretly and carved '*Gloria in Excelsis*'.

It didn't seem blasphemous, it seemed a celebration. If anyone saw it in years to come they would think it was a hymn of praise to God. They might think a priest had put it there. He would not go and score it out. That would be childish. He could finish the story, of course. He could say that the glory of the world passed by; *Sic Transit Gloria*

Mundi. Only a few would understand it and when they did they would never connect it with Gloria Darcy, loving wife of Mike Darcy, shopkeeper.

But that would be childish too.

Maura O'Sullivan and her son Michael passed them by as they stood on the bridge, Gloria and Richard who would never speak again.

'Good day Mrs Darcy, Mr Hayes,' she said.

'My daddy?' Michael ran up to him and hugged his leg.

Richard knelt down to return the hug properly.

'Go home, Gloria,' he said.

She went without a word. He could hear the sound of her high red heels tapping down the road towards the centre of Shancarrig.

'How are you, Michael? You're getting to be a very big fellow altogether,' he said and buried his head in the boy's shoulder so that no one would see his tears.

LEO

When Leonora Murphy was a toddler, her father used to sit her on his knee and tell her about the little girl who had a little curl *right* in the middle of her forehead. He would poke Leo's forehead on the word *right* to show her where the curl was. Then he would go on, *And when she was good she was very very good, but when she was bad she was HORRID.* At the last word he would make a terrible face and roar at her, *HORRID, HORRID.* It was always frightening, even though Leo knew it would end well with a big hug, and sometimes his throwing her up in the air.

She wasn't frightened of Daddy, just the rhyme. It seemed menacing, as if someone else was saying it.

Anyway it wasn't even suitable for her because she was a girl with much more than one little curl. She had a head full of them, red-gold curls. They got tangled when anyone tried to brush her hair. Her mother gave up in despair several times. 'Like a furze bush, like something you'd see on a tinker child.' Leo knew this was an insult. People were half afraid of the tinkers, who camped behind Barna Woods sometimes when they were on the way to the Galway races.

If Leo ever was bad and wouldn't eat her rice or fasten her shoes properly, Biddy would say that she'd be given to the tinkers next time one of them passed the door. It seemed a terrible fate.

But later when she was older, when she could go exploring, Leo Murphy thought that it might be exciting to go and live with the tinkers. They had open fires. The children ran around half dressed. They went through the woods finding rabbits.

She used to creep around with her friends from school, Nessa Ryan and Niall Hayes and Eddie Barton. Not daring to move they'd peep through the trees and the bushes and watch the marvellous free lifestyle of people who had no rules or no laws to tie them down.

Leo couldn't remember why she had been so afraid.

But then, that was when she was a child. Once she was eleven and grown up things could be viewed differently. She realised that there were a lot of things she hadn't understood properly while she was young.

She hadn't realised that she lived in the biggest house in Shancarrig, for one thing. The Glen was a Georgian house, with a wide hall leading back to the kitchen and pantry. On either side of the hall door were big beautifully proportioned rooms – the dining room where the table was covered with papers and books, since they rarely had anyone to dine – the drawing room where the old piano had not been tuned for many a year, and where the dogs slept on cushions behind the big baskets of logs for the fire.

There was a breakfast room behind where they ate their meals, and a sports room which had wellingtons and guns, and fishing tackle. This is where Leo kept her bicycle when she remembered, but often she left it outside the kitchen door. Sometimes the wild cats that Biddy loved to feed at the kitchen window came and perched on the bicycle. There was a time when a cat brought all her little kittens one by one and left them in the bicycle basket, thinking it might be a safe haven for them.

That was the day that Leo had watched stony-faced as her father drowned them in the rain barrel.

'It's for the best,' her father said. 'Life is about doing things for the best, things you don't like.'

Leo's father was Major Murphy. He had been in the British army. In fact, he had been away at the War when Leo was born. She knew that because every birthday he told her how he had been at Dunkirk and hadn't known if the new baby was a boy or a girl. Since there had been two boys already the news, when it did arrive, was great news.

Leo's brothers were away at school. They didn't go to Shancarrig school like other boys did, they were sent to a boarding school from the time they were very young. The school was in England, where Grandfather lived. Grandfather wanted some of his family near him and he paid the school fees, which were enormous. It was a famous school, where prime ministers had gone.

Leo knew that it wasn't a Catholic school, but that Harry and James did go to mass on Sundays. She also knew that, for some reason, she wasn't to talk about this to her friend Nessa Ryan, or to Miss Ross, or Mrs Kelly, or especially not to Father Gunn. It was all perfectly right and good, but not something you went on about.

She knew there were other ways in which she was different. Major Murphy didn't go out to work like other people's fathers did. He didn't have a business or a farm, just The Glen. He didn't go down to Ryan's Hotel in the evening like other men, or pop into Johnny Finn Noted for Best Drinks. He sometimes went for a walk with Niall Hayes's father, and he went to Dublin on the train for the day. But he didn't have a job.

Her mother didn't go shopping every morning. She didn't call to Dunne's or to the butcher's. She didn't get a blouse and skirt made with Eddie Barton's mother. She didn't get involved with arranging flowers on the altar for Father Gunn, or helping with the sale of work at the school. Leo's mother was very beautiful and gave the air of having a lot to do as she floated from room to room. She really was a very beautiful woman, everyone always said so. Mrs Murphy had red-gold hair like her daughter, but not those unruly curls. It was smooth and shiny and turned in naturally, as if it had always been like that. Once a month Mother went to Dublin and she had it trimmed then, in a place in St Stephen's Green.

Somehow Leo knew that Harry and James weren't going to come back to Shancarrig when they left school. They had been talking about Sandhurst for as long as she could remember. They were both accepted. Her father was delighted.

'We must tell everyone,' he said when the letter arrived.

'Who can we tell?' His wife looked at him almost dreamily across the breakfast table.

Father looked disappointed. 'Hayes will be pleased.'

'Your friend Bill Hayes is the only one who's heard of Sandhurst.' Miriam Murphy spoke sharply.

'Ah come on. They're not as bad as that.'

'They are, Frank. I've been the one who's always lived here, you're only the newcomer.'

'Eighteen years, and still a newcomer ...' He smiled at her affectionately.

Leo's mother had been born in The Glen, and had played as a child in Barna Woods herself. She had gone fishing down to the River Grane, and taken picnics up to the Old Rock, from which Shancarrig got its name. She had been here all through the troubles after the Easter Rising, and through the Civil War. In fact, because there were so many upheavals at that time, her parents had sent her off to a convent school in England.

Shortly after she had left it she had met Frank Murphy and, as two Irish amid the croquet and tennis parties of the south of England in the early 1930s, they had been drawn together. Frank's knowledge of Ireland was sketchy, but romantic. He always hoped to settle there one day. Miriam Moore had been more practical. She had a falling down home, she said. It needed much more money than they would ever have to turn it into a dream.

Miriam's parents were old. They welcomed the bright son-in-law with open arms. They hoped he would be able to manage their beautiful but neglected house and estate. They hoped he would be able to keep their beautiful but restless daughter contented.

They died before they could judge whether he had been able to do either.

'Is Sandhurst on the sea?' Leo asked interestedly. If Harry and James were going to a beach next year, instead of back to school, she was very jealous indeed.

Her parents smiled indulgently at her. They told her it was in Surrey, nothing to do with sand as in Sandycove or Sandymount or any other seaside place she had been to. It was a great honour to get in there. They would be officers of the highest kind.

'Will they be a higher rank than Daddy if there's another war?' Leo asked.

'There won't be another war, not after the last one.'

He looked sad when he said that. Leo wished she hadn't brought the subject up. Her father walked with a stick and he had a lot of pain. She knew this because she could hear him groaning sometimes if he thought he was alone. Perhaps he didn't like being reminded of the War, which had damaged his spine.

'You should write to them, Leo,' her mother said. 'They'd like to get a letter from their little sister.'

It was like writing to strangers, but she wrote. She told them that she was sitting in the drawing room, and that Lance and Jessie were stretched in front of the fire. She told them about the school concert where they all wanted to sing 'I've Got a Lovely Bunch of Coconuts' and Mrs Kelly had said it was a filthy song. She told them how Eddie Barton had taught her how to draw different kinds of leaves, fishes and birds, and said she might do them a special drawing for Christmas if they ordered it.

She said she was glad they were going to be high-class officers in the army, even if there was never going to be another war. She said they would be glad to know that Daddy was walking a bit better and Mother looking a lot less sad.

To her surprise they both wrote almost by return and said that they loved her news. It was strange not being one thing or the other, they wrote.

Leo had a big bedroom that looked out over the garden. It was one of four large rooms around the big square landing. Nessa Ryan was always admiring the upstairs.

'It's like a room in itself, this landing,' she said in admiration. 'It's so poky in the hotel, all the rooms have numbers on them.'

Leo said that when her mother was young in The Glen there was breakfast on the landing. Imagine, people bringing all the food upstairs to save the family going down. Sometimes they used to eat in their dressing-gowns, Mother had told her.

Nessa was very interested that Major and Mrs Murphy had different bedrooms; her parents slept in the same bed.

'Do they really?' Leo was fascinated. She broached the subject with Biddy.

Somehow, it didn't seem right to ask directly.

'Don't go inquiring about where and how people sleep. Nothing but trouble comes out of that.'

'But *why*, Biddy?'

'Ah, people sleep where they want to sleep. Your parents sleep at each end of the house, that's what they want. Leave it at that.'

'But where did your parents sleep?'

'With all of us, in one room.' So it wasn't much help.

When Harry and James came home for a very quick visit she decided to ask them. They looked at each other.

'Well, you see. With Papa being wounded and everything . . .'

'All that sort of thing changed,' James finished.

'What sort of thing?' Leo asked.

They looked at each other in despair.

'All sorts of things. No sorts of things,' Harry said. And she knew the subject was over.

Mother never told Leo anything about the facts of life. If it hadn't been for Biddy and Nessa she would have been astonished by her first period. Although she knew how kittens, puppies and rabbits, and therefore babies, were born, she had no idea how they were conceived. She very much hoped that it was nothing to do with the behaviour of the dogs and cats at certain times. She didn't see how such a thing would be possible for humans anyway, even if any of them would agree to do it. She hated Nessa Ryan being so knowing so she didn't ask her, and she knew that Biddy in the kitchen flushed a dark red when the matter was mentioned ...

When Leo Murphy was fourteen such matters had been sorted out, if not exactly satisfactorily, at least she felt that she had mastered whatever technical information there was about it from reading pamphlets and magazines.

She had agreed with Nessa and Maura Brennan that it was quite impossible to believe that your own parents could ever have done it, but then the living proof that they must have was all around.

Maura Brennan was able to add the information that a lot of it happened when the man was drunk, and Leo said it was very unfair that the woman shouldn't be allowed to get drunk as well, because it was bound to be so awful.

Maura was very nice. She never pushed herself on anyone. In ways Leo liked her better than she liked Nessa Ryan, who could be moody if she didn't get her own way. But Maura lived in the poorest of the cottages. Her father Paudie was often to be seen sitting on someone's steps with a bottle in his hand, having been out drinking all night.

Maura wouldn't go on to the convent with them next year when she and Nessa went into town on the bus to secondary school. And yet at fourteen Maura seemed to know a lot more about life than the rest of them did.

It seemed very unfair to Leo that families like Maura Brennan's and Foxy Dunne's had to live in the falling down cottages by the river and had such shabby clothes. Foxy Dunne was much brighter than Niall Hayes, much quicker when it came to giving answers in school, but Foxy had no bicycle, no proper clothes, and had never been known to wear shoes that fitted him. Maura Brennan was much kinder and more gentle than Nessa Ryan but she never got a dress like Nessa got for her birthday and she hadn't a winter coat.

Leo knew she wasn't meant to go into the cottages and so she didn't. No one ever said not to, but it was something that was unspoken.

Only Foxy ever challenged it.

'Aren't you coming in to see the Dunne family at leisure ...?' he asked.

They had learned the word leisure at school today. Mrs Kelly had written it on the board and talked about what it meant.

'No thanks. I've got to go home today,' Leo would say.

'But *I'm* allowed to come and see the Murphy family at leisure,' he would say.

Leo was well able for him. 'Yes you are, and very welcome too, when you want to ...'

It was a stand-off.

They admired each other ... it had always been like that, since they were in Mixed Infants together ...

After the end of the summer term Leo and Nessa travelled on the bus to the convent school. They would meet the Reverend Mother, get a list of books and other items they would need, details of the school uniform and probably a string of rules as well. They thought that they would also be shown around the convent, but this did not materialise. They were tempted to spend the time idling round and sampling the pleasures of freedom of a place ten times the size of Shancarrig, but they felt that somehow they would be found out. It would be told back in Ryan's Hotel that they had been skitting and laughing on a corner with an idling lad, or licking ice creams in the street.

Better by far to get the early bus home and be shown to be reliable.

Nessa went into the hotel where she felt they weren't nearly grateful enough to see her.

'Are you back already?' Mrs Ryan said without enthusiasm.

'I hope you did everything you were meant to do,' her father said.

Leo grinned at her. 'It'll be the same in my place,' she said companionably. 'They'll have fed the dogs and won't have kept anything for me.'

She strolled up the hill, pausing to talk to Eddie Barton and tell him about the convent. He would be going to the Brothers. He said he wasn't looking forward to it. It was only games they cared about.

'In this place it's only prayers they care about,' Leo grumbled. 'There's statues leaping at you out of every wall.'

She trailed her shoulder bag behind her as she passed the old gate lodge that had been let once to people, who had left it like a pigsty. Now it was all boarded up in case any intruders got in.

It was a Thursday, and as soon as she was home Leo remembered that it was, of course, Biddy's half day. There would be food left under the meat safe. They usually had something cold for supper on a night when Biddy wasn't there. Leo knew that she should help herself because there was no one to greet her. Major Murphy had gone to Dublin that morning. He had caught the early train. Her mother must have gone walking in Barna Woods. Leo planned to take her food up to her bedroom and listen to her gramophone. She had written to James and Harry about the song 'I Love Paris in zee Springtime'. She could play it over and over. Some day she would go to Paris in 'zee Springtime or zee Fall' with someone who would sing that to her. She thought it would never go out of fashion. She closed herself into her room and before she even started on her milk and chicken sandwich she put on the record.

She threw herself on her window seat and was singing along with it when, to her surprise, she heard a door bang and footsteps running up or down the stairs, she couldn't tell which.

Thinking she might be playing it too loudly, she went to take off the handle of the machine and as she did so her eye caught sight of a young man fleeing across the grass and into the shrubbery. As he ran he was pulling on a shirt.

Leo was very frightened. It must have been a robber. Could there be more of them downstairs? She didn't know whether to shout for help or pretend that she wasn't there.

Her mind raced. They must know she was there if they had heard the music playing. Perhaps one was waiting for her outside her bedroom door. She could feel her heart thumping. In the silence of the house she heard a door creak open. She had been right. There *was* someone else lying in wait for her. She prayed as she had never prayed before.

As if in direct answer to her, God had managed to make her mother's voice call out, 'Leo? Leo? Is that you?'

Mother was standing outside her bedroom door, flushed-looking and confused.

Leo ran to her. 'Mother. There were robbers ... are you all right?'

'Shush, shush. Of course I am ... what are you talking about?'

'I heard them running down the stairs ... they went through the garden.'

'Nonsense, Leo. There were no robbers.'

'There *were*, Mother. I heard them, I saw them ... I saw one of them.'

'What did you see?'

'I saw him pulling off or putting on a shirt. Mother, he ran over there behind the lilacs, over the back fence.'

'What on earth are you doing home anyway ... weren't you meant to be on a tour of that school?'

'Yes, but they didn't show us. I saw him, Mother. There might be others in the house.'

Leo had never seen her mother so full of purpose. 'Come downstairs with me this moment and we'll put an end to this foolishness.' She flung open the doors of all the rooms. 'What burglar was here if he didn't take the silver, the glass? Or here, in the sports room, all your father's guns. Each one intact. Look, they didn't even take our supper, so let's have no chats about burglars and robbers.'

'But the feet on the stairs?' She was less sure of the figure now.

'I went downstairs myself and came back up to my room. I didn't know you were back ...'

'But I was playing the record player ...'

'Yes. That's what made me come out and look for you. To know what you were doing blasting it out and then turning it off.'

Mother looked excited. Different from the way she was normally.

Leo didn't know what made her think it was dangerous, but that is exactly what she felt it was. She had to walk just as delicately here as if there really were a robber hiding in the house.

She spoke nothing of the incident to her father, nor to Biddy. When Nessa Ryan asked whether Leo's welcome home had been any more cordial than the one that Nessa had got herself in the hotel, Leo said that she had made a sandwich and listened to 'I Love Paris'.

Nessa Ryan said that life was very unfair. She had been roped in to help polish silver, since she was back.

Imagine having all the freedom in the world in a big house like that.

Imagine. She didn't notice Leo shiver as she realised that she had denied the fright, and that somehow made the fright much bigger than it had been before.

Foxy Dunne came up the drive next day. His swagger showed a confidence that many of those twice his age might not have felt approaching The Glen.

But Foxy didn't push his luck; he went to the back door.

Biddy was most disapproving.

'Yes?' she said coldly.

'Ah, thank you, Biddy. It's good to get a real traditional Irish welcome everywhere, that's what I always say.'

'You and your breed never say anything except to make a jeer of other people who put their minds to work.'

Foxy looked without flinching.

'*I'm* different from my breed, as you call it, Biddy. I have every intention of putting my mind to work.'

'You'll be the first of the Dunnes who did, then.' She was still annoyed to see him sitting so confidently in her kitchen.

'There always has to be the first of some family who does. Where's Leo?'

'What's that to you?'

At that moment Leo came into the kitchen. She was pleased to see Foxy Dunne. She offered him one of Biddy's scones that were cooling on a wire tray.

'Will you like the place inside?' He was speaking about the secondary school.

'I think so. A bit Holy Mary, but you know.'

'A lot of people around here could do with being Holy Mary,' Biddy said.

Leo laughed. Everything seemed to be back to normal again.

'You'll work hard, won't you?' Foxy was concerned.

'Imagine one of Dinny Dunne's lads laying down the law on working hard,' Biddy snorted.

Foxy ignored her. 'It's important that you work as hard as I do,' he said to Leo. 'I have to, because I come from nothing. You have to because you come from everything.'

'I don't know what you mean,' Leo said.

'It would be dead easy for you to do nothing, for you to just drift about without doing anything, and end up just marrying someone.'

'Not for ages.' Leo was indignant.

'Not any time. You should get a job.'

'I might *want* to marry someone.'

'Yes, yes. But you'd be better off with a job, whether you married anyone or not.'

'I never heard such nonsensical talk.' Biddy was banging the saucepans around to show her disapproval.

'Come on, Foxy. We'll go out to the orchard,' Leo said.

They picked small gooseberries and put them in a basket that Leo's mother had left under a tree.

'It won't always be like this here, you know,' Foxy said.

'No. It'll be term time, and a list of books as long as your arm.'

'I meant this house, this way of going on.'

She looked at him, alarmed. The anxiety of the other night came back; things changing, not being safe any more.

'What do you mean?'

She looked very startled suddenly, and he didn't like the way her face got so alarmed, so he reassured her. He told her that if he could pretend to be sixteen or over he could get taken on by a man who was raising a crew for a builder in England – all fellows from round here, fellow countrymen ... he'd start just doing odd jobs, but he'd work his way up.

'I wish you weren't going away,' Leo said. 'I know it's crazy, but I have this stupid feeling that something awful is going to happen.'

It was three weeks later that it happened. On a warm summer evening. The house was quiet. Biddy had gone on her annual summer holidays back to her family's farm. Leo had finished her letter to Harry and James, she had written how Daddy's back seemed much better and that Dr Jims had said that walking couldn't do him any harm – it couldn't hurt him any more than he had been hurt in the War – and that if he sat in a chair like an old man with a rug over his knees then he'd turn into one.

So he went off for long walks with Mr Hayes, even up as far as the Old Rock. That's where they had gone today. Leo decided to walk down to the town to post the letter. Once it was written she liked it to be on its way. It could sit on the hall table for days, with Biddy dusting around it. She found a stamp and headed off. Mrs Barton was ironing, Leo could see her through the window. She never went out to sit in her little garden. Surely she could have brought some of her sewing out of doors on a beautiful evening like this. Leo looked up to see if she could see Eddie's face at his window. He wrote almost as many letters as she did. She met him sometimes at the post office and Katty Morrissey said that between them they kept the whole of P & T going.

But there was no sign of Eddie. Maybe he was off finding odd shapes of wood and clumps of flowers to draw. She did meet Niall Hayes, however, walking disconsolately up and down The Terrace.

'God, that school I'm going to is like a prison,' Niall said. 'It's like *The Count of Monte Cristo*'.

'The convent's all right. It's choked with statues, though, all of them with cross faces.'

'Oh, I wouldn't mind if it was only the statues. You should see the faces on these fellows. All of them in long black dresses, and looking desperate.'

'Sure doesn't Father Gunn wear a long dress, and Father Barry. You're used to them.' Leo thought Niall Hayes was making heavy weather out of it all.

'They don't have faces like lighting devils.'

'Did your father go to school there?'

'Of course he did, and all my uncles. And they've forgotten how awful it is. They keep telling me of all the fun they had there.'

'Your father's gone for a walk with my father.' Leo was tired of all the gloom.

'Well, it must have been a short one then. My father's back in the house there, making some farmer's will. Leo, I don't think I could *bear* to be a solicitor here in Shancarrig.'

'You could always go somewhere else,' Leo said. There seemed to be no cheering Niall today.

She was sorry her father's walk had been cancelled, but maybe he was sitting with Mother in the orchard. She had seen sometimes they had a big jug of homemade lemonade, and they looked as if they were a bit happy.

She met Father Gunn, who said wasn't it amazing the way the time raced by. There was another whole class ready to leave Shancarrig and go out into the wide world. It was extraordinary how grown-ups thought time raced by. Leo found it went very slowly indeed.

As she came in the gate of The Glen she heard cries coming from the gate lodge, and at the same moment she saw her father hastening as fast as he was able down the drive. Leo shrank away from the sound of crashing furniture and screams.

But she knew without a shadow of a doubt that it was her mother's voice she heard screaming, 'No, no! You can't! No,' and a great long wail.

'Oh, my God, my God. Miriam. *Miriam.*'

Her father was stumbling. He had dropped his stick, and had to bend down for it.

Leo watched as if it was slow motion.

Then they heard the shots. Three of them. And at that moment

Leo's mother came staggering to the door. Her blouse was covered with blood. Her hair and eyes were wild.

'My God ... he tried to ... he was trying to ... he would have killed me,' she cried. She kept looking behind her where they could see a shape on the ground.

'Frank!' screamed Leo's mother. 'Oh, do something, Frank. For God's sake! He would have killed me.'

Leo shrank still further away from the scene which she could see unfolding, but yet could not take in.

Her father walked in exaggeratedly slow motion towards the door and took her mother in his arms.

He soothed her like a baby.

'It's over, Miriam, it's over,' he said.

'Is he dead?' Leo's mother didn't want to look.

Horrified, Leo saw her father bend to the shape on the floor and turn it over. Leo could see a man with dark hair, lying on the floor of the gate lodge. There was a big red stain all over the front of his shirt.

It was the man she had seen running towards the lilacs in the shrubbery three weeks ago, the day that she thought there had been robbers.

And now both her father and mother were crying.

'It's all right, Miriam darling. It's over. He's dead.' Her father was saying this over and over again.

Later they gave Leo a brandy too. With a little water in it. But that was well after they had come back to the house.

The door of the gate lodge had been closed. They all walked up the drive arm in arm and Mother had gone up to wash herself.

'You might need to, you know, not change anything,' Leo heard Daddy say, but Mother looked at him wildly.

'You mean ... wear this? Wear *this* on my body? All this blood? What for? Frank, use your head. What for?' She was near hysteria.

'I'll wash you,' he offered.

'No. Please let me be on my own for a few moments.'

Mother had a wash basin in her room, with a mirror and a light over it, and little pink floral curtains.

Leo didn't want to be alone, so she followed her mother into the room. Their eyes met in the mirror.

'Are you all right, Mummy?' She rarely used that word.

Mother's face softened. 'It's all right, Leo. It's over.' She said Father's words like a parrot.

'What are we going to do? What's going to happen?'

'Shush. Let me get rid of all this. We'll put it out of our minds. It'll be like a bad dream.'

'But ...'

'That's for the best, Leo, believe me.' Mother looked very young as she stood there just in her slip and skirt. She rubbed her neck and arms with a soapy flannel and warm water, even though there was no trace of blood. That was all streaked and hardening on the yellow blouse she had thrown into the wastepaper basket.

Mother was brushing her teeth, and she shook her tin of Tweed talcum powder into her hand and rubbed it into her skin.

'Go on, darling. Go down to your father. I want to finish dressing.'

Leo thought Mother only had to put on a blouse. And of course a brassiere. She had only just realised that for some reason Mother hadn't been wearing one as she stood beside the hand basin. Just the slip. Her silky peach-coloured one.

Everything was so strange and unreal. The fact that Mother had asked her to leave the room now was only one tiny fragment more in the whole thing.

Leo went into the drawing room. She felt something like this should not be discussed in the breakfast room where they lived on ordinary days. Her father must have felt the same thing. He had put a match to the fire and the two dogs, Lance and Jessie, seemed pleased. They stretched their big cream limbs in front of the grate.

Leo thought suddenly that Lance and Jessie didn't know what had happened. Then she remembered that nobody knew – not Niall Hayes, whom she had been talking to half an hour ago – nor Mrs Barton, who had waved from her ironing – nor Father Gunn, who had said that time passed so quickly.

Father Gunn? Why wasn't he here?

The moment someone died you sent for the priest. And Dr Jims, Eileen and Sheila's father, he should be here. That's what happened when people got sick or died, Father Gunn and Dr Jims arrived in their cars.

Mother was at the door. She shivered and hugged herself.

'That's lovely of you to light the fire,' she said.

They both looked up, Leo and her father. Mother sounded so

ordinary – so normal. As if it all hadn't happened out there. Down in the gate lodge.

That was when Father poured the brandy for the two of them.

'Give Leo a little, too.' Mother sounded as if she was offering more soup at lunchtime.

'Come up here to the fire. Warm your hands. I'll phone Sergeant Keane. He'll be up in five minutes.'

'No.' It was like a whiplash.

'We have to call him, we should have phoned immediately.'

Leo was sipping the horrible and unfamiliar brandy. She didn't know how people like Maura Brennan's father wanted to drink alcohol all the time. It was disgusting.

'My nerves won't stand it, Frank. I've been through enough already.'

'Sergeant Keane's very gentle. He'll make it as quick as possible. It's just the formalities.'

'I won't *have* the formalities. There's no point in asking me to.'

'A man tried to kill you, he had one of my guns. He *could* have killed you.' Father's voice broke with emotion at the thought of it.

Mother became even more icily calm.

'But he didn't. What happened was that I killed him.'

'You defended yourself against him ... the gun went off. He killed himself.'

'No. I picked up the gun and shot him.'

'You don't know *what* happened. You're in shock.'

Major Murphy made a move as if to go out to the hall to the telephone.

Mother didn't even need to raise her voice to make her seriousness felt.

'If you ring him, Frank, I'm walking out of that door and you'll never see me again. Either of you.'

He put out his arms as if to hold her again, support her as he had up the drive, console her as he had done when he was holding her, telling her it was over.

Mother really seemed to believe that it *was* over.

Leo kept moving the glass around between her hands as she listened to her parents talking about the man who lay dead in their gate lodge.

Her mother's voice was strange and unnatural. It didn't sound like a voice, it sounded like a noise, a thin even noise, with no highs and lows.

She spoke as one who is being perfectly reasonable.

Frank had told her it was over, finished. So let it be forgotten. Why drag heavy-footed policemen in, and go over it and over it, and ask questions and give answers? The man had threatened her. He had got killed himself. It was an eye for an eye. Justice had been done. Let it be left as it was.

At every interruption she gave her strange disembodied threat: 'Or else I will disappear from this house and you will never see me again.'

It was as if they had forgotten she was here. Leo watched mesmerised as her mother, by sheer force of repetition, began to beat down the rational arguments. She saw her father change from the strong man comforting his wife caught in a terrible accident and become someone hunted and unsure. She saw him bite his lip and watched his eyes widen with fear at every repeated threat that Miriam Murphy would walk out the door and never be seen again.

She wanted to interrupt, to ask Mother where she would go. Why she would leave them, her home and her family?

But she didn't dare to move.

It was when her father had said, 'I couldn't *live* without you, Miriam, you couldn't leave knowing that . . .'

'Please . . .' She looked across at her fourteen-year-old daughter, as if a lapse of taste had been committed. A man shouldn't speak of his need, of his weakness, not in front of a child.

Major Murphy came over to the window seat where Leo was sitting.

'Leo, dearest child.'

'What's going to happen, Daddy?'

'It's going to be all right. As your mother says, it's over, it's over. We mustn't . . .'

'Will we get Dr Jims? Father Gunn . . . ?'

'Leo, come with me. I'll bring you up to bed.'

'I want to stay here, Daddy, please . . .'

'You want to help us, you want to be big and brave and do the right thing . . .'

'No. I want to stay here. I'm afraid.'

Outside in the big garden darkness had fallen. The bushes were big shapes, not colours as they had been when the three of them walked back up, huddled together from the horrors they had left in the gate lodge.

He propelled her out of the door and to the kitchen where he warmed some milk in a saucepan. He took the big silver pepperpot and sprinkled some over the top of the milk when it was poured into a mug.

He walked up the stairs with her and led her to the room.

'Put on your nightie, like a good girl,' he said.

He turned his back as Leo slipped out of her green cotton dress and her summer vest and knickers, and pulled on the pink winceyette nightdress from the nightdress case shaped like a rabbit. Leo remembered with a shock that when she stuffed her nightie in there this morning nothing had happened. None of this nightmare had begun.

She got into bed and sipped the milk.

Her father sat on the bed and stroked her forehead. 'It will be all right, Leo,' he said.

'How can it be all right, Daddy?'

'I don't know. I used to wonder that in the War, but it was.'

'It wasn't really. You got wounded and you can't walk properly.'

'Yes, I can.' He stood up.

His face was so sad Leo wanted to cry aloud. She wanted to open the window in her room, kneel up on the window seat and cry out for someone in Shancarrig to help them all.

But she bit her lip.

'I have to go down now, Leo,' he said.

It was as if they were allies. Allies to protect a strange silent mother downstairs who wasn't speaking in her ordinary voice.

She used to play that game of 'if'.

If I get up the stairs before the grandfather clock in the hall stops striking then Mrs Kelly won't be in a bad mood tomorrow. If the crocuses come up in front of the house by Tuesday I'll get a letter from Harry and James.

Now she sat in the dark bedroom with her arms around her knees. If I don't get out of bed it will be all right. Dr Jims will come and say he wasn't dead at all. If he is really dead then Father Gunn will say it wasn't Mother's fault.

If I don't get out of bed at all and if I sit like this all night without moving then it'll turn out not to have happened at all.

She woke in the morning stiff and awkward. She hadn't managed to stay awake. Now the charm wouldn't work. It *had* happened, all of it.

There was no point in holding her knees any more. None of it was going to work.

How could it be an ordinary day? A sunny day with Lance and Jessie rushing around outside, with Mattie the postman cycling up the drive, with smells of breakfast coming from downstairs.

Leo got out of bed and looked at her face in the wardrobe mirror. It was grey white and there were shadows under her frightened grey-green eyes. Her curly hair stood upright over her head.

She pulled on the clothes she had thrown on the floor last night, last night when Daddy had been standing with his frightened face.

At that moment the door opened and Mother came in. A different Mother from last night. Mother was dressed in a blue linen suit, her hair was combed, she wore her pink lipstick and she looked bright and enthusiastic.

'I have the most wonderful news,' she said.

Leo felt the colour rushing to her cheeks. The man wasn't dead. Dr Jims had cured him.

Before she could speak Mother had opened the wardrobe door and started to take out some of Leo's frocks.

'We're going on a holiday, all three of us,' she said. 'Your father and I suddenly decided that this was what we all needed. Now, isn't that a lovely surprise?'

'But ...' Leo's voice dried in her throat.

'But we have to get going just after breakfast, it's a long drive.'

'Are we running away?' Leo's voice was a whisper.

'For a whole week we are ... now, where are your bathing togs? We're going to a lovely hotel on a cliff, and we'll be able to run down and have a swim before breakfast every day. Imagine.'

Her father didn't catch her eye at breakfast, and Leo knew that she must not mention the events of last night. Her father had somehow bought the right for both of them to run away with Mother. That's what was happening.

They heard a knock at the back door. All three of them looked at each other in alarm, but it was Ned, who did the garden. Leo heard her father explaining about the sudden holiday ... and giving instructions.

The glasshouses were in a terrible state – if Ned could concentrate entirely on clearing them, and sorting out what was to be done. . . .

'And what about the rockery, Major, sir?'

'It's very important that you leave that. There's a man coming down from the Botanic Gardens in Dublin to have a look at it. He said nothing was to be touched until he came.'

'I'm glad of that.' Ned sounded relieved. 'Will I fill in the hole we dug?'

'Oh, we've done that already ...'

If Ned was surprised that a man with war injuries, and his frail wife, had covered in a pit that it had taken him two days to dig, he showed no sign of it.

'I'll leave it as it is then, Major, sir?'

'Just as it is, Ned. No disturbing it at all.'

Leo felt a cold horror spread all over her.

The memory of last night, hugging her knees in the dark. The sound of footsteps, of low urgent voices, of dragging and pulling. But her mother was calm as she listened to the conversation at the back door, and even laughed when Daddy came back into the room.

'Well, I expect that was welcome news for our Ned. Anything that he hasn't to do must come as a pleasant surprise.'

Leo beat back the wild fears.

Often her dreams seemed real to her ... more real than ordinary life. This is what must be happening now. There was another knock at the door. Again the look of alarm was exchanged.

This time it was Foxy Dunne.

'Yes, Foxy?' Leo's father was unenthusiastic.

'How are you?' Foxy never addressed people by title. He wouldn't greet the priest as Father and he certainly wouldn't call Leo's father Major.

'I'm fine thank you, Foxy. How are you?'

'Great altogether. I came to say goodbye to Leo.'

Suddenly her father's voice sounded wary. 'And how, might I ask, did you know that she was going away?'

'I didn't.' Foxy was cheerful. 'I'm going away myself, that's why I came to say goodbye.'

'Well, I suppose you'd better come in.'

Foxy walked easily through the scullery and the kitchen and into the breakfast room.

'How're ya?' he said, nodding easily at Leo's mother.

She smiled at the small boy with the freckles and the red hair, the one Dunne boy that poverty and neglect had never managed to defeat.

'And where are you off to?' she asked politely.

Foxy ignored her and addressed Leo. 'I'm off to London, Leo. I didn't think I'd ever be able to do it. I thought I'd be hanging around here like an eejit, dragging a brush around someone's shop.'

'You're too young to go to England.'

'They won't ask. All they want is someone to make tea on a site.'

'Will you be frightened?'

'After my old fellow and Maura Brennan's old fellow? Both of them coming home drunk and both of them trying to beat me up ... how could I be frightened?'

He talked as if Leo's parents weren't there. It wasn't deliberately rude, it was just that he didn't see them.

'Will you ever come back to Shancarrig again?'

'I'll come home every Christmas with fistfuls of pound notes, like everyone else on the buildings.'

Major Murphy asked whether Foxy would learn a trade.

'I'll learn everything,' Foxy told him.

'No, I mean a skilled trade, you know, an honourable trade, like a bricklayer ... It would be very good to serve your time, to do an apprenticeship.'

'It'll be that all right.' Foxy didn't even look at the man, let alone heed him.

'Will you write and tell what it's like?' Leo knew her voice sounded shaky and not full of interest as Foxy would have liked.

'I was never one for the writing, but as I say, I'll see you every Christmas. I'll tell you then.'

'Good luck to you over there.' Leo's mother was standing up from the breakfast table. She was bringing the conversation to a close.

Foxy gave her a long look.

'Yeah. I suppose I'll need a bit of luck all right. But it's more a matter of working and letting them know you can work.'

'You're only a child. Don't let them ruin your health, tell them you're not able for heavy work.' The Major was kind.

But Foxy was having none of it. 'I'll tell them I'm seventeen. That's how I'll get on. Seventeen, and a bit stunted.' He was going in his own time, not in Mrs Murphy's. 'I'll see you at Christmas, Leo,' he said, and went.

Leo saw him fondling the ears of Lance, and throwing a stick for Jessie.

Other people were in awe of the two loudly barking labradors. Not Foxy Dunne.

She thought of him a few times during their holiday, that strange time in a faraway hotel, where there was nothing whatsoever for her to do except read the books that were in the library. Sometimes she walked with her father and mother along the sandy beaches, collecting cowrie shells. But usually she left Mother and Father to walk alone, with the dogs. They seemed very close together, sometimes even holding hands as Father limped along, and Mother sometimes bent to pick up some driftwood and throw it out into the sea so that Lance and Jessie could struggle to bring it back.

She didn't sleep too well at night in the small room with the diamond-shaped panes of glass in the window. The roar of the Atlantic Ocean down below the cliffs was very insistent. The stars looked different here from the way they looked in Shancarrig when she'd sit on her window seat and watch at night – the familiar garden of The Glen, the lilacs, the shrubbery down to the big iron gates and the gate lodge.

She shivered when she thought of the gate lodge. She had not been able to look at it as they had driven past on the morning they had left home. She dreaded seeing it again when she went back, but she wanted to be away from this strange dreamlike place too, this holiday that never should have been.

Biddy would be at home now in The Glen. What might have happened? What might she have found? Yet neither Father nor Mother telephoned her or seemed remotely worried.

Leo felt a constriction in her throat. She couldn't eat the food that was put in front of her.

'My daughter hasn't been well. It has nothing to do with your lovely food.'

Leo looked at her mother in disbelief. How could she lie so easily and in such a matter-of-fact voice? If she could do that she could lie about anything. Nothing was as it used to be any more.

Leo was very afraid. She wanted a friend. Not Nessa whose eyes would widen in horror. Not Eddie Barton who would retreat into his woods, and his flowers, and his drawings. Not Niall Hayes who would say it was typical of grown-ups – they never did anything you could rely on.

She couldn't tell Father Gunn, not even in confession. Maura Brennan would be more frightened than she was herself.

For a moment she thought of Foxy Dunne, but even if he were at home he wasn't the kind of person you could tell. She wondered how he was standing up to life on a big building site in London. Did he seriously think that people would believe he was seventeen? But he was always so cocky, so confident, maybe they would.

She looked away to the other side of the car as they drove back in through the gates of The Glen. It was as if she was afraid that the door of the gate lodge would be swinging wide open and that Sergeant Keane and a lot of guards would be there waiting for them.

But everything was as it always had been. The dogs raced around, happy to be home and no longer cooped up in the station wagon. Biddy was bustling around full of interest in their sudden holiday. Old Ned, who was sitting smoking in the glasshouse, busied himself suddenly.

There had been no news, Biddy said. Everything had gone fine. There was a letter from Master Harry and Master James, and some other parcel that didn't have enough stamps on it and Mattie wanted money paid.

There had been cross words with the butcher because they had delivered the Sunday joint of beef as usual and been annoyed when told that the family were on holidays. Sergeant Keane had been up to know if there was any word of one of the tinkers who had gone missing.

Biddy had given them all short shrift.

She had told Mattie that enough money had been spent on stamps to and from this house for him to feel embarrassed even mentioning the question of underpayment. He had slunk away, as well he might. The butcher had felt the lash of Biddy's tongue as she told them that the new frontage on the shop had been paid for with money that Major Murphy and his family had spent on the best of meat, they should be ashamed to grumble.

She asked Sergeant Keane what he could have been thinking of to imagine that a tinker boy could even have crossed the lawns of The Glen.

At first Leo didn't want to meet anyone. She wanted to stay half sitting, half kneeling on her window seat, looking out to where the dogs played, and old Ned made feeble attempts at hoeing, to where her father walked with his halting movements out to meet Mr Hayes, and where Mother drifted, her straw hat in her hand, through the shrubbery and past the lilacs.

No man came from the Botanic Gardens in Glasnevin to deal with the rockery that they had planned on top of the great pit that had been filled in.

When Mr O'Neill, the auctioneer from the big town, came to inquire whether they would be interested in letting the gate lodge, Leo's father and mother said not just now, some time certainly, but at the moment everything was quite undecided – perhaps one of the boys might come home and live in it.

There had never been any question of Harry or James coming back. Leo realised it was one more of these easy lies her mother told, like when she had told the people at the hotel that Leo had been unwell and that was why she hadn't been able to eat her meals.

One day Maura Brennan from school came and asked for a job as a maid in the house. She said she had to work somewhere and why not for someone like Leo, whom she liked. Leo had been awkward and frightened that day. It seemed another example of the world going mad: Maura, who had sat beside her at school, wanting to come and scrub floors in their house because that was the way things were.

But as the days turned into weeks Leo got the courage to leave The Glen. She called on Eddie Barton and his mother. They spoke to her as if things were normal. She began to believe they were. There was an ill-written postcard from London saying 'Wish you were here'. She knew it was from Foxy, though it didn't say. And one Saturday at Confession Father Gunn had asked her was there anything troubling her.

Leo's heart leapt into her throat.

'Why do you ask that, Father?' she said in a whisper.

'You seem nervous, my child. If there's anything you want to say to me, remember you're saying it to God through me.'

'I know, Father.'

'So, if there is any worry ...'

'I am worried about something, but it's not my worry, it's someone else's worry.'

'Is it your sin, my child?'

'No, Father. No. Not at all. It's just that I can't understand it. You see, it has to do with grown-ups.'

There was a silence.

Father Gunn was digesting this. He assumed that it was to do with a child's perception of adult sexuality and all the loathing and embarrassment that this could bring.

'Perhaps all these things will become clear later,' he said soothingly.

'So, I shouldn't worry, do you think, Father?'

'Not if it's something you have no control over, my child, something where it would not be appropriate for you to be involved,' said the priest.

Leo felt much better. She said her three Hail Marys, penance for her other small sins, and put the biggest thing as far to the back of her mind as possible. After all, the priest said that God would make it clear later; now was not the appropriate time to worry about it.

As she prepared for her years in the convent school in the town she tried to make life in The Glen seem normal. She had joined their game. She was pretending that nothing had ever happened on that summer evening when the world stopped.

Leo started to go down the hill to meet the people she had been at school with once more – her friend Nessa Ryan in the hotel, whose mother always found work for idle hands – Sheila and Eileen Blake, who were home from a posh boarding school and kept asking could they come and play tennis at The Glen. Leo told them the court needed a lot of work. She realised she was lying as smoothly as her mother these days. She met Niall Hayes, who told her that he thought he was in love.

'Everyone's doing everything too young,' Leo said reprovingly. 'Foxy's too young to be going to England to work, you're too young to be in love. Who is it anyway?'

He didn't say. Leo thought it might be Nessa. But no, surely not? He lived across the road from Nessa, he had known her all his life. That couldn't be what falling in love was like. It was too confusing.

She met Nancy Finn from the pub. Nancy was what they called a bold strap in Shancarrig. She was fifteen and had been accused of being forward and giving people the eye. Sometimes she helped serve behind the counter. It was a rough sort of place.

Nancy said she'd really love to go to America and work as a cocktail waitress. That was her goal but her father said it was lunacy. Nancy said her father, Johnny Finn Noted for Best Drinks, was fed up. The guards had been in every night for three weeks asking was there any brawl between tinkers and anyone, and her father said he wouldn't let a bloody tinker in the door. Sergeant Keane said that was a very unchristian attitude, and Nancy's father had said the guards would have another tune to play if he *did* let the tinkers in and took their money, so there had been hard words and the upshot was that the guards were watching Johnny Finn's pub night after night, ready to pounce if anyone was left with a drink in front of them for thirty seconds beyond the licensing hours.

The summer ended and a new life began, a life of getting the bus every day into school in the big town. The bus bounced along the roads through villages and woods, and stopped at junctions and crossroads where people came down long narrow tracks to the main road. Leo and Nessa Ryan learned their homework to the rhythm of the bus crossing the countryside. They heard each other's poems, they puzzled out theorems and algebra. Often they didn't even look out the window at the countryside passing by.

Sometimes Leo seemed as if she was looking out at the scenery. Anyone watching her would think that there was a dreamy schoolgirl looking out at the fields with the cattle grazing, the colours changing from season to season in the hedges and clusters of bushes that they passed.

But Leo Murphy's eyes might not have been focusing on these things at all. Her thoughts were often on her mother. Her pale delicate mother, who wandered more often through the gardens of The Glen no matter what the weather, with empty eyes, talking softly to herself.

Leo had seen her mother sit under the lilac tree picking the great purple flowers apart absently in her lap and crooning to herself, 'You had lilac eyes, Danny. Your eyes were like deep lilac. Your eyes are closed now.'

She spoke of Danny too when she half sat and half lay over the rockery. Every day, rain or shine, she tended it, and a weed could hardly put its head out before Mrs Murphy had snapped it away.

'At least I kept your grave for you, Danny boy,' she would cry. 'You can never say I didn't put flowers on your grave. No man in Ireland got more flowers.'

The first time Leo heard her mother speak like this she was frozen with horror. It was a known fact that the missing tinker was Danny. His family had told people that he must have a girl in Shancarrig. He used to be gone from the camp for long periods, and when he'd come back he was always smiling and saying nothing. There was the question he might have run off with someone from the locality. Sergeant Keane had assured the travellers that there were no unexplained disappearances of any of the girls of the village; he had made inquiries and there was no one missing from the area.

'No one except Danny,' said Mrs McDonagh, the sad-looking woman with the dark, lined face who was Danny's mother.

Leo heard all this from other people. Nessa Ryan heard it discussed a lot in the hotel, and reported it word for word. It was the only exciting thing that had happened in their lives. She couldn't understand why her friend Leo wasn't interested in it, and wouldn't speculate like everyone else about what might have happened.

The months went by and Leo's mother became less in touch with reality.

Leo had stopped trying to talk to her about school, and everyday things. Instead she spoke as if her mother was an invalid.

'How do you feel today, Mother?'

'Well ... I don't know, I really don't know.' She spoke in a dull voice. The woman who used to be so elegant and graceful, the mother who would plan a picnic, correct bad grammar or a mispronounced word with cries of horror ... that had all gone.

She barely touched her food, just smiled vaguely at Father, and Leo, and at Biddy as if they were people she used to know. She spoke to the dogs, Lance and Jessie, no longer the big gambolling pups, but more stately with years. She reminded them of how they had known Danny, and they would stand guard over his grave.

Biddy *must* have heard it. She would have had to be deaf not to have known what she was talking about.

But the conspiracy continued.

Mrs Murphy had been feeling under the weather, surely now the longer days, or the bright weather, or the good crisp winter without any damp ... whichever season ... she would show an improvement.

Old Ned had been pensioned off. Eddie Barton came and cut the grass sometimes, but there was nobody coming to do the gardens as they should have been done. Sometimes Leo and her father would struggle, but it was beyond them. Only the rockery bloomed. Mrs Murphy wandered outside The Glen with her secateurs in her pocket and took cuttings for it, or even dug up little plants that she thought might flourish.

In the increasingly jungle-like gardens of The Glen the rockery bloomed as a monument, as a memorial.

In her efforts to keep her mother out of anyone else's sight and hearing, Leo pieced together the story of horror, of what had happened in those weeks when she was fourteen and had understood nothing of the world. Those weeks before her world changed.

Mother remembered not only Danny's lilac eyes but his strong arms, and his young body. She remembered his laughter and his impatience and greed to have her, over and over. With a sick stomach Leo listened to her mother remembering and crying for a lost love. She hated the childlike coquettish enthusiasm in her mother's face when she spoke of the man she had welcomed on the mossy earth, in her bedroom on the rug, under the lilac trees, and in the gate lodge.

But it was when she mentioned the gate lodge that her face would harden and her questioning take a different turn. Why did he have to be so greedy? What did he need with silver? Why had he demanded to take their treasures? What did he mean that he needed something to trade, some goods to deal in as they went towards Galway? Had he not taken her, was that not the greatest treasure of all? Miriam Murphy's eyes were like stone when she went through that part of the story of the last time they had met ... of the silver he had wrapped in a tablecloth as he had roamed through the house, touching things, taking this, leaving that. She had begged him and pleaded.

'Say there was a robbery ... say you came back and found it all gone.' His lilac eyes had laughed at her.

'I told him he must not go, he had been sent to me, and he could not leave.'

Leo knew the chant off by heart, she could say it with her mother as the woman stroked the earth of the rockery.

'You wouldn't listen, Danny. You called me old. You said you had given me my fun and my loving and that I should be grateful.

'You said you'd take some guns, that we had no need of them, but in your life you'd need to hunt in the forest ... I asked you to take me with you ... and you laughed, and you called me old. I couldn't let you leave, I had to keep you here, and that was why ...' Her mother would smile then, and stroke the earth again. 'And you are here, Danny Boy. You'll never leave me now.'

Leo had known for years why her father had struggled that night, dragging and pulling with his wounds aching and his useless leg trailing behind. He knew why this woman had to be protected from telling this sing-song tale to the law. And Leo knew too.

At school they thought her a tense child. They spoke to her father about her since Mrs Murphy, the mother, never made any appearance.

Mother Dorothy, who was wise in the ways of the world, decided that the mother might have a drink problem. It had to be. Otherwise she'd have come in some time. Very tough on the child, a nice girl, but with a shell on her as hard as rock.

Leo told Father Gunn that Mother wasn't all that well, and that if they didn't see her at mass he wasn't to take any wrong meaning out of it.

Father Gunn asked would she like the sacraments brought up to The Glen.

'I'm not too sure, Father.' Leo bit her lip.

Father Gunn also knew the ways of the world.

'Why don't we leave it for the moment?' he suggested. 'And if there's any change in that department then all you have to do is ask me.'

Leo thought to herself that in Shancarrig it was really quite easy to hide anything from anybody.

Or maybe it was only if you happened to live in The Glen, a big house surrounded by high walls, with its own gardens and shrubberies and gate lodge.

It might be different trying to keep your secrets if you lived in the cottages down by the river, or in The Terrace with everyone seeing your front entrance, or in the hotel with half of Shancarrig in and out of your doors every day.

She felt watchful about her mother, but not always on edge. No long-term anxiety like that can be felt at the pain level all the time. There were many hours when Leo didn't even think about her mother's telling and re-telling the story. There were the school outings, there were the parties, the times when Niall Hayes kissed her and their noses kept bumping, and later when quite suddenly Richard Hayes, who was Niall's older cousin, kissed her and there was no nose-bumping at all.

Richard Hayes was very handsome, he had stirred the place up since he arrived. Leo felt sorry for Niall because deep in her heart she thought Niall still had a very soft spot for Nessa, and Nessa was of course crazy about the new arrival in town.

And it had to be said that Richard was paying a lot of attention to Nessa. There were walks, drives and trips to the pictures in the town. Leo thought he was rather dangerous, but then she shrugged. Who was she to know? Her views on love and attraction were extremely suspect.

Some of the girls at school were going to be nurses; they had applied to hospitals in Dublin and in Britain for places.

'Should I be a nurse, Daddy?' she asked.

They were walking, as they often did in the evening. Mother was safely talking to the rockery, and if you counted Biddy as the silent rock she had been for three long years, then there was no one around to hear the chant that had begun again.

'Would you *like* to be a nurse?'

'Only if it would help.'

Her father looked old and grey. Much of his time was spent persuading his sons not to come back to Shancarrig, and telling them that their mother was in poor mental health.

Naturally they had written and asked why was nothing being done about this. They had written to Dr Jims, which Major Murphy thought an outrageous interference. But fortunately Jims Blake had agreed with him that arrogant young men thought they knew everything. If Frank Murphy said there was nothing wrong with Miriam, then that was that. The doctor had seen the thin pale face and the over-brilliant eyes of Miriam Murphy, always a fairly obsessional person he would have thought, checking light switches, refusing to throw out old papers. This is what he had noticed on his visits to The Glen, and assumed that like many a nervy woman there was nothing asked and therefore nothing that could be answered. This was not a household where he would be asked to refer her to a psychiatrist in order to work out the cause of the unease. At least he wasn't being asked for ever-increasing prescriptions of tranquillisers or sleeping pills. This in itself was something to be thankful for.

Foxy Dunne came home every Christmas as he had promised. When he arrived on his first visit home, wearing a new zippered jacket with a tartan lining, at the back door of The Glen, he was surprised at the frostiness of his reception. Not that he had ever been warmly welcomed there, but this was out of that league ... 'Well, tell my friend Leo. She knows where I live,' he said haughtily to Biddy.

'And I'm sure, like everyone, she knows only too well where the Dunnes live and would want to avoid it,' Biddy said.

Leo had heard. She called to the Dunnes' cottage that afternoon.

'I came to ask if you'd like to go for a walk in Barna Woods,' she said.

Foxy looked very pleased. He was at a loss for words. The quick shrugging reaction or the smart joke deserted him.

'Well, I won't ask you into my house either,' he said. 'Let's go and be babes in the wood.'

He told her of living in a house with eleven men from their own country. He told her of the drinking and how so many of them spent everything they had nearly killed themselves earning.

'Why do you stay there?' she asked.

'To learn ... to save. But mainly to learn.'

'What can you learn from old men like that drinking their lives away?'

'I can learn what not to do, I suppose, or how it could have been done right.'

Foxy sat on a fallen tree and told her about the chances, the men who had made it, the small contractors who did things right and did them quickly. He told her how you had to watch out for the fellow who was a great electrician, a good plumber, a couple of bright brickies, a class carpenter. Then all you needed was someone to get them together and you had your own team – someone who had a head for figures, someone who could cost a job and make the contacts.

'And who would you get to do that?' She was genuinely interested.

'God, Leo, that's what *I'm* going to do. That's what it's all about,' he said.

She felt ashamed that she hadn't the confidence in him.

'Did you know my father was in gaol?' he asked defensively.

'I heard. I think Biddy told me.'

'She would have.'

She was torn between being sympathetic and telling him it didn't matter.

'Did he hate it?' she asked.

'I don't know, he doesn't talk to me. He should have been there longer. He hit a fellow with a plank that had nails in it. He's dangerous.'

'You're not like that,' she said suddenly.

'I know, but I didn't want you to forget where I come from.'

'You are what you are, so am I.'

'And do you have any tales to tell me?' he asked.

'No. Why?' Her voice was clipped.

He shrugged. It was as if he had been offering her the chance to trade confessions.

But he didn't know they were not equal confessions. What his father had done was known the length and breadth of the county. What her mother had done was known by only three people.

He looked at her for a while, as if waiting.

Then he said, 'No reason, no reason at all.'

She saw him looking at her, with her belted raincoat, hands stuck deep in her pockets. The wind made her cheeks red. Her red-gold curls stood out around her head like a furze. She felt he was looking straight through her, that he could see everything, knew everything.

'I hate my hair,' she said suddenly.

'It's like a halo,' he said.

And she grinned.

Every Christmas he came home. He called to The Glen and she would take him walking. For the week that he was home they would meet every day.

Nessa Ryan was very disapproving. 'You *do* know his father was in gaol,' she told Leo.

'I do,' Leo sighed. She had heard it all from Biddy, over and over.

'I'd be surprised you'd go walking with him, then.'

'I know you would.' Leo had heard the same thing from her father. But that particular time she had answered back. 'Well, if everyone knew about us, Daddy, maybe people wouldn't want to go walking with us either.' Her father looked as if she had struck him. Immediately she had repented. 'I'm so sorry, I didn't mean it ... I just think that Foxy is lonely when he comes home. I don't ask him in here. I'm seventeen, nearly eighteen, Daddy. Why can't we let people alone? We, of all people?'

Her father had tears in his eyes. 'Go and walk with whoever you like in the woods,' he had said, his voice choked.

That was the Christmas when Foxy told her that he was on the way to the big time. He was working with two others. They were setting up their own contracts, they would hire men, get a team together. No more working for cheats and fellows who took all the profit.

'I'll soon have enough saved to come back a rich man,' he said. 'Then I'll drive up your avenue in a big car, hand my coat and gloves to Biddy, and ask your father for your hand in marriage. Your mother will take out the sherry and plan your wedding dress.'

'I'll never marry,' Leo told him.

'You sure as anything didn't take my advice about getting trained for a career or a job,' he said.

'I can't leave The Glen.'

'Will you tell me why?' His eyes still had that power to look as if they could see right through her, and know everything.

'I will, one day,' she promised, and she knew she would.

This year at least she had an address for Foxy. She wrote to him, he sent a very short note back.

'Why don't you learn to type, Leo? Your writing is worse than my own. We can't have that when we're in the big time, neither of us able to write a letter.'

She laughed.

She didn't tell Nessa Ryan that she had just got a sort of proposal from Foxy Dunne.

She didn't tell her parents.

Her mother died on an autumn night. They said it was of exposure. Her lungs filled up with the damp night air and, added to a chest infection ... There was no hope for a woman whose health had always been so frail.

She had been found in her nightdress, lying over the rockery in the garden.

The church was crowded. Major Murphy asked people to come back to Ryan's Hotel for a drink and some sandwiches afterwards. This was very unusual and had never been known in Shancarrig. But he said that The Glen was too sad for him and for Leo just now. He was sure people would understand.

Then Leo went to the town every day on the bus and learned to type in the big secretarial college where Nessa had done a course.

'Why couldn't you have done it with me?' Nessa grumbled.

'It wasn't the right time.'

There had been no note from Foxy Dunne about her mother's death.

She didn't write to tell him. Surely some member of his awful family was in touch, surely there would have been a mention that Mrs Murphy of The Glen had been found dead in her nightdress, and that her wits must have been astray. Everyone else knew about it.

When he came back at Christmas it was clear that he hadn't known. He was sympathetic and sad.

She asked him in, not to the breakfast room but the drawing room. Together they lit the fire.

The old dogs lay down, pleased that the room was being opened up.

Biddy was beyond complaining now. Too much had happened in this house. That Foxy Dunne be invited into the Major's drawing room seemed minor these days.

He told Leo of his plans. He had seen so much in England of how places could be developed. Take The Glen. They could sell off most of the land, build maybe eight houses, and still keep their own home.

'I expect your father would like that,' he said.

Outside they could see the sad lonely figure of Major Murphy walking up and down to the gate and back in the darkening evening.

'We can never sell the land,' Leo said.

'Is this part of what you told me you'd tell me one day?'

'Yes.'

'Are you ready to tell me now?'

'No. Not yet, Foxy.'

'Does your mother's death not make it different?' Again that feeling that he knew everything.

'No. You see, Daddy still lives here. Nothing could be ... interfered with.'

She thought of the big diggers, the excavators, the rockery going, as it would one day, when The Glen would disappear like so much of Ireland, and make way for houses for the Irish who were coming back to live in their own land, having worked hard in other countries.

People like Foxy coming back to their inheritances.

The body of Danny McDonagh which had lain so long under its mausoleum of flowers would be disturbed. The questions would be asked.

'We're over twenty-one. We can do what we like,' he said.

'I could always do what I liked, for all the good it did me.'

'So could I,' he answered her with spirit. 'And it did me a lot of good. I never wanted anyone else but you, not since we were children. What did you want?'

'I wanted to be safe,' she said.

He promised her that was exactly what he would do for her. They talked a little that night, and more the next day in Barna Woods. He left her at the gate of The Glen, and saw her look away from the gate house.

'Something happened here,' he said.

'I always knew you had second sight.'

'Tell me, Leo. We're not people to have secrets from each other.'

Through the window of The Glen they could see her father sitting at the drawing-room fire. He must have got the idea of sitting in that room after seeing them there yesterday. She told Foxy the story.

'Let's get the key,' he said.

She went through the kitchen and took it from the rack in the hall. Together, with candles, they walked through the gate lodge, a blameless place that didn't know what had happened there.

He raised her face towards him and looked into her eyes.

'Your hair is like a halo again. You're doing it to drive me mad,' he said.

'Don't you see all the problems, all the terrible problems?'

'I see nothing that won't be solved by a load of concrete on where that rockery stands now,' Foxy Dunne said.

A STONE
HOUSE AND
A BIG TREE

The decision to close the school was known in 1969; National Schools all over Ireland were giving way to Community Schools in the towns. But still it was a shock to see the building advertised for sale in the summer of 1970.

FOR SALE
Traditional stone schoolhouse. Built 1899. School accommodation comprises three large classrooms, toilet facilities and outer hall. Accompanying cottage: two bedrooms, one livingroom/kitchen with stanley range.
For sale by Public Auction June 24th if not disposed of by Private Treaty.
Auctioneers: O'Neill and Blake.

Nessa and Niall Hayes read it over breakfast.

From their dining room they could look over at Ryan's Shancarrig Hotel and see the early tour buses leaving on their excursions. Nessa worked flexible hours across the road in her family business. Neither of her sisters had shown any interest in hotel work.

'They will when they see there's money in it,' her mother had said darkly.

'Imagine the school for sale. We'd never have thought that possible.' Niall was thirty now. Nobody ever referred to him as young Mr Hayes any more, in fact his father took the back seat in almost every aspect of the business nowadays.

'What's not possible?' Danny Hayes was four, and very inquisitive. He loved long words and would pronounce them carefully.

'That you're not going to go to the same school we went to.' Nessa wiped his chin expertly of the runny bits of egg. 'You'll go on a big yellow bus to school. You won't walk over the bridge like we did.'

'Can I go today?' Danny asked.

'After Christmas,' Nessa promised.

'Won't he be a bit young?' Niall looked worried.

'If *your* mother had had her way you wouldn't have been allowed up the road to Shancarrig school until you were twenty.' There was a laugh in Nessa's voice, but also a tinge of bitterness.

It had not been quite as simple moving into The Terrace as she had thought it would be. Although her father-in-law had handed over the reins quite willingly to his son, Ethel Hayes had been less anxious to let go the gloomy rein over the family.

There were dire warnings of pneumonia, rheumatic fever, spoiled children, temper tantrums, all directed at Nessa. Danny and Brenda

281

would suffer for it all later, was Mrs Hayes's prediction – the children were allowed too much freedom, too little discipline, and a severe absence of cod liver oil.

'Would we buy it?' Nessa asked suddenly.

'What on earth for?' Niall was genuinely surprised.

'To live in. It would be a great place for the children to play ... the tree and everything. It would be lovely.'

'I don't know.' Niall bit his lip. It was his usual reaction to a new idea, to something totally unexpected.

Nessa knew him well enough.

'Well, let's not think about it now. It's a month to the auction,' she said.

Deftly she forced Danny to finish his egg and toast by cutting it into tiny cubes and eating one alternately with him. She settled Brenda into her carrycot. Niall was still sitting at his place pondering the bombshell.

'It's only an idea,' Nessa said airily. 'But if you're talking to Declan Blake at all, ask him how much he thinks they'll get for it.'

Niall looked out of the window, and saw Nessa moving into her parents' hotel. The carrycot was taken from her at the door by the porter. Danny had run to the hotel back yard where Nessa and her mother had built a sandpit, and swings and a see-saw to entertain the children who came to stay.

It had been yet one more excellent marketing notion for Ryan's Shancarrig Hotel.

Jim and Nora Kelly read it in Galway. They were staying with Maria and Hugh. They had wanted to be away when it was announced and by wonderful chance it coincided with the very time they were badly needed. Maria's first baby was due. She wanted her parents to be with her.

'It's the end of an era,' Maria said. 'There must be people all over Ireland saying that.'

'Not only Ireland – didn't our people go all over the world?' Jim Kelly said.

He was fifty years of age, and had been re-employed in the school in the town. It wasn't the same of course, nothing would ever be the same. But he knew a great number of the children, and he came trailing clouds of respect. A man who had run his own show, even in a small village, was a man to be reckoned with.

Nora had taken early retirement. And taken many a train to visit Maria over on the Atlantic coast. They walked along the beach together, the pregnant girl and the woman who was as good as her mother, with so much to say. Jim was pleased that his wife had taken the closing of the school so well. It might have been too much of a change for her to have gone to teach in the town.

Maria patted her stomach. 'It'll be so strange that she won't know the place as a school,' she said wonderingly.

'Or he. Remember, you could have a boy.' Jim Kelly knew that none of them minded whether it was a boy or girl.

They were so happy that Maria had found the steady Hugh after a series of wilder boyfriends had broken their hearts. Hugh seemed to know how much Maria needed her background in Shancarrig; he was always finding excuses to bring her there.

'Still, when the baby's born I'll wheel her ... or him, up to the school and say that this is where Grandpa or Grandma used to live, where every child lived for a while.' Maria looked sad. 'Oh, come on. I'm being stupidly sentimental,' she said with a little shake. 'And anyway, aren't you better off by far living in that fine house near everything, instead of having to toil up and down the hill?'

The Kellys had settled in one of the cottages that had been vastly changed and upgraded. The row of houses by the Grane that had once held the most unruly Brennans and Dunnes were now what young Declan Blake called Highly Des Res material.

'I wish there were going to be children there,' Nora Kelly said. 'I suppose it's unlikely that anyone who has children could afford to buy it, but somehow the place cries out for them. Or am I the one being sentimental now?'

'There'd be nobody local who could think of it.' Jim was ticking off people in his mind.

'Maybe when Hugh makes a fortune we'll buy it ourselves ... and let little Nora play under the copper beech like I did.'

There was a lump in their throats. It hadn't been said that Maria was going to call her child after Nora Kelly.

'I thought maybe Helen after your mother.' Nora felt she should say it anyway.

'The second one will be Helen!' said Maria.

And the matter was left there.

Chris Barton read the notice out to her mother-in-law. She always called Eddie's mother Una. It was yet another bond between them, the fact that she thought of the older woman as her sister.

'Well, Una. Is this our big chance?' Chris asked. 'Is this the famous opportunity that is meant to present itself to people? A ready-made craft centre ... get Foxy to build a few more outhouses that we could rent out as studios ... is this it or is it madness?'

'You're the one with the courage. I'd still be turning up hems for people and letting out their winter skirts if you hadn't come along.' Mrs Barton declared that she said an extra decade of the rosary every single night of her life to thank the Lord and His Mother for sending Chris to Shancarrig.

'I don't know, I really don't know. I'll ask Eddie. He has a great instinct for these things. We might be running before we can walk, or we might regret it all our lives. I trust his nose for this sort of thing.'

It was true. Mrs Barton realised that her daughter-in-law really did defer to Eddie's instincts and tastes. It wasn't a case of pretending to take his advice like Mrs Ryan in the hotel did, and indeed her daughter young Nessa who was busy pushing Niall Hayes into some kind of confidence. Chris genuinely thought Eddie the brains of the outfit. It made Una Barton's heart soar.

She thought less and less about the husband who had left her all those years ago – a quarter of a century – but sometimes she wished that Ted Barton could know how well his son had done and how splendidly they had managed without him.

Eddie came in holding the twins by the hand. He laughed as he saw his wife and mother automatically reach to protect everything on the table that was in danger of being pulled to the floor.

'Can we leave them with you, Una? I want to talk to Eddie in Barna Woods.'

'The last time you did that you proposed to me. I hope this doesn't mean you're going to leave.' He laughed confidently. He didn't think it was likely.

The children were strapped into their high chairs, and fussed over by their grandmother. Chris and Eddie walked as they so often walked together, shoulders touching, talking so that they finished each other's sentences, at ease with each other and the world. There was nobody in Shancarrig who noticed that Chris had a Scottish accent now, any more than they saw that she had a lame leg and a built-up shoe. She had been there since she was eighteen or nineteen. Part of the scenery.

They sat in the wood and she asked him about the centre. Was it exactly the right time? Or was this folly? Her eyes looked at him for an answer and she saw his face light up. He would never have thought of it, he said ... to him it would always have been the school, the place that he had gone, rain or shine, where he had played and studied. Of course it was the answer.

'Would we live there, or just work there?' Chris wondered.

'It would be great for the children.'

'We could sell the pink house.' Chris had always called it that, since the moment she had arrived.

'But my mother?'

'She said she'd leave it to us.'

'Where would she go? She's so used to being beside us ...' Mrs Barton lived in her own little wing of the pink house, beside them but not on top of them.

'She'd come with us, you big nellie. We'd be building a whole lot of places and she could choose the kind of place she'd like. It's no bigger a hill for her to climb than the one that she's been on all her life.'

Eddie's eyes were dancing. 'We could invite people in ... like the pottery couple, or the weavers ...'

'We could have a small shop there, selling everyone's work. Not only ours, but everyone's.'

'Nessa would get them up here from the hotel for a start, and Leo's got all sorts of contacts all over the place.'

'Will we do it?'

They embraced, as they had embraced in these woods years ago at the thought of being married and living happily ever after.

Richard saw the advertisement.

He wondered would whoever bought it cut down the tree in the yard. What would they make of the things that were written on it? He was prepared to bet that his wasn't the only carving that told a story.

He thought about the school all day in the office.

It was a tiring journey home, a lot of traffic. He was hot and tired. He hoped that Vera hadn't arranged anything for tonight. What he really would like to do was ... he paused. He didn't know what he would really like to do. It had been so long since he had allowed himself a thought like that.

He knew what he would really *not* like to do, and that would be to go to the club. Vera might have set up a little evening, a few drinks at the bar, dinner. He would know when he got in. If she had been to the hairdresser this is what she had planned.

He nosed the car into the garage beside Vera's.

Jimmy the gardener was edging the lawn. 'Good evening, Mr Hayes,' he said, touching his forehead.

'That looks great, Jimmy. Great work.' Richard knew his voice was automatic; he didn't see what the man had done or what needed to be done. He thought that a full-time gardener was a bit excessive in a Dublin garden.

Still, it was Vera's decision. It was after all she who had bought the house, and filled it with valuable things. It was Vera who made the day-to-day decisions about how they spent the money which was mainly her money.

She was sitting in the conservatory. He noticed sadly that she had been to the hairdresser.

'You look lovely,' he said.

'Thank you, darling. I thought we might meet some of the others at the club ... you know, rather than just sitting looking at each other all night?' She smiled.

She was very attractive in her lemon-coloured dress, her blonde upswept hair and her even suntan.

She did not look in her late thirties any more than he did. But unlike him she never seemed to find their life empty. She filled it with acquaintances, parties given, parties attended, a group of what she called like-minded people at the golf club.

Vera had taken their childlessness with what Richard considered a disturbing lack of concern. If the question was ever raised between themselves or when other people were present she always said the same thing. She said that if it happened it did, and if it didn't it didn't. No point in having all those exhaustive tests to discover whose *fault* it was, as if someone was to blame.

Since Richard knew from the past, only too well from his drama with Olive, that there could be nothing lacking on his side, he wished that Vera would go for an examination. But she refused.

She had the newspaper open in front of her.

'Look! There's a simply lovely place for sale, in that Shancarrig where you spent all those years.'

'I know. I saw it.'

'Should we buy it, do you think? It has tons of potential. It would make a nice weekend place, we could have people to stay. You know, it might be fun.'

'No.'

'What do you mean, *no*?'

'I mean NO, Vera,' he said.

Her face flushed. 'Well, I don't know what you're turning on *me* for, I only thought *you'd* like it. I do everything that I think you'd like. It's becoming impossible to please you.'

He moved over to reach for her but she stood up and pulled away.

'Seriously, Richard. Nobody could please you. There isn't a woman on earth that could hold you. Maybe you should never have married, just been a desirable bachelor all your life.' She was very hurt, he could see.

'Please. Please forgive me, I've had a horrible day. I'm tired, that's all. Please, I'm a pig.'

She was softening. 'Have a bath and a drink and we'll go out. You'll feel much better then.'

'Yes. Yes, of course. I'm sorry for snapping.' His voice was dead, he could hear it in his own ears.

'And you really don't think we should pick up this little house as a weekend place?'

'No, Vera. No, I wasn't happy there. It wouldn't make me happy to go back.'

'Right. It will never be mentioned again,' she said.

And he knew that she would look for somewhere else, a place where they could invite people for the weekend – fill their life with even more half strangers. Maybe she might even pick on whatever town Gloria had settled in. He knew the Darcys had left Shancarrig not long after he had.

Leo sat in the kitchen of The Glen making a very unsuccessful effort to comb Moore's hair. He had inherited the frizz from his mother and the colour from his father. He was six years old and in the last pageant that Shancarrig school had put on he had been asked to play The Burning Bush. This was apparently his own choice.

Foxy was delighted. Leo was less sure.

Moore Dunne was turning out to be a bigger handful than anyone could have believed. Foxy had insisted on the name. While he worked in England he said that he had discovered it was very classy to use one family name added to another. Leo's mother had been Miriam Moore, this had been the Moore household.

Moore's younger sister, Frances, was altogether more tractable. 'We'll liven her up yet,' Foxy had said ominously.

Unlike many of the builders who had returned from England in the prosperous sixties with their savings and their ideas of a quick killing, Foxy Dunne had decided to go the route of befriending rather than alienating architects.

The eight small houses he had built within the grounds of The Glen had a style and a character that was noticeably missing in such similar small developments in other towns. A huge row of semi-mature trees had been planted to give the new houses privacy, but also to maintain the long sweep of The Glen's avenue.

Major Murphy had lived to see his grandchildren but was buried now in the graveyard beside his wife.

From the big drawing room of The Glen Leo ran the ever-increasing building empire that Foxy had set up. All his cousins in the town now worked for him, the cousins who had once barred his father from crossing the doors of their shops. His cousins Brian and Liam waited on his every word and his uncle treated him with huge respect.

Foxy's father was not around to see the fruits of having totally ignored his son. Old Dinny had died in the county home some years previously. Foxy's own brothers, never men to have held down jobs for any notable length of time, most of them with some kind of prison record, were now regarded as remittance men. Small allowances were paid as long as they stayed far away from Shancarrig.

The main alterations that had put Ryan's Shancarrig Hotel on the map for tourism had been done by Foxy Dunne. It was he who had transformed the cottages by the River Grane, his only concession to any sentimentality or revenge having been his own personal presence as they levelled to the ground the house he grew up in.

The church hall, which was the pride of Father Gunn's life, was built by Foxy at such a reduced rate that it might even have been called his gift to the parish.

Foxy kept proper accounts. The books that Leo kept were regularly audited. The leases to the property he bought and sold were handled by his friend Niall Hayes. Maura came up from the gate lodge every day to do some of the housework and to mind the children. As always, her son Michael came with her. Michael was growing up big and strong but with the mind and loving heart of a small child.

288

Moore Dunne was particularly fond of him. 'He's much more interesting than other big people,' Moore pronounced.

Leo made sure she told that to Maura.

'I've always thought that myself,' Maura agreed.

Leo and Maura had a cup of tea together every morning before both went to their work – Leo to cope with Foxy's deals and Maura to polish and shine The Glen. Together they looked at the advertisement offering their old school for sale.

'Who would buy it, unless to set up another school?' Maura wondered.

'I'm very much afraid Foxy wants to,' said Leo. He hadn't said it yet, but she knew it was on his mind. It was as if he could never burn out the memory of the way things used to be. Not until he owned the whole town.

They heard the sound of his car outside the door. 'How's Squire Dunne?' he said to his son.

'I'm all *right*,' said Moore doubtfully.

'Only all *right*. You should be tip top,' Foxy said.

'Well yes, but I think there's another cat growing inside Flossie.' Moore was delighted.

'That's great,' said Foxy. 'It'll be a kitten, or maybe five kittens even.'

'But how are they going to get out?' Moore was puzzled. Maura giggled.

'That's your mother's department,' said Foxy, heading for the office. 'I have to think of other things like planning permissions, son.'

'For the school?' Leo asked.

'Aha, you're there before me,' he said.

She looked at him, small and quick, eager as ever, nowadays dressed in clothes that were made to measure, but still the endearing Foxy of their childhood. She followed him into the room that was once their drawing room, where her father had paced, and her mother had sat distracted, and Lance and Jessie had slept uncaring by the fire.

'Do we need it, Foxy?' she asked.

'What's need?' He put his arms around her shoulders and looked into her eyes.

'Haven't we enough?' she said.

'Love, it's a gold mine. It's *made* for us. The right kind of cottages, classy stuff, the kind rich Dubliners might even have as a summer place, or for visiting at the weekends. Do them up really well, let Chris

289

and Eddie loose on them. Slate floors ... you know the kind of thing.'
He looked so eager. He would love the challenge.

Perhaps he was right, it *was* made for them. Why did she keep
thinking he was doing everything just to show? To show some anonymous invisible people who didn't care.

Maddy Ross thought it was wonderful that God moved so mysteriously. Look at how he had closed the school just at exactly the
right time for Maddy.

Now she could be quite free to spend all her time with the Family.
The wonderful Family of Hope. Madeleine Ross had been a member
of the Family of Hope for three years. And it had not been easy.

For one thing there had been all that adverse publicity in the papers
about the castle they had been given, and the misunderstanding over
the deeds.

There had been no intention at all to defraud or deceive, but the
way the papers wrote it all up you'd think that the Family of Hope
was some kind of international confidence tricksters' organisation.

And there had been the whole attitude of Father Gunn. Maddy had
never really liked Father Gunn, not since that time long ago when he
had been so patronising and so judgemental about her friendship with
Father Barry. If Father Gunn had been more understanding or open
and liberal about the place of Love in God's scheme of things then a
lot of events would have worked out differently.

Still, that was water under the bridge. The big problem was Father
Gunn's attitude today.

He had said that the Family of Hope was not a wonderful way of
doing God's work on earth, that it was a dangerous cult, that it was
brainwashing people like Maddy, that God wanted love and honour
to be shown to him through the conventional channels of the church.

It was just exactly what you would have expected him to say. It was
what people had said to Our Lord when he went to the temple to
drive out the scribes and the Pharisees. They had said to him that this
wasn't the way. They had been wrong, just as Father Gunn was wrong.
But it didn't matter. Father Gunn couldn't rule her life for her. It was
1970 now, it wasn't the bad old days when poor Father Barry could
be sent away before he knew his mind to a missionary place where
they weren't ready for him.

And Father Gunn didn't know about the insurance policy that
Mother had left her. The money she had been going to give to the

people of Vieja Piedra before they had been abandoned and the work stopped in midstream.

Maddy Ross still walked by herself in Barna Woods and hugged herself thinking of the money she could give to the Family of Hope.

They wanted to buy a place to be their centre.

She had wondered for a long time if there might be anywhere near here. She wanted to live on in Mother's house and near the woods and river that were so dear to her, and held so many memories. And now at last she had found the very place.

The schoolhouse was for sale.

Maura showed the picture of the school to Michael that evening in their little home – the gate lodge of The Glen.

'Do you know where it is, Michael?' she asked.

He held it in both his hands. 'Is my school,' he said.

'That's right, Michael. It's your school,' she said and she stroked his head.

Michael had never attended a lesson inside the school, but he had gone sometimes to play with the children in the yard. Maura had often stood, lump in throat, watching him pick up the beech leaves as she had done before him, and all his uncles and aunts – the Brennans who had gone away.

'We might walk up there tonight, Michael, and have a look at it again. Would you like that?'

'Will we have tea early so?' He looked at her anxiously.

'We'll have tea early so,' she agreed.

He got his own plate and mug, made of Bakelite that wouldn't crack. Michael dropped things sometimes. His mother's china he never touched. Some of it was in a little cabinet that hung on the wall, other pieces were wrapped in tissue paper.

Maura O'Sullivan went to local auctions, always buying bargains in bone china. She never had a full set, or even a half set, but it didn't matter since she didn't ever invite anyone to dine. It was all for her.

They walked past the pink house and waved to the Bartons.

'Can I go in and play with the twins?' Michael said.

'Aren't we going to look at your old school?' They crossed the bridge where the children called out a greeting to Michael, as they had done for many years. And would always do. As long as Maura was there to look after him. Suppose Maura weren't there?

She gave a little shudder.

At the school she saw Dr Jims and his son Declan. The *For Sale* sign was there in the sunset. It would look big in other places; under the copper beech it looked tiny.

'Good evening, Doctor.' She was formal.

'Hello, Declan ...' Michael embraced the doctor's son, whom he had known since he was a boy in his pram.

'Changing times,' Dr Jims said. 'Lord, I never thought I'd see this day.'

'Don't be denying me my bit of business, Dad ...' Declan laughed.

They got on so well these days, Maura realised. It must have been that nice girl Ruth that Declan had married. Some people had great luck altogether out of their marriages. But hadn't she got as much love and happiness as anyone had ever got in the whole world?

Michael was looking at the names on the tree. 'Is my name there, Mammy?' he asked.

'If it's not it should be,' Dr Jims said. 'Weren't you here as much as any child in Shancarrig?'

'I'll write it if you like,' Declan offered.

'What will you put?'

'Let's see. I'll put it near my initials. There, see DB 1961? That's me.'

'You've no heart drawn,' Michael complained.

'I didn't love anyone then,' Declan said. His voice seemed full of emotion. The two of them had made a great production of getting out Declan's penknife and choosing a spot.

Dr Jims said to Maura, 'Are you feeling all right? You're a bit pale.'

'You know me, I worry about things. Nothing maybe ...'

'It's a while since you've been to see me.'

'No, Doctor. Not my health, the future.'

'Ah. There's divil a thing you can do about the future.' Jims Blake smiled at her.

'It's like ... I wonder sometimes in case something happened to me, what would happen ... you know,' Maura looked over at Michael.

'Child, you're not thirty years of age!'

'I am that. Last week.'

'Maura, all I can say is that every mother in Ireland worries about her child. It's both a wonder and a waste. Life goes on.'

'For ordinary people, yes.'

Michael gave a cry of pleasure, and came to tug at her.

'Look at what he's written. Look, Mammy.'

Declan Blake had drawn a heart, and on one side he had *M O'S*. On the other he said he was going to put *All his friends in Shancarrig*.

'See what I mean?' said Dr Jims.

Maddy Ross invited Sister Judith of the Family of Hope to come and see the schoolhouse. Sister Judith said it was perfect. She asked how much would it cost. Maddy said she had heard in the area of five thousand pounds. With her mother's insurance policy, Maddy explained, there would be that and plenty more. She would get the deeds drawn up with a solicitor. Not with Niall Hayes. After all, she had taught Niall Hayes at school; it wouldn't be appropriate.

Maria's child was born in Galway. It was a girl. She was to be called Nora. Nora Kelly telephoned Una Barton with the good news. The old habits die hard and they still addressed each other formally.

'Mrs Kelly, I'm so *very* pleased. I'll make the baby a little dress with smocking on it,' she said.

'Maria'll bring her back to Shancarrig on a triumphal tour, and you'll be the first port of call, Mrs Barton,' she cried. The Kellys inquired about the school and was there any word about buyers.

Mrs Barton paused. She didn't know whether the children wanted it known or not. Still, she couldn't lie to a woman like Mrs Kelly.

'Between ourselves, Eddie and Chris are trying to get the money together, with grants and everything. They hope to turn it into an arts centre.' There was a silence. 'Aren't you pleased to hear that?'

'Yes, yes. It's just I suppose we were hoping there would be children there.'

'But there will. They're going to live there with the twins, and me as well. That's the hope, Mrs Kelly, but it may come to nothing.'

'That would be great, Mrs Barton. I'll say a prayer to St Anne for you. I'd love to think of your grandchildren and mine playing under that tree.'

The Dixons were just driving through when they saw the schoolhouse. They were enchanted by it, and called in to Niall Hayes to inquire more about it.

They found him singularly unhelpful.

'There's an auctioneer's name and telephone number on the sign,' he said brusquely.

'But seeing that you are the local solicitor we thought you'd know, might shortcut it a bit.' The Dixons were wealthy Dublin people looking for a weekend home; they were used to shortcutting things a bit.

'There could be a conflict of interests,' Niall Hayes said.

'If you want to buy it then why is the board still up?' asked Mr Dixon.

'Good afternoon,' Niall Hayes said.

'Terrifying, these country bumpkins,' said Mrs Dixon, well within his hearing.

'We've never fought about anything, Foxy, have we?' Leo said to him in bed.

'What do you mean? Our life is one long fight!' he said.

'I don't want us to buy the school.'

'Give me one good reason.'

'We don't need it, Foxy. Truly we don't. It'd be a hassle.'

He stroked her face, but she got up and sat on the edge of the bed.

'Things are always a hassle, love. That's the fun. That's what it was always about. *You* know that.'

'No. This time it's different. Lots of others want it too.'

'So? We *get* it.'

'No, not just rivals, real people. Chris and Eddie, Nessa and Niall, Miss Ross, and I think Maura has hopes of it.'

'Miss Ross!' He laughed and rolled around the bed. 'Miss Ross is away with the fairies. It would be a *kindness* not to let her have it.'

'But the others! I'm serious.'

'Look. Niall and Nessa are business people, they know about deals. That's what Niall does all day. Same with Chris and Eddie, they'd understand. Some things you go for, some you get.'

Leo began to pace around the room. She reminded herself of her parents. They had paced in this house too.

She shivered at the thought. He was out of bed, concerned. He put a dressing-gown around her shoulders.

'I told you. Give me one good reason, one *real* reason, and I'll stop.'

'Maura.'

'Aw, come on, Leo, give me a break! Maura hasn't a penny. We practically *gave* her the gate lodge. Where would she get the money? What would she want it for?'

'I don't know, but she has Michael up there every evening, the two of them staring at it. She wants it for something.'

*

294

'Nessa, come in to me a moment, will you?'

'Why do I always feel like a child, instead of the best help you ever had in this hotel, when you use that tone of voice?' Nessa laughed at her mother.

Brenda Ryan poured them a glass of sherry each, always a sign of something significant.

'Has Daddy gone on the tear?'

'No, cynical child.' They sat companionably. Nessa waited. She knew her mother had something to say.

She was right. Her mother said she was going to give her one piece of advice and then withdraw and let Nessa think about it. She had heard that Nessa and Niall were thinking of buying the schoolhouse as a place to live. Now, there was no way she was going to say how she had heard, nor any need for Nessa to bridle and say it was her own business. But all Breda Ryan wanted to put on the table, for what it was worth, was the following:

It would be an act of singular folly to leave The Terrace, to abandon that beautiful house just because old Ethel was a lighting devil and Nessa didn't feel mistress of her own home. The solution was a simple matter of relocation, banishing both parents to the basement.

But not, of course, describing it as that. Describing it in fact as Foxy Dunne and his architect having come up with this amazing idea about making a self-contained flat for the older folk.

Nessa fidgeted as she listened.

'It's only a matter of time,' her mother told her. 'Suppose you went up to the schoolhouse and his parents were dead next year, think how cross you'd be. Losing the high ground like that. Keep the place, don't let them divide it up with his sisters. It's the best house in the town.'

'I wonder are you right.' Nessa spoke thoughtfully, as to an equal.

'I'm right,' said her mother.

Eddie came back from his travels. He had found enough people to make the whole centre work. Exactly the kind of people they had always wanted to work with, some of whom had known their work too. It was flattering how well Chris and Eddie Barton were becoming known in Ireland.

The next thing was to visit the bank manager.

And the projections.

Eddie had asked the potential tenants to write their stories so that he and Chris could work out the costings. He also asked them to tell what had been successful or unsatisfactory in the previous places they had been.

He and Chris together read their reports.

They read of places where no visitors came because it wasn't near enough to the town, places that the tour buses passed by because there was no time on the itinerary. They learned that it was best to be part of a community, not outside it. They sat together and realised that in many ways the schoolhouse was not the dream location they had thought.

'That's if we take notice of them,' Chris said.

'We *have* to take notice of them. That's our research.' Eddie's face was sad.

'Aren't we better to know now than after?' Chris said. 'Though it's awful to see a dream go up like that.'

'What do you mean a dream go up like that? Haven't we our eye on Nellie Dunne's place after her time? That place is like a warren at the back.'

She saw Eddie smile again and that pleased her. 'Come on, let's tell Una.' She leapt up and went to Eddie's mother's quarters.

'I don't mind *where* I am as long as I'm with the pair of you,' said Mrs Barton. She also told them that she heard that both Foxy Dunne *and* Niall Hayes were said to have their eye on the school.

'Then we're better off not alienating good friends who happen to be good customers as well,' said Chris. The two women laughed happily, like conspirators.

Father Gunn twisted and turned in his narrow bed. In his mind he was trying to write the letter to the Bishop, the letter that would get him a ruling about the Family of Hope. It now seemed definite that Madeleine Ross had given these sinister people the money to set up a centre in Shancarrig schoolhouse. They would be here in the midst of his parish, taking away his flock, preaching to them, in long robes, by the river.

Please let the Bishop know what to do.

Why had he made all those moves years ago to prevent a scandal? Wouldn't God and the parish have been far better served if that half-cracked Father Brian Barry and that entirely cracked Maddy Ross had been encouraged to run away with each other? None of this desperate mess about the Family of Bloody Hope would ever have happened.

Terry and Nancy Dixon called in on Vera and Richard Hayes's house on their way back home after their ramble.

'We saw the most perfect schoolhouse. I think we should buy it together,' Terry said. 'It's in that place you worked for a while, Shancarrig.'

'We saw it advertised,' Vera said, glancing at Richard.

'And?' The Dixons looked from one to the other. Richard's eyes were far away.

'Richard said he wasn't happy in Shancarrig.' Vera spoke for him.

'I'm not surprised,' said Nancy Dixon. 'But you wouldn't have to mix all that much. It would be just the perfect place to get away from it all. There's a really marvellous tree.'

'A copper beech,' Richard said.

'Yes, that's right. It should go for a song. We talked to the solicitor but he wasn't very forthcoming.'

'That's my uncle,' Richard said.

The Dixons looked embarrassed. They said it was a younger man, must have been his son. Not someone who was going to set the world on fire? they ventured.

Richard wasn't responding. 'They all wrote their names on that tree,' he said.

'Aha! Perhaps you wrote *your* name on the tree, that's why we can't go back there.' Vera was coquettish.

'No. I never wrote my name there,' Richard said. His eyes were still very far away.

'Is there much interest from Dublin?' Dr Jims asked his son.

'No, I thought there'd be more. Maybe if we advertised it again.'

The two men walked regularly together in Shancarrig. Declan and Ruth were having a house built there now. They didn't want the place in The Terrace. They wanted somewhere with more space, space for rabbits and a donkey, for the children they would have. Ruth was pregnant. They also felt that it was time to have a sub-office of O'Neill and Blake Estate Agents in Shancarrig. Many of the visitors who came to Ryan's Shancarrig Hotel now wanted to buy sites. Foxy Dunne was only too ready to build on them.

'What will it go for?' Dr Jims had the school on his mind a lot.

'We've had an offer of five. You know that.' Declan Blake jerked his head across at Maddy Ross's cottage.

'We don't want them, Declan.'

'I can't play God, Dad. I have to get the best price for my client.'

'Your client is only the old Department of Education, son. They're being done left, right and centre, or making killings all over the place. They don't count.'

'You're honourable in your trade. I have to be in mine.'

'I'm also human in mine.' There was a silence.

If either of them was remembering how Dr Jims had bent the rules to help his son all those years ago neither of them said it.

'Perhaps they'll get outbidden.' Declan didn't seem very hopeful.

'Has Niall Hayes dropped out?'

'Yes. And Foxy Dunne – that's a relief in a way. And so has Eddie. I wouldn't want them raising the price on each other.'

'There. You do have a heart.' Dr Jims seemed pleased.

'And nobody else?'

'Nobody serious.'

'Who knows what's serious?'

'All right, Dad. Maura. Michael's mother. She says that she wants the place to be a home, a home for children like Michael, with someone to run it. And she'd help in it too. People like Michael who have no mothers ... that's what she wants.'

'Well, isn't that what we'd all want?' said Dr Jims. 'And if we want it, it can be done.'

Nobody ever knew what negotiation went on behind the scenes, how the Family of Hope were persuaded that it would be very damaging publicity to cross swords with a community which wanted to provide a home for Down's syndrome children – and had raised the money for it. Maddy Ross was heard to say that she was just as glad that Sister Judith hadn't been forced to meet the collective ignorance, superstition and bigotry of Shancarrig.

Foxy and Leo had provided a sister for Moore and Frances – Chris and Eddie a brother for the twins – Nessa and Niall a brother for Danny and Breda – Mr and Mrs Hayes had decided of their own volition to move downstairs to the basement of The Terrace and had their own front door by which they came and went – Declan and Ruth Blake had built their house and called their son James – the Kellys' granddaughter Nora was walking – when the Shancarrig Home was opened.

There were photographs of it in all the papers and nice little pieces describing it.

But it was hard to do it justice, because all anyone could see was a stone house and a big tree.

A Week in Winter

For dear generous Gordon
who makes life great every single day.

Chicky

Everyone had their own job to do on the Ryans' farm in Stoneybridge. The boys helped their father in the fields, mending fences, bringing the cows back to be milked, digging drills of potatoes; Mary fed the calves, Kathleen baked the bread and Geraldine did the hens.

Not that they ever called her Geraldine, she was *Chicky* as far back as anyone could remember. A serious little girl pouring out meal for the baby chickens or collecting the fresh eggs each day, always saying 'chuck, chuck, chuck' soothingly into the feathers as she worked. Chicky had names for all the hens, and no one could tell her when one had been taken to provide a Sunday lunch. They always pretended it was a Shop Chicken, but Chicky always knew.

Stoneybridge was a West of Ireland paradise for children during the summer, but the summer was short and most of the time it was wet and wild and lonely on the Atlantic coast. Still, there were caves to explore, cliffs to climb, birds' nests to discover and wild sheep with great curly horns to investigate. And then there was Stone House. Chicky loved to play in the huge overgrown garden. Sometimes the Miss Sheedys, three sisters who owned the house, and were ancient, let her play at dressing up in their old clothes.

Chicky watched as Kathleen went off to train to be a nurse in a big hospital in Wales, and then Mary got a job in an insurance office. Neither of those jobs appealed to Chicky at all, but she would have to do something. The land wouldn't support the whole Ryan family. Two of the boys had gone to serve their time in business in big towns in the West. Only Brian would work with his father.

Chicky's mother was always tired and her father always worried. They were relieved when Chicky got a job in the knitting factory. Not as a machinist or home knitter but in the office. She was in charge of sending out the finished garments to customers and keeping the books. It wasn't a *great* job but it did mean that she could stay at home, which was what she wanted. She had plenty of friends around the place, and each summer she fell in love with a different O'Hara boy but nothing ever came of it.

Then one day Walter Starr, a young American, wandered into the knitting factory wanting to buy an Aran sweater. Chicky was instructed to explain to him that it was not a retail outlet, they only made up sweaters for stores or mail order.

'Well you're missing a trick then,' Walter Starr said. 'People come to this wild place and they *need* an Aran sweater, and they need it now, not in a few weeks' time.'

He was very handsome. He reminded her of how Jack and Bobby Kennedy had looked when they were boys, same flashing smile and good teeth. He was suntanned and very different to the boys from round Stoneybridge. She didn't want him to leave the knitting factory and he didn't seem to want to go either.

Chicky remembered a sweater they had in stock which they

2

had used to be photographed. Perhaps Walter Starr might like to buy that one – it wasn't exactly new but it was nearly new.

He said it would be perfect.

He invited her to go for a walk on the beach and he told her this was one of the most beautiful places on earth.

Imagine! He had been to California *and* Italy and yet he thought Stoneybridge was beautiful.

And he thought Chicky was beautiful too. He said she was just so cute with her dark curly hair and her big blue eyes. They spent every possible moment together. He had only intended to stay a day or two but now he found it hard to go on anywhere else. Unless she would come with him, of course.

Chicky laughed out loud at the idea that she should pack in her job at the knitting factory and tell her mother and father that she was going around Ireland hitchhiking with an American that she had just met! It would have been more acceptable to suggest flying to the moon.

Walter found her horror at the idea touching and almost endearing.

'We only have one life, Chicky. *They* can't live it for us. We have to live it ourselves. Do you think *my* parents want me out here in the wilds of nowhere, having a good time? No, they want me in the Country Club playing tennis with the daughters of nice families, but hey, this is where I want to be. It's as simple as that.'

Walter Starr lived in a world where everything was simple. They loved each other, so what was more natural than to make love? They each knew the other was right so why complicate it by what other people would say or think or do? A kindly God understood love. Father Johnson, who had taken a vow never to fall in love, didn't. They didn't need any stupid contracts or certificates, did they?

And after six glorious weeks, when Walter had to think of going back to the States, Chicky was ready to go with him. It involved an immense amount of rows and dramas and enormous upset in the Ryan household. But Walter was unaware of any of this.

Chicky's father was more worried than ever now because everyone would say that he had brought up a tramp who was no better than she should be.

Chicky's mother looked more tired and disappointed than ever, and said only God and his sainted mother knew what she had done wrong in bringing Chicky up to be such a scourge to them all.

Kathleen said that it was just as well she had an engagement ring on her finger because no man would have her if he knew the kind of family she came from.

Mary, who worked in the insurance office and was walking out with one of the O'Haras, said that the days of *her* romance were now numbered, thanks to Chicky. The O'Haras were a very respectable family in the town and they wouldn't think kindly about all this behaviour at all.

Her brother Brian kept his head down and said nothing at all. When Chicky asked him what he thought, Brian said he didn't think. He didn't have time to think.

Chicky's friends, Peggy, who also worked in the knitting factory, and Nuala, who was a maid for the three Miss Sheedys, said it was the most exciting, reckless thing they had ever heard of, and wasn't it great that she had a passport already from that school trip to Lourdes.

Walter Starr said they would stay in New York with friends of his. He was going to drop out of law school, it wasn't really right for him. If we had several lives, well then, yes, maybe,

4

but since we only have one life it wasn't worth spending it studying law.

The night before she left, Chicky tried to make her parents understand this. She was twenty, she had her whole life to live, she wanted to love her family and for them to love her in spite of their disappointment.

Her father's face was tight and hard. She would never be welcome in this house again, she had brought shame on them all.

Her mother was bitter. She said that Chicky was being very, very foolish. It wouldn't last, it couldn't last. It was not love, it was infatuation. If this Walter really loved her then he would wait for her and provide her with a home and his name and a future instead of all this nonsense.

You could cut the atmosphere in the Ryan household with a knife.

Chicky's sisters were no support. But she was adamant. *They* hadn't known real love. She was not going to change her plans. She had her passport. She was going to go to America.

'Wish me well,' she had begged them the night before she left, but they had turned their faces away.

'Don't let me go away with the memory of you being so cold.' Chicky had tears running down her face.

Her mother sighed a great sigh. 'It would be cold if we just said, "Go ahead, enjoy yourself". We are trying to do our best for you. To help you make the best of your life. This is not love, it's only some sort of infatuation. You can't have our blessing. It's just not there for you. There's no use pretending.'

So Chicky left without it.

At Shannon airport there were crowds waving goodbye to their children setting out for a new life in the United States.

5

There was nobody to wave Chicky goodbye, but she and Walter didn't care. They had their whole life ahead of them.

No rules, no doing the right thing to please the neighbours and relations.

They would be free – free to work where they wanted and at what they wanted.

No trying to fulfil other people's hopes – marry a rich farmer in Chicky's case, or become a top lawyer, which was what Walter's family had in mind for him.

Walter's friends were welcoming in the big apartment in Brooklyn. Young people, friendly and easy-going. Some worked in bookshops, some in bars. Others were musicians. They came and went easily. Nobody made any fuss. It was so very different to home. A couple came in from the coast, and a girl from Chicago who wrote poetry. There was a Mexican boy who played the guitar in Latino bars.

Everyone was so relaxed. Chicky found it amazing. Nobody made any demands. They would make a big chilli for supper with everyone helping. There was no pressure.

They sighed a bit about their families not understanding anything but it didn't weigh heavily on anyone. Soon Chicky felt Stoneybridge fade away a little. However, she wrote a letter home every week. She had decided from the outset that *she* would not be the one to keep a feud going.

If one side behaved normally then sooner or later the other side would have to respond and behave normally as well.

She did hear from some of her friends, and had the odd bit of news from them. Peggy and Nuala wrote and told her about life back home; it didn't seem to have changed much in any way at all. So she was able to write to say she was delighted about the plans for Kathleen's wedding to Mikey, and did not mention that she had heard about Mary's romance with Sonny O'Hara having ended.

Her mother wrote brisk little cards, asking whether she had fixed a date for her wedding yet and wondering about whether there were Irish priests in the parish.

She told them nothing about the communal life she lived in the big, crowded apartment, with all the coming and going and guitar playing. They would never have been able to begin to understand.

Instead she wrote about going to art exhibit openings and theatre first nights. She read about these in the papers and sometimes indeed they went to matinees or got cheap seats at previews through friends of friends who wanted to fill a house.

Walter had a job helping to catalogue a library for some old friends of his parents. His family had hoped to woo him back this way to some form of academic life, he said, and it wasn't a bad job. They left him alone and didn't give him any hassle. That's all anyone wanted in life.

Chicky learned that this was definitely all Walter wanted in life. So she didn't nag him about when she would meet his parents, or when they would find a place of their own, or indeed what they would do down the line. They were together in New York. That was enough, wasn't it?

And in many ways it was.

Chicky got herself a job in a diner. The hours suited her. She could get up very early, leave the apartment before anyone else was awake. She helped them open up, did her shift and served breakfasts and was back before the others had struggled into the day. Chicky would bring cold milk and bagels left over from the diner's breakfast stock. They got used to her bringing them supplies.

She still heard news from home but it became more and more remote.

Kathleen's wedding to Mikey, and the news that she was pregnant; Mary walking out with JP, a farmer they used to laugh at not long ago as a sad old man. Now it was a serious romance. Brian getting involved with one of the O'Haras, which Chicky's family thought was great but which the O'Haras were a lot less excited about. How Father Johnson had preached a sermon saying that Our Lady wept every time the Irish Divorce referendum was mentioned, and some of the parishioners had protested and said he had gone too far.

Stoneybridge was, after a few short months, becoming a totally unreal world.

As was the life they lived in the apartment, with more people arriving and leaving, and tales of friends who had gone to live in Greece or Italy, and others who played music all night in cellars in Chicago. Reality was, for Chicky, this whole fantasy world that she had invented of a busy, bustling, successful Manhattan lifestyle.

Nobody from Stoneybridge ever came to New York – there was no danger of anyone looking her up or exposing the lies and the pathetic deception. She just couldn't tell them the truth; that Walter had given up the cataloguing of the library. It was so boring because the old couple kept saying he should go home for a weekend and see his parents.

Chicky couldn't see much wrong with that as a plan, but it seemed to spell aggravation for Walter so she nodded sympathetically as he left the job and she took extra hours in the diner to cover their costs in the apartment.

He was so restless these days; the smallest things upset him. He liked her to be always a cheerful, loving Chicky. So that's what she was. Inside, she was tired and anxious Chicky, too, but not showing any of it.

She wrote home week after week and believed in the fairy tale more and more. She started to fill a spiral notebook with details of the life she was meant to be living. She didn't want to slip up on anything.

To console herself, she wrote to them about the wedding. She and Walter had been married in a quiet civil ceremony, she explained. They had a blessing from a Franciscan priest. It had been a wonderful occasion for them and they knew that both families were delighted that they had made this commitment. Chicky said that Walter's parents had been abroad at the time and not able to attend the ceremony but that everyone was very happy about it. \

In many ways, she managed to believe this was true. It was easier than believing that Walter was becoming restless and was going to move on.

When the end came for Walter and Chicky it came swiftly, and it seemed to everyone else inevitable. Walter told her gently that it had been great but it was over.

There was another opportunity, yet another friend with a bar where Walter might work. A new scene. A new beginning. A new city. He would be off at the end of the week.

It took ages for it to sink in.

At first she thought it was a joke. Or a test of some sort. There was a hollow, unreal feeling in her chest like a big cavity that was getting even bigger.

It could *not* be over. Not what they had. She begged and pleaded; whatever she was doing wrong she would change it.

Endlessly patient, he had assured her that it was nobody's fault. This is what happened – love bloomed, love died. It was

9

sad, of course, these things always were. But they would stay friends and look back on this time together as a fond memory.

There was nothing she could do except go home, back to Stoneybridge to walk along the wild shores where they had walked together and where they had fallen in love.

But Chicky would never go back.

That was the one thing she knew, the one solid fact in a quicksand world which was changing all around her. She could not stay on in the apartment even though the others were hoping that she would. Outside this life, she had made very few friends. She was too closed; she had no stories, no views to bring to a friendship. What she needed was the company of people who asked no questions and made no assumptions.

What Chicky also needed was a job.

She couldn't stay on at the diner. They would have been happy to keep her, but once Walter was gone she didn't want to be around the neighbourhood any more.

It didn't matter what she did. She didn't really care. She just had to earn a living, something to keep her until she got her head straight.

Chicky could not sleep when Walter left.

She tried, but sleep would not come. So she sat upright in a chair in the room she had shared with Walter Starr for those five glorious months – and those three restless months.

He said it was the longest time he had ever stayed any-where. He said he hadn't wanted to hurt her. He had begged her to go back to Ireland where he had found her.

She just smiled at him through her tears.

It took her four days to find a place to live and work. One

of the workmen on the building next to the diner had a fall and was brought in to the diner to recover.

'I'm not bad enough to go to hospital,' he pleaded. 'Can you call Mrs Cassidy, she'll know what to do.'

'Who is Mrs Cassidy?' Chicky had asked the man with the Irish accent and the fear of losing a day's work.

'She runs Select Accommodation,' he said. 'She's a good person, she keeps herself to herself, she's the one to contact.'

He had been right. Mrs Cassidy took over.

She was a small, busy person with sharp eyes and her hair drawn into a severe knot behind her head. She was someone who wasted no time.

Chicky looked at her with admiration.

Mrs Cassidy arranged for the injured man to be driven back to her guest house. She said she had a next-door neighbour who was a nurse, and if his condition worsened she would get him to hospital.

Next day Chicky called to Cassidy's Select Accommodation.

First she enquired about the workman who had been injured and brought to the diner. Then she asked for a job.

'Why did you come to me?' Mrs Cassidy had asked.

'They say you keep yourself to yourself, you don't go blabbing around.'

'Too busy for that,' Mrs Cassidy had admitted.

'I could clean. I'm strong and I don't get tired.'

'How old are you?' Mrs Cassidy asked.

'I'll be twenty-one tomorrow.'

Years of watching people and saying little had made Mrs Cassidy very decisive.

'Happy Birthday,' she said. 'Get your things and move in today.'

It didn't take long to collect her things, just a small bag to pick up from the big, sprawling apartment where she had lived as Walter Starr's girl with a group of restless young people for those happy months before the circus left town without her.

And so began Chicky's new life. A small, almost monastic bedroom at the top of the boarding house, up in the morning to clean the brasses, scrub the steps and get the breakfast going.

Mrs Cassidy had eight lodgers, all of them Irish. These were not people who had cereal and fruit to start the day. Men who worked in construction or on the subway, men who needed a good bacon and egg to see them through until the lunchtime ham sandwich that Chicky made and wrapped in waxed paper and handed over before they left for work.

Then there were beds to make, windows to polish, the sitting room to clean, and Chicky went shopping with Mrs Cassidy. She learned how to make cheap cuts of meat taste good by marinating them, she knew how to make the simplest of meals look festive. There was always a vase of flowers or a potted plant on the table.

Mrs Cassidy always dressed nicely when she served supper, and somehow the men had followed suit. They all washed and changed their shirts before sitting down at her table. If you expected good manners, you got good manners in return.

Chicky always called her Mrs Cassidy. She didn't know her first name, her life story, whatever had happened to Mr Cassidy, even if there had ever *been* a Mr Cassidy.

And in return, no questions were asked of Chicky.

It was a very restful relationship.

Mrs Cassidy had stressed the importance of getting Chicky her green card, and registering to vote in the city council to make sure that the necessary number of Irish officials got returned to power. She explained how you got a post-office box number so that you could mail without anyone knowing where you lived, or anything about your business.

She had given up trying to persuade the girl to get a social life. She was a young woman in the most exciting city in the world. There were huge opportunities. But Chicky was very definite. She wanted none of it. No pub scene, no Irish clubs, no tales of what a good husband this lodger or that lodger might make. Mrs Cassidy got the message.

She did, however, point Chicky towards adult education classes and training courses. Chicky learned to be a spectacular patisserie chef. She showed no interest in leaving Mrs Cassidy's Select Accommodation, even though a local bakery had offered her full-time work.

Chicky's expenses were few; her savings increased. When she wasn't working with Mrs Cassidy, there were so many other jobs. Chicky cooked for christenings, First Communions, bar mitzvahs and retirement parties.

Each night, she and Mrs Cassidy presided over their table of Select Lodgers.

She still knew nothing about Mrs Cassidy's life history, and had never been asked any details about her own. So it was surprising when Mrs Cassidy said that she thought Chicky should go back to Stoneybridge for a visit.

'Go now, otherwise you'll leave it too late. Then going back would be a big deal. If you go this year just for a flying visit then it makes it much easier.'

And in fact, it was so much easier than she had thought.

She wrote and told them in Stoneybridge that Walter had to go for a week to LA on business, and that he had suggested she use the time to come to Ireland. She would just love to come back home for a short visit and she hoped that would be all right with everyone.

It had been five years since the day her father had said she would never come back into his house again. Everything had changed.

Her father was now a different man. Several heart scares had made him realise that he did not rule the world, or even his own part in it.

Her mother was not as fearful of what people thought as she once had been.

Her sister Kathleen, now the wife of Mikey and the mother of Orla and Rory, had forgotten her harsh words about disgracing the family.

Mary, now married to JP, the mad old farmer on the hill, had mellowed.

Brian, bruised by the rejection from the O'Hara family, had thrown himself into work and barely noticed that his sister had returned.

So the visit was surprisingly painless and thereafter every summer Chicky returned to a warm welcome from her family.

When she was back in Stoneybridge she would walk for miles around and talk to the neighbours, filling them in on her mythical life on the other side of the Atlantic. Few people from these parts ever travelled as far as the States – she was safe in knowing that there would be no unexpected visitors. Her facade would never be brought crashing down by a surprise arrival from Stoneybridge at a non-existent apartment.

Soon she was part of the scenery.

She would meet her friend Peggy, who told her of all the dramas in the knitting factory. Nuala had long ago left to live in Dublin and they never heard from her any more.

'We always know it's July when we see Chicky back walking the beaches,' the three Sheedy sisters would say to her.

And Chicky's face would open up into a big smile embracing them all in its warmth and telling them and anyone else who would listen that there was nowhere on earth as special as Stoneybridge, no matter how many wonderful things she saw in foreign parts.

This pleased people.

It was good to be praised for having the wisdom to stay where you were in Stoneybridge, for having made the right choice.

The family asked about Walter, and seemed pleased to hear of his success and popularity. If they felt ashamed that they had wronged him so much they never said it in so many words.

But then it all changed.

The eldest of her nieces, Orla, was now a teenager. Next year she hoped to go to America with Brigid, one of the tribe of red-haired O'Haras. Could she stay for a little bit with Aunty Chicky and Uncle Walter, she wondered? They would be no trouble at all.

Chicky didn't miss a beat.

Of course Orla and Brigid would come to visit; she was enthusiastic about it. Eager for them to come. There would be no problem, she assured them. Inside she was churning, but no one would have known. She must be calm now. She would work it out later. Now was the time to welcome and anticipate the visit and get excited about it.

Orla wondered what would they do when they got to New York.

'Your uncle Walter will have you met at Kennedy, you'll come home and freshen up and straight away I'll take you on a

Circle Line Tour around Manhattan on a boat so that you'll get your bearings. Then another day we'll go to Ellis Island and to Chinatown. We'll have a *great* time.'

And as Chicky clapped her hands and enthused about it all she could actually imagine the visit happening. And she could see the kind, avuncular figure of Uncle Walter laughing ruefully and regretfully over the daughters that they never had as he spoiled them rotten. The same Walter who had left her after their short months in New York and headed west across the huge continent of America.

The shock had long gone now, and the real memory of her life with him was becoming vague. She very rarely went back there in her mind anyway. Yet the false life, the fantasy existence was crystal sharp and clear.

It had been what had made her survive. The knowledge that everyone in Stoneybridge had been proved wrong and she, Chicky, at the age of twenty, had known better than any of them. That she had a happy marriage and a busy, successful life in New York. It would be meaningless if they knew he had left her and that she had scrubbed floors, cleaned bathrooms and served meals for Mrs Cassidy, that she had scrimped and saved and taken no holiday except for the week back in Ireland every year.

This made-up life had been her reward.

How was she to recreate it for Orla and her friend Brigid? Would it all be unmasked after years of careful construction? But she would not worry about it now, and let it disturb her holiday. She would think about it later.

No satisfactory thoughts came to her when she was back in her New York life. It was a life nobody in Stoneybridge had dreamed of. Chicky could see no solution to the problem of Orla and her friend Brigid O'Hara. It was too aggravating.

Why couldn't the girl have chosen Australia, like so many other young Irish kids? Why did it have to be New York?

Back at Mrs Cassidy's Select Accommodation, Chicky broke the code that had existed between them for so long.

'I have a problem,' she said simply.

'We will talk problems after supper,' Mrs Cassidy said.

Mrs Cassidy poured them a glass of what she called port wine and Chicky told the story she had never told before. She told it from the very beginning. Whole layers and onion skins of deception were peeled back as she explained that now the game was up: her family who believed in Uncle Walter wanted to come and meet him.

'I think Walter was killed,' Mrs Cassidy said slowly.

'What?'

'I think he was killed on the Long Island highway, in a multiple car wreck, bodies barely identified.'

'It wouldn't work.'

'It happens every day, Chicky.'

And as usual, Mrs Cassidy was right.

It worked.

A terrible tragedy, motorway madness, a life snuffed out. They were so upset for her, back in Stoneybridge. They wanted to come to New York for the funeral but she told them it would be very private. That's the way Walter would have wanted it.

Her mother cried down the phone.

'Chicky, we were so harsh about him. May God forgive us.'

'I'm sure He has, long ago.' Chicky was calm.

'We tried to do what was best,' her father said. 'We thought we were good judges of character, and now it's too late to tell him we were wrong.'

'Believe me, he understood.'

'But can we write to his family?'

'I've already sent your sympathies, Dad.'

'Poor people. They must be heartbroken.'

'They are very positive. He had a good life, that's what they say.'

They wanted to know should they put a notice in the paper. But no. She said her way of coping with grief was to close down her life here as she had known it. The kindest thing they could do for her was to remember Walter with affection and to leave her alone until the wounds healed. She would come home next summer as usual.

She would have to move on.

This was very mysterious to those who read her letters home. Perhaps she had been unhinged by grief. After all, they had been so wrong about Walter Starr in life. Maybe they should respect him in death. Her friends now understood her need for solitude. She hoped that her family would do that also.

Orla and Brigid, who had been planning to come and visit the apartment in Seventh Avenue, were distraught.

Not only would there be no welcoming Uncle Walter coming to meet them at the airport, but there would be no holiday at all. Now there was no possibility of Aunty Chicky to take them on this Circle Line Tour round the island of Manhattan. She was moving on, apparently.

And anyway, their chances of being allowed to go to New York had disappeared. Could anything have been more unfortunately timed, they wondered.

They kept in touch and told her all the local news. The O'Haras had gone mad and were buying up property around Stoneybridge to develop holiday homes. Two of the old Miss

Sheedys had been carried away by pneumonia in the winter. The old person's friend, it was called; it ended life peacefully for those who couldn't catch their breath.

Miss Queenie Sheedy was still there; strange, of course, and living in her own little world. Stone House was practically falling down around her. It was said that she seemed to have barely the money to pay her bills. Everyone had thought she would have to sell the big house on the cliff.

Chicky read all this as if it were news from another planet. Still, the following summer she booked her flight to Ireland. She brought more sombre clothes this time. Not official mourning, as her family might have liked, but less jaunty yellows and reds in her skirts and tops – more greys and dark blues. And the same sensible walking shoes.

She must have walked twenty kilometres a day along the beaches and the cliffs around Stoneybridge, into the woods and past the building sites where the O'Haras were busy with plans for Hispanic-style housing complete with black wrought iron and open sun terraces much more suitable for a warmer, milder climate than for the wild, windswept Atlantic coast around Stoneybridge.

During one of her walks she met Miss Queenie Sheedy, frail and lonely without her two sisters. They sympathised with each other on their loss.

'Will you come back here, now that your life is ended over there, and your poor dear man has gone to Holy God?' Miss Queenie asked.

'I don't think so, Miss Queenie. I wouldn't fit in here any more. I'm too old to live with my parents.'

'I understand, dear, everything turns out differently, doesn't it? I always hoped that you would come and live in this house. That was my dream.'

And then it began.

The whole insane idea of her buying the big house on the cliff. Stone House, where she had played when she was a child in their wild gardens, and had looked up at from the sea when they went swimming, where her friend Nuala had worked for the lovely Sheedy sisters.

It could happen. Walter always said it was up to us what happened.

Mrs Cassidy had always said why not us just as much as anyone else?

Miss Queenie said it was the best idea since fried bread.

'I wouldn't be able to pay you the money that others might give you for the place,' Chicky said.

'What do I need money for at this stage?' Miss Queenie had asked.

'I have been too long away,' Chicky said.

'But you will come back, you love walking all around here, it gives you strength, and there's so much light and the sky looks different every hour here. And you'll be very lonely back in New York without that man who was so good to you for all those years – you don't want to stay there with everything reminding you of him. Come home now, if you like, and I'll move into the downstairs breakfast room. I'm not too good on the old stairs anyway.'

'Don't be ridiculous, Miss Queenie. It's your house. I can't take any of this in. And what would I do with a big house like this all on my own?'

'You'd turn it into a hotel, wouldn't you?' To Miss Queenie, it was obvious. 'Those O'Haras have been wanting to buy the place from me for years. They'd pull it down. I don't want that. I'll help you turn it into a hotel.'

'A hotel? Really? Run a hotel?'

'You'd make it special, a place for people like you.'

'There's no one like me, no one as odd and complicated.'

'You'd be surprised, Chicky. There are lots of them. And I won't be around here for long, anyway; I'm going to join my sisters in the churchyard soon, I'd say. So you should really have to decide to do it now, and then we can plan what we are going to do to make Stone House lovely again.'

Chicky was wordless.

'You see, it would be very nice for me if you *did* come here before I go. I'd just love to be part of the planning,' Queenie pleaded. And they sat down at the kitchen table in Stone House and talked about it seriously.

When Chicky got back to New York, Mrs Cassidy listened to the plans, nodding with approval.

'You really think I can do it?'

'I'll miss you, but you know it's going to be the making of you.'

'Will you come to see me? Come to stay in my hotel?'

'Yes, I'll come for a week one winter. I like the Irish countryside in winter, not when it's full of noise and show and people doing leprechaun duty.'

Mrs Cassidy had never taken a holiday. This was groundbreaking.

'I should go now while Queenie is alive, I suppose.'

'You should have it up and running as soon as possible.' Mrs Cassidy hated to let the grass grow beneath her feet.

'How will I explain it all . . . to everybody?'

'You know, people don't have to explain things nearly as much as you think they do. Just say that you bought it with the money Walter left you. It's only the truth, after all.'

'How can it be the truth?'

'It's because of Walter you came here to New York. And because he left you you went and earned that money and saved it. In a way, he *did* leave it to you. I don't see any lie there.' And Mrs Cassidy put on the face that meant they would never speak of it again.

In the following weeks, Chicky transferred her savings to an Irish bank. There were endless negotiations with banks and lawyers. There were planning applications to be sorted, earth movers to be contacted, hotel regulations to be consulted, tax considerations to be made. She would never have believed how many aspects of it all there were to put in place before the announcement was made. She and Miss Queenie told nobody about their arrangement.

Eventually it all seemed ready.

'I can't put it off much longer,' Chicky said to Mrs Cassidy as they cleared the table after supper.

'It breaks my heart, but you should go tomorrow.'

'Tomorrow?'

'Miss Queenie can't wait much longer, and you have to tell your family some time. Do it before it's leaked out to them. It will be better this way.'

'But to get ready to go in one day? I mean, I have to pack and say my goodbyes . . .'

'You could pack in twenty minutes. You have hardly any possessions. The men in this house aren't great on big flowery goodbye speeches, any more than I am myself.'

'I'm half cracked to do this, Mrs Cassidy.'

'No, Chicky, you'd be half cracked if you didn't do it. You were always great at taking an opportunity.'

'Maybe I'd have been better if I hadn't seized the opportunity of following Walter Starr.' Chicky was rueful.

'Oh yes? You'd have been promoted in the knitting factory.

Married a mad farmer, have six children that you'd be trying to find jobs for. No, I think you make great judgements. You made a decision, contacted me for a job and *that* turned out all right for twenty years, didn't it? You did fine by coming here to New York, and now you're going back home to own the biggest house in the neighbourhood. I don't see much wrong with that career path.'

'I love you, Mrs Cassidy,' Chicky said.

'It's just as well you're going back to the Celtic mists and twilight if you're going to start talking like that,' Mrs Cassidy said, but her face was much softer than usual.

The Ryan family sat open-mouthed as she told them her plans.

Chicky coming home for good? *Buying* the Sheedy place? Setting up a hotel to be open summer and winter? The main reaction was total disbelief.

The only one to show pure delight in the idea was her brother Brian.

'That will soften the O'Haras' cough,' he said with a broad smile. 'They've been sniffing after that place for years. They want to knock it down and build six top-of-the-market homes up there.'

'That was exactly what Miss Queenie didn't want!' Chicky agreed.

'I'd love to be there when they find out,' Brian said. He had never got over the fact that the O'Haras hadn't thought him worthy of their daughter. She had married a man who had managed to lose a great deal of O'Hara money on the horses, Brian often noted with satisfaction.

Her mother couldn't believe that Chicky was going to move in with Miss Queenie the very next day.

23

'Well, I'll need to be on the premises,' Chicky explained. 'And anyway, it's no harm to have someone there to hand Miss Queenie a cup of tea every now and then.'

'And a bowl of porridge or packet of biscuits wouldn't go amiss either,' Kathleen said. 'Mikey saw her picking black-berries a while ago. She said they were free.'

'Are you *sure* you own the place, Chicky?' Her father was worried, as always. 'You're not just going in there as a maid, like Nuala was, but with a promise that she will leave it to you?'

Chicky patted them down, assured them it was hers.

Little by little they began to realise that it was actually going to happen. Every objection they brought up she had already thought of. Her years in New York had made her into a businesswoman. They had learned from the past not to under-estimate Chicky. They would not make the same mistake a second time.

Her family had arranged for yet another Mass to be said for Walter, as Chicky hadn't been at home for the first one they said. Chicky sat in the little church in Stoneybridge and wondered if there really was a God up there watching and listening.

It didn't seem very likely.

But then everyone here appeared to think it was the case. The whole community joined in prayers for the repose of Walter Starr's soul. Would he have laughed if he could have known this was happening? Would he have been shocked by the superstition of these people in an Irish seaside town where he had once had a holiday romance?

Now she was back here, Chicky knew that she would have to be part of the church again. It would be easier; Mrs Cassidy had gone to Mass every Sunday morning in New York. It was yet one more thing that they had never discussed.

She looked around the church where she was baptised, made her First Communion and her Confirmation, the church where her sisters had been married and where people were praying for the repose of the soul of a man who had never died. It was all very odd.

Still she hoped that the prayers would do someone somewhere some good.

There were a series of minefields that had to be walked very carefully. Chicky must make sure not to annoy those who already ran bed-and-breakfast accommodation around the place, or who rented out summer cottages. She began a ceaseless diplomatic offensive explaining that what she was doing was creating something totally new for the area, not a premises that would take business away from them.

She visited the many public houses dotted around the countryside and told them of her plans. Her guests would want to tour the cliffs and hills around Stoneybridge. She would recommend that they see the real Ireland, take their lunch in all the traditional bars, pubs and inns around. So if they were to serve soup and simple food, she would love to know about it and she would send customers in their direction.

She chose builders from another part of the country, as she wanted to avoid giving preference to the O'Haras or their main rivals in the construction business. It was so much easier than choosing one over the other. It was the same about buying supplies. Offence could easily be taken if she was seen to favour just one place.

Chicky made sure that everyone would get something from the project. She was so good at getting everyone on side.

The main thing was to get the architects in and out and the

workmen on site. She would need a manager, but not yet. She would want someone to live in and help her with the cooking but again, that could wait.

Chicky had her eye on her niece Orla for this job. The girl was quick and bright. She loved Stoneybridge and the life it offered. She was energetic and sporty, into windsurfing and rock climbing. She had done a computer course in Dublin and a diploma in marketing. Chicky could teach her to cook. She was lively and good with people. She would be a natural for Stone House. Irritatingly, the girl seemed to want to stay in London with her new job. No explanations, she just went. Things were so much easier for the young these days than in her time, Chicky thought. Orla didn't have to ask permission or family approval. It was assumed that she was an adult and they had no say in her life.

The plans went on and on. There would be eight guest bedrooms and one big kitchen and dining area where all the guests would eat dinner together. She found a huge old-fashioned table that would have to be scrubbed every day but it was authentic. This was no place for fancy mahogany and place mats or thick Irish linen tablecloths. It must be the real thing.

She got one local craftsman to make her fourteen chairs, and another to restore an old dresser to display the china. With Miss Queenie she drove to auctions and sales around the countryside and found the right glasses, plates, bowls.

They met people who would be able to restore some of the old rugs in the Sheedy home, and who could replace frayed leather on little antique tables.

This was the part that Miss Queenie loved most. She would say over and over what a miracle it was to have all these lovely treasures restored. Her sisters would be so pleased when they saw what was happening. Miss Queenie believed that they knew every detail of what was going on in Stone House, and watched it all approvingly. It was touching that she saw them settled in some happy place waiting for the hotel to open and checking the comings and goings in Stoneybridge.

It was rather more unsettling when Miss Queenie also assumed that Walter Starr would be there in heaven with the two Miss Sheedys, cheering on every development that was being made by his brave, courageous widow.

Chicky made sure to tell her family about her plans each week so that they could be well briefed and ahead of the game. It gave them great status to know in advance that the planning applications had been approved, a walled kitchen garden to grow their own vegetables planned and oil-fired central heating for the whole house installed.

She would probably need a professional designer as well. Even though she and Miss Queenie thought they knew what the place should look like, they *were* pitching for discerning people, they would charge real money and must make the place right. What Chicky thought of as elegant might well be considered tacky.

Even though she had looked at all the hotels and country houses in magazines, she had little practical experience in getting the right look. Mrs Cassidy's Select Accommodation hadn't been a real training ground for style.

There would be a lot of work ahead: she would have to have a website and take bookings online, still a very foreign world to her. This is where young Orla would be her right hand if she were to come back from London. She had telephoned her twice but the girl had been distracted and non-committal.

Chicky's sister Kathleen said that Orla was like a bag of cats and that there was no talking to her on any subject.

'She's more headstrong than you ever were,' Kathleen said ruefully, 'and that's really saying something.'

'Look at how well and sane I turned out in the end,' Chicky laughed.

'The place isn't up and running yet.' Kathleen's voice was full of doom. 'We'll see how well and sane you are when you're open for business.'

Only Mrs Cassidy, over in New York, and Miss Queenie believed it would happen and be a big success. Everyone else was humouring her and hoping it would take off but in the same way that they hoped for a long hot summer and for the Irish soccer team to do well in the World Cup.

Sometimes Chicky would go and walk the cliffs at night and look out over the Atlantic Ocean. Always it gave her strength.

People had had enough courage to get into small, shaky boats and set sail over those choppy waters, not knowing what lay ahead. Surely it couldn't be too hard to set up a guest house? Then she would go back indoors where Miss Queenie would run and make them a mug of hot chocolate and say that she hadn't been so happy since she was a girl, since the days when she and her sisters would go to a hunt ball and hope they might find dashing young men to marry. That had never happened, but this time it would work. Stone House was going to happen.

And Chicky would pat her on the hand and say that they would be the talk of the country. And as she said it, she believed it. All her worries would go. Whether it was because of the walk in the wild winds or the comforting hot chocolate or Miss Queenie's hopeful face or a combination of all three, it meant she slept a long, untroubled sleep every night.

She would wake ready for anything, which was just as well because in the months ahead there was quite a lot she had to be ready for.

Rigger

Rigger never knew his father – he had never been spoken of. His mother Nuala was hard to know properly. She worked so hard for one thing, and she said little of her life in the West of Ireland in a small place called Stoneybridge. Rigger knew she had worked as a maid in a big house for three old ladies called the Miss Sheedys, but she never wanted to talk about it nor her family back home.

He shrugged. It was impossible to understand grown-ups, anyway.

Nuala had never owned anything of her own. She was the youngest of the family so any clothes she got had been well tried out on the others first. There was no money for luxuries, not even a First Communion dress; and when she was fifteen they had found her a job working for the Miss Sheedys in Stone House. Very nice women they were; ladies, all three of them.

It was hard work: stone floors and wooden tables to scrub, old furniture to polish. She had a very small room with a little iron bed. But it was her own, more than she ever had at home. The Miss Sheedys hadn't a penny really between them, so there was a lot of fighting back the damp and the leaks and there was never the money to give the house any proper heating or a good coat of paint – both needed badly. They ate very little but Nuala was used to that. They were like little sparrows at the table.

She looked at them with wonder, as they had to have their table napkins each in its own ring and they sounded a little gong to announce the meal. It was like taking part in a play.

Sometimes Miss Queenie would ask about Nuala's boy-friends, but the other sisters would *tut-tut* as if this wasn't a suitable topic to discuss with the maid.

Not that there was that much to discuss. There were very few boyfriends around Stoneybridge. Any lads her brothers knew had all gone to England or America to find work. And Nuala wouldn't be considered good enough for the O'Haras or some of the big families in the place. She hoped that she would meet one of the summer visitors who would fall in love with her, just like Chicky, and not care that she was in domestic service.

And she *did* meet a summer visitor, called Drew. It was short for Andrew. He was a friend of the O'Haras, and they had all been kicking a ball around the beach. Nuala sat watching the girls in their smart swimsuits. How wonderful it must be to be able to go into town and buy things like that, and lovely coloured baskets and coloured towels.

Drew came over and asked her to join the game. After a week she was in love with him. After two weeks they were lovers. It was all so natural and normal, she couldn't under-stand why she and the other girls had giggled so much about it at school. Drew said he adored her and that he would write to her every day when he went back to Dublin.

He wrote once and said it had been a magical summer and

that he would never forget her. He gave no address. Nuala wouldn't ask the O'Haras where to find him. Not even when she realised that her period was late and she was most probably pregnant.

When this became more certain to be true, she was at a complete loss about what to do. It would break her mother's heart. Nuala had never felt so alone in her life.

She decided to tell the Miss Sheedys.

She waited until she had cleared and washed up their minimal supper before she began the story. Nuala looked at the stone floor of the kitchen so that she did not have to meet their eyes as she explained what had happened.

The Sheedy sisters were shocked. They had hardly any words to express their horror that this should have happened while Nuala was under their roof.

'What on earth are you going to do?' Miss Queenie asked with tears in her eyes.

Miss Jessica and Miss Beatrice were less sympathetic but equally unable to think of a solution.

What had Nuala hoped they would do? That they might ask her to bring up the baby there? That they would say a child around the house would make them all feel young again?

No, she hadn't hoped for that much but she wanted some reassurance, some pinprick of hope that the world was not going to end for her as a result of all this.

They said they would make enquiries. They had heard of a place where she might be able to stay until the baby was born and given up for adoption.

'Oh, I'm not going to give the baby away,' Nuala said.

'But you can't *keep* the baby, Nuala,' Miss Queenie explained.

'I never had anything of my own before, apart from the room you gave me and my bed here.'

The sisters looked at each other. The girl didn't begin to understand what she was taking on. The responsibility, the fuss, the disgrace.

'It's the 1990s,' Nuala said, 'it's not the Dark Ages.'

'Yes, but Father Johnson is still Father Johnson,' Miss Queenie said.

'Would the young man in question perhaps . . . ?' began Miss Jessica tentatively.

'And if he's a friend of the O'Haras, he would be an honourable person and do his duty . . .' Miss Beatrice agreed.

'No, he wouldn't. He wrote to say goodbye; it had been a magical summer.'

'And I'm sure it was, my dear,' Miss Queenie clucked kindly, not noticing the disapproval from the others.

'I can't tell my parents,' Nuala said.

'So, we'll get you to Dublin as quickly as possible. They'll know what to do up there.' Miss Jessica wanted it off her doorstep soonest.

'I'll make those enquiries.' Miss Beatrice was the sister with contacts.

Nuala's eldest brother Nasey was already living in Dublin. He was the odd one in the family, very quiet, kept himself to himself, they would always say with a sigh. He had a job in a butcher's shop and seemed settled enough.

He was a bachelor with a home of his own, but he wouldn't be anyone she could rely on. He had been too long left home to know her and care about her. She did have his address for an emergency, of course, but she wouldn't contact him.

The Sheedys had found a place for Nuala to stay. It was a hostel where several of the other girls were pregnant also.

A lot of them had jobs in supermarkets or cleaning houses. Nuala was used to hard work, and found it very easy compared to all the pulling and dragging at Stone House. She got jobs by word of mouth. People said to each other that she was very pleasant and that nothing was too much trouble for her. She saved enough to rent a room for herself and the baby when it was born.

She wrote home to her family telling them about Dublin and the people she worked for, but saying nothing of the visits to the maternity hospital. She wrote to the Sheedy ladies telling them the truth, and eventually giving them the news that Richard Anthony had been born weighing six and a half pounds and was a perfect baby in every way. They sent her a five-pound note to help out, and Miss Queenie sent a christening robe.

Richard Anthony wore it at his baptism, which was in a church down by the River Liffey at a christening of sixteen infants.

'What a pity you don't have any family there with you at this time,' Miss Queenie wrote. 'Perhaps your brother would be pleased to see you and meet his new nephew.'

Nuala doubted it. Nasey had always been withdrawn and distant from what she remembered.

'I'll wait until he's a little person before I introduce them,' she said.

Nuala now had to get jobs which would allow her to take the baby with her. Not easy at first, but when they saw the long hours she put in and how little trouble the child was she found plenty of work.

She saw a great deal of life through the households where she worked. The women who fussed about their homes as if they thought life was a permanent examination where they would be found wanting. There were families where husband and wife were barely civil to each other. There were places where the children were spoiled with every possession possible and still were not content.

But also she met good, kind people who were warm to her and her little son and grateful when she went the extra distance and cooked them potato cakes or made old dull brasses shine like new.

When Richard was three it was getting harder to take him to people's houses. He wanted to explore and run around. One of Nuala's favourite ladies was someone they all called Signora, who taught Italian classes. She was a most unusual woman: completely unworldly, wore extraordinary flowing clothes and had long hair with grey and red and dark brown in it all tied back with a ribbon.

She didn't have a cleaner for herself, but paid Nuala to clean two afternoons a week for her mother. Her mother was a difficult, hard-to-please person who hadn't a good word to say for Signora except that she had always been foolish and head-strong and no good would come of it all.

But Signora, if she knew this, took no notice. She told Nuala about a marvellous little playgroup. It was run by a friend of hers.

'Oh, that would be much too expensive for me,' Nuala said sadly.

'I think they'd be very happy to have him there if you could do a few hours' cleaning in exchange.'

'But the other parents mightn't like that. The cleaner's child in with theirs.'

'They won't think like that, and anyway, they won't know.' Signora was very definite. 'You'd like playschool, wouldn't you, Richard?' Signora had a great habit of talking to children as if they were grown-ups. She never put on a baby voice.

'I'm Rigger,' he said. And that's what he was called from then on.

Rigger loved the playschool, and nobody ever knew that he arrived there two hours before the other children while his mother cleaned and polished and got the place ready for the day.

Through Signora, Nuala got several other jobs nearby. She cleaned in a hairdressing salon where they made her feel very much part of it all and even gave her very expensive highlights for nothing. She did a few hours a week in a restaurant on the quays called Ennio's, where again she was involved in the place and they always asked her to try out a bowl of pasta for her lunch. Then she would pick up Rigger and take him with her while she minded other children and took them for walks on St Stephen's Green to feed the ducks.

Nuala's family were entirely unaware of Rigger's existence. It just seemed easier that way.

As happens in many big families, the children who left became dissociated with their old home. Sometimes, at Christmas, she felt lonely for Stoneybridge and for the days when she would decorate the tree for the Miss Sheedys and they would tell her the stories of each ornament. She thought of her mother and father and the goose they would have for Christmas and the prayers they would say for all emigrants – particularly her two sisters in America, her brother in Birmingham and Nasey and Nuala in Dublin. But it was not a lonely life. Who could be lonely with Rigger? They were devoted to each other.

She couldn't think what made her get in touch with her brother Nasey. Possibly it was another letter from Miss Queenie, who always saw things in a very optimistic way. Miss Queenie said that it was probably a lonely life for Nasey in Dublin, and that he might enjoy having company from home.

She could barely remember him. He was the eldest and she the youngest of a big family. He wasn't going to be shocked and appalled that she had a son who was about to go to big school any day.

It was worth a try.

She called to the butcher's shop where Nasey worked, holding Rigger by the hand. She recognised him at once in a white coat and cutting lamb chops expertly with a cleaver.

'I'm Nuala, your sister,' she said simply, 'and this is Rigger.'

Rigger looked up at him fearfully and Nuala looked long and hard at her brother's face. Then she saw a great smile on Nasey's face. He was indeed delighted to see her. What a waste of five years it had been because she was afraid he might not want to recognise her.

'I'm going to be on my break in ten minutes. I can meet you in the café across the road. Mr Malone, this is my sister and her little boy Rigger.'

'Go on now, Nasey. You'll have lots to talk about.' Mr Malone was kindly. And it turned out that they did have lots to talk about.

Nasey was easygoing. He asked nothing about Rigger's father, nor why she had taken so long to contact him. He was interested in the places she worked, and he said that the Malones were looking for someone to help in the house and that they were a really decent family. She could do much worse than go there. He was in touch with another nephew, Dingo, a good lad, full of dreams and nonsense. He made deliveries in his own van. He lived alone, but he always said the people he worked for made up for it, and he loved hearing about their lives. He would be pleased to know he had a new cousin.

Nasey asked about home and she was vague with details.

'They don't really know about Rigger,' she said. She need not even have said it. He understood.

'No point in burdening people with too much information,' he said, nodding soundly.

He said that he had never found anyone suitable for himself but was always hoping that he would meet someone one day. He didn't like picking up girls in pubs, and honestly where else was there? He was too old for kids' dances and clubs.

And from that meeting on, he became part of Nuala and Rigger's lives.

He was the dream uncle who knew a keeper at the zoo, who taught the boy to ride a bike, who took him to his first match. And when Rigger was eleven it was Nasey who told Nuala that the lad was mixing with a very tough crowd at school and that they had been chased out of several stores for shoplifting.

She was appalled, but Rigger was shruggy. Everyone did it; the shops *knew* they did it. It was the system.

Then he was involved in an incident where old people were threatened and forced to hand over their weekly pension. That led to the children's court and a suspended sentence.

And when Rigger was caught in a warehouse stealing television sets, it meant reform school.

Nuala had not known it was possible to cry so much. She was totally shocked. What had happened to her little boy? And when? Nothing had a purpose any more. Her jobs were just that now, jobs.

She barely listened to the chat in Katie's hairdresser's, in Ennio's restaurant or in St Jarlath's Crescent – places where she had once been so happy, so involved.

She decided she would write to him every week but she had no idea what he was interested in.

Football, probably, so she looked up the evening paper to see where the team was playing next and also to know was there any film that Rigger might like. Week after week she wrote. Sometimes he replied, sometimes he didn't, but she continued every week.

She told him how her father had got ill and died and how she had gone back to Stoneybridge for the funeral. She said it was so strange how small it seemed now after so many years away from the place. She hardly knew anyone, and her sisters and brothers seemed like strangers. Her mother looked so small and old. So much had changed, it was like going to a different place.

Rigger wrote back to that letter.

I'm sorry your da died. Why did we never see him, or go back to this place? Fellows here are always talking about their grans and their grandas.

Nuala wrote back.

When you come home I'll take you on the train to Stoneybridge and you'll see it all for yourself. It's such a long story but it's going to be easier to tell you all about it than write it down.

By the time he came back from the reform school, Rigger was sixteen and Nuala's mother had died.

Nasey went on his own to the funeral. Nuala didn't go. She

hadn't been at all easy when she had gone to see her father buried. She fancied that some of the neighbours looked at her oddly and that the sisters in America were annoyed with her for not coming back more regularly. Her brother from Birmingham had given her a very irritating lecture about it being time she settled down and had a family instead of just running around enjoying herself in Dublin.

Nasey told the family that he did see Nuala from time to time but said no more. He kept to his theory that people should not be burdened with too much information. He brought news from home. Two of the Miss Sheedys had died. Now only Miss Queenie remained.

Then came the news that Chicky Starr had come back from America and was going to buy Stone House. Miss Queenie would live there for her lifetime and they were going to make the place into a hotel.

Nuala remembered Chicky well. They had been at school together. Chicky had married an American called Walter Starr and had gone to live in New York. Nuala had written to her there. Her poor husband had been killed in a terrible car crash.

She would have her work cut out for her if she was to make any kind of a fist of that big sprawling house and turn it into a hotel where people would pay to stay.

Rigger didn't talk much about his time at the reform school when he came back. He had learned a bit of this and a bit of that, he said. But he wasn't qualified at anything. They had done a bit of building up in the school: plastering one week, digging another. Nasey said he would try to get Rigger taken on by Mr Malone in the butcher's shop, but times were hard. People were buying more and more of their meat ready-wrapped in supermarkets.

Signora asked Nuala did she know if Rigger would go back to school. She would give him some lessons to try and help him catch up, but he didn't want that.

He had had enough school, he said.

Nuala had very much hoped that he would have grown away from his old ways, that he could find new friends and a different way of living.

But Rigger was barely home a few weeks when Nuala realised that her son had indeed made contact with those boys he could find from the old days. Some of them were not around any more. Two were in gaol, one on the run – possibly in England – and the others under the fairly constant and watchful eye of the Guards.

Rigger had been warned from every side about the danger of getting a criminal record if he offended again.

He went out early and came home late with no explanation or description of how he spent his time. One night she heard shouting and running and doors banging and she lay shaking in the dark waiting for the arrival of the Guards with their sirens wailing. But nobody came.

Next morning she was drawn and anxious but Rigger had obviously slept well and seemed unconcerned. She was relieved when he told her that he was going to look for a job.

Nasey was surprised to see Rigger come into the butcher's shop with two of his friends. Surprised and not altogether pleased.

But Rigger had come to ask was there any casual work going, could they clean up the yard, for example?

Nasey was pleased to see some interest in legitimate work, and he ran to Mr Malone asking if they could have a couple of hours' work. And to give them their due, they did the job well. Nasey reported it all to Nuala with pleasure. The lads had done the job, got a few euro and gone away well satisfied.

Nuala began to breathe properly again. Perhaps she had been overanxious about nothing.

Two nights later, Nasey was taking his late-night walk and passed the butcher's shop. He looked up automatically at the burglar alarm and saw to his astonishment that it was not turned on. Never had he left the premises without switching it to 'Active'. Horrified, he let himself in and heard sounds at the back of the shop from the cold room.

As he went in he saw three men lifting carcasses of beef into a van which was parked in the back yard.

He ran towards them and one of the men dropped a great side of meat and came at him with a crowbar.

'What are you doing?' Nasey cried. As the man was about to hit him, from nowhere a voice shouted, 'Leave him, leave him, for Christ's sake.'

The blow was stopped and Nasey recognised his protector was in fact his nephew Rigger.

'I don't believe it, Rigger.' Nasey was nearly in tears. 'You were paid for your work and you came back to steal their meat.'

'Shut up, Nasey, you big eejit. Just get out of here. You were never here, do you hear me? Just go home and say nothing. No harm done.'

'I can't. I can't let Mr Malone's livelihood be taken like this . . .'

'He's well insured, Nasey. Have some sense, man.'

'You can't do this. What are you going to do with the carcasses?'

'Cut them up. Sell them along the Mountainview Estates.

Everyone round there wants cheap meat. Nasey, get out of here, will you?'

'I'm not going and I'm not going to forget it.'

'Rigger, either you shut him up or I will,' one of the others said.

Nasey felt himself being pushed out the door, and he could feel Rigger's breath hot on his face.

'Jesus, Nasey, have you an ounce of sense? They'd beat the side of your head in. Get *out*. Run. RUN!'

Nasey ran all the way to Nuala's house and told her what had happened. White-faced, the two of them sat drinking mugs of tea.

'Even if I *don't* tell Mr Malone, he'll know anyway. He's not a fool. Who else would have been able to come in and see the lie of the land and suss the place out except those three? And he knows that Rigger is my nephew.'

'I'm so sorry, Nasey,' Nuala wept.

'We have to think what to do with him. He'll go to gaol over this,' Nasey said.

'It's all my fault. I should have been able to control him. I was too busy making money for him. Saving for an education that he'll never have.'

'Stop that. It's not down to you.'

'Well, who else's fault is it but mine?'

'This is no time to be trying to work that out. We have to hide him. The Guards will come looking for him here.'

'Could we send him back to Stoneybridge?' Her face was despairing.

'But who would look after him there? And I thought you didn't want anyone to know about him.'

'I don't want him in gaol either. Who knows about him isn't important any more.'

'None of them would be able to handle him,' Nasey said. 'If there was somewhere he could live in and work . . .'

Nuala strained to think of anywhere.

'Could he work for Chicky at Stone House? Miss Queenie wrote to me not long ago that she was looking for someone to help her.'

'He'd never stick it.' Nasey shook his head.

'He will if he knows it's that or prison.'

'Ring Chicky,' Nasey said.

Nasey didn't hear the phone conversation. He was out on the street waiting for Rigger to come back. He saw the boy running down the street. Rigger was home. His face was white and his hands were shaking. He was willing to blame everyone but himself.

'If I go down, Nasey, it will all be due to you. The other lads just threw me out. They won't let me have any part of what we got. It's so unfair. I set it up. I gave them the way in.'

'Yes, you did,' Nasey said grimly.

'I *told* the others you wouldn't split on us but they don't believe me. They say you'll have gone to the Guards already. Have you?'

'No,' Nasey said.

'Well thank God for that, anyway. Why couldn't you have just backed away?'

'I did. I ran away as you said.'

'And you're not going to tell?' Rigger looked like a child.

'I don't *have* to tell, Rigger. Mr Malone will know.'

'Oh my God, it's *Mister* Malone this, *Mister* Malone that. Would you hear yourself?' Rigger was full of scorn. 'Aren't you big enough and old enough to be your own master instead of yes sir, yes sir, three bags full, to him?'

44

'They'll find you even if I were struck dumb and never spoke again,' Nasey said.

'Just shut your mouth, Rigger, and listen carefully,' Nuala spoke suddenly.

He looked at her in shock. Her face was hard and unforgiving. He had never known her raise her voice to him like this before.

'We're going to get you out of Dublin tonight. And you're not coming back.'

'What?'

'There's a truck driver taking his lorry back to Stoneybridge tonight. You'll go with him. He will take you to Stone House.'

'What's Stone House? Is it a school?' Rigger was frightened.

'It's where your mother worked when she was young. It's where she left from to have you, all those years ago. With all the pleasure and pride that was to bring her.' Never had Nasey sounded so bitter.

Rigger tried to speak but his uncle wouldn't let him say a word. 'Get your things together, give me your phone, tell nobody where you're going. You'll be in Stoneybridge by the time they open up Malone's in the morning.'

'But you said that the Guards would find me anyway.'

'Not if you're not here, they can't. Not if no one knows where you are.'

'Mam, is that right?'

'Chicky is doing me this one favour. She suggested the driver. She'll keep you for a week to see how it goes. If you get up to any of your old tricks, she'll call the Guards down there and they'll have you back here and behind bars before you know what's happened.'

'Mam!'

'Don't "Mam" me. I was never a proper mother to you. It

45

was only pretending to be a family, that's all it was, and it stops tonight.'

'Nasey?'

'What?'

'Will you get into any trouble?' Rigger asked. It was the first hint that he might care for anyone other than himself.

'I don't know. That remains to be seen. I'll tell Mr Malone that I'm very sorry about it, about getting him to let you all work in the yard. Which I am – very, very sorry indeed.'

'He won't sack you, will he?'

'Who knows? I hope not. Years of work. One mistake.'

'And the other lads . . .'

'As you said, they threw you out, ran off on you. They're not thinking about you. You don't have to think about them.'

'But if they're caught?'

'They will be, but you will be far away, starting a new job.' Nasey was calm and cold.

Things happened quickly then. Rigger's bag was packed in silence. The man with the empty lorry arrived. The wordless driver just indicated the front seat. There would be little conversation on the road across Ireland.

His mother turned away as he tried to say goodbye. Rigger's eyes filled with tears.

'I'm sorry, Mam,' he said.

'Yes,' Nuala said.

And then he was gone. He had no idea a journey could take so long. He also had no idea what lay ahead. He had been given very firm instructions to discuss nothing with his driver. He looked out the window as they passed the small dark fields on either side. How did people *live* in places like this? Sometimes there were dead rabbits and foxes on the road. He would like to have asked why these animals went out into the traffic but conversation seemed to be forbidden so instead, he listened to endless country and western songs all about losers and drunkards and people who had been betrayed.

By the time they got to Stoneybridge, Rigger felt lower than he had ever felt in his life.

The driver left him at the gate of Stone House. His mother had worked here. *Lived* here. No wonder she had never come back. He wondered had she relations around the place? Did his father live here? Married to someone else, maybe?

Rigger asked himself why had he never asked or wanted to know? What on earth was he going to do here until things died down in Dublin, if they ever would?

He went and knocked at the door. A woman with short curly hair answered immediately and placed her finger on her lips.

'Come in quietly and don't wake Miss Queenie,' she said in a low voice with a slight American accent.

Who *were* these people called Chicky and Queenie?

What was he doing in this cold barn of a place? He went into a shabby kitchen with a broken range where a small kitten sat in front, warming itself. It was white with a tiny little triangular black tail and little black ears. Seeing him, it mewed piteously.

Rigger picked it up and stroked its head. 'What's its name?'

'It only arrived today, like yourself. It came in an hour ago.'

'Will it stay?' he asked.

'It depends.' Chicky Starr was giving nothing away.

Rigger looked her in the eye for the first time. 'Depends on what?' he asked.

'If it's willing to work hard, catch mice, if it's no trouble and behaves nicely to Miss Queenie. That sort of thing.'

47

'I see,' Rigger said. And he did. 'What will I do first?' he asked.

'I think you should have some breakfast,' she said.

And so it began. His new life.

It was a mad notion, turning this house into a hotel. What kind of people did they think would come here, to this place? Still, it was the only game in town.

It was Miss Queenie who had brought the kitten into the household. The last of a litter born in one of the farm cottages down the hill, its survival had been in doubt until Miss Queenie had settled the matter by putting the tiny creature into her pocket and bringing it home. She held it in the palm of her hand and talked to it soothingly as the kitten gazed solemnly at her with its enormous grey-green eyes; she had decided, she told Rigger, to call it Gloria. He realised quickly that Miss Queenie was like something from an old black and white movie; she liked to keep to the traditions of the house as it had been, with a little gong rung to signal mealtimes and proper table settings. She never went out without a smart hat and gloves.

She seemed to think Rigger was a friend, and a very helpful person who had turned up at the right time when they needed him. She told him long, confused tales about people called Beatrice and Jessica and others long dead. She was totally harmless, but possibly not playing with the full deck.

Mindful of Chicky's advice, Rigger realised the importance of being nice to Miss Queenie. He made her a mug of tea every morning and served it in what was called the morning room. At the same time, he fed Gloria.

Miss Queenie knew that you shouldn't give cats saucers of milk, just lots of water and a little pouch of kitten food; certainly Gloria seemed to be thriving on it. She slept most of the day, and for sure was not a kitten of great brains: she seemed to have bouts of huge anxiety because she kept thinking that her tail was another animal following her. Miss Queenie said Gloria wasn't to be blamed for this entirely. After all, her tail *was* a different colour. Miss Queenie had made up a little cat bed in the corner of the kitchen by the range. As Gloria slept, Miss Queenie would watch her happily for hours.

Chicky was less forthcoming. She worked very hard and expected him to do the same. She had little time for small talk.

There was so much to do in the place.

He dug the wild, unkempt gardens of Stone House until his back ached and his face was roughened by the constant sea spray. The soil was hard and stony and the briars and the brambles were enormous. Even though he tried to protect himself he was covered with scratches and cuts. He liked it best when Gloria decided to keep him company, her triangular little black tail held high in the air as she sniffed at the ground where he dug. She pounced on leaves and chewed on twigs and more than once avoided being decapitated only by a whisker as Rigger dug through the brambles. Her curiosity was infinite and insatiable; she explored tirelessly as he worked on. And as he paused, leaning on his spade, she would solemnly roll on to her back and gaze at him upside down.

On the days when the Atlantic storms battered the house and the rain came in horizontally, there were old lofts to be cleared out, furniture to be shifted, woodwork to be painted. The old outhouses were dealt with by a couple of builders who were kept busy hacking out and making good. Rigger worked for them, carrying bricks and stones and wooden planks. He chopped wood for the fires and cleaned the grates out every morning, then poured fresh water and breakfast for Gloria and made tea for Miss Queenie.

49

She was a nice old thing, away with the fairies, of course, but no harm in her. She was interested in everything and would tell him long stories about the past when her sisters were alive. They would have loved a tennis court, but there was never the money to make one.

'Your mother was wonderful when she was here. We really missed her when she left,' Miss Queenie would say. 'Nobody could make potato cakes like Nuala could.'

This was news to Rigger. He didn't ever remember potato cakes at home.

Rigger had a bedroom behind the kitchen where he slept, exhausted, for seven hours a night. On a Saturday, Chicky gave him his bus fare, the price of a cinema ticket and a burger in the next town.

Nobody ever spoke of why he was there, or the fact that he was in hiding. There was little time to make friends around the place and that was good too, as far as Rigger was concerned. The fewer people who knew about him the better.

And then he heard the news he had been waiting to hear.

Nasey phoned him with the details. Two youths had been arrested for the theft of meat from the butcher's shop. They had been before the court and had been given six-month sentences.

The Guards had watched Nuala's house for several weeks, and when there was no sign of Rigger, and nobody knew where he had gone, the matter was dropped.

'How did they catch them?' Rigger asked in a whisper.

'Someone pointed the Guards in the area of the Mountainview Estates and there they were, as bold as brass, going from door to door selling the meat.'

Rigger knew that the 'someone' must have been Nasey, but he said nothing. 'And your own job, Nasey?'

'Is still there. Mr Malone sometimes sympathises with me on the fact that you ran away. He even told me that you might be better off out of Dublin.'

'I see.'

'And maybe he's right, Rigger.'

'Thank you again, Nasey. And about my mam?'

'She's still in a bit of shock, you know. She had been so looking forward to you getting back from that school, counting the days, in fact. She had such plans for you, and now it's all over.'

'Ah no, it's not all over. Not for ever, it's not. I can come back now that the others are off the streets, can't I?'

'No, Rigger, those fellows have friends. They're in a gang. I wouldn't advise you coming back here for a good while.'

'But I can't stay here for ever,' Rigger wailed.

'You have to stay for a fair bit more,' Nasey warned.

'I miss my mam writing to me like she did up in the school.'

'I wouldn't say she's up to writing to you. Not yet, anyway. You could always write to her yourself, of course,' Nasey said.

'I could, I suppose . . .'

'Good, good.' Nasey was gone.

Maybe Miss Queenie would help him write to his mother.

She was indeed a great help, telling him things that might interest Nuala: how this garage had been sold, the O'Haras' new houses – which were going to make them millionaires – had now lost all their value and were like white elephants with no buyers. Father Johnson had a new curate who was doing most of the work in the parish.

Rigger didn't know whether his mother found any of this interesting as she never wrote back.

'Why do you think she doesn't write back to me?' he asked Miss Queenie.

The old lady had no idea. Her pale blue eyes were troubled and sad on his behalf as she stroked Gloria on her knee. It was strange, she said, Nuala had been so proud of him and even sent pictures of his christening and his First Communion. Maybe Chicky would know.

Nervously he asked Chicky, who said crisply that he must have an over-sunny view of life if he believed that his mother had got over everything.

'It wasn't easy for her to ring me in the middle of the night. We hadn't seen each other for twenty years, and she had to tell me that I was the only person on earth who could help her. She can't have liked doing that. I would have hated it.'

'Yes, I know, but could you tell her I've changed?' he begged.

'I have told her.'

'And why doesn't she write back to me, then?'

'Because she thinks it's all *her* fault. She doesn't really want to get involved with you again. I'm sorry to be so hard, but you did ask.'

'Yes, I did.' He was very shaken.

By now Rigger had actually become interested in this whole mad plan to turn the old house into a smart guest house. The rough work and clearing of the ground had all been done; it was time for rebuilding. Real contractors would be brought in on the job. He looked on in amazement as the plans for bathrooms and central heating were laid out on the kitchen table as Gloria batted them from one side to the other. He knew there were meetings with bankers and insurance brokers, that designers were planned in the future.

He was unprepared for Chicky to change his terms of employment.

'You've been here six months and you've been a great help, Rigger,' she said one evening when Miss Queenie had gone to bed. He was very pleased with the compliment. There hadn't been many of those coming his way. Rigger waited to hear what would come next.

'When the builders move in properly in a few weeks, I'll need help to get Miss Queenie to and from Dr Dai's and the health clinic. Can you drive?'

'Yes, I can drive,' Rigger said.

'But do you have a licence? Did you do a driving test or anything?'

'I'm afraid not,' Rigger admitted.

'So that's the first thing you must do – get some driving lessons from Dinny in the garage and do the test. Can you grow things?'

'What kind of things?'

'We should have our own produce here: potatoes, vegetables, fruit. We should have hens, too.'

'Are you serious?' Sometimes Rigger thought that Chicky was certifiable.

'Completely serious. We must offer visitors something special; make them feel that this place is providing their food rather than just going into town and buying it all in a supermarket.'

'I see,' said Rigger, who didn't see at all.

'So I was thinking that if I called you my manager and paid you a proper wage you might feel you have more of a stake here. It won't just be a place where you are hiding out. It would be a real job with a real future.'

'Here? In Stoneybridge?' Rigger was astounded that anyone could see *his* future in these parts.

'Yes, here in Stoneybridge indeed. It's not as if you're likely to be able to go back to Dublin at any time in the near future. I hoped you might want to put down some roots here, make something of yourself.'

'I'm grateful to you and everything but—'

'But what, Rigger? But you see a glittering future for yourself in Dublin stealing great sides of beef and beating up decent butchers who try to protect their business?'

'I didn't beat up anyone,' he said indignantly.

'I know that. Why else do you think I took you on? You saved Nasey's life, he says. He was determined you should have a fresh start. I'm trying to give it to you, but it's difficult.'

'Do you like me, Chicky?'

'Yes, I do, actually. I didn't think I would but I do. You're very good to Queenie, you're kind to the kitten, you have a lot of good points. You're very young. I wanted to get you some skills and see that you have a bit of a life. But you just throw it back at me and say that a life here is worth nothing at all. So I'm a bit confused, really.'

'It's just not what I thought my life would be,' he said.

'It's not what I thought *my* life would be either, but somewhere along the line we have to pick things up and run with them.'

'At least your bad luck wasn't your own fault,' Rigger said.

'It probably was in some ways.' She looked away.

'But your husband being killed and all – you weren't to blame for that.'

'No, that's right.'

54

'I'd be happy to be your manager if you'll still take me,' he said, after a pause.

'We start to dig the vegetable garden tomorrow morning, and your first driving lesson will be with Dinny tomorrow afternoon. You'll start to learn the rules of the road tomorrow night. Miss Queenie will be in charge of that.'

'I'm up for it,' Rigger said.

'And I'll open a post office account for you and put half your wages in each week and give you half in cash. That way you can buy some nice clothes and take a girl to a dance or whatever.'

'Can I tell my mother and Nasey?'

'Oh yes, of course you can. But I wouldn't hold out any hopes about your mother.'

'It will be the first bit of good news she ever had about me,' he said.

'No, she was delighted with you way back when you were born. She wrote and told Miss Queenie all about it. You were six and a half pounds, apparently. But things are different now. Nasey says she needs to see a doctor; it's kind of a depression but she won't hear of it.'

Chicky thought she saw tears in Rigger's eyes but she wasn't sure.

The driving lessons went well. Dinny said that Rigger was fearless but reckless, quick to react but impatient. The rules of the road were a trial, but Miss Queenie loved testing him each evening.

'What does a sign like a circle crossed out mean on the outskirts of a town?' she would ask.

'That you can drive as fast as you like?' Rigger suggested.

'No, *wrong*, it means you can drive at the national speed limit,' Miss Queenie cried triumphantly.

'That's what I meant.'

'You *meant* drive as fast as you like,' Miss Queenie said. 'They would have failed you.'

He passed the test with no problem.

He drove Miss Queenie everywhere: to her appointments with Dr Dai, to the hospital for a check-up, to the vet to have Gloria spayed.

'It seems a pity for her not to have kittens of her own,' Miss Queenie had said as she stroked the little cat on her lap.

'But we'd only have to find homes for them, Miss Queenie. We couldn't have a house full of cats when the visitors come.' He realised that he was beginning to think of himself as part of the whole project.

'Would you like children of your own one day, Rigger?' She always asked strange, direct questions that nobody else did.

'I don't think so, to be honest with you. They seem to be more trouble than they're worth. They'd only end up disappointing you.' He knew he sounded bitter, and tried to laugh and take the harm out of it. Miss Queenie hadn't really noticed.

'We would have loved to have had children, Jessica, Beatrice and myself. We could always see our children playing around Stone House, which was silly really because if we *had* married we wouldn't have been living here any more. It was all a dream, anyway.'

'And was there ever anyone you particularly would have liked to marry, Miss Queenie?' Rigger amazed himself asking her such a thing.

'There was one young man . . . oh, I would have loved to

marry him, but sadly there was TB in his family and so he couldn't marry at all.'

'Why not?'

'Because it was a disease of the lungs and people could catch it and it would pass on to the children. He died in a sanatorium, poor, poor boy. I still have the letters he wrote to me.'

Rigger patted her hand and, embarrassed, he patted Gloria's head as well. They drove on in silence until they arrived at the vet.

'Don't worry, Gloria. You won't feel a thing, pet. And anyway, there's more to life than just sex and kittens,' Miss Queenie said reassuringly as she handed the purring cat over.

The vet and Rigger exchanged glances. This wasn't the normal conversation in the surgery.

While Gloria was being seen to, Rigger and Miss Queenie drove off to do items off Chicky's list. Rigger marvelled at how many people knew him by name in Stoneybridge and the surrounding countryside. Surely his mother would be pleased to know that he was so accepted in this place where she had grown up.

But still there was no word from her.

He had written to Nuala telling her about the day-old chicks they had bought and had to protect from Gloria, who wanted to practise her hunting skills; and how hard it was to dig potato drills. He told her about how the builder was going to charge a fortune to make a walled garden, so Rigger had built it himself, stone upon stone, and raised growing beds. How every time he dug a hole to plant something, Gloria arrived and sat in it, gazing at him seriously. Despite that, now there were shrubs and plants grown up against the wall, which was called espalier. They had runner beans and courgettes and whole rakes of salads and herbs.

He did not tell his mother about the lovely girl called Carmel Hickey, who was studying hard for her Leaving Certificate but could be persuaded to go out to the cinema or for a drive down the coast with Rigger.

Some of the neighbours, and indeed her own family, worried that Rigger lived in Stone House with the two women.

Chicky laughed. People said that it looked odd, that was all. But she dismissed it and life went on easily for the three of them, working long hours and coping with people who didn't turn up on time or at all. She taught Rigger to make the kind of meals that Miss Queenie liked: little scones and omelettes. He mastered it quickly. It was just another thing to learn.

Rigger sometimes asked Chicky's advice about what girls liked. He wanted to give Carmel a treat. What would she suggest.

Chicky thought that Carmel might like to go to the fairground that came every year to a nearby town. There would be fireworks and bumper cars, a big wheel and a lot of fun.

And apparently Carmel liked it a lot.

It was touching to see Rigger getting dressed up to take his girl out in the old van. Chicky sighed as she saw them heading off by the cliffs. Rigger didn't drink so she never worried about there being any danger ahead. She could not have foreseen the conversation a few short months later.

Carmel was pregnant.

Carmel Hickey, aged seventeen and about to sit her Leaving Certificate, was going to have the child of Rigger, who was eighteen. They loved each other, so were going to run away to England and get married. Rigger was very sorry to let Chicky down and leave her like this, but he said it was the only thing to do. There was no question of a termination and Carmel's parents would kill them both. There would be no tolerance in the Hickey family.

Chicky was unnaturally calm about it all.

First thing she said was they must tell nobody. Nobody at all.

Carmel was to do her exams as if nothing was wrong. Then, in three weeks' time when the exams were over, they could get married here, in Stoneybridge, and take it from there.

Rigger looked at her as if she was mad.

'Chicky, you have no idea what they'll be like. They'll skin me alive. They have such hopes for her: a career, a life and eventually a great catch as a husband. They don't want her married to a dead end like me. They'd never stand for it, not in a million years. We *have* to run away.'

'There's been far too much running away,' Chicky said. 'Your mother ran away from here. I ran away. You ran away. It has to stop sometime. Let it stop now.'

'But what can I offer Carmel?'

'You have a job here – a good job – you have savings already in the post office. I'll let you have that cottage beside the walled garden. You can make a home there. You will be providing all the produce for Stone House and for anyone else you can sell it to. You're a genuine businessman, for God's sake. These days they'd be hard put to find anyone so ready and able to make a home for their daughter.'

'No, Chicky. You don't know what they're like.'

'I *do* know what they are like. I've known the Hickeys all my life. I'm not saying they'll be pleased, but it beats the hell out of getting the Guards to find you in England or asking the Salvation Army to trace you.'

'Married? Here in Stoneybridge?'

'If that's what you want then yes. I think you're both too young. You could get married much later, but if you want it now then leave Father Johnson to me.'

'It won't work.'

'It will if you say absolutely nothing and just get that house done. You have to have it ready to show to the Hickeys the day you tell them that Carmel is pregnant.'

'Chicky, be reasonable. If it were going to work, we can't do all this in three weeks or a month.'

'If I tell the builders that Stone Cottage is the priority then we can. And you can take some of the furniture we have stored here.'

He looked at her with some hope in his eyes. 'Do you really think . . . ?'

'We haven't a minute to waste, and don't tell your mother either. Not yet.'

'Oh God, she's going to go mad too. More bad news.'

'Not when she hears it as a package. Not when she hears that you have a house, a proper job and a bride. Where's the bad news there? Aren't these the things she always hoped for, for you?'

Carmel Hickey proved to be amazingly practical. She swore she would focus entirely on her exams while saying that she wanted to learn bookkeeping and commercial studies as a career. She insisted that Rigger spend every waking hour getting Stone Cottage up and running. She seemed vastly relieved that they were not going to catch the emigrant ship and live on nothing in England.

Carmel had every confidence in Chicky, even to the point of keeping Father Johnson on side.

And Carmel was right to be confident. By the time the Leaving Certificate exams were over, Father Johnson had been convinced that a good Christian marriage to be solemnised between two admittedly very young and very slightly pregnant people was a good thing rather than a bad thing.

And when the Hickeys began to wail and protest, Father Johnson was reproving and reminding them not to stand in God's way.

The Hickeys were somewhat mollified after their first tour of Stone Cottage, and the evidence that Rigger appeared to be his own boss rather than just Chicky's handyman. They had to admit that the place was very comfortable and what they called 'well appointed'.

Gloria had decided to come and dress the set. She sat washing herself by the small range, giving the place an air of domesticity. Old lamps that the Miss Sheedys had once loved had been taken out and polished, rugs had been made by cutting out the better bits of old carpets and everything was brightly painted.

The wedding would be small and quiet. They didn't want any show.

Nuala wrote one short letter and made one brief telephone call to wish them well but to say that she wouldn't be able to come to the wedding.

'Ah Mam, I'd love you to be here to meet Carmel and to see our home.' Rigger hadn't believed that she would refuse to come.

'I'm not able to, Rigger. It wouldn't work. I send you both my good wishes and my hopes for the future. I'm sure I will come one day and visit you another time.'

'But I'll only have one wedding day, Mam.'

'That's one more than I had,' Nuala said.

'But why are you still against me, Mam? I did what you and Nasey said I should do. I made a life here. I worked hard. I gave up all that stupid way of going on. *Why* won't you come and see us getting married?'

'I failed you, Rigger. I gave you no upbringing. I couldn't look after you or guide you. I let you make a mess of your life. I have no part of what you have become. You did all that without me.'

'Don't talk like that. I'd be *nothing* if it weren't for you. I was the eejit who wouldn't listen. Please come, Mam.'

'Not this time, Rigger. But maybe one day.'

'And about the baby . . . if it's a girl, we were going to call her Nuala.'

'*Don't!* Please don't do that. I know you think it would please me but truly I don't want it.'

'Why, Mam? Why do you say that?'

'Because I'm not worth it. When did I ever do anything properly for you, Rigger? Anything that worked? I ask myself that over and over and I can't find an answer.'

She sent a wedding gift of an expensive glass vase with a card saying she was so sorry not to be able to be there in person.

Carmel understood.

'We should let her wait until she's ready. When the baby is born she'll be here like a flash and then we'll show her what a good job she made of you.'

The wedding day itself went better than they might have hoped. Nasey came from Dublin with Rigger's cousin Dingo.

Nasey smoothed things over with the Hickeys. Rigger's mother would definitely have been here if she could, but sadly she had not felt strong enough to travel. She sent everyone her good wishes.

Privately he told Chicky that his sister was retreating further and further.

No need to upset the boy by telling him this, but she seemed to have disengaged with her son entirely.

Miss Queenie was totally resplendent at the wedding in a dark pink brocade dress that she had last worn thirty-five years ago, and with a matching hat with flowers round the brim. Chicky bought herself an elegant navy silk dress and jacket. She got a plain straw hat and put navy and white silk flowers on the brim. The Hickeys were going to get a run for their money at this wedding.

Chicky served a delicious roast lamb for lunch in Stone Cottage, and they had made a wedding cake that was the equal to anything the Hickeys might have seen in a five-star hotel, if they had ever been to one. There was no honeymoon; the young couple were hard at work fixing up the hen runs and the new milking shed. Three cows had already been bought at the cattle market and were grazing in the fields. Stone Cottage would supply its own milk for the guests as well as yogurt and even organic butter. There was a great deal to be done.

Carmel helped Chicky to go through colour schemes for the bedrooms. She had a good eye and discovered where to source materials. She was deeply cynical about the expensive advice and taste of some of the interior designers they met along the way.

'Honestly, Chicky, they don't know any more than we do. Less, in fact, because you remember this house as it used to be. They're just trying to stamp their own image on the place.'

But Chicky said that they were spending so much already, the cost of an interior designer wouldn't make that huge a difference. At least they would know if they were going in the right direction.

Chicky's niece Orla wasn't sure but agreed. Give the designers a crack at it. Orla had come back from London after talking to Chicky again. She had committed to be on Chicky's team a few weeks ago.

'I couldn't come back to Stoneybridge now,' Orla had said, 'not after London, and my mother is driving me mad. Chicky, can I stay here with you in Stone House? There's plenty of room.'

'No, I've done enough to annoy the family in the past. I'm not going to be accused of hijacking you now. Just go home and sleep at your mother's house.'

'I can't do it. She's on my case all the time: why didn't I get engaged to a banker like Brigid O'Hara did? What was I *doing* in London that I didn't meet some thick-as-a-plank rich boy like Brigid did?'

'I don't want Kathleen on *my* case, either. Stick it out, Orla. And if you *do* decide to come and work with me, we'll find you a place of your own. There's a lot of falling-down cottages here. We can do one up.'

'That would mean saying I'm going to stay in Stoneybridge for ever.'

'No it wouldn't. We can always rent it or sell it afterwards. I'd give you great training. You'll cook like a dream when I'm finished with you. But don't stay here in this house. You need to be able to shake a place off at the end of the working day.'

'You're a miracle, that's what you are.'

'No, I'm just very experienced,' Chicky had said and the decision had been made.

*

64

Rigger and Carmel, determined to prove themselves in front of everyone, worked all their waking hours to turn their plans into reality. Rigger wanted to do deliveries to faraway farms up near Rocky Ridge, but Carmel warned that her cousins who ran the local grocery shops would resent this and claim that Rigger and Carmel were taking the bread from their mouths. So instead they made marmalades and jams and found attractive little jars for them with Stone Cottage painted on each one.

Like Chicky had done already, they had to look for business without alienating the shopkeepers who made their living around the area. They must try to provide a new service rather than replace existing ones.

Soon the hotels and tourist shops were buying from them and asking for more.

Carmel found some old cookbooks and learned to make chutneys, pickles and a particularly good carrageen moss made from the local red-brown seaweed that washed up on their shores. Chicky remembered that back when she was young people *had* made it as a dull milky pudding but Carmel's was a different dish altogether. With eggs and lemon and sugar it was as light as a feather, and she served it with a whipped cream laced with Irish whiskey.

Miss Queenie was very interested in the new baby, and she was the first to hear when Carmel and Rigger came back stunned from the hospital where they had learned that it was not going to be one baby but twins.

Dr Dai Morgan, a Welshman who had been taken on as a locum in Stoneybridge nearly thirty years before, was delighted for them.

'Twice the pleasure and half the effort,' he said to the two youngsters, who were still unable to take it on board.

'How wonderful! A ready-made family all in one go, and they'll be great company for each other.' Miss Queenie clapped her hands.

It was exactly what Rigger and Carmel needed to hear after their own reaction: that one baby was going to be hard enough to manage, two would be impossible.

It was difficult to make Carmel take things more easily. But between them they managed to get her to realise that this was a priority.

And slowly the weeks went by. Carmel had her suitcase packed and ready. Rigger jumped a foot in the air if she even took a deep breath.

It happened in the middle of the night. Rigger kept calm. He phoned Dr Morgan, who said to wake Chicky at once and tell her to get things ready. It sounded too late for the hospital. He would be there in ten minutes, and he was in the door of Stone Cottage before they had time to take in what was happening.

Chicky was there too with towels and a sense of control that calmed them down. The baby girl and boy were born and in Carmel's arms well before dawn.

When Miss Queenie came to breakfast, she found Chicky and Dr Dai having a brandy with their coffee.

'I missed it all,' she said, disappointed.

'You can go over and see them in half an hour. The nurse is there at the moment. They're all fine,' the doctor said.

'Thanks be to the good Lord. Now I think I should have a tiny brandy too, to wet the babies' heads.'

All day they went in and out to see the new babies.

Miss Queenie could see family resemblances already, even though they were only a few hours old. The little boy was the image of Rigger; the girl had Carmel's eyes. She was dying to know what they would call them.

Chicky was about to say that the parents probably needed time but no, they had the names ready. The boy would be Macken after Carmel's father, and the girl would be Rosemary. Or maybe Rosie.

'Where did you get that name?' Chicky asked.

'It's Miss Queenie's name. She was baptised Rosemary,' Rigger said.

Chicky smiled at him through her tears. Imagine, Rigger, the sulky, mutinous boy who had arrived on her doorstep, knowing that and having the kindness to think of honouring the old lady. She felt a wave of sadness that Nuala couldn't share this excitement. It was as if she herself had taken over Nuala's role as a second grandmother for the babies. Nuala should be here, wresting the power from Granny Hickey instead of living in some mad guilty fog in Dublin and working herself to death for nothing.

But it was such a pleasure to look at Miss Queenie. Nobody had ever taken to child-minding like she had.

'Well I *never* thought this would happen!' Miss Queenie would say in wonder. 'You see, our own children didn't materialise and I never had any nieces so there would have been nobody to be called after me, and now there is.'

There was a lot of nose-blowing and clearing of throats and then Miss Queenie asked suddenly, 'Is Nuala just delighted that the babies are here?'

Nuala.

Nobody had actually told her yet.

'If you'd like me to . . . ?' Chicky began.

'No, I'll call her myself,' Rigger said. He went away from the group and dialled his mother's number.

'Oh, Rigger?' She sounded tired, but then she probably *was*

67

tired. Who knew how many cleaning jobs she had taken on these days.

'I thought you'd want to know. The babies are here: a boy and a girl.'

'That's good news. Is Carmel all right?'

'Yes, she's fine. It all happened very quickly and the children are perfect. Perfect. They weighed four and a half pounds each. They're beautiful, Mam.'

'I'm sure they are.' Her voice still flat rather than excited.

'Mam, when I was being born, was it quick or did it take a long time?'

'It took a long time.'

'And were you all on your own in a hospital?'

'Well, there were nurses around and other mothers having babies.'

'But there was nobody of your own with you?'

'No. What does it matter now? It's long ago.'

'It must have been terrible for you.'

There was a silence.

'We are going to call them Rosie and Macken,' he said.

'That will be nice.'

'You *did* say you didn't want us to call her Nuala.'

'Yes I did, Rigger, and I meant it. Stop apologising. Rosie is fine.'

'She's going to run the world, Mam. Her and her brother.'

'Yes, of course.'

And then she was gone.

What kind of woman could care so little about the birth of grandchildren? It wasn't normal. But then, since that night after the episode in Malone's butcher's shop, Mam had not been normal. Had he in fact driven her mad?

Rigger would not allow it to get him down. This was the best day of his life.

It would *not* be ruined.

There was no shortage of people to help with the twins, and the babies grew to feel equally at home in their own house and in the big house. They would sleep in their pram while Chicky and Carmel went through catalogues and fabric samples at the kitchen table. Or if everyone was out, Miss Queenie sat there staring into the two little faces. And occasionally picking Gloria up on to her lap in case the cat felt jealous.

Nasey announced that he was going to get married in Dublin to a really wonderful woman called Irene. He hoped that Rigger and Carmel would come to his wedding.

They discussed it. They didn't want to leave home, and yet they wanted to be there to support Nasey as he had them. They were also dying to see this Irene. They had thought Nasey was well beyond romance. It would be the ideal way for them to meet Nuala on neutral ground.

'She'll be bowled over when she sees the children,' Rigger said.

'We can't take Rosie and Macken.'

'We can't leave them.'

'Yes we can. For one night. Chicky and Miss Queenie will look after them. My mother will. There's a dozen people who will.'

'But I want her to meet them.' Rigger sounded like a six-year-old.

'Yes, when she is ready she'll meet them. She's not ready yet. Anyway, it would be making us centre stage at the wedding with our twin babies. It's Nasey and Irene's day.'

He saw it was sensible but his heart was heavy at the mother who couldn't reach out in such a little way. He knew that Carmel was right. Not this time: it was enough that he would see his mother again. Things must be done in stages.

When Rigger saw his mother, he hardly recognised her. She seemed to have aged greatly. There were lines in her face that he never remembered and she walked with a stoop.

Could all this have happened in such a short time?

Nuala was perfectly polite to Carmel but there was a distance about her that was almost frightening. During the party in the pub, Rigger pulled his cousin Dingo aside.

'Tell me what's wrong with my mam? She's not herself.'

'She's been that way for a good bit,' Dingo said.

'What way? Like only half listening?'

'Sort of not there. Nasey says it was all the shock of . . . Well, whatever it was back then.'

Dingo didn't want to rake up bad memories.

'But she must be over that now,' Rigger cried. 'Things are different now.'

'She felt she made a total bags of raising you. That's what Nasey says. He can't persuade her that it's nonsense.'

'What can I do to tell her?'

'It's got to do with the way she feels inside. You know, like those people who think they're fat and starve themselves to death. They have no image of themselves. She probably needs a shrink,' Dingo said.

'God Almighty, isn't that desperate.' Rigger was appalled.

'Here, I don't want you getting all down about it. It's Nasey and Irene's day. Stick a smile on your face, will you.'

So Rigger stuck a smile on his face and even managed to sing 'The Ballad of Joe Hill', which went down very well.

And when Nasey was making his speech he put an arm

around Rigger and Dingo's shoulders and said that he had the two finest nephews in the western world.

Rigger looked over at his mother. Her face was empty.

Carmel noticed everything and understood most things without having them explained to her. It didn't take her long to get the picture here. She had talked to her mother-in-law about subjects far removed from Rigger and the family. One by one, however, the topics she raised seemed to run into the ground. No use asking about television programmes – Nuala didn't own a television set. She rarely went to the cinema. There wasn't time to read. She admitted that it was harder to get decent jobs because of the recession. Nobody paid you more than the minimum wage. Women didn't give you their clothes like they used to, they sold them online nowadays.

She answered questions as if it was an interview in a Garda station. There was none of the normal to and fro of a conversation. Apart from hoping that all was well back at Stoneybridge, she asked nothing about her grandson and granddaughter.

'Do you take a drink at all, Nuala?' Carmel asked.

'No, no, I never got in the habit of it.'

'Rigger doesn't drink either, which makes him fairly un-usual in our part of the world, but I do love the occasional glass of wine. Can I get you one?'

'If you'd like to, yes,' said Nuala.

Carmel brought two glasses of white wine back to their little table.

'Good luck to the bride and groom,' she said.

'Indeed.' Nuala raised her glass mechanically.

'I'm taking a big risk here but I'm just going to tell you something. I *love* Rigger with all my heart. He is the perfect husband and the perfect father. You won't know this because you haven't seen him in that role. He works all the hours God sends. There is one thing he is not – he is not a son. He is nobody's son. As a father himself now he would love to know something about his own father, but he wouldn't ask you any questions about him, not in a million years. But much more important than anything, he wants his mother back. He wants so much to share this good life he has now with you.'

Nuala looked at her, astonished.

'I haven't gone away,' she said.

'Please, let me finish then I promise that I will never mention this again. He's just not complete. You are the one piece of the jigsaw that's missing. He never thinks that you were a bad mother. Every single thing he says about you is high praise. I would die happy if I thought my son Macken would talk so well of me. You don't *have* to do anything at all, Nuala. You can forget I said any of this. I won't tell him. He wanted to bring the children up to meet you but I asked him not to. I said that one day they would meet their grandmother Nuala, but not until she was ready. You say you feel guilty about letting him run wild. He now feels guilty that he has made you unbalanced and ruined your life.'

'Unbalanced?'

'Well, that's what it is, isn't it? You've got the balance wrong. You need someone to help you to mend the scales. Like as if you had a broken leg. It wouldn't heal without someone to set it.'

'I don't need a doctor.'

'We all need a doctor some time along the way. Why don't you try it? If it's no use then it's no use, but at least you gave it a try.'

Nuala said nothing.

So Carmel decided to finish. 'We will always be ready. And

he needs to be a son again. That's all I wanted to say, really.' She hardly dared to look Nuala in the eye. She had gone too far.

The woman was not well. She lived in a world of her own. All Carmel had done was to annoy her and upset her further.

But she thought that the lined, strained face had changed slightly. Nuala still said nothing but she definitely looked less tense, her hands didn't grip the edge of the table so hard.

Was this fanciful, or was it real?

Carmel knew she had already said more than enough. She would not speak any more. She sat very still for what seemed a very long time but was probably only a minute or two. Around them, the wedding party was singing 'Stand By Your Man'.

Rigger came towards them.

'They'll be going in a few minutes, do you want some confetti to throw?' he asked.

Now Carmel realised that Nuala's face had changed. She was definitely looking at the eager, happy face of her son with different eyes. It was as if she could see that this was not someone she had destroyed but a proud, happy man secure in himself and steady as a rock.

'Sit down for a minute, Rigger, knowing Nasey it will be hours before they get going.'

'Sure.' He was surprised and pleased.

'I was just wondering who was looking after Rosie and Macken tonight?' she asked.

'Chicky and Miss Queenie. They have our mobile number. Chicky rang an hour ago to say they were all asleep except herself – Miss Queenie, the twins, Gloria . . .'

'Gloria?'

'The cat. She's a heavy sleeper.'

'The cat wouldn't sleep in the pram?' Nuala looked anxious.

'No, Gloria's much too lazy to get up to that height. Anyway, they're watched all the time.'

'Good, good.'

'Chicky wanted to know how it was all going,' Rigger said.

'And what did you tell her?' His mother was actually asking a question, looking for information.

'I said it was a great wedding,' Rigger reported.

'Will you be talking to her again tonight?' Nuala wondered.

'Oh, you can be sure we will. This is the first night we've ever left them,' Carmel said.

'Could you say to her that she's to keep a sharp eye on them, and to tell them that I'll be coming to see them myself before too long? I've just got a few medical things to sort out but then I'll be there.'

Rigger struggled for the words. He was determined not to break the mood. This was not a time for hugs and tears.

'And won't they be so pleased to hear that, Mam,' he said. 'So very pleased.'

Just then there was a rush to the door. The bride and groom really *were* leaving.

Carmel looked at Nuala. She wanted to tell her that with those words she had made her son feel complete.

But there was no need. Nuala knew.

Orla

When Orla was ten they got a new teacher in St Anthony's Convent. She was Miss Daly, she had long red hair and she wasn't remotely afraid of the nuns or Father Johnson or the parents, who were demanding that the girls get first-class honours and scholarships to university. She taught them English and history and she made everything interesting. The girls were all mad about her and wanted to be just like her when they grew up.

Miss Daly had a racing bicycle and could be seen flying across cliff roads pedalling madly. They *must* all take exercise, she told them, otherwise they would end up as little wizened old ladies crawling around. If they were fitter they would have more fun. Suddenly the girls of St Anthony's became fitness freaks. Miss Daly had an early-morning dance exercise class and they all turned up eager for new routines.

Miss Daly told them that they were very foolish to resist the computer skills classes, this was the future, this would be their passport out of a dreary life. And even the noisy, troublesome pupils like Orla and her friend Brigid O'Hara listened and thought it made sense. They became part of the fundraising drive to get more computers for the school.

Their parents had mixed feelings about Miss Daly. They were glad, and indeed astounded, that she had such an effect on the children and was able to control them like no other teacher had even begun to do. On the other hand, Miss Daly wore very short shorts on her racing bike; she was almost *too* healthy, with wet hair and a just-out-of-the-sea look in all seasons. She drank pints in the local pubs, which women didn't usually do.

It was reported that one elderly bar owner had hesitated before pulling a pint for her, saying that ladies didn't normally get served in this manner. Miss Daly is meant to have said politely that he would pour the pint or deal with a complaint to the Equality Commission, whichever he preferred, and he poured the pint.

Miss Daly was not seen regularly at Sunday Mass but she put in more hours at that school than any other staff member had ever done. She was there half an hour before lessons began with her dance exercise class, and after the bell went at four o'clock she was there in the computer room helping and encouraging. A generation of girls in St Anthony's became confident with Miss Daly as their role model. She told them there was nothing they couldn't do and they believed her utterly.

When Orla was in her last year, Miss Daly announced that she was leaving St Anthony's, leaving Stoneybridge. She told everyone, including the nuns, that she had met a fabulous young man called Shane from Kerry. He was twenty-one and trying to set up a garden centre. He was quite gorgeous, twelve years younger than her and besotted with her. She thought she'd help Shane put his garden centre on the map.

The nuns were very startled by this and sorry to see her go.

The Reverend Mother made the mistake of hinting that marriage to a much younger man might have its pitfalls. Miss Daly reassured her that marriage was the last thing on her mind and that confidentially marriage was really outdated.

Reverend Mother was shocked, but Miss Daly was un-repentant.

'But didn't you realise that yourself, Reverend Mother? I mean, you were ahead of your time deciding to give the whole thing a miss . . .'

The girls organised a goodbye picnic for Miss Daly – a bonfire on the beach one night. She showed them pictures of Shane, the young man in Kerry and she begged them all to travel and see the world. She told them to read a poem every day and think about it, and whenever they went to a new place, to find out about its history and what had made it the place it had become.

She said they should learn all sorts of things while they were still young, like how to play bridge, how to change a wheel on a car and how to blow-dry their own hair properly. These things weren't hugely important in themselves but they stopped you wasting time and money later on.

She gave them her email address and said she would expect to hear from them about three or four times a year for ever. She expected them to do great things. They cried and begged her not to go, but she told them to look at the picture of Shane again and ask themselves seriously would any sane person let him slip through their fingers.

Orla did write to Miss Daly, and told her about the course in Dublin she had done, how she had won the medal at the end of the year. She told Miss Daly that she found her mother totally unbearable, full of small-town attitudes, and when Orla came back from Dublin it was usually only three days before she and her mother had a blistering row about something totally unimportant like Orla's clothes or the time she came home at night. Her father just begged her not to cause trouble. Anything for an easy life. Her aunt Chicky, who came home from America, was so different; a real free spirit, and Orla was hoping to go out on a holiday with Brigid to New York to see her. Orla always asked about Shane and the garden centre but got no response to that. Miss Daly was only interested in her pupils' lives, not in telling them tales of her own.

Then Orla wrote and said that the whole trip to New York had been cancelled because Uncle Walter had been killed in a horrific crash on a motorway. Miss Daly reminded her that her life was in her own hands. She must make her own decisions.

Why not get a job away from home and come back for short bursts? It was a big world out there; there were even further horizons than just going to Dublin.

So Orla reported that she and Brigid were going to London.

Brigid got a job in a public relations agency which handled publicity for a rugby club, among other clients. They would meet an amazing amount of fellows. Orla got work with a company that organised exhibitions and trade fairs. It was full of variety; at any moment they might be dealing with health foods or vintage cars. James and Simon, the two men who ran the company, were both workaholics and taught Orla to be tough and to work under pressure. After a month there she found herself able to talk firmly and with great authority to people who would normally have terrified her.

To her surprise, both James and Simon found Orla very attractive and each of them made a move on her. She almost laughed in their faces – two more unlikely suitors she could not imagine. Married men who scarcely saw their families and whose main interest was beating their rival companies. All they wanted was some on-the-spot entertainment.

They took the rejection cheerfully. Orla dismissed it all as a childish mistake and went on to learn more and more.

She wrote to her teacher saying that Miss Daly should be proud of her. This job was a whole education in itself, and she was rapidly becoming expert in the world of taxation, websites and networking, as well as setting up exhibitions.

Orla and Brigid shared a flat in Hammersmith. It was all so gloriously free compared to home. And there was *so* much to do. She and Brigid went to tap-dancing classes in Covent Garden on Tuesday nights. Orla also went to a lunchtime calligraphy class every Monday.

James and Simon protested in the beginning about this. She was not fully committed to the job if she insisted on being free to learn fancy handwriting. Orla took no notice of them whatsoever. If she had to earn her living in their busy, dreary, business-obsessed world, she said it was completely necessary that she have some safety valve of a little artistic input to start the week. They didn't dare say a word against it after that.

And at night they went to the theatre or to receptions that Orla organised or to various functions at the exhibition halls. They were young, lively and unimpressed and people loved them. So far, there was nobody special for either of them but neither Brigid nor Orla were in any hurry to settle down.

Until Foxy Farrell turned up.

Foxy was the kind of man they both hated. Loud, confident, big car, big sheepskin jacket, big job in a merchant bank, big opinion of himself. But he was completely besotted with Brigid. And, oddly, Brigid started to find this less hilarious and embarrassing than it had seemed at the start.

'He's basically decent, Orla,' she said defensively.

'I know he is,' Orla spoke without thinking. 'But could you *bear* it? I mean, imagine waking up beside him in the morning.'

'I have,' Brigid said, simply.

'You never have! When?'

'Last weekend, when I was in Harrogate. He drove all the way up to see me.'

'So you made it worth his while.' Orla was still reeling from this news.

'He's very nice, really. That old showing-off thing is just the way they go on in his set.'

'I'm sure he is when you get to know him properly . . .' Orla began the backtracking, which she hoped was not too late.

'Yeah, well, I'm going to get to know him improperly next weekend. We're going to Paris,' Brigid said, with a giggle.

'We're going home to Stoneybridge for the long weekend,' Orla protested.

'I know we were *meant* to. You'll have to cover for me.'

'Couldn't you go to Paris another weekend with Foxy?'

'No, this is special.'

'So I have to cover for you and explain? What *do* I explain, actually?' Orla was annoyed. They went home together dutifully three or four times a year. This was the price they paid for their freedom. Just a long weekend.

'Oh, as little as possible at the moment.' Brigid was airy and casual about it. 'I don't want to be getting their hopes up.'

'Their hopes *up*? About Foxy?' Orla had an unflattering amount of disbelief in her voice.

'Sure,' Brigid said. 'He's absolutely loaded. I'd never hear the end of it if I let Foxy slip through my fingers.'

So Orla went back to Stoneybridge on her own with vague reports of Brigid being tied up at work.

Nothing ever changed much in Stoneybridge except that Orla had always forgotten how beautiful it was and would catch her breath as she walked along the cliff paths and looked at the sandy beaches and dark jagged rock face.

Her aunt Chicky was up to her eyes doing up the Stone House, with old Miss Queenie hovering around and chattering and clapping her hands with pleasure at it all. Rigger, who helped Chicky in the place, had become much less surly. He had learned to drive and would even stop to give Orla a lift if he saw her on the road. He asked her if she remembered his mother, but Orla didn't. She had heard of this Nuala but she had gone to Dublin before Orla was born.

'Chicky would know all about her,' Orla suggested.

'I don't ask Chicky about things,' Rigger said. 'She doesn't ask me about things either, it's good that way.'

Orla took this on board. She was on the point of asking Rigger about himself. This had warned her off in good time.

So instead they talked about the renovations at Stone House, the new walled garden, the plans. He seemed to think it was going to be a huge success and was excited to be in at the start.

Orla's mother, however, had been pouring a lot of cold water on the enterprise. Chicky was always the same, getting carried away by lunatic ideas, like the time she ran off to America without a by-your-leave.

'Well *that* worked out all right, didn't it?' Orla was defensive about the aunt who had always treated her as a grown-up. 'She had a great marriage and he left her enough money to buy Stone House.'

'It's odd he never came back here himself though, isn't it?' Kathleen was never totally at ease with any situation.

'Aw, Mam, will you stop it. Something's always wrong with everything.'

'It mainly is,' Kathleen agreed with her. 'And another thing: there's a lot of talk about Chicky living with just that young lad and the old woman above in the house. It isn't fitting, it's just not the way things should be.'

'*Mam!*' Orla was pealing with laughter, 'what a fantastic world you live in. Do you think Rigger is pleasuring Aunty Chicky in the walled garden? Maybe they have a threesome going with Miss Queenie as well!'

Her mother's face flushed dark red with annoyance. 'Don't be so crude Orla, please. I'm only saying what's being said all around the place, that's all.'

'Who's saying that all round the place?'

'The O'Haras, for one.'

'That's only because they're furious that Miss Sheedy didn't sell it to *them*.'

'You're as bad as your uncle Brian – always attacking them! Isn't Brigid your own best friend?'

'She is, but that's her uncles being greedy speculators. She knows that too.'

'Where *is* she, by the way, that she couldn't be bothered to come home to her family?'

'She's working hard for a living, Mam. As am I, which is why *you* are so much luckier than the O'Haras because I put you first always, don't I?'

And her mother really had no answer to that.

Orla spent as much time as she could with Chicky. Despite all the activity and people coming and going in Stone House, Chicky was very calm. She never asked whether Orla had boyfriends in London, and if she intended to live there permanently. She never said that people would think it odd if Orla wore short skirts or long skirts or torn jeans or whatever she was wearing at the time. Chicky wasn't even remotely aware what people were saying or thinking or wondering. Chicky never told her what she really should be doing with her life.

So it was surprising when this time Chicky asked her was she a good cook.

'Reasonable, I suppose. Brigid and I cook from recipes two or three times a week. She does great things with fish. It's different over there, not full of bones and tasting like cod liver oil like it does here.'

Chicky laughed. 'Not any more, it doesn't. Do you make pastry?'

'No, it's too hard, too much trouble.'

'I could teach you to be a great cook,' Chicky offered.

'Are *you* a great cook, Chicky?'

'I am, as it happens. It was the last thing I ever expected to be, but I do enjoy it.'

'Did Uncle Walter cook also?'

'No, he mainly left it to me. He was always so busy, you see.'

'I know.' Orla didn't know but she could recognise when Chicky was closing down a conversation. 'Why would you teach me to cook?' she asked.

'In the hope that one day, not now, but one day, you might come back home here and help me run this place.'

'I don't think I could ever come back to Stoneybridge,' Orla said.

'I know.' Chicky seemed to think that was reasonable. 'I never wanted to come back either but here I am.' That day she showed Orla how to make a really easy brown bread and a parsnip and apple soup. It seemed completely effortless and they had it for their lunch. Miss Queenie said that she had never eaten such lovely food in her life until Chicky had come to the place.

'Imagine, Orla, we grew those parsnips here in our own garden and the apples are from the old orchard, and Chicky made them all taste like that!'

'I know, isn't she a genius!' Orla said with a smile.

'She is indeed. Weren't we lucky that she came back to us and didn't stay over there in the United States? And tell me, are you having a wonderful time over in London?'

'Not bad at all, Miss Queenie, busy of course and tiring, but great.'

'I wish I had travelled more,' Miss Queenie said. 'But even if I had, I think I would always have come back here.'

'What do you like particularly about here, Miss Queenie?'

'The sea, the peace, the memories. It all seems so right here, somehow. We went to Paris once, and to Oxford. Very, very beautiful, both places. Jessica and Beatrice and I often talked about it afterwards. It was great but it wasn't real, if you know what I mean. It was as if we were acting a part in a play. Here you don't do that.'

'Oh, I know what you mean, Miss Queenie.' She saw Chicky flash her a grateful look. Orla had no idea what poor Miss Queenie had meant but she was glad she had given the right response.

Back in London, she made brown bread and parsnip soup to welcome Brigid back from Paris.

'God, you've become domesticated,' Brigid said.

'And you've got something to tell me,' Orla said.

84

'I'm going to marry him,' Brigid said.

'Fantastic! When?'

'In the summer. Only, of course, if you'll be my brides-maid.'

'Only, of course, if I don't have to wear plum taffeta or lime-green chiffon.'

'Are you pleased for me?'

'Come on, will you look at yourself, you are *so* happy. I'm thrilled for you.' Orla hoped she was putting enough enthusiasm in her voice.

'You don't think he's just foolish old Foxy?'

'What do you *mean*? Of course I don't think that. I think he's lucky Foxy. Tell me where and when did he propose?'

'I *do* love him, you know,' said Brigid.

'I know you do,' Orla lied, looking into the face of her friend Brigid who, for some reason that would never be explained, was going to settle for Foxy Farrell.

Things moved swiftly after that.

Brigid left her job and spent a lot of time with Foxy's family in Berkshire. The wedding would be in Stoneybridge.

'What a pity that Chicky's place won't be up and running in time. It would be great if the Farrells could take it over for the wedding. They'll be appalled by Stoneybridge,' Brigid said.

'I was half thinking of going back there,' Orla said, suddenly.

'You're never serious?' Brigid was shocked. 'Look at how hard it was to get out of there in the first place.'

'I don't know . . . it's only a thought.'

'Well, banish that thought.' Brigid was very definite. 'You'd only be back twenty minutes before you were on all fours trying to get out of it again. And where would you work, for God's sake? The knitting factory?'

'No, I might go in with Chicky.'

'But that place is doomed, I tell you. It won't last for two seasons. Then she'll have to sell it and lose a packet. Everyone knows that.'

'Chicky doesn't know that. I don't know that. It's only your uncles who say that because they wanted to buy it themselves.'

'I'm not going to fight with my bridesmaid,' Brigid said.

'Swear you aren't thinking of mauve taffeta,' Orla begged, and they were fine again. Apart from Orla's disbelief that anyone could want to marry Foxy Farrell.

As she often did at times of change, Orla wrote to Miss Daly for advice.

'Am I going mad, sort of wanting to go back to Stoney-bridge? Is it just a knee-jerk reaction to Brigid deciding to marry this eejit? Were you bored rigid when you were there?'

Miss Daly wrote back.

I loved the work. You were great kids in that school. I adored the place. I still look back on it with pleasure. I'm in the mountains here. It's lovely, and I can drive to the sea but it's not the same as Stoneybridge, where the sea was there at your feet. Why don't you try it out for a year? Tell your aunt that you don't want to sign up for life. Thank you for not asking about Shane. He's having a little time out with something marginally more interesting than me, but he'll be back. And I'll take him back. It's a funny old world. Once you realise that, you're halfway there.

In Orla's office, James and Simon were very tight-lipped these days. Business was not good. The economy was sluggish, it didn't matter what politicians said. They knew. People weren't booking stands at exhibitions like they used to. Trade fairs were smaller than last year. The prospects were dire. They were placing all their hopes on Marty Green, who was very big in the conference business. They were having drinks in the office to impress him.

'Ask that sexy redhead friend of yours to come and help us dress the set,' James suggested.

'Brigid's just got engaged. She won't want to be a party-party girl these days.'

'Well, tell her to bring her fiancé. Is he presentable and everything?'

'You're worse than my mother and her mother put to-gether. Very presentable, richer than God,' Orla said.

Brigid and Foxy thought it would be a laugh and turned up in high good form. Marty Green was delighted with them all and seemed to be taking the sales pitch on board. He was also very interested in Orla, who had dressed to kill in a scarlet silk dress she had found in a charity shop and really expensive red and black shiny high heels. She passed around the white wine and the tray of canapés.

'These are very good,' Marty Green said appreciatively, 'who's your caterer?'

'Oh, I did these myself,' Orla smiled at him.

'Really? Not just a pretty face, then?' He was definitely impressed, which was what this reception was all about. But Orla felt he was rather too impressed with her and not enough with the company.

'That's very nice of you, Mr Green, but I wasn't hired here to make canapés and smile. We all work very hard, and as James and Simon were saying, this has paid off. We know the market and the situation very well. It's good to get a chance to tell you about it personally.'

'And very pleasant it is to hear about it personally.' His eyes never left her face.

Orla moved away but knew he was watching her all the time. Even when James was giving statistics, when Simon was talking about trends, when Foxy was braying about great new restaurants and Brigid was asking if Mr Green was interested in rugby, as she could get him tickets.

Marty Green wondered if Orla would like to have dinner with him.

She saw James and Simon smiling at each other in relief and suddenly felt hugely resentful. She was being offered to Marty Green. It was as simple as that. She had dressed up, spent her lunchtime making finicky, awkward little savouries, rolling asparagus spears in pastry and serving them with a dipping sauce, arranging little quails' eggs artistically with celery salt on lettuce leaves, and now they wanted to send her out like a sacrificial lamb to be pawed by Marty Green.

'Thank you so much but sadly I have plans of my own tonight, Mr Green,' she said.

He was suave; she would give him that much. 'I'm sure you must indeed have plans. Another time, perhaps?'

And they all smiled different smiles: Orla's was nailed to her face, James and Simon's were like a horror mask. Brigid's smile hid her shock that Orla would pass up on a date with such a wealthy and charming man as Marty Green. Foxy's smile was vague and foolish, as always.

Marty Green left saying that he would be in touch. Orla poured herself a large drink.

'Why did you have to be so very rude to him?' Simon asked.

'I wasn't at all rude. I thanked him and told him that I had my own plans.'

'That's what I mean. You don't *have* any plans.'

'Oh, yes I do. I plan *not* to go out with some businessman as if I were an escort or a hooker.'

'Come on now, that wasn't remotely what was suggested,' James said.

'It was spelled out in capital letters.' Orla was furious now. 'Take the nice man out, bill and coo at him, get his name on a contract.'

'We are all in this together. We assumed that—'

'Why didn't you bring a pole in here and put it up in the office and I could have taken off my clothes and danced around it? That would have helped too, wouldn't it?'

'It was only dinner,' Simon said.

'Yes, and at the end of an expensive dinner I'd be able to get up and say goodbye and thank you Mr Green? What world do you live in? If I'd gone out to a meal with him and then not gone back to his hotel, I would have been a tease. I would have led him on. He'd have been more annoyed still. This way we all save face. Well, most of us do.'

'Hey, Orla, you're being a bit heavy about this,' Foxy said.

Brigid glared at him but he didn't see.

'I mean, that's what tonight was all about.'

'You never said a truer word, Foxy,' Orla said.

Next day James and Simon were prepared to be generous. They had discussed it, they *could* have given the wrong impression. The last thing they wanted to do was . . . well, what Orla had suggested they were doing.

Orla listened politely until they had finished. Then she spoke very carefully.

'This isn't just a hissy fit. I've been thinking of leaving for quite a while. My aunt is setting up a hotel in the West of Ireland. I just needed something to focus my mind, and this is it. *Please* don't take this as a sulk or as part of a campaign to make you grovel. It's far from that. It's just a month's notice, with great gratitude for all I've learned here.'

Nothing they said made any difference. Eventually they had to agree to let her go.

Orla had told Chicky it would only be for a year, just to get the place up and running.

'Maybe it's hardly worth your while teaching me to cook like a dream.'

'It's always worthwhile teaching people to cook.'

'You might run a cookery school for real people,' Orla suggested.

'The main thing we have to offer here is the scenery. They could learn to cook anywhere,' Chicky said. 'Anyway, we should keep the magic to ourselves.'

'How will I manage not to take an axe to my mother when I get back?' Orla wondered.

'Don't live at home,' Chicky advised.

'Can I live with you?'

'No. That would cause bad feeling. We'll find you somewhere to live. Rigger will do it up. Your own little place. Leave it to me. When will you be arriving?'

'Any time now. They don't need me to work my notice out. They're only going to hire someone part-time to replace me, anyway. Am I stone mad to be doing this, Chicky?'

'As you said, it's only a year. You won't notice it slipping by.'

*

By the time she arrived, Rigger was busy doing up an old cottage beside the walled garden for himself and Carmel Hickey. He said that there was an old gardener's cottage and the roof was sound, so it hadn't ever got damp. It hadn't taken much more than a good clean-out to make it habitable.

Orla's new home was ready for her.

'I hope you're not going to have the morals of Miss Daly and be the talk of the town,' Orla's mother said on her first night home.

'Oh, Mam, I do hope not,' Orla agreed fervently. She could see Chicky hiding a smile.

'Your father and I don't know what you have to go and get yourself an old, damp cottage like that for anyway. You've a perfectly good home here. People will think it's very strange.'

'You know, Mam, they won't. They won't even notice,' Orla spoke automatically.

How very wise Miss Daly and Chicky had been about being independent. Now she hoped her instinct about coming back had been right and not a foolish notion.

There was little time to wonder about it. They were plunged into work straight away. Orla began to look back on the busy days in the office with James and Simon as if it had been one long holiday. She had not believed it possible that there would be so much to organise.

Chicky's financial system left a lot to be desired. It was honest and thorough and the books were kept . . . in a fashion. But it was not computerised. Chicky had never used accounting software and instead worked on a system of ledgers and cardboard files. It was like something from fifty years ago. So the first thing Orla did was to choose a room as an office. Somewhere she and Chicky could store the computer, printer and all the reference books, drawings and filing cabinets they needed.

Chicky suggested one of the several large pantries that opened off the kitchen. Orla managed to get Rigger to leave aside a few hours from doing up his own house to impress Carmel Hickey's family in order to get the office shelved and painted.

'It'll be worth it in the end,' she insisted. 'Then we will be out of everyone's hair instead of spreading everything over the kitchen table and gathering it all up again.' She found them a computer and set up the programs she needed. Then she insisted Chicky come in and learn it from the start.

'No, no, that's your department,' Chicky protested.

'Excuse *me*. I spent two hours last night learning how to make choux pastry. I didn't say it was *your* department. Today you're going to learn to deal with the bookkeeping software. It should take forty-five minutes if you concentrate.'

Chicky concentrated.

'That wasn't too bad,' Orla approved. 'So tomorrow we'll set up a bookings system, and then the next day you'll learn how to buy and sell.'

'Are you sure that we need me to . . .' Chicky was fearful at spending too much time in the office instead of out dealing with the daily problems.

'Totally sure. Suppose you wanted to buy a piece of kitchen equipment? This will save you all the time making phone calls and going shopping.'

'I suppose,' Chicky agreed, doubtfully.

But she did agree that it was great to have everything at their fingertips, and when Orla would give her a little test like asking her how would she find someone who had made a reservation for next month and wanted to extend by another week, Chicky was soon able to summon up the bookings system on the screen. And at the same time, Orla learned how to make sauces that complemented meat dishes and ways of cleaning, filleting and serving fish straight from the sea in a way that an experienced fishmonger would envy.

One by one they beat down the obstacles.

There was the pathetic attempt of the O'Hara uncles to oppose planning permission. Chicky managed to sort it without falling out with anyone, a miracle in itself. They coped with the environmentalists' lobby, who worried lest the new hotel would disturb the habitat of birds and other wildlife. Tea and scones were served to the concerned enquirers before they were taken on walks to show how nature was being protected in every way.

They all left satisfied.

The builders were encouraged in their efforts by the thought of a home-cooked meal every day; Chicky put it on the kitchen table at one o'clock and had everyone back to work at one-thirty. Most of the men, used to bringing their own sandwiches, regarded this big lunch as the high spot of the day. They went home and told their wives that the Irish stew or bacon and cabbage was very different over at Mrs Starr's place than it was at home, and it caused a lot of resentment.

The landscaping was beginning to show results, and old Miss Queenie said the house looked like it had when she was a girl – before the money had got so short.

And away from Stone House, they could see Stone Cottage taking shape. They all enjoyed furnishing it for Rigger. Orla knew he was very nervous about dealing with the Hickeys when the plan was announced but she learned from Chicky that these things were just not discussed.

93

It was all so different from living with Brigid, where every-thing was talked about and analysed down to the bone. That was, of course, the old days. Brigid wasn't the same any more. She was obsessed by this wedding, by guest lists and wedding lists and seating plans, and she expected Orla to be some kind of wedding planner since she was on the spot in Stoneybridge.

Could Orla check the church and see what kind of bou-quets they could hang on the end of each pew near the aisle? In vain did Orla say that nobody had ever seen these in Stoneybridge. Brigid was in 'Mad Bride' mode and could not be stopped.

In despair, Orla asked Chicky's advice; Chicky gave it some thought.

'Tell her that her own family want to be involved and that *they* should be doing all this sort of thing.'

'But she doesn't trust them, she thinks they're country hicks.'

'She's probably quite right, but stress that her family are very hostile to anything to do with Stone House and that it would be awkward if you were involved. That will get you out of it.'

'You're wasted here. You should be in the United Nations,' Orla said, admiringly.

Brigid visited twice before the wedding, stressed and anx-ious.

'Can I stay in your cottage?' she begged Orla. 'My mother will be the deceased mother of the bride if I stay at home.'

Orla was reluctant to have Brigid in the house. It would indeed cause bad feeling with her family, and also it would mean that Orla would get sucked into the lunatic preparations.

'I can't have you, Brigid. Miss Daly is coming to stay.'

'Miss *Daly*? *Our* Miss Daly? From school?'

'Yes, it's all arranged.'

'Lord, you've been behaving very oddly since you got back to Stoneybridge.'

'I know. It's all that sea air.'

'Since when were you such pals with Miss Daly?'

'I always have been.'

'I think that working with Miss Queenie is bad for you, Orla. You've become a total eccentric.'

'But not quite mad enough to wear canary yellow. Have you decided the colour of my bridesmaid's dress yet?'

'Oh, wear what you like. You will anyway.'

'Good. I have the very thing: dark gold with some cream lace. Restrained but smart.'

'Is it long?'

'Yes, of course it is.'

'Well, where is it? Will we go to see it when I'm over there?'

'I have it.'

'You bought it *already*?' Brigid was outraged.

'I don't have to wear it at the wedding. Just have a look at it.'

'But what will you do with it if it's not suitable? Can you give it back?'

'It will always come in useful.'

'Useful? Washing pots in a guest house? God Almighty, Orla, what's to become of you?'

'God knows,' Orla agreed.

Her main focus was to get Brigid to see the dress without knowing that it had belonged to Miss Queenie. Sixty years ago Miss Queenie had worn it to a hunt ball where she had been a great success. It fitted Orla as if it had been designed especially for her.

*

Miss Daly looked exactly the same as she had always looked. She had brought two suitcases and her bicycle.

'You're very good to come at such short notice.' Orla was grateful that her teacher had responded to the emergency call.

'It suited me very well. Shane's passing fancy turned out to be more permanent than we had thought.'

'I'm sorry,' Orla said.

'I'm not, really. It had run its course. I needed a short sharp shock.'

'And you got one?'

'Yes, a very pregnant eighteen-year-old, and the whole we-are-delighted-about-the-baby routine. It was just the right time to have a few days out to reconsider.'

'Is that what you're going to do while you're here?'

'Yes, it's a good place to think. Out by that ocean you feel smaller, less important somehow, it puts things into proportion.'

'Wish it would work for Brigid,' Orla sighed.

'You feel you've lost her, don't you?' Miss Daly was sympathetic.

'Yes, to be honest. We've been best pals since we were ten. It's all as if it were some kind of phase. You know, like when she and I were into tap-dancing for a bit and we wore leotards and did shuffle-hop-step, tap-ball-change, over and over. But this is for life. And with Foxy!'

'Maybe she loves him.'

'No. If she loved him she wouldn't be going insane trying to impress his family.'

'Or she could just need security.'

'Brigid? She's *so* well able to look after herself.'

'And have you ever loved anyone, Orla?'

'No, not *loved*. Fancied, yes.'

96

'Well at least you know the difference, which is more than some of us. Let me give you a hand planting some stuff that will survive up in Stone House. Half those things you put in will die in the winter.'

Miss Daly cycled around and had a pint in several of the local pubs to mark her territory. And when Brigid came home, she asked all the questions that Orla didn't dare to. Like what would Brigid *do* all day after the honeymoon if she wasn't going to work? Did they plan a family immediately? Would she be seeing a lot of the Farrell in-laws?

The answers were deeply unsatisfactory and seemed to centre around going to a lot of race meetings and popping down to Foxy's sister's place in Spain. But there were some small mercies. Brigid just loved Miss Queenie's dress, describing it with approval as *vintage*. Foxy's sister was going to be wearing a vintage dress also. It would be very suitable.

The wedding was just as awful as Orla had feared. It was totally over the top, with a giant marquee and conspicuous wealth on display everywhere.

The O'Haras had pushed the boat out and even done up a few of the townhouses which they had bought during the property boom but had been standing idle since the recession. They had been given a quick paint job and refurbished for the Farrell family to stay in, which met with much approval.

Foxy's best man, Conor, another clown who had left behind his Irish roots with his Irish accent, made a speech of profound vulgarity where he said that one of the perks of being best man was that you got to shag the bridesmaid, and that this wouldn't be too great an ordeal tonight. Foxy laughed uproariously. Orla stared ahead stonily and tried not to meet Chicky's eye.

Chicky whispered to her brother Brian that he was well out of that lot. But Brian, who still smarted at his rejection by the O'Hara family, had lingering regrets about Sheila O'Hara – now separated from her gambling husband – who had once been thought to be such a good catch.

After the bride and groom had left for Shannon airport, Conor approached Orla.

'I hear you have your own place,' he said.

'Don't you have a wonderful way about you,' she said admiringly, 'I bet all the girls love you.'

'We're not talking about all the girls, we're talking about you, tonight. How about it?' he said, taking her remarks at face value.

Orla looked at him, astounded. He hadn't realised she was sending him up. If Conor and Foxy were bankers, it was no wonder the Western economy was in the state it was.

'If I were to die wondering what sex was about I wouldn't go within an ass's roar of you, Conor,' she said, smiling at him pleasantly.

'Lesbian,' he spat at her.

'That must be it all right.' Orla was cheerful.

'OK, be a ball-breaker then. I was only asking because it was expected.'

'Of course you were, Conor.' Orla's voice was soothing.

Miss Daly had been on a great trek across the mountains to avoid going to the wedding. She had met two French dentists who were on holiday there. They were heading up to Donegal tomorrow. Miss Daly was going to go with them. They had a car with a roof rack – perfect for her bicycle.

Orla sat and gaped at her.

'I know, Orla, the world is divided into people like me and people like Brigid. Aren't you lucky to walk a middle road.'

She had little time to think about it. Rigger's wedding was upcoming. This was going to be a much more normal affair.

Chicky was going to serve roast lamb in Stone Cottage, and they made a magnificent cake for Rigger and Carmel. Compared to the nonsense in the marquee and the posturing of the Farrell and O'Hara factions, this was very relaxed and full of charm.

Chicky, Orla and Miss Queenie sat and congratulated each other when it was over and the Hickeys had gone home happy.

The major building work was almost completed now on Stone House; there only remained the design and decor to be agreed. Chicky still wanted to hire professionals, and Orla insisted that nobody be paid any money until they proved they could do the job. Orla thought Chicky would be well able to do it herself. She had the original source material, after all. Miss Queenie could tell them what the place looked like in the old days.

Chicky understood comfort and style, yet she was hesitant and holding back about her own ideas.

'We are charging serious money for people to come and stay here. We don't want to have them saying that the place is phoney or tatty or anything.'

'I met a lot of these designers in London,' Orla said. 'Some of them were brilliant, I agree, but a lot of them were cowboys. Real emperor's new clothes. You'd want to watch them like a hawk.'

They settled on a couple called Howard and Barbara. They came well recommended by Brigid, who had met them with Foxy Farrell at a party in Dublin.

Orla hated them on sight. They were in their early forties, with affected accents and made lots of use of the words 'darling' and 'so', usually when dismissing something.

'Darling, you mustn't even *think* about having that grandfather clock in the hall. It will be *so* disturbing and unsettling for sleep rhythms.'

'There was always a grandfather clock in the hall,' poor Miss Queenie said, mildly.

'Hallo, we *are* talking about making this place acceptable, aren't we? That's what we're here for, darling.'

They gave Howard and Barbara one of the best bedrooms with the big windows and balcony looking out to sea. They sniffed as they looked around the room. They exchanged glances as they came downstairs. They shuddered slightly at things they didn't like, like the stone floor in the kitchen. It should be ripped out and replaced by a very good solid-wood floor. Orla said that the stone floor was authentic and had been there since the house was built in the 1820s.

'I rest my case,' said Howard. 'It's time for it to go.' But Orla won that battle. The stone floor was not negotiable.

Barbara and Howard didn't want the morning room called the Miss Sheedy Room. They said it was rather *twee*, and, darling, if there was one thing that could let a place down it was to have an element of tweeness about it. They left their own room in a great mess, with wet towels thrown on the bathroom floor and an amazing amount of dirty coffee cups, glasses and ashtrays despite the no-smoking policy that had been mentioned several times.

They didn't rate the walled garden, saying it was very amateur; the guests would be used to much bigger and more manicured landscaping. They frowned darkly at Gloria and said it was unhygienic to have a cat anywhere near food. In vain did Miss Queenie, Chicky and Orla try to convince them that Gloria was a cat with impeccable manners who would never approach a dining table when a meal was in progress. Admittedly, Gloria did mistake Howard's leg for a scratching post and, when alarmed by his screeching, tried to climb up inside his trouser leg. Barbara shouted and waved her arms at the poor cat who ran behind the sofa and hid, trembling, until rescued by Miss Queenie. By now, Orla was not the only one who hated Howard and Barbara.

Defeated by the pro-Gloria lobby, they turned their hostility towards the fact that Carmel was so obviously pregnant. They hoped that she would be kept well out of the equation when the baby was born. The last thing guests wanted, darling, was the sound of a screeching infant. It would be *so* full of bad vibes.

They never praised the delicious food that Chicky and Orla served them; instead they suggested that Stone House should have a proper wine cellar, and asked for large brandies after dinner.

Orla became very firm. After breakfast on the second day, she said that she hoped they were ready to give practical advice about the decor, materials and colours that they would suggest, together with recommendations on where they should source everything.

Barbara and Howard were slightly startled by this. They had envisaged several days soaking up the feel of the place, they said. This is what Orla had suspected. She brought a coffee percolator into the office after breakfast and sat down expectantly beside the computer.

'It's a very late Georgian house, of course,' Orla said confidently. 'I've been online to research images of this kind of house at the time, and printed some of them out for discussion. I was wondering what references *you* were going to offer us so we could compare.'

They looked at her, alarmed. 'Well, of course we all know the classic Georgian great houses . . .' Barbara began. Orla could spot somebody blustering at twenty miles distance.

'Yes, but of course this isn't a great house. It's a small gentleman's residence and almost Victorian, really, rather than what was distinctively Georgian. We wondered what colour schemes you had come up with.'

'It all depends very much on where we are coming from, darling, doesn't it? It's *so* like saying how long is a piece of string. Just asking for colours,' Howard began sonorously.

'And where do you think we should source fabrics?' Orla was shuffling a heap of further printouts. She saw Howard and Barbara exchanging glances.

Chicky joined in.

'We have our own ideas, of course, but we were anxious to have real professionals to guide us. You will have so much more experience and so many more contacts than we do.'

'I didn't realise you were so computer-savvy,' Barbara said to Orla, coldly.

'You're talking about my generation,' Orla smiled. 'I was wondering, by the way, why you don't have a website.'

'Never needed one,' Barbara said smugly.

'So how do people find you, then?' Orla's look was innocent.

'Personal recommendation.'

'Yes, that's how they find your *names*, but how do they know what you've actually *done*?'

Again, the face was innocent but the challenge was there.

By the time the meeting was over, it was clear that the parting of the ways had come.

Barbara mentioned a payment for their time and input so far. Chicky and Orla looked at each other, bewildered. Howard suggested they part as friends, no harm had been done. They wished the enterprise success. They spoke in tones of regret and disbelief that Stone House would remain open for longer than a week, *if* it ever opened at all.

Rigger drove them to the station.

He reported afterwards that they sat in complete silence for the journey. When he asked would they be coming back to supervise the decorating, they had said that it wasn't on the cards.

'Well, I hope you enjoyed your visit,' Rigger had said.

'Enjoy would be *so* too strong a word, darling,' they had said as he lifted their luggage on to the train.

Chicky, Carmel and Orla chose their colours and fabrics that night and got the show on the road the next day. It had been a lesson to them. There might well have been superb designers out there, but they had not found them. There was no time to try again. They would have to trust themselves.

Little by little the place took shape.

Their website was up and running, with pictures of the views from Stone House as well as full descriptions of what they could offer. They got many enquiries but as yet no definite bookings.

Orla set up a press release which she sent to every news-paper, magazine and radio programme. She offered a Winter Week at Stone House as a prize in several competitions, on the grounds that it would bring them publicity. She bought a big scrapbook and asked Miss Queenie to keep any cuttings that might result. She contacted airports and tourist offices, book clubs, birdwatching groups and sporting clubs; she set up a Facebook page and a Twitter account.

Chicky loved being able to access such a world from their little office in Stone House. They had perfected their menus and posted them online; now they had their daily routine, with the suppliers and deliveries worked out and timed to run smoothly. Gradually the definite bookings came in, and they were within sight of receiving their first visitors when Carmel gave birth to twins.

Miss Queenie told Orla that she had never been happier. There was so much happening in Stone House these days, and she was here at the centre of it all. The morning room was now officially called the Miss Sheedy Room. There were restored photographs from their childhood showing Beatrice and Jessica and Miss Queenie as girls. She knew everybody in Stoneybridge nowadays instead of only a very few. She had delicious meals and a warm house. Who could have guessed that life would get so much better as she grew older?

'I worry about Chicky, though, she works so hard,' Miss Queenie confided in Orla, shaking her head. 'She's still a young woman, well, to me she is, anyway. She gets a lot of admiring glances but she never thinks of looking at anyone as a possible husband.'

'And what about *me*, Miss Queenie? Don't you worry about me too?'

'No, Orla, not even a little bit. You will work here with Chicky as you promised until your year is up then you'll go off and conquer the world. It's written all over you.'

Instead of being pleased with such a vote of confidence, Orla suddenly felt lonely. She didn't *want* to go off and conquer the world. She wanted to stay here and see it through.

'I'm in no hurry to go off from here, Miss Queenie,' Orla heard herself say.

'It's dangerous to stay too long in Stoneybridge. We can't marry the seagulls or the gannets, you know,' Miss Queenie said.

'But didn't you say yourself that you were never happier than you are now?'

'I made the best of things, and I was lucky. Very lucky,' Miss Queenie said.

Next morning when Orla brought the old lady her tea, she knew from one glance at the bed that Miss Queenie had died in her sleep. Her hands were folded. Her face was calm. She looked twenty years younger, as if her arthritis and aches had gone away.

Orla had never seen anyone dead before. It wasn't very frightening.

She carried the cup of tea to Chicky's room.

Chicky was already awake. When she saw Orla she knew at once what had happened.

'There *can't* be a God. He wouldn't let Queenie die before the place opened. It's so unfair,' Chicky wept.

'You know, in a way it might be for the best,' Orla said.

'What *can* you mean, Orla? She was dying to be part of it.'

'No. She was nervous. She asked me more than once whether she would sit down to dinner with the guests or not.'

'But of course she would have.'

'She was afraid she might be too old and feathery . . . Her words, not mine.'

'How can you be so calm? Poor Queenie. Poor, dear Queenie. She had no life.'

Orla stretched out her hand. 'Come in and see her, Chicky.

Just look at her face. You'll know she had a life, and you gave it to her.'

They walked into the room where Miss Queenie had slept for over eighty years. From back in the 1930s when Ireland was only ten years old as a state.

Gloria the cat came in too. She didn't get up on the bed but looked respectfully from the door as if she knew that all was not well. They stood and looked at Miss Queenie's face. Chicky leaned over and touched Miss Queenie's cold hand.

'We'll make you proud, Queenie,' she said, and they closed the door behind them and went to tell Rigger and Carmel and to call Dr Dai.

Stoneybridge said a big goodbye to Miss Queenie Sheedy. A great crowd gathered outside Stone House to walk behind the hearse as it drove her slowly to the church.

Father Johnson said that next Sunday would be the first time there would not be a Sheedy in this church for many decades. He said that Miss Sheedy had called in to him last week and asked if they could sing 'Lord of the Dance' at her funeral, whenever that was to be. Father Johnson had said that we would all have long gone to our heavenly reward by the time Miss Queenie herself was ready to go, but the Lord was mysterious and now she had gone to join her beloved sisters, leaving behind her a memory of a life well lived.

The congregation all sang 'Lord of the Dance'. They blew their noses and wiped away a tear at the thought of Miss Queenie peering good-naturedly at them and their children for years, back as far as they could remember.

Rigger was one of the four who carried the small coffin to the graveyard. His face was grim as he remembered how the old lady had welcomed him to her home and been so excited about everything, from the walled garden to Stone Cottage to the drives around in his van and then the arrival of the twins.

He was sorry that Rosie and Macken would not have such a lovely old granny figure in their lives. They would tell them all about her. One day, when he was being carried to this grave-yard they would tell their own children about the great Miss Queenie, a good relic of an often stormy past in Ireland.

There were no Sheedy relatives, and Rigger was asked to put the first spadeful of clay on the grave. He was followed by Chicky and Orla. And the great crowd stood in silence until Dr Dai, who had a powerful Welsh baritone, suddenly sang 'Abide With Me' and they all filed back down the hill.

Tea and sandwiches were served in Stone House.

Gloria had hunted high and low for Miss Queenie and sat confused outside the front door, washing furiously.

As soon as Orla was busy passing the food around she recovered enough to realise how many people had attended. Brigid and Foxy had come over from London. Miss Daly had heard from somebody and she turned up with one of the French dentists who had now become a close friend. All the O'Haras were there, their previous animosity forgotten; all the builders, the suppliers, the local farmers, the staff of the knitting factory and Aidan, a solicitor from a nearby town, who was said to fancy Chicky.

Miss Queenie would have clapped her hands and said, 'Imagine them all turning up for me! How very kind!'

Aidan drew Orla aside to tell her that Miss Queenie had made her will last week. She had left everything she owned to Chicky apart from two tiny legacies, one to Rigger and one to Orla.

He also asked Orla whether she thought Chicky might go out with him to dinner if he asked her nicely.

Orla said that maybe he should wait until Stone House had opened to the public. Chicky was very centred on that at the moment, but she reassured Aidan that there was nobody else on the scene.

'I'd be no trouble,' he told her.

'God, isn't that a great recommendation,' Orla said, fervently looking at some uncles and the woeful Foxy.

'Must say, Barbara and Howard did a great job on this place,' Foxy said approvingly.

'Didn't they just?' Chicky agreed.

Rigger was about to open his mouth and say how unhelpful they had been but Orla frowned. Life was short. Chicky had decided to play it this way. Let it go.

Only a few days to go and the first guests would arrive. They were nearly full. Only one room remained unoccupied. Orla and Chicky sat down every evening going over the list of people. They were coming from Sweden, England and Dublin. Some by car, some by train. Rigger had been alerted to everyone's arrival times.

They went over the menus again and again checking that they had every ingredient. They tried to envisage all these people sitting around their table at night and assembling for breakfast each morning. They had left a selection of magazines and novels in the Miss Sheedy Room; they had maps and bird books and guide books at the ready. Wellington boots, umbrellas and mackintoshes were all available in the boot room.

Gloria had gradually got over her short period of mourning for Miss Queenie and returned to sit by the fire with a purr that would soothe the most troubled heart.

'You have your running-away money now, Orla,' Chicky said on the last evening.

'I *always* had my running-away money,' Orla said.

'It's just that I won't hold you back. You've delivered everything you promised and more.'

'Why is everyone trying to get rid of me?' Orla asked. 'Queenie was the same. The night before she died she said I couldn't marry the seagulls and the gannets in Stoneybridge.'

'And she was right,' Chicky agreed.

'But what about *you*? Aidan was asking after you.'

'Oh, give over, Orla!'

'I bet Walter would have liked you to marry again.'

'Yes, indeed.'

'So?'

'So what? Grab Dr Dai from his wife? Take Father Johnson out of the priesthood? Go online offering "rich widow with own business"?' Chicky laughed. 'It's *you* we are talking about. You've only one life, Orla.'

'So what's wrong with living it here for a while?' Orla asked. 'It would be more than a human could bear to go before we had the first year of running the place over us.'

Chicky sank back in her chair. Gloria stretched approvingly.

The grandfather clock in the hall struck midnight.

This was the day that Stone House would open its doors to the public. They wouldn't sit alone in this kitchen for many a night to come.

They raised their glasses to each other, and outside the waves crashed on the shore and the wind whipped through the trees.

Winnie

Of course Winnie would like to have married. Or to have had a long-term partner. Who wouldn't?

To have someone there out for your good. Someone you could share with and eventually have children with. It was obvious that was what she wanted. But not at any price.

She would never have married the drunk that one friend had – a man who got so abusive at the wedding party that the ripples were still felt years later.

She would not have married the control freak, or the miser. But a lot of the men her friends had married were good, warm, happy people who had made their lives very complete.

If only there was someone like that out there.

And if there was, how could Winnie find him? She had tried internet dating, speed dating and going to clubs. None of it had worked.

When she was in her early thirties, Winnie had more or less given up on it all. She had a busy life: a nurse doing agency work, one day here, one night there, in the Dublin hospitals.

She went to the theatre, met friends, went to cookery classes and read a lot.

She couldn't say life was sad and lonely. It was far from that, but she would love to have been able to meet someone and know that this was the right one. Just know.

Winnie was an optimist. On the wards they always said she was a great nurse to work with because she always saw something to be pleased about. The patients liked her a lot – she always made time to reassure them and tell them how well they were doing and how much modern medicine had improved. She wasted no time moaning in hospital canteens that the men of Ireland were a sorry lot. She just got on with it.

She was still vaguely hopeful that there was love out there somewhere – just a little less sure that she might actually find it.

It was on her thirty-fourth birthday that she met Teddy.

She had gone with three girlfriends – all of them married, all of them nurses – to have dinner at Ennio's restaurant down on the quays by the Liffey. Winnie wore her new silver and black jacket. She had been persuaded by the hairdresser to get a very expensive conditioning treatment for her hair. The girls said she looked great, but then they always told her that. It just hadn't seemed to work in terms of attracting a life partner.

It was a lovely evening, with the staff all coming to the table and singing 'Happy Birthday', a drink of some Italian liqueur, on the house. At the next table two men watched them admiringly. They sang 'Happy Birthday' so lustily that the restaurant included them in the complimentary drink. They were polite and anxious not to impose.

Peter said he was a hotelier from Rossmore and that his friend was Teddy Hennessy who made cheese down in that part of the world. They came to Dublin every week because Peter's wife and Teddy's mother liked to go to a show. The men preferred to try out a new restaurant each time. This was their first visit to Ennio's.

'And does your wife not come to Dublin too?' Fiona asked Teddy, quite pointedly.

Winnie felt herself flush. Fiona was testing the ground, seeing was Teddy available. Teddy didn't seem to notice.

'No, I don't have a wife. Too busy making cheese, everyone says. No, I'm fancy-free.' He was boyish and eager; he had soft fair hair falling into his eyes.

Winnie thought she felt him looking at her.

But she must not become foolish and over-optimistic. Maybe he could see that, of the four women, she was the only one without a wedding ring. Maybe it was pure imagination.

The conversation was easy. Peter told them about his hotel. Fiona had tales of the heart clinic where she worked. Barbara described some of the disasters her husband David had faced setting up his pottery works. Ania, the Polish girl, who had trained late as a nurse, showed them pictures of her toddler.

Teddy and Winnie said little, but they looked at each other appreciatively, learning little about each other except that they were comfortable to be there. Then it was time for the men to go and pick up the ladies from the theatre. The drive to Rossmore would take two hours.

'I hope we meet again,' Teddy said to Winnie.

The three other women busied themselves saying heavy goodbyes to Peter.

'I hope so,' Winnie said. Neither of them made any move to give a phone number or address.

Peter did it for them in the end.

'Can I give you ladies my business card, and if you know of any other good restaurants like this you could pass them on to us?' he said.

'That's great, Peter. Oh, Winnie, do you have a card there?' Fiona said meaningfully.

Winnie wrote her email address and phone number on the back of a card advertising Ennio's Good Value Wine. And then the men were gone.

'Really, Fiona, you might as well have put a neon sign over my head saying *Desperate Spinster*,' Winnie protested.

Fiona shrugged. 'He was nice. What was I to do, let him escape?'

'Cheesemaking!' Barbara reflected. 'Very restful, I'd say.'

'Mrs Hennessy . . . That has a nice sound to it,' said Ania with a smile.

Winnie sighed. He was nice, certainly, but she was way beyond having her hopes raised by chance encounters.

Teddy rang Winnie the next day. He was going to be in Dublin again at the weekend. Would Winnie like to meet him for a coffee or something?

They talked all afternoon in a big sunny café. There was so much to say and to hear. She told him about her family – three sisters and two brothers, scattered all over the world. She said it was a series of goodbyes at the airport and tears and promising to come out to visit, but Winnie had never wanted to go to Australia or America. She was a real home bird.

Teddy nodded in agreement. He was exactly the same. He never wanted to go too far from Rossmore.

When Winnie was twelve her mother had died and the light had gone out of the house. Five years later her father had married again; a pleasant, distant woman called Olive who made jewellery and sold it at markets and fairs around the country. It was hard to say whether she *liked* Olive or not. Olive was remote and seemed to live in another world.

Teddy was an only child and his mother was a widow. His father had been killed in an accident on the farm many years ago. His mother had gone out to work in the local creamery to earn the money to send him to a really good school. He had enjoyed it there but his mother was very disappointed that he had not become a doctor or a lawyer. That would have been a reward for the long, hard hours she had worked.

He loved making cheese. He had won several prizes and it was a good, steady little business. He met a lot of good people and was even able to give employment in Rossmore to workers who might have had to go away and find jobs abroad. His mother, who had turned out to be a superb businesswoman after her years in the creamery, did the accounts for him and was very involved in the business.

Winnie told of her life as a nurse, and explained what it meant to be registered with an agency. You literally didn't know where you were going to work tomorrow. It might be one of the big shiny new private hospitals; it could be a busy inner-city hospital, a maternity wing or a home for the elderly. In many ways it was great because there was huge variety, but in other ways it meant that you didn't get to know your patients very well – there wasn't as much continuity or involvement in their care.

They had both been to Turkey on holiday, they liked reading thrillers and they had both been the victims of well-meaning friends trying to fix them up on dates and marry them off. Either it would happen or it wouldn't, they told each other companionably. But they knew they would meet again very soon.

'I *have* enjoyed today,' he said.

'Maybe I could cook you a meal next time?'

His face lit up.

And after that he was part of her life. Not a huge part, but there maybe twice a week.

For several visits to her flat he left before midnight and drove the long road back to Rossmore. Then one evening he asked if she might agree that, perhaps, he could stay the night. Winnie said that would be very agreeable indeed.

Once or twice, they even went away for a weekend together but it had to be a short weekend. She soon learned that nothing could or would change his mother's plans. Teddy could never be free on a Friday because that was the evening that he took his mother to dinner in Peter's hotel.

Yes, every single Friday, he said regretfully. It was such a small thing, and Mam did love it so much. And when you thought about all she had given up for him over the years . . .

Winnie pondered about this to herself. He didn't *seem* like a mummy's boy, but she felt that he was nervous of introducing her to his mother. As if she might not pass some test. But this was fanciful. He was a grown man. She wouldn't rush it.

Instead, she concentrated on the idea of their taking a little holiday together.

Winnie had heard about this place that was opening in the West called Stone House. The picture on the brochure had looked very attractive. It showed a big table where all the guests would get together in the evening, a cute little black and white cat sitting beside a roaring fire; it promised excellent, home-cooked food, and comfort, with walks and birdwatching and the chance to explore the spectacular coastline.

Wouldn't that be a great place for her to go with Teddy? If

only she could prise him away and break the hold of those precious Friday nights with his mother.

His mother!

She had better get the meeting over and done with before she suggested whisking the dotey boy off to the West of Ireland! But on the other hand, this place looked as if it might be really popular. Teddy would just love the idea when it was presented to him, and if it didn't suit him she could always cancel the reservation . . .

And then it *was* time to meet her – this mother who had sacrificed so much for her boy, the mother whose Friday evenings could never be disturbed. She had asked Teddy to bring his friend Winnie from Dublin to have Friday dinner in the hotel and to join them for a lunch the following day.

Winnie took great care of what to dress in, what she thought Mrs Hennessy would like.

This old lady rarely moved from Rossmore. She would be suspicious of anything flashy.

Winnie's silver and black jacket might be too dressy. She wore a sensible navy trouser suit instead.

'I'm quite nervous of meeting her,' she confided to Teddy.

'Nonsense. You'll get on so well together they'll have to call the fire brigade,' he said.

She would take the train to Rossmore with her overnight bag. Peter and his wife Gretta had invited her to stay in their hotel as their guest. Mrs Hennessy would not be told about their sleeping arrangements, so this seemed the sensible option.

'We'll give you our best room. You'll need every creature comfort after meeting the dragon lady,' Peter had said.

'But I thought you liked her!' Winnie was startled.

'She's a great dame, certainly, and the best of company, but you never saw a mama animal in the wild as protective of its young as Lillian is. She scares them away, one by one,' Peter laughed at it all.

Winnie pretended not to hear him. Battle lines were not going to be drawn over Teddy. He was an adult, a man who could and would make his own decisions.

Teddy was at the railway station to meet her. 'Mam has made up a great guest list for lunch tomorrow as well,' he said with delight. 'She says we must make it worth your while coming all this way.'

'That's very generous of her,' Winnie murmured. 'And I get to see your home, too.' She was very pleased that she had already packed a small gift for Mrs Hennessy. This was all going to be fine.

At the hotel, Peter and Gretta were in a state of high excitement. 'Do you want to see your room now, and change for dinner?' Gretta asked.

'No, not at all. I'm fine going straight in just as I am,' Winnie said. She knew what a stickler for punctuality Mrs Hennessy was and how she hated to be kept waiting.

'Whatever you think,' Gretta said, doubtfully.

Winnie moved purposefully into the bar and dining room of the Rossmore Hotel. She would reassure the old lady and win her over. It was all a matter of letting her know that Winnie was no threat, no rival. They were all in this together.

She could see no elderly figure sitting in the big armchairs. Perhaps Mrs Hennessy's legendary timekeeping had been exaggerated. Then she saw Teddy hailing a most glamorous woman sitting at the bar.

'There you are, Mam! Beaten us to it, as usual! Mam, this is my friend Winnie.'

Winnie stared in disbelief. This was no clinging, frail old woman. This was someone in her early fifties, groomed and made-up and dressed to kill. She wore a gold brocade jacket over a wine-coloured silk dress. She must have come straight from the hairdresser's. Her handbag and shoes were made of soft expensive leather. She wore very classy-looking jewellery.

There had to be some mistake.

Winnie's mouth opened and closed. Never at a loss for something to say, she now found herself totally wordless.

Mrs Hennessy, however, was able to cope with her own sense of surprise with much more dignity.

'Winnie, what a pleasure to meet you! Teddy told me all about you.' Her eyes took Winnie in from head to toe and up again.

Winnie felt very conscious of her big, comfortable shoes. And *why* had she worn this dreary navy trouser suit? She looked like someone who had come in to move the furniture in the hotel, not to have a dressed-up dinner with this style icon.

Teddy beamed from one to the other, seeing what he had always wanted: a good meeting between his mother and his girl. And he remained delighted all through the meal while his mother patronised Winnie, dismissed her and almost laughed in her face. Teddy Hennessy saw none of this. He only saw the three of them establishing themselves as a family group.

Mrs Hennessy said that *of course* Winnie must call her Lillian, after all, they were friends now. 'You are so very different to what I expected,' she said admiringly.

'Oh, really?' Poor Winnie wondered had she ever been so gauche and awkward.

'Yes, indeed. When Teddy told me he had met this little nurse in Dublin I suppose I thought of someone much younger, sillier somehow. It's marvellous to meet someone so mature and sensible.'

'Oh, is that what I seem?' She recognised the words for what they were: *mature* and *sensible* meant *big, dull, ordinary* and *old*. She could hear the sigh of relief that Lillian Hennessy was allowing to hiss out from her perfectly made-up lips. This Winnie was no threat. Her golden son, Teddy, couldn't possibly fancy a woman as unattractive as this.

'And it's so *good* for Teddy to have proper people to meet when he's in Dublin,' Lillian went on in a voice that was almost but not quite a gush. 'Someone who will keep him out of harm's way and from making unsuitable attachments.'

'Indeed, I'm great at that,' Winnie said.

'You are?' Lillian's eyes were hard.

Teddy looked bewildered for a moment.

'Well, I'm thirty-four and I kept myself out of making any unsuitable attachments so far,' Winnie said.

Lillian screamed with delight. 'Aren't you just wonderful! Well, of course Teddy is only thirty-two, so we have to keep an eye on him,' she tinkled.

Lillian knew everyone in the dining room and nodded or waved at them all. Sometimes she even introduced Winnie as 'an old, *old* friend of ours from Dublin'. She chose the wine, complained that the Hennessy cheeses were not properly displayed on the cheese plate and eventually called the evening to an end by talking about her invitation to lunch the following day.

'I had been in such a tizz wondering who to invite with you, but now that I've met you I see you'd be perfectly at ease with anyone. So you'll meet a lot of the old buffers around here. All very parochial, I'm afraid, compared to Dublin, but I'm sure you'll find a few likely souls.' Then she was out in the foyer tapping her elegantly shod toe until Teddy walked Winnie to the lift.

'I *knew* it would be wonderful,' he said. And with a quick kiss on the cheek he was gone to drive his mother home.

In the Rossmore Hotel, Winnie cried until she had no more tears. She saw her stained face in the mirror. An old, flat face; the face that could be introduced to old buffers. Somebody no one would get into a tizz over. *Where* did the woman get these phrases?

She wept over Teddy. Was he a man at all to leave her at the lift doors and run after his overdressed, power-crazed mother? Or was he a puppet who had no intention of having a proper relationship with her?

She would *not* go to this awful lunch tomorrow. She would make her excuses and take the train back to Dublin. Let them all work it out as they wanted to. The last few months had been a fool's paradise. Winnie should have known better at her age.

And talking about age, Lillian had said Teddy was thirty-two, making him sound as if he were still a child. He would be thirty-three in two weeks' time. He was only fourteen months younger than Winnie. She and Teddy had already laughed at the age difference. To them it had been immaterial. How had Lillian managed to change it all and make her seem like some kind of cougar stalking the young, defenceless Teddy?

Well, never mind. This was the last she would see of either of them.

She fell into a troubled sleep and woke with a headache.

Gretta was standing beside her bed with a breakfast tray.

'What? I didn't order . . .'

'God, Winnie, you've had dinner with Lillian. You probably need a blood transfusion or shock treatment but I brought you coffee, croissants and a Bloody Mary to get you on your feet.'

'She's not important. I'm going back to Dublin on the next

train. I'm not letting her get to me. Believe me, I know when to leave the stage.'

'Drink the Bloody Mary first. Go *on*, Winnie, drink it. It's full of good things like lemon juice and celery salt and Tabasco.'

'And vodka,' Winnie said.

'Desperate needs, desperate remedies.' Gretta held out the glass and Winnie drank it.

'Why does she hate me?' Winnie was begging to know.

'She doesn't hate you. She's just so afraid of losing Teddy. She grows claws whenever anyone looks as if they might take him away. This side of her comes out when she's in a panic. But she's not getting away with it this time.'

During the coffee, Gretta explained that there was a wedding in the hotel that day and that a hairdresser was on hand. She would come to the room and do a quick job on Winnie and then so would the make-up artist.

'It's too late for all this makeover stuff,' Winnie wailed. 'She saw me the way I was. I deliberately didn't bring any smart clothes because I didn't want to dazzle her. *Me* dazzle *her*? I must have been mad.'

'I have a gorgeous top I'm going to lend you. She's never seen it. It's the real deal – a Missoni. Truly top drawer. I got it from one of those outlet places. You'll knock her eyes out.'

'I don't want to knock her eyes out. I don't care about her or her son.'

'None of us cares about her, but we all love Teddy. You're the only one who can save him. Go on, Winnie, one lunch. You can do it. Believe it or not, underneath she's a very decent person.'

And somehow Winnie found herself in the shower and then with a hairdresser and having her eyebrows plucked and a blusher applied to her cheekbones. Eyeshadow to match the beautiful lilac and aquamarine colours of the Italian designer blouse.

'Even if you are leaving the stage, then leave it fighting,' Gretta warned as she admired the results.

'Get back and deal with the wedding, Gretta. This is your bread and butter. Your livelihood.'

'I don't care about the wedding. I care about getting Teddy out from under that woman's thumb. Look, Winnie, she *is* our friend, but Teddy *must* be allowed to live his own life, and you are the one who will do it. I don't know how but it will come to you.'

'I'm not going to issue any ultimatums. Either Teddy wants to be with me or he doesn't.'

'Oh, Winnie, if only life was as easy. You don't do weddings every week like we do all year long; you don't know the rocky roads to the altar.'

'I'd prefer a road with no rocks, a pleasant, easy road and to walk it alone,' Winnie said.

'You can do this. Go for it, Winnie,' Gretta begged.

Lillian had gathered over a dozen people for lunch. Fresh salmon was served with new potatoes and minted peas. There were very elegant salads with asparagus and avocado, walnuts and blue cheese.

Winnie looked around her. This was a very comfortable, charming house: there were wooden floors with rugs; big chintz-covered sofas and chairs were dotted around, framed family photographs covered the little side table.

A conservatory, where a table of summer drinks was laid out, opened into a well-kept garden. This was Lillian's domain.

Winnie was impressed but she would not fawn and admire

and praise. Instead, she concentrated on the other guests. Despite herself, she found she liked Lillian's friends.

She was seated next to the local lawyer, who talked about how Ireland had become very litigious with people looking everywhere for compensation, and told her marvellously funny stories about cases he had heard about. On her other side were Hannah and Chester Kovac who had founded and ran a local health centre, and they talked about the problems in the health service. Opposite, there was a gentleman called Neddy, who ran an old people's home and his wife Clare, who was the headmistress of the local school; their friends, Judy and Sebastian, told her they had started with a small newsagent's shop in the town centre but now had a large store in the main street of Rossmore. There had been a big fuss about the bypass when people thought that it would take trade away from the town, but it turned out there had been great business in selling Dubliners second homes in the Whitethorn Woods area.

These were normal, warm-hearted people, and they seemed perfectly at ease with Lillian Hennessy. The woman must have a lot more going for her than she was showing to Winnie.

She noticed Lillian glancing at her from time to time with an air of some speculation. It was as if she realised that Winnie had changed in more than her appearance since last night. What Winnie did not notice, however, was the way the lawyer kept refilling her glass with what he said was an excellent Chablis. By the time the strawberries were served, Winnie was not thinking as clearly as she would have liked.

She found herself looking over at Teddy's face and thinking how genuinely good-natured and warm he was. She admired his courtesy with his mother's friends, and his eagerness that everyone should have a good time. He looked across at her a lot and always smiled, as if the dream of his life had been realised and that she had come home.

Lillian was a good hostess. Winnie had to give her that much.

She managed to make her guests move around so that they talked to other people. Winnie had watched the little dance, and was determined to get up and go to the bathroom to avoid being closeted with Lillian.

But she hadn't moved in time.

'What a lovely Missoni top,' Lillian said to her admiringly.

'Thank you,' Winnie said.

'Could I ask where you got it?'

'It was a gift.' Winnie closed down the line of enquiry.

'I hope you haven't been bored here. I'm sure you think it's a real country-bumpkin outing.' Lillian in her cream linen dress and jacket looked as if she were dressed for a smart society wedding.

'I've loved it, Lillian. What wonderful friends you have.'

'I'm sure you have a lot of good friends in Dublin, too.'

'Well, yes, I do. Like you, I enjoy people, so I suppose I do have a lot of friends.' Winnie felt her voice sounded tinny and faraway. She might indeed be a little drunk. She must be very careful.

Lillian's eyes seemed to narrow but the piercing look was still there. With a shock Winnie realised that Lillian quite possibly hated her. It was as strong as that. This was territorial. Winnie would not get her hands on the golden son. His mother would fight for him. She was almost too tired to fight back. The night of weeping, the exhaustion of all the morning preparations, the breakfast Bloody Mary and all this unaccustomed lunchtime wine had taken their toll. Why take on a battle she could never win?

Then she saw Teddy smiling at her proudly across the table. He did love her. He didn't think she was old and dull. He was far too good to give up without some struggle.

'Your home is very elegant, Lillian. Teddy was lucky to grow up in such a lovely place.'

'Thank you.' Lillian's eyes were as hard as they had been last night. Now there was no attempt to conceal the hostility.

'I can see why you don't want to go away on holidays. You have everything here.' Winnie hoped the smile was fixed securely to her face.

'Oh, but I do like to travel, of course, and see things, visit places. Don't you, Winnie? I mean, what are your holiday plans this year?'

Teddy had moved over to join them. He was smiling from one to the other. Things were going better than he had even dreamed. Suddenly, Winnie found herself describing Stone House to them both.

Lillian was interested. 'It does sound good, like a retreat almost. And who do you think you would go with? I'm sure you can find someone, if it's as good as you say. It's the sort of place I'd love to go to myself, and I'd have thought it would appeal to a more sophisticated clientele. Do you know anyone who would like it? One of your nursing friends? Or are they all sun-lovers?' She was not letting it go.

'Yes indeed, you're right there, but not everyone wants to escape to the sun when it gets cold here,' Winnie floundered. 'I actually *like* the wind and rain when the place is beautiful, and there's going to be a nice hot bath and a good dinner at the end of the day. I'm sure a lot of people feel the same.'

'You're bound to find someone.' Lillian was patronising.

'I was thinking that perhaps Teddy would come with me,' she said, emboldened by drink and brave as a lion.

'Teddy!' Lillian seemed as alarmed as if the name of an international war criminal had been suggested.

'What a wonderful idea!' Teddy said, delighted. 'That part of the country is very unspoiled, and winter would be much more attractive than going with the crowds in summer. Will we be able to get a booking, do you think?'

'It won't be any problem,' Winnie said.

Teddy looked as if all his birthdays had come at once.

'Why don't we *all* go?' he said. 'It sounds so wonderful, and now that you've got to know each other, wouldn't it be great if the three of us went?' He looked from his mother to his girlfriend, enchanted with the way things had fallen out.

How could he have been unaware of the stunned silence that greeted his remark? But it seemed to have passed him by.

'I can't think of anything I would like more,' he said, looking again from one face to the other.

It was Lillian who first found the breath to speak. 'Of course, as you just said it might in fact be difficult to get a booking,' she began tentatively.

It was now up to Winnie. Any intelligent response deserted her. She found herself only able to speak the truth. 'I sort of provisionally booked a week already.' Winnie looked at the ground.

'Well isn't that just *great*?' Teddy was overjoyed. 'Now it's settled. What date is that?'

Winnie stumbled out the date. This could not be happening. He could not want to bring his mother on their holiday? If they ever did marry, would he invite her on the honeymoon as well? Please God make the date impossible.

She saw Teddy's face had clouded over.

'Oh *no*! That's the week of the cheesemakers' conference. That's the only week in the year I can't make,' he said.

Winnie thanked God from the bottom of her heart, and said she would pay much more attention to Him in future.

'Oh well, it was silly of me to make a booking without checking but it was only a vague arrangement. I'll call them and tell them . . .' Winnie was apologetic, and hoped that her relief didn't show.

'And it might have been very cold – damp, even,' Lillian chimed in quickly.

But Teddy was having none of it. 'The two of *you* must go together.'

Lillian coughed, but appeared to give the matter some thought. 'No, darling, we'll wait and set it up another time.'

'It would be a bit like *Hamlet* without the Prince,' Winnie said with a terrible forced smile that she felt must look like a death's head.

'There are other weekends, other places,' Lillian pleaded.

'Let's not even think of going without you.' Winnie practically tore Lillian's good linen table napkin into shreds.

'But what would I like better when I am away than to think of the two of you having a holiday together? Getting to know each other properly. The two people I love.' He was clearly sincere, and both women were trapped.

'Well, of course we will get to know each other, Teddy, it's just that we don't want *you* to lose out on a holiday,' Lillian began.

'Your mother could come to Dublin, and I would take her on a day out while you are away.' Winnie felt a whimper in her voice.

'This place sounds so right for you both, and it's booked. You must go,' he said.

'It might be the wrong age group for us. There could just be a house full of young people.' Lillian was grasping at straws. 'It's not a holiday that would attract young people, of course,' she said eventually.

'Yes, we might be out of place.' Winnie nodded so fervently she feared her poor, tired, muddled head might fall off.

But these were just the dying gasps of beached fish. They looked at each other. They both knew that to refuse would be to lose him. And neither of them was willing to take that step. They began to backtrack.

Lillian caved in first.

'But if it's what you really want . . . Yes, all in all, it has a lot going for it. Certainly, I'd be very happy to go with you, Winnie.'

'What?' Winnie felt as if she had been shot.

'Teddy is right. We *do* need to get to know each other. I could easily go with you then. And, do you know, I think I'd enjoy it.'

Winnie felt the room tilt around her.

She must speak this very moment, or else she had agreed to go on a week's holiday with this hateful woman. But her throat was dry and she could not find her voice. She felt herself nodding dumbly. She was like a drowning woman with the waters closing overhead but she could not stop it happening. She realised that if she did *not* speak, she would end up going to the West with Lillian Hennessy.

Lillian's small, spiteful face was very near hers. She was planning this week in the West as her way to destroy whatever Teddy and Winnie might claim to have.

Winnie straightened herself up.

In her mind she said, *All right, bring it on, then let's see who wins*, but aloud she said, 'It's a great idea, Lillian. I'm sure we'll have a wonderful time. I'll confirm the booking for the two of us.'

Somehow the meal came to an end and it was time for Teddy to drive her to the station.

'We'll be in touch before we go,' Lillian called from the hall door.

'What did I tell you?' Teddy asked. 'I *knew* you two would get on together.'

'Yes, she was very kind, very welcoming.'

'And you are both going off on a holiday together – isn't that magical?'

'Yes, she said she liked the sound of this place over in Stoneybridge.'

'Mam doesn't go on holidays with anyone, you know. She is very choosy. So she must have taken to you immediately.'

'Yes, isn't it great . . .' Winnie said. She felt flat and defeated and as if her hangover was about to kick in. It was a warning to her to go easy on wine at lunchtime for the rest of her life. A warning that had come way too late.

Winnie stared out the window as the train hurtled through rural Ireland. What kind of people worked moving cattle around these small green fields, or digging those crops into hard earth? They were people who would never have had too much wine at lunchtime, or any time. They would never have agreed to go on a week's holiday with the most hateful woman in Ireland. She tried to sleep but just as the rhythm of the train was beginning to lull her into some kind of rest, she got a text message on her phone.

It was from Teddy.

I miss you so much. You lit up the whole party at lunchtime. They were all mad about you. And so am I. But you'll never know just how wonderful you were to my mother. She has talked of nothing else but her holiday with you. You are brilliant, and I love you.

It didn't cheer her. It made her feel even worse about herself. She was a grown woman. She wasn't a schoolgirl. She had messed everything up. In ten weeks' time she would go to Stone House with Lillian Hennessy. It was like the Mad Hatter's Tea Party. It was like one of those terrible dreams that are both silly and frightening at the same time.

Winnie's friends noticed a change in her. She just shrugged when they asked her about her visit to Rossmore. They hardly dared to enquire whether Teddy was still visiting. Winnie refused the idea of going on any holidays with them.

Fiona and Declan had begged her to come and stay in the holiday home they had rented in Wexford. There would be plenty of room and they would love to have her. But Winnie didn't even consider it. Nor the suggestion that she go on a bus tour of Italy with Barbara and David, who were heading that way. And Ania's pictures of the boat they were renting on the Shannon River didn't raise a flicker of interest.

'You have to have *some* holiday,' Fiona said in desperation.

'Oh, I will. I'm going for a winter week to the West. It will be great.' She managed to make it sound as if it were going to be root-canal work.

'And is Teddy going with you?' Barbara could be brave sometimes.

'Teddy? No, it's the same week as the thing he goes to every year. The cheesemakers' thing.'

'Couldn't you have chosen another week?' Fiona wondered.

Winnie seemed not to have heard.

Teddy did come to visit, and stayed over in Winnie's little flat once or twice a week. He was as cheerful and happy as ever, and seemed to take it for granted that the planned holiday was the natural result of an instant friendship between the two women. Something he had always thought likely but couldn't believe had been so spectacular. He was so endearing, and in every other way he was the perfect friend, lover and life mate. He was already talking about a wedding. Winnie had tried to keep things light.

'Ah, that's way down the road,' she would laugh.

'I've it all worked out. We need an office for the cheese in Dublin anyway, and we could live half in Rossmore and half here.'

'No rush, Teddy.'

'But there is. I'd love us to have a huge wedding in Rossmore and show you off.'

Winnie said nothing.

'Or, of course, if you prefer, we could have it here in Dublin with all your friends. It's your day. It's your choice, Winnie.'

'Aren't we fine as we are?'

Winnie knew that there might well be no future to consider by the time she and his mother got back from this ill-starred holiday at Stone House.

There were several letters, texts and phone calls with Lillian. It took every ounce of skill and self-control for Winnie not to scream down the phone that it had all been a terrible mistake.

Then Teddy set off for the cheese gathering, and the following morning Winnie drove west from Dublin and Lillian Hennessy drove north-west from Rossmore.

They met at Stone House. They arrived, by chance, at almost the same time and parked their cars. Winnie's was a very old and beaten-up banger that she had bought from one of the porters in a hospital where she worked. Lillian drove a new Mercedes-Benz.

Winnie's luggage was one big canvas bag which she carried. Lillian had two matching suitcases, which she left beside the car.

Mrs Starr was waiting at the front door. She was a small woman, possibly in her mid forties. She had short curly hair, a big smile and a slightly American accent. Her welcome was very warm. She ran out to pick up Lillian's suitcases and led them into a big warm kitchen. On the table were warm scones, butter and jam. A big log fire blazed at one end, a solid-fuel cooker stood at the other. It looked just like the brochure.

They were ushered in and seated immediately.

'You are my very first guests,' Mrs Starr said. 'The others will be here in the next hour or so. Would you like tea or coffee?'

In no time at all, Mrs Starr had discovered more about Lillian and Winnie than either woman had ever known. Lillian talked about her husband being killed when her son was only a small child, and the terrible day when she had been given the news. Winnie explained that her father was married to a perfectly pleasant woman who made jewellery and all her brothers and sisters were overseas.

If Mrs Starr thought that the two women were unlikely friends and companions for a holiday, she didn't give any hint of it.

Winnie had insisted that Lillian be given the bedroom with the sea view. It was a tranquil, warm room with a big bay window. There were several soothing shades of green, no television but a small shower room. This place had been very beautifully refurbished. Winnie's room was similar but smaller, and it looked out on to the car park.

Winnie realised how tired she was. The drive had been long, the weather wet and the roads, as she got near Stoney-bridge, had been narrow and hard to negotiate. She would indeed lie down and have a rest. The room contained one large bed and one smaller one. If they had been the friends that Lillian had managed to imply they were, they could have easily shared this room. Even made each other further tea from the tray already set with a little kettle and barrel of biscuits, looked together at the books, maps and brochures about the area that lay on the dressing table.

But Winnie was past caring what anyone thought. Mrs Starr was a hotelier, a landlady and a businesswoman. She had little time to speculate about the odd couple who had arrived as her first guests.

Winnie felt herself drifting off to sleep. She heard the murmur of conversation downstairs as further guests were being welcomed. It was reassuring, somehow. Safe, like home used to be. Years and years ago, when Winnie's mother was alive and the place was full of brothers and sisters coming and going.

Mrs Starr had said she would sound the Sheedy gong twenty minutes before dinner. Apparently, the three Sheedy sisters, who had lived in genteel poverty in this house for many years, always rang the gong every evening. The ladies often had sardines or baked beans on toast for their evening meal but the gong always rang through the house. It was what their mama and papa would have liked.

Winnie woke to the mellow sound of the gong. God! Now she had to put in an evening of Lillian patronising everyone and six more nights in this wild, faraway place. She must have been insane to allow things to go this distance. That was the only explanation.

Before she left the room, a text came in.

Have a lovely evening. I so wish I were there with you both rather than here. I used to enjoy these gatherings, but now I feel lonely and miss you both. Tell me what the place is like. Love you deeply, Teddy.

The other guests were gathering. Mrs Starr had asked them to introduce themselves to each other as she wanted to concentrate on the food. She had a young niece called Orla who helped her serve.

Winnie saw Lillian, dressed to kill as might have been expected, slipping into gear and beginning to charm people. She was explaining to a young Swedish man how she and Winnie were old, *old* friends, and they hadn't seen each other for a long while and were so looking forward to walking for miles and catching up.

She talked to a retired teacher whose name was Nell. This visit had been a gift from the staff in her school. They had said they thought it would suit her. Nell wasn't at all certain. Lillian lowered her voice and said that she also had her doubts in the beginning, but her old, *old* friend Winnie had insisted she come. So far Lillian had to admit that it all seemed very pleasant.

Winnie spoke to Henry and Nicola, a doctor and his wife from England. They had found the place online when they were looking for somewhere very peaceful. Winnie thought they might have had a bereavement. They looked pale and a bit shaken, but then she could have been imagining it.

Another couple looked vaguely dissatisfied and didn't say much. There were other people further down the table. Winnie would meet them later.

They ate smoked trout with horseradish cream and home-made brown soda bread to start, then a roast lamb expertly carved by Mrs Starr. There were vegetarian dishes as well, and a huge apple pie. Wine was poured from old cut-crystal de-canters. The Sheedy sisters used to pour their orange squash and lemonade from these very decanters. They were beautiful antiques and felt like part of the house.

Winnie couldn't help but admire the way that it was all working out. The guests seemed to be talking easily. Mrs Starr had been quite right not to fuss around introducing them to each other. Everything had been cleared seamlessly and young Orla had stacked a big dishwasher and gone home. Mrs Starr joined them for coffee.

She explained that breakfast would be a continuous buffet but if people wanted a cooked meal they must assemble at nine. A packed lunch would be supplied for anyone who needed one, or else they could have a list of pubs in the area that served light lunches. There were bicycles outside if anyone would like to use them, and there were binoculars, umbrellas and even a selection of wellington boots. She told them about the various walking routes they might try and the local points of interest. There were a number of pretty creeks and inlets which were great to explore when the weather was calm. There were cliff-top walks though the paths down to the sea needed great care. There were caves that were worth exploring, but they must check the tides first. Majella's Cave was a good one. That had been a great place for lovers in the summertime, she had explained. It was easily cut off by the tide, so the boy and girl who wandered there had to stay for much longer than they had expected to until the seas had drawn back and let them go free . . .

After dinner, Winnie texted Teddy to tell him the place was charming and very different and that they had been made very welcome. She added that she loved him deeply also. But she wondered was this actually true.

Perhaps she was living in some never-never land. Acting a role, playing a part, cast now and possibly for ever as the old, *old* friend of her future mother-in-law. She fell into a deep sleep and didn't wake until there was a knock at the door.

Lillian, fully dressed, made-up and ready to roll.

'Thought you wouldn't want to miss the cooked breakfast,' she said. 'At our age we need a good start to the day.'

Winnie felt an overpowering rage. Did Lillian seriously think they were the same age?

'I'll be down in ten minutes,' she said, rubbing her eyes.

'Oh dear, you don't have an ocean view,' Lillian said.

'I have lovely mountains, though, and I just *love* mountains,' Winnie said through gritted teeth.

'Right. Great thing about you, Winnie, is that you are easily pleased. See you downstairs then.'

Winnie stood in the shower. The week ahead seemed endless, and she had no one to blame but herself . . .

The young Swede had gone off with the small intense woman called Freda. Henry, the English doctor, and his wife were ordering grilled mackerel. Other guests looked at the map Mrs Starr had provided and talked enthusiastically about the places they might go. There was an American man called John who was suffering from jet lag and looked very tired.

The weather was bright – no need for the umbrellas or wellington boots. Packed lunches were prepared already and in waxed paper for those who wanted them. Others had the names of pubs listed.

By ten o'clock, all the guests had left Stone House and Mrs Starr's niece Orla had arrived to do the bedrooms. A routine had been established. It was as if this holiday had been up and running for years rather than taking its first faltering steps.

Winnie and Lillian had chosen the cliff walk. Four miles with spectacular views, then you would arrive in West Harbour. There they would go to Brady's Bar. And after lunch, they would catch the bus that left every hour for Stoneybridge.

Winnie looked back longingly at Stone House.

How good it would be to go back and sit with Mrs Starr at the table having further tea and fresh soda bread and talk about the world. Instead, she had hours of competitive banter with Lillian Hennessy. But by the time they got to Brady's Bar, Winnie felt her shoulder muscles had relaxed. The views had been as spectacular as had been promised. Lillian had been mercifully untalkative.

Now, however, she was back to her opinionated self.

'It was a pleasant walk, certainly, but not really challenging,' she pronounced.

'Beautiful scenery. I could look at that big sky for ever,' Winnie said.

'Oh, indeed, but we should go the other way tomorrow, take the route south. There's much more to see, Mrs Starr said. All those little creeks, inlets; we can look in the caves.'

'It looked like a trickier route. Let's see if any of the others have done it first.' Winnie was cautious.

'Oh, they're all sheep. They won't take on anything adventurous. That's what we came for, isn't it, Winnie? One last gesture to fight the elements before we settle into middle age.'

'You aren't settling anywhere,' Winnie said.

'No, but you are showing dangerous signs of becoming very middle-aged. Where's your spirit, Winnie? Tomorrow we'll take a packed lunch and hit the south face of Stoneybridge.'

Winnie smiled as if in agreement. She hadn't a notion of putting herself at risk because Lillian was playing games. But that could all be dealt with tomorrow morning. In the meantime, she would just put in the time being charming and pleasant and unruffled. The prize was Teddy.

Please, dear, kind God, may he be worth it all.

They went back to Stone House on the bus and the guests were coming back from their excursions. The log fire blazed in the hearth. Everyone was drinking tea and eating scones. It was as if they had always lived this life.

At dinner, Winnie sat across from Freda, who said she was an assistant librarian. Winnie explained that she was a nurse.

'Do you have an attachment?' Freda asked.

'No, I work through an agency; a different hospital every day, really.'

'I actually meant a love attachment.'

Lillian was listening. 'We are all a bit past love interests at our age,' she tinkled.

'I don't know . . .' Freda was thoughtful. 'I'm not.'

'Very odd woman, that,' Lillian said later, in a whisper.

'I thought she was good fun, I must say,' Winnie said.

'As I've said before, Winnie, you are totally undemanding. It's amazing how little you ask from life!'

Winnie's lips stretched into a smile. 'That's me,' she simpered. 'As you said, easily pleased.'

All the others were talking about tomorrow's weather. Storms coming in from the south, Mrs Starr said, great care needed. These creeks and inlets filled up very rapidly; even local people had been fooled by the strength of the winds and tides. Winnie sighed with relief. At least Lillian's daft plan of behaving like an explorer would be cancelled.

But when they took their packed lunch next morning, Lillian headed straight in the direction that they had been warned against. Winnie paused for an instant. She could refuse to go. But then Lillian was possibly right. Mrs Starr was being overcautious to cover herself.

Winnie could do it. She was thirty-four years of age, for God's sake. Lillian was fifty-three, at the very least. She had put up with so much already, invested so much time and patience – she wouldn't check out now.

And at first, it was exhilarating. The spray was salty and the rocks large, dark and menacing. The cries of the wild birds and the pounding of the sea made talking impossible. They strode on together, pausing to look out over the Atlantic and realise that the next land was three thousand miles away in the United States.

Then they found the entrance to Majella's Cave that Mrs Starr had told them about. It was sheltered there and the wind wasn't cutting them in half. They sat on a rocky ledge to open the bread and cheese and flask of soup that had been packed for them. Their eyes were stinging, their cheeks were red and whipped by the wind and sea air. They both felt fit and alive and very hungry.

'I'm glad we battled on and came here,' Winnie said, 'it was well worth it.'

'You didn't want to really,' Lillian was triumphant. 'You thought I was being foolhardy.'

'Well if I did, I was wrong. It's good to push yourself a bit.' As she spoke, Winnie felt a great slosh of water across her face

– a wave had come deep into the cave. Oddly, it was not withdrawing out to sea again as they thought it would; rather it was followed by several more waves coming in and splashing around their feet. The two women moved backwards speedily. But still they came, the dark, cold waters, hardly giving any time for the previous wave to recede. Wordlessly, they climbed to an even higher ledge. They would be fine here, well above the water level.

The waves kept coming, and in an attempt to scramble even higher, Lillian kicked the two canvas bags that had held their picnic, their mobile phones and the warm dry socks. They watched as the waves carried the bags out to sea.

'How long does it take for the tide to change?' Lillian asked.

'Six hours, I think,' Winnie was crisp.

'They'll come for us then,' Lillian said.

'They don't know where we are,' Winnie said.

They didn't speak any more then. Only the sound of the wind and waves filled Majella's Cave.

'I wonder who Majella was?' Winnie said after a long time.

'There was a Saint Gerard Majella,' Lillian said doubtfully. It was the first time that she had ever spoken without a sense of certainty.

'Very probably,' Winnie agreed. 'Let's hope he had a good record in getting people out of situations, whoever he was.'

'You agreed to come. You *said* you were happy we had battled on.'

'I was. At the time.'

'Do you pray?' Lillian asked.

'No, not much. Do you?'

'I used to once. Not now.'

There didn't seem to be anything more to say, so they sat in silence listening to the crashing of the waves and the howling of the wind. There was only one higher ledge, which they might have to climb up on if things got worse.

They were cold and wet and frightened.

And they were of no help to each other.

Winnie wondered would they die here. She thought about Teddy, and how Mrs Starr would have to break the news to him. He would never know that her last hours had been filled with a cold hatred of his mother and with a sense of huge regret that she had allowed herself to be sucked into this idiotic game of pretence which could only end badly. But, truly, who could have known how badly?

She couldn't see Lillian's face, but she sensed her shoulders shivering and the chattering of her teeth. She must be frightened too. But it was *her* bloody fault. Still, however they got there, they were both in it together now.

After an age, she said, 'It doesn't really matter one way or another, but why are we here together? In Stoneybridge, I mean. You hated me on sight. But we both love Teddy, that should be a bond, shouldn't it?' This was the first time that love for Teddy had ever been mentioned. Here in Majella's Cave, as they faced death by drowning or hypothermia. Up to now, Winnie had been treated as some menopausal old fool who was keeping an eye on Teddy for them both.

'I love Teddy,' Winnie said loudly. 'And he loves you, so I tried to get to know you and like you. That's all.'

'It hasn't worked though, has it?' said Lillian grimly. 'We got here by accident. I didn't want to be here with you any more than you wanted to be with me. You found the place, Stone House, you went along with coming here today. And now look at us.'

A silence.

'Say something, ask something,' Lillian begged.

'How old are you, Lillian?'

'Fifty-five.'

'You look a lot less.'

'Thank you.'

'Why do you pretend that you and I are the same age? You were twenty-one when I was born.'

'Because I wanted you to go away, to leave Teddy as he was, with me.'

Another silence.

Eventually Winnie spoke. 'Well, in the end neither of us got him.'

'Do you think we're going to get out of here?' The voice had aged greatly. This was not Lillian of the Certainties.

Some small amount of compassion seeped through to Winnie's subconscious. She tried to beat it back but it was there.

'They say you have to be positive and keep active,' she said, shifting around on the ledge.

'Active? Here? What can we do to be positive here?'

'I know that. We can't move. I suppose we could sing.'

'*Sing*, Winnie? Have you lost your marbles?'

'You *did* ask.'

'OK, start then.'

Winnie paused to think. Her mother's favourite song had been 'Carrickfergus'.

> I wish I had you in Carrickfergus,
> Only three miles on from Ballygrand.
> I would swim over the deepest ocean
> Thinking of days there in Ballygrand . . .

She paused. To her astonishment, Lillian joined in.

But the seas are deep and I can't swim over,
And neither more have I wings to fly.
I wish I could find me a handy boatman,
Would ferry over my love and I.

Then they both stopped to think about the words they had just sung.

'There might have been a more inappropriate song if I could have thought of it,' Winnie apologised.

For the first time, she heard a genuine laugh from Lillian. This was not a tinkle, a put-down or a sneer. She actually found it funny.

'You could have picked "Cool Clear Water", I suppose,' she said eventually.

'Your call,' Winnie said.

Lillian sang 'The Way You Look Tonight'. Teddy's father had sung it to her the night before he was killed on the combine harvester, she said.

Winnie sang 'Only The Lonely'. She had found the record shortly after her father had married the strange, distant stepmother who made jewellery. Then Lillian sang 'True Love', and said that she had always hoped to meet someone again after Teddy's father had died but never did. She had worked long hours and tried too hard to make them people of importance in Rossmore. There had been no time for love.

Winnie sang 'St Louis Blues'. She had once won a talent competition by singing it in a pub and the prize had been a leg of lamb.

'Are we wasting our voices in case we need to call for help?'

Lillian wondered. She asked as if she really wanted to hear what Winnie would say.

'I don't think anyone would hear us anyway. Our best hope is to keep positive,' Winnie suggested. 'Do you know any Beatles songs?' So they sang 'Hey Jude'.

Lillian said that she remembered her mother had said the Beatles were depraved because they had long hair. Winnie said that her stepmother had never known who they were and that even her father was vague about them. It was so hard to have a real conversation with them about anything.

'Do they know you're here?' Lillian asked.

'Nobody knows we're here. That's the problem,' Winnie sighed.

'No, I mean in the West of Ireland. Do they know about Teddy?'

'No. They hardly know any of my friends.'

'Maybe you should take him to meet them. He said he hadn't met your folks yet.'

'Well, you know . . .' Winnie shrugged as if to make little of it all.

'He took you to meet me.'

'Yes, didn't he?' The memory of that meeting was still bitter, and Winnie cursed her foolishness trying to take on this mother-in-law from hell, locking horns with her and pretending friendship to win the son. Look where it had ended up. In this cave, waiting for at the worst a slow death by drowning or at the very best rheumatic fever.

'I wasn't entirely overjoyed at first,' Lillian admitted after a pause. 'Neither were you, but it was you who suggested coming on this holiday.'

'I did *not* suggest you come on the holiday. I told you about

Stone House and that I wanted to come here with Teddy, that was all. You invited yourself.'

'He invited me. You went along with it.'

'It doesn't matter now,' Winnie said. There was defeat in her tone.

'Don't get all down about it, please. I'm frightened. I liked it better when you were strong. Can you think of any other songs?'

'No.' Winnie was mulish.

'You *must* know some more songs.'

'What about "By The Rivers Of Babylon"?' Winnie offered.

It turned out that Lillian had been at a wedding in St Augustine's church in Rossmore where the bride and groom had chosen this as one of their wedding hymns, and the Polish priest had thought it must be an old Irish tradition and sang along with it.

Winnie said that one year, when she was working the Christmas shift in a hospital, they had all made a conga line and danced through the wards singing this song to cheer the patients up, and even the sour ward sister had agreed that it worked.

Then Lillian said there was nothing to beat 'Heartbreak Hotel', so they sang that. Winnie said she actually preferred Elvis doing 'Suspicious Minds', but they only knew one line of that, which was something about being caught in a trap. Still, they sang it over and over until it began to sound hollow.

During an attempt at Otis Redding's 'Sitting On The Dock Of The Bay', they both noticed that the level of the water had gone down. They hardly dared to say it in case yet another huge wave would crash in. But when it was clear that the tide had turned, and their throats were raw from singing and the salt spray, they reached out their hands to each other. Cold, wet and trembling, they just held on for a few seconds. Words would have destroyed the fragile hope and shaky peace they had managed to reach.

Now it was a matter of waiting.

Mrs Starr called Rigger when it was obvious that two of her guests had gone missing. He rounded up a search party, including Chicky's brothers-in-law.

'I warned them against the south cliffs, so you can be sure that's where they went,' she said in a clipped voice. Rigger asked her if there were any specific places she had told them about and when Chicky thought about it, it was clear what had happened. She had seen the challenge in Lillian Hennessy's face as she had dismissed the weather warnings the previous night. And she had noticed how Lillian left without any hint of her direction that morning.

The men said they would go towards Majella's Cave and phone her as soon as they had any news.

Before she heard from them, however, there was a call from Teddy Hennessy, who said he was Lillian's son and phoning from England. He apologised for interrupting her but said he couldn't reach his mother or Winnie by mobile phone. They must have switched them off.

Chicky Starr was professional and guarded. No point in alerting him to any possible danger until she had proof that there was a real need to be worried. She took his number carefully.

'They've gone walking over the cliff paths and should be back soon, Mr Hennessy.'

'And they're having a good time?' He sounded anxious to hear it was all going well.

'Yes; I'm sorry they're not here to tell you themselves. They'll be upset to have missed you.'

'I got a text from Winnie last night. She said the place was wonderful.'

'I'm pleased they are satisfied with it all.' Mrs Starr felt a lump in her throat. 'It's good to see old friends enjoy themselves . . .' Please God may she not have to talk to this man in an entirely different way in a few hours' time.

'Lillian's my mother, as I said. This holiday was their way to get to know each other properly, you see. It's great to know it's working so well.'

He sounded hopeful and enthusiastic. How could she tell him that his hard, brittle mother had not been getting on at all well with Winnie, who turned out to be his girlfriend? The relationship had not even been acknowledged. How would history have to be rewritten if the worst had happened?

She stood with her hand at her throat until Orla tugged at her sleeve asking whether the meal should be served now or not. She pulled herself together and got the guests seated. They were all anxious to hear news of the missing women and an unsettled air hung over the table.

'They're all right, you know,' said Freda suddenly, 'they're fine. You mustn't worry. They'll be cold and hungry, but they'll be all right.' She said it with great confidence, but it seemed like everything was in slow motion until the telephone rang.

They were safe. The search party were bringing them first to Dr Dai's house but there seemed to be nothing worse than cold and shock. Without giving any hint of her relief, Chicky Starr told the other guests that Winnie and Lillian had been caught by the tide and would need hot baths but that everyone was to start dinner without them.

When they came in the door, white-faced and wrapped in rugs and blankets, everyone cheered.

Lillian made very light of it all.

'Now you've all seen me without my make-up, I'll never recover from this!' she laughed.

'Were you trapped by the tide?' Freda was anxious to know what had happened.

'Yes, but we knew the tide would have to go out again,' Winnie said. She was trembling but there was going to be no drama.

'Weren't you very frightened?' The English doctor and his wife were concerned.

'No, not really. Winnie was great. She sang all the time to keep our spirits up. She does a very mean "St Louis Blues", by the way. She might give us a recital one night.'

'Only if *you* do "Heartbreak Hotel",' Winnie said.

Mrs Starr interrupted. 'Your son rang, Lillian, from England. I said you'd call him when you got back.'

'Let's have a bath first,' Lillian said.

'Did you actually tell him that—' Winnie began.

'I told him you'd been delayed, that's all.'

They looked at her gratefully.

Lillian looked thoughtful. 'Winnie, why don't *you* call him? He's your fellow. It's *you* that he wanted to talk to anyway. Tell him I'll talk another time.' And she headed towards her bath.

Only Chicky Starr and Freda O'Donovan saw any significance in that remark. They both realised that some great shift had taken place during the long hours waiting for a high Atlantic tide to change. It wouldn't all be sunshine or an easy road ahead, but it wasn't only the weather that looked a lot calmer and less troubled than it had that morning.

John

John had to remember that they were talking to him when they called out his name. It had been so long since anyone had called him John, which was in fact his real name, or at least the name he had been given in the orphanage all those years ago.

Everyone else knew him as Corry.

There was a character called Corry in a children's book which the nuns used to read at bedtime. A little cherub of a toddler that everyone loved. So John thought this was a good name, and the nuns humoured him.

There was a gardener in the orphanage; an old man who came from a place called Salinas. He was always telling them that this was a great part of the world and one day, when he had enough money, he would go back there and buy himself a little place.

Corry used to say the name Salinas over and over. He liked it.

He had no name. This would be his name.

He was Corry Salinas and when he was sixteen he got his first job working in a sandwich bar.

They had a contract to do lunches for film crews, and Corry soon caught everyone's eye. It wasn't just his dark eyes above the aquiline nose, his hair which curled slightly at the temples, his intelligent eyes which always seemed to smile conspiratorially – it was the way he remembered who liked peanut butter and who liked low-fat cheese. Nothing was too much trouble; even the most tiresome and self-obsessed starlets, who changed their minds and said that he had delivered the wrong sandwich, were impressed.

'I don't know where you get your patience.' Monica, who worked with him, had a shorter fuse.

'There are other sandwich bars. We want them to choose ours so it needs a bit of extra effort at the start.' Corry was cheerful. He was not afraid of hard work. He lived in a room over a laundromat and cleaned the place each morning instead of paying rent.

He didn't have to spend any money on food since there was always something to eat in a sandwich business. His savings account grew, and every cent was earmarked for acting lessons. No way could you live in Los Angeles and not want to be a part of the industry.

He and Monica were now an item.

Corry's good looks meant that being an extra would have been easy. But that wasn't really an option. It would mean hanging around all day for what was considerably less money than he earned through the lunch trade. He would hold out until he got a speaking part, and maybe an agent.

It was all part of the dream.

Monica's dream was different. She thought they should move into a place of their own and set up their own fast-food business. Why work all the hours God sent just to make the employer even more wealthy?

But Corry was firm. His dream was to be an actor. He could not commit full-time to a catering business.

Monica was upset by this. She had seen too many people waste a lifetime chasing after a Hollywood dream. Her own father was one of them. But Corry was the love of her life, this handsome boy with the mobile face and the confidence that he would make it in the movies. She didn't want to push him and risk losing him.

And then Monica was pregnant. She didn't know how to tell Corry. She feared so much that he would say he couldn't get involved. Contraception had been her responsibility. And Monica had not deliberately forgotten to take the pill. She spent days wondering how to tell him in the way that would least upset him. In the end she didn't have to; he guessed.

'Why didn't you tell me sooner?' he seemed full of love.

'I didn't want to destroy your dream.'

'Now I have two dreams: a family *and* a movie career,' he said.

They were married three weeks later, and Monica moved in over the laundromat. They found even more work to keep up their funds. Acting lessons cost a lot of money, and people told them that having a baby didn't come cheap either.

By the time that Maria Rosa was born, Corry Salinas had an agent and had been cast as one of three singing waiters in a big musical comedy. Not a great role, his agent had explained, but it would get him on the ladder. It was a vehicle for an ageing and difficult actress who was going to make life hell for everyone during the shoot. And if they liked him, who knew what could follow?

Corry made sure they liked him. He was attentive and endlessly patient for long, long days of work. He treated the First Assistant Director as if he were God. He made special fresh juices for the difficult movie star. She told everyone that he was cute.

The other two singing waiters might let their irritation show, but Corry never did. His ready smile and willingness to please paid off. By the time the shoot was over he had been offered a part in another movie.

Maria Rosa was the most beautiful baby in the world.

Monica's family did a great deal to help as they waited hopefully for Monica's husband to get a serious job that paid properly. Corry had no family to help them out but he often wheeled the baby up to the orphanage where he had been raised, and got a great welcome. He always asked if they could tell him anything at all about his own natural parents, and always they said no. He had been left at the gates of the orphanage aged about three weeks with a letter in Italian begging them to look after him and give him a good life.

'And you *did* give me a good life,' Corry always told them. The nuns loved him in the orphanage. So many of their charges had left bitter and saddened, resentful that they had spent their youth in an institution. Times had changed now, and nuns could go out to movies and theatres. They promised Corry they would go to everything he appeared in and even start a fan club for him.

Monica said it was going to be very hard getting the baby buggy up and down the stairs over the laundromat, but Corry said they couldn't move yet. Acting was a perilous career. They would indeed have a lovely home for the baby, but not at the moment.

The second movie, where Corry played a troubled teenager and the ageing, difficult actress played his stepmother, was written off as a movie too far for the diva. Her time was over, the reviewer said, her day was done. The boy, however! Now here was a talent! And so the offers started coming in.

Corry bought the house that Monica had longed for. But by the time Maria Rosa was three, everything had begun to fall apart. He spent more and more time in the bachelor apartment the studio had provided for him. He had to be seen at receptions and night clubs and at benefit nights.

Monica read that his name was coupled with Heidi, his co-star in the latest film. The next weekend when he had come home for a whole two days, she asked him directly was there any truth in what the gossip columns were saying.

Corry tried to explain that the publicity people demanded this kind of circus.

'But is there anything in it?' Monica asked.

'Well, I'm sleeping with her, yes, but it's not important, not compared to you and Maria Rosa,' he said.

The divorce was swift, and he could see Maria Rosa every Saturday and for a ten-day vacation each year.

Corry Salinas did not marry Heidi, as had been confidently predicted in the gossip columns. Heidi behaved badly about it. She got a lot of publicity as the victim of a love rat.

Monica remained silent and gave no interviews. She was never in the house when Corry arrived to pick up Maria Rosa for his Saturday visit; either her father or mother would hand over the child with few words, a look of resentment and disappointment.

Sometimes Corry was lonely and tried to ask Monica to review the situation. The answer was always the same.

'I bear you no ill will, but please contact me only through the lawyers.'

The parts were getting better; the years rolled by.

He married Sylvia when he was twenty-eight. A very

different wedding day to his first one. Sylvia was from a very wealthy family that had made several fortunes in the hotel business. She was a beautiful and much-indulged daughter who had been denied nothing, and when she had insisted on a giant society wedding as her twenty-first birthday present, she got that as well.

Corry was stunned that this dazzling girl wanted him so much. He went along with all the arrangements that Sylvia's family suggested. One request, that his own ten-year-old daughter, Maria Rosa, be one of the flower girls was refused point-blank. So firmly that he did not mention it again.

Sylvia's lawyers arranged a series of prenup agreements with Corry's lawyers. The publicity for the wedding was intense and the photographic rights hotly fought over.

The day itself passed in a blur. If Corry remembered, a little wistfully, the small wedding party when he and Monica were eighteen and full of hope, then he put the thought far from his mind. That was then, this was now.

Now did not last long. Corry was needed for long hours at the studio, for costume fittings, for publicity tours, for foreign movie festivals. Sylvia was bored. She played a lot of tennis and raised money for charities.

For Corry's thirtieth birthday Sylvia planned another lavish event. It came at a time when he was very much in the public eye with his latest film, where he played a troubled doctor with a difficult moral choice to make. Posters were everywhere showing Corry's sensitive face pondering what he was to do. Women longed to meet him and take the tortured look from his eyes.

He went through the invitation list. The great of Hollywood and the hotel industry were well represented. His daughter's name was not there.

This time he did insist.

'She's twelve years of age. She'll read about it. She *has* to be there.'

'It's *my* party and I don't want her there. She's part of your past, not your present, or indeed your future. Anyway, I was thinking it's time for us to have our own child.' Sylvia was very insistent. She had only agreed to meet her stepdaughter, Maria Rosa, half a dozen times since the wedding, saying she wasn't good with young girls – they were all so silly and giggled over nothing.

There was something so dismissive about the way she spoke, something that sent out the message that Sylvia would always get what *she* wanted. The rosebud smile he had once thought so entrancing looked more like a pout now.

He tested the water to ask if he could include some of the people from the orphanage where he was raised.

'But darling Corry, they would be *so* out of place. Surely you can see that?'

'They will never be out of place in my life. They raised me, made me who I am.'

'Well, send them money, sweetheart, help them in fundraising – that's worth twice as much as some gesture of inviting them to a glitzy do where they will be fish out of water.'

Corry did already send money to his orphanage. He was on the board of a fundraising committee, but this was not the point. Three of those gentle plain-clothes nuns, as he called them, would so enjoy being guests at a huge catered event. How could these women, who had looked after him since he was found on their doorstep, be out of place anywhere?

He felt a vein in his forehead; a throbbing sensation. He

even felt slightly dizzy. He could hear his own voice as if it were far away. It didn't seem to come from inside.

'I don't want a party if I can't have my daughter and the people who educated me, fed and clothed me.'

'You're overtired, Corry. You work too hard,' Sylvia said.

'That's true, I do work too hard. But I am serious. I have never been more serious in my life.'

Sylvia said they should leave the matter for now.

'If you send out those invitations, *then* we can leave the matter.'

'I will not be bullied or blackmailed into doing something I don't want to do.'

'Fine,' Corry said, and the marriage ended.

It was fairly painless, all things considered. Corry's lawyers dealt with Sylvia's lawyers. Settlements were agreed. But afterwards Sylvia found that a social life without Corry Salinas on her arm was not nearly as bright as it had been. She was tempted to give interviews about their tempestuous marriage.

Corry read them in disbelief. It hadn't been at all like this.

He tried to tell his daughter, Maria Rosa, that life with Sylvia had been a series of staged events, all set in a goldfish bowl to encourage the admiration and envy of others. There had been none of these violent arguments. Corry had always given in to her. The truth was that he and Sylvia barely knew each other.

'Why did you marry her then, Dad?' Maria Rosa asked.

'I guess I was flattered,' he said simply.

Maria Rosa was wise beyond her years and, because she had heard the same explanation from her mother, she believed him.

*

During the next two decades, Corry Salinas became a house-hold name, not only in the United States but all over the world. He could raise the money for any movie he was involved in. He was seen with elegant women in and out of high-profile occasions, film premieres, Broadway first nights, art openings and on the grandest, most expensive yachts in the Mediterranean. The gossip columnists were always marrying him off to film stars, heiresses and even minor royalty, but nothing transpired.

Maria Rosa was dark-eyed and romantic-looking like Corry, practical and even-tempered like Monica. She had inherited their work ethic, trained as a teacher and did voluntary service overseas. Her father's A-list celebrity lifestyle didn't attract her remotely. When she was growing up it had been the enemy of any kind of family life.

She had spent too much of her youth fleeing from papar-azzi, refusing to talk to people in case she was misquoted in the press. Any door would have been open to her as the daughter of Corry Salinas, but she never wanted to walk through them.

She was never hostile or resentful about her father. She always called him whenever she came back to LA to suggest a pizza or a Mexican dinner in a neighbourhood restaurant, where they could sit quietly in a booth without all the attendant publicity that Corry Salinas trailed wherever he went.

He heard from his daughter that Monica had married again, a gentle guy called Harvey who ran a flower shop. Her mother had never been happier, Maria Rosa explained; the only cloud in the sky was that there was no sign of *her* upcoming wedding and maybe grandchildren. But, Maria Rosa sighed, she just hadn't met anyone, and Lord wasn't this town an awful warning about how marriage could go horribly wrong.

People often said that it was unfair how men looked better as they aged; Corry could still play passionate leading roles when women in their fifties were struggling to get character parts. But he knew this could not go on for ever.

When Corry was in his late fifties, he knew that what he needed was one utterly unforgettable part to play. Something with gravitas and sensitivity. A part that would for ever be associated with him. Yet it didn't seem to come his way.

His agent, who was called Trevor the Tireless, had been trying to direct him towards a television series, but Corry would have none of it. When he had been starting out they always thought that only old, failed actors went into television. The real arena was the movie theatre; nothing else counted.

Trevor sighed.

Corry was way behind the times, he said. They were in a golden age of television, he said. There were fabulous writers doing their best work for television. There was a part on offer which had all the gravitas he was looking for – he was going to play a President of the United States! Corry could write his own ticket. The real rule for success was to be adaptable, he kept saying. But Corry would not listen.

It wasn't a matter of changing agents. Not at this stage. Trevor was indeed tireless in his efforts to find the perfect part for his most famous client. And Corry knew the old saying that changing agents was like changing deckchairs on the *Titanic*.

Corry had always been relaxed and easy-going. Suddenly he had become stubborn, utterly certain that he knew better than agents, the studios and the whole industry.

Corry hadn't listened to the kind nuns who had wanted him to be a priest, or to the man who ran the first sandwich bar who had offered Corry a permanent position. He had turned a deaf ear to those who said his acting lessons were an expense he could not afford. He had always been his own man.

Soon he would be sixty. Trevor wanted to be able to announce something great to coincide with this anniversary, but all he came up with was yet another television offer.

'It's a peach of a part,' Trevor begged. 'You play an Italian who thinks he has a fatal illness and goes back to Italy to find his roots before he dies. Then he meets this woman. They're lining up to play her if you are going to be the lead, you wouldn't believe the names we have.'

'Not television,' Corry said.

'It's all changed, believe me. Look at the awards! They're all going to television stars now.'

'No, Trevor.'

And that's how things stood for weeks.

Corry told Maria Rosa about it all.

'Why don't you do it, Father? None of my friends has time to go out to movie theatres. They all watch TV or download things on to their computers. It's all changed. Everything has.'

She was more right than either of them knew.

Corry's business manager, who had always advised him well, had been badly stung by the recession. Investments had not paid off, so even more hasty and unwise investments were made. It all blew up the day that the manager was killed in a car wreck.

He had driven straight into a wall, leaving behind him a financial confusion that would take years to unravel.

Now, for the first time in decades, Corry had to make

a career decision based entirely on the need to make money. Most of his property had to be sold off piece by piece.

Trevor was his usual tireless self in keeping Corry Salinas's financial woes out of the papers. But he did clear his throat several times about the television series. And this time Corry had to listen.

The money people were meeting in Frankfurt. They wanted Corry to be there to say that he was interested. This would help them raise the financing. It was going to be huge, Trevor said; Corry would get his property back.

'I only want to make sure my daughter is left well provided for,' Corry said glumly as he packed his bag for Germany.

They always boarded Corry discreetly, seconds before the plane took off. He slipped into his seat in first class with the minimum of fuss. If other passengers recognised him, they gave no sign. He had the treatment and sample scripts for the new television series on his lap and opened them reluctantly. His heart was just not in the project which, according to Tireless Trevor, would turn his financial life around and make him even more of a household name than he already was. When he got to Frankfurt he would shower, change and settle himself in the hotel and only then would he make up his mind about what to do. He was tired, and after a few minutes in his comfortable seat he drifted off to sleep.

He woke to realise that the plane had not yet taken off. The cabin steward was offering him some fresh orange juice. There had been a delay, he was told, an instrument check, but all was fine and the captain said they would be taking off shortly.

Corry checked his watch; there was an announcement. This plane was going nowhere. The flight was cancelled. Arrangements were being put in place to get everyone on to the next day's flight. Anyone who didn't want to wait would be transferred to another airline, but the flight would not be direct. The next day would be too late; he'd miss the meeting entirely. So much for settling down in his hotel beforehand. Trevor would never believe it. He'd never forgive him.

At the airport, all hell was breaking loose as everyone was trying to move to different airlines; in the end it was only flying by way of Shannon airport in Ireland that he had any chance of getting to Frankfurt at all. He just had time to call Trevor who, to save time, would now pick him up. He'd arrange for the media to photograph him coming through the airport. He'd make a story about the delayed flight, a few interviews and then he'd take him straight to the meeting. Whatever happened, he had to be there. Everyone was counting on him.

Everyone was counting on him, were they? Oh well. So, he'd be late, but he just might make it. He knew he would not speed the plane or shorten the journey by worrying about it, so he slept as the plane went eastwards through the night and then they were landing in Ireland.

He looked down at the small patchwork green fields far below. He could see the coastline. Maria Rosa had been to Ireland once with a student group some years back. She said she had enjoyed it. Everyone she met had some kind of story to tell. He thought fancifully about what it would be like to go on a vacation with his daughter. She was now in her early forties – a handsome woman absorbed in her teaching, equally at ease in the flower shop with her mother and Harvey, or having drinks with her father in the top Hollywood hotels.

Still no sign of a romance in her life, but she laughed it away and so Corry stopped enquiring. She might even *enjoy* a holiday with him. As soon as he got home, he'd call her and suggest it.

He looked at his watch again. This was going to be very close. He would have to run to catch his connection to Germany.

It was, in fact, too close. Corry stood and watched the flight to Frankfurt leave without him.

Tireless Trevor would be waiting at the airport, the publicity machine would meet a plane on which he was not travelling. He called Trevor's cell phone and held his own phone away from his ear as his agent fumed, protested and raged about the news. Eventually, he ran out of adjectives and abuse and just sounded weary.

'So what *are* you going to do?' he asked.

Corry said, 'I'm tired. Very tired.'

'*You* are tired?' Trevor's voice had risen again dangerously. '*You* have nothing to be tired about. It's the rest of us that have things that are making us tired, like trying to explain what can never be explained.'

'It was the airline . . .' Corry began.

'Don't give me the airline. If you had wanted to be here, you'd have been here.'

'Can they not have the meeting tonight or tomorrow?'

'Of course they can't. Who do you think these people are? They've all flown in specially. They got on planes that didn't sit on their butts on the tarmac,' Trevor raged.

'Then I'm staying here for a week. If it's too late for the meeting, then to hell with it. I'm getting out for a while.'

'Hey, this is no time . . . I've set everything up.'

'And I tried to get there, but the airline let me down. Goodbye, Trevor, talk to you in a week's time.'

'But where are you going? What are you doing? You can't go wandering off like this!'

'I'm a grown man. An *old* man, as you never tire of hinting. I can have a week's vacation here or a month, if I like. See you back in LA.' Corry closed his phone and turned it on to message.

He went to get himself another coffee. This kind of freedom was new to him. He had escaped the meeting he had been dreading. He could now do what he wanted to without consulting any handler, manager or agent. He was actually free.

The airline had done him a favour.

But where would he go? Perhaps he should buy a tourist guide book or find a travel agent. On the tables around there were various brochures offering suggestions of what to do in the region. There was a medieval banquet in a castle. There was a tour to some spectacular cliff face called Moher, which was meant to be one of the Wonders of the World. There were golf packages. None of them appealed to Corry.

But one little sheet advertised A Week in Winter and promised a warm, welcoming house and miles of sand and cliffs and wild birds. He called the number to know if there was a vacancy.

A pleasant-sounding woman said there was indeed room for him, told him to rent a car and drive north. He should call again when he arrived in Stoneybridge for directions to the house.

'About payment?' Corry began; he didn't want to give his name, and there was a possibility that he might even go unrecognised, which would be a real treat.

'We'll sort all that out when you get here,' Mrs Starr was brisk. 'And your name is . . . ?'

'John,' Corry said, without pausing.

'Right, John, take your time, and be very careful of Irish drivers, they are inclined to pull out suddenly without indicating. Assume they are going to do that and you'll be fine.'

His shoulders felt less tense. He was an ordinary tourist going on an ordinary holiday. There was no press reception, no junket of showbiz writers following him.

It was a cold, bright morning. Corry Salinas put his bag into the back of the rented car and drove north obediently.

He must remember he was called John from now on.

The other guests seemed to have settled in. The house looked just as it had done in the brochure. John turned his collar up to shield his face partially.

He was so used to people doing a double take when they met him and shouts of, 'Oh my God, you're Corry Salinas!' But at Stone House, nobody recognised him. Perhaps Tireless Trevor had been right when he said that Corry Salinas was in grave danger of being a forgotten brand.

He told them, when asked, that he was a businessman from Los Angeles taking a well-deserved week off. And then he began to feel that there was no need to turn up his collar any more. If they recognised him, they were not going to say anything. But it was much more likely that they hadn't a clue who he was.

The food was good, the conversation was easy, but he felt very weary. He was used to putting on an act, giving a performance. It wasn't demanded here, which was a relief, but on the other hand he felt somewhat at a loss. What *was* his role?

He was the first to go to bed. He asked them to forgive him

and to believe that he hadn't invented the International Date Line. They laughed and told him to sleep well.

And indeed John did sleep well, immediately, in his comfortable bed, but jet lag meant he did not sleep long. Still on California time, he woke at three a.m., alert and ready to face the day.

He made himself tea and looked out the window at the waves crashing on the shore below. He wanted to call Maria Rosa. It was eight or nine hours earlier back home. Perhaps she would have come back to her apartment after a long day's teaching.

He picked up his mobile phone but before he dialled her number, he paused. Would she really be interested to know that he had booked into this bizarre vacation? She was always polite but distant, as if anything her father did happened in an unreal, childlike maze of ratings and reviews and column inches of publicity. To Maria Rosa it had little to do with the real world.

Then he told himself to stop analysing it.

He dialled the number.

'Maria Rosa? It's Dad.'

'Hey, Dad. How are things?'

'Just fine. I'm stuck in Ireland, of all places. I missed the connection when I was heading for Germany.'

'Ireland's OK, Dad, you could be in worse places.'

'I know. It's fine. Very wild where I am, right on the Atlantic.'

'And cold, I guess?'

'Yes, but it's a warm hotel. I'm going to stay here for a week.'

'That's good, Dad.'

Was she interested? Was she bored? It was so hard to know

165

from six thousand miles away. 'I just thought I'd call to say hi.'

'It's good to hear from you.'

There was a pause. Was she ending the conversation?

'And you.' He was loath to let her go. 'Can you hear the waves crashing outside? They're really big. They're like a sort of drum roll.'

'What time is it there?' she asked.

'Just after three a.m.,' he said.

'Hey, Dad, you need to sleep,' his only daughter said.

Corry said goodnight, and felt more lonely and lost than he had ever felt in his life.

He dozed fitfully after that, and felt sluggish and groggy as he went down to breakfast. Several people were already at the table and they commiserated with him over his jet lag. A young woman called Winnie, who was a nurse, gave him sound, practical advice and although he promised he'd follow it, he allowed himself to be persuaded to try a full Irish breakfast as an alternative remedy. Mrs Starr placed a cafetière of coffee in front of him and told him to help himself.

After breakfast, he lingered over a last cup as Orla cleared the table and Mrs Starr busied herself with maps and binoculars and packed lunches for the guests setting out on walks. As the last of them left, he saw her shoulders relax and he realised how much anxiety lay under the surface.

She caught his eye as she turned round and saw that he had been watching her.

'This is our first week,' she explained.

'But you're no stranger to the business, I can tell,' he said.

'You're right,' she said, 'but that wasn't my own business. I worked for someone else. Now I'm where the buck stops. So listen, John, what would you like to do today? Would you like another cup of coffee, and I'll tell you what's around?'

They chatted companionably over another pot of coffee; and so, refreshed, John set out in blustery sunshine for his first day's walk.

Following Chicky's advice, he chose to go inland. He walked over a lonely road, saw big sheep with black faces and twisted horns. Or were they wild goats? There had been little time to study nature when he was growing up. There were huge gaps in his understanding of so many things.

He found a small pub and went from the bright, cold sunshine into the dark interior where a turf fire burned in a small grate and half a dozen men looked up from pints, interested to see a stranger come in.

John greeted them all pleasantly. He was an American, he explained unnecessarily, staying at Stone House. Mrs Starr had suggested this pub would be a good place to visit.

'Decent woman, Chicky Starr.' The landlord was pleased with the praise, and he polished the glasses with greater vigour than ever.

'She spent most of her life in America. Did you know her from there?' an old man asked him.

'No, indeed. I just saw an advertisement yesterday in Shannon airport, and here I am!'

Was it only yesterday? He already felt completely disconnected from any other life.

A large man wearing a big cap looked at John keenly. He had a broad red face and small curious eyes.

'You know, you're sort of familiar-looking. Are you sure you were never this way before?'

'Never. This is my first visit. You people sure live in a wonderful part of the world.'

That satisfied them. John had perfected the easy transferring of the attention away from himself, coupled with praise for their having lucked out in where they found themselves living.

'Chicky Starr was married to a Yank, you know. He was killed in a terrible car crash, the poor devil,' the red-faced man said.

'The Lord have mercy on him,' said the others in unison.

'That's terrible,' John said.

'Yes, she was very cut up. But she's got great guts altogether. She came back here to her own people and bought the old Sheedy place. She took ages doing it up. You wouldn't believe all the work that went into that house.'

'It's certainly a very comfortable place to stay,' John said.

'When you get back home, will you tell your friends in America to go there?'

'Sure I will.' John wondered did he know anyone in Los Angeles who would come to an outpost like this.

They left him to his soup and his pint of Guinness. He felt oddly at ease in their company, and listened while they talked about old Frank Hanratty who had painted his old van bright pink so that he could find it without any difficulty. Frank was still driving round the place peering through his glasses, seeing nothing ahead of him or behind. He had never been in any accident. *Yet*.

Frank had never married, apparently, but had a better social life than any of them; he called here, there and everywhere and was welcome wherever he went. He was mad keen on the cinema and would drive the pink van thirty miles every week and see at least two films in the big town . . .

Their conversation drifted around John. He had an image of this peaceful, undemanding life the man Hanratty lived, happy with the way the cards had been dealt. He wondered if he should buy everyone a drink. That's what would happen in a movie. But life wasn't a movie. These men might be affronted. He gave them his big, enveloping smile and promised he would come back again.

'Great soup that, lumps of chicken in it,' he said.

He couldn't have said anything that pleased the landlord more.

'That chicken was running around the back yard yesterday morning,' he said proudly.

The day's walking did wonders for his jet lag, and he slept soundly that night. He woke at six but found himself happy to lie in bed listening to the sounds of the wind and the sea. It was louder today, he felt sure. The wind seemed to have changed direction and was battering against the windows; when eventually he got up, there was a dark and angry look to the waves.

Sure enough, Mrs Starr was issuing weather warnings to everyone over breakfast. He had thought he might try the walk down to the shoreline with the little rocky inlets, but thought better of it, given her advice. Not sure what alternative route to take, he found himself lingering over a last cup of coffee, the other guests bustling around the doorway; as the last of them left, he smiled at Chicky Starr and, raising an eyebrow, invited her to join him.

'I hear you were in New York for a while,' he said.

He started to look forward to their chats. There was something restful about being able to have a normal conversation with people who had no preconceived notions about him, no idea about his other life and no expectations. The following morning, once again, John stayed back and was the last to leave after breakfast. He watched as Orla cleared away the plates.

'You are lucky to have family to help you here,' John said.

'Yes. Orla had different plans but they didn't work out, so I think she's happy to be here, for a while anyway.' Mrs Starr never usually seemed in a hurry but this particular morning, she seemed slightly preoccupied.

'Am I keeping you from anything, Mrs Starr?'

'I'm so sorry, John, I am indeed a little distracted. My car has died on me and Dinny from the garage will be up to fix it but not until this evening. Rigger, that's our manager, has to go to the doctor with his babies – they're having inoculations. We need to go shopping, Orla and I. I'm just working out how we can . . .'

'Why don't I drive you?' he suggested immediately.

'No, that would never do. This is *your* holiday.'

Orla was at the table, listening in. 'Oh, go on, Chicky, John doesn't mind. And it's only fifteen minutes down the road. I'll go with him and get myself a lift back.'

It was settled.

They drove companionably to the town. Orla was a handsome girl with easy conversation.

'It's unfair to ask you to do this on your holidays but it's Chicky's first week ever. She has enough to think about. I thought you wouldn't mind.'

'No, I'm very pleased to help. And by the way, I'll come with you. I actually like going to the stores,' John offered. He was indeed captivated by Orla's conversations with the butcher, the cheesemaker and all the feeling and prodding of vegetables in the greengrocer's. Soon it was all packed and paid for.

Orla was very grateful. 'Thank you so much. I'll ask one of the O'Haras for a lift back now, so off you go and enjoy your day.'

'I was going to have yet another coffee,' John admitted. 'I see a place over there. Why don't you put the shopping in the car and we'll go to the café for ten minutes.'

They chatted easily. Orla told him how she had nearly gone to New York to see Uncle Walter and Chicky, but then of course there had been the accident. Poor Uncle Walter had been killed.

Orla said she had done a course in Dublin and then she and her friend Brigid had gone to London to work. It had been good fun for a while but then her friend had got engaged to and married a madman and anyway, she had been feeling restless and longed for the seas and cliffs of Stoneybridge. There would have been no work for her without Chicky. There was something healing about this place. It helped to take the ache out of her heart.

'I think I see what you mean about this place being healing,' John said. 'I've only been here a short time, and I can feel it getting to me.'

'It must be very different from the life you're used to,' she was sympathetic.

'Very,' he said, without elaborating on the life he was used to.

'I suppose you couldn't sit and have a cup of coffee in a place like this out where you live . . .'

He looked at her sharply. 'What do you mean?' he asked eventually.

'John, of course we know that you are Corry Salinas. We knew the moment we saw you, Chicky and I.'

'But you didn't say.' He was stunned.

'You came here as John. You wanted to be a private person. Why should we say anything?'

'And the others, the guests? Do *they* know?'

'Yes. The Swedish guy copped you the first night, and the English couple, Henry and Nicola, asked Chicky discreetly if you were here incognito.'

'It's true what I said. I *was* on my way to a business meeting in Germany, and I *did* come here on the spur of the moment.'

'Sure. And call yourself whatever you want to, John, it's your life, your holiday.'

'But if everyone knows . . . ?' he said doubtfully.

'Honestly, they'll respect your wanting to be an ordinary person. They're mainly concentrating on their own lives anyway.'

'It would make life easier, certainly, if they know already. It's just that I was hoping to leave that world behind, at least for a while, just spend some time without all that baggage.'

'It must be desperate having to explain everything and be asked if you know Tom Cruise or Brad Pitt.'

'It's not that so much as they have such high expectations of me. They think I actually *am* the guys I play in the movies. I always feel I disappoint them.'

'Oh, I doubt that. Everyone here thinks you're full of charm. Me too. I've sort of gone off men myself personally, but you'd put a spark back into the eye.'

'You mock me. I'm an old, old man,' he laughed.

'Oh, I do *not* mock you, believe me. But I suppose I wish you got more fun out of it: being world famous, successful, everyone loving you. If I had done all you've done, I'd be delighted with myself and go round beaming at everyone.'

'It's only role-playing,' he said. 'That's my day job. I don't want to have to do it in real life as well.'

Orla considered this seriously. 'But you can be yourself with family, can't you?' she asked.

'I don't *have* any family, apart from one daughter. I called her in California the other night.'

'Did you tell her about Stone House? Will she come and bring her family here one day?'

'She doesn't have a family. She's a teacher.'

'I'm sure she's very proud of you. Do you go to her school and talk to the kids?'

'No. Lord, no. I'd never do that.'

'Wouldn't they love to meet a film star?' Orla said, surprised.

'Oh, Maria Rosa wouldn't want that,' he said.

'I bet she would. Did you ask her?'

'No. I don't want to push myself and my kind of life on her.'

'Lord, aren't you the most marvellous father. *Why* didn't I get parents like you?'

Corry was back in listening mode, where he was always at ease.

'Are they difficult?' he asked, full of sympathy.

'Well yes, to be honest. They want me to be different, I suppose. They think it's a bit fast to have my own place to live. They think I'm wasting myself washing dishes for Chicky – that's how they put it. They want me to marry one of the God-awful O'Haras and have a big vulgar house with pillars in front of it and three bathrooms.'

'Is that what they say?'

'They don't need to say it, it's there in the air like a great mushroom cloud.'

'Maybe they just wish the best for you and don't know how to put it.'

'Oh no, my mother always knows how to put it, usually in four different ways all saying the same thing – which is that I am wasting my life.'

'And leaving what you call the God-awful O'Haras aside, do you have anybody you *do* like?' He was gentle, not intrusive; interested.

'No. As I told you, I've sort of closed down a bit on men.'

'That's a pity. Some of them are very good people.' He had a wonderful smile, slightly ironic, full of conspiratorial fun.

'I don't want to take the risk. I'm sure you know that yourself.'

'I do know. I've been married twice and involved with a lot more women. I don't really understand them but I didn't ever give up on them!'

'It's different for you, John, you have the whole world to choose from.'

'You look to me like a girl who would have a fairly wide choice, Orla.'

'No. I can't get my head around it. At best it's a kind of compromise. At worst it's a nightmare.'

'Were you never in love?'

'Truthfully, no. Were you?'

'With Monica, my first wife, yes, I am sure I was. Maybe it was because we were young and it was all so new and exciting and we had Maria Rosa. But I think it was love . . .'

'Then you had more than I had.'

'Do you set out to avoid it, the love thing?'

'No, but I do set out not to be made a fool of and not to compromise. I've seen too much of that. My mother and father have very little to talk about, supposing they ever had . . . My aunt Mary is married to a man who is about a hundred because he owns a big property, but he really doesn't know what day it is. Chicky *did* marry for love, but then her fellow was wiped off the face of the earth in a car crash. Not much of a recommendation for love, any of this!'

'Maybe you have a suit of armour up before they get a chance to know you,' he suggested.

'Maybe. I don't *want* to be a ball-breaker or anything. That's just the way it seems to turn out.'

'No, I didn't mean to suggest that . . .'

'And I suppose the *real* irritation is my parents. They are much *too* interested in my life. It's getting harder and harder not to show them how annoying it is.'

'Oh, parents always get it wrong, Orla. It goes with the territory.' John sounded rueful.

'You seem to have it sorted though with your daughter.'

'No way. I want so much for her. I want her to have the best but I *know* I'm not delivering it. I get it so wrong.'

'And what kind of parents did *you* have?'

'None. I have no idea who my father was, and my mother never came back to find me.'

'Oh, I'm so sorry.' Orla reached out and laid her hand on his. 'I'm such a clown. I didn't know. Forgive me.'

'No, it doesn't matter. I'm just telling you why I'm so hung up and holding on to family,' John said. 'I never knew any one thing about my mother except that she spoke Italian and left me wrapped up at the door of an orphanage nearly sixty years ago. The hours, weeks and years I've wondered about her, and hoped she was all right and tried to work out why she gave me away.' Orla's hand was still on his. She squeezed it from solidarity.

'I bet she was thinking of you all the time, too. I *bet* she was. And look what you did with your life! She would have been so proud.'

'Would she? OK, I got to be famous but, as you say, I don't get enough joy from it, enough fun. She might have liked me to have a good time and been happier, less restless.'

'Let's do a deal,' Orla suggested. 'I will have more of an open mind about men. I won't assume they are all screaming bores. I'll do that American thing of assuming that strangers are just friends you haven't met yet!'

'I don't think it's just American,' John said defensively.

'Possibly not. Anyway, I won't vomit at the thought of going out with one of Brigid O'Hara's awful brothers or uncles. I'll give them a chance. Does that sound reasonable?'

'Very much so.' He smiled at her intensity.

'*You*, on the other hand, are going to enjoy being who you are. People *love* to meet a celebrity, John. It does them good. We live dull lives. It's just great to meet a movie star. Be generous enough to understand that.'

'I promise I will. I didn't think of it like that.'

'Oh, and about your daughter; maybe you should tell her the kind of things you've told me about love. I'd love a father who could speak like that.'

'I never have before,' he said.

'No, but you could start now and maybe tell her that you would love to see her and meet her friends, if it wouldn't embarrass her or them. I bet she'd be pleased.'

'I guess I'm afraid she'll reject me.'

'I'm going to face men who might reject me. This is meant to be a deal, isn't it?'

'Right. And will you cut your parents some slack too? They may be driving you nuts but they *do* want what's best for you.'

'Yes, I'll try. I will probably be canonised in my own

176

lifetime, but I'll try!' she laughed. They shook hands on the deal and began to drive back to Stone House.

On the way they passed Stoneybridge Golf Club. A few hardy golfer souls were out on the course. Outside the door was parked a violent pink van.

'Oh Lord, Frank's at the hot whiskeys already,' Orla sighed.

John braked suddenly.

'I'd love a hot whiskey myself,' he said.

'You can't, you're not a member of the Club. Anyway, you've only just had your breakfast.'

But John had parked the car and was striding to the main door.

Alarmed now, Orla ran after him.

Alone at the bar, on a high stool, peering at a newspaper with a magnifying glass, sat a tousled old man. He looked up when the door opened with a crash. A total stranger came through, a man in his fifties in an expensive leather jacket.

'Well, if it isn't Frank Hanratty, as I live and breathe,' the stranger said.

'Um . . . Yes?' Frank was rarely approached by people who did know him, and scarcely ever by people who didn't.

'Well, how are you keeping, Frank, my old friend?'

Frank peered at him. 'You're Corry Salinas,' he said eventually in disbelief.

'Of course I am. Who else would I be?'

'But how do you know *me*?'

'We were only talking about you in the pub yesterday. I know you are a great film buff, and now today I find you in here.'

'But how did you know I was in here?' Poor Frank was bewildered.

'Isn't that your van outside?' John said, as if it was as simple as that.

Frank nodded thoughtfully. It made sense, sure enough. 'And will you have a hot whiskey, er, Corry?' Frank offered.

'I'm no good at morning drinking. I'd love a cup of coffee, however. And do you know my friend Orla?'

They sat and talked about movies, and the boy who served them brought their coffees to a table.

'I can't believe you came in here to see me.' Frank was happier than he had ever been.

John and Orla exchanged glances.

The bargain had been made.

Henry and Nicola

When Henry had qualified as a doctor his parents had hoped that he would go on and specialise, perhaps in surgery. His mother and father, both doctors, regretted that they hadn't studied further. Look at the worlds it could have opened up, they would say wistfully.

But Henry was adamant. He was going to be a GP.

There wasn't any room for him in his parents' practice but he would find a small community where he and Nicola would soon know everyone. They would have children and be part of the place.

Henry had met Nicola during the first week at medical school. Although they were so very young, they both knew in a matter of weeks that this was it. The two sets of parents begged them to wait, let the romance run a bit before getting married. Four years later, they said they would wait no longer.

It was a small, cheerful wedding in Nicola's home town. The guests all said that in a complicated world full of confusion and misunderstandings, Henry and Nicola stood out like two rocks in a stormy sea.

They prepared themselves well for careers in general

practice with six-month postings in a maternity hospital, a heart clinic and a children's facility. Soon they felt ready to hang up their names outside a door, and while they were looking for the perfect place to settle, they also decided to try for a child. It was time.

It was hard to find the perfect place to live, but even harder to conceive a child. They couldn't understand it. They were doctors, after all; they knew about timing and fertility chances. A medical examination showed no apparent problem. They were encouraged to keep trying, which they were certainly doing anyway. After a year they tried IVF, and that didn't work either.

They endured the well-meaning and irritating comments of their parents who were hoping to be grandparents, and of friends offering babysitting services.

It would happen or it would not happen. Henry and Nicola could weather anything. They even survived a tragedy which unfolded in front of them during a stint in an A&E department. A crazed young man high on drugs brought in his battered girlfriend and, in full view of everyone, shot her dead and then killed himself.

On the surface, they coped very well: Henry and Nicola were much praised for the way they handled the situation and protected the other patients from trauma. But inside it had been a very serious shock, and there remained a memory of the morning when, at a distance of five feet, they had watched two lives end. They were trained to deal with life and death but this was too raw, too cruel, too insane. It took its toll. They slowed down in their efforts to find the perfect place to live and to practise. Compared to the violence they had seen close up, it didn't seem so important any more.

One day, Nicola saw an advertisement for a ship's doctor

with a cruise company that sailed the Mediterranean. They laughed at it together. What a life: deck tennis, cocktails with the Captain and dealing with a little indigestion or sunburn, which would be the most likely problems. What a picnic it would be. And something seemed to click with both of them. They had worked hard always; there was never time for foreign holidays. Maybe this was what they needed.

A little sun, a rest, a change. Anything that might blot out the memory of that day and their pointless sense of regret that they had not been able to second-guess a drug addict and his intentions.

They applied and went to the interview.

The shipping line said it could only employ one doctor but that they could travel together, if the other one would be able to busy herself or himself doing something else on board.

Nicola offered to teach bridge and run the ship's library.

'Or you could be the doctor,' Henry said, 'and I will do something else.'

'They would only want you to dance with the old ladies. I think you're safer in a white coat in a surgery,' Nicola laughed.

And they signed up.

They were a very popular couple on the ship, and they took to the life easily. Cruise passengers were mainly eager and innocent; their health problems were mostly connected with old age. They needed reassurance and encouragement. Henry was very good in both areas.

Nicola went from strength to strength in her little world. She even started classes in technology, teaching passengers how to work their mobile phones, Skype and basic computing skills.

They saw places they would never have visited otherwise. What other way would they have been able to visit the souks and marketplaces in Tangiers, the casinos in Monte Carlo, the ruins of Pompeii and Ephesus? They stood by the Wailing Wall in Jerusalem and swam in the blue seas around Crete.

It was only intended to be a six-month posting but when the company offered to renew the contract, it was very hard to say no. This was the first time they had ever been totally relaxed; they had time to talk to each other, to share experiences. There was a lightness of spirit they hadn't known before. The terrible events of the shooting in the A&E department were beginning to become less sharp.

And the winter-cruise schedule they were offered would be in the Caribbean. How else would they ever see places this far away? What an opportunity! They signed on again.

As they walked through the old plantations in Jamaica, or sat among the exotic flowers in Barbados, they congratulated themselves on the good fortune they had happened upon. Sometimes they talked about going back to 'real' medicine and the business of having a family by adoption. But this was not a regular conversation. They were just so lucky to have this time out.

And it wasn't as if it was all leisure. They did what they were asked to do. They looked after the people on board. Henry saved a boy's life by spotting a burst appendix and having him airlifted to a hospital. Nicola did a Heimlich manoeuvre and saved an elderly woman from choking. Henry confirmed that a sixteen-year-old girl was pregnant and helped her break the news to her parents. Nicola sat for hour after hour with a depressed woman who had considered coming on this cruise to end her life. The woman wrote to the chairman of the shipping line saying that she had never had such caring attention in her life and that she felt much better now.

So Henry and Nicola were offered a Scandinavian cruise the following spring.

Nicola had a new idea, which she ran past the Cruise Director. Why not get a hairdresser to give the men lessons in how to dry their wives' hair?

He looked at her in puzzlement.

But she persisted. Women would like the involvement and care of a partner who knew the basics. Men would buy the idea because it would save them money.

'What about the beauty-salon business?' the Cruise Director had asked.

'They have to have one cut and style in your salon first. Believe me, they will love it. It will all even out.'

And she had been right: the blow-drying sessions were among the most popular of the ship's activities.

They both loved the coastline of Norway from Bergen up to Tromsø. They stood side by side watching the sights at the ship's railings and pointed out the fjords to each other. The light was spectacular. The passengers were the usual mix of experienced cruise folk and first-timers overawed by the amount of entertainment, food and drink on offer.

It was on the third day out that Beata, one of the stewardesses, came to see Henry. An attractive blonde, Polish girl, she said that this was a very awkward matter, very awkward indeed.

Henry told her to take her time and explain the problem. He hoped she was not going to tell him there was something seriously wrong with her but Beata, twisting her hands and looking away, told him a different tale.

It was about Helen Morris, a woman in Cabin 5347. She was there with her mother and father. Beata paused.

Henry shook his head. 'Well, those are the family state-rooms, aren't they? What is the problem, exactly?'

'The parents,' Beata said. 'Her father is blind and her mother has dementia.'

'No, that can't be possible,' Henry said. 'They have to declare any pre-existing conditions before they come on board. They have to sign a document. It's for the insurance.'

'She locks the mother in the cabin and takes her father for a walk around the deck to get some fresh air, then she locks him in and takes her mother for a walk. They never go ashore for excursions. They have all their meals in the cabin.'

'And why are you telling me this? Should you not tell the Captain, or the Cruise Director?' Henry was puzzled.

'Because she would be put ashore at the next port. They wouldn't risk having those people on board.' Beata shook her head.

'But what can I do?' Henry was genuinely at a loss.

'You *know* now, that's all. I just couldn't keep it a secret. You and your wife are very kind. You'll find a way out of it.'

'This woman, Helen Morris, how old is she?'

'About forty, I think.'

'And is *she* a normal person, a *balanced* person, Beata?'

'Yes, she is a very good person. I go to their cabin and take the meals in for her. She trusts me. She said this was the only way to give them a holiday. You will know what to do.'

Henry and Nicola talked about it that night. They knew what they *should* do. They should report that a passenger had lied about the health and incapacity of her relatives. They knew that the hefty insurance payments the company paid would not cover this deception.

But what a call to make!

'Why don't you see her, talk to her?' Nicola suggested.

'I don't want to be dragged into colluding with her.'

'No, you will do what you have to do, but don't let her be a name; a statistic. Talk to her, Henry. Please.'

He looked them up on the manifest. There was no mention of impairment or disability in either parent. Helen's address was in west London, where she lived with both of them.

He knocked at the door of Cabin 5347. She was a pale woman with long straight hair and big anxious eyes.

'Oh, Doctor?' she said with some alarm.

Henry held a clipboard. 'Just a routine call. I'm visiting all passengers aged over eighty, just to see that everyone's in good health.' He felt his voice must sound brittle and over-bright.

'They're fine, thank you, Doctor.'

'So perhaps I could meet your parents, just to—'

'My mother is asleep. My father is listening to music,' Helen said.

'Please?' he asked.

'Why are you really here?' Her face was crumpling.

'Because they haven't come to meals, and so I was afraid they might be seasick.'

'Nobody told you anything?' Her voice was fearful.

'No, no.' Henry was very definite. 'Just routine. Part of my job.' He smiled at her and prepared to be invited in.

Helen looked at him for thirty seconds, her eyes raking his face. Eventually she made her decision.

'Come in, Doctor,' she said, and opened the cabin door wide.

Henry saw an old man in an armchair listening on head-phones and tapping his foot to whatever he heard. His sight-less eyes faced across the cabin. Outside, spectacular scenery of the Norwegian fjords passed by slowly, unseen. His wife sat on the bed holding a doll in her arms. 'Little Helen, little Helen,' she said over and over, and rocked the doll to sleep.

Henry swallowed. He had no idea that it was going to be like this. 'Just routine, as I said.' He cleared his throat.

'Do you have to tell?' Her eyes were red-rimmed and beseeching.

'Yes, I do,' he said simply.

'But why, Doctor? I've managed fine for four days. There are only nine days left.'

'It's not as simple as that. You see, there's a very clear policy.'

'There's no policy that's going to help me to give them a holiday, some fresh air, a change from the flat in Hammersmith with flights of stairs up and down . . . it was my only chance, Doctor.'

'But you didn't tell us the full story.'

'I *couldn't* tell you the whole story. You wouldn't have let us come.'

He was silent.

'Listen, Doctor. I am sure you've had a happy life with nothing going wrong, and I'm glad for you, but not everyone gets that deal. I am an only child. My parents have nobody else. They were so good to me. They got me educated as a teacher. I can't abandon them now.' She paused as if to collect herself. Then she spoke again. 'I work from home correcting and marking papers from a correspondence course. It's endless and back-breaking but at least I can look after them. And they ask so little . . . So is it really some sort of a crime to take them on a little holiday? And have a rest myself, and see such lovely places?'

Henry felt humbled.

Helen was twisting her hands in her lap. Her father smiled,

listening to his music; her mother cradled the baby doll in her arms, cooing and chuckling and calling it Helen.

'I do understand, really I do,' he said, feeling useless.

'But you still must tell, and then they'll put us off the ship?'

'They won't want to take the risk . . .' he began.

'But could *you* take the risk, Doctor? You, who have had all the good luck in the world, a great education, a lovely wife. I've seen you together. You have a dream job where it's all a holiday. You haven't known anything like this. Your life has been easy. Could you find the kindness somewhere to take a risk for us? I'll be so careful, believe me, I will.'

Henry contemplated telling her that his life had not been easy. They had failed to have the children they both wanted. They had seen at close quarters two violent deaths, which they still felt that, if they had been more quick-witted, they might have prevented. They were vaguely unsettled and slightly guilty about the lifestyle on board ship. But what was this compared to the life of the woman in front of him?

'How were you able to afford . . . ?' he began.

'Dad's brother died. He left him ten thousand pounds. It seemed like an opportunity that might never come again, so I ran with it.'

'I see.'

'And up to now it's been great. Just great. Better than I even dreamed.' She was full of hope.

'It won't be easy,' he said.

Her smile was his reward. He wondered if there was anyone at all in her life able to share the burden of care and the sheer determination that kept her going.

'I'll ask Nicola to join us,' Henry said, and the deal was done.

In the end, it was not too arduous. Nicola would sit in the cabin each day while Helen took her father for a walk and even a swim. Then Henry would take his paperwork and sit with the old man while Helen and her mother took the doll for a walk on deck.

Helen was adept at managing to avoid chatting to other passengers. She was looking stronger and more relaxed every day.

Henry said nothing to Beata about the arrangement but he knew she was aware of it, and that it was appreciated.

There were a few near misses. At the daily cruise conference, the Cruise Director mentioned that someone had reported an elderly man who stumbled on deck. Was Dr Henry aware of him? Was there any problem there?

Henry lied smoothly. Yes, the old chap was a bit frail but his daughter seemed very much in control.

One day when Nicola was looking after the old lady, there was a spot check by the Cabin Supervisor. She arrived at the door unexpectedly with Beata in tow.

Nicola swallowed. She had to keep her nerve. 'I'm just doing a one-to-one computer lesson,' she explained with a big smile. Mercifully Helen's mother did not choose that moment to sing a lullaby to the doll. The Supervisor moved on to the next cabin, saying that a one-to-one computer lesson was what everyone over forty needed.

'Well, come to my office and make an appointment,' Nicola begged. 'I'll fit you in to tie in with your time off.'

Then there was the Captain's cocktail party, where they noticed that there was nobody from Cabin 5347.

'They're having an early supper,' Nicola explained.

'They like to be left on their own,' Henry added.

They got to know Helen over the nine days. She said how she missed teaching; she had loved the classroom, and the joy of making children understand something in the end. She thanked them from the bottom of her heart and said they were good people who deserved all their happiness. Henry and Nicola probed her gently about what things would be like when she returned home.

'Same as before,' she said glumly, 'but at least we will have all this to look back on. It was money well spent.'

'Any more legacies likely?' Henry tried to lighten it a little.

'No, but I still have a thousand pounds. That will buy a few treats.' Again that sad smile.

They docked at Southampton. Nicola and Henry began to breathe more easily.

Helen had hired a car to drive them to London. They would take a taxi from the disembarkation point to bring them to the car-rental place.

They exchanged addresses.

'Send me a postcard from your next cruise,' Helen said, as if they were casual shipboard acquaintances rather than accomplices for nine days and nights.

'Yes, and you tell us how things are going,' Nicola said. Her voice was hollow.

It would be, as Helen had foreseen, the same as before.

The officers and crew stood on deck to bid farewell to the passengers. Nicola and Henry embraced Helen as she left, supporting a parent on each arm. They saw her walk down the gangway, her stocky little figure steady and her head held high.

The cleaners were already at work on the ship when Nicola and Henry began to disembark. They would drive home and spend ten days catching up with their parents and friends until the next cruise, this time to Madeira and the Canary Islands.

They were just saying goodbye to the Cruise Director when they heard the news. There had been a terrible accident just outside Southampton, a car crash, three fatalities – all of them passengers just disembarked from this cruise. Henry and Nicola looked at each other, stricken. Before the Cruise Director spoke, they knew.

'It appears to be suicide, can you believe it? She got into her hired car and drove them all into a wall. A total wreck, they were all killed instantly. They found the labels for the cruise ship, so they contacted us. It must have been that woman Helen Morris and her parents from Cabin 5347, apparently . . .'

'It must have been an accident.' Henry could barely speak.

'Don't think so. Witnesses say she stopped the car and reversed a distance and then drove straight at the wall. God, why did she do that?'

'We don't *know* that she did . . .' Nicola began.

'We *do*, Nicola. The law is here, they are making enquiries. We have to talk to the police, make statements.'

The Cruise Director was crisp and to the point.

'We *are* covered, aren't we, Henry? You didn't spot anything, did you?'

It seemed to Henry like an age before he answered but it was probably only four seconds.

'No, she seemed fine. Very positive.' The Cruise Director was relieved but still worried.

'And the old folk? Were they OK?'

'They were frail but she was well able to look after them,' he said, and set in train a series of lies that he and Nicola managed for the next twenty-four hours.

Before they left the ship, Henry sought out Beata. Had she

heard the news? Yes, everyone had heard. Beata looked at Henry with a very steady, level glance.

'It is so sad for the poor lady and her family, but how good that they had a happy holiday at the end of their lives.' She was begging him to say nothing. She too would be in trouble for keeping the secret.

He kissed her goodbye on the cheek.

'Perhaps we will meet on another cruise, Dr Henry.'

'I don't think so,' Henry said. He felt his days as a ship's doctor were over. From now on he would do what he had set out to do: heal people, make their quality of life better, not bend rules for sentiment's sake and end up with the deaths of three people on his hands.

'She would have done it anyway,' Nicola pleaded as they drove back to Esher.

He stared ahead without answering.

'She would have done it in Bergen or Tromsø or wherever . . .'

Still silence.

'You know, you just gave her nine extra days of a holiday. That's all you did. All *we* did.'

'I broke the rules. I played God. There's no escaping that.'

'I love you, Henry.'

'And I love you, but that doesn't change what has happened.'

They told nobody about it. They gave no explanation to anyone about why they were giving up what sounded like the very best job on earth. They offered themselves as volunteers in programmes researching suicide prevention and coping with depression. They withdrew from friends and family. They took short-term locum positions. The dream of a small country practice had slipped away. They didn't feel they would be up to it. They had been tested and were found wanting.

Eventually, Henry's parents decided to speak their minds. It was after yet another silent, depressed Sunday lunch in their home.

'You've changed very much since you came back from that cruise ship,' his father began.

'I thought you didn't approve of it. You suggested that it wasn't *real* medicine,' Henry said huffily.

'I did say, and I'll always say that you should have specialised. You could be a consultant by now, all the chances you had open to you.'

'We just want you to be happy. That's all, dear,' his mother explained.

'Nobody is happy,' Henry said, and he went out to their garden to throw sticks for the old dog.

So Henry's parents decided to speak their minds to Nicola. They caught her in the kitchen as she was sipping a cup of tea and looking into the middle distance.

'We don't want to interfere, Nicola dear,' Henry's mother began.

'I know, you never do, you're really great,' Nicola said admiringly, wondering whether she could evade the 'but' that was approaching.

'It's just that we worry . . .' Henry's father didn't want to let the discussion end before it had begun.

But Nicola had a bright, empty face. 'Of *course* you worry,' she agreed, 'that's what parents do.'

'You've been moping around for over two years, settling to nothing. Look, I know it's not really our business but we do care.' Henry's father was begging to be heard.

Nicola turned and faced him.

'What do you want us to do? Just tell me straight out. Perhaps we just might do it.'

There was something in her face that frightened him. He had never seen her so angry. He immediately tried to row back.

'All I was saying . . . what I was going to say was that . . . that . . . you should have a holiday, a break of some sort . . .' His voice trailed away.

'Oh, a *holiday*!' Nicola sounded hysterically delighted with the idea. A holiday she could just cope with. Just. 'It's funny you should say that because we *were* talking about having a holiday. I'll talk to Henry, and we'll let you know our plans.' And she fled from their kitchen before they could say any more.

She mentioned the holiday to Henry as they drove home that evening.

'I don't think I have the energy for a holiday,' he said.

'Neither do I, but I had to say something to get them off our backs.'

'I'm sorry. Your folks don't go on nagging at us like that.'

'Yes they do, but not in front of you. They're a little afraid of their son-in-law, you know!'

'Would you *like* a holiday, Nicola?'

'I would like a week somewhere before the winter settles in but I don't really know where we would go,' she said.

'Well, neither of us wants to go to the Canaries for winter sun, that's for certain,' Henry said.

'And I don't want winter snow, either. I'd hate skiing,' Nicola said.

'And I'm not crazy about a bus tour,' Henry offered.

'Or Paris. It would be too cold and wet.'

'We've become very crotchety and difficult to please, and

we're not even forty,' Henry said suddenly. 'Lord knows what we'll be like when we really *are* old.'

She looked at him affectionately. 'Maybe we've got to get through this elderly phase first, and then eventually we might become normal.' She spoke lightly but there was general wistfulness in her voice.

'I know what we'll do,' Henry said. 'We'll go on a walking holiday.'

'Walking?'

'Yes, somewhere we've never been before; the Scottish Highlands, or the Yorkshire moors.'

'Or Wales, even?'

'Yes; we'll look up a few places when we get back home.'

'We don't have to stay in youth hostels, do we?' Nicola pleaded.

'No! I think we should find a warm hotel with lots of hot water and good food.'

Nicola sat back in the passenger seat and sighed.

For the first time in two years she believed they might really have turned a corner. A week's holiday in winter would not solve all their worries and end all their woes but it might just be the beginning of some journey back.

Later that evening, when they got back to their house in Esher, it was very cold. Henry lit a fire in the small grate, the first time he had done this for two years. He saw the surprise in Nicola's face.

'Well, if we're going to take the huge decision of choosing a holiday, let's break every other tradition as well,' he said in explanation.

Nicola brought them hot chocolate. Another first. Normally when they came back from visiting either set of parents they felt exhausted, but tonight they seemed to have more energy. They brought the laptop to a small table near the fireplace and began to search for a holiday.

There were some extraordinary places on offer. A farmhouse in Wales, miles from anywhere. But too remote. They didn't want to be quite so isolated. Log cabins in the New Forest where wild ponies might come up to your windows? Yes, maybe. But would they tire of wild ponies after a day or two? An old coaching inn near Hadrian's Wall? Certainly a possibility, but they weren't instantly convinced.

Then they saw a picture of a house in the West of Ireland. A big stone place on a cliff looking down over the Atlantic Ocean. It offered walks and wild birds and peace and good cooking. There was something about it that seemed to draw them.

'It could be just a bit overwritten . . . it might not be like that at all, of course.' Nicola was almost afraid to be enthusiastic.

'Yes, but they couldn't fake those pictures – the waves and the big empty beaches . . . all those birds.'

'Should we call them? What's her name again . . . ? Oh, Mrs Starr.'

The voice that answered had a slight American accent. 'Stone House, can I help you?'

Nicola explained that they were in their thirties, they had been working very hard and needed a holiday and a change. Could she tell them a little more about the place.

And Chicky Starr told them that it was all very simple but in her own opinion, a very restful and healing place. She used to work in New York and came back here every year for a holiday. She walked and walked, and stared out at the ocean and when she got back to America, she always felt able to cope with anything.

She hoped that her guests would feel the same way.

It was beginning to sound too good to be true.

'Will it be all sing-songs and, you know, like an Irish pub?' Henry asked diffidently.

'I very much hope not,' Chicky laughed. 'There will be wine served with dinner, of course, but if people want a more lively nightlife they can go out to the local pubs, which have music.'

'And do we all eat together?'

Chicky seemed to understand the implications of the question.

'There will be about eleven or twelve of us around the table each evening, but it won't be an endurance test. I worked in a boarding house all my life before I set up this place. I'll make sure that no one is forced into being over-jolly. Believe me.'

They believed her, and made the booking straight away.

Henry's parents were pleased.

'Nicola *did* tell us you had plans,' his mother said. 'I was afraid I had been intrusive but she said it hadn't been firmed up.'

'No, Mother. No question of you being intrusive,' he lied.

Nicola's parents were astonished.

'Ireland?' they gasped. 'What's wrong with Britain? There are thousands of places here you haven't seen.'

'It's Henry's decision,' Nicola lied. That sorted it out. They were indeed slightly in awe of their son-in-law.

They flew to Dublin and took a train to the West. They looked out of the windows at the small fields, the wet cattle and the towns with unfamiliar names written in two languages. It felt quite foreign, even though everyone spoke English.

The bus to Stoneybridge did indeed meet the train as

Chicky Starr had promised them that it would. She said she would collect them in her car.

'How will we know you?' Henry had asked anxiously.

'I'll know you,' said Mrs Starr, and so she did.

She was a small woman who waved at them immediately and chatted easily as they drove to Stone House.

The place looked exactly like the photograph on the website. The house stood four-square on a gravelled pathway; the light was already going from the day and the windows glowed with soft light. A black and white cat sat in one of the windows, curled up in an impossibly small ball of fur and paws and ears.

Behind them the creamy, frothy foam on the waves rolled in towards the shore and crashed against the stark cliffs, which were somehow both majestic and containable at the same time.

Chicky gave them tea and scones and showed them to their room, which had a little balcony looking right out to sea.

She was calming, and asked them nothing about their lives or the reasons they had chosen her hotel. She reassured them that the other guests, some of whom had already arrived, all seemed delightful people. They lay down in their big bed and drifted off to sleep. A siesta at five o'clock in the afternoon! For Henry and Nicola it was another first.

Only the sound of the gong woke them, otherwise they might have slept all night. Cautiously they came down to the big kitchen and met the others.

Already gathered was an American man called John, who looked very familiar though they couldn't at first place him. He said he had come here on an impulse because he'd missed a flight at Shannon. Then there was a cheerful nurse called

Winnie, who was travelling with her friend, an older woman called Lillian. They were both Irish and seemed an odd couple though each was entertaining company. There was Nell, a silent, watchful, older woman who seemed a bit reserved, and a Swede whose name they didn't catch.

The food was excellent; the advice about touring the area very thorough. Nobody arrived with a fiddle or an accordion and a medley of Irish songs. As Mrs Starr's niece Orla cleared the table, the group all drifted off to bed easily without speeches or explanations. Back in their room, Nicola and Henry hardly dared tell each other that it looked like being a success. Over the past two years they had been through so many false starts.

A kind of superstitious magic made them tread carefully but they slept again deeply, and the sound of the waves crashing below the cliff was comforting rather than alarming.

The next morning, they woke to scudding clouds and blustery winds and felt that this was indeed going to be the place that let the fresh air in. Their acquaintance with the other guests was close enough to be familiar but not so much as to be intrusive. When Winnie and Lillian went missing the following night, Henry offered to join the search party in case medical assistance was needed; Mrs Starr said she would rather he and Nicola stood by at the house in case the two missing women made it back by themselves. The local doctor, Dai Morgan, had been alerted and was waiting in his surgery.

'Dai Morgan? That doesn't sound very Irish,' Henry said.

'No, indeed, he came here from Wales as a locum thirty years ago when old Dr Barry was sick. Then poor Dr Barry died and Dai stayed. Just as simple as that.'

'Why did he stay?' Nicola asked.

'Because everyone loved him. They still do. Dai and Annie settled in very well here. They had a little girl, Bethan, and she loved it all here. She's a doctor too, now. Imagine!'

The next day, Dai Morgan called round to Stone House to check that the two ladies had no ill effects from their time in the cave. Chicky gave him coffee at the big kitchen table and left him there with Henry and Nicola, who were in between walks.

He was a big square man in his mid-sixties with an easy, reassuring manner and a broad smile.

'Chicky tells me the pair of you are in the same trade as myself,' he said.

Immediately they were guarded. They really didn't feel like answering questions about what they had been doing and how their careers had developed. Still, they couldn't be rude to the man.

'That's true,' Nicola said.

'For our sins,' Henry added.

'Well, I suppose there are worse than us out there,' Dai Morgan said.

They smiled politely.

'I'll miss this place,' he said suddenly.

'You're leaving?' This was a surprise. Chicky Starr had mentioned nothing about that.

'Yes. I only decided this week. My wife, Annie, has had a bad diagnosis. She would like to go back to Swansea. All her sisters live there and her mother, fit as a flea, aged eighty.'

'I'm very sorry,' Nicola said.

'Is it as bad as you think?' Henry asked.

'Yes, a matter of months. We've had second and third opinions, I'm afraid.'

'And she has accepted it?'

'Oh, Annie is a diamond. She knows what it's all about. No fuss, no drama, just wants to be with family.'

'But afterwards . . . ?' Henry asked.

'I wouldn't have the heart to come back here. Stoneybridge was the two of us. It wouldn't be the same on my own.'

'They love you here. They say you made a difference to people,' Nicola said.

'I loved it here too, but not alone.'

'So when will you go?'

'Before Christmas,' he said simply.

They talked about him later as they sat in a mountain pub where black-faced sheep came and looked in the door. Strange thing for a man and his wife to have come so far away from their roots, stay so long and then go back in the end.

They still spoke of the Welsh doctor when they were walking over a long, empty beach and were the only people there. What could have persuaded him to stay in a small, lonely place like this where he knew nothing of the patients and their backgrounds?

They talked about him at night in their room with the waves crashing beneath the cliffs.

'You know what we are really talking about?' Henry said.

'Yes, we're talking about *us*, not him. Would we find peace in a place like this, just as he did?'

'It worked for him. It mightn't work for everybody.' Henry was anxious not to get swept away.

'But there might be somewhere, some place where we could be part of things, *doing* something rather than trying to get round a system.' Her eyes were bright with hope.

Henry leaned over to her and put both his hands around

her face. 'I *do* love you, Nicola. Helen was right. I am a lucky person to have a happy life, and that's because you are the centre of it.'

They found themselves more and more drawn to talk to Dai Morgan. He seemed to like their company. They didn't give him any false comfort about his wife. They were less buttoned up, less watchful than when he had met them first, and slowly they told him of their hopes of finding a place, a community where they could make a difference; something, in fact, like he had done.

'Oh, I've left a lot undone here,' Dai Morgan sighed. 'If I had my time over I'd do some things very differently.'

'Like what?' Henry didn't sound intrusive. He sounded as if he wanted to learn.

'Like a big bully from the new townhouses over there. I was called to the place twice. His wife Deirdre had some kind of vertigo, he said. She had fallen from a ladder once and from the car another time. Broken bones and bruises. It looked to me as if he could have beaten her. I didn't like him but what could I do? The wife swore that she fell. Then the third time I knew. But it was too late. She didn't recover.'

'Oh, God . . .' Nicola said.

'Oh God, indeed. Where was my God, or her God, when that bastard came at her the last time? I didn't speak before because I only had intuition and a gut feeling. Because I didn't trust that feeling, Deirdre died.'

'And did you speak then?' Nicola's eyes were full of tears.

'I tried to but they shut me up. Her own family, brothers and sisters, said that her name mustn't be tarnished in this way. She must be buried as a loved wife and happy mother, otherwise it wouldn't make sense of her life. I couldn't understand it. I still don't understand it. But if I had it all over again I would have spoken the first time.'

'What happened to him? The husband?'

'He lived on here, a few crocodile tears, a few references to My Poor Wife Deirdre. But then he met another woman, a very different kind of person entirely, and the first day he hit her she was straight into the Guards. He was done for assault. He served six months and left in disgrace. Deirdre's family put it all down to his great grief over his wife's death. In a way, I suppose, it was a result.' He looked grim at the recollection of it all.

'And do you think about it a lot?' Nicola asked.

'I used to, all the time. Every day I pass the graveyard where Deirdre is buried. Every time I saw their house, I remembered her face as she swore to me that she fell from a ladder. But then Annie said it was tearing me apart and I would be no use to anyone else in the place unless I got over it. So I suppose I got over it, in a way.'

Dai watched them nod in such genuine sympathy and understanding that he realised they really did understand; perhaps something similar had happened to them too.

He spoke carefully. 'Annie said that in a way I was putting myself centre stage, making it all *my* problem, *my* involvement, or lack of it. There were other factors to consider: he was always going to be a cruel bastard, handy with his fists; she was always going to be a victim. Did I think I was some kind of avenging angel sent down to sort out the world? And it made sense.'

'You forgave yourself?' Henry asked.

'Something else happened just then. I was in my surgery when one of the young O'Hara children was brought in. His mother said he'd got some stomach bug and he was vomiting.

She said he was very sleepy and had a temperature. Something about it didn't seem right to me, and I gave him a thorough examination. I thought he had meningitis and gave the hospital a call. They said he needed to come in straight away for tests. It would have taken too long to get an ambulance out here, so I just picked him up and ran outside and put him and his mother on the back seat. I drove like a demon to the hospital and they were ready with the tests and the antibiotics, and we saved him. He's a great big lout of a fellow now, could drink for the county. Nice lad, though. He's very good with the youngest boy, Shay. Takes care of him a bit. Every time I pass by he says, "That's the great man who saved my life", and I ask him to tell me one good reason why I should be pleased about this. But I know I did, and that for once I made a difference.'

'I'm sure it wasn't just for once,' Nicola said.

'Maybe not, but it was a kind of redemption and badly needed at the time, I tell you.'

Henry and Nicola talked about it all as they sat in their room at Stone House waiting for the dinner gong.

'Redemption . . . that's what we have been looking for,' Nicola said.

'Maybe the Tooth Fairy might find some for us.' Henry was not dismissive or cynical; he was actually smiling, and held her hand.

They were the first in for dinner.

Chicky and her niece Orla were preparing a tray of drinks for the guests. They were talking seriously about something.

'What can they *do*, Chicky? Chain his leg to the bed?'

'No, but they can't let him wander out on his own at night.'

'Try stopping him. He's going to go out anyway . . .'

When they saw Nicola and Henry they immediately broke off. Chicky was very professional. Domestic matters were never discussed in front of guests. The place ran smoothly, almost effortlessly, though it was all down to careful preparation. They enquired about what Nicola and Henry had done during the day. They took out the bird books to identify a goose that the couple had seen strutting across the marshy fields near the lake. It had pink legs and a big orange beak.

'That's a greylag goose, I'd say.' Chicky turned the pages of *Ireland's Birds*. 'Is this it, do you think?'

They thought it was.

'They come from Iceland every year. Imagine!' Chicky paused in wonder at it all.

'It would be lovely to know all about birds, like you do.' Nicola was envious of the way Chicky could lose herself in the thought of a goose flying from Iceland.

'Oh, I'm only a real amateur. We had hoped to have a real birdwatcher for you here. There's a local boy, Shay O'Hara. He knows every feather of every bird that flies the skies. But it didn't work out.'

'It would have been the making of him,' Orla shook her head sadly.

Chicky felt this needed some explanation. 'Shay's not himself these days. He's depressed. Nobody can reach him. We're all hoping it's just a phase.'

'Depression in young men is very serious,' Henry said.

'Oh, I know it is, and Dr Dai is on the case but Shay won't take medication or go for counselling or listen to anyone,' Chicky sighed.

The others had begun to arrive in the kitchen so the matter was dropped.

*

Nicola sat beside the handsome American who was still calling himself John, and who had found a new friend in a local man called Frank Hanratty. Frank had driven him miles over mountain roads in a pink van to meet an old film director who had retired to this part of the world years back. A very pleasant and contented gentleman who had given them nettle soup.

'Did he recognise you?' Nicola asked, unguardedly.

Up to now they had never acknowledged out loud that John was in fact a film actor, a celebrity.

John took it all casually. 'Yes, he was kind enough to say he knew my work. But he was fascinating. He has hens, you know, and beehives and a goat. He has a house full of books – he's as happy as anyone I ever met.'

'Extraordinary,' Nicola was wistful. 'It must be wonderful to be happy.'

John looked at her sharply but said no more.

Before they went to bed, they went outside to breathe in the cold sea air. Orla was just wheeling out her bicycle and on her way home.

'Do you ever get tired of this view?' Henry asked her.

'No, I missed it so much when I lived in London. Some people find it sad. I don't.'

'What about the poor birdwatcher you were telling us about? Does he find it sad?'

'Shay finds everything sad,' Orla said, and cycled home.

It was at three o'clock in the morning that Henry and Nicola were wakened by the sound of birds crying out to each other. It wasn't nearly time for the dawn chorus or the early-morning gathering of the gulls. Possibly it was a bird in distress out on their little balcony.

They got up to investigate.

Silhouetted against the moonlit sea was the thin figure of a teenage boy in a thin jumper, holding his arms around himself, his head back and weeping.

This must be Shay. Shay, who found everything sad.

Without even consulting each other, they put on their coats and shoes and went downstairs. They let themselves out into the cold night air.

The boy's eyes were closed, his face contorted. They couldn't make out the words that he was still crying aloud. He was shaking, and his thin shoulders were hunched in despair. He was dangerously near the edge of the cliff.

They moved towards him steadily, talking to each other so that he would not be startled at their approach.

He opened his eyes and saw them. 'You're not going to change my mind,' he said.

'No, that's true,' Henry said.

'What do you mean?'

'You're right. I'm not going to change your mind. If you don't do it now, you'll do it later tonight or next week. I know *that.*'

'So why are you trying to stop me?'

'Stop you? We're not trying to stop you, are we, Nicola?'

'No. Lord, no. People do what they want to do.'

'So what *are* you doing then?' His eyes were huge and filled with terror and his thin body was shaking.

'We wanted to ask you about the greylag goose. We saw one today. I gather it flew in from Iceland.'

'There's nothing odd about seeing a greylag goose. Sure, the place is coming down with them. Now if you'd seen a snow goose, *that* would be something to talk about,' said Shay.

'A snow goose? Do they come from Iceland too?' Nicola

206

was moving round behind him but almost nonchalantly, and looking vaguely out to sea as if hoping to catch a snow goose in the light of the moon.

'No, they're from Arctic Canada, Greenland. You'd see them over in Wexford on the east coast. They don't come here much.'

'Have you seen them yourself?' Henry wondered.

'Oh yes, often, but as I say, not round here. I saw a bean goose last year. That's fairly rare.'

'A *bean* goose!' Henry tried to put awe and admiration into his voice.

The boy smiled.

'Could you come in and show us the bean goose in the bird book?' Nicola asked, as if the thought had just come to her.

'Ah, no. I'd only have Chicky going on and on about my going to the doctor. I hate doctors.'

'Oh, I know.' Nicola rolled her eyes to heaven as if sharing his view.

'Anyway, you could look it up yourself. She has all the books in there.'

'It's not the same. You could explain . . .'

'No, I wouldn't feel easy about it.' He was about to back away. Nicola was right behind him.

She put her hand gently on his arm. 'Please come in with us. Henry can't sleep, you see, and it would be such a help to us.'

'All right, so. Just for a bit,' he said, and came with them into the kitchen of Stone House.

They found him a big tartan jacket while his thin sweater was drying on the radiator. Nicola made them tea and they had some bread and cheese. He was still there explaining how you would tell a barnacle goose from a brent goose when the O'Haras arrived, calling out his name.

They had read the note he had left on their table; the note saying he was sorry but this was the only way out. They had been praying as they ran across the cliffs that they would be in time.

Shay's father sat down at Chicky's table and cried like a baby.

They phoned Shay's mother, who had been so deeply in shock that she couldn't come with them in the search. Chicky had come downstairs and was coping with everything as if this was to be expected in a day's work.

'We need a doctor,' Shay's sister said.

Shay looked up, annoyed at the idea.

Chicky was about to explain that there were already two doctors in the kitchen. Henry shook his head.

'I'm sure Dr Dai would come,' he said.

'He'll know what to do,' Nicola agreed.

Chicky understood.

Next morning at breakfast they didn't talk about it. Orla already knew. The whole of Stoneybridge had heard how the two English visitors had talked the boy out of the death he had planned. She looked at them gratefully as she served the food.

Some of the guests had thought they heard shouting in the night. A thing of nothing, Chicky explained, and they moved on to talk about plans for the day.

They called on Dai Morgan later in the morning.

'There's a human being alive today because of you,' he said.

'But for how long?' Henry asked. 'He'll do it again, won't he?'

'Maybe not. He has agreed to go into hospital for

observation. He says he will take his medication and he might talk to a counsellor. That's a long way further down the road than before.'

Henry and Nicola looked at each other.

Dai went on talking. 'I'm anxious to get my own move started as soon as possible. I'll start telling people today. I was wondering . . . it's a bit far out, but I was wondering . . .'

They knew what he was going to say.

'I'll need a locum for a couple of months. Would you think of it?'

'They wouldn't trust us. We're outsiders.'

'I was an outsider.'

'But that's different. They don't know anything at all about us.'

'They know you saved Shay O'Hara's life. That's as good a calling card as any,' said Dai Morgan.

And then there was a lot to talk about, as plans were made.

'It doesn't have to be for thirty years, like me,' Dai told them.

He watched them as they stood together in the winter sunshine, relaxed now as they had never been before.

'Or then again, of course, you might even stay longer,' he added.

Anders

When Anders was at school and they asked him what would he be when he grew up, he always said that he would be an accountant like his father and grandfather. He would go to work in the big family firm with its impressive office in Stockholm. Almkvist's was one of the oldest companies in Sweden, he would tell you proudly.

Anders was a very happy child with blond, floppy hair in his eyes. He loved music from an early age and could play the piano creditably at the age of five. He wanted a guitar when he was older, and learned to play without any instruction. You could hear him playing in his room night after night after he'd finished his homework; then their housekeeper, Fru Karlsson, introduced him to the *nyckelharpa*, the traditional Swedish keyed fiddle. It had belonged to her grandfather, and as she had learned how to play from him so she now showed Anders. She taught him some traditional Swedish songs to play on it, and he fell in love with its ethereal sound.

He lived with his parents, Patrik and Gunilla Almkvist, Fru Karlsson and their dog, Riva, in a beautiful apartment overlooking Djurgårdskanalen. He told people that his was the best school in Sweden, and that Riva was the best dog in the world. To praise Papa's office was only just another part of the contented world he lived in. Two of his cousins, Klara and Mats, had gone to work in the family firm already, gaining office experience as they did their accountancy studies. Mats was a bit self-important but Klara was very down to earth and already knew the business inside out. They knew that Anders, as the heir and successor, would leave his piano and his *nyckelharpa* behind and go away to university to be groomed for the job that would one day be his. Meanwhile, they would take him out for coffee and tell him stories of the clients they met.

All kinds of well-known personalities from big business, sports and entertainment filed through the big arched doors of the office. There were meetings in the boardroom, there were discreet lunches in the private dining rooms of restaurants. Everyone in the office dressed very well; Mats wore designer suits and immaculate shirts, while Klara always managed to look elegant. Although she wore understated, sober office clothes she always looked as though she was ready to step on to a catwalk. Efficiency, style and discretion were the watchwords at Almkvist's. Mats and Klara looked and sounded the part. Anders wondered whether he would ever feel comfortable in this world.

It was the style aspect Anders found the most challenging. He hardly noticed what other people wore, and always liked to dress comfortably himself. He could not begin to understand the importance of handmade shoes, precision Swiss watches and pure silk ties, and they certainly didn't figure in the world of folk music to which he was most drawn.

His mother laughed at him affectionately.

'Well-cut clothes make you look much more handsome, Anders. The girls will admire you if you dress well.'

'They won't notice clothes. Either they will like me or they won't like me.' He was fifteen, awkward, unsure.

'So wrong, so very wrong. They'll love you but first they have to look at you. It's the first impression that counts. Believe me, I know.' Gunilla Almkvist always looked elegant. She worked for a TV station where they set a high value on style. She never left the house before she was properly prepared for what the day would bring. She walked the two kilometres to work wearing her trainers; her elegant high-heeled shoes were kept in her office on the bottom shelf – seven pairs of them.

She made every effort to interest Anders in dressing more smartly, trying to build an enthusiasm where none existed. By the time he was eighteen she had stopped cajoling.

'It's not a joke any more, Anders. If you were in the army you'd have to wear a uniform. If you were going to be in the Diplomatic Service there would be rules about what to wear. You are going to work in Almkvist and Almkvist Accountants. There are rules. There are expectations.'

'I'm going to study accountancy, isn't that what it's about?'

'It's what *some* of it is about. But it's also about respecting the family traditions, about fitting in.' There was something different, something odd in her tone this time.

He looked up. 'None of that's important, surely? It's not what life is about.'

'If you remember nothing else I've ever told you, just remember this. I agree that in the great scheme of things it is *not* important, but it is one small thing you can do to make life easier. That's all. Just remember I told you that.'

Why was she sounding so strange?

'You're *always* going on about clothes and style. I don't have to remember it, you keep telling me.' He smiled at her, willing everything to be normal.

Everything was not normal.

'I won't be here to tell you,' she said, her voice sounding as though her throat was constricted. 'That's why it's important you listen now. I am going away. I am leaving your father. You will be going to university this autumn. This is the time for change.'

'Does he know you are going?' Anders' voice was a whisper.

'Yes. He knew that I would wait until you had finished school. I am going to London. I have a job there, and that's where I will set up home.'

'But won't you be lonely there?'

'No, Anders. I have been very lonely *here*. Your father and I have grown apart over a long time. He is married to the company. He will hardly miss me.'

'But . . . *I* will miss you! This can't be true! How did I not see anything or know about all this?'

'Because we were all discreet. There was no need for you to know anything until now.'

'And do you have somebody else in London?' He knew he sounded like a seven-year-old.

'Yes, I have a warm, kind, funny man called William. We laugh a lot together. I hope as the years go on you will get to know him and to like him. But for your father's sake, just remember what I said about smartening yourself up. It will make your whole life much simpler.'

He turned his head away so that she would not see his distress. His mother was going off to London with a man called William who made her laugh. And what was she talking about as she left? Clothes. Bloody *clothes*. He felt his world had turned sideways and everything had slipped out of focus.

His mother and father hadn't grown apart. They had had a dinner party last Friday. Papa had raised a glass to her across the table. 'To my beautiful wife,' he had said. And all the time he knew she was going to leave with this William.

It couldn't be true, could it?

His mother stood there, afraid to touch him in case he shrugged her off, shook her away. 'I love you, Anders. You may find that hard to believe, but I do. And your father does too. Very much. He doesn't show it but it's there; great pride and great love.'

'They are different things, pride and love,' Anders said. 'Was he proud of you too, or did he love you?' Anders looked at her properly for the first time.

'He was proud that I kept my side of the bargain. I ran the house well; I was a satisfactory escort to him at all those interminable dinners; I was a good hostess. I gave him a son. I think he was pleased with me, yes.'

'But love?'

'I don't know, Anders. I don't think he ever loved anything except his firm and you.'

'He never sounds as if he loves me. He is always so distant.'

'That's his way. He will always be like that. But I have been there for all of your life and he does love you. He just can't express it.'

'If he had expressed it for you, would you have stayed?'

'That's not a real question. It's like wishing that a square was a circle,' she said. And because he believed her, Anders held his hands out to her and she sobbed in his arms for a long time.

It all moved very swiftly after that.

Gunilla Almkvist packed her clothes, as Fru Karlsson sniffed in disapproval, but left all her jewellery behind. A cover story was devised. She had been offered this post in London working for a satellite broadcasting station. It would be criminal to let the opportunity pass. Anders was going off to university; her husband was fully supportive of the move. That way there would be no accusations about a runaway wife, a failed marriage. None of the oxygen of gossip, which would be so relished and yet so out of place at Almkvist's.

Patrik Almkvist seemed courteous and grateful. He never discussed the matter with his only child. He looked pleased that Anders had had his hair properly cut and that he'd been measured for a good suit.

He spent more and more time at the office.

The night before Anders' mother left, the three of them went out to dinner together. Patrik raised his glass to his wife. 'May you find all you are looking for in London,' he said.

Anders stared at them in disbelief. Twenty years of life together, two decades of hope and dreams ending, and his parents were still acting out a role. Was this what everyone did? He had a feeling at that moment that he would never fall in love. It was all for the poets and the love songs and the dreamers. It wasn't what people did in real life.

Next day, he set off for Gothenburg and university. His new life had begun.

He had only been there a week when he met Erika, a textile and design student. She came straight over to him at a party and asked him to dance.

Later, he asked her why she had approached him that night.

'You looked smart, that's all. Not scruffy,' she said.

Anders was very disappointed. 'Does that sort of thing matter?' he asked.

'It matters that you care enough about yourself and about the people you meet to present yourself well. That's all. I'm tired of scruffy people,' she said.

They were an item from then on, it seemed. Erika loved to cook but only when she wanted to and what she wanted to. But she loved to have people to her apartment, and when she found out that Anders could play the *nyckelharpa* she was appalled that he hadn't brought it with him to university. So the very next time he went home she insisted that he bring it back with him. And then she set about organising jam sessions at her place, and she would make the most delicious suppers.

Erika was small and funny and thought that women's rights and fashion were not incompatible. She loved to dress up for any occasion, and astonished Anders when she was the most attractive and stylish woman in the room. They made each other laugh, and quite soon became inseparable.

It was just before Easter time that she told him she would never marry him because she thought marriage was a kind of enslavement, but she would love him all of her life. She said she needed to explain this to him at once lest there be any grey areas.

Anders was startled. He hadn't *asked* her to marry him. But it all looked good, so he went along with it.

Erika asked him home to meet her parents.

Her father ran a tiny restaurant; her mother was a taxi driver. They welcomed Anders warmly, and he envied the kind of family life they all had. Her sister and brother, twins aged twelve, joined in everything and argued cheerfully with their parents about every subject from pocket money to breast implants, from God to the royal family – subjects that had never been discussed in the Almkvist household. The twins asked Erika when would she be going to meet Anders' family. Before he could answer, Erika said quickly that there was no hurry. She was an acquired taste, she explained. It would take longer for people to welcome her in.

'What's an acquired taste?' her brother asked.

'Look it up,' Erika teased.

Later, Anders said, 'I would be happy for you to come and stay at my father's house.'

'No way. I don't want to give the man a heart attack. But I might go with you and stay at your mother's in London, though.'

'I'm not sure if that would be a good idea . . .'

'You just don't want to meet William and think of him sleeping with your mother, that's all.'

'Not true,' he said and then, because he couldn't keep up the lie, 'Well, I suppose it's a little true.'

'Let's see if we can get to London. I'll try and find a project, and we can improve our English *and* see London *and* check out your new stepfather at the same time.'

It was April when they finally made the visit to London. The daffodils were out in all the parks and gardens and everything seemed alive and sparkling. Gunilla and William were living in an elegant house in a beautiful square quite close to the Imperial War Museum; from there, it was only a few minutes' walk to the River Thames and all the history and pageantry London was famous for. It was the first time they had seen the city and all the richness and bustle. The crowds and the noise were daunting at first, but they dived in with enthusiasm, determined to make the most of every moment.

Gunilla was relaxed and delighted to see them. If she had any doubts about Erika's suitability as the partner of the next head of Almkvist's, she did not even hint at them. William was very welcoming and took three days off work from his television production company to show the young visitors the real London. The first stop was the London Eye, from where they could see for miles in every direction. He had looked up a few of the folk-music clubs in the city so they could take off on their own for an evening if they wanted to. To Anders' delight, William had even found out that there would be *nyckelharpa* playing at a Scandi session in a pub not far away in Bermondsey.

Anders found that it was easier to talk to his mother than it had ever been. No longer was she complaining about how he looked. In fact, she was full of admiration.

'Erika is just delightful,' she told Anders. 'Have you taken her to meet your father yet?'

'Not yet. You know . . .'

If his mother *did* know, she didn't say so.

'Don't leave it too long. Take Erika to meet him soon. She's lovely.'

'But you know how snobby he is, how much he cares about what people do, and are. You've forgotten what he's like. She stands up for herself. She hates big business. She can't bear the kind of people he deals with all day.'

'She will be much too polite to let any of that show.'

Anders wished he could believe her.

Gunilla wanted to know about the office. Did Anders go in there much when he went home?

'I haven't been home much really,' he admitted.

'You should go and keep an eye on your territory, your inheritance,' she said. 'Your father would like that.'

'He never asks me or suggests it.'

'You never offer, you never visit,' she answered.

When they got back to Sweden, Anders telephoned his father. The conversation was formal: it was as if Patrik Almkvist was talking to a casual acquaintance. In as far as Anders could understand, his father sounded pleased that he was coming home for the summer and hoped to work in the office.

'Somewhere that I can't do too much damage,' Anders suggested.

'Everyone will go out of their way to help you,' his father promised.

And so it was. Anders noticed, with some embarrassment, that people in the firm *did* go out of their way to help and encourage him. They spoke to him with a respect that was quite disproportionate for a student. He was definitely the young prince-in-waiting. No one wanted to cross him. He was the future.

Even his two cousins, Mats and Klara, were anxious to show him how much they were pulling their weight. They kept giving him an update on all they had done so far and how well they were handling their own areas. They tried hard to understand what interested young Anders. He didn't seem to want expensive meals in top restaurants; he wasn't concerned with business gossip; he didn't even want to know of rivals' failures.

He was a mystery.

His father, too, seemed to have problems working out where Anders' interests lay. He asked courteous questions about life at university. Whether the teachers had business experience as well as academic records.

He asked nothing about whether Anders had other interests or a love life, whether he still loved music, still played the *nyckelharpa* or even who his friends were. In the evenings, they sat in the apartment in Östermalm and talked about the office and the various clients that had been seen during the day. They ate at Patrik's favourite restaurant some evenings; otherwise they had supper at home sitting at the dining table and eating cold meats and cheese laid out by the silent and disapproving Fru Karlsson. The more his father talked, the less Anders knew about him. The man had no life apart from the one that was lived in the Almkvist office.

Anders had promised his mother that he would make an effort to break his father's reserve but it was proving even harder than he had thought. He tried to speak about Erika.

'I have this girlfriend, Father. She's a fellow student.'

'That's good,' his father nodded vaguely and approvingly as if Anders had said that he had updated his laptop.

'I've been to stay with her family. I thought I might invite Erika here for a few days.'

'Here?' His father was astounded.

'Well, yes.'

'But what would she do all day?'

'I suppose she could tour the city and we could meet for lunch, and I could take a few days off to show her around.'

'Yes, certainly, if you'd like to . . . Of course.'

'She came to London with me when I went to see Mother.'

'Oh yes?'

'It all worked very well. She found plenty to do there.'

'I imagine everyone would find something to do in

London. It would be rather different here.' His father was glacial.

'I'm very fond of her, Papa.'

'Good, good.' It was as if he was trying to stem any emotion that might be coming his way.

'In fact, we are going to move in together.' Now he had said it.

'I don't know how you expect to be able to pay for that.'

'Well, I thought it might be something we could discuss while I'm here. Now, may I invite Erika for next week?'

'If you like, yes. Make all the arrangements with Fru Karlsson. She will need to prepare a bedroom for your friend.'

'We will be *living* together, Father. I thought she could share my room here.'

'I don't like to impose your morality and standards on Fru Karlsson.'

'Father, it's not *my* morality, it's the twenty-first century!'

'I know, but even with your mother's shallow grasp on reality she realised the importance of being discreet and keeping one's personal life just that. Fru Karlsson will prepare a bedroom for your friend. Your sleeping arrangements you can make for yourselves.'

'Have I annoyed you?'

'Not at all. In fact I admire your directness, but I am sure you see my point of view also.' He spoke as he would in the office, his voice never raised, his sureness that he was right never wavering.

Erika arrived by train the first week in July. She was full of stories about her fellow passengers. She wore jeans and a scarlet jacket and had a huge backpack of work with her. She said she was going to study in the mornings and then meet him for lunch each day.

'My father will insist on taking us out to some smart places,' he began nervously.

'Then it's just as well you got yourself some smart clothes,' she said.

'I didn't mean me, I meant . . .'

'Don't worry, Anders. I have the shoes, I have the dress,' she said.

And she did. Erika looked splendid in her little black dress with the shocking-pink shawl and smart high heels when they went to his father's favourite restaurant. She listened and asked intelligent questions, and she spoke cheerfully about her own family – her demon twin brother and sister, her mother's adventures in the taxi trade, her father's restaurant which served thirty-seven different kinds of pickled herring. She talked easily about the trip to London and how Anders' mother had been a marvellous hostess. She even talked openly about William.

'You probably don't know him, Mr Almkvist, because of the circumstances and everything, but he was quite amazing. He'd found a pub in Bermondsey where they were playing the *nyckelharpa* – Anders loved it – and then we went to dinner in a restaurant with the most amazing gold mosaic ceiling. He owns a television production company, did you know? Totally capitalist, of course, and against any kind of social welfare, which he called a handout. But generous and helpful as well. Proves that people can't be put in pigeonholes.'

Anders watched his father anxiously. People didn't usually talk to the head of Almkvist's in this manner. They normally skirted away from topics like inequality and privilege. But his father was able to cope with the conversation perfectly well. It was as if he was talking to a casual acquaintance. He asked nothing about Erika's studies, or her hopes and plans for the future.

Anders wondered, had he ever shown any enthusiasm or eagerness for anything except the firm he had worked for all his life?

Erika had no such worries. 'He's just blinkered,' she said. 'Lots of people are. It's that generation. My father doesn't care about anything except the taxes on alcohol and customers going off on a ferry to Denmark to buy cheap booze. My mother is fixated on the need to have women-only taxis. Your father is all hung up on tax shelters and asset management and trusts and things. It's what they *do* in his world. Stop being dramatic about it.'

'But it's not a normal way to live,' Anders insisted.

Erika shrugged. 'For him it is. Always has been and always will be. It's what *you* want that's important.'

'Well I don't want to end up like that, with no interests apart from the office. Blinkered, as you say.'

'So you de-blinker yourself. Why don't we go out and look for some good music tonight?'

Erika was totally practical about everything. She saw nothing wrong with pretending to Fru Karlsson that she slept in the guest bedroom. It was a matter of respect, she said.

Too soon the week was over, and Anders and his father sat again in the empty house speaking only of audits, new business and mergers that had been the order of the day at work. Anders found he enjoyed the business conversations and relished the debates, but he longed to be back at university and moving into his new apartment with Erika. He sensed his cousins were relieved that he would be leaving the office again. His father seemed indifferent, shaking his hand formally and hoping that he would study well and bring all today's thinking and economic theory back to Almkvist's.

Once he was back at university, the voice of his father seemed to Anders like something from a different planet.

The months flew by. He did as he had promised his mother and kept in touch with his father. He made a phone call every ten days or so; a stilted conversation where they ended up talking about personnel at Almkvist's, or new business that had come in their direction. Sometimes he told his father of a business development or an element of tax law he had come across, or the long weekend when he had gone to Majorca with Erika's parents. But he was always relieved when the call was over and felt that his father thought exactly the same.

When it came to the summer holiday the following year, Anders wrote saying that he and Erika were going to spend two months in Greece. If his father was startled that the months would not be spent in the office learning the ropes, he said nothing. Anders felt rather than heard the disapproval.

'I've worked very hard. I need a break, Father.'

'Indeed,' his father had said in a chilly voice.

They had a magical summer in the Greek islands, swimming, laughing, drinking retsina and dancing at night to bouzouki music in the tavernas.

Erika told him of her plans. When she graduated, she was going to be part of a new venture conserving ancient textiles; the funding had been put in place. It was very exciting. And where would it be based? Well, right here in Gothenburg, of course. It was going to be attached to the World Culture Museum.

Anders was silent. He had always hoped she would eventually find work in Stockholm. That they would get a little apartment on one of the islands in the city centre.

They would not marry because Erika still considered it a form of slavery but they would live together when he ran Almkvist's, and have two children.

This did not seem to chime in with Erika's plans. But he would say nothing until he had thought it out.

'You're very silent. I thought you'd be so pleased for me.'

'I am, of course.'

'But?'

'But I suppose I hoped that we would be together. Is that selfish?'

'Of course it's not, but we were waiting until we knew what we wanted to do. You haven't decided yet, so I came up with my plan first to see if you could work round it.' She looked anxious that he should understand.

'But we *know* what I'm going to do. I'm going back to run the family firm.'

Erika looked at him oddly. 'Not seriously?' she said.

'Well of course, seriously. You know that. You've been there. You've seen the set-up. I have to do that. There's never been anything else.'

'But you don't want to do it!' she gasped.

'Not like the way it is, but you told me to de-blinker myself and I did, or I am trying to, anyway. I'm not going to live for the place like my father does.'

'But you were breaking free. Isn't that why we were able to come to Greece instead of you working there all summer?' She was totally bewildered.

'But we know I have to go back, Erika.'

'No, we don't know that you have to go back. You have only one life, and you don't want to spend it there, in that little world with cousins and colleagues.'

'There's no alternative. He only had one son. If I had

225

brothers who could have taken it over . . .' his voice trailed away.

'Or sisters,' Erika corrected automatically. 'It's only fair to tell him now rather than waste his time, their time, *your* time.'

'I can't do that. Not until I've tried it, anyway. It would be an insult. You're very strong on the respect thing. I owe him that much respect.' In the warm evening air as they sat in the little taverna beside the sea, they heard other people laughing in the distance. Happy people on holiday. Musicians were beginning to tune up.

Anders and Erika sat there, aware of a huge gap opening up between them.

It was now out of their control. The future that had looked so great half an hour ago was about to disappear entirely.

They tried to salvage the rest of the holiday but it was no use. It hung over them: Anders' belief that he would spend his life at Almkvist's and Erika's belief that he had yet to find what he would do were too far apart to gloss over. By the time they got back to Sweden, they knew that there was nothing ahead for the two of them.

They divided up their records and books amicably. Anders took a room in a student block. He told his father that he and Erika were no longer together.

His father's reaction was about the same as it might have been if he had said that a train was running late. A mild and distant murmur that these things happen in life. Then on to the next subject.

He studied hard, determined to get a good degree. Sometimes on the way to and from the library he would see Erika within a laughing group and feel a great pang of regret. They always greeted each other cordially; sometimes he even joined them for a beer in the student cafés.

Their friends were mystified by it all. They had always got on so well. Nothing had changed on the outside; they just were not together any more.

His mother had emailed to say she was sorry to hear they had separated. Erika must have told her. Gunilla said she and William had thought that Erika was a delightful girl, and that Anders must remember that when doors closed they could often be opened up again. She also advised him to do something with his music, or to learn to play tennis or bridge or golf, *something* that would give him a world outside Almkvist's. Perhaps he might even go back to playing the piano. He had even stopped playing the *nyckelharpa* since he and Erika broke up.

Anders was touched, but there would be little time to spend inventing hobbies. He had his final exams to concentrate on; he couldn't take up his place at Almkvist's unless he came away with a good degree. It was time to knuckle down and just get on with it.

He went home every month and worked for a few days in the office, keeping his hand in. He learned how to express his views and how to make decisions. He had a good business head, and people had begun to take him seriously. He was no longer the son and heir of the senior Almkvist: he was a person in his own right. He found himself able to talk to his cousin Mats about his drinking, which had become a matter of some concern; as Mats was family, the problem had so far not been addressed. Anders had been firm but fair. He showed little condemnation, but gave a very clear warning at the same time. Mats pulled himself together sharply and the situation was sorted.

If his father knew of it, he said nothing. But he tended to leave more and more to Anders. Anders, in turn, leaned on

Klara. She was willing to share her experience with him, which was a great help as his final exams were now only weeks away.

On a sunny day in June, Patrik Almkvist sat next to his wife Gunilla for their son's graduation. William had stayed at home because of business commitments, he said. Privately, Anders thought that might just have been a diplomatic retreat. It might have been a miserable ordeal. Instead, Anders was pleased to see, it wasn't just good manners that kept them all smiling throughout the afternoon and into the evening. He realised that now his parents no longer lived together, they could relax. To his astonishment, a kind of friendship had emerged and they were both able to enjoy their son's achievements.

The conversation over dinner was filled with talk of the future: for a long time, it had been planned that after his graduation Anders would spend a year in a big American firm of accountants, a place with a distinguished name where he would learn a great deal in a short time. It had all been arranged with the senior partners, and Anders was hugely looking forward to it. Klara had been very helpful with her Boston contacts and had arranged everything. Gunilla had contacts there too, it emerged, and he would have a marvellous time in the city. As they strolled through the streets of Gothenburg, Anders felt that everything was falling into place.

The following morning, Patrik Almkvist collapsed in the hotel lobby.

It was a heart attack.

It was not major, the hospital told them; Mr Almkvist was not in any danger but still he had to rest. Anders and Gunilla sat by his bedside for two days and then, as his mother flew back to London, Anders took his father back home to Stockholm.

Fru Karlsson took charge immediately, and Anders knew his father would be in good hands. He was making arrangements with her for home nursing and support but his father cut straight across.

'There's no way you can go to Boston now. You have to go in at the deep end, Anders. I need you in there as my eyes and ears. It's your time now.'

It couldn't be his time yet. He was much too young. He hadn't even begun to live properly.

Boston was cancelled. Soon it seemed as if Anders had always been in charge; he welcomed the challenges, yet he knew he would not have been able to cope without Klara's expertise and loyalty. She briefed him before every meeting, gave him background information on every client. He did make time to swim at lunchtime each day rather than go to eat the heavy meals in dark, panelled dining rooms that the previous regime had favoured. Once a week he went to listen to some live music but every other evening he sat with his father as Fru Karlsson cleared away their supper, and he spoke about what had gone on at the firm that day.

Little by little, Mr Almkvist's strength returned. But never to the level it had been. When he came back to work it was for short days and mainly involved meetings in the boardroom, where his presence managed to give weight and importance to the occasion.

The weeks turned into months.

Sometimes Anders felt a bit crushed by it all; other times he felt that out there somewhere was a real world with people doing what they really wanted to do or what mattered, or both. But he realised that he was privileged to have inherited such a prestigious position. In a world of uncertainty and anxiety about employment and the economy, he was amazingly lucky to be where he was, doing a job that presented new challenges every day. Privilege brought duties with it; he had always known this. This was where his duty lay.

It was his father who suggested the holiday to him.

He said that the boy was working too hard and must go to recharge his batteries. Anders was at a loss to know where to go. His friend Johan from the folk club said that Ireland was good. You could just go there and point yourself in some direction and there was always something good to see or to join in with.

He booked a ticket to Dublin and set out with no plans. Unheard-of behaviour from anyone at Almkvist's, who normally researched everything forensically before setting out anywhere. He missed Erika desperately at the airport. They had set out from here to London, to Spain, to Greece. Now he was on his own.

Had he been mad to let her slip away?

But there had been no other decision he could have made. Anders could not have stayed for ever with Erika in Gothenburg, where she had found the perfect career. And she would not have come to live in the shadow of Almkvist's and be a complaisant company wife like his mother had done.

He had hoped that he would forget her, and it was easy to find companions for dinner or dancing. As the heir to Almkvist's he was considered a very eligible catch, but no woman ever held his interest for long. He went to all the social occasions but never cared about anyone enough to seek out their company, and he had been pleased to learn that Erika had not formed any other attachment. Now, at the airport, he wanted so much to speak to her and tell her he was going to Ireland. She answered her phone immediately and was genuinely glad to hear from him. She seemed interested in everything he had to say, but then Erika was always interested in everything and everyone. It didn't make him special.

'Are you going with friends?' she asked.

'I don't want to go with friends,' he said ruefully. 'I want to go with you.'

'No, you don't get the sympathy vote by saying something like that. You have all the friends you need. You have the life you chose.' Her tone was light but she meant it. He *had* made his choice. 'You'll make lots of new friends in Ireland. I go to an Irish bar here. They have great music. They're easy people to get to know.'

'Well, I'll send you a postcard if I find an Irish bar when I get there.'

'I believe it will be hard *not* to find one. But do that anyway.'

Did she sound as if she really would like to hear from him, or was she just being Erika – easy, relaxed and yet focused at the same time?

He walked glumly to the plane.

Erika would have loved the Dublin hotel, which managed to be both chaotic and charming at the same time. They advised him to take a city bus tour to orientate himself and to go to a traditional Irish evening in a nearby pub that night. Then, at breakfast the next morning, he met a group of Irish Americans who were discussing renting a boat on the River Shannon. It was proving to be more expensive than they had hoped. They really needed another person to share the cost. Would he like to make up the numbers?

Why not, he thought? The brochure looked attractive — lovely lakes and a wide river, little ports to visit. Before he realised it he was en route to Athlone in the middle of Ireland, going aboard a motor cruiser for a lesson in navigation. Soon they were cruising past reeds and riverbanks and old castles, and places with small harbours and long names. The sun shone and the world slowed down.

His fellow passengers were five easy-going men and women from an insurance company in Chicago. They were meant to be looking for ancestors and relatives, but this sat lightly on them. They were more interested in finding good Irish music and drinking a lot of Irish beer. Anders joined in enthusiastically.

He bought three postcards at a tiny post office and sent them to his father, his mother and Erika.

He puzzled for a long time before he wrote the few lines to his father. There was literally nothing to say that would interest the old man. Eventually, he decided to say that the economy of the country had taken a serious hit because of the recession. That at least was something his father would understand.

When the river cruise was over, the Irish Americans had gone off on a five-day golfing tour. They invited him to come with them but Anders said no. Bad as he was at manoeuvring a boat on the Shannon, he didn't want to upset real golfers by going out on the course with them.

Instead he found a coach tour of the West of Ireland.

John Paul, the cheerful, red-faced bus driver, claimed that he knew all the best music pubs on the coast, and every night they found another great session. John Paul knew all the musicians by name and told the coach party their history and repertoire before they got to the venue each evening.

'Ask Micky Moore to sing "*Mo Ghile Mear*" for you, it'll make the hairs rise on the back of your neck,' he would say. Or else he knew when some old piper was going to come in from retirement and do a turn. Anders was interested in it all.

It turned out that John Paul played the pipes himself. Not bagpipes. No, indeed, bagpipes were Scottish. Real pipes were the uilleann pipes. You didn't have to blow into them like the Scots did; instead there was a kind of a bellows under your arm which you pressed with your elbow. *Uilleann* was actually the Irish word for elbow.

The music was haunting, and Anders was mesmerised by it all.

John Paul said that if ever he got some money together he would open his own place and welcome all kinds of musicians there.

'Here, in the West?' Anders wondered.

'Maybe, but then I don't want to take the bread and butter away from the people who are already here. They are my friends,' he said.

John Paul and Anders talked about God and fate and evil and imagination. He asked John Paul how old he was. The man looked at him, surprised.

'You speak such good English, I forget you're not from round here. I was born in 1980, nine months after Pope John Paul visited Ireland. Nearly every lad who was born that year was called John Paul.'

'And will you go on driving the bus all your life?' Anders wondered.

'No, I'll have to go home to the old man sometime. The others have all gone far and wide, done well for themselves. I'm only John Paul the eejit, and my da is not really able to manage the place on his own. One of these days I'll have to face it and go back to Stoneybridge and take over.'

'That's hard.' Anders was sympathetic.

'Ah, go on out of that! Haven't I bricks and mortar and beasts in the field and a little farm waiting for me? Half of Ireland would give their eye teeth for that. It's just not what I want. I'm no good at going out looking for sheep that have got stuck on their back with their legs in the air and turning them the right way up. I hate having to deal with milk quotas, and what Europe wants you to plant or to ignore. It's life-blood for some people; it's drudgery for me, but it's a living. A good living, even.'

'But your own place with the musicians?'

'I'll wait until I'm reincarnated, Anders. I'll do it next time round.' His big, round, weather-beaten face was totally resigned to it.

On the last night of the coach tour, the passengers all clubbed together to take John Paul out for a meal. And as a thank you, he played them some airs on the uilleann pipes. He got a group photograph taken and everyone wrote their names and email addresses on the back.

Anders had a cup of coffee with John Paul on the last morning.

'I'll miss your company,' Anders said. 'Nobody to discuss the world and its ways like you.'

'You're making a mock of me! Isn't Sweden full of thinkers and musicians like ourselves?'

Anders felt absurdly flattered to be thought of as a musician and a thinker.

'It probably is. I just don't meet them, that's all.'

'Well they're out there,' John Paul was very definite. 'I've met great Swedes travelling here. They can play the spoons, they can all sing "Bunch Of Thyme". And wasn't Joe Hill himself from Sweden?'

'Maybe you're right. I'll let you know when I find them.'

'You keep in touch, Anders. You're one of the good guys,' John Paul said.

Anders wondered if he really was one of the good guys when he went back to work at Almkvist's. He learned within an hour of his return that his cousin Mats, who had had the problem with alcohol, had apparently revisited that part of his life in spectacular fashion. Moreover, one of Almkvist's most prestigious clients had absconded with a very young woman and a great deal of assets weeks before a major audit.

His father looked more grey-faced and concerned than ever. Only a few hours after he was back, Anders felt the benefits of his holiday in Ireland slipping away from him. He played some of the music he had brought home with him. The lonely laments played on the uilleann pipes, the rousing choruses where everyone had joined in, reminded him of the carefree days and the easy company, but he knew it was only temporary. It was like a child wanting a birthday party to last for ever.

His father showed no interest in any stories of his trip, no matter how he tried to tell them.

'Why don't you let me show you some of the photographs I took?' he suggested. 'Would you like to listen to some of the music with me? We were listening to some marvellous traditional Irish music . . .'

'Yes, yes, very interesting but it was just a holiday, Anders. You're like Fru Karlsson who wants to tell you what she dreamed about last night. It's not relevant to anything.'

He decided at that moment that he would move out of his

father's apartment. Get himself a small place of his own, break this never-ending cycle of discussing work from morning to night.

He hoped he would have the energy to make the move. Everyone was going to resist it. Why leave a perfectly comfortable, elegant place which would be his one day anyway? Why disrupt Fru Karlsson and her ways? Why leave his father alone instead of being his companion in these latter years?

Anders thought of John Paul going to look after *his* father, setting sheep back on their four legs again and abandoning his dream of a musicians' haven in order to do his duty. But even John Paul would have some time off to himself. Maybe he could go and play his pipes of an evening. He didn't have to discuss farming with his father as the moon rose in the sky.

If Anders ever had a son of his own he would tell the boy from the outset that he must follow his heart, that he would not be expected to play his role in Almkvist's. But it didn't seem likely that he would have a son. He could never see himself settling with anyone but Erika. And he had thrown that away.

Nevertheless, he telephoned to tell her about his trip to Ireland.

Erika was interested in everything and knew a lot about Irish music already. She had bought a tin whistle and was teaching herself to play.

'Come and stay for a weekend and I'll take you to The Galway. You'd love it,' she suggested.

A weekend away from Almkvist's; away from dramas about his cousin's rehab, the client who had absconded with funds and girlfriend, his father's anxiety, the general downturn in business . . . it was just what he needed.

As he drove towards Gothenburg, where he had been so

happy as a university student, Anders wondered if he would stay at Erika's apartment. Nothing had been said. She might have booked him into a hotel. If he *did* stay at the flat, then would they share a room? It would be so artificial if she made up a mattress for him on the floor. And after all, Erika didn't have any partner or companion these days – nor did he, so there would be no question of cheating on anyone.

But then he couldn't expect things to return to the way they had once been. He sighed, and knew that he would have to wait and see.

Erika looked wonderful, her eyes dancing and her words tumbling over each other as she told him about how successful the conservation project was; they had got serious recognition and an important grant. She cooked supper for him, the Swedish meatballs which had always been their celebration meal. The apartment hadn't changed much – new curtains, more bookshelves.

After supper they went to The Galway, the bar where Erika was greeted as a regular. She introduced Anders to people on both sides of the bar, and then they settled in for a music session. Suddenly he was back in the West of Ireland, with the waves beating on the shore and a new set of faces bent over fiddles, pipes and accordions every night. The music swept him away.

Later, he talked to the people who had played. Particularly to a man called Kevin, the piper.

'Do you know the theme from *The Brendan Voyage*?' he asked.

'Indeed I do, but I don't usually play it because whenever I played it in the London pubs it made people cry.'

'It made me cry too,' Anders said.

Erika looked up, surprised. 'You never cry,' she said.

'I did in Ireland,' he said wistfully.

'We have a habit of upsetting people,' Kevin said ruefully. 'Come in tomorrow night and I'll play it for you, then we can have a bawl over it together, and a pint.'

'That's a date,' Anders agreed readily.

Later, back in Erika's flat, they drank beer and picked at some of the leftover food. She lit candles on the coffee table and they sat opposite, suddenly acutely aware of each other. She gazed at him seriously.

'You've changed,' she said.

'I haven't changed about being very fond of you,' he said.

'Me neither, but you are still sleeping in the spare room,' she laughed.

'It seems a pity.' He smiled.

'Yes, but I'm not going to spend yet more weeks and months regretting what might have been.'

'*Did* you spend weeks and months regretting it?'

'You know I did, Anders.'

'But you still wouldn't consider coming to live with me and just putting up with Almkvist's.'

'And *you* wouldn't consider giving up Almkvist's and coming to live with me. Listen, we've been through all this before. It's well-trodden ground.'

'You know I had responsibilities. Still do.'

'You don't like it, Anders my friend. You're not happy. You have told me not one word about your life there in the office. That's my one complaint. If I had thought that it was what you wanted then I might have considered it.'

'You call me your friend . . . !' he said.

'You are. You will always be my friend, when you and I are long married to other people.'

'It won't happen, Erika. I've looked around. There's no one out there.'

'Well, then we will have to look harder. Tell me more about Ireland.'

He told her about the Irish Americans on the Shannon, and about John Paul who had to go back to look after his father. And then he went to bed in the brightly painted guest room. He stayed awake for a long time.

At The Galway next day, Anders and Erika sat and listened while Kevin played the pipes. As he listened, Anders again heard the waves breaking on the wild Atlantic shore and he felt a surge of misery overwhelm him. He suddenly saw his life stretching in front of him in an unending straight line: getting up in the morning, putting on a suit, going to work at the office, coming home to a lonely apartment, going to bed, getting up the following morning . . . Responsibility. Loyalty. Duty. Rules. Expectations. Family tradition. And when the musicians took a break, Anders tried to explain to Erika why he had to stay with his father, but the words weren't there. He found his sentences trailing away.

'It's just that . . .' he began, then faltered. 'It's the family tradition. I mean, if I don't . . . There are these expectations . . . It's who I am. And I can do it. I *am* doing it. I am the next Almkvist. They're all waiting for me. All my life . . . And in any case, if I'm not that, who am I?'

'Anders, stop, please. Look, it isn't that you are in your father's business that I don't like. It's that you hate it and always will. But you won't do anything else. It's your decision, not theirs. It's your life, not theirs. You can do anything with your life. At least think what else you might do. When you find what the something else is, then you will consider leaving.'

She leaned over and stroked his hand. 'Leave it for now,' she suggested.

'Which means leave it for ever,' he said sadly.

'No, you've gone as far as you can down the road and you always reach the same fork. Maybe something will happen. Something that you will want more than that office. Then when that day comes, you can think about it again.'

He ached to say that he wanted Erika more than he wanted the office, but it was not strictly true. He could not walk away, and they both knew this. They hugged each other before he set out on the long drive home.

His heart was heavy as he played his music in the car. It was only a dream, a holiday memory. It was childish to think it might be another life for him.

The weeks went by, and his father was cold and distant about Anders moving into his own apartment. Fru Karlsson was bristling with resentment. She tried to exact a promise that he would turn up at his father's every night.

Often he ate alone in his flat, putting a ready meal into the microwave and opening a beer. Back in the big apartment, his father would also be dining alone.

Once a week Anders turned up for dinner, already armed to cope with the resentment and the pressures which would be there to greet him. Either his father or Fru Karlsson would remind him that his room was there and ready should he wish to stay the night. There was heavy sighing about the size and emptiness of the family apartment. His father said how hard it was to know what was going on in the office these days since he himself only went in for three hours a day, and Anders was off enjoying himself every evening and not there to discuss the day's events.

He often wondered how John Paul was faring in the

months since he had seen him. Had life on the farm turned out better than he had feared, or was it worse? Had the sacrifice been worthwhile? John Paul might have regretted the intimate revelations of his reluctance to go and look after his father. He might not relish having it all brought up again.

One evening Anders looked up Stoneybridge, the place where John Paul was going home to live. On his laptop he saw that it was a small, attractive, seaside town that clearly only came to life for the summer months and would be fairly desolate in these winter days. Yet he read that a new venture had begun there; a large place on a cliff called Stone House, offering a winter week on the Atlantic coast with spectacular scenery, good food, walking and wild birds. There would be music in the pubs if guests cared to seek it out. It was a ludicrous idea and he knew it was, but still he went online and booked a week there.

He told his father little about the trip – just a winter week's holiday. His father, of course, asked nothing, only registered vague disapproval of his sudden decision to go.

And Anders did not tell Erika about the trip. Their last meeting had been a kind of watershed. There was no point in telling her he was going to Ireland again; she wouldn't come with him. She would just go on about him wasting his life. She couldn't understand that he simply had no choice in the matter. He didn't want to have that conversation again.

He flew to Dublin and caught a train to the West.

Chicky Starr met him at the station. She seemed to see nothing odd about a young Swedish accountant flying over to spend time in this deserted place. She complimented him on his excellent English. She said that Scandinavians were wonderful at learning languages. When she had lived in New

York, she had been astounded at how new arrivals from Denmark, Sweden and Norway adapted so quickly.

He was relaxed and comfortable long before they arrived at the wonderful old house and he met his fellow guests. The American man was the absolute image of Corry Salinas the actor, even spoke like him too. Anders found himself wondering what on earth Corry Salinas would be doing here. He found himself exchanging glances with the English doctor, who had also spotted the actor. But so what? If the man wanted a rest, a change, he'd be no different from all the other people who had gathered there. No one would bother anyone else.

Over dinner, he found himself in conversation with a nice woman called Freda, who seemed surprised to hear of his interest in music. He'd come to the right place, she said; music was in the very air they breathed in this part of Ireland. She'd be keen to hear some good music herself.

'You play an instrument yourself,' she said. It was a statement rather than a question. Anders found he was telling her about the *nyckelharpa* and about his love of music.

'And what do you do for a living?' she asked.

'I'm just a boring accountant,' he said with a wry smile.

'Accountants are no more boring than anyone else,' she replied, 'but if your heart is elsewhere, would you not want to follow your destiny?' As she spoke, her eyes looked into the distance.

'Ah, no,' he said wistfully, 'I know perfectly well where my destiny lies. I will take over from my father very soon and run the business which was his life's work. And once or twice a week I will go to a tiny club and play music to half a dozen people. And that will be my life.' And then, as if to take the bleakness out of his words, he smiled and added, 'But this is my holiday, and I'm going to find the best sessions in the county. Care to join me?'

It was agreed. The very next day they would meet after breakfast and go off in search of the best music to be found.

It was all totally undemanding and he was glad that he had come. When he went to bed and looked out on the crashing waves in the moonlight, he knew he would sleep properly. He would not wake twice, three times during the night, restless and unsure. That alone made it worth coming to this place.

The following morning, Anders asked Chicky Starr about music venues.

She knew of two pubs, both of them known locally for their sessions. One of them did terrific seafood at lunchtimes, if he was interested in sampling the local food.

As they were talking, Freda joined them, ready and eager for the day. The weather looked set fair and, with high spirits, the two set out in the direction of the town, Anders carrying his small rucksack on his back with his maps and guides inside. They passed whitewashed cottages, farmhouses and out-buildings. For a while, the road followed the coastline, and high as they were on the clifftop, the wind and spray stung their faces. Even the trees were bent double and stunted by the Atlantic gales. Then the road took them inland so that the sea was out of sight. As they got nearer to the town, the fields disappeared, ploughed up and replaced with new housing, row after row looking eerily empty.

The main street in Stoneybridge was lined with two- and three-storey houses, each one painted a different colour. The pubs were easy to identify, but the two explorers made the little café their first stop. They talked easily, comparing notes on their first impressions of their fellow guests at Stone House.

Freda, Anders noticed, gave little away about her own reasons for coming to Stone House but she had observed everyone else quite closely. The doctor and his wife, she said, shaking her head a little, were very sad – there had been a recent death, she could tell. Quite how she could tell she didn't say. And that nice nurse – what was her name? Winnie, was it? – was having a dreadful time with her friend Lillian, but it would all be worth it in the end.

They went for lunch into the larger of the pubs: great bowls of steaming, succulent mussels and fresh crusty bread. And then, as if in response to some silent cue, a small, red-faced man sitting in the corner produced a fiddle and started to play. The session had started . . .

At first, musicians outnumbered audience but gradually more people arrived. Most would arrive in the evening, it was explained, but some liked to play in the afternoons and every-one was welcome to join in. The music, at first gentle and haunting, grew faster and faster. At one side of the room, a couple started dancing and Anders himself borrowed a guitar and played a couple of Swedish songs. He taught everyone the words of the songs and they joined in the choruses with great gusto.

He had, he admitted rather shyly, brought a traditional Swedish instrument with him on his holiday and he could bring it in the following day. Only if they'd like him to, of course . . .

Freda looked at him oddly as he returned to their table. 'Once or twice a week, to an audience of six people?' she said, so quietly he could hardly hear her over the cheering. 'No, I don't think so.'

Anders began to feel as if he had lived nowhere else. The American man actually *was* Corry Salinas, obviously here in hiding and calling himself John. The two women, Winnie and Lillian, were nearly drowned on their second day there and had to be rescued from a cave: Anders had missed all the excitement as he had stayed on in the town for the evening sessions. This time he had taken his *nyckelharpa* with him and had found himself called upon time and time again to play and sing along. Of John Paul there was no sign, although Anders did move between both pubs.

Eventually, on one of his visits, he asked a craggy-faced man who played the tin whistle did he know a piper from the area called John Paul?

Of course he did. Everyone knew him, very decent lad. Immediately, four other musicians joined in the conversation. They all knew poor John Paul. Stuck up there in Rocky Ridge with his old divil of a father whom no one could please. A discontented man who wished he had taken the emigrant's ship years back and blamed everyone but himself that he hadn't.

'And does John Paul play the uilleann pipes anywhere round here?'

'He hasn't been in here in months now,' one of the men said, shaking his head sadly. 'A group of us went up for him in a van one day but he said he couldn't leave the old fellow.'

The following morning, Anders asked Chicky how to get to Rocky Ridge and she packed a lunch for him.

'I'm sure John Paul would make a meal for you, but just in case he's not there you'd want to be prepared,' she said.

It was a longer walk than he had expected, and he was weary when he arrived at the big, untidy farmyard. There seemed to be nobody around. As Anders approached the door some hens ran out clucking, annoyed to be disturbed.

An old man sat at the table trying to read a newspaper with a magnifying glass. A big sheepdog lay at his feet. It looked more like a rug than a dog.

'I was looking for John Paul . . .' Anders began.

'You and half the country are looking for him. He went out of here God knows how many hours ago and no sign of him. I'm his father Matty, by the way, and I haven't even had my dinner and it's gone three o'clock.'

'Well, I'm Anders and I brought a picnic with me, so we might as well have that,' Anders said, and opened the waxed paper in the little bag that Chicky had packed.

He got two plates and divided the cold chicken, cheese and chutney. He made a pot of tea and they sat and ate it as normally as if it was quite commonplace for John Paul's father to be served a meal by a passing Swedish tourist.

They talked about farming and how it had changed over the years, about the recession and how all the townhouses that the uppity O'Haras had built were standing empty like a ghost estate because people had been greedy and thought that the Celtic Tiger would last for ever. He spoke about his other children, who had done well for themselves abroad. He said that Shep the dog was blind now and useless but would always have a home.

He wanted to know about farming in Sweden, and Anders answered as best he could but said that he wished he could tell him more. He was really a city boy at heart.

'And what brings you to this place, if you are a city boy?' Matty wanted to know.

Anders explained how he had met John Paul on the bus tour.

'He loved that old bus, dead-end job, in and out of shebeens the whole time, happy as a bird on a bush. Even thought of setting up his own shebeen, but he thought better of it and decided to row in here to try to get the last few shillings out of this place,' he said, shaking his head in disapproval.

Anders felt his gorge rising in anger. This was the thanks that the old man was giving for his son's sacrifice. Could life be any more unfair?

In a reasoned way he tried to explain that perhaps John Paul had wanted to help his father.

'You don't want to buy the place here, by any chance?' Matty peered at him through half-closed eyes.

'No, indeed, are you selling?'

'Oh, if only we could. I'd be out of it by this evening.'

'And where would you go, Matty?'

'I'd go into St Joseph's. It's a sort of a home in the town. I'd have people calling in to see me there, and company. I wouldn't be stuck up here on Rocky Ridge with John Paul working all the hours God sends, and for what? For next to nothing.'

'Did you tell him this?'

'I can't. He thinks there's a living in the place. He did nothing for himself in life but he's got a good heart, and he deserves a crack at making the place work. I couldn't go and sell it over his head.'

Anders sat there silently for a while. Matty was a man who was used to silences. Shep snored on. Maybe life was full of these misunderstandings.

John Paul was out there on mountain tops dealing with things he hated, his father was yearning to live in a nice warm, safe place where people could call in to him and his dinner would be served at one o'clock every day. They each thought the other was desperate to keep the farm going.

Could it be the same situation in Sweden?

Did Anders' father wish that he could hand the firm over to others, release his son from a life which he did not enjoy? Was this only wishful thinking? A false parallel?

Problems don't solve themselves neatly like that, due to a set of coincidences. Problems are solved by making decisions. Erika had always said that, and he had thought she was being doctrinaire. But it was true. Deciding not to change anything was a decision in itself. He hadn't fully understood this before.

The light went from the sky and Shep stirred in his dreams. Anders made more tea and found them some biscuits. Matty told him about Chicky marrying this man who was killed in a car crash in New York, and how he had left her money to come home and buy the Sheedy place. Matty said Chicky was a real survivor; she didn't expect anyone to fight her battles for her. Many a man had shown an interest in her, but she was fair and square with all of them. She was her own woman, she told them.

But you never knew what the Lord had planned for you. Maybe some nice American man might come for a holiday and sweep her off her feet again. Was there anyone among the guests that looked suitable?

Anders thought not. There *was* a pleasant American there, all right, but he hadn't seen any sign of a romance.

'Oh, is that Corry Salinas? I heard he was staying there,' Matty said.

'You did?'

'Yes, he was trying to keep it a secret but everyone here recognised him. Frank Hanratty was only telling some daft story that he came into the golf club to buy Frank a drink because he saw his pink van outside the door. Frank had better take a hold of himself.'

Just then they heard the van arrive and John Paul ran into the house.

'Da, the cattle had got through a fence up in the top field. They were wandering all over the road. Dr Dai was trying to get them back into the field through the gap with one of his golf clubs. He was worse than myself. And by the time we got someone to fix the fence—' He broke off when he saw Anders. His big face lit up with pleasure.

'Anders Almkvist! You came to see us!' he said, delighted. 'Da, this is my friend . . .'

'Don't I know all about him. We've had a long chat waiting for you to get back, and I know all about why the Swedes are better off with their krone than the euro,' Matty said.

John Paul looked on, open-mouthed.

'*And* he brought me my dinner as well,' his father pronounced. The final accolade. Anders got another mug and poured out tea for John Paul.

There was no rush. There would be plenty of time to explain everything.

John Paul drove Anders back to Stone House. 'Imagine you coming back here and up to Rocky Ridge to see me!' he said.

'I was hoping to hear you playing in one of the local pubs, but they say you work too hard. You're too tired.'

'I was hoping that *you* had come to tell me that you'd left that office of yours,' John Paul said.

'No. Not just yet.'

'But you might . . . ?' John Paul looked pleased for his friend. 'So miracles do happen.'

'Wait until I tell you about what *your* father really wants, and then you'll think twice about miracles,' said Anders.

Anders was most apologetic when he slipped in at Chicky's big dining table. 'I'm sorry I'm a bit late,' he said as he sat down next to the doctor and his wife.

'No problem. It's duck tonight. I kept it hot for you. Everything all right with John Paul?'

'Fine, fine. What's St Joseph's like as a place to stay?'

'As good as they come. If they could only persuade Matty to go in there, he'd love it. I have an aunt in there, and she barely has time to talk to you when you visit.'

'No, he *wants* to go in. It's John Paul who has the doubts.'

'We can sort him out on that. And you tell John Paul he should go away and travel a bit, let some of the other brothers and sisters come back and pull their weight here. Visit Matty from time to time, instead of leaving it all to John Paul.'

'I do have an idea at the back of my mind.'

'If it means giving John Paul a bit of a chance in life, I'm all for it.'

'I was thinking of opening an Irish bar in Sweden. Asking him to come and set up the music side of it for me. I can deal with the business side.'

'So *that* is what you were doing here. I did wonder.' Chicky seemed pleased to have found out without interrogating.

'No, it wasn't what I intended. It just sort of evolved.'

'Things *do* evolve around here. I've seen it over and over. There's something in the sea air, I think.'

'I haven't spoken to my father about it yet.'

'And if he is against the idea?' Chicky was gentle.

'I will explain it to him. I will be clear and courteous, as he has always been. I will not pour any scorn on *his* dreams; just point out that they are not mine.' His voice sounded very much more confident.

Chicky nodded several times. It was as if she could see it happening. 'And when you're hiring, you might ask my niece Orla out there, for a season anyway, to do the food for you. It would be the making of your pub, and prevent her from growing old and mad with me.'

'There are worse places to grow old and mad,' Anders laughed. He hoped he could explain all this to his father, and that he would not be too disappointed. Klara would take over Almkvist's. The company was in her blood just as much as it was in his. She knew and loved the business in a way he never would. Now all he had to do was persuade his father that a woman could head up a prestigious company like Almkvist's. He sighed and settled back in his seat. And who could he get to help him persuade his father? He pulled out a pencil and pad and started to make lists of things that he had to do. Calling Erika was top of the list.

The Walls

They never introduced themselves as Ann and Charlie, they always said, 'We are The Walls'.

They signed their Christmas cards *from The Walls* also, and when they answered the phone they would say, 'Walls here'.

Possibly it was an act of solidarity. You rarely saw one without the other, and they always stood very close to each other. They apparently never tired of each other's company, which was just as well as they worked together in their Dublin home correcting and marking papers as postal tuition for a correspondence college. They had both been teachers, but this was much more companionable and less stressful. They had a little study in their house where they went in at nine a.m. and came out at two. The Walls said it was very important to have total self-discipline when you worked from home. Otherwise the day ran away from you.

Then, in the afternoons, they would walk or garden or shop, and at five o'clock settle down to what was the high spot of the day – entering competitions.

They had won many, many prizes. Anything from choosing

a name for a chocolate Easter bunny to writing a limerick in praise of garden sheds. They had won a holiday in the South of France because they wrote a slogan for a new perfume; they got a set of heavy cast-iron cookware for guessing the weight of a turkey. They had won the latest television, a top-of-the-range microwave oven, his-and-hers sports bikes, velvet curtains and a whole range of smaller items like trendy electric kettles and leather-bound photo albums. It was a poor week when they didn't win *something*. And they so enjoyed the fun of the chase as well as the extra comforts that came from the prizes.

They had two sons who seemed to play very little part in their lives. This had always been the way. When the boys were at school they always went to play in other boys' houses: The Walls weren't into entertaining groups of children. Then one son, Andy, was taken on by a major English football club and became a professional soccer player; the other boy, Rory, had become a long-distance lorry driver and drove for hours on end all over Europe.

Both of these careers bewildered The Walls, who could not fathom why their sons didn't want to go to university, and the boys, on their part, could not begin to understand a mother and father who raked the newspapers and magazines in search of winning something like an electric toaster.

But the years went on peacefully for The Walls. They were very satisfied with the life they lived. They chose their competitions carefully and only entered for something where they felt they had a reasonable chance of winning. They scorned the kind of competitions they saw on television: a multiple-choice question asking if *Vienna was the capital of a) Andorra b) Austria or c) Australia. Choose option a, b or c.* These were not *real* competitions, they were only schemes to make money from premium-rate call lines. No self-respecting competition entrant would consider them.

They knew also that you must not make your jingles or rhymes too clever. They had seen that the middle of the road was the way to go. They would examine each other's solutions looking for puns or references that might be beyond the ordinary punter. They must beware of stepping outside the mainstream. And so far, it had all worked very well.

As they sat one summer's evening on the garden seat that had been theirs because they had matched twelve garden flowers with the months in which they bloomed, and drank from Waterford Glass tumblers that had come from the competition to write an ode to crystal, The Walls congratulated themselves on their twenty-five years of happy marriage. They were in a great state of excitement this evening: they planned to win something quite splendid to celebrate their silver wedding anniversary in a few months. There was a cruise to Alaska, for one thing. That would be heavily subscribed. Competition entrants from all over the world would be trying for that one, so they should not be too confident of winning. There was a residential cookery course in Italy, which would be nice. There was a week in a Scottish castle. The possibilities were endless. It was not a question of being mean or careful with money; The Walls could well afford a holiday abroad, but the thrill of winning one was much more satisfying, and they filled in forms and made up slogans with great vigour.

Then they found the dream prize. It was a winter break in Paris, a week in a luxury hotel. There would be a chauffeur-driven car at their disposal with an outing planned for each day of the week: Versailles, Chartres, as well as city tours, meals in internationally known restaurants. It was a once-in-a-lifetime experience.

It looked a very good bet. They had seen it in a rather elegant magazine with a small circulation; this was helpful. It meant that it would not have caught the eye of millions of readers. The task was to explain in one paragraph why they *deserved* this holiday.

The Walls knew not to make it jokey. The judges were the editor of the magazine, a travel agent and a couple of hoteliers in Ireland and Britain who were offering second and third prizes. These were people who took their product seriously. No satire or disrespect would win. The question must be addressed with equal seriousness.

And they were pleased with their entry. The Walls explained quite simply that after twenty-five years of contented partnership, they would love to bring back a little romance into their lives. They had never been people with a glittery lifestyle but, like everyone, they would love it if some magic was sprinkled on their lives. They had used words like 'sprinkle' and 'magic' before in captions or slogans, and they had worked well. They would work again.

They were now quite certain that the prize was theirs, and were unprepared for the shock of hearing they had won *second* prize – a holiday in some remote place on the cliffs over the Atlantic at the other side of the country. They looked at each other, dismayed. This was a poor reward for all the effort they had put into composing the burningly sincere essay about the need to have a little stardust shaken over them!

The woman on the telephone expected them to be very excited that they had won a week in this Stone House place, and because The Walls were basically polite people they tried hard to summon up some degree of enthusiasm. But their hearts were heavy as they thought of someone else in what had started to become *their* chauffeur-driven car in Paris, and *their* reservation at a five-star restaurant.

Ann Wall had been laying out the wardrobe she would pack. It included a designer handbag and a Hermès silk square that they had won in previous competitions. Charlie had reluctantly put down the guide book he had bought so that they would appear well informed about the Paris buildings and art treasures when they got there.

They both fumed with rage and annoyance that they had been so wrongly confident about winning the first prize. They were desperate to know what the winning essay had been about, and were determined to find out.

The Walls telephoned Chicky Starr, proprietor of Stone House, to make the arrangements for their visit. She was cheerful and practical as she gave details of train times and arranged to have them collected at the station. She was, they had to admit, perfectly pleasant and welcoming. If they had intended to win this holiday, they would have been delighted with her, but Mrs Starr must never know how very poor a consolation this holiday was going to be for The Walls.

She checked if they were vegetarians and advised them about bringing warm and waterproof clothing. No place here for designer scarves and bags, they realised. She said she would post them brochures and reading matter about the area so that they could decide in advance what they would like to do. There would be bicycles to ride, wild birds to see and a group of like-minded people to have dinner with in the evenings.

Like-minded? The Walls thought not.

Nobody else would be going there with such an aura of second best.

Mrs Starr said she would not mention to anyone that they

were competition winners: it was up to them to discuss it or not. This puzzled The Walls. Normally they were very pleased to tell people they had won a competition and had got there by their wits rather than by handing out money. Still, it was thoughtful of Mrs Starr.

With heavy hearts they agreed on the train and bus times, and said insincerely that they were looking forward to it all greatly.

Their two sons came back to Ireland to celebrate the silver wedding. They took their parents to Quentins, one of the most talked-about restaurants in Dublin.

The Walls marvelled at how sophisticated the boys had become. Andy, who was used to a high life now as a soccer player in a Premier League team, went through the menu as if he were accustomed to eating like this every night; even Rory, who mainly dined in transport cafés and places where long-haul drivers met to eat quickly and get back on the road, was equally at ease.

They asked with baffled interest about their parents' recent successes in the competition stakes. There had been a set of matching luggage, some colourful garden lights and a carved wooden salad bowl with matching servers.

Andy and Rory murmured their approval and support. They spoke about their lives, and The Walls listened without comprehension as Andy spoke of transfers and relegation in the League, and Rory told them about the new regulations which were strangling the whole haulage business, and the money that they were constantly offered to bring illegal im-migrants in as part of their cargo. Both boys had love lives to report. Andy was dating a supermodel, and Rory had moved into an apartment with a Spanish girl called Pilar.

The Walls said that they were going to the West of Ireland in a week's time. They described the place and listed all its good points. They said that Mrs Starr, the proprietor, sounded delightful.

To their surprise, the boys seemed genuinely interested.

'Good on you for doing something different.' Andy was admiring.

'And it's something you chose yourselves, not just something you won,' Rory approved.

The Walls did not enlighten them. It wasn't exactly lying, but they just didn't say it – that it had indeed been a competition. Partly because they still felt so raw about the loss of the Paris trip, but mainly because they were flattered by the way their sons unexpectedly seemed so pleased with their decision to go to this godforsaken place.

They wanted to bask for a bit in that enthusiasm rather than diminish it by giving the real reason why they were heading West.

Andy said that his supermodel girlfriend had always wanted to go to the wilds for a healthy walking holiday, so they were to mark his card. Rory said that Pilar had seen the old movie *The Quiet Man* half a dozen times, and was dying to see that part of the world. Possibly this hotel might be the place to go.

For the first time for a long while The Walls felt on the same wavelength as their children. It was very satisfying.

A week later, as they crossed Ireland on the train, the depressed feeling returned. The rain was unremitting. They looked without pleasure at the wet fields and the grey mountains. At this very moment some other people were arriving at Charles de Gaulle airport in Paris. They would meet the chauffeur who should have been meeting The Walls. They would have rugs in the car in case it was cold; he would take them to the superb five-star Hotel Martinique where the welcome champagne would be on ice in the suite. It wasn't just a bedroom, it was an actual *suite*. Tonight those people would eat at the hotel, choosing from a menu that The Walls had already seen on the internet, while they were going to some kind of glorified bed and breakfast. The place would be full of draughts and they would possibly have to keep their coats on indoors. They would eat, every night for a whole week, in Mrs Starr's kitchen.

A kitchen!

They should have been dining under chandeliers in Paris.

The fields seemed to get smaller and wetter as they went West. They didn't need to say all this to each other. The Walls shared everything already; they each knew what the other was thinking. This was going to be one long, disappointing week.

At the railway station they recognised Chicky Starr at once from her picture on the Stone House brochure. She welcomed them warmly and carried their bags to her van, talking easily about the area and its attractions. Chicky explained that while she was in the town, she had a few more things to collect, and The Walls saw their expensive matching suitcases being loaded on to the roof. They looked quite out of place compared to the more basic bags and knapsacks belonging to Chicky Starr.

She seemed to know everyone. She asked the bus driver whether there had been a big crowd at the market, and greeted schoolchildren in uniform with questions about the match they had played that day. She offered a lift to an elderly man but he said that his daughter-in-law would be picking him up, so he'd be fine sitting here watching the world go by until she arrived.

The Walls looked on with interest. It must be extraordinary

to know every single person in the place. Sociable certainly, but claustrophobic. There had been no mention of a Mr Starr. Ann Wall decided to nail this one down immediately.

'And does your husband help you in all this enterprise?' she asked brightly.

'Sadly he died some years ago. But he would have been very pleased to see Stone House up and running,' Chicky spoke simply.

The Walls felt chastened. They had been intrusive.

'It's a lovely part of the world you live in,' Charlie said insincerely.

'It's very special,' Chicky Starr agreed. 'I spent a long time in New York City, and I used to come home for a visit every year. It sort of charged my batteries for the rest of the year. I felt it might do the same for other people.'

The Walls doubted it, but made enthusiastic murmurs of agreement.

They were pleasantly surprised by Stone House when they arrived there. It was warm, for one thing, and very comfortable. Their bedroom had great style and a big bow window looking out to sea. On the little table by the window were two crystal glasses, an ice bucket and a half-bottle of champagne.

'Just our way of congratulating you on twenty-five years of happy marriage. You were very lucky to have it and even luckier to realise it,' Chicky said.

The Walls were, for once, wordless.

'Well we *have* had a very happy marriage,' Ann Wall said, 'but how did you know?'

'I read your entry in the competition. It was very touching, about how you got pleasure out of ordinary things but you wanted a little magic sprinkled on it. I *do* hope that we can provide some of that magic for you here.'

Of course, she had read their essay.

They had forgotten that she was one of the judges. But even though she had been touched and moved, she hadn't voted for them to have the holiday of their dreams.

'So you read all the entries?' Charlie asked.

'They gave us a shortlist. We read the final thirty,' Chicky admitted.

'And the people who won . . . ?

'Well, there were five winners altogether,' Chicky said.

'Yes, but the people who won the first prize. What kind of an essay did they write?' Ann Wall had to know. What kind of words had beaten them to the winning post?

Chicky paused as if wondering whether or not to explain.

'It's odd, really. They wrote a totally different kind of thing. It wasn't at all like your story. It was more a song, like a version of "I Love Paris In The Springtime" but with different words.'

'A song? It didn't *say* a song. It said an essay.' The Walls were outraged.

'Well, you know, people interpret these things in different ways.'

'But words to someone else's song – isn't that a breach of copyright?' Their horror was total.

Chicky shrugged.

'It was clever, catchy. Everyone liked it.'

'The original song may have been catchy and clever but they just wrote a parody of it and they got to go to Paris.' The hurt and bitterness were written all over them.

Chicky looked from one to the other.

'Well, you're here now, so let's hope you enjoy it,' she said hopelessly.

They struggled to get back to their normal selves, but it was too huge an effort.

Chicky thought it wiser to leave them on their own. It was so obvious that for The Walls, this holiday was a very poor second best.

'If it's any consolation to you, everyone, all the judges, thought that even if the Flemmings got the first prize, *your* story was totally heart-warming. We were all envious of your relationship,' she tried.

It was useless. Not only had they been disappointed but The Walls knew now that they had been cheated too. It would rankle for ever.

They made an effort to recover. A big effort, but it wasn't easy. They tried to talk to their fellow guests and appear interested in what they had to say. They were an unlikely group: an earnest boy from Sweden, a librarian called Freda, an English couple who were both doctors, a disapproving woman with a pursed mouth called Nell, an American who had missed a plane and had come here on the spur of the moment and a pair of unlikely friends called Winnie and Lillian. What were they all doing here?

The food was excellent, served by Orla, the attractive niece of the proprietor. Really, there was nothing to object to. Nothing, that is, apart from the fact that the Flemmings, whoever they were, had stolen their holiday in Paris.

The Walls didn't sleep well that night. They were wakeful at three in the morning and made tea in their room. They sat and listened to the wind and rain outside and the sound of the waves receding and crashing again on the shore. It sounded sad and plaintive, as if in sympathy with them.

Next morning, the other guests all seemed ready and

enthusiastic about their planned trips. The Walls chose a direction at random and found themselves on a long, deserted beach.

It was bracing, certainly, and healthy. They would have to admit that. The scenery was spectacular.

But it wasn't Paris.

They went to one of the pubs that Chicky had suggested and had a bowl of soup.

'I don't think I could take six more days of this.' Ann Wall put down her spoon.

'Mine's fine,' Charlie said.

'I don't mean the soup, I mean being here where we don't *want* to be.'

'I know, I feel that too, in a way,' Charlie agreed.

'And it's not as if they won it fair and square. Even Chicky admits that.' Ann Wall was very aggrieved.

'Wouldn't you love to know how they are getting on?' Charlie said.

'Yes. I'd both hate to know and love to know at the same time.' They laughed companionably over it.

The woman behind the bar looked at them with approval.

'Lord, it's grand to see a couple getting on so well,' she said. 'I was only saying to Paddy last night that they just come in here, stare into their drinks and say nothing at all. Paddy hadn't noticed. They probably have it all said, was what he thought.'

The Walls were pleased to be admired for having a good relationship twice in twenty-four hours. They had never before thought that it might be unusual. But then Chicky had said that the judges had been envious of them. Not envious enough, of course, to give them the main prize . . .

They said they were on a holiday from Dublin and staying at Stone House.

'Didn't Chicky do a great job on that place,' the woman said. 'She was a great example to people round here. When her poor husband, the Lord have mercy on him, was killed in that terrible road accident over there in New York, she just set her mind to coming back here and making a whole new life for herself, and bringing a bit of business to this place in the winter. We all wish her well.'

It was sad about Chicky's husband, The Walls agreed, but in their hearts it didn't make them feel any more settled in this remote part of Ireland when their dreams were elsewhere.

They didn't mention that they had won the holiday in a competition until dinner on the fourth night. Everyone was more relaxed around the table in the evenings; by that time they realised that no one had been quite what they looked. The two women, Lillian and Winnie, weren't old friends at all and they had almost drowned and were rescued; the doctors seemed more relaxed and Nicola chatted happily with the American who was revealed to be a film star; the Swedish boy had a passion for music and Freda the librarian seemed to be uncannily right in her pronouncements about people's lives. Nell was still disapproving – at least that hadn't changed. But they did feel like people who knew each other, rather than a group of accidentally gathered strangers.

They were all fascinated by the idea of winning competitions. They had thought that they were all fixed, or that so many people entered you just had no chance.

The Walls listed some of the items they had won and were gratified by the fascination that it seemed to hold for everyone.

'Is there a knack to it?' Orla wanted to know. She'd love to win a motorbike and travel around Europe, she explained.

The Walls were generous with their advice; it wasn't so much a knack, more doggedness and keeping it simple.

They were all fired up and dying to enter a competition. If only they could find one. Chicky and Orla ran to collect some newspapers and magazines, and they raked them to find competitions.

There was one where you had to name an animal in the zoo. The Walls explained that it was in a section aimed at children, and so every school in the country would be sending in entries. The odds were too great against them. They spoke with the authority of poker players who could tell you the chances of filling a straight or a flush. The others looked on in awe.

Then in a local West of Ireland paper they found a competition, 'Invent a Festival'.

The Walls read it out carefully. Contestants were asked to suggest a festival, something that would bring business in winter to a community in the West.

This might be the very thing. What kind of festival could they come up with for Stoneybridge?

The guests looked doubtful. They had been hoping for a slick slogan or a clever limerick. Suggesting a festival was too difficult.

The Walls weren't sure. They said it had possibilities that they must explore. It had to be a winter thing so a beauty pageant made no sense – the poor girls would freeze to death. Galway had done the oyster festival, so they couldn't do that. Other parts of the coast had taken over the surfing and kayaking industry.

Rock climbing was too specialist. There was traditional

music, of course, but Stoneybridge wasn't known as a centre for it like Doolin or Miltown Malbay in County Clare, and they didn't have any legendary pipers or fiddlers in their past. There already *was* a walking festival, and Stoneybridge could boast no literary figures that might be used as a basis for a winter school.

There was no history of visual arts in the place. They could produce no Jack Yeats or Paul Henry as a focus.

'What about a storytelling festival?' was the suggestion of Henry and Nicola, the quiet English doctors. Everyone thought that was a good idea, but apparently there was a storytelling event in the next county which was well established.

Anders suggested a Teach Yourself Irish Music seminar but the others said the place was coming down with tourists being taught to play the tin whistle and the spoons, and the Irish drum called the *bodhrán*.

The American, who seemed to be called John or Corry alternately, said that he thought a Find Your Roots festival would do well. You could have genealogists on hand to help people trace their ancestors. The general opinion was that the roots industry in Ireland was well covered already.

Winnie suggested a cookery festival, where local people could teach the visitors how to make the brown bread and potato farls, and particularly how to use the carrageen to make the delicious mousse they had eaten last night. But apparently there were too many cookery schools already, and it would be hard to compete.

They all agreed to sleep on the problem and to bring new ideas to the table the following night. It had been an entertaining evening and The Walls had enjoyed it in spite of themselves.

Once back in their bedroom, their thoughts went again to

Paris. Tonight was when they should have been going to the Opéra. Their limousine would have been gliding through the lights of Paris; then they would have purred back to the Martinique where they would be welcomed by the staff, who would know them by this stage. The maître d' would suggest a little drink in the piano bar before they went to bed. Instead, they were trying to explain the rules of competition-winning to a crowd of strangers who hadn't the first idea where to start.

As always, just thinking about it made them discontented.

'I bet they don't even appreciate it,' Charlie said.

'They probably called off the opera house and went to a pub.' Ann was full of scorn.

Then suddenly the thought came to her.

'Let's telephone them and ask them how they are getting on. At least we'll know.'

'We can't ring them in Paris!' Charlie was shocked.

'Why not? Just a short call. We'll say we called to wish them well.'

'But how would we ever find them?' Charlie was dumbfounded.

'We know the name of the hotel; we know their name – what's hard to find there?' To Ann it was simple.

The Walls had already written all the details of the Paris holiday in their competition notebook, including the telephone number of the Hotel Martinique. Before he could think of another objection she had picked up her mobile phone, dialled the number and got through.

'*Monsieur et Madame Flemming d'Irlande, s'il vous plaît,*' she said in a clear, bell-like voice.

'Who are you going to say we are?' Charlie asked fearfully.

'Let's play it by ear.' Ann was in control.

Charlie listened in anxiously as she was put through.

'Oh, Mrs Flemming, just a call to ask how the holiday is going. Is it all to your satisfaction?'

'Oh, well, yes . . . I mean, thank you indeed,' the woman sounded hesitant.

'And you are enjoying your week at the Martinique?' Ann persisted.

'Are you from the hotel?' the woman asked nervously.

'No, indeed, just a call from Ireland to hope there are no problems.'

'Well, it's rather awkward. It's very hard to say this because it *is* a very expensive hotel. We *know* that, but it's not quite what we had hoped.'

'Oh dear, I'm sorry to hear that. In what way, exactly?'

'Well . . . It isn't a suite, for one thing. It's a very small room near the lift, which is going up and down all night. And then we can't eat in the dining room – the vouchers are only for what they call *Le Snack Bar.*'

'Oh dear, that wasn't in the terms of agreement,' Ann said disapprovingly.

'Yes, but you might as well be talking to a blank wall for all the response you get. They shrug and say these arrangements have nothing to do with them.' Mrs Flemming was beginning to sound very aggrieved.

'And the chauffeur?'

'We've only seen him once. He is attached to the hotel, and apparently he's needed by VIP customers all the time. He's never free. They gave us vouchers for a bus tour to Versailles, which was exhausting, and there were miles of cobblestones to walk over. We didn't go to Chartres at all.'

'That's not what was promised,' Ann clucked with disapproval.

'No indeed, and we hate complaining. I mean, it's a very generous prize. It's just . . . it's just . . .'

'The top restaurants? Have they turned out all right?'

'Yes, up to a point, but you see it only covers the *prix fixe*, you know, the set menu, and it's often things like tripe or rabbit that we don't eat. They *did* say we could choose from the fine-dining menus, but when we got there we couldn't.'

'And what are you going to do about it?'

'Well, we didn't know *what* to do, so that's why it's wonderful you called us. Are you from the magazine?'

'Not directly, but sort of connected,' Ann Wall said.

'We don't like to go whingeing and whining to them; it seems so ungrateful. It's just so much less than we expected.'

'I know, I know.' Ann was genuinely sympathetic.

'And individually the people in the hotel are very nice, really nice and pleasant, it's just that in general they seem to think we won much more of a bargain-basement prize than the one that was advertised. What would you suggest we do?'

The Walls looked at each other blankly. What indeed?

'Perhaps you could get in touch with the public relations firm that set it up,' Ann said eventually.

'Could *you* do that for us, do you think?' Mrs Flemming was obviously a person who didn't want to make waves.

'It might be more effective coming from you, what with your being on the spot and everything . . .' Ann was feverishly trying to pass the buck back to the Flemmings.

'But you were kind enough to ring us to ask was everything all right. Who are you representing, exactly?'

'Just a concerned member of the public.' And Ann Wall hung up, trembling.

What were they going to do now?

First they allowed the glorious feeling to seep over them

and through them. The dream holiday in Paris had turned out to be a nightmare. They were oh so well out of it. They were better by far in this mad place on the Atlantic, which they had thought was so disappointing at first.

Everything that had been promised was being delivered here. Perhaps they had won the first prize after all.

They decided that the following morning they would call the public relations firm and report that all was not as it should be at the Hotel Martinique.

For the first time they slept all through the night. There was no resentful waking at three a.m. to have tea and brood about the unfairness of life in general and competitions in particular.

The Walls took a packed lunch and walked along the cliffs and crags until they found an old ruined church, which Chicky said would be a lovely place to stop and have their picnic. It was sheltered from the gales and looked straight across to America.

They laughed happily as they unpacked their wonderful rich slices of chicken pie and opened their flasks of soup. Imagine – the Flemmings would be facing another lunch of tripe and rabbit in Paris.

Ann Wall had left a cryptic message with the PR agency, saying that for everyone's sake they should check on the Flemmings in the Martinique or some very undesirable publicity might result. They felt like bold children who had been given time off at school. They would enjoy the rest of their stay.

That night, everyone at Chicky's kitchen table was ready with their festival suggestions; they could barely wait for the meal to finish to come up with their pitch. Lillian, whose face had softened over the last couple of days, said that the essence of a festival nowadays seemed to be, if everyone would excuse the use of that *horrible* phrase, a 'feel-good factor'. Sagely they all nodded and said that was exactly what was needed.

Chicky said that a sense of community was becoming more and more important in the world today. Young people fled small closed societies at first, as well they should, but later they wanted to be part of them again.

Orla wondered about organising a family reunion. They liked the notion but said it would be hard to quantify. Did it mean the gathering of a clan, or the bringing together of people who had been estranged? Lillian thought that an Honorary Granny Festival might be good. Everyone wanted to be a grandmother, she said firmly. Winnie looked at her sharply. This had never been brought up before.

Henry and Nicola wondered if Health in the Community might be a good theme. People were very into diets and lifestyle and exercise these days. Stoneybridge could provide it all. And Anders said suddenly that you could have a festival to celebrate friendship. You know, old friends turning up together, maybe going on a trip there with an old pal, that kind of thing. They thought about it politely for a while. The more they thought about it, the better it sounded.

It didn't exclude family, or anything. Your friend could be your sister or your aunt.

Most people must have felt from time to time that they would love to catch up with someone that they hadn't seen as much as they would have liked.

Suppose there was a festival which offered a variety of entertainments, like the ideas everyone had suggested already but done in the name of friendship? They were teeming with ideas. There could indeed be cookery demos, keep-fit classes, walking tours, birdwatching trips, farmhouse teas, sing-songs, local drama, tap-dancing classes.

The Walls watched with mounting excitement as the table planned and took notes and assembled a programme. They had a winner on their hands.

They checked the newspaper again to see what prize was being offered.

It was a 1,250-euro shopping spree in a big Dublin store.

The Walls worked it out. They would share it equally between them, with extra for Anders as they had chosen his idea. Would that do?

Everyone was delighted.

What would they call themselves? The Stone House Syndicate? Yes, that seemed perfect. Orla would type it out and give everyone a copy. They would watch for the results, which would be published the week before Christmas.

When the festival was up and running, they would all come back and celebrate here again. And best of all, they still had the rest of the week in this lovely house with the waves crashing on the shore. A place that had not only lived up to its promise but had delivered even more.

It wasn't *exactly* romance and stardust sprinkled all over them like magic, but it was something deeper, like a sense of importance and a great feeling of peace.

Miss Nell Howe

The girls at Wood Park School thought that Miss Howe was ninety when she retired. She was actually sixty. Same difference. It was old. They didn't pause to think how she would spend her days, weeks and months afterwards. Old people just continued to boss and grumble and complain. They had no idea how much she had dreaded this day, and how she feared the first September for forty years when she wouldn't set out to begin a new school year full of hope and plans and projects.

Miss Howe had been there as long as anyone could remember. She was tall and thin with hair combed straight back from her forehead and held there with an old-fashioned slide. She wore dark clothes under an academic gown. She had taught the mothers and aunts of these girls in the past but in recent years, as headmistress, she had been rarely in the classroom and mainly in her office.

The girls hated going to Miss Howe's office. For one thing, being there always meant some kind of disapproval, complaint or punishment. But it wasn't just that. It was a place without soul. Miss Howe had a very functional and always empty desk: she was not a person who tolerated chaos or mess.

There was a wall lined with inexpensive shelving holding many books on education. No handcrafted bookcases, as might have seemed suitable for a woman whose life had been involved for decades in teaching. Another wall was covered in timetables and lists of upcoming functions, details of various rosters and plans. Two large steel filing cabinets – presumably holding the records of generations of Wood Park girls – and a big computer dominated the room. There were dull brown curtains at the window, no pictures on the walls, no hint of any life outside these walls. No photographs, ornaments or signs that Miss Howe, Principal, had an interest in anything except Wood Park School. This is where she interviewed prospective pupils and their parents, possible new teachers, inspectors from the Department of Education and the occasional past pupil who had done well and had returned to fund a library or a games pavilion.

Miss Howe had an assistant called Irene O'Connor who had been there for years. Irene was round and jolly and in the staffroom they always called her the 'acceptable face of the Howe office'. She didn't appear to notice that Miss Howe barked at her rather than spoke to her. Miss Howe rarely thanked her for anything she did, and always seemed slightly surprised and almost annoyed when Irene brought tea and biscuits into what was likely to be an awkward or contentious meeting.

There were no plants or flowers in Miss Howe's office, so Irene had introduced a little kalanchoe in a brass pot. It was a plant that needed practically no care, which was just as well as Miss Howe never watered it or apparently even noticed it. Irene wore brightly coloured t-shirts with a dark jacket and skirt. It was almost as if she was trying to bring a stab of colour into the mournful office without annoying Miss Howe. Irene was quite possibly a saint, and might even be canonised in her own lifetime.

She worked in a little outer office which was full of her personality, as indeed was her conversation. There were trailing geraniums and picture postcards from all of Irene's friends pinned to her bulletin board; there were framed photographs of her on the desk. On her shelves were souvenirs of holiday trips to Spain and pictures of herself wearing a frilly skirt and a big sombrero at a fiesta. Here was a record of a busy, happy life, in contrast to the bleak cell that was Miss Howe's pride and joy.

She went home every day at lunchtime because she had an invalid mother and a nephew, Kenny, who was her late sister's child. Irene and her mother had given Kenny a good home and he was growing up to be a fine boy.

In the staffroom they marvelled at Irene's patience and endless good humour. Sometimes they sympathised with her, but Irene would never hear a word against her employer.

'No, no, it's only her manner,' she would say. 'She has a heart of gold, and this is the dream job for me. Please understand that.'

The teachers said to each other that people like Irene would always be victimised by the Miss Howes of this world. What did Irene mean, 'it was only her manner'? People *were* their manner. How else were we to know them?

Miss Howe was rightly named Her Own Worst Enemy. They giggled over the cleverness of this, and somehow it tamed her. She was less frightening when they could call her this behind her back, though they made very sure that the children never got wind of their name for her.

In the year before Miss Howe retired there was much speculation about her successor. None of the current staff appeared to have the seniority or authority to replace her. That was the way Miss Howe had run things, with never a hint of delegation. The new appointment would most probably be someone from outside. The staff didn't like that idea either. They were used to Her Own Worst Enemy. They knew how to cope and they had Irene to soften the edges. Who knew what the new person might want to introduce? Better the devil you know than the entirely new and imposed devil that you didn't know at all.

They also wondered about Irene. Would she stay and serve the new Tsar? Would she find excuses for the next principal and her manner? Suppose the new person didn't want Irene?

It was change. They feared change.

Then there was the matter of the presentation to Miss Howe. None of them had the slightest clue as to where her interests lay. Even desultory conversation at the beginning of term had failed to discover anything. Miss Howe had no holiday story to tell, nothing like that was ever mentioned, or any family gathering, or repainting of a house, or digging of a garden. Eventually they had given up asking.

But what could you give to this woman to celebrate all her years at Wood Park? There was no question of a cruise or a week in a spa or a set of Waterford Crystal or some beautifully crafted piece of furniture. Miss Howe's taste had been seen to be completely utilitarian: if it functioned, it was fine.

The teachers begged Irene to come up with an idea.

'You see her every day. You talk to her all the time. You must have *some* notion of what she would like,' they pleaded.

But Irene said that her mind was a complete blank. Miss Howe was a very private person. She didn't believe in talking about personal things.

The parents' committee was asking Irene the same question. They wanted to mark the occasion and didn't know how. Irene decided that she really must stir herself and find out more about her employer's lifestyle.

She knew Miss Howe's address, so the first thing she did was go and look at her house. It was in a terrace of houses called St Jarlath's Crescent. Small houses once thought of as working-class accommodation, which had later been redefined as townhouses and were now, of course, dropping in value again because of the recession. Most of the small front gardens were well kept, many with window boxes and colourful flower beds.

Miss Howe's garden, however, had no decoration. There were two flowering shrubs and a neatly mowed lawn. The paint on the door, gate and windowsills needed to be refreshed. It didn't look neglected, more ignored. No hints there.

Irene decided she must be brave and get to see the interior. With this in mind, the following morning she slipped Miss Howe's reading glasses into her own handbag and then called round to the house to deliver them, pretending that she had found them on the desk.

Miss Howe met her at the door with no enthusiasm.

'There was no need, Irene,' she said coldly.

'But I was afraid you wouldn't be able to read tonight,' Irene stumbled.

'No, I have plenty of replacements. But thank you all the same. It was kind of you.'

'May I come in for a moment, Miss Howe?' Irene nearly fainted at her own courage in asking this.

There was a pause.

'Of course.' Miss Howe opened the door fully.

The house was clinically bare, like the office back in Wood Park. No pictures on the walls, a rickety bookcase, a small old-fashioned television. A table with a supper tray prepared with a portion of cheese, two tomatoes and two slices of bread. Back in Irene's house they would be having spicy tomato sauce and pasta. Irene had taught Kenny how to cook, and tonight he would make a rhubarb fool. They would all play a game of Scrabble and then Irene and her mother would watch the soaps and Kenny, who was now eighteen, would go out with his friends.

What a happy home compared to this cold, bleak place.

But since Irene had come so far she would not give up now.

'Miss Howe, I have a problem,' she said.

'You have?' Miss Howe's voice was glacial.

'Yes. The teachers *and* the parents have asked me to tell them what would be a suitable gift for you when you retire this summer. Everyone is anxious to give you something that you would like. And because I work with you all day, they wrongly thought I would know. But I don't know. I am at a loss, Miss Howe. I wonder, could you direct me . . . ?'

'I don't want anything, Irene.'

'But Miss Howe, that isn't the issue. *They* want to give you something, something suitable, appropriate.'

'Why?'

'Because they value you.'

'If they really value me then they will leave me alone and not indulge their wish for sentimental ceremonies.'

'Oh, no, that's not how they see it, Miss Howe.'

'And you, Irene. How do *you* see it?'

'I suppose they must think I am a poor friend and colleague if I can't tell them after twenty years' working for you what would be a good farewell present.'

Miss Howe looked at her for a long moment.

'But Irene, you are *not* a friend or colleague,' she said eventually. 'It's a totally different relationship. People have no right to expect you to know such things.'

Irene opened her mouth and closed it several times.

When the teachers in the staffroom had railed against Miss Howe and called her Her Own Worst Enemy, she had stood up for the woman. Now she wondered why. Miss Howe was indeed a person without warmth or soul; without friends or interests. Let them buy her a picnic basket or vacuum cleaner. It didn't matter. Irene didn't care any more.

She picked up her bag and moved to the door.

'Well, I'll be off now, Miss Howe. I won't disturb you and keep you from your supper any longer. I just wanted to return your glasses to you, that's all.'

'I didn't leave my glasses on my desk, Irene. I never leave *anything* on my desk,' Miss Howe said.

Irene managed to walk steadily to the gate. It was only when she was a little way along the road that her legs began to feel weak.

All those years she had worked for Miss Howe, shielded her from irate parents, discontented teachers, rebellious pupils. Tonight Miss Howe had told her face to face that she must not presume to call herself a friend or a colleague. She was merely someone who worked for the Principal.

How could she have been so blind and so sure of her own position?

She held on to a gate to steady herself. A young woman came out of her house and looked at her with concern.

'Are you feeling all right? You look as white as a sheet.'

'I think so. I just feel a little dizzy.'

'Come in and sit down. I'm a nurse, by the way.'

'I know you,' Irene gasped, 'you work at St Brigid's heart clinic.'

'Yes; you're not a patient there, are you?'

'I come with my mother, Peggy O'Connor.'

'Oh, of course. I'm Fiona Carroll. Peggy's always talking about you and how good you are to her.'

'I'm glad someone thinks I'm good for something,' Irene said.

'Come in, Miss O'Connor, and I'll get you a cup of tea.' Fiona had her by the arm and Irene sank gratefully into a house that was so different to Miss Howe's that it could have been on another planet. Between them, Fiona and her two little boys provided tea, chocolate cake and a lot of encouragement.

Irene began to feel a lot better.

Always discreet and loyal, she resisted the temptation to unburden herself to this kindly Fiona, who must know her difficult neighbour and might even be able to give her words of consolation.

But old habits die hard.

Irene felt that you could not be someone's assistant and bad-mouth them to others. She said nothing at all about her upsetting encounter with Miss Howe. She assured Fiona that she felt strong enough now to get her bus home, but at that very moment a man called Dingo arrived at the house delivering topsoil and trays of bedding plants. The Carrolls were going to have a gardening weekend, they told Irene. The boys were going to have a flower bed each.

'Dingo will drop you home, Miss O'Connor,' Fiona insisted, 'it's on his way.'

Dingo was perfectly happy with this suggestion.

'They're a delightful family,' Irene said to him as she settled into his van. 'Are you a family man yourself, Dingo?'

'No, I've always been a believer in travelling solo,' he said. 'Believe me, Miss O'Connor, not every marriage is as good as Fiona and Declan's. Some of the couples you meet are like lightning devils. You never married yourself then?'

'No, Dingo, I didn't. I did have a chance once but he was a gambler and I was afraid, and then my mother needed me, so here I am.' She realised she sounded defeated, which was not her normal response. Miss Howe had done this to her today.

Dingo drove on, unconcerned.

'My uncle Nasey is just the same. He says he fancied someone years back but missed his chance. He's always asking me to look out for someone in their forties for him. Are you in your forties, Miss O'Connor?'

'Just about,' Irene said. 'Don't ask me next year. I'd have to say no.'

'Right, I'll tell him about you now before it gets too late,' Dingo promised.

Irene went home and prepared the supper. She never mentioned the events of the day to her mother or to Kenny. They could have no idea that all Irene's work for Miss Howe had been dismissed in one cold, cruel sentence.

Nor did they know that at the very moment they sat down to supper, efforts to find Irene a husband were under way. Dingo had called to see his uncle Nasey with the news that there was a very pleasant woman of forty-nine on the market. And he was so convincing, so persuasive, that Uncle Nasey was very interested in finding out more about Irene . . .

Over the next few weeks, the teachers at Wood Park School noticed that something about Irene had changed. She became shruggy rather than eager when they tried to discuss what kind of leaving ceremony they could arrange for Miss Howe, and what gift should be chosen.

'I don't think it matters, really,' Irene would say, and change the subject. Possibly she was worried about her position there, they thought. Maybe the next Principal would want to choose her own assistant.

Irene continued to do her work as reliably as always but without any warmth and enthusiasm. If Miss Howe noticed, she gave no sign of having seen anything amiss. Irene stopped serving tea and biscuits at awkward meetings. She retrieved the little kalanchoe, fed it plant food and nursed it back to glowing health in her own office. Gone were the days when Irene would tell cheerful tales of the world she lived in.

But now Irene had a social life of which Miss Howe was totally unaware. Nasey had called, and said that his eejit of a nephew had spoken very highly of her, and perhaps she might accompany him to the cinema on the odd occasion. Then they went bowling and to a singing pub. His real name was Ignatius, he explained, and at least it was better than being called Iggy, which another lad at school had been named. He worked in a butcher's shop for a Mr Malone, who was the most decent man ever to wear shoe leather.

He took to calling at Irene's house and bringing best lamb chops, or a lovely pork steak. Irene's mother Peggy loved him and lost no opportunity to tell him what a wonderful woman Irene was.

'I know that, Mrs O'Connor. You don't have to sell her to me. I'm hooked already,' he said, and Peggy was pink with pleasure about it all.

Nasey came from the West of Ireland and had little family of his own in Dublin. He had two nephews: Dingo Irene had met already; he drove a van and did odd jobs for people. There was his sister, Nuala, and there was his sister's boy, Rigger, who had been unfortunate in his life and spent a lot of time at reform school. He'd been sent away to the West of Ireland, and it looked as though he'd fallen on his feet over there. He had found a nice girl, grew vegetables and kept chickens. He had a job as a sort of manager for a place that was just setting up; a kind of small Big House, if you could understand that. It was perched on a cliff and the view would take the sight out of your eyes. Nasey promised that one day he would drive Irene and her mother to see the whole set-up. They'd love it.

Kenny liked having Nasey around too, and was always on hand to keep an eye on his gran if the two lovebirds, as he called them, wanted to go out on the town.

Then, just before the end of term, after six months of courtship, Nasey proposed to Irene. A small wedding was planned, and when she told him, Kenny offered to give his aunt away. But Irene had something else on her mind. She waited until Peggy had gone to bed.

'I have something to tell you, Kenny,' Irene began.

'I've always known,' he said simply. 'I knew you were my mother when I was nine.'

'Why did you never say?' She was astounded.

'It never mattered. I knew you'd always be there.'

'Do you want to ask me anything?' Her voice was small and she started to cry.

'Were you frightened and lonely at the time?' he asked, sitting down next to her and putting his arms around her.

'A bit, but he wasn't free, you see. Your father was already married. It wouldn't have been fair to break up everything he had. Then Maureen died in England and so we pretended you were hers. For Mam's sake. Mam got her grandchild, I got my son – we all did fine.' By now Irene was smiling through her tears.

'Does Nasey know?'

'Yes, I told him early on. He said you had probably guessed, and imagine, he was right.'

'Will Nasey come and live here?'

'If you don't mind,' Irene said. 'He's great with your gran.'

'Don't I know it? I love the way you play three-handed bridge at night like demons. Watching you is better than being in Las Vegas.' He said that he was delighted Nasey would be there, since he had been hoping to travel. There was a chance of a trip to America. Now he felt free to make his plans.

For eighteen years Irene had been dreading the day she must tell Kenny this news, and now it had passed almost without comment. Life was very strange.

Irene wore her engagement ring to work; Miss Howe made no comment and Irene did not bring the subject up. All the teachers noticed it, of course; Irene told them that her mother was going to be her matron of honour, and that Nasey's nephew Rigger was coming over from Stoneybridge and that Dingo was to be his best man, and that they would be having sandwiches and cake in a pub on the last Saturday in August and she would love all the teachers to come to that. They got into a fever of excitement planning a wedding present.

With Irene, it would be easy: she liked everything. It could be a holiday in Spain, a garden shed, a painting of Connemara, a weekend in a castle, a set of luggage with wheels, a croquet set, a big, ornate mirror with cherubs on it. Irene would love any one of them and praise the gift to the skies.

They were still no nearer any decision about Miss Howe's retirement gift.

There was a lot of pressure on Irene to make a decision on what it should be; she in turn didn't care one way or the other but she felt that for the teachers and students, she had to come up with some sort of an idea and she didn't want to disappoint them. It was so wonderful to be able to tell Nasey everything when she finished work in the evenings.

Nasey said he'd give the matter some thought. In the meantime, he had news of his own. His nephew Rigger had been on the phone.

'They're in a panic over at Stone House. They don't have any proper bookings for the week that it opens. He and Chicky are afraid it's going to be a flop after all their hard work.'

'Well,' said Irene, 'we should ask Rigger for some brochures, and I can hand them around at school. It's the sort of thing some of the teachers would enjoy.'

'Why don't you send Miss Howe there?' Nasey said triumphantly.

'But if she's so awful, should we inflict her on them?'

'She mightn't be too bad outside the school. I mean, she could go walking; she wouldn't annoy too many people.' Nasey's optimism wouldn't allow him to think too badly of Irene's boss.

'I'll suggest it. It might be the perfect solution,' Irene said.

'Let's keep our fingers crossed that she doesn't close the

place down overnight,' Nasey said with a big smile. Then they put their minds to their wedding.

The teachers noted that Her Own Worst Enemy was even more buttoned up than usual these days, more unforgiving about high spirits at the end of the school year than ever before. More concerned about examination results than the children's future, and if possible even more ungiving of herself on any front.

They reported that her car was seen later and later at night in the school yard, and arrived there earlier in the mornings. Miss Howe must only spend seven or eight hours out of Wood Park every day.

It was not natural.

Finally she spoke to Irene about the wedding.

'One of the parents tells me that you are thinking of getting married, Irene,' Miss Howe said with a little laugh. 'Can she be serious?'

'Yes indeed, Miss Howe, at the end of August,' Irene said.

'And you never thought to tell me?' There was disapproval and sorrow in her voice.

'Well, no. As you said, I am not your colleague or your friend. I merely work for you. And as it will all take place during the holidays, I didn't really see any point in telling you.'

Although it was not exactly discourteous, there was something abrupt in Irene's tone that made Miss Howe look up sharply. This was the time for her to say that she was very pleased and wished Irene happiness. This was even the time when she might say that indeed she *did* consider Irene a friend and a colleague.

But no; years of being her own worst enemy clicked in, and so she laughed again.

'Well, I don't suppose you have any intention of starting a family at this late stage of your life,' she said, amused at the very thought of it.

Irene met her look but without smiling. 'No indeed, Miss Howe. I already have been blessed with a son, who is eighteen now. Nasey and I do not hope to have any more children.'

'Nasey!' Miss Howe could hardly contain herself. 'Is that his name? Goodness!'

'Yes, that's his name, and goodness is a very good way to describe him. He is *very* good. To me, my son Kenny and my mother. He works as a butcher, in case you find that funny too.'

'Please calm yourself, Irene. You are being hysterical. I have just discovered two extraordinary things about you. You were always showing me photographs of Kenny, and said he was your nephew.'

'I thought it more discreet since I was not a married woman.'

'But this Nasey will make you respectable, is that it?'

Irene wondered how she could have worked for this woman for twenty years, not to mention made excuses for her that it was just her manner. Miss Howe had no heart, no warmth.

'I always considered myself respectable, always. And everyone who knows me thinks I am too. But then you don't know me at all, Miss Howe, and never have.'

'You will presumably want to continue working here after I am gone and after this . . . er . . . marriage?' Miss Howe's eyes were full of anger.

'Certainly I do. I love this school, the staff and the pupils.'

'Then you would want to watch your tone, Irene, if I am to

write you a good reference. My successor would not necessarily like the legacy of someone who is secretive and has a bad attitude.'

'Write what you like, Miss Howe. You will anyway.'

'You are being very short-sighted over all this, Irene.'

'Thank you, Miss Howe. I'll get back to my work, while I still have a job.' And Irene walked out without looking back.

She sat at her desk, shaking, and had barely the strength to answer her mobile phone.

It was her mother, with wonderful news. Nasey had been around to the house at lunchtime and had shown her how to go online and look at outfits for Mother of the Bride. She was going to choose a navy and white dress and jacket. Would that suit Irene's plans?

Soon the goodwill and excitement began to seep back. The toxic, cold loneliness of Miss Howe beyond the door in her prison-like office was ebbing away.

The new Principal had already been chosen. She was a Mrs Williams, a widow who had run a large girls' school in England but who now wanted to return to her family in Ireland. Apparently she was bringing her own furniture to the Principal's office, and was happy to keep the present level of administration. Irene would work for July and part of August helping her to get installed. She had been informed that Irene would then be on holiday for three weeks but back in the office for the first day of term.

The school assembled to say goodbye to Miss Howe. She stood on the raised dais of the school hall as she did every morning. Still wearing her black gown, her hair held by the same slide. Her face was still totally impassive.

Various teachers read out their words recognising Miss Howe's achievements; the head girl made her speech and the chairman of the parents' committee expressed gratitude on behalf of all the girls who had succeeded so well at Wood Park, thanks to Miss Howe. There was no mention of a well-deserved rest, or assurance that her real life was just beginning. Finally the envelope was handed over as a token of everyone's appreciation. It was a voucher for a holiday in the opening week of Stone House, a new hotel in the West of Ireland. Miss Howe made no attempt to thank anyone, and her face registered nothing when the gift was announced. But no one really expected any other reaction.

Mrs Williams had been invited to the farewell ceremony for Miss Howe but had refused. She did not want to be a distraction, she said. This was Miss Howe's day.

In fact, people would have been glad of Mrs Williams' presence. She would have helped the torturous ceremony and the endless wine-and-cheese event that followed. People looked at their watches begging for it to be an acceptable time to leave. Had time ever moved so slowly? Was there ever such a joyless speech deploring modern trends in education, stressing the need for discipline in schools and learning by rote, pleas that so-called creativity never take the place of good old-fashioned basics?

The audience of teachers who had done their best to make the curriculum interesting as well as draconian; the parents who were guiltily relieved that their daughters got good points and university places; the pupils who couldn't wait for the school holidays . . . everyone was praying for it to be over.

Irene went back to her office to collect her things. She was dying to get home and tell Nasey about the wedding gift which had been arranged for them by the teaching staff at Wood Park. It was not only one of those fabulous gas-fired barbecues, but also a garden firm were going to lay a little patio for them and build a special wall to enclose the area. All they needed now was a lifetime of good summers to enjoy eating out of doors!

To her surprise, she heard a sound from Miss Howe's office. She knocked on the door. Miss Howe stood there alone behind her desk, which was empty apart from her car keys. Behind her the window, framed with the heavy dark brown curtains, looked out on the empty school yard.

'I just wanted to make sure that it wasn't an intruder.' Irene started to back out again.

'Stay for a moment, Irene. I want to give you a wedding present.'

This was certainly not something she had foreseen.

'That's very kind of you, Miss Howe. Very kind indeed.'

Miss Howe handed her a fancy bag with a lot of glitter on it. Not at all the kind of thing you would have expected from Miss Howe. Irene was at a loss for words.

Her immediate response was guilt. She had paid not one euro towards the going-away voucher for Miss Howe; she had signed no card and given no good wishes. Now she was ashamed.

'Not at all. Just a little something to remind you of me.'

'I won't forget working for you, Miss Howe.'

'And I very much hope that Mrs Williams will see her way to keeping you.'

'Yes, indeed. And thank you again for the gift. Will I open it now?'

'Oh, please, no . . .' Miss Howe withdrew in a sort of

fastidious distaste, as if opening the gift would somehow sully this empty office.

The books had all been removed but the cheap hardboard shelves stood empty, ready to be removed in the next few days, although Miss Howe didn't know this. There was no trace of anyone having worked here for so long.

'Well, I will open it tonight, and let me thank you in advance for going to the trouble of choosing something for us. I do so appreciate it.' There was sincerity radiating from all over Irene.

Miss Howe gave a little shudder at the familiarity of it all.

'Well, I hope it will be suitable. One doesn't know what to get, really. Especially when it's a late marriage.'

'Sorry?'

'I mean, you probably *have* everything already, not like young people excited about setting up a new home.'

Irene would not let the light go out on the good feeling of the gift.

'No, of course not, but to us it's still very new and exciting. Neither of us has ever been married before.'

'Quite.' Miss Howe's lips were pursed in disapproval.

'Anyway, I wish you all the best, Miss Howe. I'm sure you have plenty of things planned for the years ahead.'

Miss Howe could have thanked her for the kind remark. She could have said vaguely that there was indeed a lot to do. But Nell Howe didn't do vague and pleasant. Instead she said, 'What a wonderful fairy-tale world of platitudes you live in, Irene. It must be very restful not to think things through.' Then she took up her car keys and left.

Irene watched from the window as Nell Howe got into her small car and drove out of the only life she had known for years. She stood there for a while after the car had driven through the gates of Wood Park. What *would* Miss Howe do tonight, and during the many other days and nights to follow? Would there always be a tray laid in that cold room? Was there anyone to share it with her?

There had been not one friend or relative at the gathering held in her honour. Who goes through life with *nobody* to invite to her retirement party?

Irene was a very generous person. She could not think all bad of the woman who had insulted her, and who even now at the very last was trying to ridicule her. Miss Howe had bought her a wedding present, after all. And even more important, if Irene had not gone to visit Miss Howe that day she would never have met Dingo, who had found his uncle Nasey for her.

She sighed and caught the bus home, clutching the shiny glittery bag with the wedding present.

They opened it at suppertime. It was a lace-trimmed tray cloth. There were little rosebuds on it. Irene looked at it in wonder. She could hardly believe that Miss Howe had gone to a shop and chosen this. Not at all practical, and rather old-fashioned, but such a kind thought.

Then she saw that at the bottom of the bag there was a card in an envelope. Irene opened it and read: *To Miss Howe, Thank you for getting our girl to study and turning round her life.* It was signed by the parents of a child who had recently won a major scholarship to the university. Miss Howe had passed the gift on unopened. She hadn't even opened the card to read the gratitude it contained.

Irene crumpled up the card quickly.

'What did she say?' Peggy O'Connor loved every detail, every heartbeat.

'Just wishing us well,' Irene said. In her heart she decided that she would never think about Miss Howe again. She would just exclude her from her mind and her life. The woman was a shell. She was not worth another thought.

But a week later, when Mrs Williams was in place, Irene was forced to think about Miss Howe once more. Mrs Williams had changed the Principal's office so much that it did not look remotely like the same place.

A small laptop replaced the huge, bulky computer; the hand-carved desk held attractive raffia trays, brightly coloured files and a photograph of the late Mr Williams. The new bookshelves were filled but with spaces for ornaments and little flower pots. Mrs Williams even kept a tiny watering can at hand to make sure the plants got attention.

The hard chairs had been replaced by less daunting furniture. She had established a routine that seemed more normal and less driven than her predecessor's. She seemed to be delighted with Irene, and constantly thanked her for her efficiency and support. This was a personal first for Irene, who had been used to the grim silence of Miss Howe as the best that could be hoped for.

They were going through the day's agenda when Mrs Williams looked up and said, 'By the way, why didn't you tell me you were getting married?'

'I didn't want to bore you with all my doings. I'm inclined to go on a bit!' Irene said, and smiled apologetically.

'Well, if we can't go on a bit about our wedding day, what *can* we go on about?' Mrs Williams seemed genuinely interested. 'Tell me all about it.'

Irene told her about Nasey, and how he had served his time in a butcher's shop and was going to sell his flat and come and live with her and her mother. They were going to put an extra bathroom in the house . . . she bubbled on full of enthusiasm, hoping that the day itself would be a great one, and not silly or anything.

Mrs Williams looked at the photograph on her desk and said she remembered her wedding day as if it were yesterday. Everything had gone right.

'Was the sun shining?' Irene wondered.

Mrs Williams couldn't remember the weather it was so unimportant. Everyone had been so happy, that was the main thing.

At that point, the direct telephone line rang. Irene was a bit nonplussed. She had never known calls to come in on that line. It was for the Principal's convenience, in case she wanted to make a quick call out rather than going through the whole system. At a nod from Mrs Williams, Irene took the call.

A man asked to speak to Nell Howe.

'Miss Howe has retired as Principal and no longer works here. Do you want to talk to Mrs Williams, the current Principal, and if so, perhaps you can tell me in what connection?'

'Tell me where she lives,' he said.

'I'm afraid we never disclose staff addresses.'

'You just said that she was ex-staff.'

'I'm sorry, but I'm not able to help you. We are not in touch with Miss Howe, so I am not in a position to pass on any message,' Irene said, and the man hung up.

Irene and Mrs Williams looked at each other, bewildered.

A week before the wedding, Irene saw Nell Howe across a street. Irene couldn't help herself. She ran across to her.

'Miss Howe, how good to see you.'

Nell Howe looked at her distantly and then, as if after a great effort, she said flatly, 'Irene.'

'Yes, Miss Howe. How have you been? I have been meaning to contact you.'

'Have you? Then why didn't you?'

'Could we have a cup of coffee somewhere, do you think?' Irene suggested.

'Why?' Miss Howe was surprised at the overfamiliarity of the request.

'I need to tell you something.'

'Well, there is hardly anywhere suitable around here.' Miss Howe sniffed at the area.

'This little café does nice coffee. Please, Miss Howe . . .'

As if giving in to the inevitable, Miss Howe agreed. Over cups of frothy Italian coffee, Irene told her about the wedding plans and the honeymoon they had decided on. She asked Miss Howe if she was looking forward to going away in the winter.

'Why would anyone want to go to such a remote place at any time?' was the only response.

Irene changed the subject. There was the man on the phone and his odd behaviour.

'Have you any idea of who it could be?' she asked. 'He didn't leave any message, and wouldn't give a number.'

'It must have been my brother,' Miss Howe said.

'Your brother?'

'Yes, my brother Martin. I haven't seen him for a long time.'

'But why?' Irene felt her heart racing. It was the casual way Miss Howe spoke that was so disturbing.

'Why? Oh, it all goes back many, many years ago.' Miss Howe's face was non-committal and unmoved. 'And none of your business, anyway. Is that it? Is that all?' And with a chilly nod of her head, Miss Howe left the café.

It was a wonderful day for the wedding. Kenny gave the bride away, and Peggy looked as though she might burst with pride. Dingo, all dressed up in a new suit, was the best man and in his speech said that he was very proud of being the match-maker who had brought the happy couple together.

Carmel and Rigger had managed to get time off for the occasion; Rigger's mother, Nasey's sister Nuala, was there. The sun shone from morning until late evening. Mrs Williams joined them in the pub and mingled with the teachers, the butchers from Malone's shop and all the friends and neighbours. In a million years poor Miss Howe would never have been able to mix like this.

There was a honeymoon in Spain and then back to work at Wood Park, where life promised to be much easier and more pleasant than in the previous regime.

Rigger and Carmel kept in touch all the time about Stone House. The voucher they had designed for Miss Howe had given them more ideas, and a week at Stone House was now going to be one of the prizes for a competition in a magazine. The list was filling up nicely; it looked as if Chicky Starr would have a full house for her opening week. There was great excitement all around the place. Rigger said his mother was going to come and visit soon. It would be her first time in Stoneybridge since she was a girl.

She didn't want to stay in the big house but Rigger and Chicky were insisting. It would be such a great return for her.

Irene did try to warn them that Miss Howe might be difficult to please.

'We can handle it,' said Rigger cheerfully. 'It will be great practice for us. We saw off Howard and Barbara; your Miss Howe will be no problem for us, you'll see.'

Miss Howe travelled by a late train, and so Rigger went to meet her. He saw a tall, stern-looking woman with one small case looking around the station impatiently. This must be the one.

He introduced himself and took her suitcase.

'I was told that Mrs Starr would meet me,' the woman said.

'She's at the house, welcoming the other guests. I'm Rigger, her manager. I live in the grounds,' he said.

'Yes, you told me your name already.' From the tone of her voice she seemed highly disapproving of it.

'I hope you will have a wonderful week here, Miss Howe. The house is very comfortable.'

'I would have expected no less,' she said.

Rigger hoped he would have a moment to warn Chicky that it was time to fasten the seatbelts.

Chicky didn't need the warning. The body language alone was enough to alert her that Miss Howe was not going to be a happy camper. She stood stiff and unyielding in the group that had gathered in the big cheerful kitchen. She refused a sherry or glass of wine, asking instead for a glass of plain tonic water with ice and lemon. She nodded wordlessly when introduced to fellow guests.

She said she didn't need to see her room and freshen up; since she was one of the last to arrive, she wouldn't delay the meal by absenting herself. She had a knack of bringing conversations to an end with her pronouncements.

She showed no interest in the itineraries and options that Chicky laid out for them. One by one the guests gave up on her.

The American man asked her what kind of business she was in, and she said that, unlike in the United States, people here didn't judge others on what occupation they had or used to have.

A Swedish boy told her that it was his second visit to Ireland, and he barely managed to reach the end of his first sentence before she made her boredom clear.

A nurse called Winnie wondered if Miss Howe had toured in the West before, and she shrugged, saying not that she could remember. Two polite English doctors told her that they were astounded by the spectacular scenery. Miss Howe said that she had arrived in the dark and hadn't seen anything remarkable so far.

When Orla, who served at the table, asked her if the meal was satisfactory, Miss Howe replied that if it hadn't been she would certainly have mentioned it. It would be doing the establishment no favours not to speak her mind.

As Chicky Starr showed Miss Howe to her room after dinner, she waited for some small expression of pleasure at the beautiful furniture, the fresh new linen on the bed, the tray with the best china tea things . . . everybody else had admired them.

Miss Howe had just nodded briefly.

'I'm sure you're tired after the journey,' Chicky Starr said, biting back her disappointment and trying to forgive the lack of response.

'Hardly. I just sat in a train the whole way from Dublin.' Miss Howe was taking no prisoners.

And for the days that followed, alone among the guests Miss Howe found nothing to praise, no delight in the wild scenery, no appreciation for the food that Orla and Chicky served every night.

Chicky sat beside the strange, uncommunicative woman in order to spare the guests from the ordeal of trying to talk to her. Even for Chicky, with a background of years working in a New York boarding house with a room full of men dulled by work in the construction industry, this was hard going.

Miss Howe never asked a question or made an observation. Whatever had gone wrong in her life had gone very wrong indeed.

On the fourth morning when Miss Howe had yet again shown no interest in exploring the coastline, Chicky begged Rigger to drive her to the market town with him.

'Oh God, Chicky, do I have to? She'll turn the milk sour.'

'Please, Rigger, otherwise she'll just sit staring at me all day and I've a lot of cooking to do.'

Rigger was good-natured about it. Apart from Miss Howe, the week was going so very well. All these people were going to praise the place to the skies. Stone House would take off as they had always believed it would. One day with Miss Howe wouldn't kill him.

Any questions about how she was enjoying the holiday met with a brick wall, so he chatted away cheerfully about his own life. He told Miss Howe about his two children: the twins, Rosie and Macken, and nodded proudly at their photographs stuck up on the dashboard of his van.

'They get their looks from their mother,' he said proudly. 'I hope they get their brains from her too! Not too many brains on their dad's side.'

'And were your parents stupid?' she asked. Her voice was cold, but it was the only time she seemed interested in a conversation.

'My mother wasn't. I never knew my father,' he said.

Most people would have said they were sorry, or that was a pity, but Miss Howe said nothing.

'Were your parents bright, Miss Howe?' Rigger asked.

She paused. It was as if she was deciding whether to answer or not. Eventually she said, 'No, not at all. My mother was a very unfit person to be anywhere near children. She left home when I was eleven and my father couldn't cope. He lost his job and died of drink.'

'Aw God, that was a poor start, Miss Howe. And did you have brothers and sisters to see you through?'

'One younger brother, but he didn't do well, I'm afraid. He made nothing of his life.'

'And there was no one to look out for him?'

Again a pause.

'No, there wasn't, as it happened.'

'Wasn't that very sad. And you were too young to do anything for the lad. I was lucky. I hit a bit of a rough spot but I had my mam always looking out for me, writing to me every week even when I got sent to the reform school. She tried her best for me, even if it took coming here to sort me out properly. I'd fallen behind on the old reading and writing, you see. It took me a while to catch up. I didn't get any exams or anything, but I got my head together and everything.'

'Why didn't she make you do exams?'

'Ah, she knew I was never going to be a professor, Miss Howe. She worked all the time to put food on the table but still, it wasn't easy to see everyone else with money when I didn't have any.'

'Did you get into trouble again?' Miss Howe's lips were pursed as if she had expected him to go to the bad.

'I met all the fellows I used to know. They were all doing

well but not legit, if you know what I mean. They said it was dead easy and you couldn't get caught. But my uncle Nasey put the fear of God into me. He thought I should get a fresh start in the country. I didn't want that at all. I was afraid of cows and sheep, and it was very dull compared to Dublin. But my mam had lived here when she was young, and she said she had loved it.'

'Why did she leave then?' Miss Howe hated grey areas.

'She got into trouble, and the man wouldn't marry her.'

'And did she bring you back here?'

'No, she has never been back herself but she is coming. Soon, as it happens.'

The market was busy. Miss Howe watched as Rigger sold eggs and cheese made from goats' milk. He heaved bags of vegetables out of the back of his van and carried large amounts of meat back into it, ready for the freezer. He bought two little ducks, which he said would be pets for the children rather than food for Chicky's table.

He seemed to know everyone he met. People asked about Chicky Starr, about Rigger's children, about Orla. Then Rigger had to call on his wife's family and drop in some eggs and cheese. Miss Howe said she'd stay in the van.

'They'll offer me tea and apple tart,' he said.

'Well then, eat it and drink it, Rigger. Leave me to my thoughts.' She watched people looking out the window of the farmhouse, but she had no intention of going into a small, stuffy kitchen and making small talk with strangers.

As an outing it was hardly a success, but Chicky was grateful to Rigger.

'Did you learn anything about her?' she asked.

'A bit, but it was like the confessional of the van. She probably regrets having told me.'

'Let it rest, so,' said Chicky.

The following day, Miss Howe called on Carmel in Rigger's house at the end of the garden. Carmel, knowing of the situation, welcomed her more warmly than she might have if left to her own devices. She introduced Miss Howe to the babies, who smiled and burbled good-naturedly; together they went to see the rabbits, the tortoise and the new ducks, who were called Princess and Spud.

Miss Howe drank tea from a mug and refused to be drawn into giving any praise for Stone House or for the holiday in general. Carmel struggled on, even when Miss Howe lectured her on the merits of learning poetry by rote.

Suddenly Miss Howe asked to look through what books Carmel and Rigger had in their library.

'We're not really the kind of people who'd have a library,' Carmel began.

'Well then, what a poor example you will be giving your children,' Miss Howe snapped.

'We will do the best we can.'

'Not if you have no dictionary, no atlas, no poetry books. How are they going to see the point of learning if there is no sign of learning in the home?'

'They'll go to school,' Carmel said defensively.

'Yes, that's it, leave everything to the school, and then blame them when things go wrong.'

Miss Howe's tone was hectoring. It was as if she were speaking to a disobedient child in her school rather than a kindly woman who had tried to help her to enjoy her holiday.

'We wouldn't blame the school; we're not like that.'

'But what have you to offer them? What is the point in anything unless the next generation get a good grounding and

302

a proper start? You don't want them ending up uneducated and in a reform school like your husband.'

Carmel could take it no longer.

'I'm sorry, Miss Howe, but I cannot have you insult my husband like this. If he told you about his past, and he must have because Chicky wouldn't have told you, then he did so in confidence, not to have it hurled back at us in accusation.' Carmel was aware that her voice was sounding shrill, but she couldn't help herself. What was wrong with this woman?

'I'm sorry but I'm going to have to ask you to leave. Now. I'm too upset, and I'll say something I might regret. I know nothing about you or your life and why you are so horrible to everyone, but someone should have shouted stop long, long, long ago.'

Without warning, Miss Howe's face crumpled. Suddenly, she put her head down on the table and cried so hard her whole body shook.

Carmel was astonished. For a moment, she didn't know what to do, but then she tried to put a comforting hand round Miss Howe's shoulder.

Stiffly, Miss Howe brushed it aside. There were two spots of red on her long, pale face.

Carmel made a fresh pot of tea and then sat down in front of her unwanted guest and gazed at her in silence.

Slowly, hesitantly at first, Miss Howe started to talk.

'It was 1963. I was eleven; Martin was eight. There were just the two of us. President Kennedy came to Ireland that year, and we all went out to line the route to see him.'

This was all unreal, Miss Howe talking about her private life fifty years ago.

'I remembered that we hadn't locked the downstairs windows at home. That was my job. The house was empty. Dad was at work, and my mother was going to her sister's and they were very strict about locking up. So even though I didn't want to, I had to leave the grand place I had and run home. In the house I heard noises like someone was being hurt, so I ran upstairs and my mother and a man were on the bed, naked. I thought he was killing her and I tried to drag him away . . . and then my mother went down on her knees to me and begged me not to tell my father. She said she'd be good to me for the rest of my life if I would keep this little secret between us, and the man was getting dressed and she kept saying, "Don't go, Larry. Nell understands. She's a big, grown-up girl of eleven. She knows what to do." And I ran out of the house and I telephoned my dad at work and said to come back quick because a man called Larry was hurting my mother and she wanted me to keep it a secret and he came home and . . .'

'You were only a child,' Carmel said soothingly.

'No, I knew. I knew what she was doing was wrong and that she had to be punished. I wasn't going to be part of any secrets. I *wanted* her to be punished. I didn't know Larry was Dad's great friend. But even if I had known, I'd still have told. It was wrong, you see.'

'And what did your father do?'

'We never knew, but when Martin and I got back from waving at President Kennedy, our mother was gone and never came back again.'

'Where did she go?' Carmel tried to keep the horror out of her voice.

'We never heard, and Dad looked after us but he was no good and then he took to drink. And he kept thanking me for exposing his whore of a wife and he would hit Martin over nothing. And Martin got in with a tough crowd at school and did no study whatsoever. I just put my hands over my ears and studied all the hours God sent. I got scholarships all the way and when my father died of drink, I managed on my own. Martin said I'd ruined his life twice. First I'd sent his mother away and now I'd lost him his father.'

'And he never forgave you?'

'No. He made nothing of himself. I haven't seen him for years. He rang the school not long ago, I don't know why. I don't want to see him again.'

'So he has not been part of your life since then?' Carmel asked sadly. The best she could hope for was to escape from this situation before she heard any more; already she knew that Miss Howe would never forgive herself for the loss of self-control, nor would she forgive Carmel. She must have looked anxious to end the conversation because Miss Howe spotted it.

'All right, so you want me to leave now. I'll leave. I don't care!'

Carmel reached out to shake her hand. 'I will bid you farewell, and wish you well in the future.'

'You will bid me farewell, *bid me farewell*, no less,' Miss Howe sneered. 'What a great line of clichés you will teach those unfortunate children. I weep for them and for their future.'

'Then go and weep over them. We will love them and look after them always and give them a great life,' Carmel said sadly.

'I suppose you and your husband will spread this all over the country before the night is out,' said Miss Howe bitterly.

'No, Miss Howe, that is not how we behave. Rigger and I are people of dignity and decency, not of gossip and accusations. What you have told me is your business and will go no further.'

As Miss Howe left, Carmel sat at the kitchen table shaking. Rigger would be furious; Chicky would be annoyed. *Why* couldn't she have held on to her temper? Miss Howe would never forgive her for knowing about her past.

'I don't want that Miss Howe in our house again,' she told Rigger when he came home. 'She said we were ignorant parents, and that she wept for Rosie and Macken.'

'Well, she's the only one who does,' Rigger said. 'Everyone else is delighted with them. And who the hell cares what Miss Howe says?'

Carmel smiled at him. It was quite true. She would comb her hair and they would go for a walk on the beach; they would walk along the damp sand and gather shells as the salt air stung their faces. They would give their son and daughter the best life they could.

Later that day, Rigger whispered to Chicky that it was only fair to warn her that words had been exchanged between Carmel and Miss Howe.

'Don't worry,' Chicky said. 'She was never likely to get us any business. She's just told me she's going back to Dublin tonight. In a while she will be gone and out of our lives. Tell Carmel not to give it a second thought.'

'You're great, Chicky.'

'No, I'm not. I'm lucky. So are you. Miss Howe was not.'

'We made a bit of our own luck.'

'Perhaps, but we listened when people tried to help us. She didn't.'

Before dinner, Chicky carried Miss Howe's small case to the van.

'I hope *some* of it was to your liking, Miss Howe,' she said. 'Perhaps when the weather is better, you might come back to us again?' Chicky was unfailingly courteous.

'I don't think so,' Miss Howe responded. 'It's not really my kind of holiday. I spent too much of my life talking to people. I find it quite stressful.'

'Well, you'll be glad to get back to the peace and quiet of your own place,' Chicky said.

'Yes, in a way.'

The woman was brutally honest. It was her failing.

'Did you discover anything here? People often say they do.'

'I discovered that life is very unfair and that there's nothing we can do about it. Don't you agree, Mrs Starr?'

'Not entirely, but you do have a point.'

Miss Howe nodded, satisfied. She had spread a little gloom even as she left. She would sit alone on the train back to Dublin and then get the bus back to her lonely house. She looked straight ahead as Rigger drove her to the railway station.

Freda

When Freda O'Donovan was ten, Mrs Scully, one of her mother's friends, read everyone's palms at a tea party. Mrs Scully saw good fortune and many children and long, happy marriages ahead for everyone. She saw foreign travel and small inheritances from unexpected quarters. They were all delighted with her, and it was a very successful party.

'Can you tell my future too?' Freda had asked.

Mrs Scully studied the small hand carefully. She saw a tall, handsome man, marriage and three delightful children. She saw holidays abroad – did Freda think she might like skiing? 'And you will live happily ever after,' she said, smiling down at Freda.

There was a pause. After what seemed a long time, Freda sighed. Although her mother seemed pleased about what she was hearing, Freda was confused. She just knew that none of it was true.

'I want to know what's going to happen,' she insisted, and she started to cry.

'Whatever's the matter? It's a good future,' said her mother, pleading with her daughter not to make a fuss about silly fortune-telling.

But Freda wouldn't listen and just cried harder. She was having no part of this prediction. It just wasn't right. She knew. Sometimes, she thought she knew what was going to happen, though she had already learned to keep quiet about it.

She didn't see a husband and three children. And she certainly didn't see herself living happily ever after. She cried all the more.

Freda's mother just didn't understand why Freda was so upset. Never had she regretted anything as much as persuading Mrs Scully to tell a child's fortune, and she would make sure it never happened again.

Mrs Scully wasn't invited to tell fortunes after that. And Freda never told anyone what she saw about the future.

Life at home was quiet and a bit frugal for Freda and her two older sisters. Her father died young, and there was no money for luxuries like central heating or foreign holidays. Mam worked in a dry cleaner's, and Freda had a very undramatic time at school, where she was bright and worked hard and got scholarships. She had her heart set on becoming a librarian; her best friend, Lane, wanted to work in theatre. The two were inseparable.

Freda couldn't remember when she got the first inkling that she might have some unusual insights. It was hard to describe them. The word 'feelings' didn't quite cover them because they were more vivid than that. Nor did she recall when it had been that she realised not everyone had the same insights; but over the years, she had learned not to talk about them to anyone. It always upset people when she mentioned anything, and so she had kept quiet; she didn't even talk to Lane about it.

There was no passionate love life: as a student, Freda went to clubs and bars and met fellows but there was nothing there that made her heart race. Mam was inclined to be overcurious about Freda's private life, and yet at the same time disappointed to hear that there was no love interest at all.

Freda loved books, and felt she had everything she ever wanted when she got her library certificate and was lucky to find a place as an assistant at the local library. Her sisters, though, were dismissive about her lack of love.

'Well, of course you can't find a fellow. What do you have to talk about except books,' Martha said.

'You could have bettered yourself if you had tried,' Laura had sniffed.

Freda looked very defeated, and her sisters felt remorseful.

'It's not as if you're a *total* failure,' Martha said encouragingly. She had a very stormy relationship with a young man called Wayne, and was not predisposed to believe the best of men.

'You did get taken on as a library assistant, and now you could earn a living anywhere.' Laura was grudging but fair. She was going out with a very pompous banker called Philip, to whom style and reputation meant everything.

Theirs was not neutral advice.

It was during the run-up to Christmas that Freda got another of her 'feelings'. They were having a family lunch to plan the Christmas festivities. Freda was coming for the day for sure, but Laura would be going to Philip's parents' big Christmas Eve do. Martha was very irate because Wayne would make no plans. What kind of person made no plans for Christmas?

Their mother edged the conversation back to the turkey. They would have their Christmas lunch at three p.m. with whoever wanted to join them, and that would be fine.

Laura fidgeted; she had something she wanted to share. She wasn't absolutely certain but she thought that Philip was going to propose to her on Christmas Eve. He had been very vague about his parents' party. Normally he put a lot of store by these events, and would tell her in advance who everyone was. No, there was something much bigger afoot. Laura was pink with excitement.

And totally unexpectedly Freda knew, she didn't just suspect but she *knew* that Philip was going to break off his relationship with Laura before Christmas; he was going to tell her that he was expecting a child with someone else. It was as clear as if she had seen a newspaper headline announcing it, and Freda felt herself go pale.

'Well, say something!' Laura was annoyed that her huge news and confidence was not meeting with any reaction.

'That would be wonderful,' her mother said.

'Lucky you,' Martha said.

'Are you *sure?*' Freda blurted out.

'No, of course I'm not sure. Now I'm sorry I told you. You're just saying that because I dared to say you couldn't get a fellow of your own. It's just spite.'

'Did you and Philip ever talk about getting married?' Freda asked.

'No, but we talked about love. Leave it, Freda. What do you know about anything?'

'But you might have it wrong.'

'Oh, don't be such a sourpuss.'

'Are you going to be talking to him before the party?'

'Yes, I'm meeting him this evening. He's coming round to my flat at seven.'

Freda said nothing. Tonight was when he was going to tell her. It was there in her chest like indigestion all day, as if she had eaten something that she couldn't swallow properly. At nine o'clock she called her sister.

Laura's voice was unrecognisable.

'You knew all the time, didn't you? You *knew*, and you were laughing at me. Well, are you happy now?'

'I didn't know, honestly,' Freda begged.

'I hate you for knowing. I'll never forgive you!' Laura said.

In the weeks and months that followed, Laura was very cold towards Freda. She cried when Philip's engagement was announced on Christmas Eve: his marriage to a girl called Lucy would take place in January.

Martha said that Laura would never believe to her dying day that Freda had not known about Lucy way in advance. There was no other explanation.

'I got a feeling, that's all,' Freda admitted.

'Some feeling!' Martha sniffed. 'If you ever get a *feeling* about me and Wayne just let me know, will you?'

'I don't think I'll ever let anyone know about a feeling ever again,' Freda said fervently.

The Friends of Finn Road Library will hold their first meeting on Thursday September 12th on these premises at 6.30 p.m. All are welcome, and we hope to have ideas and suggestions about what you want from your Library.

Freda knew within minutes of printing out the notice in the library that all was not well. It didn't take a psychic to see it: Miss Duffy's face was stern with disapproval, peering over her shoulder. This Library did not need Friends, the look said. It was not a dating agency. It was a place where people came to borrow books and, even more importantly, to return them. This kind of thing had no place in a library. It was, to use the worst criticism possible, *quite inappropriate.*

Freda fixed a smile very firmly on to her face. In advance, she had tied her long dark curly hair back with a ribbon to make herself look more serious in preparation for this encounter. This was a time to look businesslike. It most definitely was not the time to get into a serious battle. And if she lost, then she would just wait and try again.

She must never let Miss Duffy know how very determined she was to open up the library to the community, to bring in those who had never crossed its threshold. Freda wanted passionately to make those who *did* come in feel welcome and part of it all. Miss Duffy came from a different era, a time that believed people were lucky to have a library in their area, and should want no more than that.

'Miss Duffy, you remember you telling me when I applied to work here that part of our role was to bring more people in . . . ?'

'As library users, yes, but not as *Friends.*' Miss Duffy managed to use the word as a term of abuse.

Freda wondered had Miss Duffy always been like this, or had there ever been a time when she had hopes and dreams for this fusty old building.

'If they sort of thought of themselves as Friends, they might do a lot more to help,' Freda said hopefully. 'They might help with fundraising, or getting authors to donate books . . . Lots of things.'

'I suppose, as you say, that it can't do any harm. But where will we get seating for them all if they *do* come?'

'My friend Lane has lots of fold-up chairs in her theatre. She won't need them that night.'

'Oh, the theatre, yes.' Miss Duffy's interest in the small experimental playhouse down the street was minimal.

Freda waited. She couldn't put the notice on the board until she had Miss Duffy's agreement; she was nearly there, but not quite.

'I'd be happy to sort of run the meeting, I mean, I'd sort of introduce you as the Librarian, and then when you had spoken I could throw it open to them . . . the Friends, you know.' Freda held her breath.

Miss Duffy cleared her throat. 'Well, seeing as you're so keen on it, then why not put up that notice and let's see what happens.'

Freda began to breathe properly again. She fixed the paper to the notice board. She forced herself to move slowly and not to show her excitement at having won. When she was quite sure that Miss Duffy was safely installed at her desk, Freda took out her mobile phone and called her friend Lane.

'Lane, it's me, I have to speak very quietly.'

'And so you should. It *is* a library that you work in,' Lane said sternly.

'I got the Friends idea past Miss Duffy. We're in. It's going to happen!'

Halfway down the street, Lane paused in the middle of writing begging letters for support of her little theatre.

'Fantastic, well done Freda! The killer librarian.'

'No, don't even *say* that, it could be such a disaster. Nobody might turn up!' Freda was delighted that she had got this far, and yet terrified that it would all collapse on her.

'We'll get them in somehow. I'll get all our team here to go, and we can put up a notice about the meeting and pull in our audience as well. Listen, will we go for lunch to celebrate?' Lane was eager to seize the moment.

'No, Lane, I can't, no time. I have work to do on the budget allocations.' Imagine – people thought there was nothing to do in a library except stand around! 'But we're meeting at Aunt Eva's tonight as planned, aren't we?'

Eva O'Donovan was pleased that Freda and Lane were coming to supper. It meant that she had to galvanise herself and get into the day. First she must finish 'Feathers', her weekly birdwatching column in the newspaper. Eva had found that if she was very reliable about getting her copy in early, typing it neatly into her laptop, she could get away with outrageous views.

Then she must find something in the freezer that those girls could eat. They never had a proper lunch and were always hungry. Besides, she didn't want them reeling around after a few Alabama Slammers. She studied the contents of her freezer with interest.

There was a sort of fish and tomato bake. She would put that in the oven when they arrived with some fresh tomato and basil. She defrosted some French bread. Nothing to it; people made such a fuss about cooking when all it took was a bit of forward thinking.

When she had pressed Send on her article about the great flocks of waxwings that had come in from Northern Europe, then she would choose a colourful stole and a hat and would lay out all the drinks ingredients on her little cocktail table. This was the best part of the day.

Chestnut Grove was a house that would have suited nobody except Eva: it was in poor repair with a wild, rambling garden, very shaky plumbing and unreliable electrical works. She really couldn't afford the cost of maintaining it properly, and it might have seemed sensible to sell the place – but when had Eva ever done the sensible thing? Besides, the garden was full of birds that nested there regularly and were great material for her column.

The walls of her study were covered with pictures of birds and reports from various conservancy and birdwatching groups around the country. There were shelves full of magazines and publications. Eva's laptop computer was there, half buried in papers. In this room, as in every room in the house, there was a divan bed ready to be used at a moment's notice if someone wanted to stay overnight. And someone often did.

There were clothes hanging in every room; on almost every wall there were hangers holding colourful, inexpensive dresses, often with a matching stole or hat. Eva would pick them up at markets, car-boot sales or closing-down sales. She had never bought a normal dress in what might be called a normal shop. Eva found the price of designer clothes so impossible to understand that she had refused to think about it any more.

What were women *doing*, allowing themselves to be sucked into a world of labels and trends and the artificial demands of style? Eva couldn't begin to fathom it. She had only two rules of style – easy-care and brightly coloured – and was perfectly well dressed for every occasion.

Eva took out her highball glasses and lined up the Southern Comfort, amaretto liqueur and sloe gin. She had a very well-stocked bar but drank little herself. For Eva, the serving and making of cocktails was all in the preparation, the theatrics and the faint whiff of decadence.

Freda and Lane let themselves in through the back gate of Chestnut Grove and walked through the large sprawling garden. There were no formal flower beds, no lawns, no cultivated patios or terraces; instead it was a mass of bushes and brambles ready to trip the unwary in the dark. Here and there, some late roses peeped through. But mainly it looked like a site which was going to be cleaned up for a makeover on television.

'It's so different to my parents' garden,' Lane said, avoiding some low-hanging branches filled with vicious thorns. 'Their garden looks as if it's auditioning for some prize all the time.'

'Still, they do have it in great shape. You wouldn't put your life at risk like here,' Freda said.

'Yes, but Dad isn't allowed to have his vegetables anywhere that they can be seen. What would the neighbours say if they saw drills of potatoes and broad beans?'

As they reached the house, Eva ran to meet them. She was wearing a dark orange-coloured kaftan and had tied her hair up in a scarf of the same material. She looked like a very exotic bird that you might see in the aviary at the zoo. She could have been heading out for a Moroccan wedding, a fancy-dress party or the opening of an art gallery.

'Isn't the garden just wonderful right now?' she cried.

Wonderful wasn't the first word Freda and Lane would have chosen to describe the great wilderness they had just ploughed their way across, but it was impossible not to get caught up in Eva's enthusiasm.

'It's got lovely bits of colour in it, certainly,' Lane said.

'Just the way the branches look against the sky, that's what I love.' Eva guided them into the front room and began to mix the cocktail.

'Here's to the library, Freda my dear, and to all the many, many Friends waiting to join in its celebration.'

She was so genuinely delighted that Freda felt choked.

Nobody else except Lane and Aunt Eva would understand and care that she had made this great step. How lucky she was to have them. Most people had nobody to share excitements and celebrate with.

The cocktail nearly took the roof off her head. Freda placed it down carefully. Eva didn't expect you to knock the drink back in one go; she liked you to appreciate its different flavours. There must be about five things in this, Freda thought, all of them alcoholic except for the orange juice. She treated it with great respect.

Eva wanted every detail of the new scheme in the library. Was Miss Duffy grudging? Was she hostile? Had she given in with a bad grace? What did Eva want the Friends to do, once she had assembled them?

She was so eager and enthusiastic that Freda and Lane felt dull and slow in comparison. If Eva had been running the library, there might be fairy lights around it, and music blaring from inside. She could have set up a cocktail bar in the foyer. Her life was like her house – a colourful fantasy where anything was possible if you wanted it badly enough.

Miss Duffy was dealing with people who wanted to be Friends of the Library, and she was not dealing with them very well. She handed them the leaflet that Freda had prepared and had said there was a welcome for everyone at the Friends' meeting, but she was vague when people asked what it was going to involve.

Some people with anxious faces asked would there be money involved, like an admission fee, or a collection. No, nothing like that, Miss Duffy said. But then she wondered. Had Freda suggested there might be a fundraising aspect?

A man asked would there be advice about what books they

should read. Miss Duffy didn't know. Two girls asked would there be an entrance test, or could anyone at all come? Miss Duffy said there was no test, but she knew she had frowned at the expression 'anyone at all'.

A nervous young man arrived, saying he had written a lot of poems which had won prizes when he was at school, and wondered would there be a chance that he could give a reading. He was shy and awkward and kept looking as if Miss Duffy was going to order him off the premises for such a suggestion.

Miss Duffy was starting to feel it was all a bad idea.

'Oh, *there* you are, Miss O'Donovan,' she cried, even though Freda was over half an hour early.

Freda looked at her watch anxiously.

'It's just there were so many enquiries about this Friends business, it's beginning to upset our routine.'

Freda's face lit up. 'I am sorry, Miss Duffy, but isn't that great news! It means that people *are* interested.' Freda had hung up her coat and was down to work at once.

Miss Duffy relented. It was hard not to be pleased with this attitude, and even though the silly girl was inviting more enquiries, more trouble and distraction on herself, she seemed perfectly happy to do the work associated with it.

'Did you have a good weekend, Miss O'Donovan?' she asked, to show that her irritation was not serious.

Freda looked up at her, surprised. She smiled and said that it had been very good but she was happy to be back here in Finn Road. It had been the right answer.

Miss Duffy didn't want any details, only a sense of commitment.

Freda went through the list of enquiries: she telephoned the man who wondered would there be advice about what books to read and said yes, there would if people wanted it. She called the girls asking was there an entrance examination, and she said it was going to be a fun evening – they should bring all their friends. She invited the young poet, whose name was Lionel, to come in and see her.

She ignored the nagging feeling that something really important was about to happen.

The next meeting of the Friends of Finn Road Library will be on the history of this area, and admission is free. Please bring photos and stories. All are welcome!

They would be talking about the Friends evening for days. It had been such a success on so many levels despite the rain that night. Even Miss Duffy was enthusiastic.

They had all come: the young poet, Lionel, had read some beautiful poems about mute swans. He was elated at the response, even more so when Freda introduced him to her aunt Eva. The author of 'Feathers', no less!

Miss Duffy had been suspicious when around half a dozen young girls had turned up, but they had turned out to be full of suggestions for reading groups.

'I must say, I was surprised that they held us in such esteem,' she said the very next day. Lane and Freda had cleared the place up perfectly and had returned the chairs to the theatre. There was nothing that Miss Duffy could complain about, so instead she decided to be pleased, gratified even.

Freda had long ago decided that she would accept no credit for it all, even though she would have had to take all the blame if it had turned out badly.

'It's only what you deserve,' Freda said, as if it had all been

Miss Duffy's idea. 'You have been here for years building this place up; it's only right they should honour you and say how much the library means to them.'

Miss Duffy accepted it all graciously as her due.

That was good: it left Freda time to get on with things. There was so much to organise in an ordinary working day. They would have to check the Issue, the list of items currently out on loan. Then there were the notes to borrowers of books that were overdue. They would go through the Issue looking for requested items and report on their status. Then today there was the Stock Selection meeting, where they all sat down with Miss Duffy to choose what new titles they could order. They would examine books sent to them as approval copies, and look at notes from the book magazines as well. There was little enough time to think about this Friends meeting, never mind organise the next one. It was curious that she felt so deflated. Whatever it was she had been so sure was going to happen just hadn't materialised.

Miss Duffy was surprised to see the great bunch of very expensive flowers that had been delivered. The message was simple. *I am already a Friend of the Library . . . Now I want to be a Friend of the Librarian.* The evening had been a success, of course, but who would have sent these as a thank you? The only person that ever sent flowers to Miss Duffy was her sister, and she was more of a potted violet sort of person. So who could have sent her this bouquet? She admired the flowers once more. Miss O'Donovan might arrange them for her if they could find a big enough vase.

Freda, of course, found a vase. She went into the store room and brought out a huge glass jar. Those flowers must have cost a fortune. Who on earth would have sent them?

Miss Duffy was vague, and said they were from a friend. She looked at her reflection in the glass doors and patted her hair several times. There was a thoughtful look in her eye.

Freda gave up.

When she was separating the long roses from the green ferns to arrange them better, she found the card that had come with the flowers.

. . . *Now I want to be a Friend of the Librarian.* They were for her. She realised it with a shock that was almost physical. But who was it? And what did he mean? And why had he not put Freda's name on them, instead of letting Miss Duffy think they were for her? She felt everything slowing down and becoming slightly unreal. There were far too many questions. She wanted to be alone to think about why she felt so uneasy and slightly shaky.

Lane had been on the phone to Eva to ask her what colour were a puffin's legs.

Eva hadn't hesitated. 'Orange,' she said. 'Why?'

'And the beak? We're painting scenery. Tell me about the beak, I know the shape and everything but what colour is it?'

'Blue, yellow and orange. But you have to get the colours in the right order.'

'I don't mean an exotic puffin like in an aviary, I mean just an Irish puffin.'

'That's it, that's a home-grown puffin. Come into the library – I'm just on my way there myself. I'll point you to the books.'

'I think I'd better. Birds with a blue, yellow and orange beak! You'd have to be on something very attitude-changing to see that in Ireland.'

They met on the steps.

'We're painting these huge backdrops for the next production,' she explained. 'I need to be sure about the puffins' beak and legs. Are they really all colours of the rainbow, or were you having me on?'

'Beaks have three colours, legs are orange – mostly during the breeding season. Much duller in winter,' Eva confirmed.

'Merciful God, in Ireland, birds like that!'

'Well, if you ever came with us over to the Atlantic coast, you'd see them for yourself, whole colonies of them,' Eva said reprovingly. 'There's a place called Stoneybridge. You should come along.'

And as they went in, they saw Freda at the counter talking to someone. She was pointing at a brochure and Freda was laughing and shaking her head. Her eyes were bright and she looked so young, so animated and alive in this old, grey building. Miss Duffy wore her usual navy wool cardigan with a small white lace collar; she was demure and full of gravitas. Freda in contrast wore a red shirt over black trousers. She had her black curly hair tied back with a big red ribbon. She looked like a colourful flower in the middle of it all, Lane thought. No wonder they were all queuing up to talk to her.

Waiting next in line was a man in a cashmere scarf and a very well-cut overcoat. He was looking at Freda intently.

Lane held back suddenly. She didn't know why, but she felt faintly uneasy.

'What is it?' Eva asked.

'That man, waiting to speak to Freda,' Lane whispered.

'I can't see him,' Eva complained.

'Come this way, so. You'll see him then and you won't distract her.'

They both saw the way Freda was looking at the man who

had approached her. It was just too far to hear what she was saying but her face had changed completely.

Whoever he was, he was significant.

Lane disliked him on sight.

'Did you like my flowers?'

'The ones for Miss Duffy, the Librarian? They're lovely. Shall I get her for you?'

He paused to smell one of the roses. 'They were for you, Freda.' He was very good-looking, and there was such warmth in his smile.

She couldn't help smiling back, though if Freda had ever known how to flirt she had forgotten the technique.

'You weren't at the Friends evening,' she said. 'I'm sure I'd have remembered you.'

'Oh but I was here. I didn't know about the meeting, I just came in when the rain came on. I stood at the back, over there.' He pointed to a pillar beside the back door.

'You didn't sit down?'

'No, I only wanted to miss the worst of the downpour, and I thought a talk in the library would be boring.'

'And was it?' She felt as if she were probing a sore tooth.

'No, Freda, it was a great evening, there was warmth and enthusiasm and hope all here in this very room. That's why I stayed.'

This was exactly what she had felt. She thought that people had been given some kind of lifeline that night. They were dying for something new, something to get involved in; they were all so anxious to help. She looked at him wordlessly.

'I came to ask you to have dinner with me.' She saw his neck redden slightly. Suddenly he looked uncertain. 'I mean, it doesn't have to be dinner, it could be a walk, a coffee, a movie, anything you like. Oh – no, wait – my name is Mark. Mark Malone. Will you come out with me?'

'Dinner would be nice . . .' she heard herself say.

'Good. Can I book somewhere tonight?'

Freda didn't trust herself to speak at first. 'Well, yes, tonight is good,' she said eventually.

'Where would you like to go?'

'I don't know . . . anywhere. I like Ennio's down on the quays, I go there with my friends sometimes for a treat.'

'Well, I don't want to muscle in on your special place for you and your friends. What about Quentins, that's good too, isn't it? Is eight OK with you?'

'Eight o'clock it is,' Freda said.

He grinned, and then ostentatiously took her hand and kissed it.

When he had gone, Freda raised her hand to her cheek and held it there. She didn't know it but she was being watched by her aunt Eva, her friend Lane, Miss Duffy, Lionel the poet and a young girl who happened to be looking for a job as a cleaner.

They all saw Freda's face as she moved her hand slowly to her lips. The hand that the man had kissed. Something momentous had just happened in front of their eyes.

The rest of the day passed. Somehow.

Lane said, 'Have you anything to tell me?'

Freda had asked, 'About puffins?'

'No, about men coming in and kissing your hand.'

Tomorrow, Freda had promised.

He was already there when Freda went into Quentins. He wore a dark grey suit and a crisp white shirt. He was very

325

handsome. He grinned and stood up to welcome her as Brenda, the elegant owner and manager, led Freda to the table.

'I thought you might like a glass of champagne, but I didn't order for you,' he began.

'Right on both counts,' Freda said, smiling. 'I would indeed like a glass of champagne, but thank you for not assuming.'

'I wouldn't do that, I hope,' he said. 'I'm so pleased to see you – you look terrific,' he said.

'Thank you,' she said simply.

'Well you do, you are very beautiful, but that's not just why I asked you to dinner.'

'Why did you ask me?' she genuinely wanted to know.

'Because I can't get you out of my mind. I loved what you said about that man's poetry, the elegant sadness of it. Someone else would have taken twice as many words to say it. And then you got all excited about those schoolgirls and their reading groups; you enthused them all and you have so much energy, so much life radiating from you. Since the first moment I saw you in the library I noticed it; I see it here. I wanted to be part of it. That's all.'

'I don't know what to say. I've been lucky; I'm very happy in my job, and life and everything . . .'

'And are you happy to be here? Now?'

'Very,' Freda said.

They talked easily.

He wanted to know everything about her. Her school, her college, the home she lived in with her parents and sisters. How she had got her job at Finn Road Library. Her little flat at the top of a big Victorian house. Her eccentric aunt who wrote the long-running 'Feathers' column in the newspaper, and took Freda on birdwatching outings.

326

'Sounds like a lark,' he said solemnly.

'I can't top that,' she snorted. 'It's your tern again.' And they both collapsed laughing.

He seemed interested in every single thing she had ever done in her life. The conversation moved towards holidays, and whether it was worth all the hassle of going away to the sun just for one week, or whether you had to be an athlete to go skiing. Wasn't that amazing – he had been to the very same Greek island, wasn't the world a very small place? They liked the same movies, the same songs. He had even read some of Freda's favourite books.

Freda asked him about his life too. After all, it was like a blind date; they knew nothing about each other, yet here they were, sitting having dinner in one of Dublin's best restaurants. He had been brought up in England, in an Irish family. His parents still lived there, and his brother. No, he didn't see much of them, he said sadly. He shrugged it off, but Freda could see that it hurt him.

He had been to university in England, studied marketing and economics but it wasn't nearly as important as all he had learned through his experience in the leisure industry. He had been in car hire, in yachting charter, in mass catering, all the time learning about what made business tick. He had worked in London, New York and now Dublin; even though he had come here as a child on holidays it was still a new city to him. He was now working for a leisure group that was going to invest in Holly's Hotel; they wanted to develop it into a major leisure complex.

'I'm sure it all sounds dull to you but it's really exciting, and it's not all about money,' he said eagerly. 'And I would love to know more about the history of the area. You could be very helpful.'

He hadn't found a proper place for himself yet, so he just had a room in the hotel. It was good to be on the premises, as it meant he could see what kind of business the place was. It was such a personal hideaway, the kind of place people believed they had actually discovered for themselves. The staff remembered your name, they seemed eager for you to enjoy the experience of being there. No wonder they were successful.

On the day of the rainstorm, he'd been in a meeting with the developers which had run late, and he'd been dashing along Finn Road just as the downpour was at its worst. It was only a happy accident, pure chance that he'd seen the library was open and decided to take shelter for a while. That's when he'd spotted her. Suppose he'd just gone on down the street? Suppose the meeting had ended on time and he'd got away before it had started raining?

'You and I might never have met.' He laughed, and gave a mock shiver to think this could have been on the cards.

Freda felt her shoulders relax. She loved Holly's Hotel just as it was; it was a great place for a celebration, and the idea of it being turned into a 'leisure complex' sounded awful. But it didn't matter by what chance she had been introduced to this exciting man, who for some impossible-to-understand reason seemed to fancy her greatly. She gave a sigh of pure pleasure.

He smiled at her and her heart melted.

Freda hoped that he wouldn't want to come home with her. The flat was in a total mess, and there was all the business of it being a first date and being thought a slapper, and if he were going to come to her place she would need a week getting it ready. Suppose he suggested going to Holly's Hotel?

But he wouldn't, would he, he had too much class.

Or maybe he didn't want to all that much?

They were the last people to leave the restaurant. Quentins arranged a taxi for them. Mark said he would see her home. When the cab stopped, he got out and saw her to the door.

'Lovely place, as I would have expected,' he said, and he kissed her on each cheek and got back into the taxi.

Freda climbed the stairs and went into her little flat, which looked as if it had been ransacked by burglars but was actually just the way she'd left it. She sat on the side of her bed, not knowing whether to be relieved or disappointed that he hadn't come in.

When she had been telling him about the library, he had listened to every word as if she was the only person in the room. But what if he was that way with everyone? Did he really like her? Of course not, how could he? She was just a librarian; he was so smart and had travelled everywhere.

She felt suddenly lonely here tonight. She might get a cat to talk to.

Eva had advised her against it; she said that cats were the natural enemy of birds, and anyway, if you became fond of them it stopped you from travelling. Still, if she had a cat it might purr at her, be some kind of presence in this empty place, perched at the top of a big house.

She fell into a troubled sleep and dreamed over and over that she was trying to get on to a ferry but it kept leaving the shore before she could get on board.

'Come on, Freda, we don't *do* vague,' Lane said over coffee in the little theatre the next morning.

'I'm not being vague, I'm telling you every single detail of

the menu down to the chocolate shaped like a Q at the end.'
Freda was indignant.

'But what about *him*? Did you like him? Was he easy to talk to?'

'He was fine, very smooth, very charming. He's in what they call the "leisure industry . . ."'

Lane snorted in derision.

'. . . and he's here to discuss investing in Holly's. They want to do a major expansion.'

'Holly's doesn't need expanding. It's fine as it is. Did you . . . ?'

'No.'

'And did he want to . . . ?'

'Again, no. So now, does that answer every interrogation on the sexual front?' Freda wondered.

Lane looked hurt. 'We always tell, that's why I asked.'

'Well, I *have* told. Nothing, nada, zilch.'

'Ah yes, but will you tell when there *is* something to tell?' Lane speculated.

'We'll never know, will we?' Freda sounded more light-hearted than she felt.

'Suppose I were to warn you off this guy Mark,' Lane looked serious. She couldn't put a finger on what it was, but there was something about him that worried her. 'Suppose I said I didn't trust him. Suppose I said you don't know anything about him, that he's just spinning you a line. If I were to do that, would I lose you as a friend?'

'Nothing to warn me off – one bunch of roses which went to Miss Duffy, one dinner . . . hardly an affair.'

'Early days,' Lane said darkly. 'He'll be back. I feel sure of it.'

*

Joe Duggan, a man Freda had last met in college five years ago, rang to ask her to a party that night. Freda had no intention of going to a group of strangers with a fellow she barely remembered, but polite as always, she asked him what he was doing these days.

'Lecturing in technology, mainly to dummies,' he said. 'You know, people who are afraid of gadgets and who don't want to miss out. I'm not too bad at it, actually; I tell them machines are stupid and that calms them down.'

'Joe, I may have a great job for you. Can you come and see me in the library on Friday,' Freda said. This could be the next Friends meeting settled.

Perfect.

Miss Duffy had a face that would stop a clock.

'When you have quite finished organising your social life, Miss O'Donovan, I wonder can I ask you to help with the Library Fines? And there are several people waiting for your attention at the counter.'

The first in line at the counter was Mark Malone. He said nothing, just looked at her.

'Do you have any work to go to?' she asked him to keep the conversation light and to break his stare.

'I work very hard,' he said. 'Way into the night often, but I made time this morning to come and see you.'

'Thank you so much for dinner,' Freda said. 'I was going to write you a little note, in fact, to say how much I enjoyed it.'

'What would you have said?'

'That it was a very warm and generous evening and to thank you.' She kept an air of finality to the way she spoke, as if she thought it was a one-off and that she was just being grateful without regrets.

'You said you have a day off tomorrow,' he said.

Normally on her day off, Freda would do what she and Lane called the everyday business of living: she would bring her sheets and towels to the launderette, do some shopping at the supermarket, maybe persuade Lane to take a long lunch. Sometimes she went to an art exhibition or did window-shopping in the boutiques. She might tend her window boxes, filling them up with bulbs for the spring, and in the evening she might go to a wine bar with friends.

But not tomorrow. That would be a very different day.

Mark had wondered if Freda would like to go down to County Wicklow with him. He had to go to a meeting with Miss Holly, and maybe they could have lunch there. In the shower, Freda planned the day. They could go for a walk in the afternoon, then they would go home and she could get his supper ready. Maybe they would stay at Holly's. In any case, he would say she looked very beautiful. He would take her in his arms.

'We don't have to wait any longer,' he would say; or maybe, 'I wouldn't have been able to get through tonight without you.' Something. Anything. It didn't really matter.

She wondered what it would be like. She hoped she would be attractive enough for him. Please him properly. She wasn't very experienced, and certainly no one recently.

The last time must have been nearly two years ago when she had had a holiday romance, a lovely guy called Andy from Scotland who had promised to stay in touch and said he would come to Ireland to see her. But he didn't stay in touch and he hadn't come to Ireland. It hadn't been a big deal. Andy already had a life planned for himself: it involved banking, living near his parents and his married brothers, playing a lot of golf.

Freda didn't know why she was even thinking about Andy now, except to worry that she might not have been any good at it, which was possibly why he might not have kept in touch. Perhaps as a lover she had been useless. She had quite enjoyed it all herself, that magical summer holiday, and thought that Andy had too. But then, you never really knew.

It would have been lovely to have had some reassurance about that side of things. Freda smiled to herself wryly at the thought of telephoning Andy at his bank, years after the fling, and asking for reassurance about her performance.

But then Mark wasn't looking for some kind of sexual athlete. Was he? Women must have been throwing themselves at him since he was a teenager. She wished she knew more about him, and what he wanted.

And then, when she least expected it, Freda got one of her feelings. She saw as clearly as if it were an advertisement in an estate agent's catalogue a book-lined apartment with a living room and kitchenette, two big bedrooms and a study with an overflowing desk. There was a view of the sea from the window. At the door was a small woman with short blonde hair, reading glasses around her neck on a chain and a vague, worried smile.

She was saying, '*There* you are, darling. Good to have you home!' to whoever was coming in the door. But who was the woman? And who was she talking to? The breath left her body with a great rush, and she felt light-headed and as if her legs had turned to paper. Was it Mark?

*

It couldn't be. It was wrong, the *feeling* must be wrong. She hadn't seen a man, she hadn't seen who it was arriving at the door. It couldn't be Mark. It couldn't be.

Shaking, she got dressed and, hands still trembling, applied mascara and lipstick. She put up her hair, found her good boots and she was ready. She felt a shiver. She felt very glad she had told nobody about this date.

The shrill bell of the intercom buzzed. He was on the doorstep.

'I'll come straight down,' she said into the receiver.

He looked at her with great admiration as she came down the steps to the hall. 'You look so beautiful,' he said.

Freda still felt shaken. She wanted to make a jokey remark to take the intensity out of it all. She wasn't used to saying thank you and accepting such praise as almost her right. She said the first positive thing that came into her head.

'And you look very handsome, just terrific, actually.'

He threw his head back and laughed. 'Aren't you *so* kind to say that! Now, let's stop admiring each other and get into the car, out of the cold.' He held open the door of a dark green Mercedes.

The drive down to Wicklow passed in a blur. Freda could scarcely remember how they got there, what they talked about. All she could see was Mark's face as he concentrated on driving, as he smiled at her from time to time.

While Mark went to have his meeting with Miss Holly and her senior staff, Freda sat in the lounge by the fire in a big chintz-covered chair, a magazine unread on her lap, a cup of coffee untouched on a little table beside her. Instead, she looked into the flames and thought about what had been happening; and as she did so, from nowhere the pictures started forming in Freda's mind. She fought them back, closed her eyes and opened them but still the pictures were there. Mark was in a room with people who were shouting. Miss Holly was sitting in a corner, weeping. Mark was looking calm and dismissive; he was telling her something very unwelcome and frightening. Whatever it was, it was wrong, it was all wrong.

Shakily, she pushed the vision aside. It was nonsense; it didn't mean anything. She'd just dozed off and had a silly dream. She sighed, and again tried to rid herself of the images. But she felt dizzier and more confused.

Soon he was back.

'How did it go?' she asked.

'Don't ask. I'll tell you when we are well out of range. Let's go. You and I are free agents, nobody waiting for us; we don't have to be anywhere except where we want to be.'

'I have to be back. I open the library tomorrow, and I have to be in before eight.'

He smiled back. 'Right. We'll go for a meal, and no talk about work for either of us – is that a deal?'

'It's a deal,' Freda said.

In the car they were quiet; Freda studied his face but Mark looked relaxed and happy. Freda began to feel that it had just been a mad dream. As he helped her out of the car, he kissed her, and all through dinner she could think of nothing else.

That night, they made love for the first time.

The following night, they went to the cinema. Freda didn't even remember the film afterwards, just the sensation of sitting with her shoulder touching his. Later they went back to her flat.

On Friday he asked her to go to a concert but she had set up the meeting with Joe Duggan, the computer expert, and she hesitated. Mark's face clouded over and he looked so disappointed, she knew she had to do something.

She called Lane.

'I will do anything for you for the rest of my life. *Anything*. Scrub floors in your theatre . . .'

'Who do I have to kill?' Lane asked.

'No, it's this guy, Joe Duggan, who's going to give the talk next week. I can't meet him tonight at the library. Could *you* do it, tell him everything?'

'Freda. No.'

'I'm begging you on my knees.'

'I can't, I run a theatre. You're the librarian.'

'It's only an old talk; you know the kind of thing they want.'

There was a silence.

'Lane?'

'It's not like you, and it's *not* only an old talk. It's something you set up, and a lot of people are depending on you.'

'Never again, just this once! I'll tell Joe that I'll contact him on Monday morning.'

'And if I don't?'

'I don't know what I'll do.' There was a catch in Freda's voice.

'I think this is the shabbiest thing I have ever heard,' Lane said.

'But you'll do it.'

'Yes.'

'Thank you, Lane, from the bottom of my heart . . .' Freda began.

'Goodbye, Freda.'

Freda called Mark.

'Well?' he asked.

'I'm free this evening,' she said.

'I was so hoping you might be,' Mark said.

The concert was heaven and at dinner afterwards, he told her that there was no one like her. He said how much he admired her work, and even gave her some ideas for a Friends night; he wanted to spend all his time with her, and make up for lost time. She couldn't help herself: he was so sweet and caring, and she melted at his touch.

It was too sudden, too quick, she told herself. But then everyone had to meet somewhere and somehow. Would it have been any different if they had met at a dance, a club, in a crowded bar? But still she was nervous about letting herself go with the tide. But whenever he called, or they were together, she forgot all about her misgivings.

The Friends of the Library welcome all those who don't know a thing about computers but want to learn. Joe Duggan will be here on Friday night to help all ages who want to be part of the tech world.

When Mark suggested they go away for a weekend, she hesitated once again. He couldn't go away with her if he was married, it wouldn't be possible. But the dreams kept coming. The face of the woman with the short blonde hair would not go away. She just knew it was Mark the woman was welcoming, and she could see the wedding ring in the dream.

If he were married, what would he be telling his wife as he headed off to the Dublin mountains with Freda? Freda was very confused. But she wasn't about to give up the chance of such happiness.

When she called Lane to cover for her again with Joe, Lane

didn't have much to say. She listened to her friend and then agreed.

'For Joe's sake, not yours,' she added icily.

Freda felt bad for her friend, but then thought about her weekend with Mark. Mark needed Freda on many levels, that was obvious. He wanted her for company, for friendship and for support as well as for sex. He loved her; he told her so. The marriage could only be one of convenience, she was so sure of that.

Eva hoped that this romance would settle down soon so that Freda could concentrate on other things apart from Mark Malone. She did seem besotted with the fellow and in a way, Eva could understand why. He was such a charmer, such an enthusiast. In many ways very suited to Freda. But Eva thought they were also very different. Mark was tougher, and he was going to get there, wherever it was, taking no prisoners. Freda was happy with life the way it was now.

He had got off on the wrong foot with Lane, but that would sort itself out in time. Lane had taken against Mark in a big way; she complained that Freda had lost interest in every-thing – her work, her friends, her whole life. 'It's as if a sort of mist or fog or something settled on her,' she had said. 'He controls her every move.'

They'd met him a number of times now but Lane still didn't trust Mark.

Silly, foolish Agony Aunt, Eva told herself. Useless trying to work these things out logically, rationally. Still, it was a worry, all right. There was a possible storm gathering. Lane didn't like him and didn't trust him. He was the first man who had threatened such a solid friendship. Usually they encouraged each other about boyfriends and gave enthusiastic, supportive advice.

Freda would say that Lane had an army of brooding young men who fancied her. Lane would laugh, and say that these were all out-of-work actors; all they fancied was two weeks' work in her theatre. Lane said that she knew of at least three people who went in to that library just to talk to Freda rather than to open a book. They were always wanting to ask Freda out, but she never seemed to understand this and kept finding books for them instead . . .

This strong reaction both for and against Mark Malone had been so out of character for both girls.

Due to the success of Joe Duggan's 'Don't Fear Technology' lecture last week, the Friends of Finn Road Library have decided that there should be twice-weekly sessions on this topic.

Freda called to Eva to borrow a black beaded jacket. She had been invited to a drinks party at Holly's Hotel in a couple of weeks' time. Mark had gathered some journalists and tour operators for what he called a social drink. It was really part of his long-term plan to get the press on board over the plans for the hotel.

Eva had hoped Freda would stay for lunch.

'You see, Eva,' said Freda, guiltily, 'I don't really have all that much time . . . I have so many things to do just now.'

Eva looked at her directly.

'What, exactly?'

'Oh, you know, all the stuff at the library; this Friends thing has really taken off due to Joe Duggan, and they can't get enough of him.'

'No thanks to you, though.'

'What do you mean?' Freda was startled.

'Well, you weren't there to show him round the library, Lane and I did that. And then you took off for a weekend with Mark the actual night of his talk.'

'Yes.' Freda looked at the ground.

'So he had an elderly twitcher like myself, and the manager of an experimental theatre to help him set up. Lord knows what he would have been able to achieve if he'd had a real librarian on the case.'

'You were great, you and Lane, I thanked you, you did brilliantly.'

'You weren't there.' Eva was stern.

'Look, you know . . . you know the way things are.'

'No, I don't, actually. Why don't you come looking for woodpeckers with me? And why don't you ask Mark along too?'

'Thank you so much, Eva, but when I said I was busy, I really am. I have a few fences to mend, if you know what I mean.'

'I know what you mean.'

Freda knew Aunt Eva was right. As far as Lane was concerned, it was as if a curtain had fallen over their friendship. She would put on her polite face, which was more unsettling to Freda than her angry face. It was so distancing, so chilly.

Lane had not forgiven Freda for disappearing the night of Joe Duggan's talk.

To Freda, it was really most petty and unfair of Lane to take this attitude. Joe had been a huge success; he was going to have his own series. In all her years at the library, Freda had never taken any time off like this before. And this was not even real regular library hours: this was something she had arranged as a volunteer, for heaven's sake.

And Joe had understood. He had said that she was very kind to have arranged such a pleasant person to greet him. It wasn't as if she had abandoned him or anything.

Such a fuss over nothing.

Mark had to be in London for a few days, so Freda felt easy about inviting Lane and Eva to have dinner at Ennio's. She hoped that they would understand how she felt. It would be all right.

It was a happy evening as Freda, Lane and Eva sat in Ennio's restaurant eating pasta and catching up.

Eva was organising her next birdwatching trip to the West of Ireland. There was a new hotel opening in a couple of weeks' time, up on the cliffs above Stoneybridge. Perfect for birdwatchers. Eva was already planning her visit.

She paused dramatically and then proposed a toast. 'You two are not to have a fight,' she announced, 'I won't allow it. Especially over something as foolish as a man.'

By this stage, both Freda and Lane were laughing.

'You're such a stirrer, Eva, there's no row,' Freda said.

'I'd never fight with Freda,' Lane promised.

'Great, that's sorted, then.'

Lane and Freda looked at each other helplessly.

'My aunt, the drama queen!' Freda said.

'Whatever made her think that we were going to have a row?' Lane asked.

'My saying I love Mark Malone, you saying he is a shit . . . that might have given her food for thought.'

'I'll never say anything like that about him again. I just thought you would have wanted to be there for Joe and his talk. But as it happens, it has worked out – he has asked me out on a date, so I forgive you,' Lane said.

Freda leaned over and patted her on the wrist. And then, right in the middle of the meal, Freda was called to the phone. The waiter led her to a little desk which had the reservations book and handed her the phone.

'Hallo?' Freda had no idea who knew she was here.

'*Ciao, bella*,' the voice on the phone said.

'Mark!'

'Just wanted you to know I miss you, and it is quite ridiculous that I am at one boring dinner and you are at another when we could be together.'

'Mine's not a boring dinner, I told you – it's friends,' she said. 'And anyway, you're back tomorrow, aren't you?'

'No, sadly not. I have to stay on here. More meetings. It won't take much longer; I'll get away as early as I can.'

The smile vanished from her face. 'Oh no, but I've booked to have some time off!'

'Well, I won't make so many arrangements in future. Is that OK? Would you like me to cancel my business meetings?' He sounded angry.

'I'm sorry. I didn't mean anything.' Freda was confused.

There was a pause.

'All right,' he said eventually. 'I'm sorry, I'm under a lot of pressure here. We'll speak tomorrow. I'll know more then.'

'Tomorrow, then,' she agreed, shaken. And then as a thought just struck her, she asked, 'Mark, why didn't you call me on my mobile?'

'I didn't bring mine with me so I don't have the number,' he said smoothly. 'I remember you said Ennio's, so I looked it up in the book.'

'Tomorrow, then,' she said.

Back at the table, Lane asked her, 'Was that him?'

Freda smiled. 'It was, as it happens.'

'Why didn't he ring you on your mobile? Was he checking up to see if you were really where you'd said you'd be?'

Eva looked up sharply.

Lane's tone had been light, but Freda found herself feeling very tense. After all, she had asked Mark the very same question herself. But she would admit none of this to Lane.

'Oh, definitely, that's it, a martyr to jealousy he is,' she said with a very insincere little laugh.

'What's worrying you?' Eva asked.

'Nothing,' Freda said. 'He's just having to stay on in London.'

For the very first time since she had gone to work there, Freda didn't want to go in to the library. There were too many calls on her time. Lane still didn't understand Mark; even Eva had lost patience. They just didn't understand. Miss Duffy was being so demanding about categories. 'A misfiled book is a lost book,' was her great mantra.

There was that bossy woman who had complained that some book was sheer pornography and that she had mistakenly recommended it to her book club up in Chestnut Court. Someone else had thrown a tantrum about the lack of Zane Grey books. She needed to find Joe Duggan, and apologise again for not being at the library for his talks.

And she could deal with it all if she didn't feel so uneasy after their conversation the night before. She had dreamed about the blonde again, and now she was sure Mark was married. But she didn't care. He loved Freda. He told her so many times.

She straightened her shoulders and walked slowly up the steps that normally she took two at a time when she went into work.

A few days later, Eva invited Lane to come for lunch with her.

'There's a report of a great flock of Common Scoters over the other side of Howth, and there might be some rare ones among them.'

'Uncommon Scoters?' Lane suggested.

'Well, Velvet Scoters, they're called actually.'

'Velvet? Sounds good.'

'They're sea ducks, the males are all jet black with yellow bills, the females have white necks and dull grey bills. Winter visitors. Come with me in the car and we'll have a sandwich in a pub out that way,' Eva suggested.

'And what will I wear?'

'Nothing too bright that would alarm them. Don't know what the weather's doing but, you know, lots of waterproof anoraks and scarves and sweaters and maybe a backpack or lots of pockets.'

It was the best offer Lane had had. Freda was like a weasel, with Mark making plans and then cancelling them at the last moment; when he wasn't around, she just sat staring at her phone waiting for him to ring. Lane said she'd love the drive.

As they left the main roads behind and headed towards the sea, Eva pointed out the migrating birds newly arrived: flocks of white-fronted geese as well as the ducks, swans and wading birds that came down from the Arctic. Now they would have plenty of things to see.

Eva concentrated hard on the busy traffic.

'Will we go somewhere there's easy parking?' she suggested, and that was why they chose the dark wine bar near the sea.

Which was where they saw Mark Malone, who was meant to be in England at a conference.

He was sitting at a table over by the window. Opposite him was a blonde woman in jeans and a thick Aran sweater. Between them was a little girl. She looked very young and very happy. They were the perfect happy family, as if there was nobody but the three of them in the place.

Mark and the woman were feeding each other forkfuls of pasta and then laughing after each mouthful. The little girl was laughing at them gleefully. The three of them shared such affection and closeness, there was no doubt that they all belonged together.

Eva and Lane looked at them, stunned.

They were unable to back out of the restaurant before being seen. As Mark looked up and caught sight of them, his face froze into an angry mask.

Eva and Lane looked at each other and at exactly the same moment they both said, 'The bastard!' Then without another word they walked out, got into Eva's car and began to drive back to the city.

As they drove off, Lane asked, 'Do birds do that, you know, cheat all round them?'

'It's complicated.'

'I bet it is.'

'Do we say anything?' Eva wondered aloud.

'Of course we do. The question is, to which of them? To Freda or to Mark?'

'If we hadn't gone in there . . .' Eva began.

'That's no use – we *did* go in. And we saw him. She can't be made a fool of like this.'

'But it would humiliate her if we said—' Eva was protective.

345

'Well, it would humiliate her more if we didn't say,' Lane countered angrily.

'We don't actually know . . .'

'Of course we know. That wasn't his office colleague or his sister. That child was his. Let me tell you that if you saw my lover with his wife and daughter, I'd say you were a poor friend not to tell me.'

'You say that now, but you might think differently if it really *was* the case.'

'Well, I'm glad we cleared *that* up, anyway, because I would most definitely want to be told. That puts the ball back in my court, gives me the right to make a decision.'

'But we can't tell her, Lane. Come on, think about it.'

'It's important enough for him to lie about it, tell her that he's in London, and be holed up in a wine bar where he's not going to meet anyone.'

'Or so he thought,' Eva said. 'Don't tell her, Lane, it would destroy her.'

'She should be told. Let her take him back if she wants to, but she has the right to know.'

'Leave it, just for a bit, anyway.'

In the end, neither of them had to tell Freda. Mark got there first.

It was the night of the reception at Holly's. She hadn't heard from Mark all day but she knew he was busy. She hoped she would be a credit to him tonight. Eva's black jacket looked very well on her; she would wear a scarlet silk skirt and her good black and red shoes. She knew Mark would have to circulate and that she would have to manage on her own, but later they would be together.

The reception was in full swing when Freda arrived at the

hotel. There was a buzz of conversation, and trays of elegant canapés were being passed around.

She slipped in without acknowledging Mark. He was at the centre of a laughing group near the window. Freda moved to the other side of the room and watched him talking. He was animated and able to include everyone around him in whatever it was that they were talking about. His easy smile rested on one person and then the next. And then he moved on seamlessly to another group.

She must not stand here like part of the furniture, looking at him. She was an invited guest.

She recognised a few faces. A man who ran a TV chat show, a woman columnist, a well-known television reporter. He had certainly the kind of people he needed. He would be in good form later on.

She chatted easily to people around her, and drank little from her glass so that it could not be topped up. She met a man who was in charge of IT for a large company. He agreed with Freda that there was an almighty waste with technology being updated every week and systems becoming obsolete in a year or two. Freda wondered what they did with their old equipment, and made a very strong case for him to consider Finn Road Library. She explained about the computer classes, and he seemed very interested. Then she saw Mark looking across at her oddly and hastily changed the subject to the splendours of the hotel. It was such a jewel of a place, and everyone felt that it was their own little secret.

'That's why it would be insanity to change it,' the man said.

'But to make sure it survives, to get a steady flow of visitors . . . ?' she was repeating Mark's words now.

'There are dozens of hotels with big conference facilities,

spas, entertainment for the busloads. Holly's is different; it should stay different,' he said.

'And what if it gets squeezed out, if it just gets crushed by all the others because it was afraid to expand?'

'You've bought the line,' the man said. 'You're well indoctrinated already, you don't even need to stay for the speeches.'

'I'm not sure I know what you mean.'

'Oh, the spiel, disguised as a nice warm welcome, lovely to see you all in this old-fashioned place, now we plan to change it and ruin it.'

'And will they?' Freda could hardly breathe.

'Don't know yet,' he said. 'A few of us on the board want things to stay as they are, the others all see a great glittering future and a franchising of the Holly brand abroad. They're obviously going to tear it down, and this little circus is to get their friends in the press to help them get planning permission. Anyway, don't get me started. What's your library called, in case we can send a few computers your way?'

They exchanged details. At that moment, Mark appeared at their elbows.

'You're never cruising the room looking for help for your library, Miss O'Donovan?' he said.

'My suggestion entirely, Mark. This young lady is doing something worthwhile with her life, and that's a rare treat these days.'

Mark steered her away firmly.

'Who was he?' Freda whispered.

'Never mind who was he, what the hell is going on?' Mark hissed at her. 'What do you think you're doing, trying to sabotage my event? Who put you up to it? No, don't tell me, you and those bitches . . .'

348

'*Mark?*' Freda was bewildered. The look on his face alarmed her. What on earth had happened?

'What did you think you were going to do?' His eyes raked her face. 'Stand up here and make accusations? Wreck my chances?' His voice sounded clipped and furious, though his face wore a forced smile as he continued to steer her towards the door.

'I don't know what you're talking about,' she said with spirit, trying to free her elbow from his grip. 'I don't know what's gone wrong, but why don't I call you tomorrow, and we'll fix that nice relaxed evening we were going to have for tomorrow night instead? Right?' Her voice sounded doomed and hollow inside her own head. 'Or perhaps you could come round to my place later tonight and tell me what this is all about?' She hoped she didn't sound as if she was begging.

'I don't think so,' he said derisively. 'It's too late for all that. Sending your friends to spy on me! Why couldn't you leave things alone? You fool, you stupid fool . . .' He was hardly able to get the words out. 'How could you have been so stupid? You've wrecked everything. And when I think how much I loved you, and the risks I took for you.'

She was frightened now. 'Tell me, what *is* it? What did I do? Whatever it was, it was a horrible accident. And whatever I did wrong, I'm sorry . . .'

By now, they had reached the front door of the hotel. Freda was distraught, but Mark's face was cold as he half dragged her outside.

'Do not contact me again. Don't call, don't text, don't email. Stay out of my life. And don't you or your friends *ever* come near my wife and child again . . .'

Freda watched him, mute and hopeless, as he turned and walked away from her, back into the hotel. The door closed.

She passed the line of taxis without seeing them. Her eyes were blurred with tears. Then, out of sight of the hotel, she stopped and leaned on a railing to cry properly. She stood there in Eva's black beaded jacket and wept.

Passers-by looked at her, concerned. Some even stopped to ask could they help, but Freda just cried more. Then she felt an arm on her shoulder and realised that it was the IT man she'd been talking to earlier.

'Have you anyone to go to?' he asked kindly.

She was fine; it was only something personal and silly, she would get over it, she reassured him through her sobs.

Did she want him to call someone for her?

And even though she always thought of herself as someone surrounded by friends, tonight there was literally nobody she could ring.

He put her into a taxi; later, she realised, he had paid the driver. In the back of the cab, she sat staring ahead of her for twenty minutes. In her little flat, everything was perfect: candles arranged carefully on tables and in the grate that would barely take minutes to light; the food and wine in the refrigerator, a big bowl of scented lilies on the windowsill.

A warm and welcoming place. It mocked her for all her hopes and confidence.

Then the walls seemed to be closing in on her, and it was as if she couldn't breathe.

Sometimes when she woke suddenly at night, she wondered had she imagined the whole thing. Maybe it was all a dream, a fantasy, everything about that night at Holly's Hotel. She thought she had known him so well. He was gentle, funny and loving. He could not have been with her all this time unless he did love her as he swore he did.

Eventually, the story had emerged from Eva and from Lane. The day out, the lunch, Mark, the blonde woman, the child. *The child.* He had a daughter. She turned over in her mind all the visions she had tried to repress: at no stage during these visions had there been any sight of a daughter. But then she had seen his wife, hadn't she? The blonde woman in her vision really was indeed his wife. Freda had seen her and done nothing.

Over the days that followed, Freda lost weight and her face became drawn and lined.

Eva was seriously worried, and turned from sympathy to bewilderment and then to genuine concern. 'I feel so power-less to help you,' she said sadly.

'I have no idea what to do,' Freda wailed. 'I loved him so much. I thought he loved me. How would I know what to do?'

'You are full of guilt,' Eva said. 'You probably don't need to be, but you are. You are trying to make amends, to make things right somehow, but you can't. You have to look to the future now.'

Eva made a decision. Freda needed to get away; she needed a change of scene. She needed to be somewhere where she wasn't reminded of Mark every day, where she could see clearly once again. She made two phone calls: one to a Mrs Starr at Stone House in the West of Ireland to change her reservation, and the other to Miss Duffy. Freda wasn't feeling very well. She was going to need a few days to recover . . .

As she drew near to the house, Freda wondered had she made a great mistake. This place would do her no good at all. She knew nobody here; all she could do was think about the time she had felt so happy and then so devastated. Why was she here? There weren't any ghosts to lay. Just very real memories of her great love.

Mrs Starr was very welcoming. She showed Freda to a pretty room at the side of the house, and said that Eva had said to be sure to mention all the birdwatching opportunities. Freda stared dully out of the window and watched as the wind caught the branches of the tree outside her window. Holm oak, she thought, sadly. *Holly* oak. The memory of her humiliation came flooding back.

Oddly, the wind seemed to be shaking only one of the branches of the tree. Freda watched transfixed as a small black and white face emerged from the leaves and stared in at her quizzically for a moment, before disappearing into the foliage again. She held her breath as the little cat clambered further and further up the tree, patches of black and white appearing every now and then.

'Don't worry,' said Chicky Starr, following her anxious gaze. 'That's Gloria. She's fine. She's afraid of nothing. Whatever it is she thinks she's chasing will be long gone and she'll make her way down again. I'll introduce you, if you like. Come down to the kitchen and I'll give you the cat treats she loves. Three pieces, mind, no more than that.'

Downstairs in the kitchen, Chicky opened the side door and whistled. Within seconds, Gloria appeared looking hopeful, wound herself around Chicky's legs then sat down abruptly for some urgent leg-washing.

'Three pieces,' reminded Chicky, passing the box of treats to Freda. 'Don't believe her when she tells you she should have more.'

Freda sat down by the fire and immediately Gloria jumped up on to her lap, purring loudly with anticipation. One by one, Freda dispensed the little pieces of dried food; delicately, Gloria accepted them. Then she curled up in a very tight ball and promptly fell asleep.

If only, Freda thought wistfully as she stroked the top of Gloria's head, if only she could stay here by the fire all week with this warm little bundle of fur in her lap. If only she didn't have to move, to meet anyone else, to make small talk. She dreaded meeting her fellow guests.

The feeling intensified when she met the others as they gathered for pre-dinner drinks in Chicky Starr's kitchen. They were all perfectly pleasant: Freda looked from one face to another and felt that each and every one of these fellow travellers had some deep secrets; her heart felt heavy at the thought of having to talk to any of them. Perhaps if she kept herself totally to herself, they would just leave her alone.

Of course, in the end it wasn't like that at all. Chicky Starr's welcome was warm, and they gathered around the roaring log fire; the atmosphere was generous and relaxing and soon the conversation rose to a much higher pitch. Suddenly Freda found no difficulty in talking to these total strangers, and for a while she recovered her old animation.

She talked to a nice young Swedish man who turned out to be interested in Irish music. Before she realised what she'd done, she had agreed to go off to the town with him the next morning and find a music pub. On her other side, she had a spirited debate with a retired schoolteacher about standards of literacy among the young people of today. To her surprise, Freda felt her spirits lift as she told Miss Howe about the Friends of Finn Road Library and the young girls' reading group.

That night as she lay in bed, she thought about the events

of the day. On an impulse, she got up and opened her door quietly. A small lamp on the hall table showed her there was no one around. Softly she whistled. At first there was no response, but after a moment she heard a soft thud and then the purposeful padding of small feet.

Freda slept that night with Gloria curled up beside her. In the morning, she set off with Anders and let herself be carried along with his enthusiasm. She found herself laughing out loud at his stories at lunchtime; and then moved to tears by the plaintive sounds of the music they listened to in the afternoon.

Freda was slowly starting to feel better. Dinner that night was even easier than the night before. She said nothing when she dreamed about storms, but pushed aside any notion of trying to warn anyone. She was relieved when Winnie and Lillian were found safe and sound.

It was on the fourth day that Chicky found Freda and Gloria curled up together by the fire in the Miss Sheedy Room. Gloria was dreaming, her pink little paws were twitching and she was making snuffly noises; Freda was stroking her fur and daydreaming.

Chicky was carrying a tray with a teapot and two cups. As she set it down on the small table, Freda looked up at her, startled. Gloria, affronted, jumped down on to the floor where she lay on her back with her feet in the air and surveyed the room gravely.

'I thought you might like some tea,' Chicky began. 'Gloria knows she's not supposed to be in here, but the two of you have definitely bonded.'

It was true: Freda and Gloria had by now become inseparable. The little black and white cat followed Freda throughout the house and escorted her on her walks through the garden.

The two of them were seen admiring Carmel's twins and being formally introduced to the two new ducks, Spud and Princess. Gloria had considered them from a safe distance; then she had jumped up on to a fence-post and washed her face thoughtfully.

Chicky told Freda about Miss Queenie and how she had rescued Gloria and carried her into the house in her coat pocket. Rigger had thought her quite mad at the time, but like everyone else, he doted on them both. This room, she said, was named after Miss Queenie.

'I don't know if it's true or not,' she said, 'and I never asked her about it, but apparently some woman from the travellers had told all three sisters years back that she saw three unhappy marriages ahead, so they all refused whatever offers they got . . .'

That was when Freda told Chicky Starr about the second-sight experiences, about the times she had spoken out and had regretted it, and how she had tried to suppress her knowledge ever since. Even if she had a feeling, she had learned to keep it to herself. She couldn't change anything by speaking up; she would only have people shun her or be angry about what she saw. Whether she said anything or not, she couldn't win.

Then she told Chicky about Mark Malone, and how she had pushed aside the notion that he might have been married.

Chicky listened carefully. She passed no judgement; she seemed to understand totally that Freda could have loved Mark and put aside her fears.

'Why are you worried about talking about seeing these things?' she asked.

Freda loved her for accepting totally that she *had* seen them; there was no attempt to persuade her that they were imagination, dreams, coincidences.

'Because they've brought nothing but grief.'

'Suppose you had one about me now? Would you tell me?'

'I don't think so, no.'

'You'd let me blunder on? Even if it's something avoidable, you'd be afraid to tell me?'

'But I myself don't want to accept that I have them. If I don't tell anyone, then I don't have to face it. I never know when they're going to come, that's what's so unnerving.'

Chicky listened to Freda and shook her head. She had more to say, but there was a commotion in the kitchen; Rigger had just arrived with the vegetables for tonight's dinner and she had work to do. She patted Freda on the arm and left her with Gloria, who had decided that the fringe on the fireside rug was in need of serious chastisement.

The next night, the entire table gave a cheer when Henry and Nicola announced that they would be staying on as doctors in the town. Freda was happy to be part of such a cheerful group, and she went to bed feeling relaxed and content.

There had been something of a fuss earlier on when Miss Howe had suddenly decided to leave. Rigger had been called to drive her to the station, and she had gone without a word to the other guests. There had been something very sad about the droop of her shoulders as she got into the van. It was all a bit unsettling.

All the same, the holiday was turning out to be a great success, each day bringing something new: wild scenery, the trip into town for music with Anders, good food and conversation at night and always at least eight hours' sleep. Freda felt stronger and better every day.

*

356

And it was on the last day of her holiday that, just before dinner, Chicky beckoned Freda into the kitchen.

'I wanted to talk to you because I've worked out what you should do about, you know, your problem.'

'You have?'

'I think you should change your tactic,' said Chicky as she laid the table for dinner. 'You say you are afraid that people will know you have this power, so you have been keeping it all a secret.'

'I don't want to admit to anyone, even myself, that what I say might come true.'

'This is the problem, Freda. I think you should tell everyone you meet that you are a psychic, say you can see the future and know what's going to happen. Offer to read their palms, tea leaves, cards. Then it's all out in the open.'

'And how would that help?'

'It would take the magic out of it, the secrecy, the power. People might think you are flaky but it sort of devalues the whole thing. That's what you want, isn't it?'

'Yes, it is, in a way.'

'Then this is the way. This devalues it. This way, nobody will think it's serious, no matter what you see or what you say.'

'You want me to *tell* people that I have second sight?'

'Call it what you like. Tell them any kind of vague, hopeful things about the future to cheer them up – that's all people really want from their horoscope, anyway. It will tame it for you, make it harmless. The way I look at it is that you are full of guilt over these visions. You have to try to make them insignificant. They were just thoughts, like anyone has thoughts, that's all.'

Freda stood there in the kitchen of Stone House and felt

357

everything shift slightly. There was a huge sense of relief as well as the sense of loss. She always thought that Mark had loved her. But why should she have believed this when there was absolutely no evidence that she had been anything except a pleasant distraction? It was both liberating and sad.

'I'll tell them over dinner,' she said. 'I'll tell them all that this is what I do.'

'Let's see how you get on,' said Chicky. 'That's it, Freda. You go and knock them out.'

As Chicky Starr's guests sat down for the last dinner of their winter week together, Freda heard herself telling this group of strangers that she was a psychic. They murmured their response with varying degrees of interest.

John, the American, said that many of his friends in the States consulted psychics regularly; the two doctors looked less enthusiastic but curious all the same. Winnie said cheerfully that she would love to book a session with her, while Lillian said it was a pity that so many so-called psychics, present company excepted of course, were charlatans. Anders said that they had a client in his father's accountancy firm who wouldn't make a single investment without consulting astrologers.

It proved to be just an easy conversational topic. So much more open to discussion than when she had said she was a librarian. The feeling of dread began to recede.

The evening was becoming very animated. The guests were still busy with the competition to set up a great Irish festival, and then someone asked Freda if she would tell their fortune. She looked around her wildly. This had not been part of the plan. Chicky Starr came to her rescue.

'Perhaps Freda might have come on a holiday to escape from her work. We shouldn't impose on her.'

They all looked disappointed; then Freda remembered Chicky saying that all people wanted from psychics was vague good news and promises about the future. She looked around the group. It would be harmless and even easy to tell them that life ahead looked good.

She held their hands and saw all kinds of good things: success and challenges and peace and long relationships.

For Winnie, she saw a wedding in the near future and great happiness in store. Lillian would meet someone at the wedding, possibly for love but certainly for friendship. Lillian's face was pink with pleasure.

So far, so good.

In Henry's hands she saw a new beginning, a happy life.

In Nicola's there was a child. Really, Nicola wondered. A child? Definitely, Freda was certain. And then, suddenly, Freda found herself saying, 'You're pregnant now. A little girl. I can see her. She's lovely!' She could see the little girl wrapping her arms around Nicola's neck. And when she saw the tension disappear from Nicola's forehead and the huge smile break out over her face, Freda realised for the first time that she could bring real joy to people's lives.

For John, or Corry, as they knew him, she foretold a whole change of direction, different kind of work and a different place to live. A much less complicated lifestyle, and a grandchild who would be part of his life. She was moved when she saw tears spring to his eyes.

Anders had a great love in his life; he must go home and ask her to marry him very soon. Only then would he be successful in his business.

For The Walls, she saw a cruise. Somewhere warm; she could see sunshine on the water.

She turned to Chicky Starr last. Freda took her hand and concentrated. Nothing. She paused, and then said hesitantly that Stone House would be a great success and that there would be a man, perhaps someone she had already met.

And then Freda knew. There had been no accident. There had been no wedding. But it didn't matter; Chicky was going to be fine. She smiled. It was *all* going to be fine.

They were delighted with her. It seemed to end the week well for everyone.

Names, phone numbers and email addresses were exchanged. A toast was proposed to Chicky, to Rigger and his family, to Orla and to Stone House.

They all signed the visitors' book with warm messages. The timetable for the next day was arranged. For those going home by train, Rigger and Chicky would provide a taxi service to the station. Carmel had made a small pot of Stone House marmalade for each guest.

And that night, Freda stroked a gently purring Gloria as she stood at her window looking at the patterns the clouds made going across the moon. She would call Lane and Eva as soon as she got back. Time for dinner at Ennio's. They had a lot of catching-up to do.

It was a scramble in the morning to see everyone off on time. Chicky Starr finally waved goodbye to each of her guests, but she saved a special hug for Freda, who now looked so much happier than when she had arrived.

It was time to get ready for the new guests, who would arrive in just a few hours. Carmel had come in to help clean the rooms, change the bedding and get everything ready for the new intake. Chicky would make a casserole that would cook slowly and be ready whenever they needed it. There would be freshly baked bread, and chocolate mousse for dessert.

Chicky knew she would miss the people who had made her first week at Stone House such a success, but she was looking forward to greeting the newcomers with all their new challenges and demands. She took a deep breath of sea air. She was ready for them.

Gloria wound herself around Chicky's feet. Chicky picked her up and scratched her ears. Then the two of them went back into Stone House.